W9-AQU-540

DATE DUE

			PRINTED IN U.S.A.

VOL. ONE

A PROMISE UNBROKEN

A HEART DIVIDED

AL LACY

Multnomah Publishers

BATTLES OF DESTINY, Volume 1
published by Multnomah Publishers
A division of Random House Inc.

Compilation of:
A Promise Unbroken © 1993 by ALJO PRODUCTIONS, INC.
ISBN 0-88070-581-7
A Heart Divided © 1993 by ALJO PRODUCTIONS, INC.
ISBN 0-88070-591-4

Cover Photography by Steve Gardner, www.shootpw.com

Multnomah is a trademark of Multnomah Publishers
and is registered in the U.S. Patent and Trademark Office.
The colophon is a trademark of Multnomah Publishers.

Printed in the United States of America

For information:
MULTNOMAH PUBLISHERS
12265 Oracle Boulevard, Suite 200
Colorado Springs, Colorado 80921

07 08 09 10 11 12 13 14 — 10 9 8 7 6 5 4 3 2 1 0

Novels by Al Lacy

JOURNEYS OF THE STRANGER SERIES:
Legacy
Silent Abduction
Blizzard
Tears of the Sun
Circle of Fire
Quiet Thunder
Snow Ghost

ANGEL OF MERCY SERIES:
A Promise for Breanna
Faithful Heart
Captive Set Free
A Dream Fulfilled
Suffer the Little Children
Whither Thou Goest
Final Justice
Not by Might
Things Not Seen
Far Above Rubies

Novels by Al and JoAnna Lacy

HANNAH OF FORT BRIDGER SERIES:
Under the Distant Sky
Consider the Lilies
No Place for Fear
Pillow of Stone
The Perfect Gift
Touch of Compassion
Beyond the Valley
Damascus Journey

MAIL ORDER BRIDE SERIES:
Secrets of the Heart
A Time to Love
The Tender Flame
Blessed Are the Merciful
Ransom of Love
Until the Daybreak
Sincerely Yours
A Measure of Grace
So Little Time
Let There Be Light

SHADOW OF LIBERTY SERIES:
Let Freedom Ring
The Secret Place
A Prince Among Them
Undying Love

ORPHAN TRAINS SERIES:
The Little Sparrows
All My Tomorrows
Whispers in the Wind

FRONTIER DOCTOR SERIES:
One More Sunrise
Beloved Physician
The Heart Remembers

DREAMS OF GOLD SERIES:
Wings of Riches
The Forbidden Hills
The Golden Stairs

A PLACE TO CALL HOME SERIES:
Cherokee Rose
Bright Are the Stars
The Land of Promise

BOOK ONE

A PROMISE
UNBROKEN

BATTLE OF RICH MOUNTAIN

For my darling wife, JoAnna (Joni to me),
whose tender love has been the inspiration
for romance in all my novels,
and whose ideas, suggestions, and help
in historical research over the years have been invaluable.

PROLOGUE

When that first Confederate shell arched through the predawn sky and exploded behind the walls of Fort Sumter on April 12, 1861, it touched off one of the greatest points of crisis in the history of America. Not only did the Civil War quickly develop into a bloody conflict between two societies with opposite views on slavery, but it moved inexorably toward something almost unthinkable—a tragic clash between families. Brothers battling brothers.

In the century between the end of the Napoleonic Wars and the commencement of World War I, the most catastrophic military conflict fought anywhere was the American Civil War. Some historians have alluded to the Civil War as a combination of "The Last Medieval War and the First Modern War." I agree. As the first modern war, it ominously foreshadowed the horrors of warfare that have followed in the twentieth century.

The Civil War introduced trench warfare, propaganda, warfare of psychological attrition, aerial observation, naval blockade, economic warfare, iron-clad ships, and the Gatling gun, as well as the horrible impeding influence of filthy, disease-ridden, prisoner-of-war camps. Compulsory enlistment for military service was also put into use for the first time in American history.

The Civil War brought about many other firsts. It was the first war to have photographers taking pictures on the battlefield. It was the first war to employ repeating rifles and to use railroad artillery, naval torpedoes, flame throwers, land mines, electrically exploded bombs, telescopic sights for rifles, fixed ammunition, the wigwag signal code, and periscopes for fighting in the trenches. During the Civil War, the bugle call "Taps" was first played, naval camouflage was invented, and the Congressional Medal of Honor was introduced.

With all of its firsts in modern warfare and the hatred that raged between the North and the South, the Civil War cost more American lives in the four years from Sumter to Appomattox than the two World Wars, Korea, Vietnam, and Desert Storm combined. The carnage that took place between April 1861 and April 1865 was appalling. Of the three million men who saw action afloat and ashore—Union and Confederate—more than a million were casualties. Well over 600,000 lost their lives as a direct result of combat (including those who were wounded, then died of infections and various diseases). Another 400,000 were wounded, but lived to tell of the horrors of the war.

This caldron of blood was spread wider than the casual follower of the Civil War realizes. According to government authorities, there were some 95 major battles, 310 minor battles, and over 6,000 skirmishes, some of which the soldiers themselves called "squabbles" or "dust-ups." If a man died in a dust-up, he was just as dead as if he had been killed in a major battle. The bulk of the fighting took place on Southern land. However, a few battles were fought on Union soil, including two of the bloodiest—Gettysburg and Antietam. Blood was shed in land-fighting as far north as Vermont, and as far west as the Pacific coast. California saw 6 skirmishes, Oregon 4, and 19 occurred in New Mexico Territory. There were other skirmishes in the territories of Washington, Utah, and Idaho.

The fighting in Vermont was a result of Confederate raiders striking the town of St. Albans. Other Rebel raiders shed blood in

Illinois, Minnesota, and New York. The southernmost fighting happened between Union and Confederate forces on a sandy beach in Florida known today as Cape Canaveral.

The seeds of war over slavery were planted in this country long before the first shot was fired upon Fort Sumter. When Spain conquered a large part of South America in the late fifteenth century, they made slaves of the Indians and forced them to work in the mines and in the crop fields. The Indians, however, began to die off quickly because of exposure to European diseases and harsh working conditions. To remedy this problem, Spanish king Charles I began to import slaves from Africa in 1517. The idea slowly caught on in other lands. The first African slaves arrived at the English colony of Virginia aboard a Dutch ship early in 1619.

Almost immediately pressure began to build between northern and southern colonists over slavery, and it grew worse as the decades passed. During the Revolutionary War, slavery was a hot issue amongst the colonists, and it did not subside when the thirteen colonies declared their independence on July 4, 1776. For the sake of unity political leaders on both sides of the issue agreed to not allow their ideologies to divide them. This worked fairly well until the mid-nineteenth century, when a fatuous abolitionist zealot named John Brown led a band of men on a killing spree in Kansas, murdering proslavery leaders in cold blood. Although Brown controlled his thirst for blood in the months after the Kansas ritual murders in May of 1856, he was anything but inactive. He gained more recruits for his crusade against slavery as time passed, and moved eastward. His scheme was to set up a base in the Alleghenies from which he could invade Virginia, free a multitude of slaves, and make them part of his army.

It took Brown over three years to prepare his small band of men for the invasion. On the night of October 16, 1859, Brown and his men took over the Union arsenal at Harper's Ferry and held several hostages. Word of Brown's plan had been sent to thousands of slaves, whom he expected to rally around him. Once he had armed them with the guns and ammunition from the arsenal, he would lead them in a march of liberation.

The slaves did not show up, but the United States Marines did. When the fighting was over, only John Brown and four of his men remained. They were captured and were hanged in Charles Town, Virginia, on December 7, 1859. Southerners angrily accused the North of plotting to end slavery by instigating a giant slave rebellion. The accusations flared tempers in the North. When the Northerners disclaimed any connection with Brown, Southerners called them liars…and the situation grew worse.

News of the Harper's Ferry incident spread to every state, including Massachusetts, where famed poet Henry W. Longfellow resided at the time. On the same day John Brown was hanged, Longfellow penned these prophetic words:

> This will be a great day in our history; the date of a New Revolution—quite as much needed as the old one. Even now as I write they are leading old John Brown to execution in Virginia for attempting to rescue slaves! This is sowing the wind to reap the whirlwind which will come soon.

When John Brown was being escorted from the Charles Town jail to the public place of execution, he handed a note to one of the guards that incredibly coincided with Longfellow's presage of the national calamity that Brown had done so much to make inevitable. It read: "I, John Brown, am now quite certain that the crimes of this guilty land will never be purged away but with blood."

One hundred and twenty-six days later, the whirlwind of blood had its beginnings at Fort Sumter, South Carolina.

Events might have been vastly different had the nation been more mature. At the time John Brown was inciting civil unrest, the United States was less than a hundred years old, barely an adolescent as nations go. The people of the two philosophies concerning slavery had much to learn about each other.

The economy in the northern states was much stronger and more stable than the economy in the South. The Northerners, according to southern leaders, failed to understand the situation.

At the close of the eighteenth century, profound economic changes were taking place in Great Britain and all over Europe. There was an increasing demand for cotton, but the climate in that part of the world prevented the growth of the product. Hence, clothing manufacturers from the Continent crossed the Atlantic Ocean and met with southern cotton producers, placing large orders. The plantation owners were elated with the new business opportunities, but found that the only way they could make what they felt was a fair profit was to use slave labor.

The South was already providing virtually all of the cotton needed by the growing textile mills in the northern states. The added demand from the Europeans meant the need for expansion in cotton production in the South, which also meant the expansion of slavery. Cotton and slavery became inextricably intertwined. Apathetic about the economics of it, northern newspapers and periodicals were concerned only with the baneful practice of slavery. They blasted the southern cotton producers, saying in essence, "To sell cotton in order to buy Negroes—to produce more cotton to buy more Negroes—is immoral, and the practice should be outlawed by the Congress of the United States."

The attitude of the North embittered Southerners, who retorted in their own publications that the rich Northerners were ignorant and should mind their own business. Thus, the adolescent nation, driven by the winds of bitter debate over slavery, took a set course toward bloody conflict.

Fuel was added to the fire by reports that filtered northward concerning the brutal treatment of slaves by the southern plantation owners. Political leaders in the South readily admitted that there were slave owners who were short on compassion toward their slaves, feeding and housing them poorly and often abusing them physically.

They were quick to point out, however, that such slave owners were in the minority.

The same politicians hastened to denounce the arrogant Northerners for being in the dark about the constant danger of slave revolt. Even the decent and compassionate slave owners found it necessary to exercise strict discipline on their human chattel to keep them in line.

The plantation owners remembered the slave revolt near Charleston, South Carolina, in September of 1739, when twenty-five white people were killed before the rebellion was crushed. They also had not forgotten the massive slave revolt in Haiti between 1791 and 1804 when a collective army of six thousand vengeful slaves, brandishing guns, machetes, spears, knives, and clubs created a massacre. Marching behind a standard—the body of a white baby impaled on a spear—they killed their white masters, violated their wives and daughters, and shed the blood of whites anywhere on the island who stood in their way.

Also remembered were conspiracies to revolt that occurred at Richmond, Virginia, in 1800 and at Charleston, South Carolina, in 1822. Although these two plans were thwarted, it caused the slave owners to take precautionary measures. Fresh in the minds of plantation owners was the slave revolt in the summer of 1831 at South Hampton County, Virginia, when fifty-seven whites were killed, resulting in the hanging of nearly a hundred slaves.

When southern newspapers tried to make it clear to Northerners that slave owners lived in the shadow of revolt and had to use "fear tactics" to keep their slaves in subjection, the northern newspapers answered back, "Free the slaves and your impending danger will be gone!"

Thus, the contentious exchange between North and South raged until John Brown came along and lit the fuse that exploded the verbal conflict into full-scale war. The four years of carnage brought about an acceleration of maturity. America grew up.

The conflict ended at Appomattox Court House, Virginia, on

Sunday afternoon April 9, 1865. Slavery ended in the United States later that year with the passage of the Thirteenth Amendment to the Constitution.

When General Robert E. Lee mounted his horse and rode away from the McLean house that fateful day, followed by hundreds of weeping Confederate soldiers, the Civil War was over. The bitter memories and deep sorrows of the four-year struggle, however, lived on. As time passed, it eased the sorrows, but the memories were rooted in the soil where the blood was spilled. Although the guns were silent, in the minds of both Northerners and Southerners, the war would never end. The memories would continue to burn in their hearts until, like their brothers and friends who died in the conflict, they too passed through death's dark door.

Having laid this brief historical foundation, I now tell my version of the Civil War's first major battle, which took place on July 11, 1861, at Rich Mountain in western Virginia.

ONE

Web Steele whipped his head around as the flat report of the shot carried to him through the cool mid-October air. Jerking hard on the reins, he drew horse and buggy to a halt in the middle of the road. While the breeze carried the small dust cloud away, he peered past the imposing archway on his left that housed the gate to the Jason Hart plantation.

Letting his gaze follow the narrow, winding road that led to the mansion and its complex of buildings nestled in a thick stand of trees, he listened for any further sound of trouble. The gunshot seemed to have come from that way, but the pounding of the horse's hooves and the whir of the wheels had suppressed the report enough to make it impossible to be sure.

Pulling his gaze from the Hart mansion, Steele looked up the road ahead of him as his horse blew and stamped a hoof. The Virginia sky was clear, and the brilliant light of the early afternoon sun revealed no movement in that direction. The John Ruffin plantation lay two miles further on, but the shot was too loud to have come from there.

Turning around on the seat, he looked down the road behind him. The Steele plantation—from which he had just come—was nearest, but it also was too far away to have been the source of the shot. There was no sign of life except for the birds that hopped about in the branches of the towering trees that lined both sides of the road. Sunlight danced on the orange and golden leaves as they fluttered in the autumn breeze.

Steele looked to his right across the rolling hills toward Richmond, but saw nothing moving.

Suddenly there was a second shot, followed by a third. This time he knew it was coming from the Hart place. The gate beneath the archway was open. Snapping the reins, he sent the horse galloping under the archway, following the narrow, winding road. Another shot rang out, and Web felt a vast hollow in his stomach. Instinct told him that what he had been expecting to happen on both the Ruffin and Hart plantations was now in progress directly ahead of him.

The mansion was a quarter-mile from the road. As the buggy bounded into the spacious yard, another shot reverberated through the air, the sharp sound coming from the rear. Guiding the horse along the path to the backside of the house, Steele saw Jonas Hart and his two sons hunkered behind an overturned wagon, facing the tool and wood shed, which was close to the barn, about forty yards from the rear of the mansion. There were splintered places on the wagon where bullets had chewed wood.

Drawing the buggy to a sudden stop, Steele saw Mabel Hart, her oldest daughter, Mary Ann, and daughter-in-law, Chloe, collected on the back porch of the mansion with the butler and the maid. All were wide-eyed with fear.

As Web Steele jumped out of the buggy, he saw that Jonas was holding a revolver with one hand and a bleeding shoulder with the other. Sons David, twenty-two, and Daniel, twenty-one, were not armed. A group of slaves could be seen at the edge of a clearing some fifty yards further back, where their small cabins huddled in a circle. They too looked frightened.

Steele knew his instincts were correct. Hart had a slave revolt on his hands. Some of them were holed up in the tool and wood shed, and were armed. The absence of Hart's sixteen-year-old daughter and fourteen-year-old son might mean they were being held hostage.

Jonas Hart shouted, "Web, take cover! We've got real trouble here!"

Steele took one look at the open window next to the shed's only door and saw the barrel of a revolver glint in the sunlight. He dashed to where Jonas and his sons were clustered behind the overturned wagon. "Please tell me that Darrel and Melissa aren't in there!"

A gray pallor was on Jonas Hart's pain-pinched face. Even his lips were colorless. At forty-four, he owned the large plantation and had done well, but Steele knew that Jonas was sometimes unnecessarily harsh with his slaves. He had come close to warning Jonas about it on several occasions, but the man was sixteen years his senior, and he could not bring himself to do it.

Jonas's voice was tight as he replied, "They're in the shed, all right, Web."

"How many slaves in there?" Web asked.

"Two."

"Do I know them?"

"Yeah. Dexter and Orman."

Eyeing the blood that was running between Jonas's fingers as he gripped his shoulder, Web said, "You'd better get to the house and let Mabel tend to that wound."

"Naw," growled the plantation owner, "it's only a scratch. It'll be all right. Main thing right now is to bring this situation to an end."

Looking back toward the shed, Steele said, "Dexter and Orman, eh? What do they want?"

Gritting his teeth in pain, Jonas replied, "To go free. They say if we'll let them go, they'll release the kids when they're a safe distance from here."

"What brought this on?"

"Nothing special, they just—"

"Tell him the truth, Pa," butted in David, who was slave over-seer for his father. "I've been warning you this was going to happen."

"Shut up!" snapped Jonas. "If you'd be a little more stern with these lazy whelps, it wouldn't make me look so mean when I have to discipline them."

David Hart had been developing a distaste for slavery for the past two years. He and his father had had many heated discussions about it. Jonas accused him of becoming an "abolitionist Yankee" in his heart.

Before David could respond, a voice came from within the shed. "We's gettin' tired of waitin', Massa Jonas! We want those horses, and we want 'em right now!"

Web Steele recognized the voice of Dexter, whom he had known for several years. In a half-whisper, he said, "Jonas, Dexter knows me well. So does Orman. Do you think it would help if I talk to them?"

"Couldn't hurt, that's for sure," spoke up Daniel. "Both of them like you."

"What about it, Jonas?" pressed Steele.

"Go ahead. Talk to them. Like Dan said, it can't hurt for you to try."

"Massa Jonas!" bellowed Orman. "We saw Massa Web come in. You can do yo' talkin' later. We want those horses, or we's gonna be forced to hurt dese chillin o' yo's!"

Jonas's anger broke. "You harm my kids and you'll wish you'd never been born, Orman!"

There was no response from the shed. Setting his gaze on Steele, Jonas said, "Well, do your talking."

"First I have to know what David meant when he told you to be truthful with me."

"Aw, I just found it necessary to give them both a good belt-whipping, that's all. They've been getting lazier by the day. David won't chastise them, so they just get continually worse."

"How bad did you whip them?"

"Not too bad."

"Did you draw blood?"

"A little."

"Pa, you expect too much of them," said David. "Their bodies get tired like ours do. If you'd only ease up on the load—"

Jonas swore, cutting off his elder son. "Young and strong as they are, they oughtta be able to do a whole lot more than they've been doing! There are other slaves on this place who put out more work."

"Yes, and there are other slaves who'll be doing this same thing shortly, too," responded David.

"Not if I make an example of these two," Jonas growled, sending a heated glance in the direction of the shed.

At that moment drumming hoof beats were heard in the direction of the road, and seconds later two riders came thundering around the corner of the mansion. The Hart men and Web Steele recognized Reed Exley, slave overseer of the neighboring John Ruffin plantation, and one of the Ruffin slaves, a handsome young man named Mandrake.

David Hart mumbled, "The last person we need here right now is Exley."

Web agreed. As with most people in the Richmond area, he harbored a deep dislike for Exley, who was married to wealthy John Ruffin's oldest daughter, Elizabeth. Web was engaged to Ruffin's next-oldest daughter, Abby. While courting her for the past year-and-a-half, he had gotten to know Exley quite well...much to his sorrow.

At thirty-one, Reed Exley was three years older than Web. He was short, stocky, blond, and somewhat good-looking; he was also self-centered, greedy, and unprincipled. He had a mean, hair-trigger temper, shifty, ice-blue eyes, and a perpetual cocky smirk. His vile soul was exposed further by his vicious and cruel treatment of the Ruffin slaves. It was because of this treatment that Steele expected an all-out slave rebellion. There had been a few runaways in the past several months, but so far, no actual uprising.

It was Exley's job to oversee the slaves and to handle the buying and selling of them. Web, who had the same job on his father's plantation, was kind and compassionate with his slaves. His observation of Exley's merciless, inhuman handling of the Ruffin slaves had led him to discuss it on one occasion with Abby's widower father, but it had done no good. John Ruffin had a blind spot when it came to his son-in-law, and because Exley had never abused the slaves before his eyes, he refused to believe it ever happened. Even when Abby and her younger sister, Lynne, told their father of seeing Exley mistreat the slaves, he would not believe it.

Daniel Hart, who was courting Lynne Ruffin, also disliked Reed Exley. When he saw Exley and Mandrake ride up, he noticed that Exley was wearing a sidearm.

"Better get your head down, Reed!" called Jonas. "We've got a couple of slaves with their noses out of joint, and they've been doing some shooting."

Exley and Mandrake ran in and hunkered down. "Yeah, I heard it," said Reed. "I decided to come and see if I could help." As he spoke, he drew his gun, then looked at Jonas's bleeding shoulder. "You shot bad?"

"No. Mabel can fix me up once this is over."

"So what's going on?" queried Exley.

Jonas gave Exley a brief explanation, naming the two black men who were holding his daughter and son hostage.

Looking around at the others, Exley saw that the only weapon in the bunch was the revolver in Jonas's hand. "Well, why don't we get some more guns and rush 'em?"

"Web's about to try talking them out," said Jonas.

Exley gave Web a cold stare. "Talk?" he spat incredulously. "These beasts don't understand talk!" Then to Jonas, "They both have guns?"

"Yes."

"Where'd they get 'em?"

"I have no idea."

"I say let's lay our hands on some more guns and rush 'em."

"That's a good way to get Darrel and Melissa killed," Web said. "Dexter and Orman are desperate. Put your gun away, Reed, and let me handle this."

"Massa Jonas!" came Dexter's strained voice. "What's goin' on? Why's Reed Exley here?"

"He just came because he heard the shooting," Steele answered for Jonas.

"Yeah? Then why'd he bring that black man with him?"

Web knew Mandrake well. He smiled at him, then turned to Exley and said, "That's a good question. Why did you bring Mandrake along?"

A wicked grin spread over Exley's face as he set his icy eyes on Mandrake. In that brief moment, Steele saw a subtle and fleeting manifestation of the man's cruelty. Reed held his hard gaze on Mandrake and replied, "Simple, Webster. When I heard the shots, I figured it could be something like this. Mandrake, here, has shown a little too much starch to suit me. The other slaves sort of look to him as their leader. I suppose it's because he's young, full of fire, and has all those muscles. Anyway, I made him come along so if some of Jonas's beasts were gonna get disciplined for startin' trouble, he could see first-hand what happens to black boys who revolt against their white masters."

Trepidation showed on Mandrake's dark features. Daring not to look Reed Exley in the eye, he drew in a long, gravelly breath, passed a glance at Steele, and looked at the ground.

Suddenly a shot was heard inside the shed. Melissa Hart screamed. A harsh voice blared, "Nobody's hurt, Massa Jonas! I jus' shot through the roof! But Orman and I are tired of waitin' for you to let us go. We want those horses now! If'n we don't get 'em, somebody in dis shed is goin' to get hurt...an' it ain't me or Orman!"

"Jonas, you gonna do somethin'?" asked Reed Exley. "Or you

just gonna sit here and let them animals kill your kids?"

Jonas licked his lips. "I've got to let Web see if he can talk them out. They like Web. Maybe he can do something with them."

"I doubt it," snarled Exley. "But so he talks 'em into lettin' your kids loose and throwin' their guns out. What you gonna do then?"

"I don't know," said Jonas. "Let's just cross one bridge at a time here. Most important thing is to get Melissa and Darrel out of there."

"Well, they oughtta be hanged or shot through the head in front of the rest of your slaves," grunted Exley. "If you don't make an example of 'em, the next time you whip one, you'll go through this kind of nonsense again."

"Dexter!" called Steele, unwilling to stretch the ordeal out any longer. "Can we talk?"

"We's listenin'."

Web Steele left his crouch and stood to his full height, exposing his empty hands. The Hart brothers set admiring eyes on him from their low position. Wealthy plantation owner Dudley Steele's handsome son stood three inches over six feet, with a muscular frame. He had thick, wavy black hair, matching well-trimmed mustache, medium-length sideburns, and coal-black eyes.

As Web was about to speak, Mabel Hart's high-pitched voice could be heard from the back porch of the mansion. "Jonas! Do something! They'll kill our children!"

"We are!" Jonas shouted back. "Just stay calm!"

"Dexter!" called Steele.

"Yassuh?"

"There is nothing to gain by doing harm to Melissa and Darrel. Let them come out, and we'll talk."

"Cain't do that, Massa Web! If'n we let the kids go, Massa Jonas will beat us again! 'Specially now that we done shot 'im. We ain't gonna have no mo' of those beatin's! We ain't lazy like he say. We works hard. But we cain't keep up the kind o' workin' he's puttin' on us."

"Dat's right, Massa Web!" came Orman's voice. "We knows

about yo' slaves. Ain't none o' them gets treated like us."

"Well, I'm sure if you'll let Mr. Hart's children loose, he'll not beat you. His wound is not serious. I'm sure he'll not punish you for it, and will be more tolerant from now on."

"We wants to hear him say dat!" shouted Orman.

Steele looked down at Jonas Hart. "Well?"

Jonas's face flushed and his eyes had fire in them. "Web, I can't tell those two I'll be more tolerant! You can't expect me to just over-look this and tell them all is forgiven!"

"I think you're going to have to if you don't want to get those kids hurt...or killed," replied Steele.

"What's the matter with tellin' 'em everything's all right so they'll let the kids go...then blast 'em when they show their faces?" suggested Exley.

Web scowled at him. "You fool, Reed! There are more than thirty men in that crowd of slaves standing out there watching us. If we shoot Dexter and Orman, they just might decide to swarm in here and tear us apart."

"We got two guns," parried Exley.

"And how many bullets will you have after blasting Dexter and Orman?" clipped Steele. "Even if you could cut a few of them down, what about the rest? There'd still be enough of them to tear us limb from limb. You're not using your head, Reed."

Reed's temper flared. "They ain't gonna do no such thing! Even if they started for us, when they saw some of their black pals drop, they'd back off."

"You think so?"

"I know it."

Turning to the slave beside Exley, Steele asked, "What about it, Mandrake? Would they back off?"

Mandrake cleared his throat nervously. "Well, Massa Web, I cain't say fo' sure. If they's thinkin' straight, they'd prob'ly not come rushin' into a couple of blazin' guns. But seein' two of their own shot down after they had been tol' they was forgiven just might make 'em crazy-blind mad. If'n that was to happen, wouldn't be a white person left alive on this place."

Exley was livid. "Mandrake, you keep outta this! I don't want to hear another word outta you! You got that?"

Mandrake flicked a fearful glance at Steele, who glared at Exley and snapped, "I asked for his opinion, Reed! You had no right to jump him. Why do you have to be such an idiot?"

Exley bristled. His hot glare met Steele's. The message passed between them—a mute understanding of their mutual dislike.

Reed's teeth clamped together as he hissed, "I resent bein' called an idiot!"

"Then quit acting like one."

Steele looked down at Jonas and said, "Are you going to tell Dexter and Orman they're forgiven, and that you'll be more tolerant from now on?"

"Better do it, Pa," put in David. "Something's going to happen in that shed pretty soon if you don't."

Jonas pulled the bloody hand away from his wound and saw that the bleeding had stopped. Taking off his hat and throwing it angrily on the ground, he said in a hoarse half-whisper, "I can't let those two get away with this! If I do, others will be encouraged to rebel. I'll do anything to get Darrel and Melissa out of there safely, but after that, there has to be severe punishment."

"More beatings?" asked Steele.

"Yes! More beatings! They're not going to get away with this!"

"Pa," said David, "if you hadn't beaten them in the first place, we wouldn't be having this problem now. If you make it sound like everything is forgiven just to free Darrel and Melissa, then whip Dexter and Orman, that will really incite a rebellion. The best thing is for you to stand up right now and talk to them. Admit that you've been working them too hard, and that you were wrong to belt-whip them. You take any other course, and there'll be disaster."

Mabel's high-pitched voice pierced the air. "Jonas! What are you doing? Why are you taking so long?"

"I'm working on it!" Jonas shouted toward the house.

"Well, I say we rush 'em," interjected Reed. "Those black dogs deserve to die."

Mandrake licked his lips as anger welled up within him, but he did not set eyes on Exley.

"You're talking like an idiot again, Reed!" growled Steele. "You couldn't rush them fast enough to save those kids' lives."

"We'll do it my way," said Jonas. "I'll tell them they're forgiven. When Darrel and Melissa are safe and those beasts have thrown down their guns, we'll tie them to a tree and put the fear of God into them."

"Then I want no part in this," said Web, turning to walk away. He froze when another gunshot came from the shed.

Melissa's scream curdled the air and Mabel darted off the porch toward the shed, emitting a wordless wail. Darrel's voice was heard above his sister's scream, calling for his father to help them.

Web intercepted Mabel and guided her toward her husband and older sons hunkered behind the wagon.

David saw his wife coming a few steps behind Mabel, and shouted, "Chloe! Go back!"

Chloe Hart was frightened and did not heed David's command. Reaching the wagon, she dropped to her knees and threw herself into his arms, sobbing.

Dexter's desperate voice rang out from inside the shed, "Time's up! We want those horses right now!"

Jonas's ragged emotions flooded to the surface. "Dexter," he bawled, "I want my children out of there this instant!"

"No!" came the defiant reply. "You give us the horses, and like we already tol' you, we'll let Darrel and Melissa go when we think we're far enough away!"

"You'd never get far enough away!" boomed Hart. "You can't pull this kind of stuff on me and get away with it! You're not getting any horses! Now give it up! Let those kids out of there!"

"No! They're gonna get hurt if you don' do as we say!"

Web said, "Jonas, you've got to apologize for beating them and tell them you'll lighten their work load."

"I don't have to do any such thing."

Another plea came from Darrel, begging his father to help them.

"Jonas!" wailed Mabel. "What is wrong with you? Don't you care what happens to your children?"

"Of course I care, but nobody does this to Jonas Hart. They're not going to get away with it!"

David looked his father in the eye and said heatedly, "Pa, your pride is going to get Darrel and Melissa killed! Dexter and Orman trust Web. Why don't you just tell them you'll set them free right now, and let them ride out of here in Web's buggy with him? After this episode, they'll never be worth their salt around here any more. Let them go. We can get along without them."

"I paid good money for those two, David!" snapped Jonas. "They're not getting out of here! They're going to get what's coming to them!"

"I still say we rush 'em!" blurted Reed.

Ignoring Exley, Jonas looked toward the open window of the shed and bellowed, "Dexter! Orman! If you harm a hair of either one of my kids, you'll die! I'll kill you myself…personally!"

"We'd rather die than have to live like we've been livin'!" came Dexter's reply. "We've talked it over, Massa Jonas. If'n you don't let us ride out of here with Darrel and Melissa like we tol' you, den yo' gonna have to come in after us. We'll die, but so will yo' chillun!"

Mandrake glanced cautiously toward Reed, then said to Hart, "Massa Jonas, they means what they's sayin'. B'lieve me. They is desperate, and they's gonna do what they's sayin' if'n you don' let 'em go."

Reed Exley cursed and slapped Mandrake's face. "You shut up!" he blared. "I said I didn't want to hear another word outta you!"

Mandrake's head whipped sideways from the blow. He took a step back, placing a hand to his smarting cheek.

Web wanted to knock Exley rolling, but the situation at the shed was about to explode. He could tell by the stubborn set to Jonas's jaw that the man was not going to give in. Mabel was whimpering, trembling with fear, and appeared on the verge of collapse. Glancing at the slaves gathered by the cabins, Web saw them watching intently and talking among themselves. Something had to be done, and it had to be done quickly.

Turning to Hart, he said, "Jonas, will you sell Dexter and Orman to me? Right now?"

"What? Why would you want to buy black devils like them?"

"David's right. After what's happened here today, neither of them will be worth their salt around this place any more. I know Dexter's not married, and I assume Orman isn't either."

"Right."

"I'll give you a thousand apiece. "

"A thousand?" Jonas gasped. "Web, you know those two will bring a good eighteen hundred apiece at an auction."

"This isn't an auction, and you've got the lives of a son and daughter at stake. Time's running out. Just agree and I'll take them off your hands this minute. I'll be back with a check to cover payment within an hour."

Jonas rubbed his chin, pondering the offer.

David spoke up. "Pa, what are you waiting for? Tell the man he's got a deal!"

Jonas threw a scornful look at his oldest son, then said to Steele, "All right, Web. They're yours for a thousand apiece. Take them and get them out of my sight."

Mabel sobbed a sigh of relief.

"Dexter! Orman!" called Steele.

"Yassuh?"

"Do you trust me?"

"We does," said Dexter.

"Then you'll believe me when I tell you I've just made a deal with Jonas. He's going to sell both of you to me right here and now."

"He is? You mean we can ride outta here with you and be yo' slaves from now on?"

"That's right. I can't give him a check to pay for you until I get back home. He'll have to draw up the papers while I'm gone, and we'll close the deal later this afternoon. But you will have to conduct yourselves from this moment on as if you are my slaves. Do you understand?"

"Yassuh!" replied Dexter.

"Suits me jus' fine!" came Orman's lilting voice.

"All right. Now, how many guns do you have in there?"

"Two, Massa Web."

"You wouldn't lie to me?"

"No, suh!"

"All right, throw them both out the window."

There was a brief pause, then the two revolvers sailed out the open window.

"Oh, God bless you, Web!" Mabel said with a quaking voice.

Steele gave her a compassionate smile, then called toward the shed, "Fine! Now, open the door and let Darrel and Melissa come out."

The shed door swung open, and neither slave could be seen as first Melissa then her younger brother emerged. Sobbing, Mabel ran toward them and Jonas followed. Daniel was next, with David and Chloe behind him. Mary Ann had left the porch and was close by. She quickly joined the group.

Exley breathed a curse and mumbled something under his breath. Mandrake looked on with interest.

The faces of the two slaves were barely visible at the window as they observed the family embracing Darrel and Melissa. When Jonas was sure they were unhurt, he returned to Web's side. Web waited until the tight-knit group had passed the overturned wagon on its way to the mansion, then said, "All right, boys. I want you to come out now."

"Massa Web?"

"Yes, Dexter?"

"If'n we belongs to you now, then Massa Jonas cain't hurt us, right?"

"Right. Tell them, Jonas."

Hart shuddered and clenched his jaw, looking hard at Steele.

"You backing out now?" Steele half-whispered.

"I'd like to," came the heated reply, also in a half-whisper.

"You're a man of your word, Jonas. Answer Dexter's question."

Looking toward the dark faces at the window of the shed, Jonas said with sand in his voice, "Web and I have each other's word on the sale. I'm not going to harm his slaves."

"Come on," said Steele. "I'll take you to my father's plantation."

With fear evident in their faces, Dexter and Orman emerged slowly from the shed and walked cautiously toward the overturned wagon.

Jonas gripped his wounded shoulder once more and set burning eyes on the slaves. "You two better thank your lucky stars Web Steele happened along. Otherwise, you'd have gotten a beating like you've never seen in your worst nightmares. And if you had harmed my children, you'd have died at the end of a rope!"

"They still oughtta be strung up, Jonas!" thundered Reed Exley. "These two have more than over-stepped their bounds, and the way I see it, they deserve to die! When word gets out that they pulled this on you, there'll be more incidents just like it all over this county! Letting them get by with it isn't right. They need to pay for what they've done!" Even as he spoke, Exley whipped out his revolver, swung it on the slaves, and fired twice.

TWO

The first shot struck Orman at the base of his throat. He made a gagging sound, threw both hands to the wound, and pitched to the ground head-first. The second shot hit Dexter on the left side, just under the armpit. He stopped, stiffened, and teetered for an instant, then fell on his back.

In the same instant the shots were fired, Web Steele bolted toward Reed Exley and toppled him with a flying tackle, knocking the wind from Exley's lungs. Exley rolled on the ground gasping for breath as Steele leaped to his feet. Bending over, Web sank strong fingers into Reed's shirt and jerked him to a standing position. Cocking his right arm, Web unleashed a sledgehammer blow that connected with Exley's jaw. Exley's head whipped sideways and he landed on his back, unconscious.

Jonas Hart looked toward the others, who stood dumbfounded, and said, "Dan and David, you two stay here. The rest of you get inside the house."

Jonas turned about to see Web kneeling beside Dexter. Glancing at the unconscious Exley, Jonas set his attention on the group of male slaves coming across the field, carrying garden tools and clubs. There was anger in their eyes. A steel band of fear tightened around his heart.

Unaware of the angry slaves, Steele looked up at Jonas and said, "Orman's dead, Jonas. The slug Dexter took is in his left side, but it's not too deep. I don't think it pierced his lung. I'll get him into my buggy and take him to the doctor."

David and Daniel drew up as Jonas, eyes fixed on the approaching mob of over thirty black men, stammered, "I...I don't think you'll get the chance, Web. We've got real trouble brewing."

Steele stood and set his gaze toward the oncoming slaves as Jonas said to his sons, "Boys, run to the house and get the rifles."

"That would be foolish," Web said.

"Well, what do you suggest?" Jonas blurted, panic evident in his voice.

"You're going to have to talk your way out of this. You try using guns, and they'll kill all of us, including your family and servants."

Web quickly turned back to Dexter and knelt beside him. He pulled his large bandanna from his hip pocket, wadded it into a ball, opened Dexter's shirt, and stuffed the bandanna next to the wound, using it as a compress to stay the flow of blood. Dexter looked at him with glazed eyes and tried to smile.

"You just hold on, Dexter," Web told him. "I'm going to take you to my doctor in Richmond."

Gritting his teeth in pain, Dexter said, "Massa Web, no Richmon' doctor will work on a lowly slave."

"Mine will," Steele said.

Web caught sight of Reed Exley out of the corner of his eye. Exley was sitting up, holding his jaw. At that moment, the fierce-eyed slaves drew up. Cletus, a big man in his early fifties, was two steps ahead of the others. He carried a length of broken tree limb in one hand. His deep booming voice cut a swath across the yard as he blared, "We saw the whole thing, Massa Jonas! We aims to see that nuthin' like this ever happens again! Is both them slaves dead?"

"Orman is," Hart replied shakily. "Dexter took a slug in his side, but I think he'll be okay."

Cletus glanced at Dexter, then glared at Jonas. "De Good Book say vengeance belong to de Lord," he said cryptically, "but fo' dis one time, maybe it belong to us blackies."

The words sent a chill through Jonas. "Now, Cletus," he said with strain in his voice, "any violence will only bring trouble down on all of your heads. You remember the slave revolt over in South Hampton County nearly thirty years ago. Almost a hundred slaves were hanged. It won't be any different in 1860 than it was then, Cletus. They'll hang you just as quick today as they hanged those rebellious slaves then."

Cletus showed his white teeth in an angry grimace. "Yeah, I know. But I remind you, nearly sixty whites died befo' those slaves was hanged."

Stiffening, Jonas countered, "Do you think those slaves thought it was worth it when they felt the nooses around their necks?"

A young slave who stood close to Cletus cut in, "None of us slaves minds dyin' if'n it'll stop you rich white plantation owners from bein' cruel to our black brothuhs."

"If'n we don' get some satisfaction right now, I say we start bashin' heads!" shouted another.

Raising their clubs and garden tools over their heads and shaking them in a threatening manner, the others began shouting their agreement.

Jonas looked fearfully at his sons. David said in a low tone, "Pa, you'd best swallow your pride and beg their forgiveness."

Jonas's features hardened. "This is ridiculous!" he hissed. "I bought and paid for these beasts! Why should I have to kowtow to them?"

Web was close enough to hear the exchange. The slaves were still shouting, their clamor building to a fevered pitch. Having dealt with slaves all of his adult life, Web knew they had held off attacking for a reason. They really did not want to shed Hart family blood, but they did want the cruelty to stop. They knew that to wipe out the Hart family would only bring white men from all over the county with blood in their eyes. They would hang for sure.

Web thought of what the young slave had said only moments before. *We don' mind dyin' if'n it'll stop you rich white plantation owners from bein' cruel to our black brothuhs.* He knew the issue here was Jonas Hart's cruelty to his slaves. Orman was dead, and Dexter was seriously wounded as a result of the beating Jonas had given both of them earlier in the day. This, along with Jonas's past mistreatment of many of them, had them ready to shed blood unless they received assurance it would stop. Jonas was too hard-headed and blinded by his ego to see the true picture.

Realizing the danger of delay, Steele left Dexter's side, brushed past Jonas and his sons, and stood within three steps of Cletus. Shouting above the angry voices, he cried, "Cletus, let me talk to you! Quiet them down!"

Cletus raised his empty hand shoulder high, and the noise stopped. "All right, Massa Web," he said levelly, "I's listenin'."

Web motioned for Jonas to join them, then said, "Cletus, I want you to tell Master Jonas why you didn't just storm in here and start bashing heads after you saw Dexter and Orman shot down. All of you are mad enough to crack every white man's skull in sight. Why did you stop when you reached us? You've all got something in your hands that could maim or kill us."

Jonas stepped up beside Steele. David and Daniel were close on his heels.

Cletus ran his palm across his eyes and said, "We's plenty mad 'bout Massa Jonas beatin' Dexter and Orman dis mo'nin', Massa Web. An' we don' blame them fo' tryin' to get away, even if they had to threaten Darrel and Melissa. Bein' beat on fo' runnin' out o' stren'th is wicked an' vile."

Jonas was still holding his revolver. He raised his good arm and sleeved away the sweat on his brow, feeling the pressure from Cletus's hard gaze.

Cletus went on. "We didn't pick up dese tools an' clubs till that Reed Exley over there shot our brothuhs down. De only one we really wants to bash is him."

Exley was standing close to Mandrake by the wagon. Hearing Cletus's threat, he set his eyes on his revolver, which lay near Jonas and his sons. He knew it was useless to try to reach it. The slaves would be on him before he got halfway. His mind was racing. How would he escape them? Could he make a run for it and reach his horse in time?

"So heah's what we wants, Massa Jonas," continued Cletus. "If'n you will promise us there'll be no mo' beatin's, an' de work load will be made lighter, we won't do you an' yo' fam'ly no harm. We'll go on workin' fo' you within reason. We knows de consequences if'n we revolt against you. We also knows if'n we jis' ran away, we'd have to go way up north to make a livin', an' some of us wouldn' make it that far. So—to answer Massa Web's question—we didn' barge in here an' start knockin' heads 'cause we really don' wanna do that. We jis' wants to be treated with kindness and respec'."

"An' we want that white animal who shot Dexter and Orman!" spoke up one of the slaves.

Reed Exley bolted for his horse, commanding Mandrake to follow. A half-dozen slaves ran after them, but the two men were on their horses and galloping away before they could reach them. A couple of the slaves threw their clubs at them in frustration.

The rest of the slaves shouted their hatred for Exley, saying he should die for what he had done. Cletus quieted them, "It's too late, now. He's gone and there's no way we can catch 'im. White man's law would never judge him for killin' a black man, so we'll have to fo'git about 'im."

While the slaves grumbled at Cletus's words, the big man said to Jonas, "What's yo' decision, Massa Jonas? Does we git decent treatment with no beatin's?"

It went against Jonas Hart's grain to have his own chattel lay down demands to him, but he knew the powder keg he was sitting on if he pushed them any further. "Okay, Cletus. From now on, I won't demand as much work from each slave, and I won't use the belt on any of you unless you deliberately provoke me. Fair enough?"

The slaves looked at their leader in silence, waiting for his reaction. Rubbing his chin, Cletus said, "You won' consider a man or woman's lim'tations provokin' you delib'rately?"

Jonas hated to be put in this position, but the circumstances offered him no choice. "No," he said, clearing his throat. "I'll take those limitations into consideration."

"All right," nodded Cletus. "That's all we aks. We'll take Orman, now, and bury 'im."

"Pa," David interjected, "didn't you have something else you wanted to say to these men?"

Knowing what David meant, Jonas squared his jaw and clipped, "No. That's all." With that, he hastened toward Web Steele, who was once again at Dexter's side. While the slaves picked up Orman's lifeless form and carried it away, Jonas stood over the wounded slave and asked, "He gonna make it?"

"I think so," Web replied without looking up. "The bleeding has nearly stopped. I'm no doctor, but I'd say the slug is caught in his rib cage. It'll take surgery to get it out, but young and healthy as he is, he should be all right."

Jonas looked over his shoulder to make sure the other slaves were out of earshot. Satisfied they were, he said gratingly, "Too bad."

"What do you mean?"

"Too bad he didn't die like Orman, that's what I mean. After what he put my kids through, he deserves to die!"

"So you're not accepting any blame in this at all, I take it. The whipping you gave them this morning wasn't wrong?"

"Not at all!" boomed Hart. "They got what they had coming!"

David overheard and sucked in his breath. "Pa, I don't understand you. I thought you were finally seeing that you've been expecting too much from our slaves…that you've been working them too hard."

"I had to make it look that way to appease them, but those black devils are just putting on an act. They could work a lot longer and a lot harder, and they know it. I'll find a way to get more out of them!"

David scowled at his father. "Well, don't expect me to do it. I'll have nothing to do with working them to death."

Jonas swore and banged a fist into a palm. Wincing from the pain in his shoulder, he gruffed, "You're sounding more like a stinking northern abolitionist all the time, David, and I don't like it! As long as you draw pay on this plantation, you'll make those lazy black beasts work like I tell you to!"

Father and son were the same height, and they were now nose-to-nose. Mabel was watching from the back porch of the mansion. When she saw them arguing, she headed toward them.

Jaw jutted stubbornly, David rasped, "I will not be a part of working them till they drop! Do you hear me, Pa? I will not!"

"They're not going to drop!" Jonas bit back. "Can't you see? They're pulling the wool over your eyes! You'll work them exactly as I tell you!"

"No I won't!"

"Jonas! David! Stop it right now!" Mabel shouted. "There's no reason for you two to be arguing like this."

Jonas's face was flushed with anger. Turning to his wife, he said, "It's time he learned to obey my orders, Mabel. He's too soft on the slaves, and he's got to see that. If he'll work them like I say, they'll get used to it, and we won't have any more trouble from them."

"Well," she said, "maybe David's way is best. I don't think we'd have seen what we saw today if you had let David do his job the way he sees fit."

Jonas eyed his wife dully and said, "You watch after the affairs of the house, Mabel, and I'll take care of running the plantation. This is between David and me. You go back to the house, now."

David patted her arm and said quietly, "Go on, Ma. There's no reason for you to get wedged between Pa and me."

Mabel's lower lip quivered and tears misted her eyes. Patting her son's cheek, she gave Jonas a sharp glare and walked away.

Jonas watched her for a few seconds, then turned back to David and said, "I don't want to hear any more out of you. When I say you'll work the slaves hard for sixteen hours a day, I mean for you to do just that. Do you understand me?"

David's voice was measured as he said, "I understand, yes. But I will not be a part of working them till they drop."

"They aren't gonna drop!" cried Jonas. "And if they do, it'll be an act. Their Maker gave them strong bodies because He intended for them to be slaves. You're just too soft-headed to see that."

"God never intended for anybody to be slaves," David protested. "You'll never convince me any different. Every man has a right to be free."

Daniel Hart was standing a few feet away. He swallowed hard when he saw the fury in his father's features. Jonas's cheeks were mottled and his eyes had turned the color of slate. "You don't belong here any more, David!" he bellowed. "You're through! Do you hear me? Through!"

Daniel jumped between them, strain showing on his face. "Pa, you don't mean that! David's your own son!"

Ignoring him, Jonas looked past him to David and growled, "I mean it! Get off this plantation!"

"Suits me fine!" retorted David. "Get somebody else to do your dirty work."

"Get off this property, David!" bawled Jonas. "Take your wife and get out!"

"I will!" shouted David, turning and walking toward the mansion. Over his shoulder, he warned, "You better not push those slaves any further than you already have. What you saw today from Cletus and the others is only the tip of the iceberg."

"Shut up!" snapped the irate father. "I don't need any of your stinking Yankee abolitionist advice. Just pack up and get out!"

Web Steele moved past Jonas, carrying Dexter in his arms, heading for his buggy.

"Wait a minute, Web," said Jonas, hurrying to flank him. "If you're taking him into Richmond to the doctor, when will you be back with your check?"

Daniel moved up to Web's other side as he headed toward the buggy without breaking stride. Dexter's head lay against his chest, his eyes closed and his mouth set against the pain.

Without turning to look at Jonas, Steele said, "It may be to-morrow. I'll stay with Dexter till I'm sure he's going to be okay."

"But you said you'd pay me today," argued Jonas.

"I ought to make you collect the thousand for Orman from Exley," said Steele as they drew up to the buggy.

"Oh, no you don't!" said Jonas. "You gave me your word that you'd pay me a thousand apiece for them. It wasn't my fault Reed shot them."

"It wasn't my fault, either," sighed Steele as he gently placed Dexter on the seat. "But since I'm a man of my word, I'll pay you the two thousand as soon as I can bring it to you." Finding it difficult to put Dexter in a comfortable position on the buggy seat, he turned to the younger Hart and said, "Daniel, I could use your help. Would you mind riding along with me and holding onto Dexter?"

"I'd be glad to," smiled Daniel. "Would...would you give me a couple minutes to tell my brother good-bye?"

"Sure...but hurry."

Jonas glared at Daniel as he ran toward the house, then said to Steele, "You could have asked me if it's all right for Daniel to ride into town with you."

Web had had more than enough of Jonas Hart for one day, but he kept his voice unruffled as he said, "Daniel's an adult. I didn't know he had to ask your permission."

Jonas bit his tongue to check the retort that flashed into his mind.

While he kept Dexter from falling from the seat, Web said, "Jonas, you haven't asked for my advice, but I'm going to give it to you anyhow. You ought to reconsider your firing of David. Decisions made in the heat of passion are usually foolish ones. If you don't reverse it, it'll—"

"Like you said," interrupted Jonas, "I haven't asked for your advice. So keep it to yourself."

Inside the mansion, the family and the servants were gathered around David and Chloe in the large kitchen. The women were weeping. David had one arm around his wife and the other around his mother when Daniel entered the room.

"Oh, Dan," sobbed Mabel, "I can't stand this. Your father is acting like a stubborn fool!"

Daniel took hold of her hand and said, "I know, Ma, but there's nothing any of us can do about it." Looking at his brother, he asked, "Where will you go?"

"Beverly."

Daniel knew that Chloe's parents lived in the western Virginia town of Beverly. Harvey Trench owned a successful clothing store, and over the past two years had made several offers to his son-in-law, asking him to come work for him. "You going to take your father-in-law up on his offer?"

"Yes," nodded David. "I didn't tell you that when Chloe and I visited there three weeks ago, Dad Trench added more to his offer. He knows of my growing aversion toward slavery and offered to make me a partner in the business. I'm going to take him up on it."

"Can't blame you," said Daniel. "I'm sure you'll be much happier."

"What about you?" asked David. "Pa will probably want you to take my job."

"I'll tell him I'm just not overseer material," replied the

younger brother. "I can't leave Ma and Pa, but I don't want the responsibility that you've had."

David smiled weakly and nodded.

Daniel quickly explained that he was going to ride to Richmond with Web and had to leave immediately. He embraced David and Chloe, saying he would try to come to Beverly soon and see them. Then he kissed his mother and hurried out of the house.

Web was waiting for Daniel in the buggy seat, supporting the wounded slave. Looking around for his father, Daniel asked, "Where'd Pa go?"

"Headed toward the slave shacks," replied Steele. "I tried to help him see that he was making a big mistake in letting David go, but he didn't appreciate my advice. Stomped off in that direction, muttering to himself."

With Daniel cradling Dexter in his arms, Web put the buggy in motion and headed down the shady lane to the road. He wanted to swing by the Ruffin place and tell Abby why he was late for their Saturday afternoon date, but he knew he had to get the wounded slave to the doctor in Richmond as soon as possible.

As the buggy rolled swiftly down the road toward town, Daniel said to the black man he held in his arms, "You'll be all right, Dexter. We'll have you to the doctor soon."

"Mm-hmm," responded Dexter, his pinched features revealing the pain he was experiencing. "I's glad Massa Web's doctuh will work on slaves. Lots of 'em won't."

"He'll have you fixed up good as new in no time," Web said. "When we get you to the Steele plantation, there are a couple of real pretty slave girls who'll be more than glad to nurse you back to health."

Dexter tried to smile. "Yassuh. I's jus' sorry I won't be able to work very good fo' a while, Massa Web."

"Don't you worry about it," said Web. "If Mr. Exley hadn't shot you, you'd be pulling your weight tomorrow."

"Dat's right," nodded Dexter. "No offense to Massa Daniel,

heah, but I's glad to get away from de Hart plantation."

Daniel said to Web, "What are you going to do about Exley?"

"I haven't decided yet," replied Web. "I could take him to court for destroying what belonged to me, but I may just deal with him myself."

"Will Mr. Ruffin punish him?"

"Nope. By the time I get there, Exley will have John Ruffin believing that what he did was right. It always works that way. In Mr. Ruffin's eyes, Exley can do no wrong."

Daniel was quiet for a few seconds, then he said, "I wish you didn't face having Reed Exley for your brother-in-law."

"Me too," grinned Web, "but I'd put up with anything to marry Abby."

"Well, in about eight months, she'll be your wife."

"I can hardly wait." After a pause, Web asked, "When are you going to pop the question to Lynne?"

Daniel cleared his throat. "Well, I...uh...I haven't quite decided yet. Since we've only been courting for three months, I feel I should give it a little more time."

"You are going to ask her, though?"

"Oh, yes! I'm head-over-heels for Lynne. I've never met a girl who rang bells in my heart like she does."

"You're not hesitant because marrying her will make Reed Exley your brother-in-law too, are you?"

"Not in the least. I can't stomach the man, but as you say, I'd put up with anything to marry Lynne."

Reed Exley and Mandrake galloped for a mile after reaching the road, then slowed their horses to a walk. As they rode toward the Ruffin plantation, Exley said, "Now, Mandrake, I don't want you telling anybody about what you saw me do back there. I'll make my explanation to Master John, and nothing else will be necessary. I don't want the rest of the slaves to even know about it. So keep your mouth shut. Understand?"

Mandrake was feeling good about the big bruise on Exley's

face. Deep inside, he was lauding Web Steele for putting it there. Aloud, he replied, "I undahstan', Massa Reed."

"I'm glad I took you along," said Exley. "You needed to see how I handled those two no-goods. If I'm crowded to it, I'll handle my slaves the same way. So you'd best remember what you saw today. If I get any kind of rebellion out of our slaves because of you, I'll not only shoot you, but I'll shoot them. Are you listening to what I'm saying?"

"Yassuh."

"Okay. So you'd better get the starch outta your pants and walk straight. If you show me any more resistance—even the slightest glimmer of it—I'll start by punishing Orchid for your sins."

Mandrake's mind ran to his beautiful wife. A cold chill washed over him. He would go crazy if Exley ever laid a hand on her.

"Am I getting the message across to you, black boy?" grunted Exley.

The deep hatred Mandrake felt toward Exley had grown this afternoon. He pictured himself strangling the life from the man. He knew Exley was capable of hurting or killing Orchid just to punish him. Keeping his eyes on the road ahead, he replied, "Yassuh. I got the message."

THREE

Beautiful Abby Ruffin sat on the long open porch of the Ruffin mansion, keeping a steady eye on the tree-lined lane that led to the road. Web Steele was late for their afternoon date, and it worried her. Web was always a little early for any and all engagements. Such deportment was indicative of his forceful and aggressive personality.

Abby had expected Web just about the time the sound of gunfire had erupted in the direction of the Steele plantation. She and her two sisters had been sewing baby clothes in the parlor when the firing began. Moments afterward, Reed and Mandrake rode at a gallop out of the yard. John Ruffin had entered the room to find his daughters collected at the window, watching Reed and the slave ride out.

Abby had expressed fear that the shots had come from the Steele plantation, but her father had calmed her quickly by saying the gunfire had come from much closer, perhaps from the neighboring Hart place. He explained to them that Reed had armed himself and was on his way to investigate.

The cool breeze that swept across the front of the mansion raised goose bumps on Abby's skin. Shuddering slightly, she lifted the shawl that lay beside her and wrapped it around her shoulders. The front door of the mansion opened and her two sisters joined her on the porch. Elizabeth, who was six months pregnant and weakened by her condition, sat down beside Abby and sighed. "No sign of him yet?"

"No," Abby sighed in return. "He should have been here forty minutes ago. It's not like Web to be late."

"Maybe he was on his way when those guns were fired and did like Reed," suggested Lynne. "Maybe he went to investigate."

Abby looked up at Lynne and smiled. "That's probably it, honey. I'm sure he'll be along pretty soon. I just hope he didn't get himself involved in some kind of trouble."

"I hope Reed didn't either," put in Elizabeth. "Papa seemed so sure the shots came from the Hart place. Reed is so brave and valiant. If there's a slave revolt at Hart's, he'll be right in the middle of it."

Abby felt her stomach flip. Reed Exley was anything but brave and valiant. He was arrogant and egotistical and wouldn't risk a fight unless he knew he had enough help around him to guarantee victory. Abby marveled at how blind her sister could be to what her no-good husband really was. She and Lynne exchanged furtive glances. Lynne didn't like Reed any more than Abby did.

At twenty-eight, Elizabeth was expecting her first child and had been experiencing difficulties since her third month. The family physician attributed the difficulties to her having her first baby so late in her twenties, but Abby and Lynne were certain Elizabeth's problems stemmed from the emotional stress Reed put on her. Of course Elizabeth would never admit to such a thing. Though Reed's mental cruelties kept her upset most of the time, Elizabeth did her best to conceal it. To hear her talk, Reed was a knight in shining armor.

Abby loved her older sister dearly, and wished she had shown better judgment in the man she picked for a husband. Of course, Papa John had done almost as much to ensure that Reed would become his son-in-law as Elizabeth had. Somehow, Reed had been able to wrap the old man around his little finger. The younger sisters had seen Reed for what he was the first time they met him. Their dear mother—God bless her memory—had seen through Reed, too, but her words of warning to John and Elizabeth had gone unheeded.

Elizabeth's hair was a mouse-brown, and she was quite plain. Abby did what she could to help her older sister, fixing her hair and helping her to use a little rouge on her face. With Abby's touch, Elizabeth was considered moderately pretty. She was tall and slender and, before she became pregnant, had very little shape to her figure.

Lynne, at twenty, was almost as tall as Elizabeth, but had a better figure and was more attractive. Her long hair was ash-blond, and she had the imagination and ability to style it in several different fashions. Her physical beauty and the bright spark of her personality had garnered many a would-be suitor. Lynne, however, was interested in only one man—Daniel Hart. She was living for the day when Daniel would ask her to be his wife.

Lynne moved around the bench where her sisters were and sat down on the edge of the porch. There was a worried look on her face as she said, "If Reed doesn't come back pretty soon, I'm going to ride over to the Hart place myself. I want to be sure Daniel is all right."

"I don't blame you, honey," smiled Abby. "If Web doesn't show up by just about the same time, I'm going with you."

"Might as well make it a threesome," spoke up Elizabeth. "I'm going, too."

"The two of us can do the investigating for you, sweetie," said Abby. "The one thing you don't need right now is excitement." She paused a few seconds, then added, "No sense in us getting all worked up over this situation yet. Let's give it at least another half hour."

Lynne agreed, letting her admiring gaze settle on the sister who was three years her senior. Lynne's heart carried an equal amount of love for both her sisters, but Abby had the edge on Elizabeth for admiration. Abby was the talented one of the three. She could sing and play the piano and the violin with the greatest of skill. She was bright, vivacious, warm, and compassionate. She was also the strongest of the Ruffin sisters. When their mother died almost two years ago, it was Abby who held her father and sisters together emotionally. She was the family's mainstay.

Lynne didn't mind admitting to herself that she also envied Abby for her striking beauty. Though Lynne knew she too was considered attractive, it was Abby whose elegant features turned the heads of men. Her sparkling eyes were the color of blue velvet, and her long auburn hair resembled the flame of a fiery sunset. Just under five-feet-three (some three to four inches shorter than her sisters) she carried an exquisite figure on a petite frame.

Though Abby had kept company with many young men from time to time, the only one she ever loved was the handsome, dashing son of Dudley Steele. Abby had fallen in love with Web when she was barely sixteen. Though they attended the same church and were often present at the same social functions, Web never seemed to notice her. Abby used to pray that he would notice her, and because he was five years older, she prayed that he wouldn't fall for another woman before it happened.

Abby's prayers were answered on December 4, 1858, when she was twenty-one. It was the day her mother was buried. People from miles around attended the funeral. It was at the graveside that Webster Steele set his eyes on Abby as she was comforting her father and sisters. He had known who she was for a long time, but on that day, he first took note that instead of looking at a mere girl, he was seeing a beautiful, mature young woman.

Web called on Abby a few days later and confessed that she had caught his eye at the graveside. A few weeks later, he also confessed that when she caught his eye, he fell in love with her. It was Abby's turn, then, to confess that she had fallen for him at sixteen, and had prayed that one day he would be hers. She was living now for the day they would be married.

Suddenly there was movement beneath the trees on the lane. Lynne jumped and cried, "It's a buggy! It must be Web."

Elizabeth remained seated, but Abby joined her younger sister at the edge of the porch, peering toward the horse and buggy that were winding along the lane in the dappled shade.

Seconds later, the buggy rounded the last curve, and they saw that the driver wore a stovepipe hat with bushy silver hair sticking out beneath the brim.

"Oh," said Abby, "it's Uncle Edmund."

"Well, girls," put in Elizabeth, "get ready to hear a lecture on politics, abolition, and how bad it's going to be if Abe Lincoln gets elected next month."

At sixty-six years of age, Edmund Ruffin was known in Virginia as the leading anti-abolitionist agitator in the state. A widower like his younger brother, John, Edmund lived comfortably off his two-thousand acre, eighty-slave plantation north of Richmond. When the slavery issue began to grow hot between politicians in the North and the South, he had spent much time and money in an effort to persuade the southern states to secede from the Union and form a Confederate nation of their own.

Edmund was tall and slender like John, but as a badge of rebellion against the North, he wore his silver hair so long that it rested on his narrow shoulders and fell almost to the middle of his back. He was a grim man who never laughed and seldom smiled. The slavery issue consumed him. His hatred for the abolitionists and his desire to see the South break away from the North was all he ever thought or talked about.

Edmund swung his buggy onto the circular drive in front of the mansion and drew rein. Without smiling, he greeted his nieces, alighted, and tied the reins to one of the hitching posts that were provided for guests.

As he stepped onto the porch, Abby said, "To what do we owe this visit, Uncle?"

Edmund removed his hat, arched his bushy eyebrows, and replied, "Your father invited me for supper this evening. Didn't he tell you?"

"No," smiled Abby, "but it's nice to see you."

"I came early so as to spend some time with John," said Edmund. "Is he about?"

"He's in the library, Uncle Edmund," said Lynne. "You can go on in."

At that instant, Elizabeth stood and said excitedly, "Reed is here!"

Edmund looked on as the three sisters moved to the edge of the porch, eyes fixed on Reed Exley and Mandrake as they trotted up the lane toward the mansion. As they reined in near Edmund's buggy, Elizabeth called out, "Reed, we heard more shots after you left. Were they coming from the Hart place?"

"Yes," replied Exley, dismounting.

"What happened?"

"Just a minute, Elizabeth," Reed said tartly, "you can listen and learn while I talk to your father."

As always, Elizabeth tried not to show that her husband's curt mannerisms hurt her. Abby and Lynne exchanged glances, both want-ing to slap Reed's mouth for the way he spoke to their sister.

Exley handed the reins to Mandrake, who remained mounted, and said something in a low tone. The handsome young slave nod-ded, then rode toward the barn, leading Exley's horse.

Edmund joined the women at the top of the steps as Reed began to mount them. "What's this about shots?" he asked.

"Come on in, Edmund," Exley clipped, shoving his way past the women and heading for the door. "You can listen also while I tell John."

Assuming John Ruffin to be in the library—where he spent a good deal of his time—Exley headed swiftly down the hall in that direction. Elizabeth's condition made it difficult for her to keep up. Her sisters stayed by her side, knowing it would be useless to ask Reed to slow down. Edmund walked ahead of them.

Abby called out, "Reed, did you happen to see Web on the road?"

"Not on the road," he replied over his shoulder, "but he was at the Hart place before I got there."

"Is he all right?"

"Yes."

"Is he still there?"

"I'm not sure, Abby." His tone was much kinder toward her than the one he had used on Elizabeth.

"What do you mean?" queried Abby.

"I mean, he may have taken a wounded slave into town to a doctor."

Satisfied that Web was in no danger, Abby told herself she would have to wait to learn any more from Reed.

Since there had been shots fired at the Hart place, Lynne was concerned about Daniel but refrained from asking Reed about him. Certainly he would have told her if anything had happened to Daniel.

Exley reached the door of the library and tapped lightly, saying, "John, may I see you? It's important."

"Come in," came John Ruffin's reply.

Exley opened the door and entered the library.

John was on his feet, holding a book in his hand. Concern was etched on his face as he asked, "Did you find out what the shooting was all about?"

"Yes, I did," nodded Exley, "and I want to tell you about it."

John looked past his son-in-law to see his daughters and Edmund filing through the door. Edmund had paused in the hall to allow the women to enter first.

"We want to hear it too, Papa," said Elizabeth, holding her midsection and making her way toward an overstuffed chair.

The sun had set and the western sky was a deep purple as Web Steele hauled his vehicle to a stop next to Edmund Ruffin's horse and buggy. He wondered what new avenue of attack on the abolitionists the old boy had come up with this time. It seemed he always had something new cooking over his flame of hatred for Northerners.

Web used the heavy knocker at the front door of the mansion, and it took only seconds for the butler to answer. Charles was in his late fifties, and like Uncle Edmund, never laughed and seldom smiled. Managing a weak grin, he said, "Good evening, Mr. Web. The family is just beginning their meal in the dining room."

"I'm sorry to arrive at such an inconvenient time, Charles," said Web, "but circumstances prevailed this afternoon. If I could just see Miss Abby for a moment, I—"

"Web!" came Abby's voice as she rushed into the entry way. "Come in, darling."

Web removed his hat and stepped in, allowing Charles to close the door. Charles quickly disappeared as Abby raised up on her tiptoes and planted a soft kiss on Web's lips.

Gripping his upper arms, she said, "Reed told us what happened at the Hart place. How awful! Did you take the wounded one to the doctor?"

"Yes, that's why I'm so late getting here. I...I'm sorry we missed our Saturday afternoon ride. I was just passing the Hart gate when the first shot was fired. There was nothing I could do but plunge in there and see if I could help."

"I understand," she said softly. "I'm just so thankful nothing happened to you."

"Did Reed tell your father about it?"

"Yes. He told all of us, including Uncle Edmund."

"Did he tell you that he shot the two slaves after they had thrown down their guns?"

Abby looked at Web with surprise. "I don't recall him saying they were unarmed when he shot them."

"That figures," Web said. "I wonder just how much truth you got."

"Well, if it's typical Reed Exley," she said, "the way he told it would be about half true."

"Did he tell you that before he opened fire on them, I had agreed to buy them from Jonas?"

"No."

"That figures, too."

"You mean Reed shot them, knowing they were to be your slaves?"

"Yes."

"And you're under obligation to pay Jonas even though one is dead and the other is wounded?"

"Since I'm a man of my word, I am, yes."

"Is the wounded one going to be all right?"

"Doc Simmons says he'll be fine, but it'll be about three months before he's able to do a good day's work."

"Well, I'm glad that you won't lose your money on him."

A stony look came over Web's black eyes. "I don't plan on losing the money on the dead one, either. Mr. Exley's going to pay me for killing him."

"Knowing him, that may be difficult."

"I have no doubt it will."

"I hope this doesn't cause a problem between you and Papa. You know how he is about Reed."

"I'll talk to Reed privately about it, honey," Web said quietly. "Your dad won't have to be involved. I don't expect it to come out of Ruffin money. It's going to come out of Reed's own pocket."

"I suppose what Reed told us about his heroics was a lie, too."

"Heroics?"

"Yes. The way he told it, the two slaves were holding Darrel and Melissa hostage in the tool shed and were threatening to kill them. It was his sharpshooting that dropped the slaves so the kids could escape."

Shaking his head, Web chuckled dryly, "Boy, is that a lie! Dexter and Orman had already let the kids go and thrown their guns out. On my word that I was buying them and Jonas wouldn't harm them, they came out of the shed. It was then that Exley shot them."

"Oh, my," Abby sighed. "He didn't tell it like that at all."

"Of course not. He's got to make himself look like the hero. Did he explain the bruise on his face?"

"He told us that you put it there. He said you were angry because he had handled a situation you couldn't take care of, so you hit him. I knew you probably hit him, but that it had to be for a different reason than that."

"When he opened fire on those two slaves, I tackled him to keep him from firing any more shots. I was so angry at him I punched him hard—and it felt real good, too."

"I've dreamed of belting him a few times myself," Abby snickered. "I'm sure it did feel good. Come on. I'll have Harriet set another place at the table. We've just begun eating."

"Oh, I'd better not," said Web. "You've got Uncle Edmund here. I don't want to barge in."

"You're not barging in," Abby assured him. "After all, you're practically family."

Folding her in his arms, he breathed, "Yeah! Isn't that the truth?"

After a long, tender kiss, Web said, "I *would* like to spend a little more time with you. You're sure it's all right if I stay for supper?"

"Of course," she giggled, taking him by the hand and leading him down the hallway toward the dining room.

They could hear Uncle Edmund ranting about the abolitionists as they drew near the door. He cut it short as the handsome young couple entered the room. Elizabeth and Lynne greeted Web warmly as Abby called toward the kitchen for Harriet to set an additional place at the table. Edmund saluted him without smiling, and Reed gave him a cold look. John—upset that Web had hit Reed—mumbled a less-than-enthusiastic welcome. Abby noticed it and flushed with anger.

The place was set, putting Web next to Abby and directly across from the Exleys. John sat at the head of the long table, and Edmund at the end. While food was passed and Web was loading his plate, Edmund picked up where he had left off. "Yes, sir," he said, "there's real trouble on the way. We're gonna have a fight between the North and the South as sure as shootin'. And I say, let it come."

"My sentiments exactly, Ed," nodded John. "I'm sick and tired of those pious northerners trying to make us feel guilty because we have slave labor. Just let them come down here and try to make a profit on cotton while at the same time paying all their workers. It can't be done."

"Best thing that can ever happen in this country is secession," grunted Edmund. "We don't need those yahoos butting into our business. That's why I'm voting for Abe Lincoln."

Everyone at the table seemed shocked. Web set curious eyes on Abby's uncle and said, "Pardon me, sir, but did I hear you right? I've heard you call Abe Lincoln 'that black Republican.' You're going to vote for him?"

"Of course," nodded Edmund.

"But I don't understand," said Web, picking up his fork while staring at the old man. "Why would you vote for a man you despise?"

"Simple," said Edmund, leaning on his elbows. "If Lincoln's elected, there's no doubt in my mind that South Carolina will pull out of the Union. They're poised on the edge of secession at this minute. All it'll take to push them over the edge is for Lincoln to be elected. When South Carolina secedes, the rest of the southern states will follow. We'll have our own government, our own president, and our own congress. We won't have to put up with those rooster-tail Yankees anymore. We can get on with our lives as God intended."

"That's something I've been thinking a lot about lately," Web said.

"What's that?"

"Whether God intended for one man to own another."

Reed looked at his future brother-in-law as if he had just turned green. "That's a fine thing for a southern plantation owner's son to say," he growled. "You're building a fortune by owning and working black people so you and Abby can get married, and you don't know if God intended for you to do it?"

"Of course God intended it," said Edmund. "He made 'em black, didn't He?"

"He made them black," replied Web, "but why do we take it to mean that He meant for white people to make chattel of them?"

"You'd better not let your father hear you talking this way, Web," spoke up John Ruffin. "He might not take to it very well."

"I've already talked to him about it," countered Web.

"Oh?" said John, looking surprised. "And how did he take it?"

"He's not upset. I haven't forsaken my family's age-old position on slavery. All I said was that I've been thinking a lot about it. Dad doesn't try to do my thinking for me. And there's one thing he and I absolutely agree on."

"What's that?" asked John.

"That since we own slaves, we will treat them like human beings. We keep in mind that they have limitations just like we do, and that they have feelings just like we do."

"Umm," put in Edmund. "That kind of thinking can get you into a lot of trouble. You start being soft with 'em, they'll take advantage of you. If they think they can pull the wool over your eyes, they'll act like they're sick when they're not, and they'll put on like they're just plumb tuckered out when there's plenty of work left in 'em."

"Yeah," interjected Exley. "You give 'em an inch and they'll take a mile. That's the problem Jonas Hart faced today because David has been too soft on those black beasts. Jonas tries to fix the problem by applying some discipline to a couple of real rebellious ones, and they take his kids hostage."

"I'm glad you brought the subject up, Reed," said Web, fixing the man with a hard stare. "I noticed that you turned tail and ran like a scared rabbit when that bunch of slaves decided they wanted to get their hands on you for murdering Orman. What you did could have gotten Jonas and his whole family killed, not to mention myself. I had to do some tall talking to get them calmed down."

"Wait a minute, Web," said John, pointing a finger at him. "It isn't exactly murder when two men are holding guns on a couple of innocent young people and a sharpshooter puts some hot lead in them."

"I agree, but Dexter and Orman were not holding guns on

Darrel and Melissa when Reed shot them. They had let the kids go at my word that they would not be punished, and had thrown their guns out before they came through the door of the shed."

Abby smiled to herself.

John shot a glance at Reed, then looked back at Web and said, "You aren't telling it like Reed did."

"You have that correct, sir," nodded Web. "Reed's lying."

Exley stiffened in his chair and was about to speak when John beat him to it. "Wait a minute!" snapped John. "Why would Jonas just stand there and let you give them your word that they wouldn't be punished for what they'd done?"

"He did that because he had agreed to sell them to me for a thousand dollars apiece. The deal was clinched then and there, and Jonas himself told Dexter and Orman that as far as he was concerned, they belonged to me and would not be punished."

Looking at his son-in-law, John said, "Reed, this isn't the way you told it to us a little while ago."

"Aw, he's lying to make himself look good," Exley said crustily.

"Am I?" demanded Web. "Tell you what—you sit tight while I drive over to the Hart place and bring Jonas back with me. You can tell your story to Mr. Ruffin in front of Jonas. I could bring Daniel along as an extra witness, too."

Exley's face blanched. Abby elbowed Lynne, who was seated next to her. Lynne returned the gesture.

Elizabeth turned and faced her husband. Uncle Edmund looked on impassively.

John said, "Let's get to the bottom of this, Reed. As soon as we finish eating, let's have Web go bring both Daniel and Jonas." The very tone of John's voice showed that he believed Reed's version of the story and was eager to call Web's hand.

Reed knew that Jonas and Daniel would verify Web's words. He glanced at Elizabeth. She was watching him intently, her eyes question marks. His scalp tingled and he could feel cold sweat at his hairline.

Exley hated Web for exposing him as a liar. It would be a pleasure to kill him. Thoughts were racing through his mind. The family was looking on, and his father-in-law was waiting for him to agree to settle the matter. There was only one way to save face, and Exley took it. Clearing his throat, he said, "John, I haven't exactly been up front about this. Actually, I shot those two black scum-buckets after they had thrown down their guns. But I had to. You know how word spreads in this county. By Web's buying them like he did, they were going to get away with their crime. If this got out to all the other slaves in the county, we would have a massive revolt on our hands. Others would try the same thing against their masters...including ours."

John Ruffin smiled, eyed his son-in-law warmly, and said, "Well, Reed, I wish you had told me the truth to begin with, but I can see why you reacted as you did. You're right. If those two had gotten away with their crime, it would give reason for slaves all over to try the same thing. That settles it for me. You did the right thing."

Anger was mounting steadily within Web Steele and it showed on his face. As always, Reed was able to manipulate Papa John into his way of thinking and make himself look good.

Abby sensed Web's rising anger and laid a hand on his forearm, squeezing it slightly. Web patted her hand and said to the plantation owner, "Mr. Ruffin, I realize I'm not part of this family yet, and I don't mean to cause trouble...but those two slaves had been belt-whipped by Jonas until they bled. According to David, their only offense was that they had been worked to the point of exhaustion, and when Jonas wanted more from them, they couldn't do it. This type of thing has been happening on the Hart plantation for quite some time. Dexter and Orman had simply come to the place where they couldn't stand it any longer. I understood this, and so did David. After going as far as they did to gain their freedom, it was apparent that Dexter and Orman would no longer fit in on the Hart plantation, so to avert a tragedy, I offered to buy them then and there. It would have worked, and everything would have been fine, if Reed hadn't shot them down."

John Ruffin was quite fond of Web Steele and was happy that Abby was going to bring him into the family. For Abby's sake, he wanted to keep peace. Smiling at Web, he said calmly, "I'm sure you were doing what you thought was best, Web, and I admire you for it. What's done is done, so why don't we just forget it and talk about other things?"

Web got a hold on his temper and nodded quietly. Turning to Reed , he said, "When supper's over, I want a word with you in private."

Exley had a cup of coffee in his hand, and was staring icily at Web over the rim. Web met his gaze and held it. After a long moment, Exley broke the spell and looked away.

FOUR

There was a brief lull in the conversation at the Ruffin table. Then Uncle Edmund launched into his condemnation of the "underground railroad" that was helping runaway slaves elude capture by their southern owners. Edmund lauded the Fugitive Slave Law that placed the full power of the federal government behind efforts to capture escaped slaves. He then began a verbal attack on the touring troupes that were traveling the North and performing a play based on Harriet Beecher Stowe's book, *Uncle Tom's Cabin*. The book, published eight years previously, was the ultimate piece of abolitionist propaganda. It personalized the scandal of slavery and pictured Southern society as evil. By 1860, the book had sold over a million copies.

Edmund's temper flared even more as he told how Mrs. Stowe's book had poisoned Northerners' minds with wickedly contrived rhetoric depicting the inhuman suffering of Uncle Tom, Eliza, and Little Eva at the hands of the vile slave overseer, Simon Legree. The play was having an even greater effect, tugging at the heartstrings of observers who had been previously unmoved by outspoken abolitionists. From that subject, Edmund took a bead on the upcoming presidential election, repeating his intention to vote for Abraham Lincoln.

When the meal was finished, Web leaned close to Abby and said, "Can we take a little stroll after I talk to Reed?"

"Sure," she smiled, "but try not to punch him again."

"That'll be up to him," he replied. Looking across the table, he said, "Reed, I'd like to have our little talk now."

John's face showed concern. "Web," he said cautiously, "you put one bruise on Reed today. I hope you're not planning to—"

"Smack him again?" cut in Steele. "Sir, Mr. Exley got himself punched today because he opened fire on two unarmed human beings. Unless he gets violent while we're having our little chat, he'll not feel my fist."

"Maybe you should have someone with you," suggested Edmund.

"No, sir," replied Web, shaking his head. "This is private business between Mr. Exley and myself." Rising, he said, "We can talk out on the front porch, Reed."

Elizabeth asked her husband what Web wanted to talk to him about. Pushing his chair back and rising to his feet, Reed said, "I have no idea, but I'm about to find out."

Under the gaze of everyone at the table, Web gestured for Exley to go ahead of him, then followed the shorter man down the hallway to the entry way and out onto the porch. Charles had fired two lanterns that hung on either side of the door. The combined light cast an orange glow on the porch.

When Web closed the door, Exley turned on him and snapped, "Okay, what's this private little talk supposed to be about?"

"The thousand dollars you owe me," Web replied bluntly.

"What are you talking about? I don't owe you any thousand dollars."

"You heard me make a deal with Jonas to pay him a thousand apiece for Dexter and Orman. You killed Orman, leaving me to pay for a dead slave. You owe me Orman's price. I want it, and I want it now. I mean to give Jonas that much of his money on my way home."

"I'll have to talk to John about it before I can pay you," rasped Exley. "He may not want Ruffin money going for a 'dead horse' as they say."

Steele's voice hit him like the flat of an ax. "I'm not talking about Ruffin money, I'm talking about Exley money. John Ruffin didn't kill Orman. You did."

"You're outta your mind!" Reed gusted. "I ain't payin' you nothin'!"

"You'll come up with the thousand right now or so help me, I'll hog-tie you and take you to the Hart place and plant you on the doorstep of Cletus's shack. You know who Cletus is, don't you?"

Exley's breathing was coming in short spurts. He burned Steele with fiery eyes, but did not reply.

"Don't look at me like that," warned Steele. "I mean what I say. Cletus will tear you limb from limb if you refuse."

Exley ran a dry tongue over equally dry lips. He studied Web's resolute face. Reed knew he would be at the mercy of the huge black slave and his black brothers this very night if he refused Web's demand. Exley was tough and good with his fists, but he knew he was no match for the powerful man who stood before him. Steele could back up his threat.

Resigning himself to the inevitable, Exley licked his lips again and said, "I don't have that much cash."

"A check will do. Make it to Jonas. The kind of pay you get, I have no doubt it will clear the bank. If it doesn't, then I'll take you for a little visit to see Cletus."

Exley opened the door, telling Steele he would return shortly. It took him less than five minutes to go to his and Elizabeth's quarters on the third floor of the mansion and return with a check made out to Jonas Hart for the correct amount. When Web folded it and placed it in his shirt pocket, Exley said, "You know, I'm really sorry that you're gonna become part of this family. Too bad Abby doesn't have better taste."

Steele regarded him coldly. "I don't like you, either. Now excuse me. I've got a date to take a walk with that woman who has such bad taste."

Moments later a pale moon looked down on Web Steele and Abby Ruffin as they walked arm-in-arm beneath the towering trees along the lane that led to the road. A slight breeze was blowing and leaves were fluttering to the ground around them. The air had a bite to it. Abby used her free hand to tug at the collar of her coat and said, "Did you have any success?"

Patting his shirt pocket, Web replied, "Yes'm. Your kind and sweet brother-in-law wrote out a check to Jonas Hart for a thousand dollars."

"In protest, of course."

"Of course."

Neither one spoke for a long moment, then Abby said, "Web, I'm worried."

"About what, sweetheart?"

"This secession talk. While you were on the porch with Reed, Uncle Edmund said he thinks there'll be bloodshed before it's settled…a lot of bloodshed. Civil war."

"Could be," nodded Web. "I sure hope not. An awful thing, civil war. So many families have people on both sides of the issue. Brothers will be shooting at brothers, cousins at cousins…even fathers and sons fighting on opposite sides. Horrible thing."

"Do you think Mr. Lincoln will be elected?"

"Hard to say, honey. Mr. Douglas has a lot of people behind him. And so do the men running on the other tickets. If Lincoln gets elected, it'll be by a small margin."

"Small or large, it won't make any difference. If he gets in the White House, it's going to light the fuse. At least Uncle Edmund seems sure of it."

"He's not the only one," mused Web. "Most of the political experts say the same thing."

Abby stopped, released her hold on his arm, and looked up at him in the pale light. "Oh, Web," she said with a shudder in her voice, "if war comes, you will have to fight, won't you?"

"I suppose so."

Tears filmed her eyes. "I...I can't bear the thought of you having to go into battle. If...if something happened to you, I—"

"Hey, wait a minute," Web said, taking her in his arms. "Let's not borrow trouble. Maybe the experts are wrong. Maybe there won't be a war, after all."

Abby tilted her face toward his. The tears spilled down her cheeks, turning silver in the moonlight. Web cupped her face in his hands and wiped her cheeks with his thumbs. Worry sharpened the rounded lines of her beautiful face. "I'm sorry," she said in a half-whisper. "It's just...that I love you. I can't bear the thought of watching you march off to some battlefield, knowing that...that you might never come back to me."

"I love you the same way, darling," Web said softly. "I hate the thought of such a thing, too. Let's just take our lives a day at a time and not let the possibility of war ruin our times together. Okay?"

Abby smiled and nodded. Sniffing, she said, "Okay."

They were standing where the trees were far apart and the silvery spray from the night sky was dancing in her hair and highlighting the rich loveliness of her features. Their eyes locked in a gaze of love, and an electric spark of emotion leaped between them.

Suddenly Abby's arms were about his neck, pulling his head down. Their lips molded in a velvet kiss that momentarily swept them from a care-filled world to a carefree paradise of love. Web held her tight for a few seconds, then kissed the tip of her nose and said, "We'd better get back. I've got to deliver this check to Jonas before he goes to bed."

Abby nodded and held tight to his arm as they headed down the lane toward the mansion.

Election day in 1860 was on Tuesday, November 6. The Republican candidate, Abraham Lincoln, was at his Springfield, Illinois, home that evening, awaiting the results. His family and a few friends sat in the parlor with him. A young neighbor boy had volunteered to be Mr. Lincoln's runner between the house and the telegraph office, which was only a short distance away.

By eight o'clock that night, the telegraph reported that Illinois, which had gone Democrat in the 1856 election, had gone Republican. Later, they learned that the neighboring state of Indiana had followed suit. Soon came a flood of Republican victories from other northern states. Before midnight, Pennsylvania—home of the present president, Democrat James Buchanan—fell into the Republican column.

Just after midnight the big news came that New York, the state with the largest electoral vote in the nation, had gone Republican. Abraham Lincoln's election was now certain.

The citizens of Springfield went wild. Bands played. There was dancing in the streets. Firecrackers were set off. The president-elect walked a few blocks with his family and friends to the Republican headquarters for a victory rally. The elated crowd sang to Mr. Lincoln, ending each song with cheers and applause. Among his well-wishers were people who had voted for his main rival, Northern Democrat Stephen Douglas, for Abraham Lincoln had failed to carry his own county.

Late in the afternoon on November 7, when the final returns were at last recorded, the electoral vote reflected with appalling accuracy the sectional split within the country. Lincoln had carried every free state except New Jersey, which divided its electoral vote evenly between Lincoln and Douglas. South of the Mason-Dixon line, Lincoln carried nothing. Many southern states had not even placed his name on the ballot.

Tennessean John Bell, the Whig candidate, had captured Virginia, Kentucky, and Tennessee. The rest of the South went solidly for Southern Democrat John Breckinridge. Lincoln, with 180 electoral votes, had won the majority and would be the next man in the White House.

The popular vote, however, showed the proverbial tightwire that the new man in the Oval Office would have to walk. The combined opposition outpolled Lincoln by almost a million votes. Even in the free states, his total majority was under 300,000. He would assume office with only a tenuous hold on the people of his own section of the country.

Arrayed against Lincoln were the seven states of the deep South, and there was little doubt that if secession came, the four states of the upper South would join them. No matter how the border states had voted, no one could predict which side they would take in the event of a Southern secession.

By December 1, the pendulum in the United States was swinging toward just such a secession. In a effort to keep it from happening, a committee of thirteen senators held an emergency meeting. Their mission: to reconcile the South and salvage the Union. Led by Senator John J. Crittenden of Kentucky, the committee put forth a proposal to reestablish the old Missouri Compromise line and extend it all the way to the Pacific coast, permitting slavery in the territories south of a fixed and permanent latitude. Along with this compromise to appease Southerners, the committee also attempted to mollify Northern sentiment by strengthening the Fugitive Slave Law, and to make both amendments unrepealable and unamendable for all time.

The special senate committee hoped to have the plan adopted by Congress and then put to a referendum. It was killed, however, by the Republicans in Congress, who opposed it bitterly.

Meanwhile, the South was reacting vigorously to the election of the despised "black Republican," Abraham Lincoln. Aging Edmund Ruffin, the leading secessionist provocateur, was traveling from city to city, holding rallies and giving loud, agitating speeches that whipped up Southern passions and patriotism. The flames of rebellion against the Union were being driven and enlarged by the winds of Ruffin's powerful, persuasive, and prolific words.

Dark, ominous clouds filled the sky over Richmond, Virginia, on December 12, 1860. A storm was on its way, sending a raw, biting wind through the town.

Christmas shoppers gripped their hats, bending their heads against the wind. In spite of the cold and the impending storm, the holiday season was in full swing. Shoppers greeted each other cheerfully on the streets and in the stores.

Up and down the main street of Richmond's business district, saddled horses tethered to hitch rails laid their ears back and turned their rumps windward, while those hitched to vehicles stomped their hooves and fought their bits. Naked trees swayed in the wind, their jagged branches resembling skeletal hands against the dull-gray sky.

Webster Steele and Abby Ruffin emerged from Poindexter's Dry Goods Store and moved briskly down the boardwalk. Web's arms were full of packages. Abby held onto her wide-brimmed hat and labored to keep up with him, taking two strides for every one of his.

"Hey, Goliath!" she said, squinting against the bite of the wind. "Slow down, will you? Not everyone's as long-legged as you!"

Grinning, Web eased his pace and replied, "Sorry. I forgot."

Nudging him playfully with an elbow, Abby said, "I hope you won't forget on our wedding day! After we're pronounced husband and wife, we're supposed to walk down the aisle and out the door *together*. It'll look sort of funny if you pass through the door ahead of me!"

Web laughed, his breath forming a small cloud in the frigid air. "Never fear, my love. I'll remember. When we're married, I'll stick so close to you, you'll think we're Siamese twins!"

A coldness swept over Abby that came from the thought that gripped her, and not from the icy wind. *Unless you have to put on a uniform and fight the Yankees.*

They greeted friends and acquaintances along the boardwalk and finally reached the spot where Web's horse and buggy waited at the rail. The animal snorted at the sight of him and bobbed its head. Leaving Abby on the walk, Web moved to the rear of the buggy, juggled the packages while he opened the lid of the box, and placed them inside. Returning to his beautiful bride-to-be, he smiled, took her gloved hand in his, and said, "Okay, Miss Ruffin, how about lunch?"

"I'd love it," she smiled in return. "Especially if it comes with a bucket or two of piping hot coffee. I think my blood is icing up!"

It was nearly one o'clock, and the lunch crowd was thinning out as the happy couple entered the welcomed warmth of the Blue Ridge Café. Ralph Talbot, the café's owner, greeted them from behind the counter and said, "What are we having today? A family reunion?"

Web stared at him quizzically. "What do you mean?"

Pointing across the room with his chin, Talbot said, "Over there."

Web and Abby followed the direction he was pointing and saw Daniel Hart and Lynne Ruffin seated at a table. Both were smiling at them. Daniel rose from his chair and motioned for Web and Abby to join them.

"We don't want to butt in," grinned Web.

"You're not butting in," replied Daniel. "We just got here ourselves and are about to order. We'd love to have you sit with us."

"Only if you let me pay the bill," Web insisted.

Grinning broadly, Daniel hunched his shoulders and said, "Far be it from me to pass up a free lunch."

Web helped Abby shed her coat and placed it on a wall peg nearby. He hung his own coat over it, then placed his hat on top. Web seated Abby, then sat down opposite her.

To her sister, Abby said, "You didn't tell me you were coming to town today."

"I didn't know it at the time Web picked you up," responded Lynne. "Daniel showed up about half an hour later and asked if I wanted to go Christmas shopping."

"What'd you buy me?" joked Web.

"Nothing," giggled Lynne. "You've been a bad boy."

Shrugging, Web said, "Can't argue with that, but I wish Abby hadn't tattled on me."

The foursome had a good laugh, then gave their order to the waitress.

While they drank steaming coffee, Daniel said to Web, "Lynne tells me that Dexter is doing all right."

"Sure is. He's not up to a full day's work yet, but he's doing fine." Web paused, then asked, "What do you hear from David and Chloe?"

Daniel's face went grim, and Lynne patted his hand tenderly. "Well, they won't send any mail to us because of Pa's anger toward them, but once in a while they get a letter to us through my Aunt Althea here in town. She's Ma's sister. Last we heard, which was about three weeks ago, they were doing fine. David's quite happy working with his father-in-law, and Chloe's glad to be close to her family. Chloe's the one who does the writing. She said there's a lot of talk in western Virginia about secession. Folks over there are eager to pull away from the Union."

"Same as here," Abby interjected glumly. "I'm so afraid there's going to be a civil war."

"Lynne tells me Uncle Edmund is eating fire over it," said Daniel.

"That's putting it mildly," said Abby. "Uncle Edmund should have been a preacher. He sure knows how to sway a crowd. He's been traveling all over the South, firing people up against the Union. He predicts that South Carolina will secede before the first of the new year."

"He really wants to see a war come, doesn't he?" said Daniel.

"Yes," nodded Abby. "In the worst way. As old as he is, he'll still be right there in the middle of it. He hates Yankees and everything they stand for. He'd probably be the happiest man in the world if he could fire the first shot."

"Well, I don't exactly hate Yankees," said Daniel, "but if war comes, I'll sure be willing to do my part."

Lynne blanched. Taking hold of Daniel's hand across the table, she whimpered, "I don't want you fighting in a war...any war. I can't stand the thought of you facing enemy guns and possibly getting killed."

"Lots of men go to war and come back, Lynne," Daniel replied, squeezing her hand. "If I have to go...will you wait for me? I mean...will you stay my girl even if other fellows come around?"

Tears filled Lynne's eyes. "Yes, Daniel. Yes, I'll always be your girl, and more than that if you want me."

"Maybe Abby and I should sit at another table," suggested Web.

"Oh, no," Daniel objected. "You two are family. Well, that is, Abby is. You will be pretty soon, Web. It's no secret that Lynne and I are very fond of each other. In fact, we've been just on the verge...that is, I've been just on the verge of telling her that I love her and want to ask for her hand in marriage once I get her father's permission."

"Oh, Daniel!" squealed Lynne, tears gushing. "I love you, too! And, yes, I'll marry you. Papa thinks the world of you. I know he'll give his blessing to our marriage."

"Well, Abby," sighed Web, "it looks like you and I just sat in on an engagement. Tentatively, I mean."

"Tentatively only until I can talk to Mr. Ruffin and buy a ring," laughed Daniel.

"It's as good as done, then," put in Abby. "Papa's already told me that he hopes you and Lynne will fall in love and get married. He really does think a lot of you, Daniel."

"I'm glad to hear that," said young Hart. "I'll be very proud to be related to the Ruffins. Mr. Ruffin is already like a second father to me, and I sure do love Elizabeth, and—" Daniel faltered in midsentence at the name that flashed into his mind.

Abby read it in his eyes and voiced the name for him. "Reed?"

"Yeah," he said dully. "Reed."

"Reed," echoed Web. "The original wart on the face of the human race."

Lynne snickered as she thumbed away her tears. "I agree with that a hundred percent."

"Let's talk about something else," put in Abby. "That topic will ruin my lunch."

The others agreed, and the subject was changed. When the meal was finished, Web and Abby excused themselves, saying they needed to get on with their shopping, and left the "engaged" couple to themselves.

Heads bent against the icy wind, they headed down the street toward Sarah Weatherby's Ladies' Ready-to-Wear Shop. "This is the last stop for today, isn't it?" Web asked.

"Right," responded Abby, holding onto his hand. "I'll have a little more shopping to do next week, but this is the last major thing."

Sarah Weatherby was middle-aged and gabby. She was talking a female customer's ear off when Web and Abby entered the store. She took time to smile and wave, but kept on talking. Web followed Abby to a pair of clothes racks and stood patiently while she began to examine dresses one by one.

Sarah's customer left, and the portly proprietor approached Web and Abby. "Hello, Abby. Something for yourself?"

Abby had the skirt of a dress stretched out so as to view its cut. "No," she replied. "It's for Elizabeth. Christmas present."

But Sarah wasn't listening. She was greeting Web. When Web and Sarah had exchanged a few friendly words, Sarah turned back to Abby and asked, "What did you say, dearie?"

Letting go of the dress and lifting another one, Abby responded, "I said I'm looking for a dress to give Elizabeth for Christmas."

"Oh," smiled Sarah. "I thought maybe you were coming in to order that wedding dress you'll be needing pretty soon. The wedding is still on for early June, isn't it?"

"Yes," Abby smiled in return, giving the man she loved a fleeting glance.

"My, I'm sure it's going to be a lavish wedding," sighed Sarah. "Just be sure you give me plenty of time to fit you and get the order in."

"I will," Abby assured her. Then a thought struck her. "By the way, Sarah, where do you have your wedding dresses made?"

"New York."

"I was afraid of that. What will we do if the Union splits up and Virginia sides with the South? Those New Yorkers won't want to do business with us 'troublesome Southerners.' "

"Ps-s-s-t!" said Sarah, laughing. "There ain't no civil war coming, honey. All this tough talk by the politicians on both sides is just so much hot air. Nobody can make me believe that either side wants to shed blood over this slavery issue. Once Mr. Lincoln takes office, the whole thing will cool off and soon die out. He says he wants the country united, and I believe he's got the wherewithal to bring it to pass."

"I wish I could agree with you, Sarah," spoke up Web, "but by the very fact that Mr. Lincoln was elected, the whole issue has become a lit fuse on a powder keg. Unless there's some kind of miracle that snuffs out the fuse, the North and the South are going to be at war."

Sarah bit her lip. Glancing at Abby, she said, "I don't mean no offense, honey, but if your Uncle Edmund would stay home and mind his own business, it would certainly help to snuff it out. He's doing more to bring on war than anybody else."

Abby did not reply. She would not speak against her father's brother, but Sarah had just voiced her own thoughts about Edmund Ruffin.

Noting Abby's silence, Sarah cleared her throat and said, "So you…ah…want to buy a dress for Elizabeth?"

"Yes," Abby nodded. Pointing to one that had struck her fancy, she said, "I like this one. I think it looks like her, don't you? It's her size."

Lifting the dress off the rack and holding it up to Abby, Sarah said, "It is Elizabeth to a T, honey. Would look good on you, too."

"I'll take it," smiled Abby.

As Sarah carried the hanger and dress toward the counter, she said, "Is Elizabeth doing all right, now? I knew she was having some trouble."

"She was pretty sick for a while," replied Abby, following her, "but she's doing a little better now. Still awfully weak."

"When's she due?"

"January fifteenth."

"Mmm. Just over a month."

"Yes. I want to give her the dress for Christmas. It'll be incentive after she's had the baby to get back to her previous size."

Taking the dress off the hanger and laying it on the counter, Sarah rolled a length of white wrapping paper from under the counter and cut it with a pair of scissors. "She shouldn't have too much trouble, slender as she is."

"A little more trouble than you might think," chuckled Abby. "She's put some flesh on her hips, and of course, there's always the task of getting the tummy back to size."

The dress was purchased and the young couple returned to the street and the cold wind. Turtling her head deep into the upturned collar of her coat, Abby looked up at Web and said, "I think it's colder now than when we started."

"Yeah, you're right," agreed Web.

Greeting a few more acquaintances along the way, Web and Abby soon arrived at the buggy. While Web was placing the package in the rear box, Abby's gaze strayed across the street. Parked in front of the general store was a Ruffin plantation wagon, which she recognized instantly. Sitting in the bed of the wagon amid boxes of supplies was Mandrake and his wife, Orchid. Wearing only their thin clothing, they huddled close and shivered against the cold. Orchid was pretty and smaller than Abby. Mandrake had his muscular arms wrapped around her, trying to make her as warm as possible. They were both looking down and had not noticed Web and Abby.

Web dropped the lid of the box and moved to help Abby into the buggy. She let him draw near, then pointed across the street and said, "That's the wagon Reed always uses to come into town for supplies. Look in the back."

Web could not believe his eyes. It was not normal for a plantation owner's slaves to be subjected to such severe weather without proper covering. He looked around for Exley, but there was no sign of him.

Abby saw Web's jaw muscles tighten as he growled, "So help me, one of these days I'm going to wring your brother-in-law's neck."

FIVE

Mandrake raised his head as Web and Abby halted halfway across the street, waiting for a carriage to pass. When he saw them clearly, he spoke to Orchid, and she looked up. Mandrake hopped over the tailgate, then helped his wife to the ground. As the white couple drew up, the slaves bowed their heads slightly and lowered their gaze.

"Hello, Mandrake...Orchid," said Abby.

Still looking down, Mandrake replied warmly, "Hello, Miz Abby. Good aftuhnoon, Massa Web."

"Hello, Miz Abby," echoed pretty Orchid. "Aftuhnoon, Massa Web."

"Hello to both of you," Web responded amiably.

Abby laid her hands on Orchid's shoulders and said softly, "Sweetie, I have told you before—you don't need to bow to me. And you can look me in the eye."

Orchid set her large eyes on her husband. Mandrake spoke for both of them. "Miz Abby, we loves you fo' bein' so kind to us, but we've agreed that we'd best do it anyhow. It's bettuh fo' us not to break the habit. If'n we got used to not bowin' and lookin' down in the presence of y'all white folks, we might fo'get at the wrong time with the wrong puhson."

Abby glanced at Web and said, "Might that wrong person be my brother-in-law?"

Fear etched its claw-marks on the features of both slaves. They looked at each other wide-eyed, then Mandrake nodded slowly. "Yaz'm."

"I thought so," Abby muttered.

"Did Exley bring you to town?" queried Steele.

"Yassuh," nodded Mandrake.

"Where is he?"

"At the Lamplighter Tavern."

"Where are your coats?"

"We don' got coats no mo'."

"What happened to them?"

Fear was still on Mandrake's face as he said, "I don' like to talk bad 'bout Massa Reed, Massa Web. Maybe it be bettuh if'n I don' answer you."

"You can answer him, Mandrake," Abby said.

"Yaz'm," he said, then looked at Web. "Well, suh, the las' month or so, Massa Reed has been treatin' me extra mean."

"By 'month or so,' do you mean since the incident at the Hart place when he shot Dexter and Orman?"

"Well, yassuh. It started right after that, and has got worse evuh since. He keeps findin' fault with my work, and blamin' me when somep'n gits broke...like tools. An' oncet it was the latch on the barn door...and then it was the handle on the watuh bucket. An' then... then this mo'nin' it was the winduh in the tool shed. I did'n' break none o' them things, Massa Web. Hones' I did'n'. I aks all the othuh slaves if'n it was them that broke that stuff, and ever' time, they tol' me they did'n' do it. They ain' got no reason to lie to me, Massa Web. They knows that I would'n' tell on 'em. It's like that stuff is gittin' broke jus' so's Massa Reed can punish me fo' it."

In spite of the cold, stinging wind, Web Steele's face went hot and turned crimson. Looking down at Abby, he grumbled, "Yeah, and I know who's been doing it." To Mandrake, he said, "So what about your coats?"

"Well, this mo'nin' jus' befo' noon, Massa Reed come to our shack and aks me if'n I know who broke the winduh in the tool shed. When I say I did'n' know, he call me a liar and slap my face. He say one of the slave chillun tol' him he seen me do it. When I aks him which one, he cuss me and say he don' have to tell me. Then he take my coat off the peg. Orchid was fixin' lunch. He grabbed a butcher knife off the cupboard and cut my coat to pieces. Orchid could'n he'p it, Massa Web. She started cryin'. Massa Reed tell her to shut up. She try, but she so scared she cain't stop. He grab her coat an' cut it to shreds, too."

Abby looked at the small black girl, barely nineteen years old, and said, "You poor dear."

"After Massa Reed cut up our coats," continued Mandrake, "he say we gonna ride into town wif him so's we can load the supplies in the wagon. He say to punish me fo' breakin' the winduh, me and Orchid both have to make the trip with no coats."

Steele ranged the length of the street with his angry gaze, looking toward the Lamplighter Tavern. Looking back at the slaves, he said, "I'm going to have a little talk with Mr. Exley, but first I'm taking you two over to the clothing store and buying you some new coats. Come on."

"Oh, no, we cain't, Massa Web," gasped Mandrake. "Massa Reed tol' us to stay with the wagon till he come back. If'n he should come while we was in the store, he'd really get mean."

Hearing the trepidation in Mandrake's voice, Web said, "All right. I understand." Peeling off his coat, he dropped it over Orchid's shoulders and added, "Miss Abby and I will be right back."

Abby was shedding her wrap, too. "Let Mandrake have Master Web's coat, Orchid. You take mine."

"Oh, Miz Abby," protested Orchid, "you keep yo' coat on. You'll catch yo' death."

"Don't argue, honey," Abby said firmly. "Just do as I say. We'll be back shortly."

The sharp knife-edges of the relentless wind stabbed at the couple as they hurried toward Stockton's Clothiers a half-block away. "Web," Abby said, her teeth chattering, "I don't know if you should get too rough with Reed. He's Papa's pet, and I don't want Papa getting it in for you. We are going to be married in a few months, and I—"

"Don't worry, sweetheart," Web cut in. "I'll not tarnish Papa John's image of me by bruising his pet son-in-law, but I am going to let Reed know what I think of him."

Ten minutes later, Web and Abby were back at the wagon, watching the slaves shoulder into their new coats.

"Massa Web," Mandrake said, emotion quaking his voice, "we don't know how to thank you fo' yo' kindness."

"You don't have to," smiled Steele. "It's thanks enough for me just to know you're warm. Now, Miss Abby is going to wait inside the general store while I go have a talk with Mr. Exley. You two get back in the wagon bed and see if you can't huddle down between the boxes and get out of this wind."

Orchid's comely face pinched, and she elbowed her husband, saying, "Go ahead an' tell 'im, honey."

"Tell me what?" Web asked.

Mandrake said nervously, "There's nothin' Massa Web can do 'bout it, Orchid."

"Tell 'im," she insisted. "Maybe while he's talkin' to Massa Reed, he can make 'im see how wrong he is if he goes through with it."

"But Orchid," argued Mandrake, "it ain't right fo' us to expec' Massa Web to handle our problems."

"What is Reed up to now?" Web asked.

Mandrake pulled nervously at an ear. "Well, he...he's threatnin' to sell one of us at the slave auction comin' up jus' aftuh Christmas."

"He what?" blurted Steele, scowling. "Why's he threatening to do that?"

"Jus' 'cause he knows I don' like 'im, Massa Web. He's tryin' to break my spirit."

"If he sells one of us," put in Orchid shakily, "we'll be separated forevuh!"

Putting an arm around Orchid's shoulder, Abby said, "Now, honey, don't you fret about that. Slaves who are married cannot be sold separately."

"No offense meant, Miz Abby," said Mandrake, "but they can."

"He's right, darlin'," said Web. "They can."

Abby's velvet-blue eyes widened. "Why, I've never heard of such a thing! It just can't be possible."

"Tell her about your marriage vows, Mandrake," said Web.

Looking Abby square in the eye for the first time, Mandrake said, "When we said our vows befo' that black preachuh two years ago, Miz Abby, yo' papa an' Massa Reed were both there. Massa John had tol' the preachuh to be sure to include the word *distance* in the vows."

"Distance?" said Abby. "What are you talking about?"

"You know that part where you white folk say, 'Til death do us part'?"

"Yes."

"We had to say, 'Til death or distance do us part.'"

Abby looked at Web. "Why hasn't my father ever told me about this?"

Shrugging, Web said, "He probably never thought it had anything to do with you, so why should he bother to tell you?"

"Whoever came up with such a preposterous thing?" she gasped.

"Probably whoever decided slave owners needed an ax to hold over their slaves' heads. If they get out of line, threaten them with selling their husband or wife."

The constant bite of the wind had reddened Abby's face, but her anger made it redder still. "Reed Exley!" she spat. "That low-down, dirty—"

"No cussing, now!" cut in Web.

"I wasn't going to. *Skunk* was the word I had in mind. Web, how could he be so cruel as to sell Mandrake or Orchid?"

"It's easy for him," said Web. "He's rotten to the core."

"Well, I'm not going to let him do it!"

"I wish there was some way you could stop it, darlin', but if Reed decided to do it, you'll be powerless to do anything about it."

"Then I'll have a talk with Papa."

"You and I both know that won't do any good. You're angry, Abby, and you're not thinking straight. Mandrake just said that it was your father who made sure *distance* was in the vows. You know Papa John will never reverse any decision Reed makes concerning the slaves. If Reed decides to sell Mandrake or Orchid, there'll be no stopping him."

Opening her eyes, Abby asked, "When you go over there to the tavern to talk to him, will you at least try to make him see how wicked it would be to separate them?"

"I can try, but Reed Exley will do whatever he wants."

"I'll appreciate it if you try," Abby said, sighing.

"We will too, Massa Web," said Mandrake.

"Yes," nodded Orchid. "We will, too."

"All right," said Web. "I'll be back as soon as I talk to Mr. Exley."

At the Lamplighter Tavern, Reed Exley hunched over a table, playing with an empty shot glass. There was a half-empty whiskey bottle on the table. The cold wind had driven many men off the streets, and the place was nearly full. The large room was clouded with smoke and rumbled with the garbled sound of voices, punctuated intermittently with an outburst of hollow laughter.

Exley's hat was pushed back on his head, leaving a shock of blond hair exposed and a matted clump of it dangling on his forehead. A black cigar was between his teeth and he puffed heavy clouds of smoke toward the ceiling while he waited for his friend, Bob Tally, to return to the table.

Tally was owner of the Lamplighter and had stopped by the table to chat several minutes earlier. Secession and the threat of civil war became the immediate topics of discussion. As they talked, Tally had asked Exley if he had ever seen an edition of the *North Star*, a Rochester, New York, newspaper owned and operated by Frederick Douglass, a black man who had run away from a southern plantation in 1842. Exley had heard of the paper but had never seen it. Excusing himself, Tally went to his office to fetch the latest edition.

Exley poured himself another shot of whiskey, removed the cigar from his mouth, and took a sip. Sticking the smoking cigar between his teeth again, he smiled to himself, thinking of Mandrake and Orchid outside, freezing in the cold.

Tally, a tall, slender man of sixty-five, drew up to the table with a folded newspaper in his hand. Sitting down, he flopped the paper on the table and opened it to the second page. Holding it up so Exley could see Frederick Douglass's picture, he said, "This's him. He always writes an editorial on this page. Look at the headline over the article."

Exley focused on the bold print and read it aloud, "Editor is Thief and Robber." Squinting against the smoke that was drifting into his eyes, he said, "What's he mean by that?"

"Let me read it to you. He says, 'I admit that I am a thief and a robber. Eighteen years ago I stole this head, these limbs, this body from my master, and ran off with them.' What do you think of that?"

Exley swore around the cigar and said, "Somebody oughtta go up there to Rochester and put that insolent smart-mouth in chains…drag him all the way back to the South behind a wild horse and nail his black hide to a barn wall."

Tally snickered. "Here's more of his black insolence. Old charcoal skin says, 'The other day a young Negro just coming into manhood asked me what he should do about white oppression against us colored folks. I gave him his answer in just one word: agitate!' Now, how does that tickle your spine, Reed?"

Exley jerked the cigar from his mouth, his face purple with rage. Swearing profusely, he banged a fist on the table, causing glass and bottle to jump, and roared, "If I had big-mouth Douglass on the Ruffin place for just one day, I'd teach him some manners!"

The circle of men at tables around them grew quiet, and eyes turned to view the man who had just made the loud outburst. Exley gave them a fleeting glance, then looked back at Tally and growled, quieter this time, "Give me Douglass for even one hour, and I'd make him think agitate! I'd put a whip to his back and beat him till he drowned in a pool of his own blood!"

A man at a nearby table said, "Hey, Reed! You talkin' about Frederick Douglass?"

"Yeah," nodded Exley. "His kind need to taste a little Southern hospitality for bein' a big black mouth!"

A rousing cheer went up as men raised bottles and glasses toward Exley, voicing their enthusiastic agreement.

With all the excitement, no one noticed Web Steele enter the tavern. Closing the door behind him, Steele peered through the smoke and picked out Exley in the crowded room. Listening to the tumult, he quickly picked up that Exley was the center of attention. He had evidently said something for all to hear, and they were in full agreement.

Moving aside into the shadows, Web unbuttoned his coat and waited to hear what Exley would say next.

Waving his smoking cigar, Exley said loudly, "I hate the black guts of every banjo-eyed African beast on this planet! If it weren't for the free labor we cotton producers get from 'em, I'd say put 'em all on leaky boats back to Africa!" After a loud outburst of voices agreeing with Exley's sentiments, he stood up, stuck the cigar back in his mouth, and gusted, "Tell you somethin' else, boys. Around the Ruffin place, those darkies don't get away with anything! I work 'em so hard, they don't have the strength left to sass-mouth. I also have my ways of handling 'em when they show that they're even thinkin' about gettin' stiff-necked on me. There won't be any slave revolts on the Ruffin plantation, I'll guarantee you. I keep 'em just plain scared all the time."

"That's the way to do it, Reed," spoke up the slave overseer of a local plantation. "Keep 'em scared."

"Guess you've all heard about that little shootin' incident Jonas Hart had back in October," said Exley. "Y'all noticed that right after that, Jonas's mealy-mouthed, soft-hearted, blackie-lovin' son David got himself fired and run outta the county! Jonas hired a hard-nosed overseer a couple weeks later, and they haven't had any of that kind of trouble since."

"That's right!" came an unidentified voice.

"And I'll tell you somethin' else, boys," said Exley. "That mealy-mouthed, soft-hearted, African-lovin' son of Dudley Steele is gonna learn the hard way that bein' tender and compassionate with those kinky-haired beasts ain't the way to go. It'll backfire on him sooner or later. Of course, he ain't got much sense. Only reason he's even got the overseer job is 'cause the old man knows he couldn't get a job anywhere else. Feels sorry for him."

As Exley was saying, "African-lovin' son of Dudley Steele," Web detached himself from the shadows. The men of Richmond knew Web Steele. Eyes in the crowd bulged and mouths gaped as patrons saw him through the clouds of smoke heading toward Exley, whose back was to him.

Exley wondered why no one was voicing agreement to his statement about Web. Chuckling, he said, "And what's more, Abby Ruffin is going to marry Webster because she feels sorry for him. She's gonna waste her life with that useless, no-good—"

Web had circled around Exley and stepped into view while the man was in midsentence. The shock of Steele's sudden appearance registered clear to the marrow, stealing Exley's breath. He felt his face burn.

"That useless, no-good what?" demanded Web.

A tic began to jump under Exley's left eye, and his face went ashen, replacing the deep-red of his embarrassment. He swallowed with difficulty, not only fearful of the whipping Web Steele might lay on him, but also of the shame he would have to bear if all these men were to watch it happen.

Web's voice was raw as he repeated, "That useless no-good *what*, mister? You were telling all these men that Abby was going to waste her life with some useless, no-good something, but you didn't tell them what the useless, no-good something is. Finish it."

There was a crypt-like silence in the smoky room.

Exley could feel the eyes of the crowd on him. His mind was racing. He wished Bob Tally would speak up and demand that there be no fighting in the place, but Tally was silently looking on with the rest of them.

Exley once again found himself in a corner. He dare not lose face with the men of Richmond, but it would come if he got whipped by Steele. He would also lose face if he backed down. His mind flashed back to the day Web showed him to be a liar in front of John Ruffin and the rest of the family. Steele would like to have worked Exley over then, but he refrained for one reason, and Exley knew what it was. Steele wanted to stay in the good graces of Papa John. Reed was going to have to gamble that Steele would not attack him now for the same reason he didn't do it before. It was a gamble, but he was in a corner and there was no other way out.

His heart banged his ribs as he looked Steele in the eye and retorted defiantly, "You want me to finish it? Okay. That useless, no-good, blackie lover."

Web knew what Exley was doing. He had taken a long moment to reflect on the situation before making his reply. He was gambling that Web would not batter him because it would upset Papa John. Had Exley known about Web's promise to Abby, he would have answered sooner.

Web was glad Exley had already embarrassed himself in front of the other men, but he decided Exley needed a little more embarrassment. He reached out and seized the front of Exley's shirt with his left hand and yanked him close. Exley's hat fell on the floor. Putting his nose within an inch of Exley's and fixing him with a hard stare, he hissed, "I'm in a jovial mood because it's Christmas time, bigmouth, so I won't bloody up Mr. Tally's place today. But you and I are going to have a private talk outside right now."

Making a half-turn and jerking Exley so hard his feet momentarily left the floor, Web dragged him, stumbling and groping for balance, toward the door. With his free hand, Steele pushed the door open, then saw the crowd about to follow. Pointing a stiff finger at them, he rasped, "I said private!"

The men got the message and eased back. Web shoved Exley through the doorway onto the boardwalk and slammed the door. The cold wind lanced them.

Reed was indeed embarrassed and was struggling against Web's powerful grip as he dragged him to the corner of the building. People on the street stared as Exley was forced into the six-foot space between the tavern and the next building.

Slamming the short, stocky man against the wall of the tavern, Steele said, "Now, we're going to have a little chat!"

"It's cold out here," complained Exley. "I want my coat and hat."

Steele let out a quick gust of irritation. "Aw, poor thing! It's cold out here, is it? Well, that's exactly what I want to talk to you about. Abby and I found Mandrake and Orchid sitting in the wagon in this freezing cold. When we asked them where their coats were, they were afraid to answer. Abby convinced them it was all right to tell us, and they finally did."

"Yeah? Well, you only heard their side of the story."

"I don't care about your side of it, Exley. You drove them into town like that, so I don't have to wonder where the fault lies."

"Oh, is that so? You're stickin' your nose in where it don't belong, Steele. It so happens that those two are under discipline."

"Because you broke a window and accused Mandrake of it?"

Exley was having a hard time breathing with Web twisting his shirt collar at his throat and pressing him hard against the wall. "That's a lie," he croaked.

"You and I both know better, so let's not waste time discussing it," said Web, pressing Exley against the wall a little harder. "Even if Mandrake did break the window, your making him and Orchid sit in that wagon with no protection in this cold is wicked and inhuman."

"Says you."

Web took a step back, jerked Exley toward him, then slammed him against the wall. His voice was menacing as he said, "I bought Mandrake and Orchid new coats, Exley, and I'm warning you—don't touch them."

"You got no business buyin' coats for another man's slaves," Reed countered.

"Yeah? Well how about Abby? I have an idea she'll make it her business to tell her father about finding Mandrake and Orchid freezing to death."

Suspecting by this time that Web wasn't going to beat him, Exley sneered, "She may tell Papa John about it, but it won't change a thing. I'll explain my side of things, and he'll agree that my discipline was proper."

Web knew the man was right. John Ruffin gave Exley a free hand with the slaves, and he would never believe Exley himself had broken the window. Web wanted to thrash him, but he had made Abby a promise.

The icy wind was knifing between the buildings, and Exley's teeth were chattering. "Let go of me," he demanded.

"Not until you promise me you'll let Mandrake and Orchid keep those coats and wear them."

"All right, all right, I promise. Now let me go."

Web released his hold, but did not step back. "You better not be lying to me."

The sneer returned to Exley's face. "You know what your problem is, Steele? You're just too soft. You've got as many slaves on your place as we do. You ought to have learned by now that the only way to handle slaves is to treat 'em like the animals they are. Keep 'em scared and discipline 'em hard when they get outta line."

"Too soft? Let me ask you something. In the three years you've been John's slave overseer, how many have run away?"

"Thirteen. So what?"

"It proves that you're too hard on them. We've never had even one slave run away from our plantation. They're fed and clothed well, and though we expect them to produce by working hard, they're still treated like human beings."

"Human beings! Bah! They're animals, I tell you. Nothin' but black-skinned animals."

Web was struggling to control his temper. His hands ached to pound Exley, but he had to keep his promise to Abby. He knew if he stayed much longer, he wouldn't be able to hold himself in check. "One other thing, Exley. What kind of animal are you for threatening to sell Mandrake or Orchid and tear them apart? Don't you have even one little speck of decency in that twisted brain of yours?" With a parting glare, Web turned and walked away.

"Get off my back, Steele!" Exley called after him. "What I do with the Ruffin slaves is none of your business!"

Web made his way down the street toward the general store, where Abby waited for him near the large front window. There was anxiety in her eyes.

Stepping up to him, Abby asked, "How'd it go?"

"We had a little talk."

"Is he angry?"

"You could say that."

Her eyes widened. "You...you didn't lose your temper and beat him up, did you?"

"Yes and no. Yes, I lost my temper. No, I didn't beat him up."

"Did you talk to him about his threat to sell Mandrake and Orchid?"

"Yes. He said whatever he does with the Ruffin slaves is none of my business."

"Do you think he'll really sell one of them?"

"Knowing Reed, it'll surprise me if he doesn't."

SIX

Huddled in the Ruffin wagon, Mandrake and Orchid watched Web Steele enter the general store. Pulling his wife close to him, Mandrake said wistfully, "I wish Massa Web was our massa."

"Me too," agreed Orchid. "He's such a kind and gentle man. I sho' is glad Miz Abby is marryin' him. It's Miz 'Lizbeth I feel sorry fo', bein' married to that mean Massa Reed. Sometimes I've seen him treat her so bad, she has cried and cried."

"I has, too," nodded Mandrake. "Only Massa John nevuh sees it. He nevuh sees anythin' bad that Massa Reed does."

"He's like the devil," said Orchid. "He's crafty and sly."

The cold wind whined around the wagon as neither one spoke for several minutes, then Orchid gripped Mandrake hard and said, "Oh, honey, what we gonna do if'n Massa Reed decide to sell one of us?"

"I don' know," replied Mandrake. "We jus' gotta hope and pray that he don' do it."

"But what if'n he does? I cain't stan' the thought of livin' without you. I…I'd rathuh be dead."

"Don't talk that way, Orchid," said Mandrake, hugging her tight.

Orchid was quiet for a moment, then she said, "Maybe we should run away."

Shaking his head vigorously, Mandrake said, "No, honey! Massa Reed would find us…and when he did—"

"Not if'n we had somebody like Massa Web to he'p us."

"Orchid, you gotta stop talkin' that way. We couldn' put a thing like that on Massa Web. Like I tol' you, we jis' gotta hope and pray that Massa Reed don' decide to sell one of us."

Orchid began sniffling.

Mandrake used one hand to stroke her cheek. "Aw, c'mon, now honey. Don' cry. Ever'thin' will be all right."

"But Massa Reed seems to hate you so. Why? You nevuh done nothin' to him."

"I know, honey, but he knows even though I obey 'im on the outside, I'm disobeyin' 'im on the inside. I try nevuh to show it, but somehow he knows."

"I think it also bothuhs him 'cause the othuh slaves look to you as a leaduh 'cause yo' strong in both yo' mind and body. Massa Reed mus' think you is some kind of threat."

"Well, it could be, honey, but—" Mandrake's words were cut off by the sight of Reed Exley coming up the street.

"What is it?" asked Orchid.

"It's him. Massa Reed. He's comin', and he looks real mad."

Snow was starting to fall from the low-hanging clouds as Exley drew up, eyes blazing. "You two are in real trouble! Do you hear me? *Real* trouble!"

Mandrake felt fire deep within him. He could take Exley's mistreatment of himself, but when the man turned his anger on Orchid, it was all he could do to keep from laying hands on him. Holding his voice steady, he said, "We stayed with the wagon jus' like you tol' us, Massa Reed. Why we in trouble?"

"You blabbed your big mouths off to Web Steele!" Exley

blared. "Told him about me cuttin' your coats up this morning, and got him to buy you new ones. You're gonna be sorry, black boy!"

"We did'n' say nothin' to Massa Web. *He* aks *us* where our coats were. We did'n' wanna tell 'im nothin' 'bout it, Massa Reed, but Miz Abby say we should. But we did'n' aks Massa Web to buy us new ones. That was his idea. He did'n' like seein' us freezin'."

Exley swore angrily, reached over the side of the wagon, and seized Orchid by the arm. He yanked her over the edge and flung her to the ground. Mandrake tensed and fire flashed in his eyes. Instinctively, he started toward Exley.

Taking a step back, Exley reached into his coat pocket and pulled out a small caliber derringer. Mandrake froze with his body halfway over the side of the bed. Orchid gasped from where she lay on the ground.

Eyes wild, Exley waved the derringer in the black man's face and hissed, "Come on, Mandrake! You've wanted to lay hands on me for a long time, haven't you? Well, come on! Just give me an excuse. Nothing would make me happier than to put a bullet into that muddled black brain of yours."

People on the street were gawking, but no one made a move to intervene. What a white man did with his slaves was his own business.

Staring at the gun, Mandrake eased back into the wagon bed. Tiny snow crystals were sticking to his coal-black hair.

Holding the gun steadily on Mandrake, Exley glanced down at Orchid and said, "Take your coat off, girl."

"Massa Reed," pled Mandrake, "please don' do this to her!"

"Shut up!" snapped Reed. "She'll do what I tell her!"

Fear etched itself on Orchid's face as she fumbled with the buttons on her coat. When she finally removed the coat, a gust of wind hit her like a cold fist, taking her breath. With his free hand, Exley snatched the coat and threw it on the ground. Orchid whimpered, hugged herself for warmth, and put her back to the side of the wagon.

Still holding the gun on Mandrake, Exley glared at him and said, "There's a can of kerosene in there, Mandrake. Grab it and climb out of the wagon."

Fumbling for the handle on the one-gallon can, Mandrake asked, "What you gonna do, Massa Reed?"

"Shut up! Climb outta there and take your coat off."

Under the threatening muzzle of the derringer, the black man obeyed. When his coat was off, Exley said, "Throw it down there next to Orchid's and pour some kerosene on them."

"Massa Reed, please," Mandrake pleaded. "Burn mine if'n you want, but please don' burn Orchid's. She's cold. Please let her put it back on."

Exley swore, switched the derringer to his left hand, and cracked Mandrake on the jaw with his right, knocking him down.

Quivering from the cold, Orchid broke into tears.

Switching the gun to his right hand once more, Exley backhanded the girl across the mouth, railing, "Stop that stupid bawling!"

Mandrake scrambled to his feet with murder in his eyes.

Leveling the derringer at Mandrake's face, Exley yelled, "C'mon, black boy! Try me!"

"You got no call to hit my wife, Massa Reed. Leave her alone."

Exley showed mock surprise. "What's this I hear? Is the black scum of a slave daring to tell *me* what to do?"

Mandrake held his gaze, but did not speak.

"You just wait till I get you home, black scum. You're gonna be one sorry slave!"

Mandrake bristled and clenched his fists. Orchid saw that he was at the breaking point. "No, Mandrake!" she shouted. "Don't do it!"

The muscular slave looked at her, forced his emotions under control, took a deep breath, and said, "Don't worry, honey. I won't."

"Too bad," Exley chuckled. Reaching into his shirt pocket, he pulled out a wooden match and handed it to Mandrake. "Now, do as I tell you, boy. Soak those coats with kerosene and set 'em on fire."

Obeying reluctantly, Mandrake poured the liquid on the coats, then knelt down and struck the match against the side of the metal can. Cupping the flame in his hands against the wind, he touched it to the wet fabric. The coats caught fire, and the flames spread rapidly, fanned by the wind.

While in the general store, Abby had decided to make a few additional purchases. Web was carrying the string-tied bundles as he opened the door and let Abby pass through ahead of him. Looking over her head, he noticed that a small crowd had gathered on the street. Then he saw the wind-whipped smoke and the yellow flames on the ground. When he realized the fire was beside the Ruffin wagon and saw Exley and the two coatless slaves, he knew what was burning.

Handing Abby the bundles, Web said, "He's not getting away with this. If what I'm about to do tarnishes your father's image of me, then so be it."

Abby said something that was stolen away by the wind as Steele ran toward the scene.

Exley caught a glimpse of Web just before he drew up. Pivoting, Exley aimed the derringer at him and yelled, "Hold it, Steele!"

Web skidded to a halt. "Put the gun away, Reed. Man throws a gun on me, he'll wish he hadn't."

"Just butt out!" Exley screamed. "These slaves don't belong to you, and you got no business buying 'em coats! Now, get outta my sight!"

Web stepped within reach of Exley and extended an open palm. "Give—me—the gun."

Exley was so angry at Steele that his mind slipped over the edge of sound reason. His face went purple with rage. Shaking the derringer at Steele, he spouted, "I'm gonna kill you and do Abby a favor!"

Web moved with the swiftness of a panther. Grasping the gun arm, he gave it a savage twist and the derringer flew out of Exley's hand. Like a maddened beast, Exley wailed and swung the fist of his free hand at Web's face, connecting with his cheekbone.

The blow stung Web. He let go of Exley's arm in time to avoid a second punch and countered with a hard right to Exley's mouth. Exley staggered back a couple of steps. He swore at Steele, then lunged at him, bending low. His head caught Web in the stomach, driving him against the Ruffin wagon, barely missing Mandrake and Orchid, who clung to each other in the cold.

Abby hurried to the derringer and picked it up. Jamming it in her coat pocket, she moved back to within a few feet of the wagon.

The wagon shook with the impact as the two men slammed against it, and the two horses in the harness flinched and nickered nervously. With his head still low, Exley started to pull back. But he was too slow. Steele brought his knee up in a vicious thrust, catching Exley square on the nose.

The force of the blow snapped Exley's head back and dropped him on his backside. Blood appeared instantly, bubbling from his nostrils. Steele stood over him, spread-legged, waiting for him to get up.

Cursing violently, Exley sprayed blood and leaped to his feet. He charged like a wounded beast, swinging wildly. Web dodged Exley's fists and launched a combination of blows that found flesh and bone with bruising force. Exley backpedaled and slammed into the wagon. One blow had opened a cut above his right eye and blood began to seep down, obscuring his vision. He hung there wiping blood with the back of his hand, swaying on rubbery legs.

Abby knew the cut would need a doctor's attention. She found herself not caring how her father felt about this fight. Reed had it coming.

Steele moved in for the finish, lashing out with both fists. Exley countered weakly with his right while using his left arm as a shield. Web plowed through it and connected with a right cross. Reed Exley bounced off the wagon and hit the ground face-first. He was out cold.

Mandrake and Orchid tried not to show their elation.

The crowd looked on in silence as Steele knelt down and rolled Exley over. As Abby stepped close, he said, "This cut is going to need some stitches."

"I would say so."

Rifling through Exley's pockets, Web found a roll of money and said, "Mr. Exley doesn't know it, but he's going to buy new coats for Mandrake and Orchid."

Web took enough money to cover the cost of the coats and put the rest back in Exley's pocket. Handing the bills to Abby, he said, "If you'll go buy the coats, I'll take him to Doc McKinley. I know he's not the Exley's family doctor, but he's closest. I'll be back shortly."

Hoisting the limp figure over his shoulder, Steele moved down the street toward the doctor's office while Abby led the two slaves to Stockton's Clothiers.

Ten minutes later, Web entered Stockton's to find Mandrake and Orchid smiling and wearing their new coats. Mandrake said, "Thank you, Massa Web."

"Don't thank me," grinned Web, rubbing the bruise Exley had put on his cheekbone. "Thank Mr. Exley. He paid for them."

"Mm-hmm," nodded Mandrake, smiling furtively. "In more than one way."

"So what's Doc McKinley say?" queried Abby.

"He'll live," replied Web. "Doc says it'll take four or five stitches."

"He regain consciousness by the time you got him there?"

"Not completely. He didn't know what day it was. Well, let's get you and these two people home. Reed can drive himself in the wagon."

Darkness was falling and the snow was coming down harder as the buggy pulled up to the huge white mansion. Charles was in his overcoat, lighting the kerosene lanterns on the front porch.

Mandrake hopped off the buggy and helped Orchid down. As Web was stepping down to assist Abby from the buggy, Mandrake said, "Massa Web, since you gonna be in there fo' a while, I'll take yo' hoss and buggy and put 'em in the barn. Then they won't git cov-uhed with snow."

Web thanked him and guided Abby up the snow-covered porch steps as Mandrake led the horse away with Orchid by his side. Charles greeted Web and Abby as he finished lighting the last lantern, then followed them into the house. Pausing in the entry way and removing his hat, Web said, "Just a minute, Abby. I'm going to take my hat and coat back out on the porch and shake the snow off."

Charles said, "Don't bother, Mr. Web. Just give them to me. I'll take care of that little chore for you."

"Thank you," said Web, handing Charles his hat.

While Web was slipping out of his coat, Abby said, "Darling, I'm going up to my room for a moment. I'll be right back." Suddenly her hand flew to her mouth and she gasped, "Oh, the packages! We forgot to bring them in."

"I don't know why I didn't think of them," said Web.

"We've both got our minds on this little talk we're going to have with Papa," sighed Abby.

"I can fetch them for you, Miss Abby," volunteered Charles. "Are they in the box of Mr. Web's buggy?"

"Yes, thank you, Charles. You're a dear. Just put them over here in the closet. I'll pick them up later."

"Yes'm," nodded the butler, taking Web's coat.

Web helped Abby remove her coat as they walked together into the large receiving room. Coat in hand, she moved toward the wind-ing staircase, saying, "Wait here, darling. I'll be right back."

"You really don't have to sit in on this," Web said. "I can talk to your father alone."

Shaking her head, she replied, "Huh-uh. It'll sit better if I'm there to back up your story."

Shrugging, Web smiled. "Okay. Can't argue with that."

With admiring eyes, he watched Abby mount the wide stair-case. When she reached the top, she paused at the banister, smiled down at him, then hurried down the hallway. He marveled at how she made his heart leap. No other woman had ever affected him that way.

Web waited in the receiving room in the light of the large candle-bedecked chandelier that hung overhead. The grandfather clock that stood in a nearby corner chimed once. It was a quarter of six. Dinner was usually at seven-thirty at the Ruffin mansion. There would be ample time to have his talk with Papa John. He dreaded it, but it had to be done. He thought of Reed Exley and wondered how things were going at Doc McKinley's office.

Abby returned within five minutes, having smoothed her hair. Web met her at the bottom of the stairs and said, "How'd you get to be so beautiful?"

"I take lessons," she giggled.

"Are they expensive?" Web asked, giving her his arm.

"Very."

"Well, you're wasting the money. You couldn't *get* any prettier."

Smiling up at him, she chirped, "I think I'll keep you around. You're good for my ego."

They reached the library door and found it partially open. Sticking her head in, Abby saw her father in his favorite chair, reading by lantern light. "Hello, Papa," she said cheerfully. "May Web and I come in?"

"Of course!" said John, laying the book on a small table next to the chair and rising.

Abby hurried to him, kissed his cheek, and said, "I was able to find the perfect dress for Elizabeth."

"Wonderful!" he exclaimed, sending a broad grin toward his future son-in-law. "She walk your legs off, Web?"

"Not quite, sir," Web replied, running a finger across his mustache.

"You were planning to stay for dinner, weren't you?"

"Of course he was," piped up Abby. "I invited him."

"Good," nodded Papa John, "because I did some inviting myself."

"Oh?" said Abby. "Who?"

"Well…Mr. and Mrs. Steele, for starters."

"Wonderful!" said Abby.

Web smiled his approval. His parents were well-acquainted with John Ruffin, but he wanted them to get to know each other even better.

"I figure," said Papa John, "that since Dudley and I are going to one day be grandfathers-in-law, we might as well start spending more time together."

Web and Abby laughed. Then Abby said, "Who else are we having for dinner, Papa?"

"The McLaurys."

"Oh, wonderful again!" said Abby. "We haven't had Reverend and Mrs. McLaury in some time."

"That's great," Web said. "It's almost like…an occasion."

"Well, it is sort of an occasion," replied Papa John. "Since Reverend McLaury is going to be the one to tie the knot between you two, seems to me he'll have a definite part in making Dudley and me grandfathers-in-law."

"Oh, Papa," said Abby, kissing his cheek again, "you're a sugar lump!"

John's face tinted slightly. Clearing his throat, he said, "The McLaurys couldn't make it by seven-thirty, so we're having dinner at eight." As he spoke, he noticed the purple bruise on Web's cheekbone, and squinted at it. "What happened, son? You run into a swinging door?"

"Uh…no, sir," responded Web, touching fingers to the bruise. "In fact, I want to talk to you about it."

"Oh?"

"Yes, sir. It has to do with an unpleasant incident that happened in town this afternoon."

Puzzlement showed on the older man's face. "All right. Want to sit down?"

"Sure," Web nodded, trying not to show his uneasiness.

John Ruffin sat in his favorite chair while Web and Abby took seats facing him. Wanting to get it over with quickly, Web said, "I got this bruise in a fight with Reed, Mr. Ruffin."

"Reed?" echoed John, stiffening. "What on earth did he hit you for?"

"Well, sir, this is what I want to expl—"

"You said 'fight' so I suppose you hit him back. Does he look worse than you?"

"Well, yes, sir. I left him with…uh…with Doc McKinley in town. He's—"

"Doc McKinley!" blurted Ruffin. "What on earth did you do to him?"

"Reed's not hurt bad, Papa," butted in Abby, keeping her voice low and level. "Please just let Web tell you what happened. I was there, so I can verify what he tells you."

"All right," said Papa John, frowning. "I'm listening."

The plantation owner listened intently as Web told him about finding Mandrake and Orchid sitting coatless in the back of the Ruffin wagon. Leaving nothing out, he told of the anger that grew within him while he was purchasing new coats for the slaves, and of how he then went to the tavern and dragged Exley outside for a confrontation. John paled as Web told of Reed's use of the derringer and of his ending up at the doctor's office in need of stitches. John was about to comment when Web told him of Exley's threat to sell Mandrake or Orchid and separate them forever.

Concluding, Web said, "Mr. Ruffin, in view of what I've just told you, and Abby has verified, I strongly suggest that you put a firm hand on Reed. He is quite short on temper, and in my opinion, he holds a strong dislike for all Negroes, including your own slaves."

John Ruffin adjusted his position in the chair, rubbed his slender chin, and said, "I really think you're misunderstanding Reed, son. He's a good boy, actually. Has a lot of excellent qualities."

Abby felt her stomach turn over.

Web wanted to say that he had never seen even *one* good

quality in Reed Exley, that he was *not* a good boy, and that he *did* understand him, but he could not bring himself to put it that bluntly. "Well, sir," he said, "you have your opinion and I have mine. But I am suggesting that you watch him more closely. I'm concerned that he will eventually do something that will cause real problems with the slaves."

John Ruffin forced a weak smile and said in a placating tone, "Web, I appreciate your concern, but I don't think it's as serious as all that. You see, Reed hasn't been himself lately. Elizabeth's illness has played on his nerves. This pregnancy has been as hard on him as it's been on her. He loves Elizabeth so much that he can hardly think of anything else, you understand. With his nerves stretched to the limit, he's been much quicker to fly off the handle than usual."

Abby wondered how her father could be so blind.

"But, sir," said Web, "Reed's brutality with the slaves was going on long before Elizabeth got pregnant. Abby's been telling me about it for well over a year."

John glanced at his daughter, then looked at Web and said, "Son, you must remember that Abby's a woman...a very tender and compassionate woman. What looks to her like brutality is really just firm, wise discipline on Reed's part."

Leaning toward her father, Abby said levelly, "You can tell yourself that all you want, Papa, but I'm not blind and I'm not stupid. I know brutality when I see it. Reed has been brutal with your slaves almost from the day you gave him the job. Lynne has told you about incidents she has seen also, but you turn a deaf ear. Please listen to what Web is telling you. If Reed is allowed to proceed as he has been doing, sooner or later there's going to be some kind of tragedy."

Ruffin raised his hand, palm forward, and said with a chuckle, "Don't be such a worry wart, honey. Nothing's going to happen."

There was a tap at the half-open door. John looked up to see Charles peering at him. "Yes, Charles?"

"Pardon me, sir," said the butler, "but your brother is here. Should I have him wait in the parlor?"

"Of course not," replied Ruffin, "show him in. We're just chatting about trivial things."

Web and Abby exchanged glances and shook their heads.

Charles stepped back into the hall and seconds later, Edmund Ruffin appeared, his long silver hair dangling on his shoulders. "Hello, everybody," he said in his normal boisterous voice. "Charles insisted that I wasn't interrupting anything important."

"Of course not," John chuckled. "Sit down."

Edmund greeted Abby and Web and moved to a chair beside Abby. Excitement was evident in his eyes. Standing in front of the chair, he ran his gaze over the three faces and said, "I've got good news, and I just had to come over here and tell it."

"So what's the good news?" asked John.

"South Carolina's going to secede from the Union!"

John's jaw slacked. "Are you sure?"

"Absolutely. You know I stay in touch about these things. I received a telegram two hours ago from my good friend Dave Jamison in Columbia. He's the richest plantation owner in South Carolina and a leader in the state. There's going to be a convention in Columbia a week from today, and he has been chosen to preside over it. The one and only reason for the convention is so the government leaders of South Carolina can vote to take their state out of the Union. Delegates will be there from all the other southern states. Dave wants me to make a speech and stir them up to go home and lead their states to do the same."

"I have no doubt that you'll be quite persuasive, Edmund," said John, smiling. "You've said all along if South Carolina pulled out, the rest of the southern states would too."

"It's bound to bring on a war," Web said with conviction.

"I have no doubt that it will," Edmund said flatly. "And if this is what it takes to make those thick-headed Yankees leave our bread and butter alone, then I say let it come."

Abby's face lost its color as she turned and looked at the man she loved. She knew if war came, Web Steele would be in the thick of it.

SEVEN

Web and Abby went to the parlor, leaving the Ruffin brothers to discuss the details of the upcoming secession convention. Charles had built a fire in the fireplace and the room was warm and cozy. Closing the double doors behind them, they held hands as they crossed the room and stood close to the crackling, popping flames.

Two lanterns glowed softly in the room, and the flames from the fireplace cast dancing shadows on the walls. Those same shadows were on Abby's exquisite features as she turned to face Web, her eyes radiating her adoration.

Their lips fused together in a lingering kiss giving vent to the love they felt for each other. After a long moment, Abby rested her head against Web's muscular chest. She drew a shuddering breath and said, "Oh, darling, I can't bear the thought of you going into battle. If war comes, you'll be expected to enlist...and I know that's what you'll do."

"I'll have to," he breathed, pressing her head tighter to him with the palm of his hand. "As a loyal son of the South, I must...even though I'm struggling over this slavery business."

Lifting her head to look at him, she said, "It's really bothering you, isn't it?"

"Yeah. Especially when I see the kind of treatment Mandrake and Orchid receive from your brother-in-law. I know that other slaves are being mistreated in the same manner all over the South. It's inhuman, and it's dead-wrong."

"But there are lots of slave owners like you and your father who treat their slaves well."

"I know. But I'm still not sure it's right for one human being to own another."

"Well, since Reverend McLaury will be here for dinner, why don't you ask him about it? As far as I know, he has never broached the subject from the pulpit, but I'm sure he'd tell you his view. It would be good for him to express it with Papa and Uncle Edmund at the table."

"I don't know," said Web. "If Pastor McLaury views slavery as wrong, Papa John might take it quietly, but your uncle is liable to lose his temper and start a fight. You know how he is."

"I guess you're right. Maybe you should just ask if you can talk to him in private. At least then you'd know how a man of God views the issue."

"Okay. I'll do it that way. After dinner, I'll ask him if we can talk privately for a few minutes."

Hatred toward Web Steele burned hot in Reed Exley as he guided the heavy-laden wagon up the winding drive toward the Ruffin mansion. Cursing the falling snow, he noted the presence of Edmund Ruffin's horse and buggy in front of the house. He was happy to see that Web's buggy was not there. Moving past the mansion, he drove the wagon to the first slave shack and hollered, "Lenox!"

It took only a few seconds for the door to come open, casting a rectangle of yellow light on the snow-laden ground in front of the shack. "Yes, Massa Reed?" said the slave from the doorway.

"Come out here and take the wagon to the supply shed. Unload it and be sure to wipe the snow off the boxes."

"Yassuh," nodded Lenox, reaching for his hat and coat.

Exley slid from the wagon and walked gingerly through the snow toward the front of the mansion. His face was swollen from the beating Web had given him, and a small bandage covered the stitches over his right eye. It throbbed with pain.

He mounted the steps and crossed the porch. Pushing through the door, he slammed it behind him and moved across the entry way into the receiving area, scattering snow as he went.

Having heard the door slam, Charles emerged from the hall and said, "We're having guests for dinner, Mr. Reed. We won't be eating until eight o'clock. What happened to your face? May I take your coat?"

Without replying, Exley threw his hat on the floor, scattering more snow, and quickly removed his coat, dropping it before the butler could get a hand on it. "John in the library?" he snapped.

"Yes, sir," responded Charles, leaning over to pick up the hat and coat. As Exley headed down the hall, Charles called after him, "Miss Elizabeth isn't feeling well, Mr. Reed. I think you should go up and see her."

He was sure Exley heard what he said, but the man ignored him. At the same time, the parlor door came open. Web Steele looked at the snow on the floor and recognized Exley's hat and coat in Charles's hands. "Reed's back, eh?"

"Yes, sir," the butler replied with lack of emotion.

"Sounded like he slammed the door right through the frame."

"If it weren't so sturdily built, he would have, sir."

"Upset, eh?"

"To put it mildly," came the butler's dull answer.

Exley found the library door closed and burst through it without knocking. The Ruffin brothers were seated and in conversation, which broke off immediately as they turned and looked at the intruder.

Unruffled, John looked at Exley's bruised, swollen face and asked, "Are you all right, son?"

"I'm fine."

"Web told me about the altercation you two had," said Ruffin. "I hope you're not too badly cut."

"My cut will be fine," grunted Exley. He glanced at Edmund without greeting him, then looked back at John. "I want to talk to you, and I want to do it right now."

Gesturing toward a chair, John said, "Sit down."

"A *private* talk."

"Edmund's my brother," countered John. "We can talk in front of him."

Remaining on his feet, Exley rasped, "I don't know what Steele told you, but for no reason at all, he attacked me on the street there in town!"

"No reason at all?" echoed Ruffin.

"That's right! You should break up the relationship between him and Abby right now. The man is a troublemaker. If Abby marries him, she'll lead a miserable life. Hotheaded and violent as he is, he's liable to get mad at her some time and beat her up good. She tries not to show it, but I know she's afraid of him. He's got her intimidated."

John rubbed his chin. "Now, son, I've never seen any indication of anything like that."

"Of course not," huffed Exley. "Steele is not gonna let you see him for what he is. And poor little Abby…like I said, she tries not to show the fear she has of him. But, Papa John, I've seen enough to know that it's there. I don't know what kind of hold he's got on her, but she's terrified of him. I'm tellin' you, you've got to break that relationship off before they get married."

"I'll have a talk with Abby," said John. "She'll tell me if she has any reason to be afraid of Web. Now, he told me about the situation over Mandrake and Orchid's coats. Did you actually cut up their coats?"

"Yes I did. Mandrake has been a mule to handle lately, Papa John. I haven't told you about it because I didn't want to bother you with such matters, but he's showing rebellion and he's a leader among the slaves. I've applied discipline in order to correct his attitude. Cuttin' up their coats was part of that discipline."

"Well, I can't fault you for that," John said, "but making them sit in the back of the wagon exposed to the cold…they could catch pneumonia."

"Exposed to the cold? What do you mean?"

"I mean being out in this cold weather with no coats."

"Oh, so that's it. I see Mr. Steele forgot to tell you they were wrapped in blankets. The only time they were exposed to the cold was when I had them loading the supplies into the wagon at the general store. I didn't think a few minutes would hurt them."

"But why did you burn the coats Web bought them?"

"Why did *I* burn the coats? It wasn't me who burned them! It was Mandrake. Apparently he didn't like Steele stickin' his nose into Ruffin business any more than I did. I was in the general store talking to some friends, and all this coat business happened while I was in there. When I came out, here was Mandrake setting the coats on fire after pouring some kerosene on 'em from the supplies in the wagon. I was reprimanding Mandrake for burning the coats when big boy Steele came from out of nowhere and attacked me. I got in one good lick, but I don't fight dirty like he does, and—"

"Exley, you're a liar!" boomed Web Steele from the open door.

The Ruffin brothers looked up, and Exley's jaw dropped.

Abby followed Web as he stepped into the room.

Exley's open mouth began to frame a word, but Steele cut him off. "You weren't in the general store all that time. Why don't you tell the truth? You were in the Lamplighter Tavern drinking. You're the one who told Mandrake to burn the coats, and you threw a gun on him when he was ready to jump you for manhandling his wife. I didn't attack you and you know it. You pointed that derringer at me and I told you to hand it over. When you shook it in my face and threatened to kill me with it, I took it away from you. You swung first. I told you if a man throws a gun on me, he'll wish he hadn't.

From the looks of you, I'll bet you wish you hadn't."

Exley framed another word, but Steele cut him off again. "Abby and I have been standing here since you told Mr. Ruffin that for no reason at all I attacked you today. Since that first lie, you've done nothing but pile more lies on top of it. Mandrake and Orchid did not have blankets, and you know it."

"And what's more," spoke up Abby, "Web doesn't have some strange hold over me, I am not intimidated by him, and I do not fear him. That is a concoction of your own wild imagination."

Pointing a stiff finger at Exley, Steele said tightly, "I'm going to say to you what I said to Mr. Ruffin. It is obvious that you have a strong dislike for all Negroes, including those slaves who live and work on this plantation. If he doesn't get a firm hand on you, you're going to cause some real problems with the slaves. And while I'm getting this off my chest, there's something else I want to say. Only a heartless fiend would separate a man and his wife like you've threatened to do to Mandrake and Orchid."

Exley turned to John Ruffin and growled, "I don't have to stand here and take this abuse!" With that, he whirled and headed for the door. He avoided Steele's hard glare as he passed him, but gave Abby a lingering, wanton look as he moved past her and out the door.

Abby burned the back of his head with flaming eyes.

John Ruffin sighed, rubbed the back of his neck, and stood up. Edmund, who had remained silent throughout the heated exchange, also rose to his feet.

John drew a deep breath and let it out through his nose as he moved slowly toward Web and Abby. To Web he said, "I wish you and Reed would get along. After all, when you and Abby marry, you'll be part of this family, just as Reed already is. You two are going to have to lay aside your differences and work at keeping peace in the family."

Web looked him in the eye, wondering if he was still blind to the truth. He and Abby had both showed Exley to be a liar, but

John's last words made it sound as if he had not heard any of it.

Just then Lynne Ruffin and Daniel Hart appeared at the door, giving everyone in the library a cheerful greeting. Lynne had been at the Hart plantation all afternoon and had invited Daniel home for dinner, unaware that the Dudley Steeles and the McLaurys were coming. When she explained this to her father, John clapped a hand on Daniel's back and told him they could set another place at the table just as they were going to do for Uncle Edmund.

Abby suggested that she and Lynne look in on Harriet in the kitchen and see if she could use some help. They also needed to advise her of the two extra dinner guests.

The men sat down in the library. Edmund was eager to tell Daniel the news of South Carolina's upcoming secession from the Union.

Arriving in the kitchen, Abby and Lynne found Harriet busy preparing a lavish meal. Harriet informed them that Elizabeth had not been feeling well most of the day, and that she wasn't going to eat dinner with the family. Abby was concerned and decided to go check on her. When Lynne offered to go too, Abby suggested that she stay and help Harriet. Lynne agreed, asking Abby to give Elizabeth her love.

Climbing the stairs, Abby wondered if Reed had gone to the Exley quarters on the third floor. She doubted it. He was probably pouting. Usually when Reed pouted, he went off somewhere by himself. She hoped he had done so this time. At the moment, she would rather see Elizabeth alone.

Topping the stairs at the second floor, Abby thought about the salacious look Reed had given her while leaving the library. She was glad Web hadn't seen it, or there would have been more Exley blood shed. She thought of the many times Reed had made passes at her since he had married Elizabeth and moved into the mansion. Such incidents had become more frequent since Elizabeth's pregnancy.

Abby had scolded her brother-in-law each time, and each time Reed had laughed it off, saying he should have married Abby in the first place. Showing her temper, she had shamed him for talking that way. The last time it happened—just a week ago—she had told him angrily that she never would have married him under any circumstances.

Reaching the third floor and moving slowly down the hall, Abby's heart went out to her older sister. She could not fathom what Elizabeth had ever seen in the egotistical, self-centered Reed. Sooner or later he was going to break her heart.

Abby would never tell Elizabeth of Reed's advances toward her. It would serve no purpose. Reed would deny it and probably try to drive a wedge between the two sisters. Neither would she tell Web. That kind of trouble the family could do without. In a few more months, Abby would be married to Web and out of the Ruffin house. She would no longer be vulnerable to Reed's advances. For the sake of everyone involved, she could tolerate him a little longer.

Much to her relief, Abby entered the Exley quarters to find Elizabeth alone. Reed had not been there since arriving home.

Elizabeth was lying on her bed. She was pale and feeling weak. Abby filled her in on Uncle Edmund's news of South Carolina's upcoming secession, and they discussed the probability of war between the North and the South. Elizabeth showed deep concern that if war came, her husband would have to enlist in the military. Abby said she had the same fear about Web.

The two sisters talked for quite some time, then Abby kissed Elizabeth's forehead and said she would send Harriet up with a tray of food. Elizabeth thanked her for the visit and asked that she greet the Steeles and the McLaurys for her.

When Abby reached the second level and started down the winding staircase, everyone except Reed had gathered in the receiving area. Charles was taking coats, and there was much chatter as Edmund eagerly made his announcement of South Carolina's impending secession.

Web looked up and saw Abby descending the stairs. He smiled at her and said, "There you are, darling. How's Elizabeth?"

"She's not feeling very well, but at least she's going to try to eat a little."

When Abby reached the bottom of the stairs, Dudley and Cora Steele embraced her. Dudley planted a kiss on her cheek and said, "Just a few more months and you can call me Dad."

Smiling, Abby kissed him back and said, "I think I'll just start calling you that right now."

Dudley laughed, hugged her, and said, "Honey, you just go right ahead!"

Dudley Steele was two inches shorter than his son, but had the same build except for a slight paunch that was making itself more evident than he preferred. His thick head of hair was salt and peppered, and the lines at the corners of his eyes were deepening. Abby told herself that if Web were as handsome at fifty-seven as his father, she would have no complaints.

Web's mother was two years younger than his father. She stood five-feet-four, and in spite of a few wrinkles and silver streaks in her light-brown hair, was very attractive. She and Abby loved each other dearly, and were looking forward to an even closer relationship when Abby also became "Mrs. Steele."

Turning from her future in-laws, Abby welcomed the family's pastor and his wife. Benjamin McLaury did not fit the mold of a preacher. At forty-three, he was rawboned and muscular with a rugged, steely look in his blue eyes. Like Web Steele, he was square-jawed and every inch a man. There was compassion in him, as was needed for a man of his profession, but there was also the temperament of a man who would not avoid a fight. Standing straight-backed and six feet tall, he commanded respect from men and women alike.

Dorothy McLaury, quiet and reserved, was a perfect complement to her husband. She was about Abby's height and quite pretty. Though she would soon turn forty, no one would suspect it. She was often mistaken to be an older sister of her twenty-two-year-old daughter.

John Ruffin led the group into the dining room, where Harriet and Charles were ready to serve the meal. As everyone was gathering around the large table, Reed Exley appeared. The guests immediately noticed his bruised face and the bandage over his right eye, but nothing was said. Exley acted as if he looked normal.

Before Reed found a seat, Harriet said, "Mr. Exley, I have a tray of food made up for Elizabeth. Would you like to take it up to her?"

Looking surprised, Exley said, "Why isn't she coming down to dinner?"

The maid had little liking and less respect for Reed. Giving him a disdainful look, she said, "If you would take the time to look in on her occasionally, you would know how she was feeling. She's been doing poorly today and doesn't have the strength to leave her room."

Abby wanted to applaud Harriet. John Ruffin's face tinted slightly; he conveniently discovered lint on his dark suit coat and began brushing it off. Web nudged Abby and was nudged in return. Lynne and Daniel exchanged furtive glances, grinning at each other. The Steeles and the McLaurys looked at their plates, and Uncle Edmund was busy adjusting his chair to a choice position at the table.

Though angry at the lowly maid's insolence, Reed masked his feelings and said, "I've had a rough day myself, Harriet. How about you or Charles taking the tray up to Elizabeth? I'll look in on her later."

Harriet's face was like granite as she replied, "Very well, sir."

Web shoved his chair back and said, "I'll take it up to her, Harriet. You and Charles are going to have your hands full serving the meal, here."

"That would be appreciated, Mr. Web," nodded the maid, smiling. She gave Reed a sharp glare and said, "The tray is on the center counter in the kitchen."

Reed looked a bit uncomfortable as Web left the room, but was spared momentarily while Reverend McLaury prayed over the food.

As soon as McLaury said, "Amen," Edmund began talking about the secession convention in Columbia, South Carolina, and with his loud voice, dominated the conversation. Web returned and took his seat beside the woman he loved. Exley quickly looked the other way.

When Edmund paused a moment to eat, Daniel Hart spoke to John and asked if he could talk to him some time soon. John was nodding his assent when Edmund butted in and said, "You'll have to get it done before the seventeenth, Daniel—or wait until after John and I get back from the convention."

Feeling confident of the subject young Hart wanted to discuss with him, John asked, "Is it important, Daniel?"

"Quite important, sir."

"Is it something that can wait until Edmund and I return from the convention?"

"Well, perhaps it could, but I'd rather talk to you before you go."

Smiling, John said, "I think I can make it quick and easy for you."

Daniel met his gaze and swallowed hard. "You can, sir?"

"Mm-hmm. Right here in public. The answer is *yes*. You have my absolute blessing to take Lynne for your wife."

Everyone laughed—except for Reed Exley, who remained stone-faced. Lynne's eyes filled with tears as she took hold of Daniel's hand.

Daniel wiped a shaky palm over his brow and said, "Whew! You sure made that easy, sir."

"Yeah, a lot easier than you made it for me!" chuckled Web.

There was laughter again, but Reed said nothing about the time he had asked John for Elizabeth's hand in marriage.

Reverend McLaury leaned past his wife to look at Daniel and said, "You two have a date in mind?"

"We really haven't discussed it yet, sir. I just asked Lynne today. Come to think of it," he added, looking at Web and Abby, "it was sort of public when I did that, too."

"Well, let me know when you decide on a date and we'll make plans accordingly," said the preacher.

"We'll do it," nodded Daniel.

"Papa," said Abby, "I didn't know you were planning on going to the convention with Uncle Edmund."

"Well, I made that decision after you and Web left the library. I think I should go and lend my support. Besides, I've never taken the time to attend one of my brother's anti-abolition rallies. I've heard he's a right fiery speaker, and I want to be there when he makes his speech at the convention."

Web remembered that he was going to ask Pastor McLaury for an appointment. He was eager to find out what the man thought of slavery. He would ask him for the appointment in private after dinner.

Reed spoke up. "I'd like to go to the convention too, Uncle Edmund, but since John's going, I'll need to stay here and look after things."

"I understand," nodded Edmund, brushing the long hair from his face.

Exley broke into laughter, as if he had heard something funny.

"What are you laughing at, son?" asked John, speaking in a tender tone that made Abby's stomach turn.

"I was just thinkin'," replied Exley. "I'd love to see the look on ol' Abe Lincoln's face when he hears that South Carolina's finally gonna cut the dog's tail off!"

"He already knows it," said Edmund. "There are plenty of people in South Carolina, as well as the rest of the South, who are Lincoln lovers. They've gotten the news to Washington already, and you can be sure the president-elect has heard about it in Illinois."

Deviltry showed on Exley's puffy face as he said, "It'd be good if somebody put a bullet in ol' Abe's black Republican brain before he takes the oath of office. With him outta the picture, that war everybody's talkin' about could be averted. It'll be Lincoln's fault if the North and the South get into it."

Benjamin McLaury set hard eyes on Exley and said, "This slavery issue has been going on since Abraham Lincoln was teaching himself to read by firelight as a boy, Reed. If civil war comes, it'll not be his fault, nor the fault of any one man. Mr. Lincoln was elected by the abolitionists in the North, yes, but if somebody murdered him as you have so coldly suggested, they would simply put in another man with the same views."

Exley looked at his father-in-law, expecting support, but none came. John Ruffin was a true Southerner, but he would not advocate the murder of any man.

Edmund spoke up next. "Do I detect some abolitionist leaning in you, Reverend? I've never heard you preach, but I'm wondering if you're a true son of the South. Have you preached in behalf of slavery in your pulpit?"

"No, I haven't," replied McLaury quickly.

"Weren't you born in the South?"

"Yes, I was. Right here in Virginia."

"Then you've got to be for slavery."

McLaury's jaw jutted. "Who says?"

"I did!"

"Now, gentlemen," cut in John Ruffin, "we're here to enjoy a nice meal together and be sociable. Let's not get into an argument."

"You used the word *gentlemen*, Mr. Ruffin," said Daniel. "Since they are gentlemen, certainly they can discuss this issue without arguing. I've had discussions with my brother about slavery. He's dead-set against it. In fact, he and my father had a severe falling out over it and he moved to western Virginia."

"Where in western Virginia?" Edmund asked.

"Over by Rich Mountain. Town called Beverly."

"Mmm," nodded Edmund. "Know right where it is. Held a rally at Philippi, which is near there, a couple of weeks ago. If your brother feels that way about slavery, why doesn't he move north?"

"There are a lot of people in the South who are against slavery, Mr. Ruffin," Daniel replied levelly. "A man doesn't have to cross the

Mason-Dixon line just because he has his own opinion about the subject." Turning to McLaury, he said, "Since we are ladies and gentlemen here, Reverend, I'd like to know your opinion on it. What does the Bible say about slavery?"

"That's a good question," put in Web. "Dad and I have discussed it several times. I was going to talk to you about it in private, Reverend, but since the subject is on the table, how about telling us your opinion?"

"Yes," spoke up Dudley Steele. "I'd like to know, if war comes between the North and the South, whose side will God be on?"

EIGHT

Benjamin McLaury could feel the eyes of everyone at the table on him as he looked at Dudley Steele and said, "I'll be glad to discuss with you what Scripture says about slavery, but I'm not convinced that God will choose sides if there is a war. He loves all of His children, and there are believers on both sides. This is exactly why I haven't addressed the subject from the pulpit. There are people on both sides of the issue in my congregation, as most of you know. And as you will see, the Bible leans toward every man being a free man, but does not actually condemn slavery."

"So you haven't preached on it because it could divide the people of our church just as it is dividing the people of the North and the South?" asked Dudley.

"Basically, yes," nodded the pastor. "However, I do not shun controversy where the Bible is clear-cut and definitive. I'm willing to fight for what I believe. I have in the past, and will do so in the future." Looking at John Ruffin, he asked, "May I borrow a Bible, John?"

Abby jumped up, saying, "I'll get mine, Reverend."

While Abby was out of the room, Web said, "Reverend McLaury, you are a good judge of humanity, since humans are your business. Do you think either side in this North-South split is willing to go to war? Some are saying that in spite of all the war talk, neither side really wants to shed blood over it. They say America will simply become a divided nation."

"That kind of talk is ridiculous!" blared Edmund. "Of course we're willing to shed blood over it! I certainly am! It's time we sever ourselves from those pious snobs up north who condemn us slave owners. They won't take their noses out of our business until we shoot them off."

McLaury said to Web, "I agree with Edmund that there are people in the South who are willing to shed blood. Like him, some are even eager to do it. I don't think the Northerners will start a war over it. When war comes, it'll be initiated by Southerners."

"You say when war comes, Reverend," spoke up Cora Steele. "Are you actually expecting it to happen?"

"Yes. As Web said, some political leaders are saying America will simply become a divided nation. I don't think so. Once South Carolina secedes next week, the other Southern states will soon follow. When a confederacy of Southern states is created, there will be an immediate controversy over some Union real estate located south of the Mason-Dixon line. Like the forts off the coast of South Carolina. The South will say it's their property, and the North will balk. When the war starts, that's probably where it will happen. Mark my word, the South will fire the first shot."

"Amen!" gusted Edmund. "And I'll be there to see it happen!"

Abby returned and handed McLaury her Bible.

While thumbing his way to an Old Testament passage, McLaury said, "To keep this from getting too lengthy, let me simply state a few facts, then I'll read you some Scripture." When he had found the place he wanted, he shoved his plate aside and laid the open Bible before him. "The Hebrew word for slave is *evedh*. The Greek word is *doulos*. It is interesting that in our English Bible the word slave is only found twice, once in the Old Testament and once in the New Testament. Jeremiah 2 and Revelation 18. All the other times, the words *bondservant, bondman,* or *bondwoman* are used...or

BATTLES OF DESTINY

122

even the word *servant*. Of course *servant* did not always mean *slave*. There are many instances in both Testaments when you find the term *hired servant*. This, of course, was a servant who was paid."

"So when we read the word *servant* in the Bible," spoke up Daniel, "it means *slave* unless we're told he or she was hired?"

"Correct," nodded McLaury. "In the Old Testament, God allowed slaves to be acquired in a number of ways. One was when Israel's enemies were taken as prisoners of war. This is found in Numbers 31. Another way was by gift, such as when Laban gave his daughter Leah a young woman named Zilpah for her handmaid. A handmaid was a slave."

"But not to be whipped and beaten into submission, right, Reverend?" spoke up Lynne.

"That's right, Lynne. Slaves among the Hebrews were more kindly treated than slaves among other nations, since Mosaic laws governed their treatment. Remember that Moses got his instructions from the Lord, and He would never advocate harsh treatment and cruelty by one human being to another."

Abby looked at Reed, hoping he was listening.

"This is what I wanted to read to all of you," said McLaury. "I said a moment ago that God allowed slaves to be acquired. In Leviticus 25, He made it clear that no Israelite was to own another Israelite. Listen to verse thirty-nine and a portion of verse forty: 'And if thy brother that dwelleth by thee be waxen poor, and be sold unto thee; thou shalt not compel him to serve as a bondservant: but as an hired servant.' We know that by the word brother, the Lord means another Israelite, because in verse forty-six, He speaks of 'your brethren the children of Israel.' "

"But what about owning slaves who were not Israelites?" queried John .

"God did allow that," nodded McLaury. "In verse forty-four, He says, 'Both thy bondmen, and thy bondmaids, which thou shalt have, shall be of the heathen that are round about you; of them shall ye buy bondmen and bondmaids.' "

"Aha!" gusted Edmund. "See there! We Southerners are in the right."

"Let me hasten to point out that three times in this chapter God warns against ruling with rigor," said McLaury. "The dictionary will tell you that *rigor* is 'severity.' Too often slave owners—in that day and today as well—tend to forget that their slaves are human beings, and treat them with severity."

"Maybe there wouldn't be such strong objection to slavery on the part of abolitionists if all slave owners were kind and caring to their slaves," said Dudley.

"I'm sure that would make a difference," nodded McLaury, "although there would still be opposition against one human being owning another one."

"Well, if God commanded it," spoke up Edmund, "how can anyone be against it?"

"God didn't command it in the sense of requiring or demanding it, Mr. Ruffin," replied McLaury. "Since slavery was a practice in Bible days, He allowed it. But in so doing, He laid down some restrictions on how slaves were to be treated."

Edmund seemed displeased.

"I said earlier," proceeded McLaury, "that God allowed slaves to be acquired in a number of ways. I mentioned that they could be taken as prisoners of war, and that they could be acquired as a gift. They were also acquired by birth as the offspring of slaves already possessed. Exodus 21:4 deals with that. In the very next chapter, we find that if a man stole something from another and was caught, the man from whom he stole could own him as a slave if he couldn't make restitution."

"Good enough for him," grunted Reed.

Ignoring Exley's comment, McLaury went on. "In Exodus 21, we learn that a person could volunteer to be someone's slave if they so chose. Which brings me to an important point. In the laws that God laid down concerning slaves, He set it up so they could gain their freedom in a number of ways. I won't take time to read them to you now, but you can find them in Exodus 21, Leviticus 25, and Deuteronomy 15. Now, let me show you something from Exodus 21, imbedded in the very context of slaves gaining their freedom. In verse two, God says, 'If thou buy an Hebrew servant, six years he shall serve: and in the seventh he shall go out free for nothing.' So God put a restriction on how long a Hebrew slave could be held as a slave. After six years, he was free. The next verse tells how the slave's wife can be freed.

"Sometimes a slave owner would decide he wanted to make a maidservant his wife, and he would betroth her to himself. If he changed his mind later and took another woman for his wife, the maidservant was to be set free. Verses ten and eleven say, 'If he take him another wife; her food, her raiment, and her duty of marriage, shall he not diminish. And if he do not these three unto her, then shall she go out free without money.' So you can see that the context here is slaves getting their freedom.

"Then notice verse twenty-three: 'And if any mischief follow, then thou shalt give life for life, eye for eye, tooth for tooth, hand for hand, foot for foot, burning for burning, wound for wound, stripe for stripe. And if a man smite the eye of his servant, or the eye of his maid, that it perish; he shall let him go free for his eye's sake. And if he smite out his manservant's tooth, or his maidenservant's tooth; he shall let him go free for his tooth's sake.' The context here is slavery, and slaves going free. Catch these words: Eye for eye, tooth for tooth. Now, the same words are used elsewhere in the Old Testament in a different context, but that does not nullify this one.

"Now watch a change in attitude on this eye for eye, tooth for tooth position by the Lord Himself in the New Testament." Flipping pages, McLaury found the passage he wanted. "Jesus said in Matthew 5:38, 'Ye have heard that it hath been said, An eye for an eye, and a tooth for a tooth: But I say unto you, That ye resist not evil: but whosoever shall smite thee on thy right cheek, turn to him the other also.' Down in verse forty-three, He said, 'Ye have heard that it hath been said, Thou shalt love thy neighbour, and hate thine enemy. But I say unto you, Love your enemies, bless them that curse you, do good to them that hate you, and pray for them which despitefully use you, and persecute you.' "

Reed Exley was squirming on his chair as McLaury ran his gaze in a quick sweep across the faces around the table and said, "Seems to me that since Jesus changed the eye for eye and tooth for tooth approach, and that it is found in a slavery context in Exodus 21, that His approach to slavery just might be different in the New Testament, also. Slavery did continue in New Testament times, but the love of Christ seemed to militate against its continued existence."

"You say *seemed* to, Reverend," said Edmund. "So the New Testament doesn't come right out and condemn slavery?"

"No, but I do think it leans toward all men being free, as I said a little while ago. Let me read something from Colossians 4. The servants spoken of here are not hired servants but slaves. Verse one: 'Masters, give unto your servants that which is just and equal; knowing that ye also have a Master in heaven.' In my mind, that which is just and equal would have to be wages. It seems to me that God is saying to abolish slavery and hire your slaves as paid workers."

"But it doesn't exactly say that," argued Edmund.

"I know," nodded the preacher. "That's why I haven't preached on this subject from the pulpit. However, it implies it. But let me show you some more." Wetting his thumb with his tongue, he flipped back a few pages, found the proper spot, and said, "Listen to this in Ephesians 6: 'Servants, be obedient to them that are your masters according to the flesh, with fear and trembling, in singleness of your heart, as unto Christ; not with eyeservice, as menpleasers; but as the servants of Christ, doing the will of God from the heart; with good will doing service, as to the Lord, and not to men: knowing that whatsoever good thing any man doeth, the same shall he receive of the Lord, whether he be bond or free.' So the servants Paul is writing about here are definitely slaves—bondmen."

"Can't argue with that," put in Web Steele, who was showing great interest.

"Now listen as Paul addresses the slave owners: 'And, ye masters, do the same things unto them, forbearing threatening: knowing that your Master also is in heaven; neither is there respect of persons with him.' Since there is no respect of persons with God, the slave and his owner are on the same level in God's eyes."

"Can't argue with that, either," grinned Web. "And…uh…that part about forbearing threatening—that means to refrain from threatening them, doesn't it, Reverend?"

"Exactly," nodded McLaury.

Web looked at the puffy-faced Exley. "You hear that?" Exley did not reply. John Ruffin ran his gaze between the two men, showing his discomfort over the strain between them.

Benjamin McLaury noticed this but did not let on. Instead, he said, "So it is clear that if a man has slaves, he should treat them kindly, remembering that he and his slaves are on the same level in the eyes of God." Turning pages again, he added, "Over here in Philippians 2:3, it says, 'Let nothing be done through strife or vainglory; but in lowliness of mind let each esteem other better than themselves.' I can see a man accomplishing this command when he compares himself to his employees, but it seems to me it would be extremely difficult to esteem a slave better than yourself. This is why I believe the Bible leans toward every man being a free man. But as I said, since it does not come right out and condemn slavery, I don't censure men such as yourselves for owning them."

"But you would censure us if we mistreated them, right?" said Web.

"Most assuredly," replied McLaury, "and so would God."

Again, Web threw a sharp glance at Exley. Then looking at the preacher, he said, "Thank you, Reverend, for being willing to discuss this with us. It's obvious that you've studied this issue thoroughly, and you have answered a lot of questions for me. I tend to agree with you that the Bible leans toward every man being a free man. However, since my father is a slave owner and he treats his slaves with kindness and compassion, I will not turn away from him. I also want to say here and now—if war comes between ourselves and the Yankees, I will fight for the South. The Northerners have no right to force abolition on us."

"That's the way I feel, too," spoke up Daniel Hart. "As a true son of the South, I'll fight for the South."

"I don't want any of our men to have to fight in a war," Cora Steele said with a pained expression.

"None of us do, Mrs. Steele," McLaury said in a tender tone, "but I'm afraid the bloody conflict is coming."

"Well, if it does," piped up Reed Exley, "I'll be the first to sign up in the Southern army. It will be my pleasure to help wipe the stinkin' Northerners off the map."

"Amen!" blurted Edmund , slapping a palm on the table top. "I say let's get on with it and stomp the Yankees into the dust!"

Charles and Harriet had waited in the kitchen until the discussion on slavery was finished, then carried the dessert to the table. While fresh apple pie was being consumed, the wind began to howl outside, pelting the windows of the mansion with snow and sleet. The storm was definitely getting worse.

Edmund announced that he would head for home right away. It was eleven miles to his place, and he wanted to get home before the storm became even more severe. Cora told her husband that she wanted to head for home, also. Daniel decided his parents would be worried about him if he was much later getting home. Web told his parents he wanted to spend a few minutes with Abby, then he would be right behind them.

When all the guests except Web were gone, Reed announced that he was going upstairs to look in on Elizabeth. John went to the library, Lynne to her room, and Web and Abby sought privacy in the parlor.

When the couple entered the parlor, they found that Charles had added logs to the fire. Abby sat down on the love seat that faced the fireplace while Web stirred the logs. Then he made his way to the love seat and sat beside her. They looked deep into each other's eyes for a long moment without speaking, then he took her into his arms and kissed her.

The kiss was long and lingering. Before their lips parted, Web felt moisture on his cheeks. Drawing back, he saw the tears spilling from Abby's eyes. The conversation at the dinner table had left her with the awful dread that war could not be avoided. She had suffered nightmares recently, dreaming of Web going off to war and never coming back. Each time, she had awakened with relief, knowing that it had been only a bad dream. She had dared to hope that the two sides would settle their differences peacefully. But now hope was an island, speedily succumbing to the tides of reality.

Clinging to him, Abby sobbed, "Oh, darling, I can't let you go to war! I can't! I just can't!"

Wrapping his arms around her once again, Web held her close. "I wish we weren't facing this awful thing, Abby," he said in a half-whisper, "but there it is, confronting us like a ferocious beast. All we can do is meet it head-on. I know you would not want me to run from the fight when it comes. I'll have to do my part, along with all the other able-bodied men of the South. Like it or not, we just have to accept what comes."

Sniffling, she said into his ear, "I...I'm sorry. Of course I wouldn't want you to play the coward and run from the war. It's just...it's just that I love you so much. I want us to have our lives together."

"And I love you very much too, sweetheart," sighed Web. "There's nothing I want more than to spend my life as your husband."

Trembling as she clung to him, Abby said, "Oh, Web, you have to make me a promise. You must promise to come back to me! If...if you didn't come back, I wouldn't want to live! You are my life, darling. You must promise to come back!"

Web Steele knew there were no guarantees when a man went into battle. Some would live through it, and others would die. But at the moment, the woman he loved needed something to cling to. She needed to hear him say it. Pulling back, he looked into her tear-filled eyes and said, "I promise, Abby. I promise that no matter how hot the battles, and no matter how long the war goes on, I'll come back to you."

After another kiss, Abby walked her man to the door, kissed him goodnight, and watched him vanish into the storm as he headed for the barn and his horse and buggy. She waited at the window until he drove away, then went upstairs to her room.

Reed Exley entered the bedroom to find his wife sitting up and reading a book by the light of the kerosene lantern on her bed stand. She had brushed her hair in anticipation of his appearance, and had applied some powder and rouge to make herself more presentable.

Elizabeth focused on his battered face as he shut the door and leaned against it. Closing the book and dropping it beside her, she asked, "What on earth happened to you?"

"Got into it with Web—and I don't want to talk about it."

"Okay," she shrugged. "Does Abby know about it?"

"Yeah. Why?"

"Well, she was up here earlier, and she didn't mention it."

"Why should she? She knew you'd see it when I came up here."

"Web brought my dinner tray up to me. He didn't say anything, either."

"Probably for the same reason," Reed said flatly. "You notice the bruise I put on his face?"

"Yes, but I didn't say anything about it. Of course, I didn't know you had put it there. What were you fighting about? Is that a cut above your eye?"

"I said I don't want to talk about it," he grunted, pulling away from the door.

As he approached the bed, she smiled weakly and asked, "Did you enjoy the discussion at dinner, honey? Harriet told me about it when she came up to get my tray."

"Aw, it was all right," he grunted. "The reverend seems to think God's sittin' up there in heaven frowning at us for owning slaves."

"Well, maybe He is. I've often wondered if it was right to own another human being."

Reed chuckled and said, "Elizabeth, those black animals aren't human beings. There isn't a thing wrong with us owning 'em. If we can own horses, we can own blackies."

Elizabeth didn't feel like arguing. Smiling up at him, she asked, "Don't I get a kiss?"

Mechanically, Reed leaned over and pecked her on the forehead. As he walked toward a chair, he said, "It's snowing pretty hard out."

Elizabeth did not comment. She only observed him with hurt in her eyes as he sat down and began to untie his shoes. After a few seconds she said in a tight voice, "Am I ever going to get a real kiss again?"

Reed pulled off both shoes before answering. "You probably will when you have the kid and look like your old self again."

Tears welled up in Elizabeth's eyes and her lower lip quivered as she said, "A woman can't give birth to a child without her body changing. I'm sorry that I'm big, but you had something to do with it, Reed. It's your baby. If you loved me enough, my appearance wouldn't matter."

Reed carried his shoes to the closet and tossed them on the floor. He took a moment to remind himself that he must feign love for Elizabeth. As long as he was married to her, he would be part heir to the plantation. One day he would come into a great deal of money. He secretly wished it was Abby he had married, but told himself that some day it would all work out. Somehow the time would come when Elizabeth would no longer be in the picture, and both Abby and a huge chunk of the inheritance would be his. Web Steele loomed large in his mind as a barrier between himself and Abby. I'll find a way to remove Mr. Steele from the picture, too, he thought.

Forcing himself, Reed walked back to the bed and sat down beside Elizabeth. He took her in his arms and kissed her passionately. When he released her, he said, "I don't know what's the matter with me, Liz. I didn't mean what I said a minute ago. Forgive me?"

"Sure," she nodded, "if you'll kiss me like that one more time."

Reed forced himself to comply, and after the kiss he patted her shoulder and said, "You have my undying love, Liz."

The next morning, Reed Exley stepped out of the mansion after breakfast into the bright sunlight. The air was frosty, and nine inches of snow lay on the ground. The plantation's male slaves were already busy shoveling snow from the walks around the mansion and from the wide porch. Mandrake and a slave named Schyler were removing snow from in front of the mansion where the guests parked their vehicles.

As he stepped off the porch and headed toward the barn, Exley gave Mandrake a sidelong sneer. Plodding through the snow, he entered the barn and moved to a rear corner where a small cubicle was built beneath the hayloft. Turning the key in the padlock that held the door secure, he entered the tight space and removed a wicked-looking metal apparatus from a hook on the wall. There were two others just like it on the opposite wall.

Smiling to himself, he examined the apparatus, which he called his "Beast Collar." Made of heavy iron, the collar was constructed to lock around a victim's neck. Four prongs, eighteen inches in length, extended horizontally from the circular collar, or neck ring. The prongs were made with two upturned hooks on their tips, and prevented the slave who wore it from lying down. Its weight caused the head, neck, shoulders, and back to ache severely.

Stepping out of the cubicle, Exley leaned the collar against the wall and padlocked the door. Chuckling, he reached into his coat pocket and pulled out the derringer. Before breakfast, he had asked Abby if she knew what had happened to the gun. When she told him, Exley demanded that she return it. Reluctantly, she went to her room and returned with the gun. When Exley took it from her, he smiled and told her she was especially beautiful when she was angry. She had stomped away and refused to speak a word to him at breakfast.

Checking the chamber of the small pistol, Exley found that it was still loaded. Smiling to himself, he slid it back into his coat pocket, picked up the heavy collar, and left the barn. Trudging through the snow, he called to the men who were shoveling and told them all to gather around.

As the black men made a circle around him, their eyes showed fear at the sight of the "beast collar," which now lay at Exley's feet. Mandrake was on the outside of the circle. Fixing him with a cold glare, Exley snapped, "Mandrake, come here!" The owl-eyed slaves cleared a path for Mandrake.

"Take off your coat!" commanded Exley.

The young slave's face went rigid. "Massa Reed," he said, "you ain't got no call to make me wear that thing."

"I'll be the judge of that," clipped Exley. "Get that coat off!"

While Mandrake looked Exley square in the eye and unbuttoned his coat, Exley said, "Didn't I tell you yesterday I was gonna make you one sorry slave for tellin' me what to do?"

"Yes," mumbled Mandrake.

"Well, now's the time." Speaking to the others, Exley said, "I want every one of you to pay attention, here. This belligerent beast had the nerve to give me a command yesterday. Nobody with black skin tells me what to do! Do you all understand?"

There was a chorus of "Yassuhs."

Reaching into his pants pocket, Exley produced the small wrench that served as the key to the iron collar. Inserting it, he opened the collar and said to two of the slaves, "Dariel—Hector— pick it up and put it on Mandrake."

Dariel, who was a large man, bristled. He said in a deep basso, "Massa Reed, I cain't do it. Mandrake is my frien'. I cain't put no pain on 'im."

Exley's pale blue eyes took on a diabolic look. He whipped out the derringer and pointed it between Dariel's bushy brows and ground out his words. "Dariel, you do as I tell you this minute, or the rest of these blackies will bury you before sundown."

Dariel looked at Mandrake sadly, then bent over and picked up the collar by two of the prongs. Hector quickly took hold of the other prongs and helped Dariel guide the collar over Mandrake's head till it rested heavily on his neck and shoulders. Breathing hotly, Exley stepped up and used the wrench to lock the collar. When he was finished, he said, "This'll teach you, black boy. Now get back to work."

Dariel turned to Exley and said, "Massa Reed, I don' mean no disrespec', but if'n Mandrake don' wear his coat, he gonna catch his death."

Grinning wickedly, Reed replied, "That'd just be terrible, wouldn't it?" Wheeling, he trudged toward the mansion, then stopped, looked over his shoulder, and said, "Oh, well. Go ahead and put his coat on him."

Exley watched Dariel pick the coat up and put it on Mandrake. Scowling, he said, "All right. Now, all of you get back to work." After a few seconds of silence, he laughed, "Hope you have a miserable day, Mandrake. I guarantee you'll have a miserable night!"

NINE

The next morning, Elizabeth Exley was sitting in a chair by one of the bedroom windows, observing her husband down below as he gave work orders to a group of male slaves. The sky was cloudy, and it looked like it could start snowing again at any time.

There was a knock at the door, followed by her father's voice. "Elizabeth, may we come in?"

"Yes, Papa."

John Ruffin entered the room with Abby and Lynne on his heels. As they gathered around her, Abby said, "You look much better today. Harriet said you ate all your breakfast."

"Mm-hmm," smiled the expectant mother, adjusting her uncomfortable body on the chair. "I feel much better."

"We came up to tell you that we're going into town," said Papa John. "We'll probably be gone till late afternoon. Is there anything we can get you?"

"I could use some new rouge and face powder, Papa," she replied. "Abby and Lynne know what kind."

"We'll take care of it," Abby assured her. "Anything else?"

"Not that I can think of. My purse is over there in the top dresser drawer."

"That's all right, honey," said John. "I'll buy it for you."

"That's not necessary, Papa," protested Elizabeth. "You shouldn't have to pay for my needs."

"It's all right," he said with a wave of his hand. "You and Reed will be putting out plenty of money when my grandchild is born." Leaning down, he kissed her cheek. "See you later, honey. Papa loves you."

"And I love Papa," she chirped.

Abby and Lynne both kissed Elizabeth and followed their father toward the door. Just as John was about to pass into the hall, Elizabeth called out, "Papa?"

"Yes, honey?"

"Did you know that Mandrake is wearing one of the iron collars?"

"No, I didn't," replied John, walking toward her, puzzlement showing on his face.

Abby and Lynne hurried behind him and peered over his shoulders as he looked through the window at the collection of slaves just beyond the barn near the first row of shacks. The distance was only some forty yards, and the pain on Mandrake's face was quite evident. Reed was standing in front of Mandrake, making him remove his coat.

"I wonder what Mandrake could have done?" mumbled John. "Has to be a pretty serious offense before one of my slaves wears a collar."

"Not since Reed's been your overseer," said Abby, almost without thinking. "He's put them on several slaves since you gave him the job. You just haven't seen them."

John pulled away from the window and said, "Well, if Reed sees fit to use that degree of discipline, they must need it."

"I can tell you why Mandrake's wearing the collar," said Abby in a tone of disgust. "He's being punished for that incident in town day before yesterday."

"You mean that incident over the coats?"

"Yes."

"How can you be so sure that's what it is?"

"Didn't you just see Mandrake's coat coming off?"

"Well…yes."

"Your son-in-law delights in freezing your slaves' blood, Papa. I've tried to tell you before—he's cruel to them." Noticing the pained look on Elizabeth's face, Abby laid a hand on her shoulder and said, "I'm sorry, Sister, but it's true."

Elizabeth reached up and squeezed her sister's hand. "I know it appears that way sometimes, Abby, but Reed can be quite tender when he wants to."

"Oh. Guess I've never seen him want to."

"Abby," said John, standing tall and straight over her, "is Web's little feud with Reed turning you against him?"

"Not in the least, Papa," she replied, meeting his gaze without blinking. "Reed is doing that all by himself." Again, to Elizabeth she said, "I'm sorry, but that's the way it is."

Elizabeth squeezed Abby's hand once more and said, "I'm sorry, too. Everything will be all right once the baby's here. Reed's been under a great strain with me being sick."

Abby knew Elizabeth's sickness had nothing to do with her husband's meanness, but she said no more.

Lynne looked out the window again, and said, "Papa, certainly Reed shouldn't make Mandrake work out in the cold without his coat."

"Don't worry, Lynne," responded John, patting her shoulder. "Reed knows what he's doing. He won't let Mandrake work without the coat for very long. He doesn't want a sick slave on his hands. Come along, girls. We need to head for town."

When her father and sisters were gone, Elizabeth looked back down at her husband, standing in the snow with the slaves. A mixture of emotions stirred within her. She loved the man, but she hated him. When she first met him, Reed had swept her off her feet. He was handsome in his own way and could turn on the charm when he wanted to. Soon after they were married and Reed was made slave overseer by her father, it became evident that he had married her to get close to the Ruffin money. Elizabeth would not admit it to herself at first, but she finally faced the truth. Reed Exley was a greedy man.

When she announced to Reed that she was pregnant nearly seven months ago, what little affection he had been showing to her began to fade. Half of her loved him because he was the father of her unborn child, and that half needed his love and affection.

The other half despised the man because he had proven to be greedy, cold-hearted, and cruel. Abby's words had struck close to home, because Elizabeth had entertained the very same thoughts.

As she watched Reed treating young Mandrake cruelly, she wondered what could be done to stop him. At times Elizabeth was frightened by her husband. He was cool and calculating, and had a way of torturing her mentally without anyone else being aware of it. She was sure that the only reason he had not harmed her physically was because it would show, and John Ruffin would then see him for what he really was. She had often thought of talking to her father and baring her soul about her fear of Reed, but each time she had not gone through with it because she knew he would not accept it. He would dismiss it as a figment of her imagination and shame her for having such thoughts. Reed had his father-in-law totally blinded.

Elizabeth observed as one of the slaves drove a horse and buggy out of the barn and headed around toward the front of the mansion. This was the vehicle that would carry her father and sisters into Richmond.

She struggled to a standing position, waddled across the room to the bedstand, and picked up her book. Returning to the chair, she sat down and began to read.

The women and children watched from inside the shacks as Mandrake stood coatless, bearing the heavy collar on his neck and shoulders. His whole body was shivering. Orchid looked on with tears spilling down her cheeks.

Pacing back and forth in front of Mandrake and the gathering of male slaves, Reed noticed John Ruffin drive away from the mansion with Abby and Lynne beside him. He was lecturing the black men on the consequences of disobedience and the awful mistake Mandrake had made in daring to give him an order.

Mandrake felt the need to defend himself and boldly said, "Massa Reed, I wouldn' have spoke to you the way I did 'cept'n that you hit my wife fo' no reason."

"No reason!" blared Exley in a knife-keen tone. He stopped pacing and glared heatedly at Mandrake. "What do you mean, no reason? She was bawlin' her head off, and female bawlin' grates on my nerves!"

"She was cryin' 'cause she was scared and cold. You dragged her out of the wagon and throwed her on the ground. Then you made her take her coat off. Orchid couldn' he'p cryin'. That's when I said you had no call to hit her, an' I tol' you to leave her alone. Wouldn' you have gone to Miz 'Lizbeth's defense if'n a man had done to her what you done to Orchid? Ain' a man got a right to defend his wife?"

Face flushed beet-red, Exley screamed, "Black-scum slaves don't have any rights!" Even while the words were spewing from his mouth, he aimed a punch at Mandrake's jaw and knocked him down.

When the prongs on the backside of the collar stabbed into the snow, jerking his neck hard in the fall, Mandrake ejected a pained cry. Cursing like a madman, Exley railed at him to shut up and kicked him in the side.

Still at her window, Orchid broke into sobs. When she saw Exley kick Mandrake a second time, she bolted from the shack, stumbling through the snow.

Exley had kicked Mandrake a fourth time when he heard Orchid's voice screeching at him to stop. Breathing hard, he turned around to see her coming toward him, sobbing.

Unaware that Elizabeth was watching, Exley turned to meet Orchid, his eyes blazing. The slaves looked at each other, blinking, as

Exley pointed at her and bellowed, "Get back in your shack, girl!"

Still stumbling toward Exley, Orchid ignored his command, screaming, "Don' kick 'im no mo', you filthy devil! Don' kick 'im no mo'!"

Exley swore and turned back to Mandrake, who was still lying on his back, holding his ribs. Orchid's use of the words "filthy devil" infuriated Exley. In retaliation, he kicked Mandrake in the face.

Orchid was on him like a wildcat, clawing and scratching. Exley fell and swung his arms to protect his face from Orchid's fingernails. "Get her off me!" he wailed. "Get her off me!"

Lenox, Schyler, and Hector seized the anger-crazed woman and pulled her off. "This won' do no good, Orchid," said Lenox as they held her tight.

She struggled against them, hissing, "Let me go! That filthy devil ain' gonna kick my man no mo'! I'll kill 'im!"

Mandrake was dazed by the blow from Exley's foot, but he was conscious enough to know what was happening. The ground seemed to be reeling beneath him as he tried to get up. The collar was a hindrance, and with his head spinning, he kept falling back in the snow.

Exley scrambled to his feet. Angrily sucking for air, he glared at Orchid and said to the slaves, "Let go of her!"

The men obeyed and backed away as Exley stood like a menacing beast, shoulders hunched, and roared, "Filthy devil, huh? You'll kill me, will you?"

Orchid's wrath had stolen away all her fear. Yelling wildly, she lunged at Exley, clawing at him. Sidestepping her, he struck her square in the face with his fist. She went down hard. Exley sent a swift kick into her side. The slaves were tense, eyeing each other as if trying to decide what to do.

Mandrake struggled to rise as Exley kicked Orchid again. He was drawing his foot back to kick her once more when he heard Elizabeth screaming at him to stop. He turned and looked at her as she leaned from her third floor window.

"Reed, stop it! You'll kill her!"

Pointing at her, he shouted back, "You shut up! I'll handle this my way!"

As he whipped around to resume his punishment, he found a huge dark form standing between him and Orchid, who was still on the ground. Dariel loomed over him. His features were grim and his deep voice steady as he said, "Massa Reed, I cain' let you hurt Orchid no mo'."

Exley looked him up and down, then whipped his derringer from his coat pocket. He took a step back to be out of Dariel's reach, aimed the small pistol at his face, and growled, "Try to stop me, Dariel, and I'll drop you where you stand!"

"Reed!" came Elizabeth's harried voice again. "Papa won't take it lightly if you kill Dariel! He paid a lot of money for him. Come in the house and cool down before you do something you'll be sorry for!"

Without looking her direction, Exley retorted, "I told you to shut up, Elizabeth. Get back in there and close that window. Now do as I tell you!"

Then to Dariel, Exley rasped, "I can kill you and get away with it, big black dog. The choice is yours. Get out of my way, or die! I'm gonna count to three. If you aren't outta my way, I'll drop you like a brain-shot bull."

"I ain't wantin' to die, Massa Reed," Dariel said levelly, "but it ain't right fo' you to treat Orchid like this. I'm askin' you to stop hurtin' her."

"You're gonna learn who's boss around here! If you're not clean outta my way by the time I count to three, you're a dead man." He paused for effect, and said loudly, "One…two…th—"

Reluctantly the huge man angled his body and backed away. Exley then saw that Orchid was still lying on the ground, but an elderly slave named Jedidiah had draped his frail body over her for protection. Mandrake was now on his feet, a bit glassy-eyed and unsteady, but preparing to go after Exley if he looked like he was going to hurt Orchid anymore.

Orchid was groaning in pain. Covering her as much as possible, the skinny old man braced himself, looked up at Exley and said, "Please, Massa Reed. Don' hu't her no mo'. If'n you gotta beat on somebody, beat on me."

For a moment it appeared that Exley would do just that. He drew a deep breath, then looked at Dariel and said, "You and Schyler take Orchid to her shack."

Speaking words of comfort to Orchid, Jedidiah rolled off of her, keeping his weary old eyes on Exley. While the two men picked Orchid up and carried her toward the shack, Mandrake started to follow.

"Hold it, Mandrake!" blared Exley, pointing the derringer at him. "You stay right here!"

Mandrake stopped and used his hands to support the heavy iron collar. He glowered at Exley, his body quivering from the cold.

As Jedidiah struggled to get up, Exley spat, "Stay right where you are, old man. I'm not through with you yet." Then to the others, he said, "You all have your work assignments. Get going."

Slowly the slaves began to move away. Scowling, Exley snapped, "Today! I want it done today!" Looking over their shoulders, they hastened their pace.

Exley slipped the derringer into his coat pocket, then reached under his coat and unbuckled his belt. Sliding it through the loops at his waist, he gripped the buckle and wound the belt around his hand twice, leaving the rest of it to dangle like a whip.

Standing over the old man, who was kneeling in the snow, Exley said, "So you want me to beat on you rather than Orchid, eh?"

A look of horror flashed over Jedidiah's wrinkled face.

Mandrake, still supporting the collar with his hands, took a step toward Exley, saying, "I'm askin' you not to hurt 'im, Massa Reed. All he done was try to protect Orchid. He didn' raise a hand against you. Besides, he's old and feeble. It ain't right fo' you to beat 'im."

Exley's mouth turned downward with irritation. "Did I hear you right, Mandrake? Are you correcting me?"

Before Mandrake could reply, Exley darted to him and lashed his face with the belt. The popping sound echoed among the mansion and the outbuildings. Mandrake staggered backward and fell. A large welt appeared on his face. Pulling the derringer from his coat, Exley pointed it at Mandrake and barked, "If you get up before I tell you to, I'll kill you!"

Elizabeth had closed the window against the cold, but remained there watching the scene below. She saw the slaves walk away at her husband's command, but noticed that while Reed was making a whip out of his belt, the slaves slipped around the corner of the barn. Two dark faces then appeared down low at the corner. No doubt the two "spies" were keeping the others informed of what was happening. She knew if Reed found out, he would be furious.

Elizabeth sucked in a quick breath and put her hand to her mouth when she saw Reed lash Mandrake across the face. Even with the window closed, she could hear the crack. She emitted a shrill whine and bit her forefinger when she saw Reed savagely lashing Jedidiah. The old man's hat had fallen off and he was in a fetal position in the snow, using his hands and arms to protect his head.

Elizabeth was so upset that her breath was coming in short, dry gasps. Suddenly she threw the window open and screamed, "Reed! Stop it! Stop it! How can you be so cruel?"

Exley had hit the old man several times when he heard Elizabeth's shrill voice. Pausing, he bellowed at her, "I told you to shut up!"

"But you'll kill him!"

"That's my business! You butt out!"

Elizabeth began to weep as Reed continued to whip the aging black man unmercifully. She could hear Jedidiah's pained cries each time the belt struck flesh. There was blood on his gnarled old hands and in his short-cropped silver hair.

As the belt continued its lashing, an unearthly wail came from the old man's lips. With a mounting panic, Elizabeth knew if Reed did not quit soon, Jedidiah would die.

Her mind went into a frenzy. She screamed at her husband to stop. Caught up in her passion, she leaned far out of the window—too far. Suddenly she felt the window sill press hard against her unborn baby, and then she was falling.

A helpless cry cut the cold morning air as she plummeted three stories to the ground.

Sitting obediently in the snow, Mandrake saw Elizabeth slip from the window and plunge to the ground. Exley had turned at the sound of the ear-splitting scream and watched his wife as she fell. But like an insane man, he kept lashing Jedidiah with the belt.

Adrenaline surged through Mandrake's body. Unable to contain himself any longer, he rose to his feet and charged Exley, hitting him with a flying tackle. Pain shot through his neck and shoulders because of the iron collar. Exley was momentarily stunned, but he quickly rolled over and scrambled to get up. When Exley was halfway on his feet, Mandrake landed a rock-hard fist to his jaw. Exley went down and lay still.

Mandrake was aware of the other slaves—men and women—rushing from the barn and the shacks as he reached into Exley's pocket for the wrench that would unlock the collar. Most of the slaves stopped to see about Jedidiah, while Orchid and Lenox drew up to Mandrake.

While Lenox helped Mandrake remove the collar, Orchid said shakily, "Oh, Mandrake, I'm 'fraid Miz 'Lizbeth is hurt bad."

"Me too," Mandrake said, his body numb from the cold. He ran toward Elizabeth and Orchid followed, slipping and stumbling in the snow. The rest of the slaves remained with Jedidiah, doing what they could to stop the flow of blood. Warily, they observed Exley, who was beginning to stir.

Mandrake knelt beside Elizabeth. She had hit the ground facing downward, but somehow had rolled onto her back. Blood was seeping from her nose and mouth and spreading on the lower part of her dress. She was hemorrhaging internally. She was barely conscious, and moaned incoherently, rolling her head slowly from side to side.

Looking up at Orchid, who stood over him wide-eyed and frightened, Mandrake said, "Run to the front door of the mansion and tell Charles what has happened. Harriet will need to make Miz 'Lizbeth comfortable while I ride into town and bring the doctuh. Hurry on, now. I'll carry her right behind you."

Orchid's face revealed her fear that Elizabeth would die. Without expressing it, she turned and ran toward the front of the mansion.

Gently Mandrake placed his hands under Elizabeth and said softly, "I'm gonna take you in the house, Miz 'Lizbeth. Harriet will take care of you while I ride into town and bring the doctuh."

Elizabeth did not respond. She had stopped moving her head and was no longer moaning. Were it not for the weak rise and fall of her breast, Mandrake would have thought she was dead. With his knees planted in the snow, the muscular slave hoisted her into his arms, cradling her like a baby. Her head and arms hung limply. Rising to his feet, Mandrake headed for the front of the big house.

He had taken only a few steps when he saw Reed Exley stumbling toward him with a few of the slaves following. Most of them were still collected around Jedidiah.

Mandrake was almost to the corner of the mansion when Exley's sharp voice bawled, "Mandrake! Stop right there!"

Mandrake stopped and looked at the wild-eyed man as he drew up with the derringer in his hand. He was angry and a muscle in his right cheek was twitching just below the eye. Mandrake wondered how long it would be before Exley went totally insane.

Exley glared at Mandrake and hissed, "You're in big trouble, black boy! You would dare lay a hand on me? And on top of that, you took the collar off without my permission. You are in big trouble!"

"Massa Reed," Mandrake said calmly, "you were beatin' on

Jedidiah like a madman. I had to stop you. And I had to take the collar off so's I could come and take care of Miz 'Lizbeth. She's hurt bad. I'm takin' her in the house so's Harriet can tend to her while I ride into town and bring the doctuh." As he said this, Mandrake began moving toward the porch.

Exley hurried around in front of him, aimed the derringer at his head, and thundered, "Stop! Put her down!"

"Massa Reed, she's hurt bad. We gotta hurry and get her in the house."

The tic on Exley's cheek twitched rapidly as he shook the gun at Mandrake and growled, "Get your dirty black hands off her. I said put her down!"

Mandrake looked down at the woman in his arms and saw that she was no longer breathing. Her body was a lifeless weight. Tears filled his eyes. Looking at Exley, he said, "She's dead, Massa Reed. Miz 'Lizbeth is dead."

It was like the angry man had not heard what Mandrake said. Gritting his teeth, he hissed, "I told you to get your dirty black hands off her! Put—her—down!"

Slowly and gently, Mandrake placed Elizabeth's body on the snow. As Reed bent down beside her, the butler appeared on the porch. Harriet and Orchid were behind him. The servants had been working on the opposite side of the mansion and had not heard any of the disturbance.

Reed bent his face into a mask of grief as Charles came up behind him. Rising and trying desperately to produce tears, he said in a quivering voice, "Elizabeth is dead, Charles. She fell from the bedroom window up there. I don't know how it happened, or why she even had the window open. Would you carry her into the house?"

Harriet let out a whimper and covered her mouth.

"Yes, sir," nodded Charles, bending down to pick up the body. He struggled for a moment, then rose to a standing position. Mandrake wanted to help him, but knew he mustn't put his "dirty black hands" on Elizabeth.

"Thank you, Charles," said Reed, still putting on a show of grief. "Lay her on one of the couches in the parlor and cover her with a blanket. I'll be in later. Right now I have to have a talk with the slaves."

Charles moved unsteadily toward the porch with Harriet beside him. When they had vanished from view, Exley instantly lost his mask of grief and said, "All right, all of you, let's go see about Jedidiah."

All of the slaves gathered in a circle around the bloodied old man, where four black women were tending to him. Jedidiah was conscious, but lay quite still. Exley bent over him, made a quick examination, and standing erect, said, "Jedidiah will be all right. In a moment, some of you can carry him to his shack and wash him up. Once he's removed from this spot, I want you men to get your snow shovels and dispose of this bloody snow. When that's done, replace it with some of that snow behind the barn. Understand?"

There was a familiar chorus of "Yassuhs."

"All right. Now listen good. If any one of you ever breathes a word of what happened here today to anybody, I'll kill you! Master John will learn that Elizabeth fell from the window—nothing else. None of you saw anything. You did not see Miss Elizabeth leaning out of the window, nor did you hear her screaming. Nobody knows why she fell. Do you understand?"

Again came the chorus of fearful "Yassuhs."

"I mean what I say. If one word of what happened ever comes from one of you, I'll punish all of you, and I'll kill the one who told. Do you all understand?"

Knowing that Exley would carry out his threat, every slave assured him they would never tell what happened. If Master John, Miss Abby, or Miss Lynne should question them about it, they would not divulge the truth.

Reed was waiting in the parlor when John Ruffin and his daughters arrived home late that afternoon. Feigning grief once more, he met them at the door and solemnly told them that Elizabeth had fallen from the window and died.

The three of them were overcome with grief and clung to each other as they wept. Charles and Harriet came in to offer their sympathy. When the shock began to wear off, Exley said he had no idea why Elizabeth was leaning out the window. He could not figure out why she would even have it open on such a cold day. He told them he had questioned the slaves about it, but none of them had noticed her until she fell.

Elizabeth was buried with her unborn baby still in the womb on Sunday afternoon, December 16. People came from miles around to attend the funeral and offer their sympathy to the family. Web Steele was a strong pillar to John and Lynne, as well as to Abby. Though he detected a facade of grief on Reed's part, he offered his condolences. Exley only gave Steele a cold stare.

Edmund Ruffin stayed close by his brother throughout, and as they walked from the grave toward the waiting funeral coach, he asked John if he was still going with him to Columbia the next day. John hesitated, saying that he shouldn't leave Lynne and Abby so soon after their sister's death. But Edmund urged him to go, saying that it would help take his mind off his own grief. Abby had Web to lean on, and Lynne had Daniel. John discussed it with his daughters, and they both urged him to go, agreeing with Uncle Edmund that it would help ease his grief.

Feigning the role of a mourning husband, Reed remained beside the grave as everyone else walked slowly away. He laughed within himself. Now that Elizabeth was out of the way, he could pursue Abby—after a proper time of mourning, of course. He was sure Abby felt an attraction for him, but in respect for Elizabeth she had always put up a front. Things would be different now, he told himself.

There was one obstacle in his way, however: Webster Steele. Somehow Reed had to get Web out of Abby's life.

TEN

On Monday morning, December 17, 1860, Edmund and John Ruffin boarded a train for Columbia, South Carolina, at the Richmond depot. Edmund was excited about the speech he was to give at the convention, and though John was not as enthusiastic about the secession as his brother, he was pleased that Edmund was considered a leader among the Southern patriots.

On the evening of that same day, Web Steele and Daniel Hart took the Ruffin sisters into Richmond for dinner at an expensive restaurant. They talked a lot about Elizabeth and what a bright light she had been in the Ruffin home when the girls were growing up. Abby and Lynne both shed a few tears as they revived old memories, some that hadn't been thought of in years.

When the discussion became too painful, Daniel brought up the pending war between the North and South. Lynne and Abby were soon on the verge of tears once more with the prospect of the men they loved having to enter the fight.

Web suggested they talk about their future, ignoring for the moment the war clouds that hung over their heads. Soon the conversation was lighter as the women brought up names they had considered for the children they would bear in the future. Web and Daniel suggested silly names just to keep the evening joyful.

During the frosty ride home in the Steele buggy, Lynne and Daniel were in the back seat, and Abby rode beside Web in the front seat as he handled the reins. Both couples were dressed warmly and were wrapped in buffalo-hide blankets.

When the lights of Richmond were behind them, Web turned so Lynne and Daniel could hear him and said, "I don't mean to freshen your grief again by talking about Elizabeth's death, but I have a strange feeling about it."

"You, too?" said Abby. "Lynne and I haven't been able to accept the story Reed is telling, either."

"When I heard it, there was an odd smell about it to me," put in Daniel. "Why would Elizabeth have the window open in the first place? Nobody opens a window this time of year unless there's a good reason."

"Certainly not to let the wintry air in, that's for sure," said Lynne.

"Elizabeth saw something outside that either frightened or excited her," Web said. "Something that had her attention enough that she wanted to hear what was going on, or something that she wanted to call out to someone below."

"Had to be," agreed Abby. "But Papa talked to some of the slaves, and they say they saw and heard nothing until Mandrake caught sight of her falling."

"I didn't tell you, honey," said Web, "but Saturday morning when I came to see you?"

"Yes?"

"Before I came to the house, I walked over to Mandrake and Orchid's shack. They were cordial as usual, but when I asked about the incident, they froze up. They tried not to show it, but they were scared to the bone. I didn't push it any further, but I've got a hunch Mr. Exley's holding an ax over their heads."

"Them and the other seventy-seven slaves," said Abby. "I asked

Papa what he thought after he had talked to some of them, and he was willing to let the question die right there."

"Sure," said Lynne, "because if Reed is guilty of something, Papa really wouldn't want to know it."

"I know," said Abby, shaking her head. "And another thing—those scratches on Reed's face."

"Yeah, I noticed those at the funeral," interjected Daniel.

"Well, I asked him about them," Abby said. "He said it was none of my business how he got them. Later I asked Papa to question him. He refused, saying if Reed didn't want to tell me, I shouldn't pry."

Web sighed, shaking his head. "I love your father dearly, girls, you both know that. But I wonder if he'll ever see that snake-in-the-grass for what he is."

"It may take awhile," responded Lynne, "but I think the day will come."

"Really?"

"Yes. Do you remember that sermon Reverend McLaury preached, oh, about four months ago? The one about 'Be Sure Your Sin Will Find You Out'?"

"Sure do," said Web. "That was a powerful one."

"Well, my ex-brother-in-law isn't immune to God's laws. One day, sooner or later, his sin will catch up to him. When it does, Papa will finally see him for what he is."

"Your *ex*-brother-in-law?" said Daniel.

"Certainly," replied Lynne, tilting her head back to look at him in the dim starlight. "He was my brother-in-law when Elizabeth was alive, but he's not married to her any more, so he's no longer related to me."

"I guess we could say that's the only good thing about Elizabeth's passing, honey," sighed Abby. "Even though Reed's still slave overseer, at least he's not in the family any more."

"Hallelujah!" said Web.

"Amen!" agreed Daniel.

An hour later, Abby was in her bedroom brushing her hair and thinking about the sweet goodnight kiss she had received from Web before he and Daniel had driven away.

Clad in a dark-red silk robe, she looked at herself in the mirror and smiled. "Abby," she said to her reflection, "you are the luckiest woman in all the world. The handsomest, most charming, most wonderful man is in love with you, and you are going to become his wife. The Lord in heaven certainly has smiled down upon—"

Abby's soliloquy was interrupted by a knock on her door. Laying the hairbrush on the dresser, she went to the door and called, "Yes?"

"It's me," came Lynne's voice.

When the door swung open, Lynne gave her a wistful look and said, "I came to kiss you goodnight."

Abby cocked her head. "Sweetie, you kissed me goodnight ten minutes ago."

"I know, but I don't have Elizabeth to kiss goodnight anymore, so I've got to kiss you twice."

Abby's eyes moistened and she took Lynne into her arms. Together they cried for a few moments, then kissed each other goodnight.

Abby closed the door, wiped away her tears, and sat down once more in front of the dresser. Picking up the brush, she ran it through her long, thick auburn hair. There was another knock at the door. "Yes?"

"It's Harriet, Miss Abby," said the maid.

"Come on in."

"Just thought I'd check and see if you needed anything before I go to bed."

"Not a thing, Harriet. Thank you."

"All right, mum," nodded Harriet. "See you in the morning."

"See you in the morning," echoed Abby. "Goodnight."

Abby finished brushing her hair. It was full and beautiful, lying in swirls about her shoulders. Rising from the stool, she started to unbutton her robe when she heard a light tap at the door. *Charles?* she thought. *He never comes to tell me goodnight.*

"Yes?" she said through the door.

"It's Reed, Abby. I need to talk to you."

Abby felt a quick gust of irritation come over her. "I'm getting ready for bed."

"I'm really sorry to bother you, but it's important."

"Can't it wait till morning?"

"No. I have to talk to you now."

Abby sighed, buttoned her robe, and opened the door.

Without waiting for an invitation, Exley bowled past her into the room. She caught a whiff of liquor on his breath.

"Just a minute!" she snapped. "This is my bedroom. I did not invite you in here."

Exley ran his gaze over her and said, "You are one gorgeous woman, Abby."

Fire flashed in her eyes. "You said this was important, Reed. State your business and leave."

A lecherous leer curved his mouth. "You're irresistible with your hair down like that," he breathed, moving toward her.

Abby backed up, saying firmly, "Don't you touch me. I opened the door because you said it was important that we talk. All right, what is it?"

Still leering, Reed replied, "I was gonna wait a little longer beyond Elizabeth's passing before I came to you, but I can't wait. You're the most beautiful and desirable woman I've ever seen, and—"

"Get out of my room!"

Exley lunged for her, laying hold on her upper arms. Before she could free herself, he was kissing her. Revulsion sent a wave of nausea through her. Struggling against him, she finally broke free and sent a stinging slap across his face. "I said get out!"

"I'll go," Exley said quietly, "but I won't give up. I think deep down, you're attracted to me."

Abby's mouth bent down with loathing. "That's what you get for thinking when you're not used to it, Reed. I never gave you any reason to think that."

"How about the times I've made a pass at you, and you never even once told Elizabeth about it? Or Web, either? If you'd told him, I know he'd have been at my throat."

"I never told Elizabeth because it would have broken her heart. It most certainly was not because I enjoyed your passes or felt an attraction toward you. And as for Web, I didn't tell him because he would have pounded you senseless. There's been more than enough trouble between you and him already. I've been trying to keep some semblance of peace in the family."

"Well, some women just won't reveal their true feelings."

"I've just revealed them to you, mister. And while we're having this little talk, I want to tell you how angry I am for the way you treated my sister. Elizabeth loved you, Reed. I don't know why, but she did. You were not only wrong to make passes at me when you were married to her, but I saw many things you did to hurt her. You showed her little consideration, and as far as I could tell, you showed her no love at all."

"Don't you know why I didn't show her any love, Abby? Because I have always been in love with you. I would have made my play for you in the first place, but you were barely seventeen at the time. It wouldn't have set well with Papa John, and he might have run me off."

"So you married Elizabeth because your abominable greed couldn't wait to marry into Ruffin money!" Abby snapped. "Get out of here, right now! I'm in love with Web Steele, and I'm going to become his wife. If you ever make a pass at me again, I *will* tell Web."

Backing into the doorway, Exley grinned "I have to tell you, Abby, you are so beautiful when you're angry."

Exley took another backward step, which put him in the hall. The door banged shut in his face. Turning and walking toward the staircase that led to the third floor, he smiled to himself. He would win gorgeous Abby to himself once Web Steele was out of the picture.

Edmund and John Ruffin stood up to stretch their limbs when the train stopped in Wilmington, North Carolina. It was evening, and they had been on the train all day. Just before the train took on its Wilmington passengers, the conductor entered the car and announced that those passengers who were going to Columbia for the Secession Convention would need to get off the train and catch another one that was leaving for Charleston the next morning. The conductor explained that the convention had been driven out of Columbia because of an outbreak of smallpox. It would convene in Charleston on Wednesday morning, December 19, as planned.

The Ruffin brothers made the appropriate change of trains and arrived in Charleston just after sunrise on December 19. They were fortunate to find accommodations in a small, unheated room with two single beds in the Charleston Hotel.

The town was alive with enthusiastic Southern patriots. Cockades of South Carolina palmetto fronds were worn on every hat to symbolize the South's defiance of the Union. Bands played, and one parade followed another along the town's main streets to the loud cheers of thousands of "Southrons." Flags of many colors—except the Union's colors—were displayed everywhere. Merchants, bankers, and businessmen throughout Charleston lent themselves to the cause.

In addition to the South Carolina Convention delegates, the entire state government was on hand, along with many visiting dignitaries from all the other Southern states, including the governor of Florida, official representatives of Alabama and Mississippi, and one former United States attorney general.

In the hotel lobby, on the streets, and at St. Andrew's Hall where the Convention was held, Edmund Ruffin encountered scores of old friends and fellow "fire-eaters" who had been leaders in the battle to break up the Union. They were the cream of Southern society—bankers, lawyers, plantation owners, clergymen, judges, and newspaper publishers. To a man, they were delighted to meet Edmund's brother, and John was impressed with the confidence they all showed in his brother as champion of the fight for secession.

Edmund's friend and president of the Secession Convention, David Jamison, found him before time to start the proceedings and informed him that his speech would come just before the lunch break. Jamison welcomed John and gave him a seat of honor on the platform next to Edmund.

Edmund's fiery speech had the entire crowd whooping, shouting, and applauding. At times, he had to stop and wait for them to quiet down before he could proceed.

At the beginning of the afternoon session, Jamison told the excited crowd that the exact language of the South Carolina Ordinance of Secession was still being worked on in committee. Then he read a telegram from the governor of Alabama urging the convention delegates to let nothing delay them from seceding, adding that his state would not be far behind.

Jamison then explained that with secession, many important things remained to be settled. At the moment the Ordinance of Secession was adopted by all 169 delegates, South Carolina would cease to be bound by Union law, and a complete new code of law for the newborn Republic of South Carolina would have to be put together. South Carolina patriots had to be appointed to take over the functions previously performed by United States' government officials. There would have to be a new postal service, and customs agents would have to be appointed to handle incoming foreign travelers and foreign goods at Charleston's port.

Jamison then focused on a critical question. What would be done about United States properties inside the territorial limits of South Carolina? The most prominent of these were three federal military installations in Charleston Harbor: Fort Moultrie, Castle Pinckney, and Fort Sumter.

A resolution was passed instructing the newly established Committee on Foreign Relations to send three commissioners to Washington, D.C., to negotiate for the transfer of all such real estate to the new Republic of South Carolina.

By late afternoon, the committee preparing the Ordinance of Secession sent a representative to the platform in St. Andrew's Hall to inform David Jamison that they needed more time. Everyone in the hall was disappointed that the day ended without a formal declaration of secession.

Though the Convention convened at midmorning the next day, the Ordinance of Secession was not ready for a vote until one o'clock that afternoon. The product of the committee's anxious travail was read aloud from the platform by the committee chairman, and at a quarter past one, all 169 delegates voted to adopt the Ordinance as read. The document was then placed in the hands of South Carolina's attorney general for safekeeping. The public signing ceremony was scheduled to take place in Charleston's Institute Hall at seven o'clock that evening. The size of Institute Hall would allow a great number of Charleston's citizens to attend.

At seven, the Convention delegates filed through excited crowds of celebrants to the platform. The signing ceremony took a full two hours. When it was done, David Jamison gave his friend Edmund Ruffin ten minutes to make an impromptu speech, which brought on a thunderous roar of "Southron" patriotism.

Jamison then quieted the massive throng, held up the signed secession document and shouted, "I proclaim the Republic of South Carolina an independent commonwealth!"

The happy clamor that followed shook the hall.

Jamison then honored Edmund Ruffin by presenting him with the pen used to sign the Ordinance of Secession. This gesture was met with an enormous roar of approval, and the convention was adjourned.

When Edmund and John Ruffin took to their beds in the Charleston Hotel that night, they found it impossible to sleep.

Church bells rang all night in celebration, cannons were fired hour after hour, military companies paraded, rifle salutes were fired, fire-crackers were set off, and the milling crowds shouted.

On the train home the next morning, Edmund told John that he was going to watch closely the situation at the three Union forts in Charleston Harbor. He had a feeling the federal leaders in Washington were not going to give up their Southern real estate eas-ily. The inevitable war just might start in Charleston Harbor, and if it did, Edmund Ruffin wanted to be there when it happened.

Word of South Carolina's bold break with the United States reached Richmond by telegraph in the middle of the afternoon on December 20. The news spread quickly through the city and into the rural areas.

That evening, Abby Ruffin was a dinner guest in the Dudley Steele home. While the Steeles, their son, and future daughter-in-law enjoyed a delicious meal of roast turkey and all the trimmings, they talked of secession and the threat of war.

"I'd like to know what's going on in the minds of President Buchanan and the rest of the government leaders in Washington right now," Cora said.

"And Abraham Lincoln in Illinois," put in Abby.

"Well, ladies," said Dudley after swallowing a mouthful of sweet potatoes, "you can bet Washington is a hot box right now. Neither the president nor the president-elect are happy about the news, I'm sure. Of course, Buchanan knows he won't have to worry about the big mess much longer. It'll be Lincoln's problem in a few more weeks. But I can tell you this much, those Northerners regard secession as a serious crime against the United States. I don't know how it can result in anything less than armed conflict."

"I don't either," said Web. "But I tend to agree with Reverend McLaury that it will be the South who fires the first shot."

Silence prevailed for a few seconds, then Abby said, "One thing for sure…if war does come, it will come before June. Which means our wedding will have to be postponed. Web will be off fighting who knows where come June."

Dudley shook his head. "Not necessarily, Abby. If there is a war, it'll be short-lived. Those hard-headed Northerners will learn quickly that we cannot be conquered nor dominated. A long war would be senseless."

Abby reached beside her and took hold of Web's hand. Sighing, she said, "I sure hope you're right, Dad."

On Saturday, December 22, Edmund Ruffin drove his buggy from the stable where he had left it near the depot in Richmond and headed for John's plantation to take him home. As they turned onto the road that led to the plantation, they found themselves following a surrey with three male occupants. To their surprise, the surrey left the road at the Ruffin lane and headed for the mansion.

The three well-dressed men were alighting from the surrey at one of the hitching posts when Edmund pulled his buggy to a halt at the front porch. John stepped to the ground, thanked his brother for taking him along to the convention, and bid him good-bye. As Edmund drove off, John moved toward the three men, holding his small suitcase. "Good afternoon, gentlemen," he said amiably. "I'm John Ruffin. May I help you?"

The one who seemed to be the leader introduced himself as Horatio Clements, and the others as Dean Faulkner and Wesley Denton, his business partners. They were slave traders from Harper's Ferry, and had an appointment with Mr. Reed Exley.

"Ah, yes," smiled Ruffin. "Reed must be going to do some buying or selling. He handles all of the slave business for me."

"Greetings, gentlemen!" came Exley's voice from the front door of the mansion. "Which one of you is Mr. Clements?"

Clements identified himself, then introduced Faulkner and Denton. Exley stepped off the porch and joined the group. He thanked Clements for his speedy reply by telegram, and for making the trip so soon.

"Had to," chuckled Clements. "The female you described sounds like exactly what I'm looking for."

"You selling one of the young girls, Reed?" inquired Ruffin.

"Yes," nodded Exley.

"Which one?"

"Orchid."

"Orchid? Aren't you selling Mandrake with her?"

"No, Papa John. I figure to sell Mandrake at the big auction in Richmond on the twenty-eighth."

"You're separating them?"

"Well, Mr. Clements isn't looking for any male slaves right now. He wants a young woman to mate with some of his choice men in order to produce the best-looking Negroes possible. I figure Orchid is perfect for what he wants, and I'll get you a good price for her. I haven't bothered you about the trouble I've been having with Mandrake lately, but he's been a real problem."

"I know about the coat incident that you and Web had some trouble over," said John.

"Well, there's a whole lot more you don't know, so I figured simply to get rid of him. When he's gone, the trouble will stop. He's developing into a leader, and I think he's dangerous."

"Rebellion?" asked Clements.

"Yeah...and other problems," Exley replied levelly.

Hunching his shoulders and heading for the porch, Ruffin said, "That's why I've got you, Reed. You're my man. Do with the slaves as you see fit. All I care is that we keep enough of them on hand and get our fair share of work out of them."

When John had entered the mansion, Exley said, "Well, gentlemen, let's go take a look at our fine specimen."

The sun was shining and the temperature had risen above what it had been for the past several days. The snow had begun to melt around late morning, and the ground was getting a bit sloppy.

While Exley led Clements and his partners toward the slave shacks, he laughed within himself. Orchid would now learn what a grave mistake she made when she attacked him. He wouldn't be able to tell her so in front of the slave traders, but Orchid was intelligent. She would figure it out. Threaten to kill Reed Exley, would she? Well, that opportunity was now gone. Within a matter of minutes, she would be on her way to Harper's Ferry.

Exley had assigned Mandrake an all-day job cutting firewood behind the barn. He wouldn't be around to make things difficult. Orchid would be gone before Mandrake came to the shack for the night. And when Mandrake learned she'd been sold to an unknown slave trader, he wouldn't need it spelled out for him, either. He'd know why, all right. Being separated from Orchid for the rest of his life was what he deserved. Sure, he'd stir up a fuss over it, but the fuss wouldn't last long. Mandrake himself was going on the block in less than a week.

A few slave women and their children were moving about the shacks when Exley and the three men drew up to the one occupied by Mandrake and Orchid. They stared at the small group of white men, wondering what was going on.

Knocking on the rickety door, Exley called, "Orchid! It's Master Reed. Come out here."

Presently the door came open a crack, then widened a bit more until two big eyes stared fearfully at Exley and the men who stood behind him.

"I want you out here right now," Exley said sternly. "There's someone who wants to see you."

Orchid swung the door wide enough to allow her slim figure to pass through, and moved into the warmth of the sunshine. Her features showed a combination of fear and distrust as Clements and his partners looked her over.

"Well, what do you think?" Reed asked Clements.

"Exactly what I've been looking for!" exclaimed Clements. Turning to his partners, he asked, "Don't you fellas agree?"

"Exactly, boss," nodded Faulkner.

"Couldn't do better anywhere, I'd say," put in Denton. "She has just the right amount of pigmentation, the right build, and she is a pretty one."

Orchid knew that Exley had put her up for sale. A look of horror flashed across her face. Her mouth went dry, and her heart drummed her ribs.

"I'll give you twelve hundred for her," offered Clements.

Exley chuckled. "You're kidding, of course."

"Not at all. She's perfect."

"No, I mean, you're kidding to be making such a low offer."

"Low?" gasped Clements. "Why, Mr. Exley, the average female her age goes for nine hundred, or at best a thousand. You know that."

"I also know that Orchid's not average. You said it yourself. She's perfect. And Mr. Denton said she's the right shade, has the right build, and that she's pretty. For what you want, I agree. She's perfect. I told Mr. Ruffin I'd get a good price for her, and you plenty well know she's worth a good price. Sixteen hundred."

"*Sixteen hundred?* Why, I've never paid that much for a female!"

Patting Orchid's shoulder, Exley said, "You can go on back inside. Mr. Clements has decided he doesn't want you."

"Now, wait a minute!" blurted the slave trader. "I...I'll give you fourteen hundred."

"Sixteen."

"Fifteen!"

"Sixteen," Exley held firm.

"Oh, all right," sighed Clements.

"Cash, like I told you in the telegram," said Exley.

"Yeah, sure, sure," said Clements, digging into his coat pocket for his wallet.

"I'll get you her papers at the house," Exley told him, smiling.

The shock that registered all the way to Orchid's marrow had stolen her breath. Terror and disbelief overwhelmed her. Working her mouth, she was finally able to speak. Shaking her head rapidly, she cried, "No! Massa Reed, you cain't do this." To Clements, she wailed, "I cain't be yo' slave, mistuh. I have a husbin. I cain't leave Mandrake!"

"Don't worry, little lady," chuckled Clements, handing a wad of bills to Exley. "I'll give you two or three husbands. You'll produce a lot of fine-looking slaves for me."

"No-o-o!" Orchid screamed as she plunged into the shack, slamming the door.

Exley jammed the money into his pocket and hit the door with his shoulder, causing it to swing open with a bang. The impact knocked Orchid down, and Exley quickly had a grip on her arms, dragging her back outside. Forcing her into the hands of the slave traders, Exley said, "Hold her. I'll get her coat."

Several female slaves looked on as their frightened children huddled close to their skirts.

"All right," Exley breathed heavily, "let's get her into your surrey. I'll run in and grab her papers, and you can be on your way."

Orchid dug her heels into the slushy snow, but to no avail. The three slave traders each had a hold on her, and she was being dragged away. Opening her mouth wide, she took a deep breath and screamed, "Mandra-a-a-ke! Mandra-a-a-ke!"

Freeing one hand, Denton clapped it over Orchid's mouth as she was about to scream again. Orchid found a finger, quickly had it between her teeth, and clamped down savagely. Denton let out a wild yelp and tried to jerk loose, but Orchid bit down harder and held on.

Exley saw movement in his peripheral vision. Turning, he saw an angry, muscular Mandrake charging like a wild bull from the direction of the barn.

ELEVEN

eed Exley stiffened when he saw Mandrake coming his direction full-speed, his whole countenance suffused with anger. He shoved his hand into his coat pocket, expecting to grip the derringer. Then he remembered that he had taken it out and laid it on a table in his quarters. The best he could do was try to stop the charging black man with a command.

Wesley Denton was howling with Orchid's teeth deep in his finger, and the other two slave traders were attempting to break her hold on him as Mandrake closed in. Exley leaped into his path and hollered, "Stop, Mandrake!"

The muscular slave rammed into Exley, knocking him rolling. Breaking stride only briefly, Mandrake caught up with the slave traders and drove a shoulder into Horatio Clements, sending him reeling in the melting snow. Gaining his balance, the angry husband turned on Dean Faulkner, striking him with a left and a right. Faulkner staggered backward, swearing.

Orchid let go of Denton's finger and pushed away from him, spitting blood. Mandrake went after him. Denton threw up his left arm in defense, but Mandrake batted the arm aside and landed a stiff right jab, followed by a roundhouse left. Denton went down hard.

Mandrake was turning about to see to Orchid when Exley and Faulkner both jumped him. The three men went down in a heap, rolling and thrashing about in the snow. Mandrake lashed out wildly, catching Exley on the mouth. Rising to his knees, he drew back a fist to strike Exley again. But before he could unleash the fist, Faulkner and Clements threw their bodies into him, knocking him flat. Exley's lip was split and numb as he swore at Mandrake and jumped in to help the two men subdue him.

Denton was shaking his head and struggling to get up. Orchid leaped on his back and began digging her fingernails into his face. Cursing her, Denton reached back, got a grip on her hair, and flipped her over his body. The breath was knocked from her as she slammed to the ground. Denton pounced on top of her and pinned her down.

When the three men were finally able to get Mandrake spread-eagled on the ground, Exley cast a glance toward the slave shacks and saw several of the slaves standing in a bunch, looking on. Shouting to them, he told them to go into the barn and bring leg and wrist irons.

Reluctantly, the slaves obeyed. Moments later, Mandrake was jerked to a standing position with his wrists and ankles in chains. Denton released Orchid, who dashed to Mandrake and threw her arms around him. "Oh, Mandrake, Massa Reed has sold me to these men! Don' let 'em take me! Please don' let 'em take me!"

Mandrake embraced her as best he could and set hate-filled eyes on Reed Exley. His nostrils flared. "You have no right to do this!"

Exley laughed. "I have all the right in the world, blackie! Orchid was Ruffin chattel. Master John has given me power to buy and sell his chattel. In my estimation, you two needed to be broken up. So I sold her." Wiping blood from his split lip, he added, "You deserve a good beatin' too, slave scum. But you're not gonna get one. In exactly six days I'm sellin' you at the auction in Richmond. Any marks on you would lower your price."

"No-o-o!" wailed Orchid, clinging to Mandrake with all her might.

"Put her in the surrey," Exley told Clements. "I'll go in the house, sign her papers, and bring them right out."

Orchid was pulled from her husband and dragged to the surrey, sobbing. Mandrake knew it was useless to try to follow. The chain between his ankles was very short. He could move only inches at a time. He watched as the slave traders put Orchid in the surrey, seating her between Faulkner and Denton.

Orchid continued to sob and cry for Mandrake while Exley was inside the mansion. After a few minutes, he emerged and handed the papers to Clements. Mandrake wept silent tears as the surrey drove away and disappeared among the trees.

With a look of triumph, Exley returned to Mandrake and chuckled, "Rebel against me, will you, black boy? I bet you're sorry, now. I'd put that neck ring back on you, but I want you lookin' fresh and fit as a fiddle when I put you on the block next Friday."

Mandrake kept his tear-filled eyes pinned on the spot where he had last seen the surrey.

Exley snapped, "Okay, slave scum, you can still cut wood with those chains on your wrists. Get back behind the barn and finish your job."

Leaving Mandrake to shuffle his way back to work, Exley walked toward the house, counting the money he had received from Clements. He stuffed two hundred dollars into his shirt pocket and smiled to himself. *The old man will never know the difference,* he thought. *He'll be happy thinkin' I got fourteen hundred for the little black wench.*

On Friday, December 28, Web Steele rolled his buggy to a halt at a hitching post beside the big barn in Richmond where the slave auction was being held. He had arrived an hour before sale time in order to look over the slaves as they were being brought in. He had orders from his father to buy one or two males if he could find good ones.

A few slave owners were already inside the barn, looking over what few Negroes were in the "pen" for observation. Web made his way across the barn floor, greeting the white men that he knew. After looking over the slaves in the pen, he stationed himself where he could get a look at the other slaves that would be brought in. He had been there about a quarter-hour when to his surprise, he saw Reed Exley appear at the door, leading Mandrake, who wore wrist chains.

Web could read the sorrow in Mandrake's eyes as he approached and asked, "You're not selling Mandrake, are you, Reed?"

"As a matter of fact, I am."

"Tell you what," Web said quickly, "you haven't registered him yet. I'll buy Mandrake and Orchid both from you right here. It'll save you the auctioneer's fee. I'll give you two thousand for Mandrake and twelve hundred for Orchid."

Reed laughed. "Orchid's gone, Steele. I sold her to a slave trader last Saturday."

"Who? Where'd he take her?"

"None of your business."

Web eyed him with naked aversion. "Since you were going to sell both of them, couldn't you at least have had the decency to sell them as a pair?"

"No, I couldn't."

"Exley, I've never known anything that called itself human to slither as low as you do. You're absolutely despicable."

Feeling safe with the crowd nearby, Exley grated, "Well, mister, let me tell you somethin'. I couldn't care less what you think of me. And let me tell you somethin' else—what I do with John Ruffin's slaves is none of your stinkin' business. So you're worried about Mandrake and Orchid being separated. You're afraid their feelings might be hurt. When you gonna wake up, big man? What's it gonna take to get it through that thick skull of yours that these blackies are nothin' but animals? Animals don't have feelings. Now, as for this animal in chains, here, he ain't for sale straight out. He's going on the block."

With that, Exley led the slave to the auctioneer's desk.

Mandrake glanced over his shoulder at Steele, a look of hopelessness in his eyes.

Web took a seat in the makeshift bleachers among some of his friends, and soon the auction began. For over two hours Negroes were led from the pen to the block singly, in pairs, and in small family groups as the auctioneer sold them to the highest bidders. It soon became evident that the auctioneer was saving Mandrake for last because of his fine physique and evident strength. He would go for a high price.

None of the slaves that crossed the block gained Web's attention. His mind was fastened on young Mandrake.

Exley sat a few feet away, holding the wrist chains that had been on Mandrake. He purposely refrained from looking at Steele. Web's cutting words were burning within him, and his hatred for Steele was growing by the minute.

A young couple was led to the block, leaving Mandrake alone in the pen. One of the auctioneer's assistants removed Mandrake's coat and shirt. Moments later, when the stalwart young slave was ushered to the block, there were many favorable comments as the bidders admired his muscular body.

When the auctioneer was ready to start the bidding, he smiled, pointed at Mandrake, and said, "Take a look at this one, gentlemen! Your eyes will tell you that he can do the work of two men. Let's start the bidding at two thousand dollars."

Exley gloated as the bidding for Mandrake immediately went higher. He would get a good price, then alter the sales slip so he could pocket a nice bundle for himself. He'd done it many times before. John Ruffin was so trusting, he would never question Reed's honesty.

Exley was also feeling relief to get rid of Mandrake. Turning his head for a glimpse at Web, he grinned and thought, *You're next, big man! I'll be rid of you soon.*

As the price of Mandrake went higher and higher, Web looked at him with compassion. Mandrake's heart was broken at his loss of

Orchid. When most of the bidders had dropped out, Web would enter the bidding.

Soon the bidding narrowed to two wealthy plantation owners. Web knew both of them. Harley Adams and Jack Wyatt loved to bid against each other. It happened at every auction.

They were countering each other ten dollars at a time, and the bid was up to $2,340.

"All right," said the auctioneer, "we have twenty-three forty! Do I hear fifty?"

"Twenty-three fifty!" called out Adams, lifting a hand.

"Twenty-three sixty!" countered Wyatt.

There was a pause. "Do I hear twenty-three hundred and seventy?" asked the auctioneer.

Exley was pleased with himself. For sure he was going to get a lot more than the two thousand Steele had offered him before the auction began. Besides, he didn't want the Steeles to own Mandrake.

Adams met the auctioneer's figure.

Wyatt quickly went to $2,380.

The men in the bleachers sat on the edge of their seats. Very few male slaves had ever gone for an amount edging up to $2,400.

"Twenty-three ninety!" said Adams.

"Twenty-four hundred!" responded Wyatt.

Slouching in his seat, Exley grinned wickedly. This was going better than he had expected.

Adams sighed and shook his head. He was through bidding.

The auctioneer said, "Going for twenty-four hundred dollars. Going once! Going twi—!"

"Twenty-five hundred!"

Mandrake's head came up.

The wicked smile drained from Exley's face.

Jack Wyatt turned and eyed Web Steele with disbelief.

The auctioneer said, "Twenty-five hundred is my highest bid. Do I hear twenty-six?"

Wyatt began shaking his head. Quickly Exley jumped to his

feet and hurried to the auctioneer, saying in a low voice, "Don't let it stop here. I don't want Steele to buy him."

The auctioneer looked at him askance. "Mr. Exley, you put no restrictions on the sale of your slave when you signed him in. He must now go to the highest bidder, no matter who it is. Of course, you can make top bid and take him back home with you."

Exley cursed under his breath and walked away, mumbling to himself. His desire to be rid of Mandrake was stronger than his objection to having him bought by Web Steele.

"Do I hear twenty-six hundred?" repeated the auctioneer.

Steele looked at Wyatt, who shook his head again. The auctioneer saw it, and said, "Going for twenty-five hundred dollars. Going once. Going twice. Sold for twenty-five hundred!"

Mandrake's face showed the elation he felt as he watched Web Steele go to the desk and write out a check. Exley stood close by the desk and observed the transaction. He did not speak as Web stepped past him carrying Mandrake's papers, but quickly moved in to collect the twenty-five hundred, insisting he be paid in cash.

Mandrake had put his shirt on and was slipping into his coat when Web approached him. A wide smile exposed his white teeth as he said, "Massa Web, I'll make you glad you paid that much fo' me. Really I will. I'll work extry hard ever' day, an' I'll—"

"C'mon, my friend," cut in Web. "Let's go."

When Reed Exley swung his buggy from the lane toward the front of the Ruffin mansion, he was surprised to see the Steele buggy parked next to the porch with Mandrake seated in it alone. What was Web doing here? Surely he wasn't making a social call on Abby while leaving his newly purchased slave sitting outside.

Mandrake watched Exley drive by and head for the barn. He heaved a sigh of relief, knowing he would never have to knuckle under to the wicked man again. He was curious, however, why Web had driven to the Ruffin place instead of going straight home. When

Web had turned off the road onto the Ruffin plantation, he had noticed the strange look on Mandrake's face. He reassured Mandrake that he needed to see Abby for just a few minutes, and would soon be taking him home.

Exley disappeared into the barn when Web came out of the house. Abby stood in the doorway, smiling. She waved at Mandrake, and he waved back, giving her his warm smile.

During the fifteen-minute drive between the Ruffin plantation and the Steele place, Web spoke to Mandrake of his anger toward Exley for selling Orchid. Though Mandrake was thrilled at now being owned by the Steeles, his sorrow over the loss of his beloved wife remained.

Web pulled the buggy to a halt at the porch of the Steele mansion. As a slave came to take the horse and buggy, Web said, "You can get out here, Mandrake. You're going inside with me."

Expecting to be taken immediately to his new quarters among the slave shacks, Mandrake blinked and said, "Yassuh, Massa Web."

Web was met by his parents as he entered the mansion. He made a quick explanation about purchasing Mandrake and told them of Exley's having sold Mandrake's wife to an unnamed slave trader. Cora spoke kind, comforting words to Mandrake, and Dudley Steele welcomed him as part of the Steele plantation. To give a slave such a welcome was unusual, but Dudley could see that his son had a special liking for Mandrake, and treated him accordingly.

Web then said, "Dad, I need to talk to you for a minute."

Dudley agreed. Cora said she would escort Mandrake to the library, where he could wait while father and son had their brief talk.

Mandrake was all eyes as he took in the lavish furniture, tapestries, and plush carpet while following Cora through the house to the massive library. While seated alone, he gawked at the hundreds of books that lined the long shelves of one entire wall, floor to ceiling. He thought Dudley Steele must own half the books in the world.

Presently Web appeared, still carrying Mandrake's papers, and sat down behind a large oak desk. Flattening the papers out on the desk top, Web set his dark eyes on the handsome young Negro and said, "Mandrake, I just explained to my father that the check I wrote for your purchase today was not a Steele Plantation check. It was my personal check."

Puzzlement showed on Mandrake's ebony features. He blinked and asked, "What does that mean, Massa Web?"

Picking up a pen and dipping it in the desk's inkwell, Web began writing on the papers before him. He had made a couple of notations and was signing his name at the bottom when he replied, "What it means, my friend, is that I personally bought you today. Dudley Steele owns all of the slaves on this plantation, but he does not own you. *I* own you."

Confused, Mandrake nervously pulled at an ear and said, "I guess I don' quite unduhstan', Massa Web."

Letting the ink dry, Web queried, "Would you like to get Orchid back?"

"Well, yassuh. Yas, of course! But how am I gonna do that? I don' know where she is."

"Do you know where Harper's Ferry is?"

"Yassuh. I been there a couple times."

"Think you can find it from here?"

Mandrake's heart was pounding. "Yassuh. I sho' can. Is Orchid at Harper's Ferry?"

"Yes. Those men who took Orchid are from Harper's Ferry. The man who bought her is Horatio Clements."

"How did you find out?"

"From Miss Abby. That's what I was doing when I was in the Ruffin house. She did a little searching in Reed's desk and found the record of Orchid's sale. There it was, plain as day."

"This Horatio Clements' place is right there at Harper's Ferry?"

"Right. I've heard of Clements. He's a ruthless and greedy man."

"Sort of like Reed Exley, huh?"

"Yeah," nodded Web, grinning. "A whole lot like Exley."

Squinting and tilting his head, Mandrake said, "Orchid's at Harper's Ferry, Massa Web, but...I's here. How do I get her back?"

"Well," said Web, "if it weren't Clements we were dealing with, I'd simply go there and offer the owner more than he had paid for her, buy her, and bring her back. But this wouldn't work with Clements. He didn't buy Orchid to use her as a slave."

"He didn'?"

"No. He intends to make her a breeder. The man is known for matching and mating the best-looking Negroes in order to produce even better-looking slaves."

Steele's words hit Mandrake like a battering ram. His eyes were round and hot, and his trembling fists were clenched. His voice quivered as he hissed, "It's that dirty Massa Reed's doing! He is the devil hisself!"

"I can't argue with that," responded Web.

"Massa Web, how am I gonna get Orchid back? She's got to be rescued befo'... befo'..."

"I know, Mandrake. I've just made it so you can go after her." Folding the documents before him and inserting them in an envelope, Web asked, "Do you know what manumission papers are, my friend?"

Mandrake looked at him questioningly and nodded.

Reaching across the desk, Web handed him the envelope and said, "That's what these are, Mandrake—your manumission papers. I told you that I bought you today. As your legal owner, I have just signed your release. Nobody owns you now. You are a free man. I'm going to give you a horse and provisions so you can ride to Harper's Ferry and find Orchid."

Tears filled the black man's eyes. He could not believe this was really happening. "Massa Web, yo' tellin' me that I's no longer a slave?"

"That's it exactly," grinned Steele. "You're your own man now. Be sure you carry those papers everywhere you go. You'll need them to prove you're a free man."

While Mandrake sleeved away his tears, Web said, "Now, be sure you understand, Mandrake. You will have to *steal* Orchid away from Clements. He bought her legally and paid for her. This is why I can't go along and help you. The law will consider it a crime. Do you understand?"

"Yassuh," nodded Mandrake, sniffing again. "I wouldn't break the law fo' no othuh reason 'ceptin' to get Orchid back."

"I know that. The *real* crime in all of this belongs to Exley and Clements. You'll have to hide out with Orchid until Clements gives up looking for her."

"Yassuh."

"And it'll be dangerous. If Clements catches you, he'll kill you."

"I unduhstan', Massa Web, but it's my only chance of gettin' Orchid back."

"I knew you wouldn't hesitate. I'll have the horse and the provisions ready before sunup in the morning. You can ride out at dawn."

"Yassuh," said Mandrake, smiling broadly. Then looking at the envelope in his hand, he blinked at fresh tears and choked, "Massa Web, there ain't no way I can thank you fo' makin' me a free man."

"You don't have to," smiled Steele. "It'll be thanks enough just to know that you and Orchid are back together and happy. Once Clements gives up the search, I want you to come by here and let me know that you're both all right. Okay?"

"How long do you think that'll be, Massa Web?"

"Probably not more than a week or two. Clements and his men won't have much time to spend on trying to hunt Orchid down."

"Well, then there's somethin' I want to say."

"Yes?"

"Since I's a free man, I can make my own choices, right?"

"Right."

"Then I choose to bring Orchid back here to the Steele plantation an' be yo' willin' slave fo' the rest of my days."

After swallowing the lump in his throat, Web said, "It might not work out that way. If we go into a civil war and the North wins, there'll be no more slavery in this country. We Southern plantation owners will have to hire all our labor."

"Then I'll be yo' hired han', Massa Web. I want to make a home fo' Orchid here, an' work fo' you the rest of my life whether it be as hired han' or willin' slave."

"That would make me very happy, Mandrake," said Web. "Let's plan on it."

"Yassuh!" exclaimed the black man. Then rubbing his chin, he said, "Massa Web, now that I's a free man, and 'specially since Massa Reed no longer have power over me, there's somethin' I want to tell you. It's about Miz 'Lizbeth's death, Massa Web. It was her husbin' who caused her to die. The reason she open the winduh was to holler at Massa Reed. He was beatin' on ol' Jedidiah with a belt. Miz 'Lizbeth was yellin' at him to stop when she lost her balance an' fell."

Web Steele ran a finger through his mustache and said, "Just as I thought. It *was* Reed's fault."

"Yassuh. None of us slaves ever tol' the truth 'bout it 'cause Massa Reed threaten us, an' we know'd he'd carry out his threat if'n we ever tol' on 'im."

"I appreciate you telling me this, Mandrake. It's important that we know the truth."

"I jus' hope he gits what's comin' to 'im," Mandrake said tightly.

"I do too." After a pause, Web said, "Tell you what, my friend. You can sleep here in the mansion tonight, and we'll get you on your way to Harper's Ferry before the sun is up."

Mandrake had never slept in a feather bed. Alone in one of the guest rooms that night, he nestled himself deep in the soft mattress and went to sleep thinking of Orchid.

The next morning Mandrake rode out before dawn, heading north. Avoiding towns and villages as much as possible, he stayed on course with only one thing in mind. He must find his wife and steal her from Horatio Clements.

Twice that first day he was accosted by white men who thought he was a runaway slave. They were eager to collect the reward money slave owners paid for the return of their chattel and were disappointed when Mandrake produced his manumission papers.

Late in the afternoon on the second day, Mandrake came upon beautiful Lake Anna. The sun was going down and he was tired, so he decided to make camp along the shore. There was a natural brush enclosure that would protect him from the night wind and also give him a measure of privacy. Web had provided him a warm bedroll.

Dismounting and giving the horse ample opportunity to graze on the tawny grass near the water's edge, Mandrake gathered enough twigs and sticks for a small fire. He was about to light the fire when he heard his horse nicker. Looking up, he saw two young white men walking toward him along the shore.

Harry Binder and Cletus Hicks were in their early twenties. They had scraggly beards and their dirty hair hung down over their ears beneath greasy hats. They approached the black man with their hands in their jacket pockets and a wicked gleam in their eyes.

Mandrake stood beside his pile of sticks, sensing trouble.

TWELVE

Horatio Clements and his men arrived at Harper's Ferry midday on December 29, having spent several days en route. Clements had stopped at plantations along the way taking orders for a new crop of his specially bred slaves who were coming of age.

Sitting in the back seat of the surrey with Dean Faulkner, Orchid rode in silence, pining for her husband. She had spoken very little during the entire trip.

The surrey skirted Harper's Ferry on the south edge of town and ran parallel with the Potomac River for about a mile. The Clements place was situated on the south bank of the river. The huge compound of unpainted frame buildings was surrounded by an eight-foot-high stockade fence, resembling a military fort.

A cold shudder ran through Orchid as they pulled up to the gate, which was manned by an armed guard. The guard swung the gate open and greeted the three men warmly. As he set curious eyes on Orchid, he grinned and said, "You did yourself right proud on this one, Mr. Clements."

"I think so, too," replied Clements, and drove the surrey through the gate.

The worm of dread that had been eating at Orchid's insides

continued its gnawing as the surrey crossed the compound and drew up in front of a flat-roofed frame structure with a weathered sign over the door that read: Clinic. Unlike most slaves, Orchid had learned to read.

Hopping out, Clements said, "You fellas take the horse and surrey to the barn."

"Will do," nodded Denton.

Clements reached a hand toward Orchid and said, "This is where you get out."

Orchid's heart was pulsing in her throat. "Why do I have to go to a clinic?"

"Because I want Doc Tuttle to examine you, that's why," Clements said stiffly. "Come on."

Orchid's mouth was dry as she let Clements take her hand and help her from the surrey. She clenched her teeth, fighting the panic that wrapped itself around her.

Clements led her through the door of the clinic, which was a large one-room affair with a half-dozen cots, an examining table, and a medicine cabinet. In one corner stood four straight-backed chairs. Three of them were occupied by black women in various stages of pregnancy. All three turned their heads and stared at Orchid with lifeless, impassive eyes.

Standing over a woman on the examining table was a thin, elderly man in a white frock. His frail hands were pressing on her distended abdomen in an attempt to establish the position of the baby.

Dr. Henry Tuttle quickly finished his examination, informed the expectant mother that she would no doubt deliver within a week, and told her she could go. He then went to Horatio Clements like a puppy would hurry to his master. His back was bent and there was a gimp in his walk. Orchid figured he had to be in his late seventies.

Tilting his head back so as to view Orchid through the half-moon spectacles that rode the end of his narrow nose, he smiled and said, "Ah, Mr. Clements, you did bring us a pretty one this time, didn't you?"

"Mm-hmm," nodded Clements. "Give her a good going over and bring the report to my office when you're finished."

"It'll be a while. I've got these other three to examine first."

"Fine. Just let me know what you find."

"Yes, sir."

Orchid sat down with two of the women while Tuttle began examining the third. Neither one spoke to her, nor did they speak to each other.

Over an hour passed before Orchid was directed to lie down on the examining table. Aware that she was frightened, Dr. Tuttle kept up a steady chatter while he checked her over. He explained that he had been in practice in Leesburg for forty years when young doctors began opening offices in the town and taking his patients. He finally had to close his practice two years ago. Horatio Clements learned about it and offered him the job of taking care of his slaves.

When the examination was completed, Orchid was left alone in the clinic while Tuttle took his report to Clements. The room was chilly. She put her coat on, then made her way to a dirty, fly-specked window and looked out on the compound. The stockade fence loomed before her like a towering prison wall. To go over it would be impossible. The only way out was the gate. Somehow she had to get through the gate and escape...and she must do it before Clements put her with one of his black men.

The thought of such a horrible thing sent a chill down her spine. She must escape and make her way back to Richmond. She would go to the Steele plantation for help. Massa Web would do something so she could again be with Mandrake.

Orchid saw Clements and Dr. Tuttle emerge from one of the buildings across the compound. They were headed toward the clinic. Fear pushed her back from the window. A trembling hand went to her mouth, and she heard herself whimpering as she backtracked across the room. She heard the footsteps of the two men just before the door came open, and felt her mouth go dry.

Clements entered ahead of Tuttle, who gimped in behind him.

Clements spotted Orchid braced against the back wall and moved toward her, saying, "Doc tells me you're in good physical condition, Orchid. That's good. Now come with me. I have a special room for you to stay in. After supper tonight, the man I have chosen to sire your first child will visit you."

The dreadful repulsion Orchid was feeling gave birth to blind panic. Her heart pumped so hard she could feel her eyes pulse. Shaking her head, she cried, "No!" and bolted, using the wall as a springboard. Clements grabbed for her as she shot past him, but missed. Tuttle made a weak effort to lay hold on her, but his reflexes were too ancient, and she was quickly out the door.

Once she was outside, Orchid looked toward the gate. Escape was the only thing on her mind. Two guards stood at the gate, chatting. A chilling fog of fear clouded her terrified brain. Suddenly she found herself running toward an open door in one of the buildings. She had to hide quickly. Clements's voice cut the air behind her as he shouted for her to stop.

Paying him no heed, she dashed for the open door. Just as she reached it, she glanced over her shoulder. Clements was running after her, and another white man had joined the chase. Orchid slammed the door, bolted it, then hurried down a hallway. Taking the first door she found open, she plunged through it and found herself in a large kitchen. Two pots of stew were cooking on the stove, and she could smell the aroma of bread coming from the oven.

There was a thunderous sound at the front of the building. Clements and the other man were trying to break the door open. Orchid dashed for a door a few feet away, pulled it open, and found herself staring at pantry shelves loaded with jars of food and sacks of flour and sugar.

Next she ran to a door at the rear of the kitchen that seemed to lead outside. She slid back the bolt and twisted the knob furiously, but it wouldn't budge. She heard the front door splinter open.

She was trapped. Suddenly her eyes fell on a butcher knife with an eight-inch blade that lay on the counter. Heavy footsteps were pounding down the hall as she picked up the knife and slipped it into her coat pocket. Seconds later Clements and Wesley Denton barged into the kitchen.

Clements's face was crimson with anger as he seized her arm roughly and snapped, "I want no more of this kind of thing, Orchid! There's nowhere to run, and the quicker you realize it, the better. I paid good money for you, and you're going to do as I say."

Orchid slid both hands into her coat pockets as Clements and Denton ushered her out of the kitchen. Her right hand closed around the handle of the knife. Somehow it comforted her. She didn't know how yet, but if she had her way, the knife was going to be her ticket to freedom.

The sun was lowering in the sky as Orchid was taken to a two-story building and led to a small room on the second floor. The furniture consisted of two wooden chairs, a rickety old bed, and a small table. On the table were wash basin, water pitcher, and a rusty kerosene lantern.

While Denton fired up the lantern, Clements said to Orchid, "Your supper will be brought to you about six o'clock. At eight, I'll bring you a nice gentleman friend."

Orchid stood next to the table as Clements and Denton stepped into the hall and closed the door. A key rattled in the lock, then their footsteps faded away.

The room was chilly. Deciding to leave her coat on, Orchid sat down on one of the chairs, buried her face in her hands, and wept, calling Mandrake's name over and over.

After crying for some time, Orchid used a towel that hung on a rack above the table to dry her face. She then walked to the room's single window, pulled back the worn, dusty curtains, and looked down on the compound. It was getting dark. An elderly black man was using a candle on a long stick to light the kerosene lanterns that hung on eight-foot poles about the grounds. Orchid guessed that the open area of the compound covered about one-and-a-half acres. The lanterns were far enough apart to leave wide, dark areas between them.

Huddling in her coat, the frightened young woman was looking at the building that housed the kitchen when the door came
open, and a white man she had not seen before came out carrying a
tray of food. She assumed it must be six o'clock, for he was heading
her direction.

At the same moment, she heard doors opening and closing
within her own building, and she saw black men and women emerging from other buildings. Many of the women were obviously
pregnant. All of them were headed for a low-roofed frame structure
attached to the building that housed the kitchen. Orchid told herself
it had to be the dining hall.

She turned from the window when she heard a key rattle in the
lock of her door. The door swung open and the man she had seen
below stepped in, carrying the tray. He was young—probably no
more than three or fours years older than she. He set the tray on the
table and raised his face into the light of the lantern. Pushing his hat
back, he said, "So you are Orchid."

Orchid nodded silently, noting that the young man strongly resembled Horatio Clements.

"I'm Harland Clements, Orchid," he said in a kind manner.
"I'm the youngest son of your new master."

When Orchid did not reply, Harland looked down at the tray
and said, "Here's your supper. The food is very good here. Father sees
to that because he wants all of his breeders to be robust and healthy."
Noticing that she was wearing her coat, he added, "I'm sorry about the
chill in here. You'll only occupy this room tonight. There are plenty of
covers on the bed, so you can make yourself warmer if you want to."

Orchid nodded, biting her lower lip. Her hands were in the coat
pockets, and her right hand gripped the handle of the butcher knife.

There was a touch of compassion on Harland's young features
as he said softly, "Orchid, I know you're frightened. It's always this
way when the new ones come here. You're also very unhappy to be
here. Right?"

Orchid nodded again.

"Let me give you a little advice. My father can get quite mean if he loses his temper. Don't fight this thing. It's going to happen in spite of the fact that you don't want it to. You seem to be a very nice young woman. And I might add, a very pretty one, too. I don't want to see anything bad happen to you. Please, just cooperate. Some Negro women my father has bought have defied him. They are no longer living. Do you understand what I'm saying?"

Orchid felt an icy chill in her stomach. She nodded again.

"And I should tell you this, too. The man my father is going to bring to you tonight can get quite short-tempered when the women he is to mate with show resistance. He has been known to become uncontrollably violent."

When she only stared at him, Harland took a step closer and asked, "Am I getting my message across, Orchid?"

"Yes," Orchid said, taking a step backward and tightening her grip on the knife.

"Good," he smiled. "That's good. I'll be here early in the morning to take you to your permanent quarters. There's a fireplace to keep you warm. You'll like it. Okay?"

Defiance was abounding within her, but disguising it, she said, "Yes."

"Good. Very good," Harland said, heading for the open door. Pausing with his hand on the knob, he added, "Hope you enjoy your supper." With that, he moved out and closed the door. The lock rattled, and the sound of his footsteps faded away. Orchid pulled her hands from her coat pockets, clenched her fists, and squeezed her eyes shut, fear and rage merging into one seething groan.

Just after eight o'clock the lock rattled again and the door swung open. Orchid was seated on one of the wooden chairs next to the table. She rose to her feet and pushed her hands into her coat pockets as Horatio Clements came in, followed by a massive black man. He stood a head taller than Clements (who was six feet tall) and had shoulders so wide, they almost touched the door frame on each side.

A strange, almost electric sensation surged through Orchid. Her blood went cold and her heart beat wildly, sending a weak, watery feeling to her knees.

The mountain of a man moved up beside Clements, who said, "Orchid, this is Theodore. I'm going to leave him with you now. He'll return to his quarters later."

Theodore smiled and said in a deep, guttural voice, "Hello, Orchid."

The terrified woman thought of what Harland Clements had told her about Theodore being short-tempered and violent when he met resistance. He was not wearing a coat. The shirt that covered his upper body pressed tight against a powerful, muscular frame. She knew if he was of a mind to do it, he could kill her. "H-hello," she said, fearing the consequences if she did not reply to his greeting.

Clements looked down at the food on the tray and said tartly, "Orchid, you haven't touched your supper. Now, we can't have this. If you're going to make my investment in you worthwhile, you must eat the food we give you. It will be the same when you eat in the dining hall with the rest of the Negroes."

"I...I jus' wasn't hungry," she said weakly.

"Well, hungry or not, when we give you food, you're to eat it. Do you understand?"

Nodding slowly, she replied, "Yassuh."

"All right," grunted Clements. He handed the skeleton key to Theodore, and said, "Be sure to lock her in when you go."

"Yes, Massa Horatio," nodded Theodore. He waited till Clements was in the hall, then closed the door and locked it. Turning about, he pocketed the key and set his eyes on Orchid. The yellow glow of the lantern cast shadows in the hollows of his face, giving him a hellish, diabolical appearance.

Theodore took a step toward Orchid, moistening his heavy lips, and said in his deep basso, "If you're thinkin' 'bout puttin' up a fight, Orchid, you'd best forget it."

Orchid's fingers tightened around the handle of the knife in her coat pocket. Never had she experienced such fear. Her heart began to pound like a mad thing in her chest.

She thought of Mandrake, telling herself that unless she escaped this awful place, she would never see him again. The knife was her only hope. Maybe she wouldn't make it, but she would rather die than give in to this giant.

"Let's get your coat off," said Theodore, moving toward her.

Orchid could hardly breathe. Theodore's hands were reaching toward the buttons on her coat when she whipped out the knife and plunged it with all her might into his belly, just above his belt buckle. It went in, full haft.

Theodore groaned, his eyes bulging, his mouth gaping with shock. Acting on instinct, Orchid yanked the knife out and rammed the blade in again, higher up this time. The knife buried itself in Theodore's chest.

Orchid wanted to jerk it out and stab him again, but the handle slipped from her grasp as Theodore stumbled away from her and fell heavily on the table, knocking it over. Pitcher and basin went flying. The lantern hit the floor, shattering the glass chimney and spilling kerosene. Instantly the flame found it.

Theodore lay on his back, struggling to remove the knife from his chest. Orchid knew the door key was in his pocket. She had to have it to escape. Fire was rapidly spreading over the dry floor.

In desperation, Orchid grasped a chair and brought it down savagely on Theodore's head. The blow stunned him, and his hands fell away from the knife. Theodore's eyes rolled back in their sockets so only the whites showed. He coughed once, spewing blood, then his crimson teeth showed in a grimace of death. Knowing she may have to use the knife again, Orchid yanked it from his chest and searched his pocket for the key. It took only seconds to produce it.

The fire had reached the bed and flames were licking their way up the bedspread. A cloud of smoke pressed against the ceiling and would soon fill the entire room.

Orchid could hear loud voices coming from the compound as

she coughed and unlocked the door. Peering into the hall, she saw that a lone lantern burned halfway toward the rear of the building. It was enough for her to see that there was a door at the other end of the hall, which she assumed led to a staircase outside, identical to the one she had mounted at the front when forced into the building. There was no one yet in sight.

She had enough presence of mind to reason that if she locked the door, it would lead them to believe that both she and Theodore were still inside. The more people occupied with the fire, the better her chances of escape.

Just as she turned the key in the lock, Orchid heard footsteps on the front stairs and the sound of excited voices. Thrusting the key in a coat pocket, she held the knife and ran toward the rear of the building. When she passed through the door, she found that it did lead to a landing and stairs that went all the way to the ground.

It was pitch dark, but she found her way to the bottom and headed along the side of the building toward the dimly lit compound. More people were running toward the burning building.

Keeping to the shadows, Orchid made her way along the edge of the compound toward the gate. She was determined to make good her escape. As she neared the gate, she paused in the shadows and looked back across the compound. A large crowd of Negroes, sprinkled with a few whites, was gathered at the blazing building. The fire had the attention of everyone. Men were dashing to the spot with buckets in hand, and the crowd was forming a bucket brigade from the water trough some forty yards away.

Orchid turned toward the gate. Two guards stood together, looking at the blaze. As Orchid inched closer, she heard one guard say to the other, "You stay here. I'll go help fight the fire."

The lone guard watched his friend hurry toward the burning building and was unaware that a small, dark form was moving up behind him. When the knife was plunged into his back, he let out a loud cry, but the sound was swallowed up in the clamor on the compound, and no one heard it.

The guard lay on the ground, moaning, the knife burning like a red-hot iron. He raised up to see a woman fumbling with the heavy latch on the gate. Determined to stop her, he struggled to his knees and pulled his revolver from its holster.

Suddenly the gate was open and the woman was dashing to freedom. The guard fired. He heard a pained cry and saw her stagger against the gate frame, then disappear. The guard stumbled to the gate and was able to make out the woman's form weaving toward the bank of the Potomac River. When she reached it, there was a slight pause, then a distinct splash.

THIRTEEN

Mandrake's muscles tensed as Harry Binder and Cletus Hicks drew up. Both of the unkempt young men had smirks on their faces. Hicks, who was tall and slender, said, "Hello, boy. What's your name?"

"Mandrake," replied the black man levelly, distrust showing in his eyes.

Hicks read it. Looking at his short, thick-bodied partner, he said, "S'pose this African boy has a last name, Harry?"

"Well, if he don't," chuckled Binder, "he's got to be a runaway slave. We could pick us up a right handsome reward if that's the case."

"Yeah," replied Hicks, casting an appreciative glance at Mandrake's horse. Looking back at Mandrake, he asked, "You steal that horse and run away, boy?"

"No. I have manumission papers. The horse is a gift from the man who used to own me."

The dirty, long-haired men exchanged glances and laughed.

"You believe that, Clete?"

"Naw. You cain't trust a black-skinned African. I say he either produces them papers or we take him to the law and let them find out where he run away from."

Without a word, Mandrake walked to the horse, opened a saddlebag, and pulled out the envelope that held his manumission papers. Removing the papers, he unfolded them and held them up so Binder and Hicks could see them. "You satisfied now?" asked Mandrake. "I's as much a free man as either one o' you."

The two men looked at each other, nodding.

"Okay," chuckled Hicks, "so you ain't no runaway slave. But me and Harry really do need us a good horse. We'll just take that one."

Mandrake bristled. While replacing the papers in the envelope, he retorted, "You won' be doin' anythin' of the kind."

The stocky Binder's features hardened. He stepped close to Mandrake and growled, "Who's to stop us? You think you can handle both of us, boy?"

Mandrake countered, "I'm on an important trip, an' I gotta get where I'm goin' soon as possible." He wheeled and returned to the animal, placing the envelope back in the saddlebag.

Suddenly a strong arm was around Mandrake's neck, clamping it in a scissor-lock. Harry Binder bore down hard on Mandrake's throat, choking him. At the same time, Hicks grabbed Mandrake's ankles and they carried him toward the lake. He twisted and squirmed, but both men were strong, and he couldn't break free.

Binder and Hicks waded into the lake, heading for deep water. They were going to drown him.

In desperation, Mandrake made an abrupt twist of his upper body and grabbed for Binder's head. It worked. Binder lost his grip, stumbled, and went to the bottom in four feet of icy water. Hicks then lost his hold on Mandrake's ankles, stumbling slightly himself. Mandrake went to the floor of the lake, quickly righted himself, and stood up. When he rose out of the water, Hicks was waiting for him. But Mandrake dodged Hicks's haymaker and countered with a hard right to the jaw. Hicks went down just as Binder jumped on

Mandrake's back. The impact sent both of them into the water.

Mandrake bobbed up first and gained his footing. When Binder surfaced, the angry black man unleashed two rapid blows to his face, sending Binder back down again. Mandrake felt a fist strike him in the right kidney, sending a streamer of pain through his body. He spun around, ducked a second punch, and lashed back with one of his own. Hicks flopped backward from the impact, and at the same time, Mandrake heard Binder come out of the water behind him, gagging and choking.

In one fluid motion, Mandrake whirled and punched Binder again, sending him under the surface. He quickly spun around, expecting Hicks to be on him again, but was surprised to see him dashing for the shore. Fearful that Hicks was going after his horse, Mandrake ran after him and tackled him just as they reached the shoreline.

Both men came to their feet. Hicks swore at Mandrake and swung at him. Mandrake ducked and answered back with three rapid, forceful blows. Hicks staggered back, trying to keep his footing. But Mandrake was after him like an angry beast and cracked him with two more hard blows. Hicks went to his knees, then sprawled forward on the sand.

Mandrake stood over him for a few seconds, breathing heavily. He looked toward the lake, expecting another assault from Binder, but there was no sign of him. Perhaps he had hightailed it while Mandrake had been occupied with Hicks. Mandrake made his way to his campsite, mounted the horse, and rode northward along the shore. His mind went to Orchid. Nothing was going to stop him from finding her and taking her away from the vile man who had bought her.

Mandrake rode at a steady trot all night and reached the north edge of Lake Anna just before dawn. He decided to hole up during the daylight hours and ride at night. It would take him longer to cover the miles to Harper's Ferry, but he didn't need any more confrontations.

Just before sunrise, Mandrake found an abandoned barn and took his horse inside. After eating some cold biscuits and beef jerky provided by Web Steele, he lay down and slept.

That night he traveled again, stopping to water the horse periodically and allowing it to graze a bit. At dawn, he found a secluded spot beside a small creek just south of Warrenton. He ground-reined the horse so it could get to the creek for water and munch on the tawny winter grass. He had been asleep about two hours when he was awakened by a sharp male voice shouting, "Hey, black boy, wake up!"

Mandrake came awake instantly and sat up. Blinking against the bright Virginia sunlight, he could see a tall man standing over him with a cocked revolver in his hand. A badge pinned to the man's waist-length coat read: Sheriff, Louisa County, Virginia.

"Come on, get up!" barked Sheriff Ned Langley.

Mandrake rose to his feet and looked around at the half-circle of armed men who faced him. A half-dozen black muzzles were trained on him. Mandrake then saw Cletus Hicks astride a horse in the background.

"You're under arrest for the murder of Harry Binder," Langley said gruffly.

Mandrake was taken to Louisa and locked up in jail. His manumission papers were confiscated by a deputy and locked in the safe at the sheriff's office.

During the ride to town, Mandrake did not speak a word in his defense. Hicks had told Sheriff Langley that the newly freed Negro had assaulted him for no reason, leaving him lying on the shore of Lake Anna with a broken jaw. Harry Binder had come on the scene just as Mandrake was leaving, and tried to stop him. The ex-slave overwhelmed Binder, dragged him into the lake, and drowned him.

Mandrake knew that free or not, he didn't stand a chance. He was black. No one would believe the true story.

After locking Mandrake's cell, Langley pressed his face close to the bars and told him that because he was a free man, he would be entitled to a trial. The trial would be held in about six weeks when the circuit judge showed up in Louisa. Then laughing as he walked away, the sheriff told him the trial would only be a formality; Cletus's testimony would put a rope around Mandrake's neck.

During the next six weeks, Mandrake languished in the cell, yearning for Orchid and wishing he could get a message to Web Steele. Massa Web would believe Mandrake's story and come to his rescue; but there was no way to contact him.

One day in early February, 1861, Sheriff Langley told Mandrake that the circuit judge had taken ill and would not be able to come to Louisa until he recovered. There was no way to know when that might be.

Late in the afternoon several days later, Mandrake was lying on his bunk thinking of Orchid. He feared that by now she had been forced to mate with one of Horatio Clements's choice black males. He was fighting tears when the jail door banged open and two deputies came dragging a white man down the narrow corridor, followed by the sheriff.

Langley unlocked the door to Mandrake's cell and pulled it open, saying, "Got some company for you, black boy. No sense putting him in another cell. That'd just mean two to keep clean."

The new prisoner was thrown into the cell and landed on the floor in a heap. Langley locked the door and walked away with his men.

Mandrake left his bunk and helped his new cell mate to the bunk on the opposite side of the barred cubicle. The man had been beaten severely. His lips were cut and there were bruises all over his face.

Sitting up on the bunk, he dabbed at the cuts on his mouth and said, "Thank you, my friend."

"Looks like they done work you over good," remarked Mandrake.

"Yeah. You might say that."

"What'd you do?"

"Killed a man."

"Murder?"

"Yep."

"Oh," nodded Mandrake. "The man you killed do somethin' bad to you?"

"Not to me. He beat up a friend of mine and crippled him for life. I was just takin' out vengeance for my friend."

"I see."

Extending his hand, the bruised man said, "Name's Jess—Jess Dorman."

Meeting the hand with a solid grip, Mandrake said, "Glad to meet you, Jess."

When their hands parted, Dorman asked, "What's your name?"

Mandrake had a sudden thought. Now that he had been freed by Web Steele and was no longer a slave, he needed a last name. It took only seconds for him to reply, "Mandrake Steele."

"You a runaway slave?"

"No!" Mandrake replied. "I was a slave, but my massa set me free."

"So what are you in here for?"

"Same thing as you."

"Murder?"

"Yassuh."

"Who'd you murder?"

"Nobody. I killed a white man in self-defense."

"How'd it happen?"

"You sure you wants to hear it? It's a long story."

Scooting back on his bunk so he could lean against the wall, Dorman said, "Sure. Ain't got nothin' else to do. I'd like to hear it."

Mandrake took a half hour to tell his story, beginning with Reed Exley's treatment of Orchid and himself. He explained how and why Exley sold Orchid to Horatio Clements, then described how Web Steele had bought him and set him free so he could go after her. Finally he told how he had been attacked and forced to defend himself, resulting in the apparent accidental drowning of the man he was now accused of murdering.

When the story was finished, Dorman shook his head and said, "Well, even though it was self-defense, Mandrake, you'll die just as dead when you hit the end of your rope as I will when I hit mine."

"Yassuh," Mandrake said, bowing his head, "but that's not the wo'st part of all this. The wo'st is what Orchid's facin' at Harper's Ferry. I don' want to hang, Jess, but more'n anythin' I don' want my wife sufferin' what she's sufferin'."

Dorman was quiet for a moment, then he said, "I haven't told you much about myself, Mandrake. I'm no angel, believe me. I've been in trouble with the law plenty of times. And...ah...I've broken outta jail before."

Mandrake's heavy eyebrows arched. "You have?"

"Yeah. Three times. Neither one of us is gonna hang. Let me think on it a while, and I'll figure a way to bust both of us outta here."

Just before midnight the following day, young deputy sheriff Alvin Sparks was seated in the office alone. He had come on duty at eleven o'clock, checked on his two prisoners, and returned to the office for the night. He had a newspaper spread out on the desk and was reading of the heated battle in Congress over slavery.

In the small cell block behind the office, Jess Dorman whispered through the darkness, "It's been nearly an hour since he was in here, Mandrake. That oughtta be enough time. You ready?"

Unable to see his cell mate in the pitch black, Mandrake sat up on his bunk, took a deep breath, and said, "Yassuh. Let's git this thin' over with. I's got to head fo' Harper's Ferry."

"Be sure to hit him plenty hard."

"Don' worry, Jess. I'll put 'im out."

Rolling to his knees on the bunk, Dorman stuck his forefinger down his throat, gagged, and began giving up what was left in his stomach from supper.

Mandrake shouted toward the office door, "Deputy! Hey, deputy! We gots trouble in here!"

The office door came open and Deputy Sparks appeared, carrying a lighted lantern. Dorman kept gagging and heaving as Sparks hurried to the cell door and asked Mandrake, "What's the matter with him?"

"I don' know," replied Mandrake, looking worried, "but he's really sick. Must've been somethin' in the food that disagreed with 'im."

"Well, you aren't sick, and you ate the same stuff he did."

"Yassuh, but he was tellin' me befo' supper that he gots a stomach problem. If'n somethin' ain' done, he could die."

Sparks set the lantern on the floor, pulled the key from his belt, and began to unlock the door. "Let me take a look at him. Doc Smithers don't appreciate bein' called out in the middle of the night if it isn't a matter of life and death."

Sparks drew his revolver from its holster, pointed it through the bars at Mandrake, and said, "Get over there against the far wall."

When Mandrake had obeyed, Sparks swung the door open and entered the cell. He was trying to keep one eye on Mandrake while leaning over Dorman, but for a brief instant, he put his full attention on the sick man. Mandrake moved with the swiftness of a cougar and chopped the deputy behind the ear.

Sparks crumpled to the floor, then tried vainly to rise, knowing he was in trouble. Mandrake bent over and struck him savagely on the jaw. Sparks collapsed and lay still.

Dorman had been careful not to soil his clothing. Leaping from the bunk and wiping his mouth, he said, "Good job, pal! Let's go!"

Leaving the deputy locked in the cell, the two men hastened to the street and ran down the block. Finding a dark spot between two buildings, they slipped into the shadows, breathing hard.

"Okay," gasped Dorman, "this is where we part company. Like I told you, I'm headin' for Ohio. It's been good knowin' you."

"Same here," responded Mandrake. "Thanks fo' helpin' me break out."

"I was helpin' me as much as I was you. Hope you get your wife outta there."

"Thanks," said Mandrake, then wheeled and darted across the street.

Moments later, Mandrake was out of town, heading due north for Harper's Ferry, which he knew was some ninety miles away. Without his papers, he would have to be very careful.

For two days and nights, Mandrake worked his way north-ward, staying clear of towns and villages. He kept to the brush on the farm land as much as possible, and though he hated to do it, he stole food from farmers' storm cellars at night. On the morning of the third day, he skirted a cotton plantation by bending low and darting between clumps of bushes and huge oak trees. While halting to catch his breath, he saw the slaves working among the buildings. The sight made him feel a warm spot deep inside toward Web Steele. Massa Web had set him free. He thought of Orchid at that awful place near Harper's Ferry and longed for the day they could be together on the Steele plantation, willingly serving the man who had paid such a high price to free him.

Unaware that he was being watched, Mandrake moved furtively another hundred yards or so and found that he was ap-proaching the Rappahannock River. He would follow the bank till he found a safe spot to cross. Maybe there would even be a bridge.

He drew within twenty yards of the river bank, moving slowly through dense brush. He was about to come to a small clearing when two men in their mid-twenties suddenly appeared, aiming shotguns directly at him.

"Hold it right there, blackie!" shouted the taller one.

Mandrake froze.

The short man, who had a cocky look to him, ran up and said, "Where you from, boy?"

The other one hastened to flank his companion. Keeping his eyes on Mandrake, he said, "Hughey, looks like we've got us a runaway. I'll bet there's a plantation owner somewhere south of here who'd pay a handsome sum to get him back."

"Maybe, but I'll tell you what, Bobby. My pa might like to keep him for himself."

Mandrake felt as if a spear of ice had pierced his chest. "I…I used to be a slave," he said cautiously, "but I was set free by Massa Web Steele down by Richmon'."

"Oh?" said Hughey. Keeping the shotgun trained on Mandrake, he held out his free hand and clipped, "Let me see your papers."

Mandrake swallowed hard. "I…I don' got 'em no mo'."

"What happened to them?" asked Bobby.

Mandrake didn't dare tell them the truth. Sheriff Langley might be willing to give a reward for getting him back. "I…uh…I lost 'em," he said weakly.

"Humpf! Likely story," said Hughey. "Let's take you to see my pa. He's always looking for black boys built like you."

"Wait a minute, Hughey," cut in Bobby. "Your pa won't pay us anything for him. We could make some money if—"

"Shut up!" snapped Hughey. "If this black boy was old or skinny or something like that, we'd try to make some money on him. But even with his coat on, I can tell this African has what it takes to do a real day's work."

Mandrake was taken at gunpoint to the very plantation he had been skirting. Wealthy owner Todd Morrison emerged from the mansion at his son's call and smiled broadly when he set his eyes on Mandrake. Looking him up and down, Morrison asked, "Where'd you come from, boy?"

"I was a slave on the John Ruffin plantation down by

Richmon', suh," answered Mandrake. "Then his slave foreman—"

"He any kin to Edmund Ruffin?" cut in Morrison.

"His brother, suh."

"I see. You said you *were* a slave on the John Ruffin plantation?"

"Yassuh," nodded Mandrake. "But I'm a free man now."

"You have papers to prove it?"

"Nossuh. I did have, but I lost 'em."

"Lost them?" repeated Morrison, his face displaying his disbelief. "You know what, boy? I think you're lyin'. I'd bet my last dollar you're a runaway."

"Nossuh," said Mandrake, shaking his head. "I's tellin' you the truth. Like I started to tell you, Massa John's slave foreman sold my wife to a man in Harper's Ferry fo' a breeder, then took me to the auction in Richmon'. Massa Web Steele bought me, give me my manumission papers and a horse, and tol' me to find Orchid and take her away from that place. My papers was in the saddlebags, but somebody stole the horse and I lost 'em."

Todd Morrison smiled to himself. He figured the story was probably true, but seldom did a man get a chance to lay hold on a Negro like the one who was standing before him. Turning to Hughey, he said, "Son, keep your shotgun trained on this boy. Don't let him take a step."

Mandrake felt the pressure of the shotgun's twin bores as he watched Morrison walk part way across the yard and hail a passing slave. He commanded the black man to go to a shed and bring a pair of leg irons, then returned and said with a smile, "Looks like we picked us up a nice piece of chattel for free, Hughey. Just in case he gets any ideas about running, we'll hobble him good."

"Please, massa," said Mandrake, his face pained. "I needs to get to Harper's Ferry an' save my wife. Please don' do this!"

Morrison sneered. "You don't really expect me to believe that cock-and-bull story, do you? You're my slave now, and I don't want to hear any more about it."

A PROMISE UNBROKEN

201

Despair washed over Mandrake like a cold ocean wave. As long as he was kept in leg irons, there would be no hope of escape. Somehow, some way, he had to convince the plantation owner to trust him and remove the irons. When he did, Orchid's husband would resume his relentless journey to Harper's Ferry.

FOURTEEN

The North and the South passed the point of no return in early February 1861 when secessionist delegates met in Montgomery, Alabama. Six other Southern states followed South Carolina in seceding from the Union to form the Confederate States of America. Virginia, North Carolina, Tennessee, and Arkansas were making plans to join them.

On February 8 the Provisional Constitution of the Confederate States of America was adopted. Each state was declared sovereign and independent, and the charter guaranteed the right to own slaves anywhere within the bounds of the Confederacy.

Jefferson Davis of Vicksburg, Mississippi, who had been a U.S. senator prior to secession, was appointed president of the Confederate States, and on February 18 he took the oath of office and gave a dynamic and stirring inaugural address.

Two weeks later another inaugural address was heard that was just as dynamic and stirring. On March 4 Abraham Lincoln became president of the United States. In his speech, Lincoln rejected any prospect for negotiation concerning the three federal forts in Charleston Harbor: Moultrie, Sumter, and Castle Pinckney. They were Union property, and they would stay Union property. When word came of Lincoln's refusal to even consider negotiation over the forts, Southern tempers flared.

At the same time, tension was building between separatists and Union loyalists in Delaware, Maryland, Kentucky, and Missouri. West of the Mississippi River, all of the organized territories had spoken out in opposition to slavery and were favoring their admission to the Union as free states. This prospect further angered leaders in the Southern movement and added impetus toward open hostilities. The roiling tide of anti-Union sentiment was cresting in the South by the last days of March.

Ominous clouds of war were gathering.

There was a private war raging in the twisted soul of Reed Exley. Desiring free rein to pursue Abby Ruffin, Exley was searching for a way to remove Web Steele from the picture. He had to do it in a manner that would not implicate himself and that would allow him to look good in Abby's eyes.

One night in early April, Exley was sitting alone at a table at the Lamplighter Tavern in Richmond. While periodically pouring whiskey into a shot glass and downing it, he worked at coming up with a foolproof plan.

In a far corner of the tavern, a painted-up woman was singing a jovial song beside an upright piano played by a silver-haired man in striped shirt and arm garters. The patrons on that side of the place were attentive to the songstress. Those on Exley's side were engaged in quiet conversation.

Exley had been there about half an hour when a shabbily dressed man came in and sat at the table next to him. Reed gave him a casual glance as the man ordered a glass and bottle from the waiter. Some ten minutes later, another shabbily dressed man came in. The new man ran his gaze to the bar, and noting that it was jam-packed, looked around for an empty table. Seeing that all the tables were occupied, he began making his way toward the two tables that were each occupied by only one man. Exley was relieved when the man drew up to the table next to him and asked his neighbor if he could use some company. He was immediately asked to sit down.

Exley overheard the new man introduce himself as Wilbur Yates from a small town in southern Virginia. He had come to Richmond in search of a job. The other man, Exley learned, was Hec Wheeler. Like Yates, Wheeler was down on his luck. He was passing through Virginia from Tennessee, on his way to Carlisle, Pennsylvania. His brother John owned a carriage business in Carlisle, and Hec was hoping John would give him a job.

The two men confided in each other that they were getting low on cash, then the conversation turned to the strife between the North and the South. While they were agreeing that if war came, they would fight on the Confederate side, Exley's evil plan was quickly taking shape.

Rising from his chair, Exley stood over the next table and said, "Excuse me, gentlemen. I couldn't help overhearing your conversation. My name is Reed Exley. I'm slave overseer on the John Ruffin plantation just outside of town, and I perceive that you could both use a little cash in your pockets."

Yates and Wheeler stood and introduced themselves to Exley, asking him to join them. They knew by the cut of his clothes that Exley was well-to-do.

As they sat down, Yates said, "You're right about our pockets being short on cash, Mr. Exley. What do you have in mind?"

"Well, I want to play a little joke on a friend of mine, but I need some help. It'll take a day or so to set it up, so here's what I'll do. I'll put you both up in a nice hotel and pay for your meals while you're here, and I'll give you each fifty dollars for helping me. How does that sound?"

Wheeler had carrot-red hair and a face that always looked like it was sunburned. Smiling, he replied, "Sounds great to me, Mr. Exley. Exactly what is this joke?"

"I'll come to the hotel tomorrow after I get things set up. I'll explain it to you then."

Exley took the two men to the Virginia Hotel, which was only

A PROMISE UNBROKEN

205

a half-block from the tavern, and got them each a room. They could eat at the hotel's restaurant and charge the meals to their rooms. Telling them he would see them some time the next day, he left the happy men to enjoy a good night's rest.

The next morning, Exley positioned himself at one of the windows in his bedroom on the third floor of the Ruffin mansion. The window allowed a view of the lane that came from the road. Abby was expecting Web to come and pick her up so they could spend the morning together in town. Exley wanted to intercept Steele before he entered the house.

It was exactly nine-thirty when Exley caught sight of the buggy coming up the lane. He dashed down the two flights of stairs and was on the porch as Web drove up.

Webster Steele alighted from the buggy, wondering why Exley was standing there almost smiling at him. As he mounted the porch steps, Exley stood between him and the door and said, "Web, I've been wanting to talk to you. I know you're here to take Abby to town and won't have time to see me now, but how about late this evening? We could have a drink at the Lamplighter."

"You know I don't drink, Reed."

"You could have some coffee. They've got good coffee at the Lamplighter."

"How would you know? Seems to me you always smell like whiskey when you come from there. Besides, you and I don't have anything to talk about."

As he spoke, Web started to walk around Exley, but the shorter man laid a gentle hand on his arm and said, "Please, Web. I really do need to talk some things over with you." Feigning a sheepish look, he added, "I've been…well, I've been wrong about some things. I need to get them off my chest. How about it?"

Web was skeptical, but in case the man had actually undergone a change of heart, it would make things much better within the family if they could patch up their differences. "Okay," he nodded. "What time do you want to meet?"

"How's ten o'clock?"

"A bit late, but I guess that'd be all right."

"Good!" exclaimed Exley, showing relief. "See you at the Lamplighter at ten tonight."

Elated that his plan was working well so far, Exley left the porch and headed toward the back of the mansion. He waited in one of the sheds until Web and Abby had driven away, then hitched his wagon to a horse and headed for town.

Meeting with Wheeler and Yates in the privacy of Wheeler's room, Exley found them eager to get on with the joke. They thought it was grand being in on it while getting paid, too.

Exley told them he wanted to make his friend, Web Steele, think he was helping to thwart a robbery. He explained that Steele was the gallant hero type, and without a doubt would fall for it. After they staged the "robbery" and Steele had been suckered in, they would laugh and tell him it was all a joke.

Exley carefully laid out the robbery plan to Yates and Wheeler, then went over the details several times to make sure they knew exactly what to do. Telling them to meet him in front of the Lamplighter at nine o'clock so they could do a little practice before Web showed up, Exley left the hotel and hurried to a small house three blocks from the town's main thoroughfare. He was glad to see that a lantern was still burning in the parlor window.

Stepping onto the creaky porch, he knocked on the door. He heard muffled footsteps, and the door swung open. A short, stout man of fifty squinted at him and said, "Reed? That you? Don't have my specs on."

"Sure is, Stan. You busy?"

Stan Frye laughed, flinging the door open, and said, "You know an old bachelor is just like a housewife, Reed. There's always somethin' to keep me busy. But come on in. I was just cleanin' out some drawers in the bedroom. They can wait."

Frye closed the door and asked, "You want some coffee? I can heat some up real quick-like."

"Sure. While it's heatin' up, I can tell you why I stopped by."

Reed Exley would leave no stone unturned. He must make sure his scheme against Web Steele was air-tight. He was certain Stan Frye would be willing to help him.

A few years before, Stan's older brother Arnie had been a successful slave auctioneer in Richmond. One day Arnie had hitched a mule he had just purchased to his wagon and had gone to town to do some business at one of the banks on Richmond's main street. When he climbed into the wagon to head for home, the mule refused to budge.

Arnie Frye, like his brother Stan, was known for being short-tempered. People on the street were looking on as he stood before the mule, cursing it and lashing it mercilessly in the face with a whip. Just then Web Steele came out of a nearby barber shop. When he saw what was going on, he moved in and shouted for Arnie to stop. Already aflame with anger, Arnie turned the whip on Web.

Web defended himself with his fists and unintentionally broke Arnie's jaw. The doctors were unable to set the fracture correctly, and Arnie was hardly able to talk after that. He lost his job as an auctioneer. He took his wife and moved to Roanoke, where he was given a job as a stable keeper by an old friend. The pay was quite small compared to what he had made as an auctioneer, and his wife left him.

Arnie turned to the bottle. He soon became a drunken sot, and even lost the stable job. Things went from bad to worse, and finally Arnie drank himself to death.

Web had never known what happened to Arnie, but nonetheless Stan blamed Web for it all and held a bitter grudge. Reed Exley had few friends, but Stan was one of them. He had often shared with Exley his smoldering hatred toward Steele. Stan was prime material for aiding Exley in his scheme.

As they sat down at the kitchen table, Exley complained that Steele had done him wrong and needed to be punished. Frye was immediately interested, and was soon happily involved in the scheme. Vengeance would be sweet.

While they sipped their coffee, Exley carefully instructed Frye, emphasizing that timing was of utmost importance. When Frye was able to repeat his part of the plan perfectly, Exley said, "Be sure that you're in the Lamplighter by eight o'clock. I'll come in about twenty after. Don't come near me. I don't want anyone to be able to say they saw us talkin' in there. Understand?"

"Got it," nodded Frye.

"Okay. Be sure you join up with some friends as soon as you get there."

"No problem."

"Good. I'll leave the tavern a little before nine to do a short rehearsal with Wheeler and Yates and return within fifteen or twenty minutes. Just in case Steele should show up a bit early, be sure you're on the street by nine thirty. Tell your friends you need to get some fresh air, and that you'll be back shortly. I'll keep an eye on you. Once you're outside, hide in the shadows till you see me come out of the tavern. I'll be at the door watchin' for Steele and move out to meet him when he pulls up. While I'm talkin' to him, you slip back inside. Stay with your friends till everybody in the place learns that there's trouble out on the street. When you come out with them, give the police the story I've gone over with you."

"Will do."

"Remember—you'll have to tell the story again in court. You've got to tell it exactly the same on the witness stand."

"Don't worry. I'll keep the story straight." Laughing wickedly, he added, "I can't wait to see that dirty skunk Steele get what's comin' to him."

There was little traffic on Richmond's main thoroughfare and only a few people were on the boardwalks when Web Steele pulled up and parked his buggy in front of the Lamplighter Tavern at five minutes before ten. Web had pondered just what Reed Exley might have to say. Perhaps he was going to apologize for the times he had done

Web wrong. Would he also admit his guilt in Elizabeth's death? Web doubted the man would go that far.

As he was tying the reins to a hitching post, Web saw Exley emerge from the tavern. By the light of the street lamps, he could see a wide smile on his face.

Knowing that his two accomplices were watching from the dark space between the tavern and the next building, Exley approached his victim amiably and said, "Web, I sure appreciate your meeting with me. It's time to bury the hatchet."

"Well, I'm glad you feel that way," Steele said warily. "Even though Elizabeth's gone, Papa John still considers you a part of the family. And since I'm marrying into the family shortly, you and I need to do what we can to get along."

Exley made it sound like he was in full agreement with Web as he waited for a wide break between people on the boardwalk and vehicles moving along the street. The break came quickly. Exley gave his accomplices the preset signal by raising his coat collar and saying, "Let's go inside, Web. The air's a bit nippy tonight."

Steele and Exley were almost to the door of the tavern when a cry came from between the buildings, "Help! I'm being robbed!" followed by the sounds of a scuffle.

Exley, relieved that no one else was on the street to hear it, looked that direction and said, "Sounds like somebody's in trouble, Web!"

True to form, Web Steele said, "C'mon!" and made a dash for the ten-foot-wide space between the buildings.

Making sure to stay a few steps behind Steele as they ran, Reed pulled a length of lead pipe from his coat pocket. There was an alley at the rear of the buildings with a lantern burning on a pole. By the dim light, Steele could see two men on the ground scuffling. Just as he drew close, Exley cracked him on the back of the head with the heavy pipe. When his accomplices heard the blow and saw Steele go down, they stopped scuffling and leaped to their feet, staring wide-eyed at Exley.

"Hey, what's goin' on?" gasped Yates. "What'd you do that for?"

"That's no way to treat a friend!" Wheeler said accusingly.

While Steele lay unconscious on the ground, Exley slipped the pipe back into his coat pocket and pulled a hunting knife from its sheath on his belt. Moving close to Yates, he said, "This was no joke to begin with, pal," and in a swift, violent move, drove the knife into Yates's heart.

Wheeler's mouth flew open in shock. He felt he was in a nightmare standing transfixed, unable to move.

Yates collapsed to the ground, dead, with the knife protruding from his chest. Exley pulled the lead pipe from his coat pocket, moved close to Wheeler, and said, "Hec, I planned it exactly this way. I killed Wilbur and not you because you're by far the smartest. Cooperate with me and you won't get into trouble."

The light from the lantern in the alley revealed Wheeler's terror-stricken features. The usual redness of his skin had faded to an ashen-gray. Swallowing hard, he struggled for a moment to locate his voice, then stammered, "Wh-what do you want fr-from me?"

Pointing toward Web's crumpled form, Exley said, "This man is my worst enemy. He's done me wrong a hundred times. I had to trick him to get him here, but finally I can have my revenge."

Licking his lips, Wheeler said, "Y-your worst enemy?"

"Yeah. He's rotten to the core. Will you help me?"

"Well, I...I..."

"It'll be worth a lot of money for you if you do."

Wheeler scrubbed a shaky hand across his mouth. "Money?"

"Yeah. A generous sum. Will you do it?"

"Wh-what do you want me t-to do?"

"I hit Steele plenty hard. He'll be out for a few minutes. Before he comes to, I'm gonna put this sheath on his belt to make it look like he was carryin' the knife. Then we'll call the police. I'll give them the story. You just back me up. We'll tell them that you and I were standin' on the boardwalk in front of the tavern when we heard this call for help from back here. We ran back to investigate and came on the scene just as Steele was plungin' the knife into Yates's chest. Got it? You just back up whatever I say."

"Just go along with whatever you say?"

"Right. You'll have to testify to it in court, too. But I'll make it worth your trouble, Hec. I'll give you a thousand dollars if you'll help me."

"A thousand dollars!" gulped Wheeler.

"That's right. You'll get five hundred tomorrow, and five hundred after you testify at the trial. How about it?"

Wheeler quickly appraised the situation. He hardly knew Wilbur Yates…and besides, there was no way he could bring the man back to life by refusing to help Exley. He had never even seen a thousand dollars in his whole life. Exley was a scary man, and he was still holding the lead pipe. Why not go along with him? Nodding, he said, "Okay, Mr. Exley. I'll help you."

"Good!" said Exley. "This is your lucky day, wouldn't you agree, Hec?"

"Sure," said Hec, nervously wringing his hands. "My lucky day."

Exley had stolen the hunting knife and sheath from a local gun shop while the proprietor was in a back room looking for extra ammunition for his derringer. There was no way the knife could be traced to him. Working fast, he placed the sheath on Web's belt, then told Hec to go shout for the police.

Before obeying, Hec said, "There's somethin' I don't understand, Mr. Exley."

"What's that?"

"Well, if you wanted to get back at this Steele fella, why didn't you just put the knife in his chest?"

Exley grinned. "I have my reasons, pal. I want his woman, too. She's sorta been down on me, but I'm gonna make ol' Reed Exley look like a saint in the courtroom, and my act will draw her to me like a magnet when Steele goes to prison…or maybe the gallows."

Web Steele's head was throbbing when he came to and heard voices all around him. Opening his eyes, he saw where he was, then remembered running into the dark space between the buildings to help a robbery victim.

"He's comin' around," said a familiar voice.

Several lanterns sat on the ground to give light on the scene. Web focused on the face of Richmond's chief of police, Frank Crabbe. Steele and Crabbe had been acquaintances ever since Crabbe had joined the force some ten years before. Leaning over Steele, he said, "Webster, I never would've guessed you could do such a thing."

Sitting up, Steele winced, rubbed the back of his head, and looked at the policemen who surrounded him. He was aware of a large knot on the back of his skull, and that it was bleeding.

Looking at Crabbe, Web said, "You never would've guessed that I could do what?"

"Murder a man," the chief replied flatly.

"What are you talking about?"

Crabbe shifted his position, giving Steele a clear view of Reed Exley and Hec Wheeler, who stood behind him. Pointing with his head, he said, "Mr. Exley told us how he and his friend were chatting on the boardwalk in front of the tavern when they heard a cry for help coming from back here. When they ran between the buildings, they saw you drive your knife into this man's chest."

Following Crabbe's finger, Web saw the corpse a few feet away with the knife still buried in its chest. Crabbe was waiting for the coroner to arrive before disturbing the body.

The truth came home to Web Steele like a punch to the solar plexus. Reed Exley had set him up. The whole thing about wanting to talk was a farce. Exley no doubt had both men working with him, then stabbed one of them to death in a wickedly devised scheme to frame him.

"They're lying, Frank," said Web.

"That won't work, Steele!" Exley snapped. "That's your knife that's stuck in him."

Web looked at Crabbe and said, "He's lying, Frank. I've never seen that knife before."

"Well, I'd say it would fit that sheath on your belt perfectly," countered Crabbe.

Web found the sheath on his belt and lanced the smirking Exley with hot eyes. Then he said to Crabbe, "The truth is, Frank, that Exley lured me to the tavern tonight, saying he wanted to make amends for the trouble he has made for me. Then he tricked me into running to help some poor victim who was supposedly being robbed. This 'friend' of his was scuffling with the poor guy who's now dead. Exley hit me over the head with something, then he or this other man stabbed him. While I was unconscious, they put the sheath on my belt."

Exley pulled the pipe from his coat pocket and waved it at Steele. "This is what I hit you with, you murderer! Only it was just after you had rammed your knife into that man's chest. As I told Chief Crabbe, I always carry this piece of pipe with me when I come into town at night…for my own protection. Good thing I was carryin' it tonight, or you might have gotten away."

Web struggled to his feet and stood swaying while he used his handkerchief to stay the trickle of blood from the cut on his head. To Crabbe he said, "Exley wouldn't know the truth if it slapped him in the face. It happened like I told you, Frank. You've got to believe me."

Shrugging his shoulders, Crabbe replied, "Whether I believe you or not isn't important, Web. It's what the jury believes that matters." Then pointing to Stan Frye, who stood with the group of policemen, he said, "This is the man they're liable to believe."

Peering at Frye, Steele asked, "What do you have to do with this, Stan?"

"Plenty," responded Frye. "I've been at the Lamplighter since about eight o'clock. I came outside to get some fresh air around nine thirty, and I saw you and that dead man over there standin' at the corner of the buildin' and goin' at each other real angry-like. I could tell from what was said that the two of you had had some kind of serious disagreement previously and that you'd come into town tonight to settle it. I figured it was none of my business, so I went back into the tavern. Looks like you wore that knife into town to do that poor man in. You did a good job of it."

Web looked at Crabbe and said with strained voice, "Frank, I'm telling you, this whole thing is a crock of lies!"

"You're the one that's lyin', mister!" spoke up Hec Wheeler. "The jury will believe Mr. Frye here, and they'll believe me and Mr. Exley, because we're tellin' the truth."

Taking hold of Steele's upper arm, Crabbe said, "You're under arrest, Web, for the murder of this man we'll identify when the coroner arrives. Take him to the jail, men."

"Frank, you're making a mistake. I'm telling you this is Exley's setup."

"We'll let the jury decide. Right now, you're being booked for murder."

Setting fiery eyes on Exley, Web said, "You won't get away with this."

Exley shrugged, cocked his head, and said, "Web, I'm not tryin' to get away with anything. Hec and I saw you murder that poor man. We had to call the law on you."

To Crabbe, Web said, "Will you see that somebody let's my parents know about this? They'll be expecting me home soon."

"I'll send a man out right away," nodded the chief.

"Tell him to have Dad let Abby Ruffin know too, will you?"

"I'll see that it's done," Crabbe assured him. "But understand—none of them can visit you till morning."

The sun was barely up the next day when Web Steele heard the door to the cell block swing open. Presently a guard appeared at his cell and said, "You've got a passel of visitors wanting to see you, Steele. Only other prisoner we've got right now is the fella next to you. He's sleeping off a drunk, so I guess he won't mind a crowd in here. You want to see them all at one time?"

"Sure," nodded Web.

The guard disappeared, and seconds later Abby Ruffin was the first to come running into the cell block. Tears were on her cheeks as she pressed herself up to the bars and choked, "Oh, Web! This just can't be happening. It's…it's like a bad dream."

Web reached through the bars and embraced her. "It's Reed's doing, honey," he said. "He set the whole thing up. Even murdered that poor man just to get back at me."

Web looked up to see his parents, Lynne Ruffin, Daniel Hart, and the family attorney, Thomas Bean. Abby moved aside so the others could approach Web. Cora embraced her son, speaking words of encouragement, followed by Lynne and Daniel. Then father and son gripped hands.

Dudley Steele said, "I brought Thomas with me, Web. He'll take your case and see that justice is done."

Bean stepped forward and shook Web's hand. "This whole thing is preposterous, Web," he said with anger in his voice. "I'll do everything in my power to see that you're cleared."

"I know you will," replied Web.

Everyone wanted to hear Web's side of the story. Abby stepped close and held his hand through the bars as he told of Reed's treachery. While the group talked with Web, Thomas Bean went to Chief Crabbe's office. He returned an hour later, informing Web that his trial was set for Monday, April 15, at ten o'clock in the morning. This gave Bean nearly two weeks to work on Web's defense. He asked that the others give him some time with Web so they could talk. They all assured Web of their full support. Last to leave was Abby, who spoke words of love and kissed him soundly through the bars.

FIFTEEN

In late November of 1860, President James Buchanan assigned ex-West Point instructor Major Robert Anderson to head up the Union forces at Forts Moultrie, Sumter, and Castle Pinckney in Charleston Harbor. Secession was a genuine threat, and Buchanan wanted the federal forts in the best of hands.

When South Carolina seceded from the Union on December 20, Anderson knew that he and his men were in a dangerous position, just a stone's throw from the very spot where the secession had taken place. The major knew war was now inevitable. He also knew that neither President Buchanan nor President Abraham Lincoln, when he took office, would negotiate a sale of the three forts to the Southerners. It was Anderson's job to defend the federal positions the best he could.

As the days passed after South Carolina's secession, Anderson had a growing concern over his vulnerability in the harbor. He had only sixty soldiers to man all three forts. Anderson's main base, Fort Moultrie, on big Sullivan's Island, commanded the northern entrance to Charleston Harbor. It was vulnerable to land attack from the rear. Fort Castle Pinckney, lying less than a mile off the coast of Charleston, was poorly armed, and unless subsidized with more men and arms, would fall quickly in an attack.

Clearly the most advantageous place for Anderson to make a stand was Fort Sumter, located on a small island a little over three miles from Charleston. Although hasty efforts to strengthen Fort Sumter were still underway, the major's predecessor had laid in enough supplies to last sixty men several months. Sumter's guns could answer any attack by closing the harbor to Southern shipping to and from Charleston.

When Anderson sent a message to Secretary of War John B. Floyd asking for more men, he was turned down. Floyd believed the forts were in no danger.

Concerned for the lives of his men, Anderson decided to gather them all in one place to face the attack he was sure would come. They would take their stand in Fort Sumter. Keeping his plans quiet, the major and his men spent all Christmas Day packing movable goods in Forts Moultrie and Castle Pinckney. A cold, hard rain postponed the transfer to Sumter that night, but the next night the soldiers ferried their gear to Sumter, and no one in Charleston was aware of it until dawn on December 27.

That morning the people in Charleston saw smoke rising across the harbor waters from the wooden gun carriages that Anderson and his men had set afire at Moultrie and Castle Pinckney to deny the Southerners use of the cannons. It was not until noon, however, that they realized that Fort Sumter was now fully garrisoned. *The Stars and Stripes were being raised on the mast atop the ramparts.*

Major Robert Anderson's message was clear. Fort Sumter was a federal installation in enemy territory, from which the United States would not retreat.

During the next three months, Major Anderson and his men lived on the supplies that had been laid up in the fort while Southern leaders attempted to bring about a diplomatic surrender of Sumter. It was to no avail. Washington would not budge. When Abraham Lincoln became president the first week in March 1861, he immediately tried to get supplies through to Anderson and his men. This infuriated the Southerners. They blocked the boat carrying the supplies, denying it entrance to the harbor.

This move by the Federals prompted President Jefferson Davis to immediately contact his commander at Charleston, a handsome, dapper Louisiana Frenchman named Pierre G.T. Beauregard. The brigadier general was ordered to begin building up his artillery on the islands around the harbor.

Beauregard worked feverishly to comply with President Davis's orders. By early April he had brought overwhelming firepower to bear on Fort Sumter, including eight-inch, long-range columbiad cannons, eight-inch high-trajectory howitzers, twenty-four and forty-two pounders, smoothbores that fired thirty-two-pound balls, and squat, wide-mouthed ten-inch mortars designed expressly to crumble fort walls. Beauregard had well over five thousand men stationed in his various fortifications, ranging in age from boys in their mid-teens to silver-haired oldsters in their late sixties. A few would man the guns, while the others stood by to storm Fort Sumter if the general deemed it necessary.

As recruits continued to arrive from all over the South, they were given a rousing welcome by the citizens of Charleston and the thousands of loyal Southerners gathered in the city.

Among those who arrived at the Charleston dock on April 9 was Edmund Ruffin. Three ferries were carrying the recruits to the islands, assigned by Confederate captains George S. James and Stephen D. Lee. Ruffin approached one of the captains, introduced himself, and asked to be ferried to wherever General Beauregard was stationed. Captain James was delighted to meet the man who was known as the "father of secession," and gave him a warm handshake. He informed Ruffin that General Beauregard had set up his head-quarters at Fort Johnson, which was located on James Island, and that the general would welcome him with open arms.

Ruffin said he was sure the impending war would start in Charleston Harbor, and that he wanted to be there for the occasion. He had never met General Beauregard, but earnestly desired to do so.

When the ferries were loaded with new recruits, the men were delivered to the various islands. The ferry occupied by the two captains and Edmund Ruffin let fifty-four men off at Fort Moultrie, then cut across the harbor of James Island. Ruffin's long gray hair whipped in the breeze as the captains escorted him inside Fort Johnson. They introduced him to several uniformed men as they made their way to the upper level of the fort where the Charleston Harbor commander had his temporary office.

The office door stood open as the three men drew up. Captain James rapped on the door frame and said, "General Beauregard, sir, we have a very distinguished guest who would like to see you."

"Well, bring him in," came a resonant voice.

Edmund Ruffin entered the stone-walled room, which had been used in days gone by as the fort commander's office. Beauregard was standing behind his desk, and two other officers got up from their chairs to meet Captains James and Lee and their guest.

When Beauregard saw the old man, he smiled and said, "You gentlemen don't need to introduce this great Southerner to me. I've seen his pictures in the newspapers." Rounding the desk, the tall, stately general extended his hand. "Mr. Edmund Ruffin. I am more than pleased to make your acquaintance."

"Thank you, general," smiled Ruffin, "likewise, I'm sure."

By Beauregard's mature features and the deep-set lines of his face, Ruffin knew he had to be in his fifties. The man was strikingly handsome, with a thick head of jet-black hair and a heavy mustache that drooped at the corners of his mouth. Ruffin wondered that there was not some gray mingled in the black of his hair and mustache.

When the two men had shaken hands, Beauregard gestured toward his other two officers and said, "Mr. Ruffin, I would like you to meet Colonel Jim Chesnut and Colonel James Chisholm."

Both Chesnut and Chisholm had also seen Ruffin's picture in the papers. They shook hands with him, expressing their appreciation for his courage and determination in leading the South to break with the North.

Additional chairs were produced, and when all were seated,

Beauregard asked, "To what do we owe this visit, Mr. Ruffin?"

Ruffin smiled. "Well, sir, as I told Captain James and Captain Lee, with all this military buildup, it sure looks to me like things are going to come to a head between our Confederate forces here in the harbor and those few foolhardy men out there in Fort Sumter. I figure the war's going to start right here, and I want to be on the scene when it happens."

"You're probably right," nodded the general, "but as of yet, President Davis and his cabinet have not given me the command to launch an attack. There's one man in the cabinet who's holding things up."

"Who is that?"

"The secretary of state."

Ruffin lifted his bushy silver eyebrows. "What's Robert Toombs got against us attacking Sumter?"

Beauregard toyed nervously with his mustache. "He's warning that if we fire upon Major Anderson and the men in Sumter, we'll inaugurate a civil war greater than any the world has ever seen."

"He could be right, sir," spoke up Captain James. "I'm a true and loyal son of the South, and I hate the thought of burying thousands upon thousands of our men. I'm just fearful that it's going to be bloodier than any of us have imagined. I believe Mr. Lincoln senses it, too. When he sent that supply ship down here for the men in Sumter, he was very careful to point out that there were no weapons aboard and no reinforcements. He doesn't want war."

"If Lincoln doesn't want war, why did he refuse to negotiate with us on the sale of these forts?" spat Ruffin.

"Seems to me," put in Colonel Chesnut, "Lincoln wants his forts sitting here in our harbor with their guns pointed at us, and at the same time he wants us to act like there's no problem between the Union and the Confederacy."

"Yeah," agreed Ruffin. "The situation's a little lopsided, I'd say." Then turning to Beauregard, he said, "General, it's my understanding that the cabinet needs only a majority vote to authorize an attack on Sumter. Why doesn't President Davis just bypass Toombs and give the order?"

"I don't know," replied Beauregard. "It's not for me to know how politicians think. All I can do is sit here and wait for my orders."

Ruffin quietly accepted the answer, then asked, "Who is this Major Robert Anderson the Union's put in charge of Sumter?"

"Well, this is the irony of all ironies," said the general, scratching at an ear. "Major Anderson was my artillery instructor at West Point twenty-three years ago. He and I became close friends after I graduated, and have been all these years. We went on a hunting trip together in the Smokies a year ago last fall. He's only a few years older than me, and we've got a lot of interests in common." The general paused to swallow a lump that had risen in his throat, then added with a quiver in his voice, "Now…now all of a sudden, we're enemies."

Captain Lee leaned forward in his chair and said softly, "General, sir, does President Davis know of your past friendship with Major Anderson?"

"No. He has no reason to be aware of it."

"When the order is given to fire the first shot, will he expect you to be the one to do it?"

"No. I have already been instructed *not* to be the one to yank the lanyard. I am to give the order to the man I choose, but Davis feels that the man to start the war should not be the officer in charge of this operation."

There was a tap at the open door. Beauregard looked up to see one of the enlisted men silhouetted against the growing darkness outside. "Yes?" he said.

"General, I'm here to advise you that the meal will be served in twenty minutes."

"Thank you, Wilson. Tell the cooks we have a guest who will be dining with us this evening. We'll need an extra setting at the officers' table."

"Yes, sir," said the soldier, and was gone.

Then to Ruffin, Beauregard said, "If you want to stick around until my orders come, Mr. Ruffin, you're more than welcome. We've got some spare cots. You can sleep in the officers' quarters with us."

A broad smile spread over Edmund Ruffin's weathered face. "I'll just take you up on that offer, sir."

On Wednesday, April 10, 1861, General Pierre G.T. Beauregard was standing on the eastern tip of James Island with Edmund Ruffin shortly after they had eaten lunch in the fort. Both men were discussing the impending conflict when they saw a rowboat coming from the mainland.

Beauregard lifted his hat, ran fingers through his hair, and sighed shakily, "I've got a feeling this boat may be bringing me my orders from the president."

The rowboat pulled up to the shore with four men aboard, each handling an oar. One man stepped out and hurried to Beauregard with an envelope in his hand, saying it was a telegram from Montgomery, Alabama. The general signed for it and noticed his four officers hastening toward him from the fort as the messenger was returning to the boat.

Beauregard opened the envelope and read the message silently. Ruffin saw his features tighten and lose color. At that moment, officers Chesnut, Chisholm, Lee, and James drew up, anticipation showing on their faces.

When Beauregard looked at them with dismal eyes, Colonel Chesnut asked cautiously, "Are those your orders, sir?"

The general nodded solemnly. "Yes. Directly from the secretary of war. I am to draw up a written surrender ultimatum and have it delivered to Major Anderson. Fort Sumter is to be evacuated within a short time after Anderson has the document of surrender in his hands. Secretary Walker is leaving the length of that short time to me. If Major Anderson refuses for any reason, or he and his men do not leave Fort Sumter by the deadline, we are to open fire on their position with all our artillery batteries."

Captain James glanced toward Sumter and asked, "Do you think the major will surrender and evacuate without a fight, sir?"

General Beauregard's face was gray and stony. "I know the man well, Captain," he replied evenly. "He will not surrender and evacuate without a fight."

James looked around at the others, then set his gaze on Beauregard and said with furrowed brow, "Once we fire on Sumter, sir, there'll be no turning back. We'll be at war with the Union."

Beauregard nodded and looked wistfully in the direction of Fort Sumter.

The officers exchanged glances, then Colonel Chisholm said, "General…"

Beauregard brought his head around slowly, "Yes, Colonel?"

"It…it's Major Anderson you're concerned about, isn't it?"

Beauregard brushed a hand over his mustache and replied with feeling, "I'm concerned first and foremost about commencing a war that will scar this great country of ours in a way that it may never recover, Colonel. And yes, I am concerned about bombarding the very fortress where stands one of the best friends I have ever had—a man I love and admire."

"Well, sir," said Chisholm clearing his throat, "if you want to find some reason to go ashore, as one of your officers, I will take the orders and fulfill them."

Beauregard laid a hand on Chisholm's shoulder and said, "I appreciate your offer, but these orders were sent to me. President Davis put me in command of this operation, and I cannot allow my personal feelings to cloud my thinking. Secretary of War Walker has laid out my orders. I must obey them to the letter."

"How long will you give Major Anderson to evacuate, sir?" queried Colonel Chesnut.

"I don't know yet. I'll have to work on it." Turning toward the fort with a sigh, the general said, "I'll be in my office if you need me, gentlemen."

The five men stood and watched Beauregard until he vanished inside Fort Johnson's walls, then Captain Lee said, "It would be a mighty hard thing to give the order to unleash all our firepower on one of your best friends."

The other officers were nodding their agreement when Edmund Ruffin spoke up. "That's just part of the price of war, gentlemen. But war must come. Those Yankees couldn't keep their big noses out of our business. Well, now they're going to pay for it. I say the quicker we fire that first shot, the better. We'll teach those Yankee dogs a lesson they won't forget!"

The men at Fort Johnson saw very little of their commander until ten o'clock the next morning. At that time, he gathered all of them in the exercise area at the center of the fort and explained his orders from Secretary Walker. He informed them that he had drawn up a written surrender ultimatum to be delivered to Major Anderson. The ultimatum demanded that the Union soldiers lay down their arms and evacuate the fort by four o'clock that afternoon. If they refused or delayed beyond that time, they would be fired upon from every direction.

Beauregard then spoke to Captain James. "Take two men with you in one of the rowboats and convey this message to the other artillery installations. Tell them about my ultimatum to Major Anderson and to be on the alert at four o'clock. If the signal gun is fired from here on James Island, they are to begin bombardment within one minute."

"And what if…well, sir, if there should be some kind of unforeseen delay? What then?"

"Tell them to stay on the alert until they hear differently, even if they have no contact from us until tomorrow. If and when we fire the signal gun from here, they are to follow with bombardment as ordered."

"Yes, sir," responded James, and with a snappy salute, he approached two soldiers he knew well and told them to follow him.

Turning to Chesnut, the general said, "Colonel, you will take the ultimatum to Major Anderson. I have it in my office. Take Colonel Chisholm and Captain Lee with you"

"Yes, sir. Ah…sir?"

"Yes?"

"Is there any personal message you want me to give to Major Anderson?"

"No," replied Beauregard, slowly shaking his head. "All that—" he cleared his throat—"all that needs to be said is in the ultimatum."

Chesnut quickly appointed two soldiers to man a rowboat and be ready to shove off in five minutes. As they rowed away from the shore moments later, General Beauregard stood like a statue atop one of the ramparts and watched them. In the boat, Captain Lee looked back at the general and said to the others, "I wouldn't want to be in his shoes right now."

When the rowboat touched shore on the small island that bore Fort Sumter, a half-dozen armed soldiers were waiting to meet it. A number of men observed the scene from inside the stone walls.

Chesnut stood up in the boat and said to the Union soldiers, "I am Colonel James Chesnut, army of the Confederacy. I have a written message from General Pierre Gustave Toutant Beauregard that I am to deliver personally to Major Robert Anderson."

"You may come ashore," a young lieutenant informed him.

"I also have Colonel James Chisholm and Captain Stephen Lee with me," said Chesnut. "May they come ashore, also?"

"Permission granted," nodded the lieutenant.

The three Confederate officers were escorted inside the fort and presented to Major Anderson, who was at a crude desk in his makeshift office on the first level, next to the barracks.

Anderson rose and greeted the Southerners with a polite nod. He was a tall, slender man in his late fifties. His hair was dark, but on the sides had turned silver-gray. The deep lines in his face and the bags beneath his eyes showed the strain he was bearing.

Chairs were brought in and Anderson invited the Confederates to be seated. Several Union soldiers waited just outside the closed door. Though his comrades sat down, Chesnut remained on his feet, as did Anderson. The colonel produced an envelope from inside his coat and extended it to the major, saying, "I have a written message for you, sir, from General Beauregard."

Anderson's face was grim as he accepted the envelope and said, "Please be seated, Colonel." Easing onto his own chair, he fixed weary eyes on Chesnut and asked, "How is my old friend, Pierre?"

"His health is fine, sir, but at the moment, he is bearing a heavy load."

Anderson closed his eyes, then opened them slowly, acknowledging that he understood. Asking the men to excuse him, he opened the envelope and silently read the ultimatum. When he finished, he folded the paper, and said, "I will have to discuss this with my officers. You gentlemen wait here."

Anderson left the door open behind him as he departed from the office. He was gone less than ten minutes. Returning to his chair, he ran his tired gaze over the faces of the Confederate officers and said solemnly, "My officers have agreed with me, gentlemen. We reject General Beauregard's ultimatum. We refuse to evacuate the fort."

While the Southerners exchanged heavy glances, Anderson took a sheet of paper and an envelope out of a small box on top of the desk and said, "I will put it in writing for the general."

When the response had been written and placed in the envelope, the major placed it in Chesnut's hand and said, "I will walk you gentlemen to your boat."

As they approached the Confederate boat, Anderson asked, "Colonel Chesnut, will General Beauregard open his batteries without further notice to me?"

"It is my understanding, sir, that the only notice you will get will be the signal shot from Fort Johnson. Exactly one minute after that, the batteries are to open up full force."

Nodding slowly, Anderson said, "Then I shall await the first shot at four o'clock, Colonel." After a brief pause, he added quietly, "If you do not batter us to pieces, we shall be starved out in a few days."

Returning to Fort Johnson, the officers met with Beauregard and gave him Anderson's note. After the general had read it, Chesnut said, "Sir, just before we left him, Major Anderson said something that I think might have been a hint."

"And what was that?" queried the general.

"He said that if we didn't batter them to pieces, they'd be starved out in a few days. You know him, sir. Do you think it was a hint that if we didn't fire on them, they'd have to give up shortly anyway because they'll be out of food?"

"I'm not sure, but it's worth giving it a little time. I'll wire Secretary Walker, explain the situation, and see if he'll grant us a few days to starve them out."

Immediately a wire was sent to Montgomery with Beauregard's request. Hours passed with no response. While eager Confederate soldiers waited at the battery installations, four o'clock came and went. Finally, just after midnight on April 12, the message from the secretary of war arrived. Walker replied that he did not desire to bombard Fort Sumter if it could be avoided, and if Major Anderson would state the date when he would evacuate, Beauregard could hold his fire.

The general went to his office and by lantern light composed another message. Handing the envelope to Chesnut, he said, "Colonel, I want you to take this message to Sumter immediately. I'm on touchy ground, now, with the powers that be in Montgomery, so this has to be the final message to Major Anderson. I am giving you the authority to act on the spot according to the major's response. If you're satisfied with it, then you speak for me in making the arrangements for a quick and smooth evacuation on the date he has chosen. If, however, you are not satisfied with his response, you also speak for me in refusing his terms."

"If the latter should be the case, sir," said Chesnut, "am I then to give warning as to when bombardment will start?"

Beauregard paused briefly before replying, "That is exactly what you will do."

The other officers and Edmund Ruffin were standing close by.

Ruffin observed as Beauregard assigned Chisholm and Lee to go along with Chesnut once again. Eager to be in on as much of the action as possible, Ruffin stepped up to Beauregard and said, "General, would you mind if I went with them?"

"I don't see any reason you can't," replied Beauregard. Then to Chesnut he said, "You don't mind, do you, Colonel?"

"It's fine with me. Let's be going."

Again, two soldiers were employed to do the rowing, and the boat glided through the dark waters of Charleston Harbor toward Fort Sumter.

It was nearly 1:00 A.M. when the envoys were met at the shoreline by several Union guards. When Chesnut explained their purpose, they were led to the dining area next to the kitchen and seated at one of the tables. A sleepy-eyed Anderson entered five minutes later and greeted them courteously. When he had read Beauregard's message, he left the Southerners, saying he would get his officers out of bed and discuss a response with them.

When Anderson had not returned after nearly two hours, the Confederate officers began to murmur amongst themselves. Ruffin saw their agitation and said, "Gentlemen, I realize I'm not part of the official party here, but for what it's worth, I think our Major Anderson is stalling. Seems to me we need to call his hand."

"I agree," said Chesnut. "It's time he gave us an answer. I'll go put his feet to the fire."

Chesnut left the dining hall and headed for Anderson's office. The officers were just wrapping up their discussion when the impatient Colonel Chesnut interrupted them. It was shortly after 3:00 A.M. when Anderson handed Chesnut his response in writing.

The major followed Chesnut back to the dining hall and stood by as the colonel read the response aloud to the others. The message was that Anderson would evacuate the fort on April 15, holding his fire in the meantime unless fired upon, or unless he detected some act of hostile intent that would endanger his men or the fort. Further, his agreement to hold fire might be altered if he received other instructions from his superiors, or if somehow a Union boat could get through to him with additional supplies.

When Chesnut finished reading the response to his companions, they could tell he was unhappy.

Pulling a pad of paper and a pencil from his coat, the colonel said, "Major, this is unacceptable. I have been authorized by General Beauregard to—"

"Why is it unacceptable?" cut in Anderson.

"You're allowing yourself too many ways out," Chesnut replied tartly. "I have been authorized by General Beauregard to advise you that your response is indeed unacceptable. If you will give me a moment, I will write out a formal declaration."

When Chesnut had finished writing, he said, "I will read it to you, Major, then it is yours to keep."

Holding the paper to the lantern light, Colonel Chesnut read, "By authority of General Pierre G.T. Beauregard, commander of Confederate military operations at Charleston Harbor, I have the honor of notifying you that we will open fire with all of our batteries on Fort Sumter in one hour. Signed, James Chesnut, Colonel, Army of the Confederacy."

At 3:30, Anderson escorted the Confederates back to their boat and shook hands with each one. As they climbed into the small craft, he said, "If we never meet in this world again, gentlemen, God grant that we may meet in the next."

The bells of St. Michael's Church in Charleston were chiming 4:00 A.M. as Chesnut's party rowed up to James Island. General Beauregard and Captain James met them as they climbed from the boat. When Colonel Chesnut announced Anderson's response, the general took it silently. As the officers and Edmund Ruffin moved back into the fort, Beauregard finally spoke. "Captain James, prepare the twenty-four pounder. I want the shell to arch over Sumter and strike water on the other side. The artillery that follows will do proper damage."

At precisely 4:30, there was a slight hint of dawn on the watery eastern horizon. Every man in Fort Johnson stood near the big twenty-four-pound cannon in a semicircle. There was electricity in the air. Their hearts beat with anticipation.

Captain James stood beside the cannon and said to Beauregard, "The gun is ready to fire, sir. It is aimed and elevated to send the ball over Fort Sumter and strike water on its opposite side, as you commanded."

Beauregard swallowed hard. "All right. Fire it, Captain."

James's face paled in the dim light. "*Me*, sir?"

"Yes. It's four-thirty. Yank the lanyard."

The captain trembled as he said, "General Beauregard, sir, I do not mean to be insubordinate, but I keep thinking of what your secretary of state said: *If we fire upon Major Anderson and the men in Sumter, we'll inaugurate a civil war greater than any the world has ever seen.* Please, sir. I respectfully request that I be relieved of the duty of pulling the lanyard. I…I just can't fire the first shot of the war."

The general's features showed no anger. "All right, Captain," he replied softly.

No one in the group said a word or moved a muscle. Beauregard gave his mustache a quick stroke, and turned toward Edmund Ruffin. "Mr. Ruffin," he said briskly, "you have fought harder for secession from the Union and independence for the South than any man I know. Would you like to be the man to fire the first shot of the war?"

Without hesitation, the old man stepped forward and snapped, "Yes, sir! I'll be glad to do it."

Ruffin had been around big guns before. He knew exactly what to do. With every eye on him, he took hold of the lanyard and jerked it. The deep-throated roar of the cannon echoed across the harbor as the fiery signal shell arced high into the lightening sky, sailed over Fort Sumter, and struck the water. Within sixty seconds, the harbor was alive with booming cannons and bright, yellow-red flashes of fire.

Now no one could stem the tide of war. America was out of control.

SIXTEEN

At a quarter of ten on Monday morning, April 15, 1861, a crowd was gathering in the main courtroom at the Henrico County courthouse in Richmond, Virginia. The topic of discussion was General Beauregard's attack on Fort Sumter on Friday, and General Anderson's surrender on Saturday afternoon. The Confederate guns had fired 3,341 projectiles at Fort Sumter during thirty-three hours of bombardment. All the barracks were in ruins and the main gate was destroyed. The outer walls had been blasted heavily. Incredibly, the Confederate artillery had injured only four Union soldiers and had killed none. The Confederates also had only four men injured by return fire, all at Fort Moultrie. Major Anderson and his men had evacuated the Sumter garrison at four o'clock on Sunday afternoon while thousands of Southerners looked on from Charleston's wharf, and General Beauregard observed from a boat in the harbor.

The rumble of voices in the courtroom carried one common thought: The time for words and accusations between Northerners and Southerners had run out. There was no doubt the Union would retaliate for the attack on Fort Sumter. Now, instead of talk, there would be fire, smoke, blood, and death. The dreaded war between the states was a grim reality.

As Abby Ruffin and her father entered the courtroom, they were discussing the newspaper article they had read just that morning, which named Edmund Ruffin as the man who had fired the first shot at Charleston Harbor. Though John and his daughter were loyal Southerners, neither was happy about Edmund's deed.

Abby insisted that they sit on the front row so she could be near the table where Web Steele would sit with attorney Thomas Bean. Directly behind John and Abby came Dudley and Cora Steele. Their faces showed the strain they were feeling over the commencement of the war, but even more, their concern over Web's fate. Daniel Hart and Lynne Ruffin followed them. Lynne's eyes were puffy from weeping. Daniel was going to enlist in the Confederate army, and though Lynne understood why, she feared for his life.

John Ruffin sat on Abby's right, Cora Steele on her left. They looked at each other tenderly and joined hands. Next to Cora was Dudley, and beside him were Lynne and Daniel.

Stan Frye had arrived early and was seated with some of the men he had been drinking with in the Lamplighter Tavern the night Wilbur Yates was murdered. Reed Exley came in with Hec Wheeler and sat on the front row across the aisle. Abby burned Exley with a hot glare when their eyes met. Exley had told her that very morning that he was sorry he had to testify against Web, but he was only doing his civic duty. He would have to take the stand and tell the truth. Web had murdered a man, and he would have to suffer the consequences. Men who committed murder had to be dealt with to the fullest extent of the law.

Knowing who the real murderer was, Abby had wanted to slap his smug face, but she had refrained. It would have accomplished nothing except to make her feel good. She hated Reed Exley. He had wickedly connived the murder and framed Web. Even if Web were acquitted, Exley would still never pay for his crime.

Abby felt a wave of anxiety as Web was led by a deputy from a side door to the table, followed by Bean. The attorney had already told Web and the family that he was concerned about the outcome. The case against Web was tight, and the prosecutor was pushing for the death penalty. If the jury convicted Web, Bean would plead for a sentence of life imprisonment based on Web's clean record up until the night of the murder.

As Web sat down at the table, he set his worried but loving gaze on Abby. Tears brimmed her dark-blue eyes as she forced a smile.

At precisely ten o'clock, Henrico County Judge William B. Tenant took his place at the bench and brought the court to order. While the charges against Webster Steele were being read, Reed Exley let his gaze stray past Hec Wheeler to the captivating redhead. She was the most beautiful woman he had ever seen. He told himself that after the little speech he was going to make on Web's behalf, Abby would look upon him more favorably. Once Web was either dead or locked up for life, in time she would forget him. She would be lonely. Reed Exley would be there to fill that loneliness and take her in his arms. One day in the not-too-distant future, lovely Abby would be his.

Stan Frye was first to take the witness stand. He gave his false testimony under oath without blinking an eye. As he related the story exactly the way he had told it to police chief Frank Crabbe, Web Steele felt something cold slide next to his spine. Reed Exley had done an expert job of coaching. Could Stan Frye really hate him enough to do this to him? Sure he had broken Arnie's jaw, but it was while trying to stop him from abusing a defenseless animal. Web thought of Stan's brother, wondering where he had gone. He hadn't seen Arnie around town for a long time.

Attorney Thomas Bean did his best in cross-examination to trip Frye up, but Exley had him well-schooled. Bean's attempt proved fruitless. As Frye left the witness stand, Abby tried to read the faces of the jurors. Sensing that the men of the jury were moved at Frye's testimony only increased her anxiety.

Hec Wheeler was next on the stand. He explained that he was on his way to Carlisle, Pennsylvania, in hopes of getting a job with his brother, who owned a carriage business there. He then testified that he saw Web Steele take the life of Wilbur Yates in cold blood. Thomas Bean's attempt to break Wheeler's story was as futile as it had been with Stan Frye.

Next, Reed Exley graphically told his version of the story, which made Yates's murder appear to have been coldly premeditated. He pictured Web Steele as a heartless man who had it in for the victim and lured him to a dark alley where he took his life. Thomas Bean tried to break Exley under stiff cross-examination, but Exley was too good a liar. Again, Bean was unsuccessful.

When Exley left the stand, the mood of the spectators was definitely against Web Steele. Web felt it and feared the jury was probably leaning the same way. Web was then called to the stand to give his side of the story. Though he denied committing the murder and showed the feasibility of Exley's setup, it did not impress the twelve men who sat on the jury. They were honest men who were trying to withhold judgment until they had heard all the evidence, but the testimonies of Frye and Wheeler and Exley's ability to capture their imaginations and evoke sympathy for the victim had left an indelible mark.

It took the jury only twenty minutes to return after retiring to a side room for deliberations. When the judge asked for the verdict, the jury foreman replied that they had found Webster Steele guilty as charged.

A cold hand clawed at Abby Ruffin's heart at the foreman's words, and she broke into heartrending sobs. Lynne tried to comfort her as Dudley Steele held Cora, who also wept uncontrollably. The judge banged the gavel and called for order. Abby saw Web looking at her as she fought to bring her emotions under control. His face was ashen and his eyes were filled with despair.

When order was restored, Thomas Bean stood and asked if he could address the judge. Judge Tenant granted his request and listened intently as Bean reminded him that Webster Steele had never before had a brush with the law. Based on his past record, Bean pled for the sentence to be life in prison rather than execution.

Tension was high in the courtroom as Bean sat down. Judge Tenant commanded the defendant to rise and approach the bench for sentencing. Before Steele and his attorney could leave their chairs, Reed Exley stood up and said, "Your honor, would you allow me to say a few words before you pass sentence? I realize this is a bit abnormal, but I respectfully request that you allow me to address you before these spectators and the court."

Judge Tenant was visibly annoyed at the interruption, but replied, "All right, Mr. Exley. You may speak your piece. But I caution you—be brief."

All eyes in the courtroom were fixed on Exley as he told of having known Webster Steele for several years. He concurred with Bean's statement that until his arrest, Steele had been a model citizen. Exley went on to explain that he and Steele had experienced some differences between them, but that he still respected and admired him.

John Ruffin sat with folded arms, feeling deep appreciation toward Reed for what he was trying to do. Abby glanced at her father, saw the look in his eyes, and read his thoughts. Her hatred for Exley only increased.

"And so, your honor," concluded the eloquent liar and murderer, "I ask you to show leniency to Mr. Steele. If you were of a mind to pass the death sentence on him, I implore you to make it life imprisonment instead. Mr. Steele made an awful mistake when he took the life of Wilbur Yates, and I think he realizes that now. During his years in prison, he could be an influence for good to his fellow inmates. Thank you for allowing me to speak on his behalf."

As he walked back to his seat, Exley glanced hopefully at Abby, whose gaze locked with his. Her scathing look made him shudder. He wondered why she hadn't appreciated what he had just done.

The judge then called Webster Steele to stand before the bench. Web felt as though he was in a nightmare from which he couldn't wake up as he stepped to the bench with Thomas Bean at his side.

Judge Tenant looked Web in the eye and said, "Mr. Steele, you have been duly tried in this court of law and found guilty of murdering Wilbur Yates in cold blood. Do you have anything to say before I pass sentence on you?"

"Yes," nodded Web. "The testimonies you heard from Mr. Frye, Mr. Wheeler, and Mr. Exley were nothing but well-planned lies. I did not kill Wilbur Yates. What has happened in this courtroom today is a travesty and a total miscarriage of justice. Reed Exley contrived this whole thing, and there is no doubt in my mind that he put the knife in Wilbur Yates. He only asked you just now to show lenience to me to make himself look good to all these people."

The judge waited a few seconds, then asked, "Is that all you wish to say, Mr. Steele?"

"Yes."

"All right," said Judge Tenant, clearing his throat. "Weighing the fact of your spotless record before this incident, I hereby sentence you to life imprisonment in the Virginia state penal facility at Lynchburg. You will be transported there tomorrow to begin your sentence." With that, the judge banged the gavel and pronounced the court dismissed.

Several of Web's friends tarried in the courtroom while Abby and his parents embraced him. While Abby and Cora clung to him, Web looked at John Ruffin and asked, "Do you think I'm guilty, Mr. Ruffin?"

John's face crimsoned. He looked at Abby, then at Web and said weakly, "I...uh...I must accept the verdict of the jury." Abby gave her father a cold, unbelieving stare. Unable to bear it, he turned and headed for the door, where he was met by Reed Exley.

The deputy stepped in and said, "Mr. Steele, I have to take you back to the jail now."

Thomas Bean laid a hand on Web's shoulder and said, "I'm sorry I couldn't get you acquitted."

"I'm not blaming you," replied Steele. "Exley had this thing too well planned. It's my own fault for believing him when he said he wanted to make amends."

"He'll get his, Web," spoke up Dudley. "Sooner or later, he'll pay for what he's done to you."

"Yes," nodded Abby. "And the sooner the better."

Dudley turned to the deputy and asked, "What time will my son be leaving for Lynchburg tomorrow?"

"I'll be taking him by train, sir. It leaves at ten o'clock in the morning."

Suddenly Cora burst into tears and wrapped her arms around Web. He tried to comfort her, saying that maybe after a few years they would consider letting him out on parole for good behavior. Dudley embraced Web, saying they would be at the depot in the morning to see him off. Lynne and Daniel expressed their sorrow at the miscarriage of justice, and walked away with the Steeles.

Weeping, Abby flung herself at Web, holding him tight. Web wrapped his arms around her and said, "I love you, darling. I will always love you."

"And I will always love you," Abby sobbed. "I know it's a hundred miles from here to Lynchburg, but I'll come and visit you often. I promise."

"Listen to me, Abby," said Web, gripping her shoulders. "We're at war now. Soon it won't be safe for anyone to be traveling. I don't know when the fighting will begin, but it will come. Most of our leaders don't think the war will last very long, so please—don't try to come until the war's over and it's safe to travel. Promise?"

Abby thought on his words for a long moment, then nodded. "All right. I'll do as you say."

The deputy took hold of Web's arm, said, "Let's go, Mr. Steele," and led him away.

With grief and anger churning deep within her, Abby left the courthouse and found her father waiting outside in the buggy. When he saw her coming, he stepped out and offered his hand to help her up. "I can get in by myself, thank you!" she blazed.

John Ruffin felt the wall between his daughter and himself as he drove down the street. Abby stared straight ahead, biting her lip to keep from bursting into tears. Finally John said, "Honey, I know this has been a terrible blow for you. It grieves me to see you so upset and unhappy."

Abby maintained her stiffness, staring and saying nothing.

"Now, Abby, you must face the facts. With Web behind bars—"

"I must face the facts! What about you facing the facts? Reed is the murderer, not Web. Nobody's as slick and slimy as your little pet snake. Even when Satan slithered into the Garden of Eden and beguiled Eve, he was no more scaly-bellied than Reed Exley!"

"The jury found Web guilty," John said defensively.

"Yes!" she spat. "Because Exley's as cunning as the devil himself. If you weren't so blind, you'd see him for what he is."

"Now Abby, you—"

"Just let me finish! Let's see if I'm right. You started to say that with Web behind bars for life, I should find another man, right?"

"Well, I—"

"Come on, Papa! That's what you were going to say, wasn't it?"

John Ruffin cleared his throat. "Well...yes. Yes, I was."

"And you were going to suggest that I consider making your pet snake that man, weren't you?"

"Honey, you shouldn't call Reed—"

"I'm calling him what he is, Papa! Come on. You were going to suggest that I make a stab at striking it up with Reed, weren't you?"

"Well, yes. I feel like since he's already part of the family and—"

"Well, you can forget it! Don't you ever even hint at it again!"

John Ruffin took a deep breath and let it out slowly through pursed lips. "All right," he breathed.

"And I'm going to tell you something else, Papa. When I visited Web in jail a few days ago, he told me that Mandrake gave him the lowdown on why Elizabeth had her window open, and why she fell."

"Oh?"

"While we were in town that day, Reed was beating unmercifully on old Jedidiah. Elizabeth opened her window and screamed at Reed to stop. He yelled back at her to shut up and kept beating Jedidiah. Elizabeth was so upset—she kept shouting at Reed and lost her balance. Reed threatened the slaves not to tell you or anyone else what had happened. Your little pet is the one who caused my sister to die."

"Now, Abby, it's only Mandrake's word against Reed's."

"I know, and you'll take Reed's word every time. How can you be so blind?"

John Ruffin did not answer, but even he had to admit to the beginning of some doubts about Reed Exley. No more was said between father and daughter the rest of the way home.

That night Abby lay in her bed shedding hot tears. Her spirit broken, she hugged her pillow and said, "Why, God? Why have you allowed such an injustice to happen to Web, and to me? We love each other, and You gave us that love. I don't understand. How can You let Reed get away with this? You know he's the one who killed that man, so why is Web going to prison? Why are we being torn apart?"

After tossing and turning for hours, Abby finally got out of bed, fired a lantern, and sat at her desk. Taking out a slip of paper, she took pen in hand and began to write a note to the man she loved.

The next morning, Abby rode into town with Dudley and Cora Steele. Daniel Hart had picked up Lynne in a buggy, and they were waiting on the platform at the depot when Abby and the Steeles arrived. As people milled about, they talked of the blow Web's conviction had dealt them.

Soon they saw a police wagon draw up, carrying Web and the deputy who was to escort him to Lynchburg. The prisoner wore handcuffs. As lawman and prisoner came onto the platform, Abby rushed to Web and embraced him. Looking down at her tenderly, he asked, "Have you heard about Stan Frye?"

"No," she replied, shaking her head.

"He died last night about nine o'clock. Chief Crabbe told me about it this morning—said it was heart failure. Frye was at the Lamplighter last night, drinking hard and celebrating my conviction. Witnesses in the place said he suddenly clutched his chest and keeled over. He was dead within minutes."

Dudley Steele pulled at an ear and remarked, "I would like to say he got what he deserved, but I know it's not right for me to feel that way. The Lord says vengeance is His."

"That's right," said Daniel, "but seems to me the Lord must've decided to call Stan to account real quick. Exley and Wheeler will get theirs in due time."

"I hate to butt in, folks," said the deputy, "but you'd best be making your parting remarks to Mr. Steele. I've got to get him on the train shortly."

It was five minutes before departure time when all but Abby had said their good-byes. The Steeles sat in their buggy near the platform, as did Daniel and Lynne, giving Web and Abby a few minutes alone.

Web looped his cuffed hands over Abby's head and folded her into his arms. They kissed tenderly several times, then held each other for a long moment. The engine's whistle blew, and the deputy said, "I'm sorry, Mr. Steele, but we've got to get on board."

The sorrowful couple kissed again, then handed each other envelopes. Abby was deeply touched that Web had also written a note to her. She stood on the platform and through a wall of tears, watched the train pull out of the depot. When it had vanished from sight, she opened the envelope and wiped tears as she read:

My Darling Abby,
    What I am about to say, I could not do in person. I had to put it in writing. I love you with everything that is

in me, and your happiness is my greatest concern. That is why I must tell you that I release you from all promises. It is not right that you should live a life of visiting me periodically in prison. You deserve better than that. You have a right to happiness and a normal life. So I am asking you to forget me and find someone else.

To do this breaks my heart, but it is the only right thing for you. For the rest of my life, there will never be a day when you are out of my thoughts.

Love always, Web

Holding the note close to her breast, Abby Ruffin wept and whispered, "Never, my darling. I will never even consider another man. You will always be the only one I love."

Aboard the train, Web Steele sat next to the window with the deputy at his side. Richmond had just passed from view when he pulled the envelope from his pocket and took out the neatly folded slip of paper.

My Dearest Web,

I am writing this at three o'clock in the morning of the day they will take you away from me.

Words sometimes fall short of conveying what is really in the heart. Such is the case at this moment. I can only say, my darling, that I love you more than I could ever tell you, and I always will.

As you have requested, I will not try to visit you until the war is over. But you will see me just as soon as it is safe once again to travel!

What R.E. has done to you is a tragedy, and I pray that he will pay for it. I feel so sick at heart for what you must endure in that prison because of his wickedness. I know you well, Web Steele, and if I am correct, you will

begin thinking about me going through life with you behind bars. You will have thoughts about telling me to
find happiness by cutting you out of my life and finding
someone else. When those thoughts come, dismiss them
immediately.

I will never want anyone but you. Never. You will
always be the only one I love. That is my solemn
promise. I mean it with all my heart and soul. I love you
desperately.

Your Abby

The deputy turned and looked at Web Steele as he clutched
Abby's note in one hand, covered his eyes with the other, and wept.

SEVENTEEN

During the month of March, Mandrake Steele wore leg irons at all times on the Todd Morrison plantation. He was sick at heart for Orchid's sake, assuming that she had been forced to mate with one of Horatio Clements's choice Negroes. Yet he was determined to run for Harper's Ferry and steal Orchid from Clements once his leg irons were removed.

On the night of March 21, two male slaves had run away from the plantation because of the cruel treatment they had been receiving from Morrison and his two sons, especially Clifford, who was his father's slave overseer. Aided by men from neighboring plantations, Clifford had gone after the runaways and caught them in the next county before noon the following day.

They were brought back to the plantation and whipped brutally by Clifford while the rest of the slaves were forced to watch. During the beating, three slaves jumped Clifford, took his whip, and turned it on him. Todd Morrison heard the ruckus, came running with a revolver, and shot the three slaves.

From that incident on, Clifford wore a revolver at all times, making sure the other slaves understood that he would use it if there was any more trouble.

Mandrake played the part of the model slave. While the days passed into weeks, he acted as if he were intimidated by Clifford's new hard-line approach, and said things to make the Morrisons think he would be afraid to ever try running away.

Since the day he had been forced to become a slave for the Morrisons, Mandrake had bunked in a small, windowless shack with three other men. When he told them his story, they sympathized with him and said they would help him escape once his leg irons were removed.

Then came the escape of the two slaves on March 21.

When the escapees were beaten and the slaves who tried to stop the beatings were killed, Mandrake's roommates changed their minds about helping him escape. To make matters worse, the following day Clifford started locking the slaves in their shacks at nightfall.

Mandrake knew his only chance of escape was at night. He would have to overpower Clifford and render him unconscious when he came to padlock the door of his shack. He would take Clifford's revolver and dash to the corral while the other slaves in his shack ran to the house to report what had happened. Even if they still wanted to help him, they couldn't do it without incriminating themselves. Mandrake did not want to get them in trouble, so he would make the move on his own without telling them ahead of time, and expect them to act accordingly.

Timing would be of the essence. When he got to the corral, he must take a horse for himself and scatter the rest of the horses into the open fields. Since it would be dark, it would take the Morrisons till daybreak to gather the horses. This would give him a good head start. They would know he was headed for Harper's Ferry. He needed enough time to get to Clements's place, break Orchid free, and be gone before either Morrison or Clements could catch them.

The whole thing was a long shot, but Mandrake felt he had no choice but to try it. He must try to get Orchid back no matter the risks. The first glimmer of hope that his scheme might work came on

Saturday, April 13—Clifford rewarded Mandrake's good behavior by removing his shackles.

News of the attack on Fort Sumter came to the Morrison plantation the next day. The country was now in a civil war. Mandrake knew this could complicate things for him. The Morrisons talked about the military buildup that would take place in both the North and the South. People would be on the alert. The fifty miles that lay between Morrison's plantation and Harper's Ferry would be more difficult than ever to travel.

Clifford left the plantation on April 15, adding a further complication. The nightly lockup of the slaves would be done by Todd Morrison and his younger son, Hughey. Mandrake doubted he could overpower two men. He would have to wait until Clifford returned in two weeks.

On the afternoon of April 29, Clifford came riding in on horseback and was greeted by the family in the yard. That night, when Clifford came alone to lock the slaves in their shacks, Mandrake looked to make sure he was still wearing his revolver. He had to have that gun. It would give him the edge he needed to steal Orchid away from Horatio Clements.

The next night Mandrake put his plan into action. He surprised Clifford, knocking him unconscious with a heavy stick, and took his gun. His roommates were also surprised, but told him they would wait till Clifford started coming to before they alerted the family.

Mandrake selected a horse, scattered the rest, and raced away bareback into the night. He rode the back country toward Harper's Ferry, and though he was on horseback, the going was slow. He arrived at the edge of Harper's Ferry on Saturday morning, May 4. The town was a beehive of activity. Mandrake wondered if it had something to do with the war. While he was trying to figure out how to find Clements's place, he saw an elderly black couple emerging from town on foot, moving his direction.

Leaving the stolen horse in the brush, he approached the couple and asked what was going on in town. They explained that Harper's Ferry had been made the induction center for Virginia men to join the Confederate army. Hundreds were arriving every day. Mandrake then asked for directions to the Clements place, and was told to simply follow the Potomac River northwestward and he would come to it. He couldn't miss it, for it was the only place surrounded by a high stockade fence.

Shortly afterward, Mandrake was hunkered in a ditch across the road from Clements's gate. The horse was secured in a deep gully nearby. His heart fluttered as he thought of being so close to Orchid, who had to be somewhere inside the formidable fence.

Observing the coming and going of white men at the gate, Mandrake told himself he would have to wait till Horatio Clements came out, get the drop on him, and with the revolver held to his head, force him to command the guards at the gate to send Orchid out. He would then hold Clements as a hostage until the three of them were a long way from Harper's Ferry. Once he felt he and Orchid were safe, he would leave Clements and they would head for Richmond.

It was early afternoon when Horatio Clements appeared. He was riding in a wagon, sitting next to Dean Faulkner, who held the reins. The gate closed behind them, and the wagon headed toward town. Mandrake hopped on the horse and followed at a safe distance.

The sun was slanting toward the hills to the west when Clements and Faulkner drove out of Harper's Ferry with a load of supplies under a tarp in the bed of the wagon. They rounded a bend in the road that was skirted by a steep, brush-covered embankment. Both men had belted down a few drinks. They were laughing and joking when suddenly they heard a heavy thud behind them.

Mandrake had jumped into the wagon bed from the embankment and was holding a cocked revolver on them, his eyes bulging.

"Stop the wagon!" snapped the black man.

Clements and Faulkner both recognized Mandrake immediately. Their faces paled as Faulkner pulled rein, halting the wagon.

Waving the gun at Faulkner, Mandrake said, "Get out."

"Wh-what are you gonna do?" stammered Faulkner.

"I'm gonna kill you if'n you don' get out!" rasped Mandrake.

The man obeyed quickly, fear framing his features as he touched ground. Mandrake pressed the muzzle of the gun against the back of Clements's head. "Now drive, mistuh. No fast moves, or this gun'll go off."

With shaky hands, Clements took the reins, saying, "Th-this isn't going to do you any good, blackie. There's something you need to—"

"Shut up and drive!"

Clements made sure the horses eased forward slowly, then held them at a steady walk. Holding the revolver firmly against Clements's head, Mandrake said, "We gonna pull up in fron' of the gate at yo' place, and you gonna tell yo' guards to sen' my wife out. If'n they don' do it, I'll kill you."

"I…I can't tell them to send her out," replied Clements. "We don't have her anymore."

"Liar!" boomed Mandrake. "You jus' wanna keep her fo'—"

"No! I'm telling you the truth."

"Then where is she?"

"She…she's dead."

The words hit Mandrake like a blow to the chest. "Stop the wagon!" he commanded.

Clements drew rein and the wagon rolled to a stop. If Clements was telling the truth, Mandrake's life was pointless. Orchid was all he had lived for. Pressing the muzzle hard against the man's skull, he breathed through clenched teeth, "Yo' lyin'!"

"No," said Clements, his mouth dry. "I…I put her with one of my choice men the very first night, but somehow she had gotten her hands on a butcher knife. She stabbed the man to death and made her way to the gate. There was only one guard at the gate, and she drove the knife into his back and let herself out. The guard told us this before he died. He was able to draw his gun and fire just as she passed through the gate. He hit her, but she kept going. He groped his way to the gate in time to see her staggering toward the river. She reached the bank and fell in. He heard the loud splash."

"This cain't be!" cried Mandrake.

"I'm sorry, but it's true," Clements said with a quiver in his voice. "The next morning we followed a trail of blood to the edge of the river. It left no doubt that she fell in. She's dead, boy."

Mandrake shook his head, refusing to believe it. "Yo' lyin' so's I'll go 'way and you can keep her to have slave babies. I know what yo' doin'."

"I...I understand why you'd think so, but I'm telling you the truth."

"How do I know yo' tellin' me the truth?" demanded Mandrake.

Cold sweat was a sheen on Horatio Clements's face. His breathing was ragged as he answered without the slightest turn of his head, "Go back and ask Faulkner. Is he following us?"

"He's a ways back, but he's comin'," replied Mandrake. "But how do I know you two didn' cook this story up?"

"Why would we do that? How would we know that you would ever show up? Think, boy."

Mandrake realized there would be no reason for Clements and his men to make up such a story. They had no one to answer to concerning Orchid. The chance that her husband would ever find where she had been taken was remote. Certainly Reed Exley would never tell him.

"All right," said Mandrake after a brief pause. "Tu'n the wagon 'round."

When they met up with Dean Faulkner, Mandrake asked him where Orchid was. When he got the same story about her escape and death, he knew it was true. His heart became heavy as lead.

Mandrake's grief clawed his insides as he made Faulkner drive the wagon to the spot near where he had stashed his horse. Leaping from the wagon, he told them to drive on, and dashed into the brush. He watched to make sure they kept going, then hopped on the horse and rode hard for the hills with tears streaming down his face.

When darkness fell, Mandrake was in a low-lying gulch ten miles southwest of Harper's Ferry. Dismounting, he prostrated himself on the ground and gave full vent to his grief. After weeping hard for some time, he sat up, wiped his face with a sleeve, and let his mind travel to the man responsible for Orchid's death. He felt the flame of vengeance burning in him.

Mandrake would return to the Ruffin plantation and kill Reed Exley. Nothing else mattered. With Orchid gone, he didn't care what happened to him. He had only one thing to live for now—to make Reed Exley pay with his life for what he did to Orchid.

On the morning of May 5, Reed Exley emerged from John Ruffin's library, where they had discussed Exley's desire to enlist in the Confederate army. He wanted to kill Yankees and do his part to bring the war to a quick end. Ruffin, being a loyal Southerner, agreed. He would hire an older man to take Reed's place temporarily. The experts were saying in the newspapers that the conflict would be short-lived. Once the Northerners realized they could not dominate the Southerners, nor take away their right to own slaves, it would all be over. Exley would tie up a few loose ends and board the train for Harper's Ferry in a couple of days.

Exley had delayed paying Hec Wheeler the second half of the thousand dollars he owed him, and Hec was becoming difficult about it. He wanted to be on his way to Pennsylvania, especially with the war developing. Exley hated the thought of parting with another five hundred dollars. Now that he had used Wheeler to help him frame Web

Steele, he decided to simply kill him and keep the money. Wheeler would die the night before Exley left for Harper's Ferry to enlist.

Exley went out onto the front porch of the mansion and found Charles talking to a young man who wanted to see Abby. Now that Web was in prison, the young man hoped Abby would agree to spending time with him. The butler explained that Miss Abby was seeing no one. She was still in love with Web and had made it clear that she always would be.

Exley waited till the young man drove away in his buggy, then chuckled, "I figured this would happen."

"There was no doubt in my mind that it would," commented Charles. "Miss Abby is the most beautiful young woman in this county. Now that it appears she is available, they're going to be beating down the door. This is the fourth one I've turned away since Mr. Web has been gone."

"Really? Well, just keep turning them away, Charles."

"I will, sir. Miss Abby told me she made Mr. Web a promise that she would love only him for the rest of her life."

Leaving the porch and heading for the barn, Exley said to himself, *We'll see about that, Miss Abby.*

Daniel Hart hauled his buggy to a halt at the hitching post in front of the Ruffin mansion just as Reed Exley was driving away from the barn. Exley looked at him but did not greet him.

Young Hart mounted the steps beneath the great white pillars and rattled the big brass knocker. Lynne Ruffin had been watching for him from her bedroom window and opened the door.

Daniel looked around to make sure no one was watching, then took her in his arms and kissed her. There were tears in Lynne's eyes as she said, "I hope you understand, darling, why I can't come to the depot to see you off. I just couldn't bear watching that train pull away."

"I understand. This isn't easy for me either, but I have to go."

"I know you do," she said with a tremor in her voice. "All loyal young Southern men must rally to the call. I just hope the experts are right, and this war will be over in a few months."

"Me, too," sighed Daniel. "I want us to be married and spend the rest of our lives together."

They embraced and kissed again.

Daniel cupped Lynne's pretty face in his hands, thumbed away the tears, and half-whispered, "I love you, sweetheart. You take care of yourself."

"I will," she sniffed. "And you take care of yourself. I couldn't stand it if something happened to you."

"I'll be fine. You'll see me coming down the lane before you know it."

Lynne walked Daniel to his buggy, where they kissed again. As he climbed aboard, he said, "Tell your sister I'll be thinking of her. What a horrible thing she's going through."

"I'll tell her," nodded Lynne, her eyes glistening with tears.

They exchanged "I love yous" again, and Daniel put the horse to a trot. Lynne stood and watched the buggy roll up the lane. Just before he passed from view, Daniel leaned out from the cab and waved. Lynne waved back, broke into sobs, and ran into the house.

On the morning of May 7, the birds were singing in the trees while the Ruffin slaves worked around the yard and the corral. The slaves were watching Reed Exley talking to Master John on the front porch of the mansion. A horse and buggy waited at one of the hitching posts. The slaves smiled at each other furtively, happy that Exley was leaving. Old Jedidiah whispered to a slave next to him, "I sure hopes theuh's a Yankee bullet waitin' fo' 'im."

"Yeah, me too," whispered the other slave. "Nuthin' would make me happier than to git the good news dat Massa Reed done lef' dis worl' an' wen' to his reward."

"I's not too shuah it'll be a reward," said Jedidiah.

The slave chuckled softly. "You knows what I means, Jedidiah.

When he faces de Lord, he'll git what's comin' to 'im."

On the porch, John looked toward the open door of the house and said, "Reed, you did tell Abby what time we were leaving for town, didn't you?"

"Yes."

"Well, I don't understand why she's not down here to tell you good-bye."

Exley shrugged, pleased that John wanted Abby and Reed to get together. He hadn't said so, but Exley knew the desire was there.

Perturbed at Abby, John called toward the door, "Charles! Go up to Miss Abby's room and tell her Mr. Reed and I are leaving. He has to catch his train."

"Never mind, Papa John," Exley said. "I'll just run up to her room and tell her good-bye."

"Better make it snappy! That train doesn't wait for anybody."

"I'll be right back."

Moments later, Exley tapped on Abby's door. She opened it and gave him a bland look.

"Abby," he said, smiling, "aren't you going to tell me good-bye?"

"Good-bye!" she snapped, swinging the door to slam it.

Exley checked the swing of the door, and said, "I'm going away to fight in the war. Don't I at least deserve a good-bye kiss?"

As he spoke, he seized her and planted a hard kiss on her lips. When he released her, she slapped him across the face with both hands. Exley grabbed her wrists.

"Let—go—of me," she hissed.

Savoring the kiss, he grinned and obeyed. Abby held him with a hard glare and wiped her mouth with a sleeve. Exley was about to speak when John's voice came from the bottom of the stairs, "Reed, you'd better hurry! You'll miss your train."

Backing toward the door, Exley smiled and said, "At least you'll remember that kiss for a while."

"Yes!" she spat. "It takes a long time to get the taste of venom out of your mouth."

Exley stopped halfway out the door and his smile vanished. Giving Abby a malevolent look, he wheeled and hurried down the hall.

When he reached the bottom of the stairs, he smiled at John and said, "She kissed me good-bye."

"Really?" gasped John, smiling as he followed. "Wonderful!"

"It sure was, Papa John," laughed Reed, hoping John would not notice the redness of his smarting cheeks.

John drove the buggy, snapping the reins to push the horse into a fast trot.

When they were about halfway to Richmond, the road took a curve around a marshy area that was surrounded by a number of large oak trees. Exley glanced at the spot near a huge oak that stood in tall grass. Grinning to himself, he knew the body of Hec Wheeler lay in two inches of water at the base of the oak.

The night before, Exley had gone to the hotel and taken Wheeler to the hotel bar for a drink. While at the bar, he told Wheeler that he had come to give him the second five hundred dollars but had forgotten to pick the money up off his dresser after changing clothes. He would take Wheeler with him right then to the plantation, and give him the money and a horse to ride to Pennsylvania.

Hec expressed his appreciation, saying this way he could head out from Richmond at sunrise. He was eager to get to Carlisle and see his brother.

When Exley's buggy had reached the spot near the huge oak, Hec felt a cold blade thrust into his side. Exley stopped the buggy, stabbed him twice more, then dragged the body into the tall grass and left it for the snakes and water creatures to feed on.

The Ruffin buggy was out of sight when there was a stirring in the tall grass at the base of the huge oak. The cold water had helped stay the flow of Hec Wheeler's blood. After being unconscious all night, he had finally come to just after sunrise. It had taken him all this time to gain enough strength to begin crawling toward the road.

EIGHTEEN

Webster Steele had been in the prison near Lynchburg for less than a week when he happened to push against the bars that covered the small window in the rear of his cell. It was a warm day, and he had to work hard to free the glassed framework so he could get some fresh air. While trying to force the framework open, he gripped the bars for leverage and found them loose.

The bars were imbedded in rotting wood. The window frame was apparently directly below a leak in the roof and many years of rain and melting snow had taken their toll. Gripping the bars and pulling hard on them, he found a great deal of play. He decided a man could work at it and finally free the bars from the wood.

The window overlooked the exercise yard, which was surrounded by an eight-foot wall. At the far corner of the wall stood a platform some fifteen feet high where armed guards watched over the prison compound. Steele knew if he was to work the bars loose and crawl through the window, it would take a miracle to ever make it across the yard and over the wall to freedom. Even if he made his escape at night, the entire place was dimly-lit with kerosene lanterns. The guards on the platform could see a man moving in the yard.

As impossible as it seemed, Web sat on his bunk day after day and tried to figure a way of escape. Every time he read Abby's note, the determination to break out grew stronger. Web thought of Reed Exley running loose when *he* should be the one in prison. Only one person could clear him of the trumped-up charge—Hec Wheeler. Web would have to break out of prison, find Wheeler, and persuade him to tell the truth.

Web thought of Wheeler on the witness stand. He had said he was on his way to Carlisle, Pennsylvania, to work for his brother who had a carriage business there. He remembered that the brother's name was John—the same as Abby's father. Carlisle was no doubt a small town. Finding a John Wheeler who owned a carriage works would be easy. Once Web got his hands on Hec, he'd scare him into telling the truth.

Every day, while there was noise and activity in the prison, Web worked the bars a little looser. Somehow he would find a way to escape. The cells in his cell block housed only one inmate apiece. Web's cell was a small cubicle six feet wide and eight feet long, and was on the second floor. The kitchen was directly below him.

Word came to the prison of skirmishes taking place in northern Virginia between Union and Confederate troops, but as of the first of May, there had been no big battles.

As tension over the war increased, the prisoners grew restless. At meals and during exercise time, there was much talk about what would happen to them if the Yankees took Virginia. Locked up in the prison, they would be sitting ducks.

On the morning of May 6, Web was sitting with five other men at a table in the mess hall, eating breakfast. Keeping their voices low, they discussed their precarious position if the Yankees decided to get rid of over two hundred Southerners cooped up within the prison walls.

A beefy man named Hugo Bond was sitting directly across from Web. Looking at the men around him, he grunted, "All those stinkin' Yankees would have to do is set this tinderbox on fire. We'd all burn to death in a matter of minutes."

"Yeah," chimed in another inmate, "Hugo's right. We'd be goners in a hurry."

"I been listenin' to some of the other guys," spoke up another. "There's talk about rushin' the guards when they least expect it and makin' a break for it."

"That could still get some of us killed," said Web. "There's always that platform—I've never seen less than two guards up there. They could cut a bunch of us down while we're trying to escape."

"Most of us would make it," said Hugo. "I guess we'll just have to decide if we're willin' to play the odds."

"Bein' shot down would be better'n burnin' up," put in a skinny little man named Ollie.

Next to Ollie sat a slow-minded, heavy-set man named Harold. Setting his dull gaze on Ollie, he asked, "If the Yankees shot a cannonball in here, would it set the place on fire, Ollie?"

"Sure would," nodded Ollie, letting his eyes roam to the walls, beams, and ceiling. "This whole prison is constructed of wood—*old* wood—and it's dry too. Once a fire started anyplace in here, it would go up fast."

"If that happened," said Harold, "would the guards let us out? Or would we be left in here to burn?"

"We're supposed to be too dangerous to live in society," remarked Hugo. "Maybe they'd just let us burn. What do you think, Web?"

"Well, I can't say for sure. No doubt the guards would try to keep us under control so we didn't run away, but I have a hard time believing they'd just save their own skins and let us die."

"I agree," said Ollie. "These guards are human. Surely they'd take us out with them."

Ollie and Harold worked as janitors in the prison. That night they were mopping the floor in the large kitchen while a guard watched them. After a while the guard left, saying he would meet them at the end of the hall when they were finished and take them to their cells.

It was late, and the other prisoners were bedded down for the night. They were about to finish up when Harold said, "Ollie, I been thinkin'. If them Yankees was to set the place on fire, and even if the guards let us go outside the walls with 'em, them Yankees would be out there in the bushes waitin' to shoot us down when we came out the gate."

"I hadn't thought about that," said Ollie, "but I think you're right. They'd shoot all of us."

Harold squeezed his mop out over a bucket of dirty water and said, "You really think Web's right...I mean that the guards would take us out with 'em if the prison was burnin'?"

"Yes."

"Then we oughtta make our break right now, before them Yankees come."

Ollie looked at him thoughtfully and said, "Right now?"

"Sure. There's lots more of us inmates than there are guards. Dark as it is out there right now, some of us could get away. And even for those who didn't, whatever happened would be better than what's gonna happen if them Yankees come."

Ollie grinned. "You know, Harold, I think you're smarter than a lot of guys around here give you credit for."

Harold returned the grin and said, "No better place to start a fire than right where we stand."

"I agree. Let's do it. There are two cans of kerosene underneath the cupboard. We'll pour it all over the room, even on the walls. Once it's burning good, we'll go running down the hall, screaming that the place is on fire. It'll be too late to do anything but let all the prisoners out of their cells and take us out of here in a hurry."

In his cell, Web was just drifting off to sleep when loud shouts met his ears. He jerked awake and sat up on his cot. The smell of smoke assaulted his nostrils, and there was a bright yellow light showing through his window.

Dashing to the window, he saw that the building was on fire

directly beneath him. The kitchen was ablaze. He saw guards running about the exercise yard, attempting to corral the inmates as other guards were letting them out of their cells. There were no guards on the platform.

There would never be a better time to make good his escape. While he was hastening into his clothes, he heard inmates coughing and shouting along the corridor. The floor was hot on the bottoms of his bare feet. His cell would be on fire within minutes. He slipped his shoes on, tied them quickly, and went to the window. It took only seconds to finish ripping the bars from the rotten wood.

Pushing himself through the window, Web dropped to the ground. In the midst of all the excitement, no one noticed him dart to a shadowed corner, grip the edge of the eight-foot wall, work his way over the top, and drop to the ground below. Moments later, he stopped to catch his breath on top of a hill, and looked back. Hugo was right. The old prison was a tinderbox. It was going up in flames fast.

As he bounded down the other side of the hill, Web had one goal in mind—get to Carlisle and find Hec Wheeler.

It was mid-afternoon on May 7 when Charles answered the sound of the knocker. Opening the door, he saw Dudley and Cora Steele standing with three well-dressed men.

"Good afternoon," said Charles, showing a faint smile.

"Good afternoon, Charles," said Dudley. Gesturing toward the three men, he said, "This is Judge William Tenant, Dr. Donald Adams, and our family attorney, Thomas Bean. We have some wonderful news for Miss Abby. Is she here?"

"Yes, sir," nodded Charles, opening the door all the way. "Please come in."

The maid was in the large receiving area, looking on with curiosity. Charles turned to her and said, "Harriet, will you fetch Miss Abby from her room while I make these people comfortable in the parlor? Mr. Steele says they have some good news for her."

"Might as well bring in John and Miss Lynne if they're around," Dudley said. "They'll be happy to hear our news, too."

Moments later, John Ruffin eased onto a couch between his two eager-eyed daughters and said to Web's father, "So what's this good news, Dudley?"

"I haven't told it yet, John," said Steele, who was the only one standing. "It'll mean most to Abby, but I wanted you and Lynne to hear it, too."

Cora sat in an overstuffed chair next to Abby, and was already dabbing at her eyes with a hanky.

Dudley took a deep breath, eyes sparkling, and said, "Web has been cleared of the murder charge and will be coming home!"

Lynne shrieked with joy, and Abby gasped and threw her hands to her mouth, wide-eyed.

"I'll let Dr. Adams tell you the rest of the story," said Dudley, and took a chair next to Cora.

Dr. Donald Adams was a prominent physician in Richmond, and though the Ruffins did not know him, they knew his reputation. He was in his early fifties and had a compassionate look about him. Easing forth in his chair, he set his eyes on Abby and said, "A man named Hec Wheeler was brought into my office this morning by a couple of men who found him on the side of the road between here and town. Wheeler had been stabbed three times and left for dead in one of the marshy areas. He was in bad shape, and at first I didn't think I could save him. He overheard me tell my nurse that I was afraid he was going to die. The knife, miraculously, had not penetrated any vital organs, but I thought he would hemorrhage to death before I could do surgery."

"Did he tell you who stabbed him?" asked John.

"Not at first. He stayed pretty mum until he heard me say he was probably going to die. He began to weep and told me there was something he had to confess before he died. He wanted to tell it to Judge Tenant. I had sent for another doctor to help me with the surgery, so I told Wheeler if we could get the judge there before the doctor arrived, he could get whatever was bothering him off his chest. It just so happened that when my nurse found Judge Tenant, he was in his chambers and was free to come. He arrived at my office before the other doctor, so I let Wheeler talk."

"And did he ever talk!" cut in Judge Tenant. "He told me, first, that it was Reed Exley who had stabbed him and left him in the marsh. This happened last night, and in the dark, Reed thought Wheeler was dead."

John Ruffin's features went white.

The judge continued. "He went on to confess that he had lied on the witness stand because Exley had paid him to go along with his story. Exley, not Web Steele, stabbed Wilbur Yates. The whole thing—including Stan Frye's testimony—had been contrived to frame Web."

Abby burst into tears, saying, "Oh, thank God! Thank God! My darling Web will be coming home to me!"

While Cora and Lynne hugged Abby, John sat pale-faced and said, "Judge, maybe this Wheeler is lying. Maybe, for some reason, he has it in for Reed. You can't convict Reed on the statement of a dying man."

"*I* can't," said Judge Tenant, "but I believe a jury will. If Wheeler had died today and wasn't around to testify, getting a conviction would have been more difficult. But he's alive to tell a jury his story. While the doctors were doing the surgery, I sent for Mr. Bean and the Steeles. The wounds weren't as bad as Dr. Adams had thought. The hemorrhaging was stopped quite easily, and when Wheeler was able to talk again, Dr. Adams told him he was going to live. Wheeler was relieved, but he still stuck by his story, knowing that it will nail him for perjury and accessory to murder. I guarantee you, the jury will buy that."

Dr. Adams said, "I told Wheeler that Web's parents and his attorney were there, but that since he was so weak, he didn't have to see them. He insisted that I let them in the room."

"We just came from there, John," said Dudley. "Wheeler told the whole story again to us."

Ruffin looked sick. "So what about Reed? He left this morning to enlist in the army."

"I know," nodded Judge Tenant. "Wheeler knew it. Exley had told someone in the hotel bar last night that he was leaving for Harper's Ferry this morning to enlist. He told it right in front of Wheeler."

"Will he be brought back for trial?"

The judge shook his head. "Not until the war is over."

"Why not?" asked Abby. "He's guilty as sin."

"I know," said Judge Tenant, "but since Wheeler didn't die, and it will be Exley's word against Wheeler's in the next trial, the army will keep him until the war is over. I wired the induction center at Harper's Ferry as soon as we were through talking to Wheeler, and got an answer right back. With this war coming on, the Confederate army needs every man it can get. Exley hadn't even shown up at the induction center yet, but when he does, they'll take him in the army and we can't touch him till the war's over."

Abby was now holding Cora's hand. Brushing a lock of auburn hair from her eyes, she asked, "So when will Web be released, Judge Tenant?"

"I'm not sure. I sent a wire to the prison superintendent right after I received the response from the induction center. I waited a few minutes for an answer, but none came, so we'll have to wait till we hear back. I'm sure they'll release him immediately on my word that he was framed."

"Will you let us know as soon as you hear?" asked Dudley. "We'll all want to be at the depot when he comes home."

Tears were spilling down Abby's cheeks again. "And what a reception he's going to get!" she exclaimed.

Cora, who was also crying again, nodded her agreement.

Abby let go of Cora's hand and wiped the moisture from her cheeks. "Mr. Reed Exley is going to get a real reception the day he returns, too. I want to be there and see his face when he's arrested."

John blinked and ran splayed fingers through his graying hair. Turning to Abby, he said, "Honey, I owe you an apology. You've tried to open my eyes to Reed, but I wouldn't let you. I'm sorry."

Abby wrapped her arms around his neck, hugged him tight, and said, "I accept your apology, Papa. I'm sorry it took all of this to open your eyes, but at least now you know the truth."

Judge Tenant assured both families that he would advise them as soon as he knew when Web would be arriving home. With that, he, the doctor, and the attorney headed back to town.

The Steeles stayed long enough to discuss the welcome all of them would give Web. When the details of the reception were agreed upon, Cora said, "The only dark thought I have now is that my boy will soon be enlisting in the army. He'll still be away from us."

"Yes, dear," said Dudley, "but at least he won't be locked up in a dingy old prison cell for the rest of his life. When the war's over, he'll come home to us. He and Abby can be married and live happily ever after, as they say in the fairy tales."

"Yes," sighed Abby. "Happily ever after."

"Daniel and me, too," chirped Lynne.

Abby hugged her. "Yes, sweetie. You and Daniel, too."

When noon came the next day without any word from Judge Tenant, Dudley Steele said to his wife, "This waiting is getting on my nerves. I'm going to ride into town and see what's going on."

"I'm sure the judge will contact us as soon as he has any word, dear. There's no need for you to make the ride."

"I *have* to. There's no reason for it to take so long to get a message through from Lynchburg."

Cora followed her husband to the entry way of the mansion. When Dudley opened the door, they both saw a buggy pulling up to the porch.

"Here's the judge, now," Cora said cheerfully. "I wonder who that is with him."

"Don't know. Never saw him before."

Judge Tenant's face was ashen-gray as he mounted the porch

steps with the tall, slender man in top hat beside him. The stranger made Dudley think of Abraham Lincoln. The pallor of Tenant's features told the Steeles that something was wrong. Cora laid a hand on her husband's arm.

"Hello, Judge," said Dudley cautiously. "Any word about when our boy will be coming home?"

Tenant cleared his throat. His voice had a somber tone as he replied, "I'm afraid I have some bad news, Mr. Steele. This is Clarence Netherling of the Virginia state penal system. May we go inside and talk?"

"Of course," responded Dudley, his brow furrowed as he glanced down at his wife.

Cora's eyes showed fearful uncertainty when she met Dudley's glance. Together they led the two men into the parlor. When everyone was seated, the judge said, "Mr. and Mrs. Steele, this…uh…this is a very difficult thing to do. I—"

"What is it, Judge Tenant?" cut in Dudley. "Has something happened to Web?"

"Yes," nodded Tenant. "I received a wire early this morning from the superintendent of the prison. He told me that Mr. Netherling here would be coming to my quarters at eleven o'clock, and would have news for me concerning your son. Mr. Netherling's office is in Richmond. I'll let him tell you what has happened."

Netherling was visibly uneasy as he began by saying, "Mr. and Mrs. Steele, there was a fire last night at the Lynchburg prison. It was a bad one. In fact, the entire place burned to the ground."

Cora began to tremble. She knew what was coming next. Seated beside her husband on a love seat, she leaned against him, drew a shuddering breath and gasped, "Oh, no! Please don't tell us our boy died in that fire!"

Dudley's arm went around Cora as he silently waited for Netherling's reply.

For a brief moment the room was quiet as a crypt. Then Netherling said falteringly, "Yes, ma'am. I'm sorry."

Cora went to pieces, sobbing incoherently while Dudley held her in his arms. She wailed for several minutes, then settled into a subdued sobbing with her face buried against her husband's chest.

Proceeding, the rail-thin man said, "The fire started in the prison kitchen, directly beneath your son's cell. The buildings were constructed totally of wood and the fire spread quickly. The guards worked feverishly, attempting to get all the prisoners out, but by the time they worked their way to the second floor, the area above the kitchen was totally ablaze."

Netherling choked up for a moment, then said, "We have accounted for all the prisoners. Your son and four other men on the second floor perished in the fire. I am so sorry to have to bring you this bad news, especially since Judge Tenant informed me that your son has been cleared of the very charges that sent him to the prison."

Dudley fought against the hatred welling up inside him toward Reed Exley. He desperately wanted the man to pay for his crimes.

Dudley stayed with Cora for a long time after the two men had gone, doing everything he could to comfort her while his own heart was filled with grief. When it seemed that she had gained control of herself, he said, "Honey, it's only right that Abby should know about Web as soon as possible. I wish she could be spared, especially because of the happiness she had just yesterday, but she has a right to know that he's...he's gone."

"Yes," nodded Cora, her face pale, "but I want to go with you. I don't want to be here alone...and Abby was practically our daughter-in-law. The two of us should break the news to her together."

"All right, if you're sure you're up to it."

She nodded, holding back the tears.

"Something else, honey," said Dudley. "Maybe we should go into town and see if Reverend McLaury will go along with us. He should be advised of Web's death, and he can be a strength to Abby in a way that we can't."

"Yes, let's do that. Abby's going to need all the help she can get."

An hour later, the Steeles and Benjamin McLaury were welcomed into the Ruffin mansion by Charles, who seated them in the parlor. Then Charles went to fetch John and Lynne, who were conveniently together in the library. When Charles advised them that Abby was upstairs in her room, Reverend McLaury told him to leave it that way. They needed to see John and Lynne first, and would like to have Charles and Harriet present also.

When the four people had collected in the parlor with McLaury and the Steeles, the pastor sadly informed them of Web's death. Lynne took it hardest, breaking down and sobbing, "Oh, poor Abby! My poor, poor Abby!"

Cora folded Lynne in her arms, speaking soothing words. Lynne suddenly stopped crying and said, "Oh, Mrs. Steele, I'm sorry. What a horrible thing for you, too. Web was your only son! I'm so sorry." Looking at Dudley, she cried, "And for you, Mr. Steele. How terrible for you to lose Web. He was such a fine man. I was going to be so proud to have him for a brother-in-law."

Cora continued to hold her while John offered his sympathy to Web's parents. Harriet and Charles then gave their condolences, telling the Steeles what a fine young man their son had been.

When Lynne had settled down, the preacher said, "Mr. Ruffin, I think it's time to let Abby know. Would you like me to break it to her?"

John bit hard on his lower lip. "Yes, Reverend. I think that would be best. Rather than call her down here to tell her, let's go to her room. The Steeles and Lynne and I will go up with you. She'll need all of us when you break it to her."

"Harriet and I will give Miss Abby our sympathy once she's over the initial shock, Mr. John," said Charles.

"Thank you," John said, forcing a weak smile for his servants.

When they reached the top of the stairs, Reverend McLaury moved out in front and led the others quietly down the hall. His heart was pounding, knowing what he had to do. When he reached the spot, he took a deep breath, let it out slowly, and tapped on Abby's door.

NINETEEN

Web Steele ran hard through the night until he reached the west bank of the James River north of Lynchburg. Exhausted, he lay in the tall grass and tried to sleep, but he was too keyed up. His mind was racing. How could he get a message to Abby and his parents? Had the prison officials thought he died in the fire? What would he do if Hec Wheeler had not shown up in Carlisle? His brother would have no idea where to find him. Without Wheeler to force into telling the truth, Web would be right back where he started.

At dawn, the fugitive was up and running again, heading due north. As he pressed on, he considered taking a horse from some farmer's field or corral and bringing it back once he had Wheeler in hand. If he stayed afoot, it was going to take a long time to get to his destination.

By midmorning, Web was growing weak from hunger. He was staying in the back country just in case some of the prisoners had escaped during the fire and local authorities had been wired to be on the alert. He spotted a small farmhouse and barn up ahead. Maybe there would be a root cellar where he could get some fruits and vegetables. And maybe they had a horse to spare that they wouldn't miss for a while.

It turned out better than he expected. The root cellar was there, and he was stuffing himself with raw potatoes when the farmer happened on to him. When Web explained his situation, the farmer believed him and put him on a horse with provisions in a gunny sack.

On May 12, Web had reached the northern tip of the Blue Ridge Mountains and was riding through the forest just west of Manassas Junction when suddenly a half-dozen men on horseback came out of nowhere and blocked his path. Two of them were in gray uniforms. Both appeared to be officers, though Web could not identify the markings on their collars. Were these the uniforms of the newly formed Confederate army?

The older man in uniform, who was about forty, nudged his horse toward Steele, and was quickly followed by the younger officer. The other four laid their muskets across their saddles and looked on with keen interest.

Web's heart thudded his ribs. Could the authorities have been alerted this far north about the fire and his escape?

"Good morning," said the older officer. "I'm Captain Philip Carney, Confederate Army. This gentleman in the uniform behind me is Lieutenant Chet Foster. These other men are new recruits and have not been supplied as yet with uniforms. Might I ask your name and where you're from?"

Web knew by their casual manner that these men did not suspect him of being an escapee from the Lynchburg prison. Smiling, he said, "My name is Webster Steele, Captain. I'm from down by Richmond. My father owns a large plantation there. I'm his slave overseer."

Carney's features were relaxed. "I see. A home-grown South'n boy, eh?"

"Yes, sir." Web was glad the prison had not made the inmates wear marked clothing.

Adjusting his position in the saddle, Carney said, "I judge by the direction you're heading that you're not on your way to Harper's Ferry."

Noting the change in tone of Carney's voice, Web said, "No,

sir. I'm headed for Carlisle, Pennsylvania. Have to see a man there about some very important personal business."

The captain's jaw jutted and he frowned. "You do know there's a war on, don't you?"

"Yes, sir."

"Then as a loyal South'n boy, you should be aiming for Harper's Ferry. That's the induction center for all Virginia men."

Acting as if he already knew that, Web said, "Before the war started, sir, I made plans to join up if it happened. And I still plan to do it, just as soon as I clear up this important personal matter."

Carney's eyes went stony. "Well now, Mr. Steele," he said, with an edge to his voice, "all of us have had to set aside important personal business in order to prepare ourselves to fight the Union. Every able-bodied man is expected to join the army. You look plenty able-bodied to me. Man refuses to jump in and make ready for the big conflict that's coming is looked upon with a high degree of scorn. You following my drift?"

Web knew he was cornered. If he rode away, saying his personal business came before the well-being of the Confederacy, they would probably shoot him off the horse. He had no choice. Clearing himself of the murder charge would have to wait. Returning to Abby would have to wait, too.

"Yes, sir," nodded Web. "I understand what you're saying. My personal business can wait."

"That's what I like to hear," smiled the captain. "It just so happens that Lieutenant Foster is going to be riding to Harper's Ferry yet today. It's only thirty miles from here. You can ride along with him. If you need to wire the folks back home, you can do that at the induction center."

"Thank you, sir," said Web. As they rode toward the army facility at Manassas Gap, Web told himself there was no way he could send a wire home. The telegraph operator in Richmond no doubt knew of Web's prison sentence. It had been written up in the local newspaper. If the operator received a telegram from Web

Steele, the authorities would be after him.

There was nothing he could do to let Abby and his parents know where he was. He had learned while in the prison that mail service had been disrupted by the Yankees and that finding men to carry the mail was becoming impossible. Several skirmishes had taken place when Confederate soldiers had come upon Federals who were attempting to stop the mail from going through. Writing letters home was out.

Abby and his parents would just have to wait till the war was over to know that he was alive and well. He hoped the experts were right about the war lasting only a few months.

On the night of May 12, elderly slave Jedidiah was about to put out the lantern and go to bed in his tiny shack on the Ruffin plantation. He was humming an old hymn while sitting on his only chair and pulling off his socks when he heard a faint tap at the door.

"Who's dat?" he asked.

"Mandrake!" came a hoarse whisper through the cracks in the door.

Jedidiah hobbled to the door and pulled it open. The yellow light from the lantern showed him the weary face of his dear friend. "Well, Mandrake, boy, come in!" he said jubilantly. "Whut you doin' heah?"

"I'm here to kill 'im, Jedidiah," Mandrake said as he stepped inside.

Closing the door, the old man asked, "Yo' heah to kill who?"

"That heartless animal Reed Exley, that's who! I figured since he treated you so mean, you'd hide me in yo' shack till mo'nin' so's I can watch fo' 'im and shoot 'im down."

Jedidiah noticed the revolver under Mandrake's belt. Rubbing the back of his neck, he said, "We all heahed 'bout Massa Web buyin' you and sendin' you off to fin' Orchid. Did you fin' her?"

Mandrake's face grew solemn. "No, I didn'. She's...she's dead."

"Daid! How?"

"It's a long story."

"Well, sit down and tell me 'bout it," said Jedidiah, gesturing toward the chair.

While the old man eased down on the edge of the bed, Mandrake sat on the chair. With his emotions running high, Mandrake told of the obstacles he faced in getting to Harper's Ferry, then of learning from Horatio Clements that Orchid was dead. He told how Orchid had stabbed the man she was supposed to mate with and even stabbed the guard at the gate in a valiant attempt to escape.

When Jedidiah heard that Orchid had been shot and had fallen into the Potomac River, he wept and said, "None of this would've happen', Mandrake, if'n dat dirty Reed Exley hadn' sold her to dat no-count Clements man."

"Yes, an' that's why I come back. That filthy devil's gonna die, and I'm the one who's gonna kill 'im!"

"If you did dat, dey'd hang you, Mandrake!"

"I don' care. With Orchid gone, I don' got nothin' to live fo'. All I wan' is to see Exley dead!"

"Well, you ain' gonna be killin' him any time soon," came Jedidiah's toneless reply. "He ain' heah. He wen' off to fight in de war."

"What! When'd he leave?"

" 'Zactly a week ago."

Mandrake stared into space for a long moment.

"Whut you thinkin'?" asked Jedidiah.

"I'm thinkin' that all Virginia men have to join up in the army at the 'duction center in Harper's Ferry. If I go to the 'duction place, they'll know where they sent 'im. Once I fin' that out, I'll go there and kill 'im."

"You gonna leave right away?"

"I need to rest a couple days. Gettin' down here with all the war stuff goin' on's been rough. Can I stay here in yo' shack?"

"Sho' nuff, but ain' you gonna let Massa John or Miz Abby an' Miz Lynne know yo' heah?"

"It's best that I don't, Jedidiah. They'd jus' try to stop me.

Massa John would, anyway. You know how he loves that low-down skunk. I'll jus' stay in here so's none of the other slaves sees me, and leave in the dark when I go."

"Whatevuh you say," nodded Jedidiah. He rubbed his hands together nervously and dropped his eyes to the floor.

Mandrake eyed him with speculation and said, "You worried 'bout somethin'?"

"Well," the old man said with a sigh, "you wouldn' call it worry. I guess you'd call it dreadin'."

"You dreadin' somethin'?"

Still looking at the floor, Jedidiah responded shakily, "Dreadin' whut I gotta tell you now."

"Tell me what?"

Raising his eyes to meet Mandrake's gaze, he said, "Dat somebody else you lubs a whole lot is daid."

Mandrake saw tears film the old man's eyes but did not venture to ask who he was talking about.

"I's talkin' 'bout Massa Web." As he said it, tears spilled down his wrinkled cheeks.

Mandrake's heart seemed to stand still. He couldn't believe his ears. It took him a moment to find his voice. "Massa Web? How? When?"

Jedidiah explained that John Ruffin had told the slaves about Web's death so they would understand why Abby was in a deep state of grief. He told how Exley had framed Web for murdering Wilbur Yates and of Web's subsequent imprisonment and death in the fire. Jedidiah followed that sad information with the news that after being stabbed and left for dead by Exley, Hec Wheeler had come clean and cleared Web of the murder charge.

Mandrake lay on the floor of Jedidiah's shack that night, weeping silently over the loss of the man who had set him free. When he thought of Reed Exley, the name seemed to burn into his mind. To Mandrake, Exley was the scum of the earth and needed to be removed. Mandrake was determined to hunt him down...or die in the attempt.

TWENTY

O n April 15, 1861—three days after the bombardment of Fort Sumter by Confederate troops—President Abraham Lincoln seized the opportunity to act without congressional encumbrance and called for seventy-five thousand men to join the Union militia and punish the Confederacy. Lincoln declared war on the Southerners, not only for their attack on Fort Sumter, but because the seven seceded Southern states had opposed and obstructed the laws of the United States.

In his campaign for military volunteers, Lincoln appealed to all loyal citizens of the Union to favor, facilitate, and aid in the vastly important effort to maintain the honor, the integrity, and the very existence of the Union. He made it clear that only by military force could they correct the wrongs of the Confederacy already too long endured by the federal government.

Lincoln gave the Southern military forces twenty days to disband and disperse. The implication was that if they did so, they would be forgiven; if they did not, his intention to "correct the wrongs of the Confederacy" would be fulfilled.

The president's bold stand stirred great enthusiasm throughout the North. In every city, town, village, and hamlet, young men turned out in large numbers to enlist, and Lincoln quickly exceeded the quota of militiamen he had wanted.

When the message came to Confederate President Jefferson Davis in Montgomery, he bristled with anger. A message quickly went to the newspapers of the South from Davis, quoting Lincoln's "bold, brash, and naked" threat, stirring up the Southern people to unite and make ready to meet that threat head-on.

Southerners of every class gave vent to their long-festering rage at the Northerners, who would dare try to force abolition on them and take away their states' rights. The Confederate enlistment drive, which had been moving nominally since early March, suddenly boiled over. Eager young men all over the South stormed the recruiting offices, ready to fight the Yankees when they invaded sacred Southern land.

Just two days after Lincoln issued his threat, a state convention was held in Richmond. The delegates passed an ordinance of secession.

On April 18, a Virginia military unit moved swiftly to take the federal arsenal at Harper's Ferry. The small Union garrison there decided to make for friendly territory and let the Confederates have the arsenal. To put up a fight when outnumbered more than ten to one would have been suicide. They retreated hastily across the Potomac River to Hagerstown, Maryland. When the Virginians marched into the arsenal, they found to their delight five thousand rifles and a healthy supply of ammunition.

After the secession of Virginia, both sides marked time. Neither had their men trained, and neither was ready to go into full-scale battle. In both the North and South, thousands of women went to work making uniforms. Progress was slow, but little by little recruits were supplied with uniforms while being trained.

Though the Confederacy was conscious that it could never muster the numerical or material strength of the North, it had a spirit and a will to fight. The South would be on the defensive. It rested its hope of victory not on conquest of the North, but in wearing down the Yankee will to fight.

The North, on the other hand, would be the aggressor. Its military objective was to invade and conquer the South, thus meting out retribution for its crimes against the United States. When the objective was accomplished, the Southern states would then be under federal jurisdiction once again, and slavery would be abolished.

On April 29, Jefferson Davis delivered to the Confederate Congress a powerful and emotional speech that stirred Southern patriotism to an even greater degree. The movement toward full secession of the Southern states moved forward rapidly. On May 1, the Tennessee legislature passed a military alliance with the Confederacy, though the popular vote to formally decide the issue would not come until June 8. Secession for Tennessee was a foregone conclusion.

Arkansas left the Union on May 6, and when North Carolina followed on May 20, the eleven-state Confederacy was complete.

Since Virginia was in a strategic position bordering the North, it was apparent to President Davis and the Confederate Congress that the heavy fighting would begin on Virginia soil. Davis and the Congress, encouraged by Virginia's zeal for battle, opened negotiations to move the Confederate capital from small, remote Montgomery to the larger and more accessible city of Richmond. The transfer was completed when President Davis and his staff arrived in Richmond on May 29. Now just a hundred miles separated the two capitals—Washington D.C., and Richmond, Virginia. Both sides went to work to secure their respective centers of government.

As the month of June came in 1861, and both sides were busy enlisting and training troops, the prime geographical region of concern was western Virginia, which did not become known as West Virginia until its entry into the Union as a state in 1863. Politically the Northern hold on that area was of major psychological importance, since the people of that region had remained loyal to the Union despite the secession of their state.

To Abraham Lincoln and the federal government, western Virginia was a strategic spot that had to be kept intact with its natural neighbors, Union states Ohio and Pennsylvania. The state governments of both Ohio and Pennsylvania looked upon western Virginia as a battleground on which to halt the Southern advance. Strategically, that region was viewed by both the Union and the Confederacy as a key position which could be used as a base for strikes deep into enemy territory.

In mid-May, the governor of Ohio put pressure on President Lincoln to order an invasion of western Virginia on the grounds that it was necessary not only to deny the use of the area to the Confederates, but to support the Union sympathizers there. The U.S. military commander of that district, General George B. McClellan, agreed that some sort of campaign was warranted.

At the time, the Confederates were disrupting trains of the Baltimore and Ohio Railroad in western Virginia, so it took little effort by Ohio's governor to persuade Lincoln to order McClellan to take prompt action.

The troublesome Confederates were bivouacked at the small town of Philippi. On June 2, McClellan dispatched a small force toward Philippi with instructions to drive off the Confederate forces and protect the railroad. On the night of June 3, an attack was launched on the Rebel camp at Philippi. The Southerners were totally unprepared, failing to even have sentries on patrol. In a minor skirmish, a few men were wounded on both sides, but the Confederates made a hasty retreat southward to the town of Beverly, located at the northern base of Rich Mountain.

The relatively easy rout gave General McClellan and his men an overwhelming air of confidence. Laughing about how fast the Rebels ran from Philippi, the federals dubbed the incident "The Philippi Races." It was apparent to the Union troops that the Confederates did not have the resolve to fight, and that the war would soon be over.

General Robert E. Lee, a native Virginian, had been appointed by President Davis as commander-in-chief of the Confederate forces on April 23. As a result of the incident at Philippi, Lee sent twenty-five hundred troops to Beverly under the command of Brigadier General Robert S. Garnett, a forty-one-year-old Virginian who was known as a dedicated family man. Garnett had served in the Mexican-American conflict with gallantry and, as a strict military disciplinarian, was considered one of the brightest officers in the old Regular Army.

Private Webster Steele had been assigned to Garnett's command upon enlistment and had been undergoing training at Harper's Ferry until General Lee dispatched the unit to Beverly. They arrived at Beverly on June 19 and set up camp between the town and the northern base of Rich Mountain.

When General McClellan's scouts reported the large number of Confederate troops that had marched into Beverly, McClellan moved toward the area, leading some fifteen thousand men to join with the small force already at Philippi.

In response to the large Union deployment, General Lee ordered an additional thirty-five hundred troops who had been training near Winchester, Virginia, to march to Beverly and join Garnett. Lee realized his regiments at Rich Mountain were still greatly outnumbered, but he had no more trained recruits that he could spare. Fear of Union attack on Richmond caused him to keep a large number of prepared men there, and another large unit had to stay at Manassas Junction to protect the vital center of the Manassas Gap Railroad.

On the morning of June 28, Private Steele was working with two other enlisted men to stabilize a twenty-four pounder cannon at the edge of the dense timber on top of Rich Mountain. The three men were sweating in the hot sun as they blocked the cannon's wheels with heavy rocks to keep it from moving when fired.

When they had finished, Web stepped behind the cannon and sighted along the barrel, eyeing the open field of grass and small trees that spread over the sharp slope on the east side of the mountain. "This ought to be about right," he said to his companions. Then running his gaze toward the dozen other cannons of like size lined across the crest of the mountain southward, he added, "Looks like we've got the entire open area covered. When those Yankees come over that grassy ridge down there and see these big guns trained on them, they just might decide to do a little backtracking."

Worry showed on the freckled face of young Private Dooley Carson. "Wish we had twice as many cannons up here," he drawled, sleeving away sweat from his brow. "From what General Garnett told us, we're gonna be grossly outnumbered."

Dooley was barely eighteen years old, spoke slowly with a heavy Southern accent, and carried an easy smile. Web had liked him from the moment they met at Harper's Ferry.

"Well, I'm glad our troops from Winchester are gonna get here before McClellan arrives with his big bunch," put in twenty-one-year-old Leroy Sheldon. "At least we can get well-fortified on top of this mountain before the blue-bellies get here."

While Sheldon spoke, all three of them looked toward the path that wound its way down the north end of the mountain. General Garnett had ordered his troops to set up camp amid the heavy timber on top of Rich Mountain. They would meet the enemy from the edge of the timber with all the fire power they could muster. Being above the Union troops would give them an advantage. Horses and mules pulled heavily loaded wagons and carts up the path, their coats shining with sweat. Some of the wagons were reaching the crest and heading for the cannons. They carried gun powder and cannonballs.

Dooley Carson moved into the shade of the trees and lifted a large canteen off the stub of a broken limb. Looking back at his partners, he called, "Hey, you Rebels want a drink?"

Steele and Sheldon looked over their shoulders at him and nodded. Carson uncorked the canteen, took a long pull, and handed it to Sheldon. While Sheldon was drinking, Web said, "Maybe these boys will have word for us about the troops from Winchester."

"Hope so," said Carson. "I'll feel a lot better when those Winchester Rebels are on top of this mountain with us."

"Won't we all?" grinned Web as he took the canteen from Leroy.

Dooley noticed there was dust on the pants of his new gray uniform. Brushing it off, he said, "Sure don't want to soil this uniform. Some Southern belle worked hard to make it."

Web was corking the canteen when the lead ammunition wagon hauled up and stopped. The mules blew as the driver set the brake and said, "Brung you boys somethin' to shoot at them blue-bellies when they come."

While the three men helped the driver unload the heavy canisters of gun powder and some sixty cannonballs, he informed them that the troops from Winchester had been spotted by one of General Garnett's scouts and would arrive within an hour. Word was that they were being led by a twenty-nine-year-old colonel named John Pegram, a graduate of West Point. Pegram had experience in fighting Indians on the western frontier.

It was nearly eleven o'clock when Colonel Pegram and his troops arrived at the base of Rich Mountain. General Garnett met them and explained to Pegram that he would be dividing the forces into two units within a couple of days. The second unit would be the largest. The Confederate scouts were reporting that General McClellan was leading his large force toward the Grafton-Philippi area to meet up with the small brigade camped there.

Acting on this information, Garnett planned to take forty-seven hundred men to Laurel Mountain, just north of Rich Mountain, and try to cripple the Yankee army by hitting them from atop the mountain. The thirteen hundred men on Rich Mountain would have to take on whatever smaller unit McClellan sent their way. Pegram would command the Rich Mountain men.

Pegram's troops then climbed to the top of Rich Mountain where they set up camp until the forces would be divided within a couple of days. The entire brigade of six thousand men was assembled in the open grassy area on Rich Mountain's east side where the tall, slender general addressed them and explained his plan.

An hour after the men had been dismissed, Web was cleaning his army-issue Springfield rifled musket in front of his tent while talking with Dooley Carson. Dooley had his right shoe off and was rubbing a sore toe.

"I think it's marvelous that Abby would be so dedicated to you that she'd promise never to consider another man," said Dooley. "Seems to me that with you in prison for the rest of your life—as she thought would be your lot—she'd want to find another man, get married, and live a normal life."

Web grinned. "You'd have to know Abby to understand. When the Lord made her, He threw away the mold. What she wrote in that note was no idle promise."

"But she may think you died in that prison fire. Maybe she'll feel that her promise can be broken since you're dead."

"Nope," said Web, shaking his head. "When this war is over and I go home, she'll still be single and unattached. Her love for me is pure, and her heart is true. She'll never love another man any more than if she died, I'd ever love another woman."

"I sure hope when I fall in love, it'll be with a girl like Abby."

Dooley was silently wondering if such a girl really existed. Maybe even now, Abby Ruffin was seeing other men. Maybe his friend was in for a shock and a broken heart when he returned home.

While Dooley was putting his shoe back on, he watched as Web picked up his bayonet and attached it to the musket. A cold shiver ran down his spine as he shuddered aloud, "Web, I don't know if I can do it."

"What's that?"

"Fight hand-to-hand with a bayonet. The idea of cold Yankee steel in my body makes my knees go weak."

Web grinned and said, "It's not supposed to be Yankee steel in your body, my friend, but Rebel steel in a Yankee body."

Dooley ran shaky fingers through his mop of sand-colored hair. "I know, but maybe those blue-bellies have been trained better than us."

"Man has to have a positive attitude," said Web. "You can't go into battle thinking you're going to die. You have to—"

"Web Steele!" came the sound of an astonished voice.

Web looked up to see Daniel Hart rushing toward him. Laying the rifle down, he stood up and met Daniel's hand in a warm hand-shake.

Daniel's features showed the shock he was feeling as he blurted, "Web, how'd you get out of prison?" He quickly covered his mouth as he realized what he had just said.

"It's all right, Daniel," chuckled Web. "He's a close friend and knows about my being in prison. Dooley Carson, meet Daniel Hart."

Carson and Hart shook hands, then Web told Daniel the whole story.

Daniel shook his head and said, "Web, from what you've told me, the authorities for sure think you died in the fire."

"That's pretty much the way I see it," nodded Web.

"Then that's what they've reported to Abby and everybody back home."

"If our assumption is correct, it sure is."

"Poor Abby! This has to be awful for her. And for your ma and pa, too."

"I know, but there's no way I can get a message through to them. No soldier is allowed to send anything personal on the tele-graph, and as you probably know, the mail service is no longer operating."

"I guess there's nothing you can do about it till this war is over and you can go home."

"That's about it," replied Web. He then explained to Dooley Carson that Daniel was engaged to Abby's sister, Lynne.

Dooley asked Daniel if Lynne was as good-looking as Abby. Daniel grinned at Web and assured Dooley that Lynne was even more beautiful than Abby.

Web laughed, "Well, I guess that's one thing we're in disagree-ment on!" Then he said, "So you came over with Colonel Pegram from Winchester."

"Yeah," Daniel nodded. His face took on a solemn look and he said, "There's somebody else you know who came with me."

"Oh? Who?"

"Reed Exley."

The distaste Web felt at the sound of the name showed on his face.

Daniel chortled, "Seems like good fortune just follows you around, Web."

"Sure!" exclaimed Dooley. "He met up with me, didn't he? And what's more, he drew me as one of his two assistants to man his cannon."

"So you're a cannon master, Web?" Daniel asked.

"He sure is," cut in Dooley. "Web took to it during training at Harper's Ferry like a duck takes to water. He can aim a cannon and hit a bull between the eyes at four hundred yards!"

"Well, let's hope it's Yankee bulls he hits this time," laughed Daniel. Clearing his throat, he said, "This is some coincidence, Web."

"What do you mean?"

"I'm in the artillery too. Trained on twenty-four pounders."

"You don't say," responded Web with a broad grin. "That's the size of my gun. You a cannon master?"

"Naw, I'm not that good at aiming one…but I'm pretty fast at getting one loaded."

"I suppose you'll be assigned to Laurel Mountain with General Garnett," said Web.

"I assume so," replied Daniel. "Sure wish I could work with you."

"Well," chuckled Dooley, "if wishes were horses, beggars would ride. Web had a dozen or more men wantin' to be on his team, but me and a fella named Leroy got the assignment."

"Guess I was born under a crooked star," groaned Hart. "Nothing like that ever happens to me." After a brief pause, he said, "I'd better get back to my outfit. Nice to meet you, Dooley. Hope to see you around, future brother-in-law."

As Daniel started to walk away, Web called after him, "Daniel!" Halting, young Hart made a half-turn. "Yes?"

"When the battle comes, you watch yourself, y'hear?"

"Yep. You too, okay?"

"Okay."

Just after breakfast the following morning, General Garnett worked with Colonel Pegram on his plan to divide up the troops. Since the Confederate scouts reported that Union General McClellan and his giant force were still several miles to the north, Garnett decided the move to Laurel Mountain would not need to be made until Monday, July 1.

Late that afternoon, the sky clouded up and rain began to fall. It was coming down heavily when Daniel Hart appeared at the tent occupied by Web Steele and his two companions. Dripping wet, he announced to Web that an opening had come up for a helper at one of the cannons on Rich Mountain. He would be working with a cannon master named Private Ed Cahill. Web was pleased to learn it. He laughed, saying they would be neighbors. Web's gun was first in the line at the north end. Cahill's gun was the very next one. Daniel stayed until the rain began to let up about half an hour before suppertime. As he was about to leave the tent, he told Web that Reed Exley had been appointed as a runner between General Garnett and Colonel Pegram once Garnett was situated on Laurel Mountain.

Web asked if Daniel had told Exley about him being out of prison and in uniform on Rich Mountain. Daniel said he had not. He was hoping that in the crowd of six thousand men, Web would not have to meet up with his hated enemy.

The next morning Web and his crew were at their cannon, making sure the powder was dry, when another ammunition wagon pulled up. They were given additional powder and cannonballs. At the same time, Lieutenant Floyd Courtman, who was in charge of artillery on Rich Mountain, rode up on a bay gelding and told Steele he wanted to meet with all the cannon masters immediately at his tent. Web left Carson and Sheldon to help unload the wagon and followed Courtman.

When the brief meeting was over, Web headed back through the timber toward his cannon. He was some forty yards from the timber's edge when suddenly a short, stocky form stepped out from behind a tree, blocking his path.

"Well, well, well," sneered Reed Exley, waggling his head. "Look who's here."

Drawing up within arm's reach, Web said, "Get out of my way."

"Or what? You'll batter me with those fists of yours? Do you know the trouble you can get into for striking a fellow soldier?"

"So what do you want?"

"I want to know how you broke out of prison."

"You going to turn me in?"

Exley laughed, rubbed the back of his neck, and replied, "Not till the war's over. Since the South needs every man it can get, Garnett wouldn't do anything about it right now. But you can count on it—when the last shot is fired, I'll see that you're back behind bars faster than a hummingbird can flap its wings."

"We both know who ought to be behind bars," Web said heatedly.

Looking around in the dappled shade of the trees to make sure no one was near, Exley remarked tartly, "Yeah, but you and I are the only ones who know."

"Not really," Web countered. "Hec Wheeler knows, and so does Abby."

Exley ignored Web's reference to Wheeler, but his straw-colored eyebrows arched at the mention of Abby. "Oh? And how is that? She wasn't there that night I killed that stupid drifter."

"She didn't have to be. She just knows you, that's all."

A mocking grin curved Exley's mouth as he said insolently, "She sure does know me. In fact, she knows me a lot better since I got you out of the picture."

"And just what do you mean by that?"

"Exactly what it sounds like. She knows her dead sister is out of the way now, and since you are too, she threw herself at me. You were only second choice, Steele. Abby really wanted me all the time. Those lips of hers are mighty sweet, aren't they?"

"Don't give me that poppycock, Exley. You've never kissed those lips."

"Oh, yes I have. You should've seen the kiss she gave me the day I left for Harper's Ferry. Said she'd be waitin' for me to come back, too. You're out of her life forever, Steele. Forever. When this war's over and I go home, she'll be waitin' for me with open arms and eager lips."

"You're lying. I know Abby and I know how she feels about you. She hates your guts almost as much as I do." Moving toward him, Web clipped, "This conversation is over."

When Web saw that Exley wasn't going to move, he slammed him in the chest with his shoulder, knocking him flat on his back.

With the wind knocked out of him, Exley rolled over, sucking for air and swearing between gasps. Looking at Web Steele's broad back as he strode toward the open area, he gasped in a half-whisper, "You ain't…ever gonna see Abby…again, Steele. I'll find a way…to put a bullet in you…before the battle on this…mountain…is over. Ha! Who'll know the difference? Confederate bullets look just like Yankee bullets."

TWENTY-ONE

On Monday, July 1, 1861, General Robert Garnett moved forty-seven hundred of his troops to Laurel Mountain, leaving the planned thirteen hundred on Rich Mountain with Colonel John Pegram in charge. When the Laurel Mountain position was fortified, Garnett kept Reed Exley busy riding back and forth between the mountains with messages.

During the next few days, the Confederates on both mountains waited nervously for McClellan to arrive and the battle to begin.

General George McClellan had moved his troops slowly toward the Philippi-Beverly area while gaining information about the Confederate strongholds on Laurel and Rich Mountains. Having left behind some fifty-four hundred men to guard the line of the Baltimore and Ohio Railroad, McClellan arrived at Philippi with over fourteen thousand troops late in the day on July 9.

McClellan divided his force into four brigades under Brigadier Generals Thomas Morris, Newton Schleich, William Rosecrans, and Colonel Robert McCook. His scouts had not seen the actual move of General Garnett and his troops to Laurel Mountain on July 1, and erroneously reported that the bulk of the Confederates were on Rich Mountain.

Acting on this information, McClellan set up his plan. He was aware that General Garnett and Colonel Pegram were each in charge on a mountain, but assumed that Garnett was with the larger force on the one farther to the south. He would use July 10 to march troops south to the town of Beverly, and to learn all he could about the terrain of both mountains by talking to local Union sympathizers. Once he knew the layout of the mountains, he would have his artillery set up at their bases under cover of darkness on July 10. At dawn on the eleventh, the cannons would cut loose on both mountains, softening them up for the infantry attack that would follow.

According to his plan, two columns would advance at the same time. General Thomas Morris would move on Laurel Mountain and McClellan would lead the other three brigades against Rich Mountain.

At three o'clock on the afternoon of July 10, the Union troops halted at the edge of Beverly and prepared to set up camp. General William Rosecrans took two officers and rode into town. Reaching Main Street, they began to ask people about the terrain of Rich and Laurel Mountains. One old timer advised Rosecrans to go to the Trench Clothing Store next door to the Beverly Bank and talk to young David Hart. David, he explained, was an enthusiastic hiker and had climbed all over both mountains. He was also a Union sympathizer.

Moments later, General Rosecrans, who was a stately man of forty, entered the clothing store alone while his officers waited on the street. A tall, slender young man came from a counter at the back of the store, smiled when he saw the blue uniform, and said, "Good afternoon, sir. I'm David Hart. How may I help you?"

The general introduced himself and explained his purpose for coming into the store. David was eager to help the Union cause. He offered to close the store early and go with Rosecrans to give a description of both Laurel and Rich mountains to General McClellan.

Rosecrans gladly accepted the offer, and within fifteen minutes, David was sitting in General McClellan's tent on the outskirts of

Beverly giving the general a description of both mountains, telling him of the most frequently used paths, and which sides were easiest to climb.

When Hart finished and had answered several questions, McClellan said, "I appreciate your help, David. It has been of the utmost value. I do want to ask you something, though."

"What's that, sir?"

McClellan stroked his heavy mustache and queried, "Why aren't you in a blue uniform?"

"I'd love to be in the Union army, General McClellan, but circumstances are standing in my way. You see, I'm a business partner with my father-in-law at the clothing store, and he had a stroke a few months ago and can't work. If I joined the army, the store wouldn't make it. My wife and mother-in-law can run it for awhile, but not for an extended time. Without the store, the family would soon be destitute. I have no choice but to stay here and take care of it."

"I understand," smiled McClellan. "You've been a great help to the Northern cause in this matter, and I thank you."

General Rosecrans asked David, "Are you a native Virginian?"

"Yes, sir. My father owns a cotton plantation over by Richmond. That's where I was born and raised."

"A cotton plantation?" said McClellan, surprised. "Your father no doubt is in sympathy with the Confederacy then?"

"Yes, sir. He and I don't get along very well."

"You have any brothers in the Rebel army?"

"I only have one who would be old enough. But I have little contact with the family, and I don't know whether Daniel has joined the Confederate army or not. I kind of think Pa might keep him home to help with the plantation."

McClellan nodded and rose to his feet. David followed suit, and so did the brigade leaders. "Thank you again, David," said the general. "You've been a real help."

Scratching at an ear, David said, "Sir, I think I can be of even more help."

"How's that?"

"I assume by what you've said that you will attack Rich Mountain from the east side, since it's not nearly as steep as the west side."

"That's right," nodded McClellan.

"Well, sir, since your scouts have told you the larger number of Confederates are on Rich Mountain, wouldn't it be good to hit them from the west, also?"

"Yes it would, but if it's as steep on that side as you say, climbing it with artillery would be impossible."

"Artillery would be out for sure," said David, "but men on foot could do it, and it would probably take the Rebels by surprise. I know a path up the west side near the north end. It's quite obscure, but if you want me to lead a detachment of men up that way, I would be happy to do it."

McClellan stroked his mustache thoughtfully. After a moment, he said, "I like the surprise idea, David, but most of my men aren't experienced in warfare. Since we're going to launch the attack at dawn tomorrow, they'd have to make the climb in the dark. I'd need them to be at the top so when our artillery finished its bombardment on the east side, they'd be ready to hit the Rebels from the west. If somehow the Rebels found out our men were coming up the west side, they'd be sitting ducks."

General Rosecrans said, "Excuse me, sir. I know it would be risky, but the unexpected sally from the west side could mean the difference between success or failure in this battle, especially since we have no idea how many troops are on Rich Mountain."

McClellan nodded slowly. "Yes, I wish we knew how many troops Garnett has." After a pause, he said, "I believe you're right, though. The element of surprise could make the difference. All right, we'll take the risk. General Rosecrans, you take your task force of nineteen hundred men and let David lead you up the west side of the mountain." Turning to Hart, he asked, "David, how long will it take that many men to make the climb up your obscure path?"

"I'd say about an hour, sir."

"And you're willing to take this risk of your own life?"

"Yes, sir. Since I can't be in your army, I'd sure like to do my part in this battle. If we can whip the Confederates here, maybe it'll be enough to make them give it up and lay down their arms. Maybe the war will start and end right here on Rich Mountain."

"The battle could get hot, son," McClellan said. "You know how to use a musket? We'll supply you with one if you do."

"Yes, sir. My brother and I have done a lot of hunting together. Pa has several Springfield muskets on the place."

"You don't mind using it if you're forced into a fight?"

"I've never killed a human being, sir, but war is war. I'll use it if I have to."

"All right," smiled the general. "Be here at three-thirty in the morning. You and General Rosecrans will lead his brigade up the mountain at four o'clock."

Just before dawn on the morning of July 11, 1861, Private Webster Steele stood at his cannon with Dooley Carson and Leroy Sheldon. They could barely make each other out in the dark. Heavy clouds had covered the sky during the night, and the scent of rain was in the air.

"Gonna be fun tryin' to kill Yankees in a downpour," mused Sheldon. "Be hard to see 'em."

"It'll be raining on us, too," said Web. "We'll be just as hard to see. Hardest thing is going to be keeping our powder dry."

"So what'll we do if it gets wet and we can't fire the cannon?" asked Dooley.

"Use our rifles," replied Web. "And if that powder gets wet, we'll have to use our bayonets."

Dooley shuddered. "Bayonets—I just don't think I can face bayonets."

"You may have to," said Sheldon. "If our powder gets wet,

Yankee powder will be just as wet. This whole battle could be won or lost with bayonets, musket butts, and fists."

"You'll be all right, Dooley," said Web. "When a man gets his back to the wall, he can do a lot of things he didn't think he could."

"Hey!" came a hoarse whisper from the darkness to their right. "You guys ready for the fight?"

It was Daniel Hart. As his vague form drew up, Web said, "Yeah, we're ready. Just show me a bunch of Yankees, and I'll send them a cannonball for breakfast."

"You really think they'll come today?" asked Daniel.

"Colonel Pegram is convinced they will," Web said. "Of course he's going by the messages that have been coming from General Garnett." When Web thought about who was delivering those messages, his stomach turned over.

The sound of hooves on dewy grass met their ears. Seconds later, Lieutenant Floyd Courtman rode up in the obscure gloom and said, "Colonel Pegram just got a report from one of our scouts that the blue-bellies are setting up artillery at the base of the mountain right in front of you. Military custom is to commence firing at dawn. We're going to beat them to it. Private Steele, I've given orders to the other cannon masters along the line to lob some balls over the edge and drop them down on top of their artillery. As you know, it's three hundred yards to the trees along the edge of the mountain at the bottom of that open field in front of you. I figure they have to be about fifty yards away from the base of the mountain to get their cannonballs up here. The slope makes the edge at the top about thirty yards inside the base line, so set your gun's range accordingly."

"Yes, sir," said Steele.

"I'll ride along the line and give orders for each gun to fire," Courtman continued. "Be ready in fifteen minutes. Load fast and fire two more shots at will. Maybe we can cut some of their fire power before they're ready to bombard us."

"We'll be ready, sir," Web assured him.

As the lieutenant rode back along the line, Daniel said, "Well, that answers my question. This is the day. I'd better get back to my cannon."

"Take care, Daniel."

"Will do. Nobody but me is going to marry the prettiest Ruffin sister."

"You've got that wrong again," Web chuckled. "I'm marrying the prettiest one."

Daniel walked away in the darkness, saying over his shoulder, "I think you need spectacles, old man!"

Web bent over the side of his cannon, placed the fingers of his left hand along the face of the range-finder, and turned the crank until the needle was on the proper mark. The muzzle of the cannon was now raised to the precise level for lobbing shells the distance Lieutenant Courtman had requested.

"You sure you've got it right?" asked Leroy.

"Are you kidding? I can aim this gun blindfolded."

"I guess that's almost what you did."

Web and Leroy could hear Dooley's heavy, unsteady breathing. Web found him in the gloom and put an arm around his shoulder. His body was trembling.

"Hey, c'mon now," Web said. "Leroy and I need you. You're our powder man. It won't do Leroy any good to drop balls down the muzzle and work the ramrod unless there's powder in the magazine. And I sure can't fire the thing unless both of you do your job."

Dooley swallowed hard. "Okay, Web. I'm sorry. It's just that—"

"I know, kid. Leroy and I are just as scared as you are. We're just better at covering it up."

"Really?"

"Yes, sir. Right, Leroy?"

"I'm probably more scared than the two of you put together," Leroy said. "My stomach is in my throat and my heart is in my stomach."

"Well, they say the waiting for battle is worse than the battle itself," said Web. "If that's true, our jitters are about to ease off."

At a quarter of five, a dull gray light appeared in the heavy clouds of the eastern sky. Leroy stood beside the cannon with two pyramids of cannonballs at his feet. The long ramrod leaned against the wheel that was blocked with rocks. Dooley, feeling better to know that his partners were also scared, was at the magazine with a full canister at his feet and the powder scoop in his hand. Web, allowing himself a private moment to think of Abby, had his hand on the lanyard. The gun was loaded and ready to fire.

"Get ready, boys," said Web, looking along the line to his right. Lieutenant Floyd Courtman could be seen at the far end, astride his mount, and every cannon crew was on the alert.

Web tightened his grip on the lanyard when Courtman moved forward and the first cannon roared. Number two cannon fired five seconds later, and one by one the others followed suit. When Ed Cahill's cannon boomed, Web tensed. Five seconds later, Courtman was adjacent and commanded Web to fire. He jerked the lanyard and quickly covered his ears as the big gun roared. As soon as the sharp sound rode away across the airwaves, Dooley was packing powder in the magazine and Leroy was picking up a cannonball.

At the same instant number one gun let loose with its second shot, the sound of artillery was heard from below. Suddenly the east side of Rich Mountain was alive with whistling shells, explosions, and the roar of Confederate cannons along the line.

Realizing that the Yankees were firing back, Lieutenant Courtman rode along the line, shouting for the cannon crews to keep firing.

As the light in the heavy clouds grew brighter, the men at the cannons noticed a great number of footmen in gray uniforms collected behind them to the far left in the thick shadows of the dense forest. Colonel Pegram was with them. Everyone knew the artillery bombardment would last only for a while, then blue-uniformed soldiers would be coming up the path and across the open fields in front of them.

Most of the Union shells were landing short of the cannon

line, digging small craters in the grass. However, two of them struck near cannons one and two, throwing dirt and rocks all over the crews and slowing them down momentarily. A third Yankee shell came down at the cannon just the other side of Cahill's and blew all three men into eternity.

Web turned to look when the shell hit, and was thankful it had not taken out Cahill's crew, which included Daniel Hart. He jerked the lanyard for the seventh time, covered his ears, then waited for Dooley and Leroy to reload. The clouds overhead were darkening and beginning to spit rain.

Just after he had fired shot number eight, Web noticed a horseman gallop up the path at the north end of the mountain and skid to a halt at the edge of the trees where Colonel Pegram was standing. It was Exley.

While Dooley was loading the magazine again, Web shouted above the thunder of cannons and shells, "Still scared, kid?"

"Yes!" nodded young Carson. "But I'm too busy to let it bother me!"

"Good! Then just keep busy!"

As Exley slid from the saddle, Colonel Pegram stepped up to meet him.

"Colonel!" Exley gasped excitedly. "General Garnett sent me to tell you that their morning started with a skirmish with the Yankees halfway up Laurel Mountain. It didn't last long, but two of our men captured a wounded Union sergeant. Before he would give the Yankee any medical help, General Garnett demanded to know the positions of all their brigades. Seems McClellan guessed that the larger number of our forces were situated here on Rich Mountain, so he sent the bulk of his troops against you. I had to ride hard to get past a huge bunch of them positioning themselves to come up the path. You already know they've got heavy artillery along the base of the mountain on the east side, but the Union sergeant also told General Garnett that there's a unit of about nineteen hundred men coming up behind you on the west! The general wanted you to know about it as soon as I could get here so you could prepare for them."

"Thank you," nodded Pegram. "I'll get right to work on it. Are you to return to Laurel?"

"The general wants to know if I got through, if possible, but he told me if it looked too dangerous to ride past the Yankee lines, I'd best stay here with you."

Exley had lied about having to ride hard past Union soldiers to make it up the mountain. He figured they would be coming up the path at some stage of the battle, but it appeared the bulk of them were going to attack from the east side once the artillery bombardment ceased. His lie would let him stay on Rich Mountain so he could get close to Web Steele when the land battle began and put a bullet in him.

"So you think it's too dangerous?" asked Pegram.

"Yes, sir," Exley lied again. "If I tried it, I'd be a dead man."

"Okay. Do this for me. Ride to Lieutenant Courtman at the far end of the cannon line and tell him about the Yankee unit that's coming up the west side. Better stay in the timber for protection. Those Union shells are hitting close to the cannons. Tell Courtman I'll send some men to help protect the backs of the men on the cannons while I send more to meet the blue-bellies head-on."

"Yes, sir," said Exley, mounting his horse.

"When you've done that," said the colonel, "come back here and you can join one of the units for the battle that's coming."

Exley nodded tightly and gouged the horse's sides. As he worked his way along the edge of the open area just inside the timber, he set hard eyes on Web Steele. The big guns continued to thunder and Union cannonballs were hitting dangerously close to Web's end of the line.

At a quarter of five that morning, General William Rosecrans and his brigade were slowly winding their way up the west side of Rich

Mountain, following David Hart. Men kept stumbling and cursing in the long line. At the head of the column, General Rosecrans was on Hart's heels. "Sure smells like rain," he said, projecting his voice so Hart could hear him above the sound of hundreds of feet tramping on dirt and small rocks.

"Wouldn't surprise me if it came a downpour any minute," David said over his shoulder. "That would make this fight we're about to get into a whole lot harder, wouldn't it?"

"Yes. I don't fancy having to carry out this bloody chore in the midst of a rainstorm. How much farther to the top?"

"Not too far, now. Another ten minutes or so."

"Good. We'll push into the woods once we're on top and wait till dawn. Then I'll send a couple of men to scout out the Reb camp and where they positioned themselves. I've been thinking, Hart…"

"Yes, sir?"

"Maybe you ought to get us on top, then head back down. Once we're close to the enemy, we won't need you any—"

The general's words were cut off by the thunder of big guns, firing about five seconds apart. Stiffening, he lifted his face toward the crest of the mountain and said, "Looks like the battle's started. Those have to be Confederate guns."

"Too close to be ours," David said.

There was a buzzing amongst the men in the column as they discussed the sudden sound of cannons.

"Hold up a minute, Hart," commanded Rosecrans. Turning to the closest men behind him, he said, "Sheffield…Manley…"

"Yes, sir," came the two voices in unison.

"Let Hart take you up to the top while we wait here. See what you can learn about what's happening. Don't take too long. If there's a chance we can be even more of a surprise, I want to know it."

"C'mon," David said to the two soldiers. "Stay close on my heels." Within seconds they had disappeared in the thick gloom."

The general told the men to pass the word along that they would halt while a reconnaissance mission was being carried out.

The Confederate cannons continued to roar for several minutes, then suddenly the distinct sound of exploding cannonballs met their ears. "Our artillery is answering back," Rosecrans said to the men just behind him. "Looks like we've got us a good fight going already."

The unseen battle raged as the Yankees waited for Hart, Sheffield, and Manley to return. The fierce discharges of artillery and the thunder of shells were incessant as the heavy-laden sky began to lighten.

Nearly a half hour had passed when the reconnaissance team became visible among the trees above them. Breathing hard as they descended the rugged path, they soon drew up, with Sheffield saying, "General, the Rebs are thick in the woods up there. We couldn't get close enough to the artillery to see how many cannons they have, but it sounds like they've got quite a few. They've got their horses and mules in a rope corral maybe sixty yards from this side of the mountain."

"We could make out their tents just past the corral, sir," said Manley. "Can't tell how many. They stretch out quite a ways. We could only see so far. The forest is quite thick up there."

The general spoke to Sheffield. "When you say the Rebs are thick up there, how are they situated?"

"Hard to tell how they're spread out over the mountain, sir, but at this end, we could tell there's a big bunch of them huddled and waiting for the ground battle."

"Can we get this unit on top without being spotted, you think?"

"If we stay low and deep in the woods, I think so, sir. Probably be best if we go up behind the rope corral. Once we're up there and get more light, we can make our surprise move."

Rosecrans looked skyward. "We're not going to get a whole lot of light the way it looks up there, but I think we'll wait till we get more than we have right now. We need to be able to see what we're doing. Once we reach the ridge, we'll go the rest of the way on our bellies."

It was beginning to rain.

✷ ✷ ✷

Just after the break of dawn that same morning, a muscular black man waited at the parlor window inside the David Hart home in Beverly. His heart quickened when he saw Chloe Hart returning on the run, holding her skirts calf-high. The thunder of the artillery battle going on at nearby Rich Mountain made the house tremble.

When Chloe stepped up on the porch, the black man moved through the door to meet her. Breathing hard, she said, "Like I thought, Mandrake, I didn't have to climb the path on Laurel very far till Rebel sentries told me to halt and identify myself. I told them I was a resident of Beverly, and that I had heard that Private Reed Exley was attached to Colonel Pegram's unit. The information the enlistment office in Harper's Ferry gave you is correct. He is."

"Good!" exclaimed Mandrake. "So you tol' the sentries you heard Exley's wife had died...that Miz 'Lizbeth was a good frien' of yours, and that you wanted to talk to Exley to fin' out if'n it was true?"

"Yes," nodded Chloe. "And I appreciate your telling me about Elizabeth's death. She and I were good friends." Her face took on a look of granite as she added, "I despised that husband of hers from the day I met him, but I despise him more since you told me he caused her death...and Orchid's...and Web Steele's, too. Poor Abby."

"Jus' 'bout ever'body who knows that rat despises 'im, Miz Chloe. Did the sentries tell you which mountain he's on?"

"He's a messenger between General Garnett on Laurel Mountain and Colonel Pegram on Rich Mountain. He's back and forth on horseback."

"Are the sentries gonna tell Exley you want to see 'im?"

"They said they would whenever they got a chance, but who knows if that'll happen now that the fighting has started."

"Yo' right. Guess the only choice I got is to sneak my way on top o' one of them mountains and try to get close enough to shoot 'im."

Chloe looked down at the revolver under Mandrake's belt. "I...I guess I have to look at this as war, right? I mean, it's not murder. David and I are on the Union side. If I'm helping you to take out a Confederate soldier during a battle, it's the way of war, isn't it?"

Mandrake smiled. "Yaz'm. You jus' keep that in mind, Miz Chloe. This is war, all right." Turning toward the edge of the porch, he said, "I'll jus' leave my horse out back with yo's, Miz Chloe, if that's all right. I can sneak up a mountain better bein' on foot."

"Of course," replied Chloe, reaching out and patting his arm. "I'll see you when you get back."

"Thank you, ma'am. An' if I don' come back, it's all right, too. My chances of killin' Exley and gettin' away without bein' shot is purty slim. But don' grieve fo' me if'n it happens. With Orchid gone, I got nuthin' to live fo' anyway."

With that, Mandrake was off, hurrying toward the road that ran between Laurel and Rich Mountains. He had hardly reached the road when he saw a rider in gray galloping toward him from the direction of Laurel Mountain.

Mandrake plunged into the brush alongside the road and ducked down. When the rider thundered by, Mandrake's jaw went slack and his eyes bulged. The rider was Reed Exley!

The hammering of the battle on Rich Mountain was heavy in Mandrake's ears. Exley was headed there, and the vengeful black man would follow.

TWENTY-TWO

The incessant roar of artillery vexed the cloudy morning as the battle raged.

The rain was still at the spitting stage two hours after the Confederate batteries had first unleashed their barrage on the Yankees at the east base of Rich Mountain. Two other cannon crews along the line had been hit. Three men lay sprawled on the wet grass, and the other three had been taken to the camp in the woods for medical attention.

Web Steele and his crew were keeping the barrel of their cannon hot as they continued to lob shells over the edge of the mountain. Web could tell there weren't as many Union cannons firing as there had been at the beginning, but the fusillade was still plenty heavy.

The thunder of artillery rolled across the top of the mountain, punctuated continually with the shriek of shells, followed by deafening explosions and the horrid humming of their dangerous fragments. Four times, shells had landed close to Steele and his crew, but so far they had escaped being hit.

The moist air was filled with the flash of fire from cannon muzzles and shell explosions, and wreaths of smoke drifted with the morning breeze. At one point, Web caught sight of Reed Exley galloping back to where Colonel Pegram and his infantry waited for the land battle that was sure to come. Leroy Sheldon pulled the ramrod from the barrel of the cannon and yelled, "Ready!"

Web jerked the lanyard while keeping his eyes on Exley, and spit.

Suddenly a Yankee shell screamed over their heads and exploded as it struck the trees behind them. Wood and shrapnel went every direction as a flash of fire sent up billows of smoke.

"That one just about took my cap off!" shouted Dooley Carson.

"Better duck next time!" Web shouted back.

While his men were reloading, Web saw Lieutenant Floyd Courtman riding hard along the rear of the cannon line. Suddenly a Yankee shell whined shrilly and struck some ten or twelve feet ahead of his mount. The concussion rocked the area, and shattered bits of cannonball struck horse and rider. The animal took it in the face and peeled over head-first. Courtman sailed forward and landed like a rag doll on the smoking spot where the shell had hit. He was directly behind Ed Cahill's cannon, a distance of about sixty feet.

Cahill yanked his lanyard and shouted at Daniel Hart to see about Courtman. Daniel wheeled and ran toward the fallen officer. Just as he knelt beside him, a shell slammed Cahill's cannon, blowing Cahill and his other helper to fragments.

The concussion slammed Dooley against his cannon and staggered Web. Sheldon was leaning over his diminishing stack of cannonballs and barely felt the shock.

Just as Web righted himself, Dooley rolled against the big gun and looked at the carnage around Cahill's broken cannon. The sight pulled a wail of terror from his mouth. His whole body shook as he looked on with fists clenched. He stood there, wailing over and over in a paroxysm of blind horror. Quickly, Web grabbed his shoulder, spun him around and slapped him. The wailing stopped instantly. Dooley's bulging eyes focused on Steele as his hand went to the burning spot on his cheek.

Grasping both shoulders hard, Web said, "Get a grip on yourself, Dooley!"

The freckle-faced youth blinked and went limp. Looking at Sheldon, Web said, "Talk to him, Leroy. I've got to check on the lieutenant."

Dashing to Daniel Hart and the unconscious Courtman, Web found Daniel weeping. Courtman had taken shrapnel in his chest, arms, and face. Though he was bleeding and his shirt was tattered, none of the metal pieces seemed to have gone deep enough to threaten his life.

Tears streamed down Daniel's face as he sobbed, "Why was I spared, Web? If that shell had hit ten seconds sooner, I'd have been killed, too!"

Web saw Courtman's horse lying on the ground, neighing in pain. To Daniel he said, "I'll carry him back to the camp. Take my musket and put that horse out of its misery, will you?"

As young Hart was rising to his feet, wiping tears, Web turned and shouted, "Leroy! You and Dooley fire the cannon where I've got it aimed! I'll be back in a few minutes!"

Suddenly there was an eruption of gunfire deep in the woods to the west. Web looked that way and said, "Daniel, now that those Yankees have topped the mountain back there, it won't be safe for the lieutenant in the camp. There's no place really safe, so let's just lay him here next to his horse."

Running to his cannon, which Leroy had just fired, Web snatched up his musket and raced for the wounded horse. Aiming the gun at its head, he cocked the hammer and squeezed the trigger. Rushing back to Daniel, he said, "Go help my guys reload. I'll be there in a minute."

Web carried Lieutenant Courtman to the dead horse and laid him as close to the animal's back as possible. Courtman was starting to come around, but Web couldn't wait. He had to get back to his gun. He would get help for the lieutenant as soon as possible.

He was halfway back to the cannon when the sky seemed to

open up and a torrent of rain came down. When he reached Daniel and his men, he cried, "We'll keep firing until it's impossible! Dooley, are you all right?"

"I'm okay, Web," replied Dooley, blinking rain from his eyes. "Thanks for popping me one. I needed it."

Web was about to tell Daniel to go back and see to Lieutenant Courtman when it suddenly struck him that there was no more artillery fire coming from the Union guns. "They've given up already on firing their cannons," he said to the others. "I've an idea we'll see infantry any second."

The musketry was going strong in the timber. Web and his companions looked back that way, then their heads jerked around as shouts met their ears from the east ridge. Hundreds of Yankees were emerging from the trees and running onto the open field. They looked like ants coming out of a giant anthill.

Turning to Sheldon, Web asked, "Is the gun loaded?"

"Ready to fire!"

Wiping rain from his eyes, Web stepped to his big gun. As he turned the crank to lower the muzzle, he heard three of the cannons along the line open up. The shells screamed down the grassy slope. None of them reached the front line of men-in-blue, but their explosions sent many of them scattering.

When he had the range-finder at the right spot, Web yanked the lanyard. The twenty-four pounder belched fire and smoke as it roared. Seconds later, the shell dropped into the front line and blew Yankee soldiers in every direction.

The three men beside him let out a whoop.

"Quick!" said Steele. "Load it again before the rain douses the powder."

As Sheldon and Carson hopped to it, Web turned to Hart and said, "Go check on the lieutenant, will you? Maybe the rain has revived him. See what you can do to stop the bleeding."

Daniel was turning to go when there were wild shouts and

whoops coming from the south end of the mountain. Through the falling rain, they saw countless blue uniforms swarming out of the timber. Just as abruptly, musket fire came from the forest to the west, and the Yankees began to fall. Men-in-gray charged at them, and the land battle was under way.

At the same time, their attention was drawn to the north, where Union soldiers were sallying up the path by the hundreds. Again, Confederate muskets opened fire. The Battle of Rich Mountain was in full force.

Daniel said, "Web, I don't have a gun. My musket went up when my cannon was hit."

"Use the lieutenant's revolver. Get down beside that horse and do everything you can to protect him."

Daniel ran toward the fallen officer. Returning to his cannon, Web turned the crank to meet the front line of Yankees, which was getting closer, and fired. The shell whined down the slope and landed in the middle of a tight-knit bunch.

Dooley said, "Web, the rain's gotten into the magazine—we can't fire the gun any more!"

A swarm of Confederate infantrymen bowled out of the timber behind Web and his men, running past them to meet the oncoming charge.

"Okay, boys!" he cried. "We're down to our muskets now! Do all you can to keep your powder dry."

The cannon crew had dug out a spot next to the big gun when they were stabilizing it. Dashing into it, they flattened out. While Web was reloading his musket, Dooley said, "None of 'em are in rifle range yet!"

"They will be soon. Be ready!"

All across the top of Rich Mountain, the thundering roll of musketry was deafening. Shouts, loud commands, and screams of dying men were barely heard in the din.

Soon the rain let up, but the fighting only intensified. Within an hour, there was no rain at all, but the sky remained cloudy and threatening.

The battle raged. Soon there was a long line of infantrymen stretched out on both sides of Web and his partners. Web kept an eye on Daniel and the lieutenant, but so far no one had gotten near them. Also of concern was Dooley. He was firing and reloading as fast as he could, but his face was showing the strain. Web knew that even if Dooley held himself together under gunfire, it was liable to change quickly if the fight got down to bayonets.

Blue-white smoke drifted across Rich Mountain like a heavy fog. The acrid smell of burnt gunpowder hung in the air.

From his prone position with Carson on his right and Sheldon on his left, Web brought down three Yankees with five shots. Bullets were chewing ground all around them and whizzing over their heads like angry hornets. More Yankees were coming over the eastern edge of the mountain.

Leroy had just fired a shot and was reloading when a bullet hissed and struck him between the eyes. He fell back, dead. Dooley saw it and began to sob.

"Nothing we can do for him, kid," Web said levelly. "Don't panic. You've got to keep firing."

Leroy had often spoken of a girl named Bonnie Sue. She was waiting for him back home in eastern Virginia. Web wondered how long it would be before Bonnie Sue would learn that the man she was waiting for was dead. His mind flashed to Abby. No doubt she thought he had died in the fire. God willing, he thought, I'll go home to her someday when this is over.

When the rain stopped, David Hart was in the woods with a Yankee corporal named Jimmy Dyer. General Rosecrans had assigned Dyer to stay with David and do what he could to keep him alive. The general didn't want the death of a civilian on his conscience if it could be avoided.

Packing the musket he had been issued, David was crawling with Dyer toward the edge of the woods on the east side. Gunfire was all around them.

When they reached a spot about twenty yards from the open field, they beheld the raging, bloody battle with awe. Presently, Dyer focused on two men in gray who were lying low behind a dead horse not more than sixty feet from the edge of the trees. One man was flat on his back. The other was up on one elbow with his back toward the woods, tending to him.

"Looks like we got one Reb taking care of another," Dyer said in a low voice. "Since it's my job to kill Southerners, this one gets it right now." As he spoke, the corporal cocked his musket and took aim.

"You're not going to shoot him in the back, are you?" asked David, feeling his stomach go cold.

"What do you want me to do? Shake hands with him?"

"No, but it's hard for me to see a man get shot in the back."

"Bet he'd do it to me," said Dyer, and squeezed the trigger.

The Confederate soldier spasmed at the impact of the bullet, arching his back. His cap fell off as he rolled over, exposing his face. David focused on the familiar features in choked-off silence. His hands palsied as he threw them to his cheeks. He found his voice and scrambled to his feet, gasping, "It's my brother! It's my brother! You shot my brother!"

Stunned at what he was hearing, Dyer leaped up as David bolted out of the trees, crying, "Daniel! Daniel!"

Bullets were splitting the air all around. Dyer darted to the edge of the timber and shouted, "Hart, come back here!"

At that instant, a Yankee bullet struck Dyer in the heart. The impact knocked him down. His right foot trembled for a few seconds before he died.

Daniel looked up with languid eyes as David knelt beside him. Lieutenant Courtman had been conscious earlier, but had passed out again shortly before Daniel was shot.

"Daniel!" sobbed David, noting that the bullet had passed through his brother's body and exited his chest. Blood was spreading over the front of his sweaty shirt.

Daniel gritted his teeth in pain, set his dull eyes on David and worked his jaw, trying to speak.

"Daniel! Oh, Daniel, I'm so sorry! I didn't know it was you!" cried David.

Daniel licked his lips, worked his jaw again, and mumbled softly, "I...I didn't know you had joined the Union army, David. Many...many brothers will kill each other in this war."

"No, Daniel! It wasn't me who shot you! It was—Daniel! Daniel!"

Daniel's eyes stared vacantly into space. His breathing had stopped.

David held Daniel in his arms and wailed, "I didn't kill you! I didn't kill you! Daniel, don't die thinking I shot you!"

Web fired a shot and lay on his side to reload his musket. Bullets were flying all around. Through the blue-white smoke, he saw David Hart holding Daniel next to the dead horse. Shocked to see David, Web shouted, "David! Get down! Get down!"

But David did not hear him for the thunder of the gunfire and the sound of his own wailing.

Laying his musket down, Web shouted above the din to Dooley, "I'll be right back!"

Dooley started to ask where he was going, but Web was already darting away. Diving flat as he reached the spot, Steele took one look at Daniel's vacant eyes and knew he was gone. David's face was dirty and streaked with tears. He stopped wailing when he recognized his old friend and shuddered, "Web, Daniel's dead. He thought I shot him. I didn't, Web! I didn't shoot him!"

"What are you doing here, David?" asked Steele. "You're not in uniform!"

"I only led a unit of Yankees up the back side of the mountain, Web. I'm not in the army."

Taking hold of David's arm, Web said, "C'mon, let's get you back into the trees. You'll be safer there."

"Not without Daniel!" David shouted.

There wasn't time to argue. "All right. Pick him up. But hurry."

The shock David was feeling had sapped his strength. Web took the limp form from him and said, "Head for the trees!"

David staggered ahead of Web, noting the body of Corporal Dyer as he passed. Once they were deep in the timber, Web laid Daniel's body down beside a fallen tree and said, "David, get down next to the tree and stay there till this battle is over."

Just as he was about to head back to his post, Web looked up to see a lone Yankee soldier taking aim at him from behind a tree. He dived for the ground in the nick of time as the bullet whizzed over his head. Rolling over and gaining his feet, he saw the Yankee charging at him with his bayonet. Web feinted as if he would leap to the right, then quickly moved left as the man-in-blue sailed past him. The Yankee cursed, pivoted quickly, and came at him again. Web spotted a broken tree limb about five feet in length lying near his feet. He snatched it up, sidestepped the charging enemy again, and cracked him on the back of the head.

The Yankee stumbled and fell. Web grabbed the musket from the man's hands and rammed the bayonet through his heart. Dashing back to David, Web told him again to stay put, and ran to his post.

The battle raged on. By three in the afternoon, Web, Dooley, Wiley Chance, and Billy Bob Hankins had moved back into the edge of the timber and were firing from a shallow draw. Dead men in blue and gray were scattered all over the open field and in the deep shade of the forest.

While Web and his companions were defending their position, Exley crept through the timber, carrying a Navy Colt .45 he had taken from a dead Union officer. He had spotted Web in the shallow draw only moments before. When he was within fifty feet to the rear of them, he wriggled into the midst of a stand of heavy brush and waited. When his opportunity came, Web would get a bullet in the back.

Steele, Carson, Chance, and Hankins had been firing from the draw for over an hour when Chance noticed six Yankees bolt from the trees to their far right, muskets blazing. He had just loaded his own gun. Swinging it on them, he fired and shouted to his companions.

One of the charging Yankees went down, but so did Chance with two slugs in his chest. Billy Bob Hankins took a bullet in the midsection, but was able to fire and drop one of the men-in-blue before he fell.

Angry bullets buzzed by Steele and Carson, one of them coming so close to Steele's right ear that he felt its hot breath. Both of them pivoted to meet the four Yankees who were coming on the run, bayonets gleaming. Dooley Carson focused on the hungry bayonets and his whole body seemed to freeze.

Web fired his gun and braced himself for the onslaught. His bullet took out one Yankee, who fell flat on his face. The other three had blood in their eyes. Two went for Steele, leaving the other one to take out Carson.

Suddenly Dooley found his courage and shot one of the two men bearing down on Web. Then he swung his bayonet on the Yankee coming at him, but the man dodged it and rammed his sharp blade into Dooley's left side. Dooley cried out and fell when the man jerked the bayonet out. He was about to finish Dooley off when he saw that his partner was in trouble. Steele had knocked him down with the butt of his musket and was about to plunge his bayonet into him.

Carson's man wheeled and bolted toward Web, bayonet poised for his back. Dooley cried, "Web! Look out!"

Web spun around to meet his attacker, parrying the bayonet thrust with his musket. Both men fought for survival, bayonets and musket butts swinging.

Gripping his bleeding side, Dooley struggled to his feet, eyes fixed on the other Yankee, who was getting up with musket in hand. Web's back was toward him, and the resolve in his eyes was obvious. He would end the fight by plunging his bayonet into the Rebel's back. The determined Yankee was moving toward Web, bayonet thrust forward. Ignoring his pain, Dooley dashed past the two combatants and threw himself between Web and the deadly bayonet.

Web had just killed the other Yankee and was turning about when he saw the cold steel of the Union bayonet being rammed full-haft into Dooley's chest. He knew what the freckle-faced kid had done. Moving quickly, Web thrust his bayonet into the Yankee's throat. The man emitted a gurgling scream and collapsed.

Dooley fell with the bayonet still buried in him. Breathing hard and oblivious to the roar of the battle around him, Steele dropped his gun, took hold of the Yankee musket, and pulled the bayonet from Dooley's chest. Tears gushed from Web's eyes as he knelt beside Dooley's lifeless form.

In the midst of the fire, smoke, and thunder of the battle, Mandrake crawled through the dense forest, his black skin blending with the deep shadows. His heart was pounding. Only moments before, good fortune had smiled upon him. He knew the odds of finding Reed Exley amid the battle were slim, but he had only one purpose left in life. Even the heavy rain that had fallen earlier, obscuring visibility on top of the mountain, had not deterred him. The search went on even though he knew that a stray bullet might find him at any moment, or some soldier on either side might mistake him for the enemy and gun him down.

Then, just moments before, Mandrake had spotted Exley. He was alone, working his way amongst the trees as if he had some destination in mind. Mandrake followed, but was forced into hiding when a small unit of Rebel soldiers came charging his way. When they were gone, Mandrake took up the pursuit again, but had lost sight of Exley.

Crawling persistently with the revolver in his hand, Mandrake maintained a set course, aiming the same direction Exley had gone. He would find him and kill him, or lose his own life in the attempt.

Mandrake was inching his way through the timber near the edge of the open field, where most of the battle was concentrated, when his attention was drawn to a hand-to-hand battle taking place in a shallow draw some thirty yards ahead. At first, he could not believe what his eyes were telling him. One of the fighting Rebels looked exactly like Web Steele. But it couldn't be! Massa Web was dead.

To get a better view, Mandrake crawled closer and positioned himself in a stand of heavy brush. The gunfire all around him was deafening as once again he set his gaze on the nearby fight and the man who so strongly resembled Web Steele.

Cold chills went all over him. It was Web! He had not died in the prison fire as Jedidiah had mistakenly told him! *Massa Web is alive!* The shock paralyzed the black man. He wanted to rush in and help his friend, but he could not make himself move.

Mandrake watched as Steele and a boyish Rebel were engaged in a life-and-death struggle with two Yankees. Just then he saw movement in the clump of brush next to him. He peered through the maze of thin branches and saw the form of a man. The man raised up, exposing his gray-capped head. Though Mandrake was lying below him, and a bit to his rear, he recognized Reed Exley.

The deafening sound of battle assaulted Exley's ears as he hunkered in the clump of brush and watched the hand-to-hand battle. He hoped the Yankees would kill Web and save him the trouble. He would like the pleasure of sending the hated man into eternity, but the main thing was to see him dead and out of the way. Exley would then have Abby for himself.

Exley was disappointed when the last of the Yankees in the draw went down. Web Steele was still alive. Swearing under his breath as Web knelt beside the young Rebel who had taken a bayonet for him, Exley eased back the hammer of his revolver. Steele's broad back was conveniently turned toward him.

Quickly Exley raised his head above the top of the bushes and looked around. The battle was still going strong all over the mountain, but no one was looking his direction. He would shoot Steele and let them think a Yankee did it. Exley grinned and drew a careful bead at a spot between Web's shoulder blades. His heart pounded with excitement as he took a deep breath, held it, and placed his forefinger on the trigger.

Web knelt over Dooley and said with quivering lips, "You took the thing you feared most to save my life. God bless you, Dooley. You're a hero, my friend—a real hero."

Though the sound of muskets continued on the open field, Web's attention was abruptly captured by the discharge of a handgun behind him. He whipped around to see a black man rising to his feet beside a stand of brush, holding a smoking revolver. He was stunned to see a Negro on the mountain at all, but when he recognized Mandrake, he was doubly stunned. He thumbed away tears and rose to his feet, so caught up in seeing Mandrake that he forgot the danger.

Suddenly two Union soldiers burst from the woods off to Mandrake's left, firing at Web Steele. One bullet hissed past Web's hip, but the other one struck him in the right leg.

Mandrake spun around. Cocking his revolver, he raised it and fired, hitting the Yankee closest to him. When the other one veered his direction with a wild yell, aiming his bayonet at him, Mandrake snapped back the hammer and shot him point-blank in the heart.

Mandrake ran to Web and found him in a half-sitting position, gripping his wounded leg above the knee. Blood was running between his fingers.

"Massa Web!" gasped Mandrake. "Is it bad?"

Gritting his teeth, Web replied, "I think the slug hit the bone and broke it, but I'll live. What are you doing here?"

"I came to find Reed Exley and kill him, Massa Web," said the muscular black man. "C'mon. Let me he'p you get back in the woods, where it'll be a li'l safer."

"You came up on this mountain to kill Reed Exley?"

"Yassuh," said Mandrake, picking Steele up in his arms, "an' I done it, too."

"You did?"

"Yassuh," Mandrake responded, carrying his wounded friend toward the thick stand of brush where Web had first spotted him.

"When?" queried Steele, still gripping the wounded leg.

"Jus' befo' you saw me. Exley was hidin' right here in these bushes, and was 'bout to shoot you in the back when I saw 'im."

Mandrake placed Web on the ground beside the heavy bush where Reed Exley's body lay half-supported by branches. His legs were still hung up inside the bush, but his torso was bent chest-up, with his head touching the ground. Web could see that Exley had been shot through the head from behind at close range. The cocked Navy Colt was still in Exley's right hand.

"That's twice my life has been saved today, Mandrake," Web told him with a quiver in his voice. "Thank you."

"No need to thank me, Massa Web," the black man said humbly. "As I tol' you, I was gonna kill him anyway. 'Course when I seen that he was aimin' to shoot you, it made it even easier. Now, let's see 'bout stoppin' this bleedin' in yo' leg."

Mandrake used a dead Yankee's belt to make a tourniquet, then tore up the man's shirt to use as a bandage. While he did, he asked Web how he escaped the prison fire and ended up in uniform on top of Rich Mountain. After Web had explained it all, Mandrake described what he had been told by Jedidiah, which confirmed that everyone at home thought he had died in the fire. Web was elated to learn of Hec Wheeler's confession, and that he had been cleared of the murder charge.

As the sun lowered toward the west, the sounds of battle began to dwindle. Web asked Mandrake why he was so intent on killing Exley that he would follow him all the way to Rich Mountain. Mandrake wept and told him of Orchid's death at Harper's Ferry, saying that without her, life had no meaning. The only thing he lived for from the moment Horatio Clements informed him of Orchid's death was to kill the man responsible.

Gritting his teeth in pain, Web asked, "So what now?"

Mandrake's eyes misted. "Well, Massa Web, I'd have somethin' to live fo' if'n you'd let me be yo' willin' slave."

"First thing we've got to do is get out of this situation alive," groaned Steele. "Then we'll make our plans. One thing, though…"

"Yassuh?"

"How about if we call you my servant instead of my slave, and I pay you wages?"

"I'll leave that up to you, Massa Web. I jus' wan' to serve you an' Miz Abby fo' the res' o' my days. An' don' you worry none. I'll get both of us off this here mountain so's we can get you an' that beautiful lady back togethuh."

TWENTY-THREE

As the sun went down over Rich Mountain, the fighting began to diminish. By dusk, no more gunfire could be heard.

Colonel John Pegram knew that he and his troops were hopelessly outnumbered. They would never survive another day of battling General George McClellan's forces. Though the gallant Confederates had killed and wounded a great number of the enemy, they had sustained the greater losses.

Even before it was completely dark, Pegram had wagons on the move, picking up as many wounded Rebels as possible. They would slip off the mountain under cover of darkness and join General Robert Garnett at Laurel Mountain.

Lieutenant Floyd Courtman was picked up still alive, along with David Hart, who insisted on taking Daniel's body with him. Though Hart had aided the Union, they would allow him to return to his home in Beverly unmolested because his brother had died fighting as a Confederate soldier.

Some time later, another wagon picked up Private Webster Steele. Mandrake refused to leave Web and was allowed to go along. They gathered some other wounded men, and made it off Rich Mountain without being detected by Union soldiers.

Concerned for the lives of his wounded men, Pegram immediately sent the wagons southeastward to the town of Mt. Meridian on the Shenandoah River. The colonel knew Mt. Meridian had a small hospital. Union sympathizers were scarce in the town. His wounded men would be welcomed and given proper medical attention.

During the night ride to Mt. Meridian, Web—with his faithful servant beside him—was able to learn from one of the wagon drivers that David Hart had been allowed to go home to Beverly and take Daniel's body with him. Web wondered if David would attempt to let his parents and Lynne Ruffin know of Daniel's death. There was no telling how long it might be before the Confederate government would be able to advise families of those killed or wounded in action. Web's heart went out to Lynne. The news of Daniel's death—whenever it reached her—would hit her hard. It would be tough on Daniel's parents also. Web hoped that somehow Daniel's death would draw David and his parents back together.

Unable to sleep because of the jostling of the wagon and the pain, Web leaned on Mandrake's shoulder and thought about Abby. Was he wounded bad enough that the army would discharge him? Or would they patch him up and send him back into the war? How long would the war last? When would he see Abby again? These were questions no one could answer.

Colonel Pegram found Laurel Mountain virtually inaccessible because of the great number of Union troops in the area. Not knowing how the battle had gone at Laurel Mountain, nor having any way to communicate with General Garnett, Pegram had no choice but to pull what was left of his unit out of the region before dawn. He hated to leave his dead men on top of the mountain, but he had no choice. To stay till morning and face McClellan's huge force would produce only more dead men.

At dawn on July 12, General William Rosecrans found that the

Confederate troops had abandoned their position on Rich Mountain without alerting his weary men on night guard duty. The enemy's whereabouts could not be discovered.

On Laurel Mountain, General Garnett's scouts soon reported the situation. Learning that Pegram had taken his men and fled into the night, Garnett knew his position was desperate. He had suffered the loss of many men in the previous day's battle. The decision was made to abandon Laurel Mountain immediately.

They had been off the mountain for only a short time, marching hastily northeastward, when General McClellan learned of it. Quickly he sent Brigadier General Thomas Morris and his brigade in pursuit.

The next morning Morris's brigade caught up with Garnett and his troops at Carrick's Ford on the Cheat River, some thirty miles from Rich Mountain. The Confederates fought hard, but lack of ammunition left them vulnerable. In the brief encounter that took place, General Garnett was shot and killed.

Because Garnett was the first Civil War general to be killed in action, and because of the way the Union army had put the Confederates to flight, the Battle of Rich Mountain constituted a victory for the federal forces. General McClellan was summoned to Washington by President Lincoln and commissioned as Supreme Commander of the Union Army.

Northern newspapers took advantage of the Union victory to heap indignities on the South, which gave Northern citizens something to cheer about. It also gave them the elated notion that the Confederates were unable to withstand Union military might, and with the war movement getting into full swing, the Confederacy would soon be defeated.

However, on July 21, the Union army suffered a much worse defeat in a bloody battle on Bull Run Creek near Manassas Junction. The Bull Run rout changed the tune of Northern newspapers, which admitted in print that it was going to be a long war, after all.

Private Webster Steele was treated at the Mt. Meridian hospital, along with the other Confederate soldiers who had been wounded at Rich Mountain. Medical doctors in sympathy with the Confederacy were called in from several surrounding towns.

Surgery was performed on Web's leg to remove bone splinters. Because the bone was shattered, he was advised by army officials that when he was ready to travel for home, he would be released from the army. His doctors said Web would walk again, but he would limp for the rest of his life.

During Web's recovery, Mandrake stayed at his side day and night. Through Southern newspapers and *Harper's Weekly* magazine, Web kept up with the progress of the war. After the Bull Run battle, there were numerous minor battles and skirmishes between the opposing forces. Everyone knew another big battle was due, but no one could predict where it might happen.

On August 17, Web's doctors released him. He was discharged from the Confederate army at Harper's Ferry on August 20 and put on a military train for Richmond that same day. With Mandrake on the seat beside him, he could hardly hold back the tears for the elation within him. Tomorrow he would hold Abby in his arms.

It was late morning on Wednesday, August 21, 1861, when Charles opened the front door of the Ruffin mansion in response to the sound of the knocker. Only a breathless gasp came from the butler when first he set eyes on the man on crutches.

Smiling, Web said, "Hello, Charles. How are you?"

"I…I'm fine, Mister Web," the butler was finally able to get out. "I'm…just shocked to see you. I…I thought—"

"That I was dead? In the prison fire?"

"Yes, sir. That's what we all thought. But allow me to say, I am certainly happy to see you alive!" Then looking at Mandrake, the butler said with a smile, "Jedidiah told us you had gone north, Mandrake."

"Yassuh. I thought Massa Web was dead too, by what Jedidiah tol' me. Was only the han' of the Lord that put me where he was so's we could meet up again. I sho' was mighty glad to fin' him alive."

"Have you seen your parents yet, Mister Web?" asked Charles.

"Yes. I stopped at my parents' place. Needless to say, they were both shocked and pleased."

"Yes, sir," said Charles.

"Is Miss Abby at home?" queried Web, his throat tightening.

"Yes, sir," nodded the butler. "She's up in her room at the moment. She's...uh...she's not been too well, Mister Web."

Web's face blanched. "She's sick? How bad?"

Charles put his hand to his forehead. "Oh, please forgive me, Mister Web. Here I am, making you stand at the door. Please come in. You too, Mandrake."

Charles closed the door behind them, then with Web hobbling on his crutches, he led them to the receiving area, where the broad staircase wound upward. Pointing to a small couch, the butler asked, "Would you like to sit down, Mister Web?"

"Not at the moment, thank you. Right now I want to know about Miss Abby's illness."

"Well, sir, it's—"

At that instant, John Ruffin appeared, having come from the library, and gasped, "Web!"

Ruffin rushed to the wounded man and embraced him. Then with tears on his cheeks, he asked how Web had escaped the prison fire and how he had hurt his leg.

Web said, "I'll explain it all to you in a moment, Papa John, but first I want to know about Abby's illness."

"Illness?" echoed John, his brow furrowing. "What are you talking about?"

"Charles said she has not been well."

"Please allow me to explain," spoke up the butler. "What I

meant was that Miss Abby has been having an awful time accepting your...death. She is not ill physically. I meant that she's not been too well emotionally." A grin spread over his face. "But she'll get well in a hurry now."

John laid a hand on Web's shoulder and said, "Abby's had such a hard time of it, Web. I knew she loved you, but I guess I never knew how much. There've been all kinds of young men here with intentions of courting her, but she won't even see them."

Web smiled. A promise unbroken, he thought to himself. Then to Ruffin he said, "I'll tell you all about my escape from the fire and all that after I see Abby. Charles said she's up in her room. May I go up and see her now?"

John looked at the old grandfather clock in the corner. "Well, you'll have to give it a few minutes, son. Right now, Abby's personal attendant is helping her with her bath."

"Personal attendant?"

John nodded and looked at Mandrake. "Excuse me, Mandrake," he said with a smile. "I haven't even spoken to you. Jedidiah told me you were here several weeks ago, and gone again. I wasn't sure if we'd ever see you around here any more. Especially since Web had set you free."

Mandrake smiled in return. "I'm still free, Massa John, but from now on, I's gonna be Massa Web's personal 'tendant. That'll be somethin', won' it? If'n Miz Abby keeps her personal 'tendant after she marries Massa Web, there'll be two personal 'tendants 'round their house."

"Oh, she'll keep her all right, Mandrake," chuckled John.

"Tell me about this attendant, Papa John," said Web.

"Nothing much to tell, son. Abby just needed another female to be close to her. Your...death left a real empty spot in her life. This young lady has been a real help to her."

Web thought of Lynne and said cautiously, "How about Lynne, Papa John? Is...is she doing all right?"

"You mean since she learned of Daniel's death?"

"Yes, sir. I saw my parents before coming here, and they told me she's spending some time at the Hart place these days."

"Lynne feels the Harts need comfort just about as much as she does. She's been there a lot since word came from the government."

"How long ago did the Harts get word?" asked Web.

"About ten days ago."

"I was with Daniel at Rich Mountain, Papa John. That's where I got this leg shot up."

"Really? Then you probably saw Reed there, too?"

Web and Mandrake exchanged quick glances.

"That's right," nodded Web.

"I got word of his death just about a week ago," said John. "Guess it takes the government quite a while to report all the deaths in battle."

"Yes, sir."

Looking serious, John said, "Web, I owe you an apology. A big apology. I was wrong about Reed, and I know it now. Did Mandrake tell you what Jedidiah told him about Hec Wheeler's confession and your being cleared?"

"Yes, sir."

"Well, Reed had me fooled, but that opened my eyes. Reed would've been convicted and hanged if he had lived to come home. I...I guess it's best that he died on the battlefield, fighting for the Confederacy. At least with him dying as a hero, it goes better for our family, wouldn't you say?"

Again Web and Mandrake exchanged glances.

"Sure. Lots better," nodded Web.

John looked at the clock and said, "Well, I know you're eager to see Abby. She should be presentable right soon, I would think. You can tell me all about how you escaped the prison fire and ended up in the army after you and she have had your reunion." Clapping his hands together, he laughed, "I sure wish I could be a fly on the wall when you walk into her room!"

There was movement at the top of the spiral staircase. Every eye flashed to the spot, thinking it might be Abby. Instead, it was Abby's attendant, clad in a brilliant white, starched dress. Her dark skin stood out in lovely contrast.

Web stood speechless at the sight of her, but it was Mandrake who was in a state of numb shock. He blinked and shook his head as if he had suddenly been swept into a heavenly dream.

At the top of the stairs, smiling and eyes brimming with tears, was the most beautiful woman Mandrake had ever seen. Orchid opened her arms and virtually glided down the stairs.

There was not a dry eye in the room as Mandrake and Orchid embraced, wept, and held each other tight. When the initial impact of the stunning surprise had eased, Orchid told Mandrake how she had escaped from Horatio Clements's place. She told about the bullet the guard had put in her side and how she had toppled into the Potomac River. Maintaining consciousness, Orchid had floated downstream a ways until she caught hold of some foliage along the bank. She was able to crawl out and make it to a small cottage near the river, where a widow woman took her in, summoned a doctor, and saw to it that she was given proper medical attention. The widow kept her until she was able to travel, then had her merchant son, who sometimes does business in Richmond, bring her home. She had arrived on July 11, the same day the battle had been fought on Rich Mountain.

Miss Abby, who was so torn up over Web's death, welcomed her, and asked Papa John if Orchid could be hired as her attendant. John was glad to do so. Since then Orchid had been living for the day her wandering husband might come home.

Holding her tight and still weeping, Mandrake looked at Web and said, "Looks like yo's and Miz Abby's household really is gonna have two personal 'tendants, Massa Web."

Smiling broadly, Web said, "I wouldn't have it any other way, my friend."

Orchid looked into Mandrake's eyes and said, "Could you let go of me long enough fo' me to give Massa Web a hug?"

"Long as it don' las' too long," grinned the happy black man.

Orchid embraced Web, then looked up at him and said, "Massa Web, that sweet lady upstairs is gonna think she's dreamin' when she sees you. But you jus' squeeze her so hard she'll know yo' real, will you?"

Balancing on his crutches, Web smiled and said, "You can count on it!"

As Orchid went back to Mandrake's arms, Web ran his gaze up the winding staircase. He could feel all eyes in the room on him as he climbed the stairs adeptly, using the crutches. When he reached the top of the landing, he looked back.

John Ruffin was wiping tears. "Sure wish I could be a fly on the wall!" he said again, lips quivering.

Web grinned, then turned and hobbled quietly down the hallway, his heart drumming his ribs. When he reached the spot, he took a deep breath, let it out slowly, and tapped on Abby's door.

EPILOGUE

When the Civil War came to an end, David Hart of Beverly, West Virginia, published a small book telling of his experience in the Battle of Rich Mountain. Still a Union enthusiast and a true patriot to the Northern cause, he wrote in part, "Our boys lit into those Rebels with their Enfield and Minié rifles, and I never heard such screaming in my life. The whole earth seemed to shake."

Edmund Ruffin, the South's secessionist leader who fired the first shot at Fort Sumter, joined the Palmetto Guard—a South Carolina militia unit—six days after Major Robert Anderson surrendered the fort to General Beauregard. At the time, Ruffin was sixty-seven years of age. He fought with that unit, facing Union guns and artillery on several occasions.

General Robert E. Lee signed the documents of surrender at Appomattox Court House on April 9, 1865. Nine days later, the seventy-one-year-old Ruffin took the rifle he had used to fight the Union and turned it on himself, committing suicide. The fall of the Confederacy was more than he could stand.

BOOK TWO

A HEART
DIVIDED

BATTLE OF MOBILE BAY

To my beloved parents, Charlie and Patty O'Brien Lacy:

It was you, Pop, who first put a Western
book in my hands...Zane Grey's *Wildfire*.
In my formative years, you encouraged me
to read and appreciate good literature about
the Old West. This developed as you hoped
it would. I soon learned to love and value
America's heritage, and eventually began to
write Western and historical novels.

And precious Mama...thank you for
believing in me, and for the unfailing love
and encouragement you showed me over
the years. You have a vital part, too, in every
novel I write. When at the beginning I
faced the seeming insurmountable
challenge of producing great numbers of
books, it was your sage words that impelled
me to take on the task. You've told people
many times, "From a very small child, Al
always was good at making up stories!"

PROLOGUE

When the first Confederate shell arched through the predawn
sky and exploded behind the walls of Fort Sumter on April
12, 1861, it touched off one of the greatest points of crisis
in the history of America. Not only did the War Between the States
quickly develop into a bloody conflict between two societies with opposite views on slavery, but it moved inexorably toward something
almost unthinkable—a tragic clash between families. Brothers fighting brothers, even fathers fighting sons.

In the century between the end of the Napoleonic Wars and
the commencement of World War I, the most catastrophic military
conflict fought anywhere was the American Civil War. Some historians have alluded to the Civil War as a combination of "The Last
Medieval War and the First Modern War." I agree. As the first modern war, it ominously foreshadowed the horrors of warfare that have
followed in the twentieth century.

The Civil War introduced trench warfare, propaganda, warfare
of psychological attrition, aerial observation, naval blockade, economic warfare, iron-clad ships, and the Gatling gun, as well as the
horrible impeding influence of filthy, disease-ridden, prisoner-of-war
camps.

Compulsory enlistment for military service was also put into use for the first time in American history during the four-year war between the North and the South. Both sides began using conscription when the War was two years old. Prior to that, and even after conscription was adopted, both armies had problems with teenage boys lying about their age in order to get in the fight. Both the North and the South had set the youngest age limit at eighteen, but often the deceitful youths were accepted because they looked to be old enough.

The Civil War brought about many other firsts. It was the first war to have photographers taking pictures on the battlefield. It was the first war to employ repeating rifles, and to use railroad artillery, naval torpedoes, flame throwers, land mines, electrically exploded bombs, telescopic sights for rifles, fixed ammunition, the wigwag signal code, and periscopes for fighting in the trenches. During the Civil War, the bugle call, "Taps" was first played, the first naval camouflage was invented, and the Congressional Medal of Honor was first introduced.

With all of its firsts in modern warfare and the hatred that raged between the North and the South, the Civil War cost more American lives in the four years from Sumter to Appomattox than the two World Wars, Korea, Vietnam, and Desert Storm *combined*. The carnage that took place between April 1861 and April 1865 was appalling. Of the three million men who saw action afloat and ashore—Union and Confederate—more than a million were casualties. Well over 600,000 lost their lives as a direct result of battlefield combat (including those who were wounded, then died of infections and various diseases contracted because of their wounds). Another 400,000 were wounded, but lived to tell of the horrors of the war. Many of them were blinded, and a great number lost limbs. Some could not tell of the war's horror because they lost their minds.

This virtual caldron of blood was spread wider than the casual follower of the Civil War realizes. According to government authorities, there were some 95 major battles, 310 minor battles, and over

6,000 skirmishes, some of which the soldiers themselves called "squabbles" or "dust-ups." If a man died in a "dust-up" he was just as dead as if he had been killed in a major battle. The bulk of the fighting took place on Southern land. However, a few battles were fought on Union soil, including two of the bloodiest—Gettysburg and Antietam. Blood was shed in land-fighting as far north as Vermont, and as far west as the Pacific coast. California saw 6 skirmishes, Oregon 4, and 19 occurred in New Mexico Territory. There were other skirmishes in the territories of Washington, Utah, and Idaho.

The fighting in Vermont was a result of Confederate raiders striking the town of St. Albans. Other Rebel raiders shed blood in Illinois, Minnesota, and New York. The southernmost fighting happened between Union and Confederate forces on a blood-soaked sandy beach in Florida known today as Cape Canaveral.

The story I am about to tell you begins on the Gulf of Mexico, just off the Florida coast at Pensacola, some six hundred miles northwest of that beach. Before we get into the story, it is important that I point out a few things about the naval part of the Civil War.

At the very beginning of the War—only days after the Union flag was lowered in surrender at Fort Sumter—President Abraham Lincoln formally ordered a blockade of the entire coast of the Confederacy, from Chesapeake Bay, whose waters lapped the shoreline of Virginia, all the way to the southernmost tip of Texas. Lincoln knew that if the North was going to win the War, it had to take control of a dozen major ports and some two hundred minor ports and inlets.

The reason was two-fold. If the Union could block the ports and inlets, it could prevent the Confederacy from receiving supplies, weapons, and ammunition from foreign sympathizers. On the other hand, by seizing the ports and inlets, the Federals would be able to float in their own troops, weapons, ammunition, supplies, mules, and horses that were necessary to conquer the Confederacy.

Lincoln's call for a Union blockade of the entire Confederate coast was a tall order. At the beginning of the War, the Federal government possessed some ninety warships, but fifty of these were sailing vessels that had been used a generation before, and were now obsolete. Of the forty steam-driven ships, half were docked at foreign harbors, and it would take time to get them back into home waters.

Ready for immediate service were five steam frigates, five first-class screw sloops, four flat-bedded steam-driven barges, a half-dozen tugboats, and a few small assorted harbor craft. With this small navy, the Federals were commanded by President Lincoln to blockade and control over thirty-five hundred miles of Confederate coast line. They had, also, to control such rivers as the Mississippi and the Tennessee, not to mention the extensive sounds along the Atlantic coast.

When the War began, the South had no navy at all. Realizing that their long coast line was vulnerable, they began improvising immediately, but they faced a gigantic handicap. Their supply source was very limited.

As the War progressed and the rival armies fought back and forth on land, the balance of power was slowly but steadily tilting in favor of the North. On the Atlantic Ocean, in the Gulf of Mexico, in the coastal sounds, and up and down the inland rivers, the Union's growing naval power was making itself felt.

In the minds of the Federals, there were three ports on the Gulf Coast that must be conquered first: New Orleans (the Confederacy's largest city) Pensacola and Mobile. These cities were railroad ports. Once they were in Union hands, the Yankees would concentrate on capturing the railroads so they could float their barges from the North, around Florida's southern tip into the Gulf of Mexico, and dock them at each of the three cities. The railroad would provide the best means of transporting reinforcements, weapons, ammunition, supplies, mules, and horses inland.

In December 1861, the Union navy was rapidly bolstering its strength with both men and ships. At that time, the U.S. Navy Department in Washington appointed veteran Rear Admiral David G. Farragut as Flag Officer of the newly formed Western Gulf

Blockading Squadron. By spring, the squadron had a sufficient amount of gun boats to begin their assault and blockade.

Aboard the flagship *Hartford*, Farragut led his strong fleet into the mouth of the Mississippi River and opened a prolonged bombardment of Forts Jackson and St. Philip, which guarded the approach to New Orleans. The mortar boats blasted the forts for a week, then in the predawn darkness on April 24, 1862, Farragut's ships went steaming up the river toward New Orleans. The commanders of both forts had run up white flags.

By the end of the day on April 25, New Orleans had surrendered, and was taken over by Union troops. Control of the mouth of the mighty Mississippi was now in Federal hands.

Admiral Farragut's fleet had sustained some damage in taking New Orleans, and found it necessary to lay up in dock while repairs were made. Early in May, the *Hartford* led the fleet into the Gulf of Mexico and steamed eastward toward Pensacola.

Just off the Pensacola coast was Fort Pickens, a Confederate stronghold. The troops who manned the fort fought hard, but were no match for Farragut's gun boats. On May 10, Fort Pickens and the city of Pensacola surrendered to Farragut and his men. Quickly, Union troops were brought in under the command of Major General Frederick Steele. While occupying the fort and the city, Steele's forces also went to work to capture the railroad.

With the fall of New Orleans and the conquest of Pensacola—along with several more minor ports—Mobile Bay assumed a position of primary importance to the Confederacy. It was the only large inlet still under Southern control.

Fully aware of that, Admiral Farragut set his sights to bowl his fleet through the mouth of the bay and attack Mobile as soon as he could muster more gun boats. The attack was delayed, however, because Farragut and his squadron were held to Mississippi River duty by the demands of the Vicksburg, Mississippi, and Port Hudson, Louisiana, campaigns. After the successful capture of Port Hudson in July of 1863, the sixty-two-year-old Farragut was physically worn out. He left his command and sailed to New York for a rest.

The U.S. Navy Department was reluctant to make an attempt at entering Mobile Bay without Farragut's leadership. They let him rest until January of 1864, then ordered him back to the Gulf with orders to move on Mobile and capture it. Upon returning to his post and studying the situation, Farragut told the Navy Department he could not capture and occupy Mobile without the aid and support of land forces. Such a campaign would take time to prepare.

Navy Department officials contacted the Senate Military Committee, asking for army help in setting up and carrying out the Mobile campaign. The Committee, by permission of President Lincoln, ordered Major General E.R.S. Canby, commander of the Military Division of West Mississippi, to provide the land forces Admiral Farragut needed.

Despite constant drains on his manpower from the Virginia theater, Canby managed to make fifty-five hundred men available for the task. They were the Union Army of the Cumberland's Fourth Corps, under the command of Major General Gordon Granger.

Farragut and Granger met aboard the *Hartford* off the coast of Louisiana in mid-February and made their plans. Mobile Bay was guarded at its mouth by two bastions of strength: Fort Morgan, a pentagonal work on the western tip of Mobile Point, and Fort Gaines on the east side of the two thousand-yard-wide channel at the entrance to the bay on Dauphine Island.

The plan was for a simultaneous attack on the forts by land and naval forces. Granger's men would move in from the Gulf on small rafts and "hit the beach" at Dauphine Island. They were to capture Fort Gaines while Farragut's navy pounded the stronger Fort Morgan with their big guns. Once the forts were out of commission, the admiral's fleet would steam up the thirty-mile length of Mobile Bay to the city.

Granger and his men would follow, and be there to help Farragut capture Mobile. When it was done, the last major Confederate port would be in Union hands. The time of the attack was set for daybreak on August 5. Both men agreed that it would take that long to be fully prepared for the battle.

In the meantime, through Confederate spies, word was sent to Major General Dabney H. Maury, commander of Rebel forces at Montgomery, Alabama, that three large, flat-topped, steam-driven Union barges had left a New Jersey harbor on May 30, on their way south. Their destination was Pensacola. The Yankees now had control of the railroad from Pensacola north, some fifty miles. This put them ten miles into Alabama, just south of the town of Brewton.

The Union barges were laden with fifty army mules and a hundred cavalry horses to replace those that had been killed in inland battles further north in Alabama. The plan was to put the animals ashore at Pensacola, place them in railroad cars built for hauling stock, and take them the fifty miles into Alabama. From there, they would herd them to Union strongholds farther upstate.

The barges had been seen rounding the southern tip of Florida on June 11, and according to Confederate intelligence were due to dock at Pensacola before sunrise on June 17. Determined to keep the much-needed Union animals from being put ashore, General Maury sent the ninety-four men of B Company, First Alabama Battalion Sharpshooters to thwart the landing.

ONE

The full moon was clear-edged and pure against the deep blackness of the night. Its silver beams danced on the rippling surface of the Gulf of Mexico.

Captain Ryan McGraw and his ninety-three men of B Company, First Alabama Battalion Sharpshooters, were huddled on the beach a hundred and fifty yards east of the Pensacola inlet where Fort Pickens stood in silent repose. It galled McGraw and his men that the Confederate fort was in the hands of Major General Frederick Steele and some two hundred Yankee soldiers.

Careful to keep themselves in the deep shadows of the towering palm trees that clustered heavily along the beach, the Sharpshooters watched two sentries patrolling atop the fort's wall. McGraw was studying the clouds being driven by gentle winds from the west. He hoped more clouds would come. The task he and his men faced would be much less dangerous if the moon's brilliance was subdued.

"All right, men," McGraw said in a low voice, "it's midnight. We'll let those clouds cover the moon, then put the plan into action. We've got to have the rafts in position before those barges show up."

Every man knew his job. Captain McGraw would take twenty men who would belly down on three makeshift rafts and paddle their way out into the gulf at a southeasterly angle until they were far enough south to observe the trio of Yankee barges coming up from Florida's southern tip. The plan was for each raft bearing seven Sharpshooters to slip quietly up behind the barges. There were reportedly five crewman on each barge.

McGraw figured the rafts should be able to get close enough to gun down the crewmen before they were spotted. Once the Yankees were disposed of, the Sharpshooters would board the barges, turn them due south, secure the rudders to hold that direction, and give them full steam. They would move back onto the rafts and head for a designated spot on shore.

Docked at the wharf some fifty yards from the fort were five boats that would easily hold twenty men apiece. As soon as McGraw and his raft team had shoved off, ten Sharpshooters were to move stealthily to the wharf, loose the boats, and row them as fast as possible to where the others waited in the shadows of the palm trees on the beach. They would all climb in the boats and row up the shoreline to pick up the raft crews and make their escape east along the beach. Once they could get safely back on land, they would beeline for Montgomery.

If the Yankee sentries on the fort walls spotted the ten Rebels who were after the boats, the rest of them were to open fire and give them cover. Once the boats were gone, General Steele and his men would have no way to go after the barges. They would hear the gunfire out on the gulf when McGraw and his men took out the crewmen, but they would be helpless to do anything about it.

None of the men in McGraw's outfit liked the idea of leaving the helpless horses and mules adrift in the broad gulf, but there was no choice. If the Union army in Alabama received the animals, more Rebel soldiers would die. It made the distasteful task easier when they realized it was better to sacrifice Union animals than Confederate men.

Knowing they had a full moon to deal with, Captain McGraw and his men had replaced their gray uniforms with dark clothing. They had also plastered their faces and the backs of their necks with mud.

Captain Ryan McGraw had placed his right-hand man and best friend, Lieutenant Judd Rawlings, in charge of the men who would stay ashore. Rawlings was twenty-three years of age, and like the rest of the Sharpshooters, well-seasoned in battle after nearly three years of fighting Yankees. He stood six feet in height on a lanky frame, but was wiry and tough. He had dark-brown hair with a handlebar mustache to match. Born and raised in Tupelo, Mississippi, he spoke slowly with a heavy drawl.

Among those men with McGraw were Sergeants Hap Hazzard and Noah Cloud. Hazzard was twenty-four, stood six-feet-one, and weighed a solid two hundred and thirty pounds. He had carrot-red hair and the temper to go with it, yet the big, tough, iron-jawed Rebel from Huntsville, Alabama, was the clown of B Company's Sharpshooters. Cloud was twenty-three, exactly the same height as Hazzard, and outweighed him a mere seven pounds. From Soddy Daisy, Tennessee, he was tough and fearless, always loving a good fight. He and Hap had become close friends, though a stranger would not believe it, for they often argued heatedly and sometimes settled their arguments with fisticuffs.

Captain Ryan McGraw, leader of the now-famous B Company Sharpshooters, was twenty-eight years old, aggressive, resourceful, and tough as pig-iron. He stood six-feet-three inches in height on a muscular frame of two hundred and ten pounds. He had thick, sand-colored hair, with medium-length sideburns, a heavy but neatly trimmed mustache, and pale-blue eyes.

As a private in the First Alabama Battalion late in 1861, McGraw had been chosen by General Dabney Maury to form the Sharpshooters unit because he had proven himself a capable fighter who could readily teach others. Upon receiving the assignment, he had been promoted to sergeant. Growing up in Hattiesburg, Mississippi, he had learned the use of both musket and revolver at the hands of his father. He could "shoot the eye out of a squirrel" with either weapon.

Ryan's father, Thomas McGraw, was a land developer in Hattiesburg, and had become quite wealthy. From the time Ryan was a mere lad, the family had a Japanese gardener, who over the years taught Ryan martial arts. By the time he was in his late teens, he was an expert and could kill a man with his bare hands if forced to do so.

By the spring of 1862, McGraw had developed his unit into a crack outfit of fighters, and had proven himself invaluable to the Confederate cause. He was promoted to lieutenant in May of that year. After leading his men in many battles and skirmishes for the next four months, and distinguishing himself under enemy fire, he was promoted to captain by a direct order from General Robert E. Lee. Known best as "McGraw's Sharpshooters," the unit had become an infamous thorn in the flesh for the North.

Each man in McGraw's Sharpshooters was highly skilled with rifle and revolver. He was also deadly in hand-to-hand combat, having been instructed in martial arts by his leader. McGraw had trained them well and whipped them into the Confederate army's toughest fighting unit. They were a close-knit, roughneck, battle-hungry bunch.

Periodically, as men in the unit were killed in battle or wounded too severely to remain in uniform, McGraw was given new recruits to train and toughen up. If a man did not immediately submit to the captain's hard discipline, he was mustered out of the unit. There was no room for men who did not fit in. They must function smoothly as a unit. Any man who rebelled against McGraw's leadership was looked upon as if he were as much an enemy as a blue-bellied Yankee.

McGraw possessed that rare ability, not learned from books, to control those fiery, turbulent spirits, and to attach them to himself with unbreakable cords. In him they recognized not only the courageous, able leader, but also the commanding officer who would not hesitate to correct a man who made a mistake, or to lay his life down for that man if called on to do it.

Captain McGraw understood the men under his command—their strong points, their weak points, and the limits of their capabilities. Though he expected his men to fight with courage and valor, he never asked a man to do more than he was able. Neither would McGraw ever ask a man to do something he would not do himself, nor would he ever expect a man to risk his life in a situation that McGraw himself would avoid. The tough leader of B Company Sharpshooters was a practical man of action, with a dauntless, fiery soul and a heart that put his men first and himself last whether in combat or out of it. He was also a God-fearing man who was not ashamed to be known as a Bible reader and a man of prayer.

When the clouds overhead had fully covered the moon, McGraw led his twenty men into the cool waters of the gulf, carrying the rafts. In the bleak stillness of the silver night, a solitary gull wailed a haunted cry from somewhere in the shadows of the palm trees.

When the men were thigh-deep in the water, they crawled onto the flat wooden surfaces of the crude vessels and began rowing southeast. Each man was equipped with two holstered six-shot .44 caliber Colt Dragoon revolvers, a long-bladed knife sheathed on his belt, and a .44 caliber Henry repeating rifle, holding sixteen cartridges.

The rapid-firing rifles were first produced in 1862 by Benjamin T. Henry and sold only to the Union. In early 1863, however, the Confederates in Virginia had managed to capture a Federal supply train. In one of the cars was a load of Henrys, along with plenty of ammunition. General Dabney Maury was able to secure enough of them to amply supply McGraw's Sharpshooters.

While the rafts moved swiftly over the relatively calm gulf waters, McGraw glanced skyward. The clouds that covered the moon would soon drift away, but there was a huge bank of them rolling in from the west.

The captain's raft was between the other two, which were no more than six feet away. Speaking to the entire team, he said, "We'll be back in full moonlight in a few minutes, men, but it looks like we've got good cover on the way."

* * *

On shore, Lieutenant Judd Rawlings gathered nine men with him, each armed like the men on the rafts. Reminding those who remained beneath the palm trees to keep an eye on the sentries, he led the nine toward the wharf, keeping to the shadows as much as possible. Rawlings was glad for the cloud cover.

Reaching the edge of the trees where they would have to scurry to the wharf in the open, Rawlings halted his men and looked toward the sky. Estimating that they would have seven or eight minutes before the moon was exposed again, he eyed the vague silhouettes of the two sentries on the wall and whispered, "Okay, men. Keep low and run like rabbits!"

Within a minute, the lieutenant and his men were flattened in the boats. There was no commotion on the fort walls. They sighed with relief, knowing the sentries had not seen them. Releasing the boats from the dock, the Sharpshooters rowed them stealthily away from the shore. They were halfway to their comrades who waited beneath the palm trees when the moon shone down in full strength. Looking back at the fort walls, they expected to hear shouting and gun shots, but all was still. At the moment, no sentries were even in sight.

The huge cloud bank was nearing the moon as Captain McGraw and his raft team bobbed quietly on the gulf. It was nearly 2:00 A.M. It appeared that the moon would be covered for the rest of the night.

McGraw had placed Hazzard and Cloud on the other two rafts as leaders. Sitting next to the captain was Private Curt Dobbs, who was looking back across the three miles of water toward the shore. In the brilliant moonlight, he could see the five boats moving slowly eastward a few yards off the beach.

"Captain," said Dobbs, "I wonder if them Yankee sentries are asleep. You'd think they'd have seen Lieutenant Rawlings and the others."

Before McGraw could reply, Hap Hazzard's deep bass voice inserted, "It ain't that the Yankees are asleep, Curt. It's just that Rawlings and those boys are good at what they do. When you've been trained by our illustrious captain, here, you're a tactical expert."

"Amen," piped up Noah Cloud, whose eyes were fixed on the eastern edge of the gulf. "If General Lee wants to win this war, he oughtta let Cap'n McGraw train *all* the Confederate troops. He's the best—"

Cloud stopped because of what he saw in the distance. "Cap'n," he breathed, rising to his knees and pointing eastward. "The barges are comin'."

Every eye was instantly fixed on the three oblong shapes in the silver light. McGraw looked above and said, "This is working out perfectly. The moon will be covered in another few minutes. Small as we are, the barge crews won't be able to see us at all. I'd say they're about two miles off shore, so we're in good shape. Let's start moving north slowly. The rate they're going, we'll be in the correct position to sneak in behind them when they reach this longitude."

A little over an hour had passed when, under the thick cloud cover, the Sharpshooters on the rafts waited for the barges to come between them and the shore. Peering through the darkness, they could make out that the barges were about thirty-five feet wide and sixty feet long. Specially constructed wooden railings lined the edges of the flat decks to keep the animals from falling off.

At the rear of each barge was a small elevated pilot's cabin. Directly below the cabin was the big steam engine. A paddle wheel the width of the barge churned water at the stern. The wooden railings ran across the deck in front of the cabin and engine, giving the crew some room to move about on either side.

The barges were running abreast of each other, and as they floated past the rafts, the Sharpshooters could tell that the fifty mules were together on the vessel closest to them. The other two barges carried the cavalry horses. The sounds of mules and horses carried clearly on the night air.

McGraw assigned Hazzard's raft to take the nearest barge, Cloud's was to attack the next one, and the captain's would go for the one closest to the shore. As they rowed hard in the wake of the paddle wheels, the Sharpshooters were not concerned about being heard. The rumble of the steam engines, the slap and grinding of the paddle wheels, and the noise of the one hundred and fifty beasts would drown out any sounds made by the men on the rafts.

The barges were about four miles from Fort Pickens and had begun to angle toward shore when the three rafts were lined up behind them. In the gloom, the Sharpshooters could make out three men on each deck, which told them that there were two in each cabin. Captain McGraw was to fire the first shot as a signal for the others to cut loose.

The men on the rafts found it relatively easy to keep up with the heavily laden, slow-moving vessels. When they were within twenty yards, McGraw drew a bead on one of the crew and squeezed the trigger. The Yankee was standing next to the cabin when the bullet hit him. He buckled and fell as Confederate rifles opened fire in a deadly salvo. Surprised crewmen were toppling to the deck. One on the center barge took a slug, staggered a few steps, then fell into the gulf.

McGraw saw one of the men in the cabin of the barge ahead of him stick his head out the window, then duck inside quickly. McGraw drew a bead on the window and waited. Seconds later, the man was at the window, aiming a rifle. McGraw's gun barked and the Yankee fell forward, dropping his weapon to the deck.

While Confederate Henrys continued to blast away at the men on the barges, Hazzard saw one of them hop over the wooden railing and disappear among the frightened mules. The other four crewmen were down. Telling his men to row up to the barge, Hazzard laid his rifle down and made ready to jump from the raft to the slow-moving vessel. Bending low for leverage, he sprang from the raft onto the barge's deck. Pulling out one of his Dragoon .44s, he made a quick check on the four Yankees, and found they were all dead.

The mules were braying and jostling about on the deck, their eyes bulging with fear, as Hazzard leaped the railing and dropped down among them. He caught sight of a dark uniform threading through the animals. The Yankee was heading for the bow.

Shoving his way forward, the big Sharpshooter raised his head and heard the report of a pistol a split second before its lead bullet whizzed past his ear. A second shot followed just as he ducked down.

The mules shrieked in panic, wheeling about and clashing with each other. The barge was rocking dangerously. Hazzard bent low and worked his way among the terrified animals in the direction of the Yankee. His gun was cocked and ready. Suddenly the shifting, wheeling mules parted, giving Hazzard a full view of his enemy. The Yankee was in a half-crouch at the front rail, bringing up his revolver. The big redhead ducked and fired, but his aim was spoiled by the swaying deck. The Yankee's bullet hissed past Hazzard and buried itself in the rump of a mule.

At the same time, another mule directly in front of the Yankee whirled about and knocked the revolver from his hand. It sailed over the rail and dropped into the gulf. Hap heard the wounded mule dig deck and hit the wooden railing behind him as he holstered his gun and headed for the weaponless man. The mule hit the railing full-force, shattering it, and plunged into the dark water.

When Hap approached him, the Yankee swore at him and swung a roundhouse haymaker. Hap batted the fist aside and chopped him with a solid blow. The Yankee staggered back against the rail. In the dim light, Hazzard could make out the man's terror-stricken features. He was going to die, and he knew it. Hazzard moved in close and locked his powerful hands on the man's head. One vicious twist, a snap, and the body went limp, falling to the deck.

The barge slowed. Hap wheeled about and saw one of the Sharpshooters from his raft in the cabin. The throttle had been eased back, and the flat-decked vessel was coming to a halt. In the deep water, the wounded mule was threshing about and bobbing below the surface. Hap pulled his revolver, cocked it, and took aim. When the mule surfaced, the Dragoon roared, and the mule went limp.

The gunfire had stopped at the other two barges. Glancing toward them, Hap saw Noah Cloud and the men with him tossing bodies into the gulf. On the other barge, Captain McGraw and his men were doing the same thing. Hazzard bent over and tossed overboard the man he had just killed.

While the engines of the barges were idling, McGraw called out above the noise of the animals and said, "All right, men. Fire up the boilers. Let's get these things turned around and headed out to sea. We've got an appointment on shore with our pals."

Major General Frederick Steele was fast asleep in his quarters at Fort Pickens when the door burst open and Colonel Arthur Benton rushed in. Shaking the general, Benton cried, "General Steele! Wake up!"

Steele moaned groggily, opened dull eyes, and stared up at Benton, who was outlined against the doorway. Someone outside the door was holding a lantern. Rubbing his eyes, the general mumbled, "What is it, Colonel?"

"The Rebels are attacking our barges, sir!" exclaimed Benton.

Steele shook his head to clear the cobwebs. "You mean the barges that are due in with our horses and mules?"

"Yes, sir! If you listen, you can hear it now!"

As the general worked his heavy body to a sitting position, the distant sound of gunfire met his ears. Cursing, he stood and shuffled to his clothes, which hung on a rack. As he struggled to get into his pants, he growled, "Those aren't big guns. Sound like rifles to me. Can't be Rebel ships."

"No, sir," said Benton. "I estimate they're about three to four miles out on the gulf, and I think the stinking Rebs are using our boats to attack the barges."

"*Our* boats?" gusted the general, snapping his suspenders over his shoulders.

"Yes, sir. All five of them are gone. They must have—"

"Gone?" boomed Steele. "How did they get in close enough to steal our boats? Sentries go to sleep on duty?"

"No, sir. We...uh...we had a slight mix-up, sir."

"Mix-up! What do you mean?" rasped the general, sitting down to pull on his boots.

"The Rebs must've come in and taken the boats at the changing of the guard. When the two sentries on duty over the midnight hour were ready to go off duty at twelve-thirty, their replacements hadn't shown up. They expected them any minute, so they came inside."

"They *what?*" roared the general. "You mean they left their post before their replacements had reported in?"

"Yes, sir."

"Who are they?"

"Jenkins and Galloway, sir."

Slipping into his coat, Steele grunted, "Jenkins and Galloway are to report to me right after breakfast."

"Yes, sir."

"So whose fault is it that there were no replacements?"

"Well, sir, like I said, there was a slight mix-up. As you know, Lieutenant Madsen is in charge of sentries. It seems he thought he had told Sergeant O'Toole to assign sentry duty for that shift because he was tied up with other things. But O'Toole says Madsen never did any such thing. So we—"

"Are there sentries on the walls *now?*"

"Yes, sir."

Bowling through the door with the colonel on his heels, Steele said, "Madsen and O'Toole are to report to me right after breakfast, also."

Walking stiffly, Steele made his way outside the fort, where he found about eighty men standing in a group, looking southeastward through the gloom. The gunfire had stopped. The three barges could barely be seen, but the sound of braying mules and neighing horses could be heard.

Colonel Arthur Benton drew up beside Steele and said, "The Rebs will probably go ashore with the animals somewhere, sir. Shall I round up a unit of men and head up the beach?"

"Forget it," mumbled the general. "I doubt that's what they'll do. They don't need the animals. I'm sure they've made this move simply to keep us from getting them. They're not dumb enough to—"

Steele stopped midsentence when the sound of steam engines being given full throttle met his ears. He waited silently, cocking his head and listening. Presently he said, "Colonel, they're moving away. If I was a betting man, I'd bet they're going to aim the barges seaward and let them go."

"Sounds like something Rebels would do, sir," agreed Benton.

TWO

Federal forces had been unable to take control of the Confederate railroad any farther north than Brewton, Alabama, ten miles above the Florida state line. Major General Dabney H. Maury, who commanded the Confederate Army in Alabama, had successfully blocked the Yankees from gaining more track with a stubborn artillery battery that had dug in where the tracks crossed a bridge over a deep gully a mile and a half south of Brewton. The Yankees were held at bay and were waiting for reinforcements before they attempted to overpower Maury's artillery.

Captain Ryan McGraw and his Sharpshooters had left Montgomery on a military train early on the morning of June 13. Their horses rode in cars built for carrying stock. When the train stopped in Brewton, the horses were unloaded, and the Sharpshooters rode to a large farm just east of town, owned by widow Mabel Griffin.

One of McGraw's Sharpshooters was Corporal Luther Mangus, who had grown up in Brewton and had worked for Mrs. Griffin's late husband as a farm hand when in his teens. When plans were being made by General Maury and Captain McGraw for the Sharpshooters to thwart the landing of the horses and mules at Pensacola, Corporal Mangus had suggested that since they couldn't go by rail any farther south than Brewton, they contact Mrs. Griffin. She would supply them with materials to build the rafts they needed, and a team and wagon to carry the rafts to the Florida coast.

Maury and McGraw liked the idea. Contact was made by telegraph, and Mrs. Griffin, a Southerner to the core, said she would be more than happy to supply whatever they needed. Since her husband's death in January, she had hired a middle-aged man named Ben Rice as farm foreman. Rice and her teenage son, Johnny Ray, would help the Sharpshooters build the rafts.

At midafternoon on June 13, McGraw and his men rode onto the Griffin place and were welcomed by Mabel, her son, and the foreman. The rafts were quickly constructed with husky logs and flat boards, and by midmorning on June 14, the Sharpshooters were ready to head for Pensacola. Johnny Ray Griffin, eager to have a part in the war against the Yankees, volunteered to go along and drive the wagon.

His mother objected that he was too young to be doing any such thing. The boy argued that even though he was only fifteen, he was tall for his age and looked older. He could handle the job.

Captain McGraw saw the fear in Mrs. Griffin's eyes and told Johnny Ray the job would be too dangerous. He could not take the responsibility of allowing him to drive the wagon even if his mother would allow it. Mabel gave the captain an appreciative grin.

With Johnny Ray looking on enviously, the Sharpshooters had moved off the farm and headed south. Corporal Luther Mangus drove the wagon, leaving his horse in the Griffin barnyard.

They reached the Florida coast in the early afternoon on June 15, and stashed the horses and the wagon in a heavily wooded area three miles east of Fort Pickens near the western tip of Santa Rosa Island. After dark, they carried the rafts to the beach and waited for the right time to head out onto the gulf to intercept the barges.

***

On the morning of June 17, Johnny Ray Griffin helped the farm's four male slaves do the chores, then went into the house for breakfast. The aroma of bacon and biscuits met his nostrils as he entered the kitchen from the back porch.

Ben Rice was just sitting down at the table, and Mabel was pouring him a steaming cup of coffee. Looking up, she smiled at her tall, slender son and said, "Get your hands washed, Johnny Ray. We're about ready to eat."

While the youth scrubbed his hands at the wash basin next to the cupboard, he said, "Ma, since I got my weeds cut yesterday, is it all right if I go squirrel huntin' this mornin'?"

Mabel looked at Ben, and Johnny Ray saw it. He knew it was Ben's responsibility to keep him busy, and on the farm it was an easy thing to do. Preempting what Ben might come up with on the spur of the moment, he said, "Squirrel would sure taste good for supper, wouldn't it, Ben?"

The foreman smiled and said to Mabel, "I think squirrel would taste good for supper."

Mabel set the coffee pot on the stove. "I declare. A woman hasn't got a chance when she's outnumbered by the men around her house!"

Johnny laughed and sat down at the table. His hazel eyes shined as he said, "You'll be glad I went huntin', Ma. You like squirrel, too."

Placing crackling bacon on a plate and setting it on the table, the widow smiled at her son and kidded him. "Well, I do, but first you've got to hit the squirrels when you shoot at them."

Johnny Ray laughed. "Ma, you know I never miss!"

"Never?" she chuckled, turning back to the stove.

The youth's face tinted slightly. "Well...I don't miss very often."

Ben spoke up. "I've noticed you drill them squirrels pretty accurately, boy. How do you do it?"

Raising his hands and making like he was sighting down the barrel of his rifle, Johnny Ray replied, "I just pretend they're Yankee soldiers, Ben. Makes it real easy to hit 'em."

Mabel placed a platter of hot biscuits on the table and eased onto her chair. "Johnny," she said levelly, "I don't like the Yankees any more than you do, but it bothers me to hear my fifteen-year-old son talking so casually about killing them."

"They're our enemies, Ma," Johnny Ray said defensively. "If I was three years older so's I was of enlistment age, I'd already be out there on a battlefield somewhere shootin' blue-bellies by the dozen." He paused a few seconds, then added, "When I turn eighteen, I want to join up with McGraw's Sharpshooters!"

Mabel's face went rigid. Through tight lips, she said, "I hope by the time you're eighteen, this horrible war will be over." Tears filmed her eyes. "I don't want you out there on a battlefield, son. I want you right here on the farm, safe and secure."

"But Ma, lots of mother's sons are out there fightin' so's the war can end. If I could go fight right now, I'd do my part to end it by killin' lots of Yankees!"

Mabel wiped away the tears with the back of her hand and said, "No more talk about killing Yankees, Johnny Ray. Now it's time to thank the Lord for the food. I want you to pray."

Young Griffin bowed his head and gave thanks for the food God had provided, and was eagerly talking about his squirrel hunt as soon as he said, "Amen."

When breakfast was over, Johnny Ray went to his room and loaded his Springfield musket. Replacing the ramrod in position beneath the barrel, he strapped on his ammunition kit, clapped the battered straw hat on his head, and returned to the kitchen. He kissed his mother's cheek and received the "be careful" routine that mothers always recite. Telling her he would be back with a dozen or so squirrels on a string by noon, he left the house.

Ben was just coming out of the wood shed as the youth passed by on his way to the hunt. Ben had an armload of wood he was taking to Mabel for the cookstove.

Johnny Ray smiled and said, "Set your mouth for some scrumptious squirrel, Ben. I'll be back with plenty, later."

"Hold up, boy. I need to talk to you before you go."

The bright-eyed youth halted and smiled. "Yes, sir?"

Moving close to him, Ben said, "Johnny Ray, I know I'm not your pa…and I'm not tryin' to be…but I think you need a little fatherly advice."

"About what, Ben?"

"Well…it's the war talk. Seems the war is just about all you talk about any more. I understand how you feel. I'm a true Southerner myself. But mothers have a real tender spot in their hearts when it comes to their boys goin' off to war. I don't know if you've ever thought about it, son, but when a woman brings a child into this world, she has to go right up to the very edge of death to do it. This makes her offspring mighty precious to her. So…when you talk about wantin' to go off to the war and kill Yankees, you're cuttin' awful close to that tender spot. Do you know what I'm sayin'?"

Johnny Ray was quiet for a moment. Then he answered, "Yes, sir. I know what you're sayin'. And I wouldn't hurt Ma's heart for nothin' in this world. But there's somethin' I need to make you understand, Ben. The main reason I wish I could go and fight Yankees is because I want to stop 'em before they get to my mother's door. I've heard what those stinkin' blue-bellies do to Southern women…and I ain't never gonna let 'em get close to Ma. I want to get this war over so's what Yankees ain't dead will be sent hightailin' it back north where they belong. I don't want anything bad ever happenin' to her."

Ben smiled. "I'm glad you want to protect her, son. Only thing I'm sayin' is, don't talk about the war and wantin' to fight in it in front of your ma, okay?"

"I got the message, Ben. She won't hear it from my lips any

more. But if the war's still on when I turn eighteen, I'm joinin' up. Wouldn't be right for me to sit back and let other fellas my age go off and fight, would it?"

"Of course not, son. I'm just prayin' this thing'll be over soon, and all the mothers' sons—Confederates and Yankees—can go home."

"Me, too," grinned the youth. Moving away, he said over his shoulder, "See you about noon."

Johnny Ray made his way across the fields and through the woods, keeping an eye open for squirrels, both in the trees and on the ground. He spotted a couple of them as he walked, but both were too far away. He didn't want to waste rifle balls or gun powder. He came to a creek that rambled over the countryside, lined with trees and brush, and he knew that squirrels liked to play there. Many times he had bagged a number of them along the creek, which was some two miles south and west of his house.

At that time of the year, the creek ran three feet deep at a width of about twenty feet. Johnny Ray came to a familiar spot where there was a break in the heavy brush that lined the creek, and slipped between the branches. The bank was steep, so he sat down and scooted toward the water's edge.

Suddenly he heard voices. Somewhere nearby, some men were talking. Leaning out over the water to see past the brush, he looked downstream. About sixty feet away, he could see booted feet and dark-blue trousers at a clearing on the bank.

Dark-blue trousers!

Yankee soldiers? Possibly. The gully where the Yankees and the Confederate artillery were at a standoff at the railroad bridge wasn't but a mile or so from the creek. Maybe the blue-bellies were on some sort of scouting mission.

Swallowing hard, young Griffin worked his way up the bank through the brush the same way he had gone down. When he reached the top of the bank, he carefully rose to his feet and moved slowly toward the men in blue. He could hear them talking as he crept nearer, keeping close to the heavy stand of brush.

Reaching another break in the thick foliage, Johnny Ray found his assumption to be correct. Three Union soldiers—a corporal and two privates—were seated on the creek bank, chatting. There were no horses around, so Johnny Ray knew they had come on foot. His heart pounded like a triphammer as he heard them discussing their mission. They were to scout out the area and see if there was a safe way to bring troops around behind the artillery battery dug in near the railroad bridge. They had decided to take a short break before moving on.

Johnny knew what he had to do. As a loyal Southern boy, he must capture these blue-bellies and take them home. Captain Ryan McGraw and his Sharpshooters would be returning soon. Johnny Ray would turn them over to Captain McGraw.

A thought passed through the youth's mind: Maybe I shouldn't try this. It's plenty dangerous. No one would expect a mere fifteen-year-old boy to attempt to capture three enemy soldiers. He wouldn't be blamed at all if he reported seeing them but had not tried to take them prisoner.

Johnny Ray bit down hard on his lower lip and shook his head. No! he thought. It's my duty! And besides, when I take them in as prisoners, it will show everybody that I am old enough to be a soldier!

Licking his lips, the determined youth switched the musket from hand to hand as he wiped sweat from his palms. Easing the hammer back to firing position as quietly as possible, he kept his eyes on the Yankees. Their voices and the rippling sound of the creek had prevented them from hearing the dry, clicking sound. Assessing the situation, he saw that the Yankees wore no sidearms or knives. Each had a Henry repeating rifle beside him on the bank.

Johnny Ray looked around to make sure there were no other Yankee soldiers near. Seeing no sign of anyone, he took a deep breath and squared himself with the path that led down to the water's edge. The soldiers were facing the creek with their backs toward him. Just as the determined youth started to move, one of the privates turned his head. He was looking back into the brush along the creek, but Johnny Ray feared he might be in the Yankee's peripheral vision.

He froze on the spot. To move would draw the man's attention. He felt a faint pins-and-needles sensation along his spine.

Suddenly a thrush fluttered out of the thicket and took flight. The other soldiers laughed at their comrade as they watched the bird fly away. The corporal said, "What's the matter, George? You spooked? You thought some Rebel was sneaking in on us, didn't you?"

George laughed it off, saying he was just smart for being cautious.

The other private chuckled, "Sometimes a fella can become too cautious, George. You know…get to where he jumps at everything that moves."

George mumbled something as he picked up a stone and threw it into the creek. Johnny Ray knew it was time to make his move. Gripping the musket in ready position, he headed down the steep bank.

The Yankees heard him coming and jerked their heads around. Johnny Ray was still within the edges of the brush above them as he stopped and shouted with a squeak in his voice, "Hold it right there!"

The Yankees sat within a dozen feet of him, their faces registering their surprise.

"On your feet!" snapped the farm boy, waving the muzzle of his musket threateningly.

Corporal Leonard Halsey slowly moved his hand toward the rifle next to him as he spoke sternly, "You'd best put that gun down, kid. You're dealing with well-trained soldiers, here. By the looks of you, I assume you're from some farm nearby. Go on home. You've got no business throwing a gun on us."

Johnny Ray ground out the words, "You dirty Yankees are trespassin' on South'n land. That makes it my business." Noting that

Halsey's hand was nearing the rifle, he rasped, "Touch that gun and you'll die!"

The corporal pulled his hand away and slowly stood up. Privates George Calkins and Eddie Smith followed suit.

"Now look, kid," Halsey said levelly, "your fooling around like this is gonna get you killed."

"I'm not foolin' around!" spat the youth. "I'm takin' you as my prisoners. Captain Ryan McGraw will see to it that you go to the prison camp up by Montgomery. All right, now…I want you two privates to throw your rifles in the creek, one at a time."

Smith looked at his partners and said with a paper-thin laugh, "This local yokel really thinks we're gonna do what he says."

"You first!" Johnny Ray snarled at Smith. "Toss your rifle in the creek!"

"Sonny," spoke up Corporal Halsey, "you're not thinking too clearly. That old musket can only fire once. You shoot one of us, the other two will get you. We'll kill you for sure."

"Maybe you're not thinking too clearly, either, Corporal," countered Johnny Ray. "If I shoot one of you, I'll shoot to kill. Are you willin' to be the one to die, so your two yahoos can finish me off?"

While Halsey glared at him, young Griffin fixed Smith with steely eyes and hissed, "I told you to throw your rifle in the creek."

Jutting his jaw angrily, Smith growled, "We're gonna kill you, kid."

"Where do you get that 'we' stuff?" asked Johnny Ray. "If you make the first move toward me, you'll be dead." The youth's stomach was fluttering, but he kept up his tough stance. "Now, either throw your gun in the creek as I told you, or come after me."

Smith glanced at his companions. They could offer no help. Cursing under his breath, he picked up his Henry by the tip of the barrel and threw it in the stream.

Johnny Ray's muzzle swung on George Calkins and he commanded, "You next."

Calkins reluctantly followed Smith's example. When the rifle splashed in the water, young Griffin said to Halsey, "Now, Corporal, I want you to pick up your gun very carefully, keeping the muzzle aimed at the ground, and lever a cartridge into the chamber. Then I want you to hand it to me butt first."

"Kid," Halsey breathed hotly, "before this is over, you're gonna be dead."

"Just do as I tell you," retorted Johnny Ray, "or you're the one who'll be dead."

The corporal bent over and picked up his Henry, thinking there had to be a way out of this predicament. It would be bad enough to become a prisoner of the Confederates, but what shame he and his two comrades would face when it got out that they had been captured by a lone farm kid. Careful to keep the rifle's muzzle pointed groundward, he worked the lever. The cartridge slid into the chamber, and the hammer was cocked.

Holding the musket in his right hand with the butt braced against his hip and the muzzle pointed dead-center on Halsey's chest, Johnny Ray extended his left hand and said, "Gently, Corporal. Place it gently in my hand. If you make any kind of a quick move, this musket will go off."

When it was done, Halsey took a step back and grunted, "You said Captain Ryan McGraw would see to it that we go to the prison camp at Montgomery. Are you talking about *the* Ryan McGraw of McGraw's Sharpshooters?"

"The same. Now I'm going to back up the bank, here, and I want the three of you to follow me, single file. Anybody makes a questionable move, he dies."

When young Griffin had them on level ground, he made them walk side by side in front of him with their hands cupped behind their necks.

As they moved across a grassy field, Halsey asked, "So where's McGraw and his Sharpshooters camped out?"

"You'll find out," replied Johnny Ray, not wanting to tell them that the Sharpshooters had been on an assignment in Florida.

The three Yankee soldiers looked at each other with concern. Hoping that the rustling of their feet in the grass would drown out his whisper, Calkins said, "Len, we gotta do something. Once this hayseed turns us over to McGraw, we're done for. I don't want to spend the rest of the war in that stinking Rebel prison camp!"

"Well, I don't either," whispered Halsey, "but what can we do? I know about these Southern farm boys. They learn to handle a gun as soon as they can pick one up. If we'd tried to take him back there by the creek, one of us would be dead."

"So what do we do, now?" whispered Smith. "We've got to get away from this hick before he takes us into McGraw's camp."

Johnny Ray's voice cut the air. "You Yankees think us hayseed hicks are deaf, do you? I'm warnin' you…try any tricks on me, and I'll kill you."

"You're just a kid," countered Halsey over his shoulder. "You shouldn't be putting a gun on someone and threatening to kill them."

"You kill Rebels, don't you?" pressed young Griffin. "Then what's wrong with a Rebel killin' you?"

"We're soldiers," argued Calkins. "Soldiers are supposed to kill the enemy. That's what war's all about."

"I am a soldier, too!" snapped Johnny Ray.

"You're lying!" Smith said. "You aren't old enough to be a soldier. And besides…where's your uniform?"

"Don't need a uniform to be a soldier."

"Then what proof have you got that you're a soldier?"

"I've got three prisoners of war. Isn't that proof enough? Only soldiers take other soldiers prisoners of war, don't they?"

When no answer came, Johnny Ray said, "You Yankees would rather it was a soldier who captured you than a hayseed Southern farm kid, right?"

The men in blue exchanged despairing glances. It was going to be embarrassing when the day came that their fellow-soldiers learned of their capture by a mere boy.

Looking past his prisoners, Johnny Ray could see the uneven roof-lines of the house, barn, and outbuildings on the Griffin farm in the distance. "Not much farther, now, enemy soldiers," he said advisedly. "You're doin' fine. Just don't get any cute ideas between here and there. By now I would've bagged me a dozen squirrels. I haven't fired a gun all day. It's so unnatural for me. So don't do anything to tempt me to pull one of these triggers."

Mabel Griffin was in her sewing room at the rear of the house when she heard the old grandfather clock in the hall chime ten.

Blending with the last few chimes was Ben's excited voice, coming from the yard. "Mabel! Mabel!"

Laying her sewing down, Mabel went to the window and looked around the yard for the foreman. When she saw him, he was near the tool shed, looking toward the south pasture. The day was warm, and the sewing room window was wide open. Sticking her head out, she called, "What is it, Ben?"

"It's Johnny Ray! He's comin' in."

"A bit early, I might say," laughed Mabel. "Does he have a string of squirrels?"

"Nope, but he's got somethin' else. You ain't gonna believe it!"

"Well, what is it?"

"You'd better come back and look for yourself."

A half-minute later, Mabel stepped off the back porch and hurried to where Ben was standing. Grinning from ear to ear, he pointed toward the pasture and said, "Look!"

Mabel's jaw slacked and a gasp escaped her lips as she saw the three Yankee soldiers with their hands clasped behind their necks, followed by young Johnny Ray, holding two rifles on them. They were about thirty yards from where she stood, moving past a cluster of apple trees.

Ben chuckled, "What do you make o' that, Mabel? That boy of yours has done got hisself three Yankee prisoners!"

BATTLES OF DESTINY

366

"You what?" exclaimed Captain Ryan McGraw, looking toward the Griffin barn, throwing his leg over the saddle.

Corporal Luther Mangus drew the wagon to a halt as the rest of the Sharpshooters dismounted. Mabel and Ben stood beside Johnny Ray at the back porch of the farm house, smiling proudly.

The bright-eyed youth stepped close to McGraw and repeated what he had said a moment earlier. "I captured three Yankee soldiers, sir, and we got 'em tied up in the barn."

Mangus climbed down from the Griffin wagon, eyes wide, and said, "Johnny Ray, did I hear you right? You captured three Yankee soldiers?"

"Yep," grinned the youth. "I told 'em I'd be turnin' 'em over to Captain McGraw and the Sharpshooters. They ain't terribly happy about it, but it's about to happen, anyhow."

"How did this come about, kid?" queried Hap Hazzard, who stood next to his friend Noah Cloud.

All the Sharpshooters gathered in a tight circle and listened as Johnny Ray told how he had stumbled onto the Yankees at the creek and caught them off guard. There was a round of laughter, then Captain McGraw said, "Well, let's get a gander at these Yankees."

Johnny Ray and Ben led McGraw and Lieutenant Rawlings to the barn. Inside, Leonard Halsey, George Calkins, and Eddie Smith were bound hand and foot, and tied together around one of the thick posts that supported the barn roof. Stepping through the wide door and viewing the prisoners by the light of the setting sun, the captain smiled and said, "Good afternoon, gentlemen. I'm Captain Ryan McGraw."

At sunrise the next morning, Mabel, Ben, and Johnny Ray stood at the rear of the house and watched the sullen-faced prisoners being placed on army horses with their hands tied behind their backs. They would ride double with three of the Sharpshooters.

Captain McGraw laid a hand on Johnny Ray's slender shoulder and said, "You did real good, son. We're all proud of you. General Maury is going to be proud of you, too. I wouldn't be surprised if you got a letter from him."

"Do you suppose since I captured those blue-bellies, General Maury would put in a good word for me to the army so's they'd let me join up?"

Shaking his head slowly, McGraw replied, "The general wouldn't do that, Johnny Ray. There's a reason the army has an age limit for recruits. You did real good in taking these prisoners, but there's a whole lot more to soldiering than that. You'll just have to wait till you turn eighteen before you can enlist."

Johnny Ray's features showed disappointment. Nodding, he said, "I understand, Captain McGraw. It's just that…well, I want to do my part to help win the war."

"You did a big part yesterday, son," smiled McGraw. "Now, your ma needs you here. You take care of her…and be all the help to Ben that you can."

"Yes, sir," said Johnny Ray.

Mother, son, and foreman stood together and watched the Sharpshooters ride away. When they were almost out of sight, Captain McGraw turned and waved. Mabel, Ben, and Johnny Ray waved back. Sergeant Hap Hazzard, who rode beside McGraw, said, "Cap'n, that there is one fine boy."

"You can say that again," grinned McGraw.

THREE

Major General Dabney H. Maury was standing in the door of his tent conversing with one of the camp's lieutenants when Captain Ryan McGraw and his Sharpshooters came riding in. The long column of riders caught his attention instantly. Confederate soldiers all over the camp stopped what they were doing to stare at the Sharpshooters and their Yankee prisoners.

Maury, who was nearing sixty and walked with a limp from a wound sustained in the Mexican War, moved toward the column with Lieutenant Foster Twite tagging along.

Raising a hand for the Sharpshooters to halt, McGraw drew rein, saluted Maury, and slid from the saddle. The general eyed the three blue-uniformed prisoners and said, "How'd it go, Captain?"

"As planned, sir," replied McGraw. "I'll give you a full report in your tent at your convenience."

"All right," nodded the silver-haired general. "Since it's almost one o'clock, most of the men have already eaten, but a few are still in line over at the cook shack. I'll let you eat lunch with your men, then you can come to the tent. Lets' say…about two o'clock."

"Fine, sir."

Looking at the prisoners, Maury said, "I see you captured some."

McGraw grinned. "*We* didn't, sir, but a fifteen-year-old farm boy did."

"Maybe we need to recruit this boy."

McGraw chuckled, "That's exactly what the kid wants, sir. I'll tell you about the capture when I make my report."

"Good enough," replied Maury. Then turning to Foster Twite, he said, "Lieutenant, take charge of the prisoners and remove them to the prison camp."

Captain McGraw dismissed his men, telling them to corral their animals and head for the lunch line. Telling the general he would see him at two, he turned toward his own horse.

"Oh, Captain," spoke up Maury, "your seven new men arrived yesterday."

"Good. They seem to be Sharpshooter material?"

"They shoot like it. Be up to you to toughen them up."

"Well, given a little time, I can do that if they're made out of the right stuff."

"I think they are, but the time you have to work on them is going to be very short."

"Another mission?"

"Mm-hmm. A big one. I'll tell you all about it at two o'clock. In the meantime, if you want to meet your new men, they're settled in at the spot designated for your unit."

The Montgomery army camp was situated a half-mile north of the town. It covered some twenty acres of open meadows and wooded areas, the meadows making up about two-thirds of the camp. The horses were kept in the woods where it was easy to confine them in a rope corral. A small brook ran through the camp, threading its way through the woods and providing water for the animals. The Sharpshooters had their tents pitched close to the brook a few yards from the edge of the woods.

As Captain McGraw led his horse toward the corral, he

thought of the seven men he had lost in two skirmishes some twenty-five miles east of Montgomery. It always hurt him deeply to see his men killed. General Robert E. Lee had ordered that B Company First Alabama Sharpshooters always be maintained at an even hundred men plus their captain. It was up to General Maury to see that it was done.

The Sharpshooters deposited their animals in the corral and headed for the lunch line. McGraw put his horse among them, then headed to where his new men were waiting to meet him.

The captain shook hands with each man, and asked where he was from and how much combat experience he had. He told them he would begin their training as soon as his meeting with General Maury was over, then excused himself to go have lunch with his men.

At precisely 2:00 P.M., McGraw approached the door of General Maury's tent. The flap was open, and Maury looked up from his battered old desk and said, "Come in, Captain."

McGraw entered and sat on a straight-backed chair, facing the desk. Maury listened intently as the captain gave his report, telling how the Sharpshooters had overcome the Union barge crews, sent them to watery graves, and headed the barges out to sea at full throttle. He commended McGraw and his men for a job well done, saying the loss of the horses and mules would greatly cripple the Union cavalry and army in Alabama.

McGraw then explained to his commander how Mabel Griffin had aided them by donating materials to build the rafts and loaning them her team and wagon so they could get them to the coast. He also told Maury about young Johnny Ray single-handedly capturing the three Union soldiers.

Laughing, the general said how ashamed the three Yankees must be to have been taken by a mere boy. He would send a letter of appreciation to Mrs. Griffin for her help, and a letter of commendation to the boy for his courage and monumental accomplishment.

Taking a deep breath and letting it out slowly, General Maury leaned forward, picked up a folder from his desk, and said, "The big mission I mentioned to you earlier has been ordered by General Lee. These are the orders. You have exactly one week to whip those new recruits into shape. I'm shipping your unit to Fort Morgan at Mobile Bay on the twenty-sixth."

McGraw's mouth pulled tight. "Mobile Bay, eh? Farragut?"

Nodding, Maury said, "In person. He's building up a fleet of gunboats off the coast, south of the bay. We knew it had to come. Old 'fair-guts' has Vicksburg, Port Hudson, New Orleans, and Pensacola as feathers in his cap. If he can capture the bay and the city of Mobile, he'll have us completely blockaded, and he knows it. Mobile will be his biggest prize."

McGraw lifted his hat, sleeved sweat from his brow, and said, "He's not only thinking of blockade from the sea, but he also remembers how Mobile figured in the Stones River and Chicamauga campaigns."

Maury nodded, recalling that prior to the Battle of Stones River and, later, the Battle of Chicamauga, great numbers of Confederate troops and guns had been shifted from Mississippi to Tennessee to fight in those campaigns. The only way the Rebel warriors could get to Tennessee in time to meet the Union forces was to travel by rail from Jackson, Mississippi, to Mobile. From Mobile, they went north to Selma, where they railroaded east to Atlanta. From Atlanta, they rode the rails northward into Tennessee. If Admiral Farragut could take Mobile, that vital link could never be used again.

"You're right about that," Maury said solemnly. "There's another reason, too."

"Sherman's proposed move on Atlanta?"

"You hit the nail on the head. As you know, then, Sherman is expected to launch a drive for Atlanta some time next spring. Mobile will once again be vital, since our army in Georgia would have to receive its supplies from Mobile. The only other seacoast link for our Georgia forces is Charleston, and it is under threat at this time, too.

It is of utmost importance, Captain, that we hold Mobile. General Lee wants you and your men to join forces with General Page and his one hundred and twenty men at Fort Morgan. We must not let Mobile Bay fall into enemy hands."

"What about Fort Gaines, General?" asked McGraw. "How many men are there?"

"I'm not sure. I think about fifty. There aren't as many guns in Fort Gaines. From what I understand, though, General Page is doing something to force the Union's ships closer to Fort Morgan. It has some very big guns."

"Doing something like what?"

"Well, from what I know about it, he's driving wooden pilings into the bottom of the bay from Dauphin Island, where Gaines stands, toward the other side of the bay's mouth...and he's also planning to drop torpedoes into the water between the pilings and Fort Morgan."

"Torpedoes? Pardon me, sir, I haven't been around naval warfare before. What are torpedoes?"

Maury smiled. "They're a new device for sinking ships. You're aware that our Brigadier General Gabriel Rains has developed what he calls 'land mines' for use on the battlefield."

"Yes, sir. A wicked device, but quite ingenious. I haven't seen them, yet, but I hear they'll blow a man to bits if he steps on one."

"For sure," nodded Maury. "Well, General Rains has come up with a 'sea mine.' It works on the same order, only it blows holes in the hulls of ships. He calls it a torpedo. He has invented two kinds, and I understand that General Page is going to use both of them in Mobile Bay."

"How do they work?"

"The first one General Rains came up with was simply a beer keg filled with gunpowder. Numerous little tubes project from the sides of the keg. The tubes contain fulminate, which upon contact with a ship's hull will explode. That sets off the powder in the keg. It'll blow a big hole in a hurry. The beer keg kind are anchored to the bottom of the bay—or whatever body of water you are attempting to protect—with thin rope lines. The wood of the keg makes it quite buoyant, so the torpedo rises to the surface. They're tied so they are just a bit under the surface, and hard to see. Deadly, I'll tell you."

"Sounds like it."

"The other kind are metal cones, usually tin. They simply float on the surface, but it's impossible to dodge them, even if you see them. The cones are filled with powder and attached to the ends of a tin cylinder filled with air, which gives it buoyancy. The charges in the cones are detonated by a spring mechanism connected to a trigger wire. One bump by a ship, the trigger sets off an internal spark. Makes quite an explosion, I understand."

"That'll give Admiral Farragut something to think about."

"I'd say so. There's something else for him to think about, too. Our new ram, the *Tennessee*."

"I've heard about it, sir. Must be some kind of ship."

"She's considered the strongest and most powerful iron-clad ever put afloat. As you know, I was down at Mobile a few weeks ago. The *Tennessee* was moving about just off shore. Formidable thing. Looks like a giant turtle. Her sides are covered with iron plates six inches thick, thoroughly riveted together."

"I've heard it's a floating fort."

"That's putting it mildly. Her biggest guns are the Brooke cannons. Has six of them. They fire a solid shot weighing a hundred and ten pounds."

"Whew! Farragut probably knows about her. Wonder what he's thinking."

"I'd like to know that myself," chuckled Maury.

McGraw shifted positions on the hard chair and asked, "How many vessels does Farragut have off shore from Mobile Bay, sir?"

"At the moment, about fourteen, but there are more on the way. I figure he won't attempt to move in until he's built up quite a fleet. So far, he has nothing to match the *Tennessee*, but there could be something in the making."

"What about land forces, sir? Are we bolstering up for what may come in behind Mobile?"

"General Lee and I are working on that right now. He wants you and your Sharpshooters down there by June twenty-seventh…twenty-eighth at the latest. So I've made arrangements for a special train to take you to Mobile on the twenty-sixth."

"All right, sir," said McGraw, rising to his feet and rubbing his left shoulder. "I'll have my new recruits as ready as possible by then. The rest of my men, as usual, will be eager to get to Fort Morgan when they learn that there's going to be a fight."

Maury stood and eyed the captain massaging his shoulder. "Still bothered with that?" he asked.

"A little. I'm not too sure it will ever be the same, sir. But that's war, isn't it? I guess nobody's ever the same after being in battle."

Limping around the desk, General Maury replied, "You're right about that. I'll sure never be the same. This leg gives me a lot of trouble." Extending his hand, he said, "You're a good officer, McGraw. I appreciate your excellent work. General Page is plenty glad to know you're coming down there, I'll tell you that."

"Thank you, sir," McGraw responded with a half-smile, meeting Maury's grip. Clearing his throat nervously, he said, "Well, I guess Mrs. McGraw's son better get busy and whip his new men into shape." With that, he turned, passed through the tent door, and headed to where his Sharpshooters were camped.

Darkness had fallen on Sunday, June 26, 1864, when McGraw's Sharpshooters assembled at the Montgomery depot. They had left their horses in the camp, knowing their duties at Mobile Bay would not call for riding. Four supply wagons stood by, waiting for the train to pull in from the railroad yards. McGraw made sure his unit was well-equipped with weapons and ammunition.

It had rained for an hour just before sundown, and the air was warm and humid. Captain McGraw stood on the platform with

Lieutenant Rawlings, discussing the situation at Mobile Bay. Lanterns on poles cast their dim light along the platform. The same subject was on the lips of the rest of the men, who were eager to do their part to withstand the impending Union aggression.

Finally, they heard the engine's deep chugging sound and turned to see a cloud of smoke belching from the stack. The big engine rolled to a halt, its firebox glowing in the inky night. Two men climbed down from the cab, and McGraw and Rawlings recognized them both. Engineer Charlie Coggins and fireman Lou Andreasen had taken the Sharpshooters and their horses to Brewton on their Pensacola mission several days before. Coggins greeted the two officers, then said, "Captain McGraw, we're pulling three coaches behind the coal car. Your men can unload the wagons into coach number three. Won't leave much room in that car, but coaches one and two will hold about fifty men apiece."

"That'll be fine, Charlie," grinned McGraw. "Lieutenant Rawlings and I will ride in the rear coach. The rest of them can divide up between the other two."

McGraw ordered the men to load the supplies in the third car, then explained the situation to Sergeants Hap Hazzard and Noah Cloud. Hazzard would be the leader in coach number one, and Cloud in number two. If the train was attacked by Union forces, the Sharpshooters were to retaliate quickly.

Twenty minutes later, the big engine hissed steam and belched smoke and they were underway. General Lee had put great stock in McGraw's Sharpshooters, depending on them to strengthen the forces at Fort Morgan. In explaining their mission to his men, Captain McGraw had relayed Lee's message as it had come to General Maury: *The fort must stand at all costs.* Neither the city of Mobile nor the strategic bay can be allowed to fall into Union hands. The results of the battle there would greatly affect the outcome of the War.

Captain McGraw sat pensively next to a window in the third coach, watching the burning cinders from the engine filtering against the dark night like fireflies. Lieutenant Rawlings sat next to him, writing a letter by the light of the overhead lanterns. He had slid a keg of gunpowder between his knees and was using its lid as a table.

After a while, McGraw pulled his attention from the window, looked at his friend, and said, "Another letter to your pa?"

"Yeah, he's been awfully lonesome since Ma died. I know Sis and her family are there, but he needs to hear from his soldier-boy son, too."

"I'm sure that's true. I hope you can get a letter through to Tupelo."

"All I can do is try. I don't know if any of my letters have been getting to him. The way we've moved around, there's no way Pa or Sis can get a letter back to me. I just hope they've gotten mine."

McGraw looked back out the window. The steady rocking of the coach and the rhythmic click of the wheels was almost hypnotic. Moments later, he was startled as Judd's voice interrupted his sleepy state.

"I bet I know who you're thinking about!"

Ryan straightened on the seat, yawned, and said, "Wrong, ol' buddy. Not this time. I've come to the place that I won't let myself dwell on her any more. No use torturing Mrs. McGraw's only son. She's probably fallen for some other patient and married him by now."

Rawlings shrugged. "Maybe...then maybe not."

"I'll probably never know, anyhow. It's best that way. She deserves someone better than me."

The lieutenant licked the envelope and sealed it. Giving his friend a mock-scowl, he said, "What're you talking about, Ryan? There's nobody better than you."

McGraw chuckled hollowly. "If you could talk face-to-face with the Lord in heaven about that, He could fill you in on that subject."

"Look," pressed Rawlings, "you need to quit punishing yourself for something that wasn't your fault."

"Maybe if I'd been a better husband, Tori wouldn't have—"

"Oh, yes she would! From all you've told me about her, no

matter how good a husband you'd been, she'd have run out on you. Some women are just that type, and Victoria is one of them."

"She didn't seem to be when we first met and married."

"So she changed. Sometimes people do that. You can't lash yourself for what happened. You're still young. When this war's over, you need to find yourself the right gal, marry her, and have a happy life. You deserve it."

There's only one gal that I want, thought McGraw, *but I can never have her. She was kind and warm to me, but there was nothing to indicate she felt anything more than friendship. However, I'll never forget that sweet kiss she planted on my cheek when she said, "Maybe someday we will meet again."*

Judd used his foot to slide the powder keg back across the aisle, then placed the sealed letter to his father in his small valise, telling himself he would mail it in the morning at Mobile. Stretching his arms, he yawned and said, "Well, Cap'n McGraw, I think I'll saw a few logs."

"Yeah, me too," Ryan said, yawning.

Rawlings lifted his lanky frame off the seat and doused all the lanterns but one. He lowered the flame on it, then sat down, stretched out his legs, crossing them at the ankles, and tipped his hat over his face. "G'night, boss," he mumbled.

"G'night, lowly subject," said McGraw.

The lieutenant chuckled and was snoring in less than a minute.

Ryan looked out the window. With the single lantern burning low, he could see the world outside. The clouds were breaking up, and there was pale moonlight showing through. A thin mist from the ear-lier rain was creeping over the Alabama countryside, spreading itself over the fields and through the woods like a blanket of cobwebs. *Eerie*, thought Ryan, then drifted off to sleep.

As the Confederate troop train cut its swath through the misty night, engineer Charlie Coggins sat in the cab with his head out the window, watching the track ahead by the light of the huge headlamp. Fireman Lou Andreasen finished shoveling a new batch of coal into the firebox and was just closing the iron door when he saw one of the Sharpshooters moving along the catwalk on the coal car. Andreasen had noticed his muscular body and carrot-red hair before.

Smiling as he entered the rear of the cab, Hap Hazzard said, "Evenin'."

"Evenin'," echoed the fireman above the thunder of the engine. "Somethin' I can do for you?"

"Naw. I just couldn't sleep. Thought I'd come and see how this bucket o' bolts works."

Andreasen grinned and glanced over his shoulder at the engineer, who was not yet aware of Hazzard's presence. "Don't let Charlie hear you call it that," he chuckled. "This engine is his baby."

Extending his hand, the fireman said, "I'm Lou Andreasen."

Hazzard shook his hand. "I'm Sergeant Hap Hazzard."

"I've noticed you before," smiled Andreasen. "You were on the train when we took the Sharpshooters down to Brewton. Hear you boys sent some Yankees into the gulf as fish food on that mission."

"You might say that," grinned Hap.

"You think it's gonna be a real battle when ol' 'fair-guts' comes tootin' into Mobile Bay, Sergeant?"

"It'll be a hot one, I figure."

Charlie Coggins turned around on his window-side seat and smiled, then looked past both men at another husky figure moving along the catwalk. Noah Cloud stepped into the cab, looked hard at Hazzard, and said, "I came into your coach to kiss you goodnight, and you weren't there."

"I'd rather be kissed by a suck-egg mule than you!" Hazzard growled.

Cloud laughed. "I was only joshin'! I wouldn't kiss you, and neither would a suck-egg mule!"

While Coggins looked on with a wide grin, Andreasen said, "I see you two are good friends."

"Friends?" chortled Cloud. "Hah! Ol' carrot-head here is just one notch from bein' a Yankee!"

Hazzard's ruddy face went beet-red. "A *Yankee?* Why, I oughtta throw you off the train right here and let the night-crawlers eat you!"

"Hmpf-f-f!" snorted Cloud. "Maybe you oughtta, but you ain't man enough!"

Hazzard jutted his jaw and started for him. Thinking they were serious, Andreasen leaped between them, saying, "Wait a minute, you two! There's no reason for violence, here. You men are on the same side!"

Both sergeants broke into hearty laughs, each throwing an arm around the fireman's shoulder.

"You're okay, pal," said Hazzard. "Sorry to have scared you. We go on like this most of the time."

"Most of the time?" asked the fireman, eyes wide.

"Yep," put in Cloud, "unless we're fightin' Yankees."

"Otherwise we'd go crazy," said Hazzard.

Cloud turned to Coggins and asked what time they would get into Mobile. The engineer pulled out his pocket watch and angled it toward the light from a small window in the iron door of the firebox. "Well, it's 1:15, now. We'll be comin' up on the Sepulga River in another forty to forty-five minutes. Mobile's another three hours after we cross the Sepulga, so we'll pull into Mobile just about five o'clock. It'll be dawn about the same time."

Hazzard and Cloud decided to look the cab over, showing interest in every detail. Coggins, delighted to show off his engine, took the time to explain how everything worked, while keeping an eye on the track ahead.

When Coggins had finished educating the sergeants on the engine, Andreasen said, "Will you gentlemen excuse me? I've got to shovel some more coal. Got to keep the boiler hot."

"We've got to get back to our men," said Hazzard. "Thanks for the hospitality." Cloud followed the big redhead along the catwalk on the coal car.

Captain McGraw was jolted from a deep sleep when the train suddenly braked. By the dim light of the lantern, he saw Judd Rawlings rolling in the aisle where he had been thrown from his seat.

Leaping to his feet and shaking his head to clear the cobwebs, McGraw stepped over his lieutenant and bolted through the door. Entering the next coach, he found the men tossed about from the sudden stop. Noah Cloud was picking himself up off the floor. Dashing past him, McGraw said, "Something's wrong, Sergeant! Get these men awake and alert. Be ready for anything!"

Charging into the next car, he found the same thing, only Hap Hazzard was about to open the front door.

"You stay in here!" shouted the captain. "Get the men awake and alert. Be ready for anything! I'll see what's going on."

"Yes, sir," nodded Hazzard, opening the door and stepping aside to make room for McGraw to pass.

When the captain was darting along the side of the coal car on the catwalk, he saw immediately why Coggins had stopped the train. The Sepulga River lay before them in the moonlight, but the trestle that supported the bridge over the river was ablaze.

Coggins was hanging out one side of the cab, and Andreasen the other. They both eyed McGraw as he drew up. Coggins said, "Looks like the Yankees set fire to the bridge, Captain! Sorry to make the stop so sudden, but we were on a curve and you can't see the bridge till you're almost on it."

McGraw's attention was fixed on the burning trestle. It was afire on both sides of the river, but the flames had not yet joined in the middle. The river was about seventy feet wide where the bridge crossed, and both banks were sloped so that the bridge that spanned it was about a hundred and twenty feet long.

"What do you think, Captain?" asked Coggins. "Should we try to cross it?"

"Better get inside the cab," said McGraw. "Could be the

Yankees are waiting out there in the brush to snipe at us."

As engineer, fireman, and McGraw moved inside the cab, Lieutenant Rawlings came off the catwalk, eyes wide as he noted the blazing bridge. "Yankees!" he gasped.

"No doubt," replied the captain, "but I'm wondering if setting the bridge afire wasn't just a random thing. Since they've been unable to capture and control this line between Montgomery and Mobile, about all they can do is try tearing up track or burning bridges. The latter is by far the easiest. This train was on nobody's schedule. There's no way the blue-bellies could have known it was coming. At this point we can't be sure, but if it *was* a random thing, they won't be hanging around to shoot at us."

"I hope that's the case," breathed Rawlings.

Turning to the engineer, McGraw said, "Charlie, you asked if we should try to cross the bridge."

"Yes, sir. My thought was that maybe it hasn't been burning long enough to weaken the superstructure. The flames are almost up to the top, but they climb pretty fast on wood like that. There's a good chance we can still get the train across."

"I was thinking the same thing myself." Looking back at Rawlings, McGraw said, "Lieutenant, we've got to get this unit and our supplies to Fort Morgan. I realize to move the train onto the bridge is taking a chance, but I've got to risk it. Since there's a possibil-ity that the superstructure could collapse, I want you to take the men and walk across the bridge right now. They'll need to be alert in case there *are* snipers waiting."

"Yes, sir," nodded Rawlings, "but I think you should let us surround you for protection as we cross."

"I won't be with you. I'll be here in the engine."

"But you said yourself that the bridge could collapse," argued the lieutenant.

"That's right, Captain," interjected Coggins. "It's gonna be plenty dangerous aboard this train when it's on the bridge. If it collapses, it's about ninety feet down to the water. Not much chance of surviving that kind of fall."

"Exactly," said McGraw. "That's why you and Lou are going to walk across with my men. Yours truly will take the train over. You can show me how to handle the throttle and the brake."

The old man opened his mouth to argue, but McGraw cut him off. "There'll be no discussion on it, Charlie. While Lieutenant Rawlings is getting the men off the train, you can give me instructions." To Rawlings, he said, "Go, man! The flames are climbing to the trestle!"

Within three minutes the Sharpshooters were assembled on the ground beside the train. Coggins and Andreasen reluctantly left the cab and joined them. Smoke from the blazing trestle was billowing skyward.

Rawlings stepped up beside the cab and said, "Captain, I think you should let me run it across."

Flanking him were Hazzard and Cloud. Both asked to take the captain's place, but McGraw quickly commanded all three to move the men onto the bridge and get across.

Waiting in the cab, Captain McGraw watched his one hundred Sharpshooters bend low, rifles ready, and hasten onto the bridge. The crackling flames below gave off ample light so that he could watch them all the way across. Keeping the engineer and the fireman tight amongst them, the Confederate soldiers trotted across the bridge, coughing from the smoke clouds that rose from below.

McGraw was relieved that no shots came from out of the dark to pick them off. When the last man was safe on the other side, Lieutenant Rawlings took off his hat and waved it, signaling the captain. The Sharpshooters huddled together and looked across the river, concerned for the safety of their leader.

The flames were now licking close to the track bed on top of the bridge. Soon the rails would be red hot. Ryan McGraw released the brake, shoved his hat to the back of his head, and laid his hand on the throttle. Easing it forward, he felt the big engine move beneath his feet. The couplings between the cars creaked, and the train moved toward the blazing structure that spanned the river.

Sweat clung to McGraw's forehead, and his lips were a tense, straight line.

FOUR

Moving slowly, the big engine rolled onto the burning trestle. Captain Mc Graw could see flames now leaping up around the edges of the bridge and licking through the cross-bars beneath the tracks.

Smoke was filling the cab. He cupped one hand over his mouth and gripped the throttle with the other. His eyes smarted from the smoke and teared up. Heat waves seemed to surround the cab. Blinking to clear his vision, McGraw coughed and leaned out the window, looking for his men. The Sharpshooters were standing together in the firelight, but with the heat waves and the smoke, he could barely make them out.

The massive superstructure moaned and swayed slightly as it bore the full weight of the train. Fear swept over McGraw and sent icy streamers all the way to his joints and marrow. His heart was pounding his ribs.

The captain gritted his teeth and willed a veil of calm to settle over him. The engine was moving, but it seemed to be inching forward at a snail's pace. He wanted to give it more throttle, but Charlie had cautioned him not to give it too much steam at once. It could cause the huge steel wheels to spin, which would jar the weakened framework of the trestle.

McGraw knew it should take less than two minutes to get the train across the bridge, but the seconds seemed like hours. He sleeved sweat from his face and felt a cold trickle down his back.

The ravenous flames were eating away at the wooden super-structure, and the roaring of the fire made the whole experience seem like a wild dream. Suddenly the bridge began to sway dangerously. Giant timbers were cracking beneath him like rifle shots…and Ryan McGraw knew it was no dream.

He couldn't see them through the smoke at all now, but McGraw could hear his men shouting frantically for him to hurry. His nerves were stretched taut, and he was aware of pain in his left shoulder as he urged the throttle forward ever so slightly, hoping to gain more speed without jarring the bridge.

The locomotive picked up speed, but still it seemed to be crawling. McGraw wiped smarting tears from his eyes as he contin-ued to lean out the window and look for the end of the bridge. The smoke cleared briefly, and he caught a vague picture of the Sharpshooters bunched up beside the track, shouting that the bridge was about to go. A few more hour-long seconds passed and finally the engine was on solid ground, followed by the four cars.

McGraw cut the throttle and applied the brakes. The steel wheels shot sparks in every direction. When the train ground to a halt, McGraw could hear the Sharpshooters whooping and sending up a cheer. His knees felt watery. He leaned against the side of the cab, heaved a sigh and said, "Thank you, Lord."

Hap Hazzard was first in the cab, with Judd Rawlings, Noah Cloud, Charlie Coggins, and Lou Andreasen on his heels. The big redhead laid a steadying hand on McGraw's shoulder and said, "Nice job, Cap'n! You drove like a professional engineer, but I hope you don't ever have to do it again."

"I'll let you do it next time, Hap. One of those trips is enough for a lifetime."

Just then, the gigantic superstructure gave a death moan and the blackened trestle cracked and popped, giving way to the flames. It buckled, sending out a horrendous splitting sound, and collapsed with a mighty roar. Hundreds of timbers sailed downward like flaming torches, hissing and sending up billows of steam as they plunged into the deep waters of the Sepulga.

The Sharpshooters stood in silence until the last section of the bridge had come apart and dropped into the dark waters below, then their captain said, "All right, men, all aboard! In spite of Yankee skullduggery, this train's going to Mobile. Let's go!"

There was an exultant shout, and the rugged men of B Company piled back into their coaches. Captain McGraw and Lieutenant Rawlings returned to the supply car, and soon the train was rolling south once again.

As McGraw and Rawlings sat side by side in their "private" car, the lieutenant said, "I don't mean to be mushy or anything, but I'm sure glad you got across."

McGraw looked at him and grinned. "Thanks, ol' buddy."

After a few seconds, Rawlings asked, "While you were on the bridge, did you think of a little southern honey-blonde?"

McGraw eyed him levelly in the dim light. "You writing a book?"

Rawlings grinned. "No, but I was just wondering. Sometimes when a fella thinks his number might be up, his mind goes to the person who means the most to him."

The captain chuckled evilly. "It did. I thought of you!" As he spoke, McGraw rubbed his left shoulder.

"Aw, go on!" chortled Rawlings. Then noting what the captain was doing, he asked, "That shoulder still bothering you?"

"Yeah. It's been giving me some pain lately. I think I was pretty tense up there on that bridge. I'm sure my nerves and muscles were stretched plenty tight."

"I can understand that. Tell you what. Why don't I move to another seat and let you have this one all to yourself? That way you can at least lie down on your back...and I can do the same thing. Maybe we can get a little shut-eye if we're lying down. Okay?"

"Sure. It's worth a try."

When the lieutenant was on the seat in front of him, McGraw stretched out with his head next to the coach's side and his feet touching the floor in the aisle. He lay with his arms folded across his chest, listening to the steady clicking of the wheels beneath him. When he closed his eyes, one image after another raced across the screen of his mind.

The image that repeated itself over and over was that of a beautiful face surrounded by honey-blonde curls. Judd Rawlings's question kept echoing through his head: "While you were on the bridge, did you think of a little southern honey-blonde?"

Sleep fled from Ryan McGraw. His heart ached for Dixie Quade, and all he could do was think about how they met. His mind flashed back to that cloudy day in November of 1862. It was cold and bleak. He and his Sharpshooters were in a battle near the southern tip of Guntersville Lake in northeastern Alabama. Under intense fire by Yankee infantrymen, they were pinned down in a heavily wooded ravine.

Muskets rattled and rifles roared in the ravine. Blue-white smoke filled the cold air, and Rebel yells and Yankee shouts made the heavens shake.

Captain McGraw was hunkered in a thick patch of brush on the ravine's steep west bank, firing his revolver at Yankee soldiers on the ridge of the east side. Next to him was a frightened Rebel soldier, eighteen-year-old Bobby Brinson, who was not part of the B Company Sharpshooters. Brinson had been in a bloody battle in the woods an hour earlier, and had seen his best friend killed right next to him. The friend's blood had sprayed Bobby's face and uniform. The shock had been so great that young Brinson wandered from the scene of the battle, moving across a field as if in a sleepwalk.

There had been heavy fighting the entire morning all over the Guntersville Lake area with two units of Alabama artillery facing off against the invading Northern army, and First, Fourth, and Sixth Alabama Infantries shooting it out with the Yankees in open fields and in the woods.

Just before noon, Colonel Derrick Pendleton of First Alabama Infantry had ordered McGraw to maneuver his men across an open field to the ravine and work their way behind a Yankee artillery battery. They were to get in close enough to pick off the artillerymen from a stand of trees nearby. It was while the Sharpshooters were working their way across the field that they spotted the young Rebel soldier moving aimlessly ahead of them. Without a word to his men, McGraw zigzagged toward Brinson in a dead-heat run and took him down with a flying tackle. McGraw was able to get him into the relative safety of the ravine, where he found it necessary to slap him to bring him out of his daze.

After a few moments, Bobby came to himself and began weeping as he told the Sharpshooters of his friend being hit with flying shrapnel from an exploding cannonball. Surprised to find himself with McGraw and his men, young Brinson told them he belonged to the Fourth Alabama Infantry. The captain then told him to stay with the Sharpshooters until they could get him back with his unit.

Keeping Brinson close to his side, McGraw led his men through the deep, winding hollow. When they were drawing close to the Union artillery unit they were to wipe out, they were suddenly attacked from both ridges by Yankee infantrymen, shooting from the heavy brush.

The Sharpshooters scattered and dived into the thickets on the steep banks of the ravine. McGraw saw young Brinson go stiff and freeze in his tracks. Snatching him by the collar, he dragged him into the brush. He noticed two of his men go down and winced at the sight of it.

As McGraw fired his revolver at the enemy across the ravine, Brinson knelt beside him, terrified. He hugged himself and trembled all over. His earlier experience had shaken him severely. While reloading, McGraw said above the noise of the gunfire, "Bobby, it'll be okay, son! We'll make it out of here! Just hold on!" Teeth chattering with fear, Bobby looked up at him and nodded shakily.

There were B Company men strung out in the brush on both sides of their captain on the west bank. The ravine was a bedlam of noise and shouts. On the opposite bank, a few Yankees were already dead. Some were on the ground and others were sprawled atop the brush along the crest of the ridge, the thick branches supporting the dead weight of their bodies. Directly below them, nestled in the thickets, Sharpshooters were shooting at Yankees on the west ridge above McGraw and the Rebels who fought from that side.

Suddenly a massive rush of blue uniforms swarmed along the west ridge. Muskets popped like firecrackers and bullets thwacked brush all around. Sharpshooters fired repeatedly from the east bank at the swarm of Yankees. Ryan McGraw pivoted and blasted away at the enemy soldiers above him, killing two before they could back away over the crest of the ridge to reload their muskets.

A third appeared directly above him, raised his musket and fired. McGraw felt the heat of the bullet as it hummed past his right ear. His own gun spit fire, and the Yankee came tumbling down the bank, rattling brush. Bobby Brinson looked up, and the dead man snagged to a stop in the bushes just above him.

McGraw heard Bobby eject a blood-curdling scream, but he was busy blasting away at another Yankee on the ridge above him. When the man-in-blue went down dead, McGraw turned to check on Bobby, but he was gone. Then, from the corner of his eye, he saw the young Rebel groping his way through the brush at the base of the bank. Just as he turned to shout at him, Bobby broke free of the entanglement and began staggering across the bottom of the ravine in mindless terror. Bullets were hissing and plowing dirt all around him.

"Bobby!" bellowed the captain. "Get back here!"

There was no response. The terrified youth continued tottering in the open, disoriented. Holstering his gun, McGraw plunged down the steep bank with ragged branches clawing at him. When he touched bottom, he bent low and dashed toward the reeling youth as fast as he could. He was within twenty feet of him when a bullet tore through Bobby's right leg, dropping him like a rock.

At the same instant Bobby went down, McGraw's chest seemed to explode high up on the left side. The powerful impact of the slug spun him around and it felt like the ground flew up and hit him in the back. The breath was knocked out of him, and his left arm and shoulder were numb.

Bullets continued to chew earth around him as he sucked hard for air and tried to get up. The ravine was filled with smoky, acrid air, and made him cough. With effort, he rolled to his knees and looked about for young Brinson. When he spotted him several feet away, Bobby was writhing in pain, clutching his bleeding leg.

McGraw had no thought for his own safety. The frightened young soldier was hurt and in danger of being killed. He had to get Bobby back into the brush. From somewhere, a strong shout rose above the thunderous din of battle. McGraw was sure it was Hazzard's voice.

Walking on his knees to Bobby, McGraw loomed over him and gasped, "C'mon, kid. I'm going to carry you out of here."

Bobby blinked and said through gritted teeth, "You're hurt, Captain!"

"My legs are okay," breathed McGraw, extending his good arm. "Let me get you on my shoulder. Hurry!"

The captain heard Hazzard shout again as he struggled to get Bobby on his shoulder. When the weight was fully on him, he took a deep breath, willed the strength into his legs, and stood up. With the wounded young soldier draped over him, McGraw headed toward the west side of the draw.

He was aware of numerous shouts amid the gunfire as he staggered beneath the weight. His men were cheering him on. As he drew near the brush, he caught a glimpse of Hazzard's ruddy face through the smoke, and Jim Henry Hankins beside him. He was within five steps of Hazzard and Hankins when he felt the raw quiver of his knees beneath him. In spite of the hot lead hitting all around, Hap was almost to him when his legs gave way under Bobby's weight. As young Brinson was lifted off him, McGraw cried, "Hap, get back into the brush!"

McGraw's head was swimming, and his own voice sounded distant and unfamiliar to his ears. He was aware of Hankins kneeling beside him when a whirling black vortex seemed to be sucking him down into a dark abyss. The gunfire began to fade away as it echoed off the walls of the abyss that was swallowing him. Then all was black…and silent.

Captain Ryan McGraw had no idea how much time had elapsed since he had passed out, but it made no difference. There was sharp pain pulsating in his left shoulder, and he was aware of a rocking sensation, accompanied by hard jolts against his back. Brilliant light assaulted his eyelids. Seconds later, the brilliance subsided. Slowly he opened his eyes and looked directly above him. He was in a moving wagon, but could see no other person. Looming over him were tree tops silhouetted against patches of blue sky, and periodically he caught a glimpse of the sun.

McGraw tried in vain to find his voice. What had happened? He couldn't remember. Who was transporting him in the wagon, and where were they taking him? Why couldn't he see anyone?

Determined to find out who was driving the wagon, McGraw tried to roll into another position. The movement shot a fiery bolt of pain through his left shoulder, and the whirling vortex was back. It took only seconds to swallow him again.

Captain McGraw had the sensation of being thrust upward dizzily and felt light against the lids of his eyes once again. He lay still, without opening them, hoping his head would stop spinning. Vaguely he recalled coming to briefly in the back of the wagon, and remembered the sharp pain in his left shoulder. This time, he felt no pain anywhere. His mouth and throat were dry. He released a tiny groan and ran his tongue over equally dry lips.

He heard footsteps, accompanied by the sound of a woman's skirt when she walks. Suddenly he was aware that someone was standing over him. A soft, sweet voice said, "Captain McGraw. Captain McGraw."

His dizziness was fading. Ryan opened his eyes, blinked a few times, and tried to focus on the object that hovered over him. It was a dull blur.

The soft voice spoke again. "Captain McGraw, can you hear me?"

Ryan's tongue was dry as sand in the hot sun, but he forced himself to answer, "Y-yes."

A cool hand touched his brow. It was soft and tender. Blinking again, he attempted to focus on the woman who was speaking to him. Little by little her face became clear. It was a young and beautiful face. She was smiling at him. The face of a goddess, he thought. It was framed in lovely swirls of hair the color of spun gold.

Her eyes were sky-blue, with long natural lashes, and her smile deepened the dimples in her cheeks.

"Well, Captain," she said, tilting her head, "I'm glad to see you are still with us. For a while there, I thought you were going to sleep through the duration of the war. Dr. Pierce will be glad to know you've regained consciousness. Your men will be happy to learn of it too."

"My men...Oh, my men!"

In a flash, it came back. McGraw was carrying Bobby Brinson toward the thick brush with guns roaring all around and bullets buzzing through the smoke-filled air like angry bees. Suddenly he was down and Hap Hazzard was lifting Brinson off him. Jim Henry Hankins was kneeling beside him, then...then came the whirling blackness.

The lady in white was saying something about his thirst and placing a tin cup to his lips. He drank lustily until she withdrew the cup, saying he must not drink too much at a time.

Swallowing what water was in his mouth, he asked, "Where am I, ma'am?"

"You're in a Confederate hospital in Birmingham."

"Birmingham? How'd I—? Oh, yes. In a wagon."

"You remember that?"

"Only a few seconds of it. I was out again pretty fast."

"They had you heavily drugged. That's why you've been so long in coming around. They gave you laudanum for your pain while transporting you here."

"How long have I been here?"

"Four days. Of course, you had surgery as soon as you arrived, but Dr. Pierce didn't have to administer much laudanum for that—you were so far under, anyway."

Ryan recalled, then, that he had been hit in the upper left side of the chest. Suddenly he realized his left arm was in a sling. Looking down at it, he asked, "How bad is it?"

"You took a bullet near enough your shoulder that it dislocated it, and high enough that it chipped your collarbone. The bullet almost went all the way through. It was so close under the skin on your back that Dr. Pierce cut through and took it out on that side."

"Will I—will I be able to use my arm and shoulder again? I mean just like before?"

"Dr. Pierce will talk to you about it," she said quietly. "Now, you need to stop talking and rest. You've been through a lot."

"But what about my men? Do you know how many were killed? What about Bobby Brinson? Where's Judd Rawlings? Is he okay? And what about—"

"Captain," the woman said, placing a finger to his lips, "I said you need to stop talking and rest."

"But—"

"I can tell you this much, then you're going to settle down. We have five Sharpshooters here in the hospital other than yourself, and they're all doing fine. I understand Private Bobby Brinson is not actually one of your men, but he is coming along real good, too. The bullet that passed through his thigh just barely chipped bone. He'll be fine. I can't tell you exactly how the battle ended, but I think our Rebels put the Yankees on the run. At least that's the way I got it from listening to your lieutenant friend tell it to Dr. Pierce."

"So Judd's okay? He didn't get hit in the battle?"

"If he did, he's hiding it quite well," she chuckled. "He's been to see you several times a day, along with about a million other of your roughnecks. A person would think you're their father or something."

"Well, in a sense I am, ma'am. I have to watch over them like a father." He paused, then asked, "You haven't heard Judd say how many of our men were killed?"

"No. I hope there were none. Do you think some might have been killed?"

"It's possible. I saw two of them fall. There was so much smoke in that ravine, I couldn't tell who they were or how bad they were hit."

"Maybe those two are among the five we have here in the hospital."

"I hope so," breathed McGraw. Brow furrowing, he said, "You haven't told me your name, ma'am."

Her dimples deepened as she gave him an appreciative smile. "Dixie is my name, Captain. Dixie Quade."

"Dixie, eh?" he grinned. "There's some south in the way you talk. Where are you from?"

Picking up the tin cup and moving it toward his mouth, Dixie said, "That's all the talk for now, Captain McGraw. Drink this."

The cup was about a quarter full. McGraw finished it and smacked his lips. "Thank you, Miss—or is it Mrs. Quade?" As he spoke, his eyes trailed down to her left hand. There was no wedding band.

"It's Miss Quade, for your information. Now, Captain, you are going to rest. I'll see that some food is brought to you shortly."

Setting the cup on the small table beside the bed, she lifted his head gently, fluffed up the pillow, and said, "Close your eyes, now. Dr. Pierce will be in to see you after 'while. I'll let him know you're back with us."

As Dixie headed for the door, McGraw said, "I want to see my men. Where are they?"

"They're close by," she called back over her shoulder. "You'll see them in due time. No more talk." With that, she closed the door behind her.

Ryan McGraw closed his eyes, wondering about his men…then about the beautiful nurse. He visualized her fascinating features, her smile, her dimples, and dwelt on the soft sound of her voice.

Soon he was dozing.

A half hour later, Dr. Jeremiah Pierce entered the sunlit room, expressed his joy that the patient had come around, then described in detail the wound and the surgery he had done. He encouraged McGraw by saying he would get the full use of his arm and shoulder back again, but might be bothered somewhat by pain from time to time. It would not hinder his work as leader of the Sharpshooters.

Relieved, the captain asked when he could see his men. Pierce told him three of them were waiting near the front entrance of the hospital, and that Private Brinson, who was four doors down the hall, was wanting to see him. The doctor added, however, that Bobby would have to wait till tomorrow, and that the three men outside would be allowed five minutes once the dressing had been changed on the wound and McGraw had eaten.

The captain was happy to see nurse Quade enter the room. She was there to help Pierce change the dressing. When that was done, the doctor told his patient that he was healing as expected.

Twenty minutes after Pierce and the nurse had left, a chubby woman with her hair done in a scarf came in, carrying a tray of hot food. She placed it on the small table beside the bed and promptly left. McGraw looked at it from where he lay flat on his back, and wondered how he was going to manage getting to it. Even if he could work his way into a sitting position on the bed, it was going to be difficult to reach it and get the food to his mouth with one hand. All he could do was try.

It took him two or three minutes to get in a sitting position, and when he did, the room was spinning around him. At that moment, the door came open and the Miss Quade hurried toward him, saying, "Captain, you shouldn't be doing that by yourself."

Grinning sheepishly, he said, "Sorry, ma'am, but the little gal left the food and disappeared. I figured it was up to me to—"

"Pauline was supposed to let me know when she was ready to bring your meal to you. I'm sorry."

She helped brace him up in the bed, then stood beside him and fed him. When he had all he could handle, she helped him lie down, picked up the tray and said, "Do you feel like seeing your three friends, now? If not, I'll—"

"Yes!" he said quickly. "I want to see them."

"You do remember that Dr. Pierce said it could only be for five minutes?"

"Yes, ma'am."

"I will warn your visitors of that, too," she said, heading toward the door. Opening it, she paused, looked at him, and commanded, "I want you to take a nap as soon as they are gone."

Ryan grinned. "Yes, ma'am."

"You have a beautiful smile, Captain. One would never think you could show such warmth to hear your men talk about how tough you are."

The captain's grin broadened. "That's because they only see my tough side, ma'am. Don't dare show them that I have a warm side. I save that strictly for pretty nurses."

Dixie's features tinted, and without another word, she was gone.

Moments later, Lieutenant Rawlings and Sergeants Hazzard and Cloud filed into the room. They greeted their leader, elated to know he would be all right. To his pleasure, McGraw learned that none of the Sharpshooters were killed in the fight, and that the five who were wounded were out of danger. Three of them were wounded seriously, and would be mustered out of the army for medical reasons.

Rawlings told him how a division of Sixth Alabama came to their rescue only moments after he and Brinson were carried into the brush by Hap and Jim Henry Hankins. The Yankees were put into immediate retreat. Several had been killed and many wounded.

McGraw asked where the Sharpshooters were camped. Rawlings informed him they were bivouacked on the south side of town, then gave him the news that General Maury had ordered them to move south to Union Grove. Federal forces were collecting there, and a battle was brewing. They were to pull out in the morning. The trio was to greet McGraw for all of the men, and wish him a speedy recovery. They wanted him back at the helm. In the meantime, Rawlings would be in charge.

The door came open and Dixie entered. Her mouth was turned down in mock anger as she looked at Judd Rawlings and said, "Lieutenant, you promised me."

Rawlings wiped a hand across his mouth, grinned, and said, "Has it been five minutes already nurse?"

Dixie placed her hands on slender hips and said flatly, "It has been thirteen minutes, Lieutenant."

"Well, time sure gets by, doesn't it?" exclaimed Rawlings, acting surprised.

Hap Hazzard gave her a wide smile and said, "Really, ma'am, if you knew just how tough Cap'n McGraw is, you wouldn't worry about a matter of a few minutes. Why, he—"

"Out!" she spat, pointing at the door. Her eyes showed that she was having fun at their expense.

"Yes, ma'am!" gulped Noah Cloud, feigning fear. "We wouldn't want to rile you. No siree! C'mon, guys. Let's vacate this place before the cute little lady decides to throw us out!"

Dixie folded her arms and fixed them with widened eyes. All three quickly shook hands with McGraw and hurried toward the door, saying they would see him soon.

Moving slowly toward the bed and smiling, Dixie said, "Some bunch, Captain. Are they like this all the time?"

"No," replied McGraw. "They're dead serious when they're fighting Yankees."

FIVE

Early morning sunlight was seeping through the window in Captain Ryan McGraw's room when he awakened at the sound of busy feet and a rustling skirt. Opening his eyes, he saw nurse Dixie Quade laying out soap, washcloth, and towel on a chair next to the bed.

McGraw was captivated by her beauty as she smiled and said, "Good morning, Captain. The night nurse told me you slept well. I'm glad."

"Me, too," he grinned. "What's going on?"

"I'm getting things ready for your bath. You'll eat breakfast first, then we'll get you washed up all nice and clean."

"My bath?"

"Mm-hmm."

"In a tub?"

"No, not yet. Just a good washing with soap, hot water, and a cloth."

"It's…ah…it's going to be sort of difficult for me to handle with one arm in a sling, but I'll do my best."

"Oh, you won't have to do it yourself. I'll take care of it."

The captain's face crimsoned. "Y-you *what?*"

There was devilment in Dixie's eyes as she said smiling, "I told you…I'll take care of it."

"Now, wait a minute. You…you're not going to give me a bath!"

Hands on hips, Dixie said, "Oh now, really, Captain. Certainly you're not *that* shy!"

Clearing his throat and looking obviously uncomfortable, Ryan replied, "No female has bathed me since my mother did when I was a baby, ma'am—and that's the way it's going to stay."

"Oh, really," snickered Dixie, about to burst into laughter. "Who do you think bathed you yesterday, and the day before, and the day before that?"

Ryan's red face suddenly drained to white. "You didn't!"

Turning toward the door and smiling to herself, she said, "Pauline will bring your breakfast in a few moments. I'll be back to feed you, then we'll take care of that bath."

Pauline came with the tray of food, laid it on the small table, and was gone in a flash. Seconds later, Dixie returned to feed him. McGraw's dread of his bath caused him to chew his food very slowly, attempting to put off the inevitable as long as possible.

When he was finished eating, Dixie picked up the tray and said, "One of the orderlies will bring in a pail of hot water in a few minutes, Captain. I'll be back shortly."

"Yes, ma'am," he said weakly.

The orderly arrived within three minutes and set the pail on the table. He was a beefy, middle-aged man with bald head, ample belly, and hulking shoulders. Smiling, he asked, "Feeling better, Captain?"

"Yes. Somewhat."

"I'm Harold Schamberg. I've been giving you your bath every day since you've been here. Glad to see you awake."

Ryan felt a sudden mixture of emotions. He was relieved to know it was Schamberg who had bathed him, but at the same time he was ashamed of himself for letting Dixie make him a victim of her sly intimidation. Laughing within, he thought, *That little scamp! She had me scared spitless, and she knew it!*

Schamberg had been gone about half an hour when Dr. Pierce came in to check on his patient. He was pleased that McGraw was looking better, commented about it, and left. Shortly afterward, the door came open and Bobby Brinson appeared in a wheelchair, being pushed by a pale, skinny orderly who looked like he ought to be a patient himself. The orderly said he would come for Bobby in twenty minutes.

The two soldiers shook hands warmly as Bobby leaned forward in his wheelchair, then young Brinson said, "Captain, I want to thank you for what you did the other day. You saved my life twice...both times at the risk of your own. Words fail me, sir, but I want you to know I appreciate it."

"All in the line of duty, Bobby," Ryan grinned.

"Not so, sir. What you did was above and beyond your duty. Please accept my apology for the way I conducted myself. There's no excuse for a soldier to let the death of his close friend push him over the edge like I did."

"Don't be too hard on yourself. You're only human. I've seen men much older than you and a lot more experienced in combat go off their keel when somebody close to them was killed." He paused, then asked, "You going to request dismissal from the army?"

Bobby shook his head. "No, sir. That experience has made a man of me, Captain. I want to fight again when this leg heals up. The doctor says I'll be able to."

"Great! I'm proud of you. You'll do all right from here on out. I'm sure of it. I assume you've linked back up with your unit."

"Yes, sir. There are some other men here in the hospital from the Fourth Alabama. Colonel Stedham—that's my commander—was here yesterday. He had already learned about the way I acted at Guntersville Lake."

"What was his attitude?"

"Same as yours, sir. He didn't scorn me at all. Said I'd be a better soldier because of it."

"Good. Doc say how long you'd be in here?"

"Couple weeks. Then I have to go easy for about another six weeks. After that, I can get back into action."

There was a brief moment of silence, then young Brinson said cautiously, "Ah...Captain McGraw, sir?"

"Yes?"

"Did you really mean what you said—that you think I'll do all right as a soldier from here on out?"

"You bet. Why?"

"Well, sir...I...ah...I would like to join your Sharpshooter unit. That is, if you'll have me."

"How good are you with guns? Rifles *and* pistols? The way this war is, I don't have time to teach men how to shoot. General Maury only sends me men who are already crack shots. They also have to convince him they're Sharpshooter material. Most of the time, he'll take the word of their commanding officer for that."

"Well, sir, I've been handling rifles—or muskets—since I was ten, and revolvers since I was fourteen. The officers in Fourth Alabama call me 'dead-eye.' I don't say this to boast, but I'm known throughout my division as being a crack shot. Even Colonel Stedham is aware of it. He'll tell you that I'm speaking the truth. I can have him come in and talk to you. And I'll give you a demonstration just as soon as—"

"Hey, hey!" cut in McGraw, raising his free hand, palm forward. "I have no reason to doubt your ability with guns. It'd be rather foolish for you to sit there and tell me all this, then be found out a liar on the shooting range. Right?"

"Yes, sir." Light danced in his eyes as he asked, "You'll let me become a B Company Sharpshooter, then?"

McGraw grinned. "I'd be proud to have you in my outfit, Bobby. Of course, the transfer will have to be approved by General Maury. He'll do that only if Colonel Stedham—"

"The colonel already said he'd recommend it, sir. Depending on if you say you want me, that is."

"You'll have to go through some pretty tough training. You ready for that?"

"Yes, sir!" responded young Brinson, eyes shining. "It'll be an honor to serve with you!"

"Then consider it done," said McGraw. "We just lost three men to irreparable wounds, so we'll need new blood. I'll have General Maury leave a spot open for you. As soon as the doctor clears you for duty, we'll sign you up in B Company Sharpshooters."

"Thank you, sir."

Bobby was telling the captain about his parents and his childhood when the skinny orderly came back to return him to his room. McGraw asked Bobby to come back and see him soon. Agreeing to do so, Bobby gave the captain a parting smile as he was wheeled through the door.

Ryan lay quietly, letting his mind drift to his lovely nurse. He had never met anyone quite like her. She was not only beautiful on the outside, but she was equally beautiful on the inside. Her sense of humor was fabulous. He recalled the devilment in her eyes when she was "setting him up" for his bath. Dixie's inward beauty also consisted of tender compassion, which he could read in her expressions. And there was a wholesomeness about her—sweet, pure, fresh wholesomeness.

The captain was dozing when a gentle hand on his arm coincided with a familiar voice saying, "Captain McGraw, time for your medicine."

Looking up at her, McGraw blinked and put a mocking stern look on his face. "Oh, it's *you*," he said gruffly. "The nurse who likes to frighten poor, wounded soldiers to death."

Dixie was holding a cup of water mixed with powders. She giggled so hard, some of the water spilled over its rim.

McGraw's stern mask melted into a warm smile as he said, "I'll find a way to get even with you, Miss Quade!"

Giggling again, Dixie said, "Better not try it, Captain. That will only cause me to reciprocate…and I don't get even. I get *ahead*."

"I'm scared."

"You *were*," she laughed. "Did you have a nice bath?"

"Lovely."

"Wonderful," she said, placing the cup to his lips. "Drink it all down like a good little boy."

Ryan looked at the cup, gave her a scowl, and obeyed. When the cup was empty, she stood over him, looking down silently. There was an ineffable something in her sky-blue eyes. Something he could not name. Was it a special admiration for him, or was he just wishing it so?

To break the silence, Ryan asked, "Miss Dixie, I've been wondering about you."

She arched her eyebrows. "What about me?"

"Well…why you're not married."

"Oh?"

"I don't mean to be nosy, but most twenty-one-year-old ladies are married."

"Twenty-one? You flatter me. I'm twenty-four."

"Really? A *young* twenty-four."

"Thank you."

"That even enhances my curiosity. How can a young woman as lovely as you not have been snatched up by some knight in shining armor?"

"Quite simple," she replied. "I've had my share of would-be suitors, but when they learn the truth about me, they run away as fast as they can go."

"And what is that?"

"I turn into a frog at midnight."

McGraw laughed and laid a hand on his wounded chest. "Oh, don't make me laugh like that. It hurts."

"It's no laughing matter," Dixie said, pushing her lips into a pout. "How would *you* like to turn into a frog every night?"

Adjusting his arm in the sling, the captain said, "Okay. Now, seriously. There's a reason why you've gone this long without some knight in shining armor getting you to the altar to make you his blushing bride."

"You're right, Captain. And that reason is…I've yet to meet my knight in shining armor. So far, every man I've met and spent some time with has a chink in his armor."

"Oh. Looking for the perfect man, eh?"

"No, just the *right* man. Maybe I've been too busy to find him."

"What do you mean?"

"When I went to nurses' school, I was too occupied to get involved with a man. And since the war started, my duties here at the hospital have put me in the same position. I have some male friends, but no serious relationship.

Dixie studied him for a moment, then asked, "How about you, Captain? I happened to see your papers in the office the other day when they were out of the file. You're not married. Now, how is it that a handsome twenty-five-year-old man like you is not married?"

"Now, who's flattering whom? I'm twenty-eight."

"Really? A *young* twenty-eight."

"Thank you."

"To quote a famous Confederate captain, that even enhances my curiosity. How can a man as handsome and dashing as you not have been snatched up by some beautiful young maiden?"

Ryan's mouth pulled tight and his features paled. "Well, it…it's like this, Miss Dixie," he replied grimly. "I was married once, but my wife left me for another man."

"Oh, I'm so sorry," she said, putting her hand to her mouth. "Please forgive me."

"It's all right. I'm the one who started this question-and-answer session."

"But, I—"

Ryan reached out and took hold of the hand that held the empty cup. "It's all right, Miss Dixie. I'm completely over her now. It's been five years since she left me."

"Do you…have any children?"

"No. Thank the Lord. Children are the ones who suffer the most when a home is broken up." Sighing, he said, "I had suspected that she was seeing someone else, but there was nothing concrete. Just little things that happened now and then. We were living in Hattiesburg at the time. That's where I was born and raised. By the way, you never told me where you're from."

"Right here in Alabama. Tuscaloosa."

"So you really are a southern belle."

"That's what they say."

"Well, anyhow, back to my ex-wife—one day I came home from work and found a note staring me in the face. It said that she had left me for a better man. They would already be out of Hattiesburg by the time I came home. I never did learn who she ran off with. Several months later I received divorce papers, along with a brief note that she was marrying the man. I haven't seen her nor heard from her since. The letter came from Fort Payne, Alabama. She might've married a soldier. I don't know. And to tell you the truth, I don't care."

Dixie spoke quietly. "It's good that you can feel that way, Captain. Saves a lot of pain. But I'm sure it hurt plenty deep at first."

"Yes. I loved that woman a whole lot. But that love is dead."

Dixie was silent for a few seconds, then she asked, "Do you think you'll ever fall in love again?"

Ryan looked up at Dixie, meeting her gaze. He wanted to say, "Dixie, I think I'm falling in love with *you*," but after a brief moment he replied, "I sure hope so. Man needs a woman to love."

That ineffable something Ryan had seen in Dixie's eyes a few minutes earlier was there again…or was he imagining it? Was she having feelings toward him like he was having toward her? Was Dixie wanting to express them like he was wishing he could?

"It's only natural," she commented softly, then took a deep breath and said, "I'd better be going, Captain. The rest of my patients will think I've forgotten them."

When she reached the door, Ryan called after her, "Miss Dixie…"

"Yes?"

"Thanks for the medicine."

Her dimples were drawing him like a magnet as she smiled and said, "You're welcome, O mighty leader of Sharpshooters."

Dixie Quade was the bright spot in Ryan McGraw's life for the next couple of weeks. When he was able to leave the bed and sit in a wheelchair, she took him for rides up and down the halls, which gave him opportunity to meet other wounded Rebel soldiers.

Word came of his Sharpshooters from time to time. They were in battles and skirmishes in many parts of Alabama and eastern Mississippi under the capable leadership of Lieutenant Rawlings.

Private Bobby Brinson was sent home as scheduled to recuperate from his leg wounds, and would become part of B Company First Alabama Sharpshooters when army doctors pronounced him ready.

At the end of his second week in the hospital, McGraw was on his feet and getting his strength back. Once he was able to move around on his own, he saw little of the lovely nurse, who was busy with newly wounded men.

On New Year's Day, 1863, when McGraw had been at the hospital for just over four weeks, he was visited by Major General Dabney Maury. The general was glad to see him doing so well, and was pleased to hear that he was due to be released from the hospital on January 4. Maury said Lieutenant Rawlings was doing a fine job leading the Sharpshooters, but he was eager to see McGraw back with his men.

On the morning of January 4, Captain McGraw was in a fresh new uniform, getting ready to leave. He would meet his unit at Montgomery, where they were taking a much-needed rest. An army wagon was waiting at the front door of the hospital to take him to the depot where he would board a train for Montgomery.

The captain's mind was on Dixie Quade as he picked up his hat and crossed the room where he had spent so many hours talking to her.

He was just reaching for the doorknob when it turned and the door swung open. It was Dr. Jeremiah Pierce, followed by the lovely nurse.

The doctor smiled and extended his hand, saying, "Well, Captain, I guess this is good-bye."

Meeting his grip, McGraw returned the smile and said, "Yes, sir. I appreciate what you've done for me. You did a good job patching me up."

"Just see to it I don't have to do it again."

McGraw chuckled. "I'll do my best, sir."

When the doctor had gone, Dixie moved into the room, closing the door behind her. She stepped close and Ryan saw that same look come into her eyes as they misted up. Did she really care that he was leaving?

Towering over her, he nervously turned his hat in his hands as he said, "Well, Miss Dixie, it's time for me to move on."

Blinking to cover the thickening moisture in her eyes, she spoke softly, "We'll miss you around here, Captain."

Ryan was wishing Dixie had said *she* would miss him. Her eyes seemed to be saying it, but she hadn't voiced it. He must not allow his imagination to give him a false impression. Yes, there were tears visible, but maybe she was this way with all the soldiers she had nursed back to health.

Trying to smile, he replied, "I'll miss all of you, too. You're a great bunch of people."

"I...I'm glad I got to know you."

From somewhere deep inside Captain McGraw there arose a strong compulsion to take her in his arms and kiss her. But he refrained, struggling against his desire. Inwardly he scolded himself for even thinking of kissing her. She had been kind to him, but he had no reason to believe he stood on special ground with her.

"Same here," he nodded, forcing a smile. He was still twirling his hat in a circle by the brim.

Dixie laid a hand on his arm and said, "Take care of yourself, won't you?"

It was like an electric current was running through him from where her hand rested on his arm. "Sure."

"Maybe...maybe someday we will meet again."

"I'd like that." Angling himself to step around her and head for the door, Ryan said, "Good-bye, Miss Dixie."

She let him move past her, then asked, "Could I walk you to your wagon?"

"I'd be honored."

Together, Dixie Quade and Captain Ryan McGraw strolled down the hall to the front of the building. The sun was shining, but the January air was cool. Ryan stopped at the door, looked through the glass at the army wagon that waited for him, and said, "You'd best not go out there without a wrap, Miss Dixie. I'll just say good-bye again right here."

A touch of sadness showed in Dixie's eyes. "Good-bye, Captain," she said, almost choking on the words.

Ryan donned his campaign hat and opened the door. He was about to pass through it when he heard her say, "Captain..."

"Yes?"

Without a word, Dixie moved close, raised up on her tiptoes, and planted a soft, tender kiss on his left cheek.

Captain McGraw was at a loss for words. Touching his hat brim, he walked to the wagon and climbed in next to the private who held the reins. As the wagon pulled away, he looked back to see Dixie waving at him through the window. He waved back, and as soon as the wagon had carried him out of sight, he touched the spot she had kissed with his fingertips.

The memory of that magnificent moment brought Captain McGraw back to the present. He was flat on his back aboard the Mobile-bound military train...and found his fingertips touching that sacred spot on his left cheek.

He breathed Dixie's name and wondered if she was still taking care of Rebel soldiers at the Birmingham hospital. It had been a year and a half since he'd last seen her. Not a day passed without her beautiful face crowding into his mind. Dixie Quade deserved love and happiness. Maybe by now that right knight in shining armor had come into her life. Maybe she had fallen in love with one of her patients and married him.

McGraw's attention was drawn to the train itself as it began to slow. He sat up and looked out the window. Darkness still prevailed. Certainly they weren't nearing Mobile yet. At the same instant, the front door of the coach burst open, and fireman Andreasen came in out of breath, saying, "Captain, we've got trouble!"

Lieutenant Rawlings stirred and sat up, blinking his eyes as McGraw rose to his feet and said, "What's the matter?"

"I think the Yankees have set a trap for us!"

"What do you mean?"

"There's a fire on the track about a mile ahead. Charlie told me to come and get you."

McGraw turned to his lieutenant and said, "Get the men awake and ready for action, then come to the engine."

"You bet," said Rawlings, following the captain and the fireman through the door.

Men were stirring and the two sergeants were on their feet as McGraw dashed through the cars with Andreasen on his heels. When they asked what was happening, McGraw said, "Do what Lieutenant Rawlings tells you!"

Plunging into the cab of the big engine, the captain found Charlie leaning out the window with his hand on the throttle. Swinging out from the rear of the cab and looking ahead, McGraw saw the flames on the track, brilliant against the surrounding darkness. Clouds had covered the moon, shutting off most of its light.

"It's Yankees, all right," McGraw said to the engineer. "They've got an ambush set up, sure as anything."

The fire on the tracks was now about half a mile away, and

Coggins had the train barely moving. "What shall we do, Captain?" he asked.

"I don't know much about trains, Charlie. Can you ram that pile of burning wood without derailing us?"

"Maybe. The cow-catcher on this engine is set quite low. It'd be better that I hit it a little more than half of full speed. Any faster, and it could jumble the timbers and throw some of them underneath us."

Lieutenant Rawlings drew up to McGraw's side and asked, "So what's the story?"

"Yankees have set up an ambush."

Swinging out to see for himself, the lieutenant breathed, "Sure enough. What's your plan?"

"Charlie's gonna ram the barrier at better than half of full speed. Tell the men to get set. There'll be bullets flying out of the darkness from both sides of the train any minute. They need to stay as low as possible and fire back through the windows. All they can do is shoot at the flashes from the enemy guns. If we should derail, and they've got a large number of men out there, this could be a bad one. If we make it through the barrier, we'll be long gone before they can do too much damage to us."

"Let's hope it's the latter," clipped Rawlings and turned to leave.

"Lieutenant..." called McGraw.

Pausing, Rawlings looked back at him.

"Better put some men in the third car. If we get derailed, we for sure have to defend our ammunition and supplies."

"Yes, sir," nodded Rawlings, and was quickly on the catwalk of the coal car.

Turning back to the engineer, McGraw said, "Give the men a few seconds to get ready, Charlie, then shoot the steam to it."

Coggins nodded his agreement, then said to his fireman, "Lou, throw some more coal in the firebox."

While Andreasen was doing so, Coggins said, "Captain, how do you suppose them dirty Yankees found out this train was coming through to Mobile?"

"Hard to say, what with that bridge on fire earlier, and now this. When we found the bridge burning, I figured it was probably just a random piece of Yankee destruction. But what we're facing here is purposeful ambush. Maybe we'll never know how they found out we were coming. War always leaves a lot of questions unanswered."

Just as Andreasen was closing the big iron door of the firebox, Sergeant Hazzard came around the side of the coal car and said, "Cap'n, we're about ready. Lieutenant Rawlings wanted me to tell you that he's distributed the men evenly in the three cars, and that he's commanding the third car."

"Thanks," said McGraw. Then to Coggins, "Okay, Charlie, let's go." Turning back to Hazzard, he said, "Hang tight back there, Hap. This could get rough."

"I'm thinkin' maybe I should send a couple men up here with you, sir."

"I don't think that'll be necessary. However, how about sending me a repeater rifle and some ammunition?"

"Will do," said Hazzard, and hopped onto the catwalk.

The train was picking up speed as McGraw said to the fireman, "Lou, I want you to climb in the coal car and keep your head down."

"I'd rather get my hands on a gun and help fight, sir," countered Andreasen.

"I appreciate that, but you're a civilian, and you're my responsibility. You'll be safest in the coal car. I'd put Charlie in there with you if I thought I could handle this thing when it hits that barrier."

"Do what the man tells you, Lou," cut in Coggins. "He's only tryin' to save your hide."

"I know," said the fireman. "I appreciate that, but I just want to do my part."

"Do your part by relieving my mind about you," came McGraw's firm words.

Saying no more, Andreasen climbed into the coal car and sat on the bottom in the black dust, behind the huge pile of coal.

Leaning out the window behind Coggins, McGraw looked at the blazing blockade on the tracks and asked, "How fast will we be going when we hit it?"

"About thirty-five miles an hour."

"Guess that'd be a little too fast for Yankees to run alongside and try to get on board."

"Yep."

"Of course if they've got horses, they could ride up and try to get on."

"Yep."

"Captain McGraw," came a voice from behind him.

Turning around, McGraw found himself looking at Corporal Bobby Brinson. Extending a Henry repeater and a small canvas sack loaded with cartridges, he said, "Sergeant Hazzard said I should bring these to you."

"Thanks, Corporal."

His features solemn, Brinson said, "Sir, I would like to respectfully request that I be allowed to stay here with you. It's not good that you should be here in the cab without some protection."

"I'll be fine. You get back to your post."

"Yes, sir."

When the corporal was gone, McGraw thought again of the day he had saved Bobby's life...and of the time in the Birmingham hospital when the bright-eyed youth had asked to become a part of the Sharpshooters. He had proven over and over again that his bloody experience at Guntersville Lake had been the making of him. Bobby had proven himself courageous and capable of operating under fire on many occasions since becoming a McGraw Sharpshooter.

The train was drawing close to the burning barrier on the track. Charlie Coggins spoke over his shoulder while keeping his eye on it and said, "Better brace yourself, Captain. Hard to tell just how big that pile of wood might be. May give us a good jolt when we hit it."

McGraw laid the sack of cartridges on the floor of the cab,

levered a cartridge into the chamber of the Henry, and went to the other window, holding the rifle in one hand and bracing himself with the other.

Suddenly there was gunfire on both sides of the cab, and bullets were ricocheting angrily off the hard metal of the cab. In the vague surroundings along the track, McGraw could see horsemen charging toward the train firing repeater rifles. He turned to tell Coggins to duck down, only to see him draped out the other window. Dashing to him, McGraw pulled him inside the cab and laid him on the floor. One of the first bullets in the volley that had come out of the night had struck him in the right temple. Charlie was dead.

McGraw caught sight of a rider drawing up beside the cab, raising his rifle. Reacting quickly, the captain fired. The Union cavalryman stiffened and peeled from the saddle as the slug tore into his chest.

McGraw hopped to Charlie's window, laid his hand on the throttle, and looked ahead on the track. The blazing pile of timber was no more than fifty yards away. The sounds of rapid gunfire behind him were forgotten for the moment as he braced himself for the impact.

SIX

The locomotive slammed into the burning timbers with a thundering roar, scattering fiery missiles in three directions. Sheets of flame fanned into the night air, along with a massive shower of bright-red sparks, some flying thirty feet above the ground.

The impact slowed the train slightly, jarring everyone on it, but it began to pick up momentum seconds later. Ryan McGraw breathed a prayer of thanks that the stack of burning wood had not been too large. The Yankees had apparently hoped to delude the engineer into thinking it would be too dangerous to attempt plowing through it. A train was a wicked thing to be aboard when it went off the tracks.

McGraw looked back where the blazing timbers were scattered, and saw the Yankees on horseback making a wide circle around the flaming debris, intending to catch up to the train. Already the Rebels in the three coaches were firing at them.

Just as McGraw squared himself with the cab, he saw more riders coming at a gallop from both sides of the track up ahead. The wide swath of the engine's single headlight showed them clearly. He hated to do it, but he called over his shoulder to the fireman, asking him to leave the coal car and come to the cab.

When Lou Andreasen reached the cab and saw the engineer lying on the steel floor, he gasped, "Charlie!"

"He's dead, Lou," McGraw said sadly. "Nothing we can do for him now. Do you know how to run this thing?"

"Yes," nodded Andreasen, unable to tear his gaze from his dead friend.

"Okay. Take over. I've got to put my gun to use. Keep down as low as you can, but watch for any more obstacles on the tracks."

With the fireman at the controls, Captain McGraw leaned out the opposite window and shouldered his rifle. Two riders were drawing near from up ahead. The one in the lead lifted his carbine and fired at McGraw. The captain pulled his head inside just in the nick of time. The bullet struck the coal car and careened off with a shrill whine. At the same time, McGraw returned to his spot and fired, hitting the rider square in the chest. The sudden lurch of the man's body threw his animal off stride, causing it to stumble. When it went down, the horse behind it was unable to avoid it. Man and beast did a somersault, slamming the ground savagely.

At the same instant, Andreasen shouted, "Captain! Behind you!"

McGraw whirled about to see a man in blue coming up the steel steps at the cab's rear on the right side. His horse was just veering away. The muscular Yankee was gripping a revolver and bringing it to bear. McGraw had levered a fresh cartridge into the chamber of his Henry, but there was no time to bring it around. He leaped aside a split second before the gun discharged and the slug buzzed past him through the glassless window.

Before the Yankee could cock the revolver for a second shot, McGraw kicked it out of his hand. It went flying into the night. The Yankee was no novice at fighting. He leaped for McGraw, gripped the Henry with both hands and attempted to wrench it from its owner. The two enemies struggled for supremacy, each knowing that if he didn't kill his man, he would be the one to die.

✴ ✴ ✴

The first volley of unexpected shots had dropped three
Sharpshooters—two in the first coach and one in the second. One of
the two in Sergeant Hazzard's coach was dead with a slug in his head.
The other lay wounded with a bullet in his shoulder. The man in
Sergeant Cloud's coach was still alive, with a mangled, bleeding ear.
A Yankee bullet had taken part of it off.

The rear door of the third coach had no window, which allowed a couple of Union cavalrymen to ride up at the rear and leap
aboard without being seen. Each wore two revolvers on his hips. One
was a corporal, the other a sergeant. The sergeant tested the door and
found it locked. "Okay," he said, "we've got about thirty seconds before the engine hits the fire. The door is plenty thin. We empty our
guns through the door, then put our backs to the rear of the car and
brace for the impact. The barrier won't stop the train, but it'll slow it
down. That's when we jump."

"Gotcha," nodded the corporal.

"Okay," said the sergeant, pulling both guns, "on the count of
three!"

Inside the third coach, Lieutenant Rawlings had his men hunkering
on the floor at the windows, between the seats, firing at the riders.
Rawlings was at one of the rear windows, using a repeater. He had
just shot one of the Yankees from his horse when he noticed the wave
of riders veering away from the train. A glance to the other side
showed him the same thing. The horsemen were easy to see now, because of the huge blaze on the tracks.

Rawlings knew the engine must be about to slam into the
burning barrier. Lifting his voice above the din, he shouted, "Brace
yourselves, men! We're about to hit that pile of timber!"

Even as the last words were coming from Rawlings' lips, a barrage of shots came plowing through the rear door, scattering splinters

everywhere. The lieutenant saw one of his men near the front of the coach take a slug that came through the door. Rawlings flattened himself on the floor and began firing through the door as fast as he could work the lever on the Henry. While he was peppering the door, suddenly the coach seemed to skid on the tracks, throwing every man forward.

Sheets of flame, sprays of sparks, and flying pieces of blazing timber could be seen through the windows. Every man in the coaches knew the train had survived the impact against the barrier and had come through without being derailed. Already it was picking up momentum.

In coach number three, Lieutenant Rawlings scrambled to his feet, drew his revolver, and eased up to the bullet-riddled door. He slid the bolt and jerked it open. By the dim light of the lantern behind him, he saw two Union soldiers lying dead on the small platform. Rawlings was about to throw the bodies off the train when more riders came thundering in, guns cracking. He leaped back inside, slid the bolt to lock what was left of the door, returned to his window, and picked up the Henry.

Inside the second coach, the Sharpshooters were readjusting their positions after being thrown forward when the train hit the flaming barrier. Sergeant Cloud looked around and asked, "Everybody all right?" There was a chorus of yeses.

Corporal Jim Henry Hankins was at a window reloading his repeater rifle and saw the dark forms of Union horses and riders drawing close to the train once more. "Sergeant!" he called out. "Here they come again!"

"Over here, too, Sergeant!" shouted Luther Mangus on the opposite side.

"Let 'em have it, boys!" bellowed Cloud, gripping his rifle and diving for the window he had occupied before the train hit the barrier. Rifles began to bark and bullets slammed into the coach. The rocking and swaying of the train made it difficult to hit the riders, especially in the dark, but from time to time the vague form of a Yankee could be seen falling from his saddle.

Private Brad Thacker squatted down to reload his rifle when he saw the rear door of the coach come open. At first he thought it was one of the Sharpshooters from the third coach, but when he caught sight of a gun muzzle being thrust through the opening and a blue uniform behind it, he realized that one of the Yankees had boarded the train from the back of his horse.

Thacker's heart froze. His rifle was out of service. The door was ten feet from where he was positioned between two seats. Reacting by instinct, he threw his weapon at the protruding gun barrel and shouted, "Back door!"

The Yankee's gun discharged, but its slug went wild because Thacker's rifle slammed against it. It took a couple of seconds for the other Sharpshooters in the car to respond. Several guns roared, sending hot lead through the opening and into the door.

When the firing stopped, Sergeant Cloud dashed to the door, but the Yankee was not in sight. He picked Thacker's rifle up, handed it to him, and said, "That was fast thinking, pal."

"Thank you, sir," grinned Thacker.

"Don't call me 'sir', boy. I'm not an officer."

"Yes, sir. I...I mean, yes, Sergeant."

Suddenly there were heavy thumping sounds directly above them. Cloud knew where the Yankee had gone. Raising his rifle, he shot through the ceiling of the coach. Working the lever rapidly, he fired several more times. A "whump" sounded overhead, then a corpse tumbled onto the small platform where the rear door stood open.

"Got him!" shouted Cloud, moving onto the platform. Using his foot, he shoved the dead Yankee off the train.

A new wave of riders was coming in, guns blazing. Two slugs chewed wood near Cloud's head. Dashing inside, he slammed the door and slid the bolt. The Sharpshooters quickly resumed their positions at the windows.

Brad Thacker, who had been with McGraw's Sharpshooters since October of 1862, returned to his window and bent low to finish loading his rifle. The sound of booming guns was deafening. Bullets were striking the coach from both sides. Suddenly a slug ripped through the wall of the coach and hit Thacker in the right side. He groaned and doubled over on the floor.

In the first coach, Sergeant Hazzard and his men were blasting away at the shadowed horsemen who came and went in waves. Several riders had come up close, fired point blank into the coach, then swept away quickly. Two of the Yankees had left their horses and grabbed onto the platform just behind the coal car. They found the door locked. One turned to the other and said, "Let's get 'em from the side!"

The platform was built so a person hanging onto its railing could swing out and look into the windows. The closest window on either side was a mere two feet from the vehicle's front end.

With revolvers in hand, the Yankees each took a side and swung out far enough to hang onto the rail with one hand and stick his gun through the window with the other.

Sergeant Hazzard happened to be at the first window on the right side. The Yankee on the left side was in position first and fired. The Sharpshooter at that window took the slug through the head and keeled over.

While the same Yankee was drawing a bead on the next Rebel inside the coach, the one on the other side stuck his hand through Hazzard's window. The Sergeant had just witnessed the shooting of his man across the aisle and was bringing up his gun to fire at the enemy who had shot him when some sixth sense caused him to turn toward his own window. The muzzle of the Union revolver was just coming inside.

Hazzard dropped his weapon, seized the revolver, and swung it upward. It fired and the bullet went through the ceiling. Hazzard's powerful hands twisted the gun from the man's fingers, and he put a steely grip on his wrist.

Across the aisle, the other Yankee fired again, hitting another Sharpshooter in the back. A split second later, Corporal Brinson's rifle fired through the window of the coach and tore into the Yankee's forehead. He dropped instantly from sight.

While the other Sharpshooters were firing at the riders, an angry Hap Hazzard had pulled the Union soldier halfway through the window. Gripping the man's arm, Hazzard stood up and brought it down violently against his up thrust knee. Bone snapped loudly. The Yankee released a blood-curdling wail, and Hap let him fall to the ground.

In the engine, Lou Andreasen stood at the controls and watched the death-struggle between Captain McGraw and the enemy soldier. Andreasen wanted to jump in and help subdue the big man, but to do so would leave the engine unattended. Such a move could result in a disaster to the entire train.

While guns popped beyond the coal car, McGraw and his enemy grappled for control of the Henry on the steel floor of the engine. They moved in jerky circles, stumbling repeatedly over the lifeless body of Charlie Coggins.

The Yankee was heavier than McGraw, and was trying to use his weight to proper advantage. He found, however, that the smaller man was a mountain of strength. Only by his bulk had the Yankee been able to stay in the fight. McGraw's shoulder wound was giving him pain, but he ignored it. He must overcome the big man and kill him.

At one point, the Yankee was able to swing McGraw around, putting his back toward the coal car. He was trying to shove McGraw backward so that he would fall off the engine and be ground to death beneath the wheels. He would gladly let go of the rifle to let it and the Rebel captain fall to the tracks.

McGraw knew what the man had in mind. When he felt himself being forced toward the edge of the cab, he stiffened and dug his heels into the engine's floor. They were again meeting strength for strength. When the Yankee saw that he could not break McGraw's stance, he suddenly jerked backward to throw him off balance. It didn't work. The seasoned Sharpshooter planted himself quickly, and drove the bigger man against the firebox, pinning him there. Their hands quivered as they gripped the Henry between them.

The husky man did all he could to force McGraw backward, but found himself without leverage because he was flattened against the firebox. The struggle continued while the engine picked up speed. Within thirty seconds, the Yankee was well aware of the rising heat on his back side. Sweating, he growled and grunted, trying to push away, but the smaller man seemed to be made of raw steel.

When the Yankee's blue pants began to smoke, he let out a howl. McGraw took advantage of his pain to wrest the rifle from his hands, let it fall, and surprise him by chopping him savagely on the throat and the left side of the neck with the edge of his hand, a move he had learned from the Japanese gardener of his childhood.

The Yankee gagged from the throat chop and went numb on the left side of his body. Momentarily defenseless, he felt himself hurled across the steel floor of the cab. A wild scream came from his lips as he sailed over the edge, bounced off the coupling between the engine and the coal car, then went under the merciless wheels.

The moon had reappeared and was spraying the land with silver light. Sucking hard for breath, McGraw looked back along the train and saw that the Union cavalrymen had given up the chase. The train was now traveling at nearly fifty miles per hour.

Picking up his rifle, the captain found Andreasen smiling at him. "That was some kind of fighting, sir."

"Not the kind I'd want to do every day," gasped McGraw rubbing his aching shoulder. "Keep this choo-choo steaming toward Mobile, Lou. I'm going back to check on my men."

When Captain McGraw had been in all three coaches and totaled up the damage, he found that three of his men were dead and four wounded. Four lives had actually been lost with the death of engineer Charlie Coggins.

At 5:20 A.M., the train pulled into Mobile's depot. McGraw had been told by General Maury that a unit of men would be there from Fort Morgan to meet them and transport them south to the fort.

The unit of twenty men had camped nearby and were on hand when the train pulled in. Their leader was Lieutenant Wesley Hall, who was pleased to meet the famous Captain Ryan McGraw, but saddened to learn of the ambush and its drastic results. The bodies of the dead Sharpshooters would receive proper burial at Fort Morgan's cemetery.

When Andreasen advised McGraw that Charlie Coggins had no surviving family, Hall said he could be buried with the soldiers. The bodies were placed in an army wagon. Another wagon would take the wounded men to Mobile's hospital, where Rebel soldiers wounded in other battles were recuperating. The army had hired a steam-engined barge to transport the wagons carrying Sharpshooters, weapons, ammunition, and supplies the twenty-eight miles south on Mobile Bay to Fort Morgan.

When Captain McGraw told Hall that he was going to deliver his wounded men to the hospital, the lieutenant said, "Oh, that won't be necessary, sir. I'll send one of my sergeants with them."

"I appreciate your willingness to offer the sergeant's services, Lieutenant, but this outfit operates a little different than the rest of our Confederate army units. These men look to me as a father. Now, would a father just send his boys over to that hospital, or would he *take* them there?"

Hall cleared his throat. "He would take them there, of course, sir. I understand."

"I appreciate that."

Hall forced a smile. "It's all right, then, for the rest of your men to go on down to the fort?"

"Yes. My lieutenant, Judd Rawlings, here, will remain with me."

A HEART DIVIDED

4 2 3

"Very well, sir," nodded Hall. "The same wagon that takes you and your men to the hospital will be here to carry you down to the dock at whatever time you choose. The army has a couple of ferry boats that move us up and down the bay whenever needed. I'll make sure one is waiting for you. I'll explain all of this to General Page and tell him you'll be along as soon as possible."

"Thank you," said McGraw.

"Yes, sir. We're mighty glad to have you and your men at Fort Morgan with us, sir."

"We're honored to be a part of the team," nodded the captain.

McGraw stood before his men and explained the situation. Others wanted to stay with the wounded, but the captain told them it was best if they went on to the fort. He assured them he would see to it that the wounded men received the very best of care, and that he would not leave them until he was completely satisfied.

Captain McGraw delivered Corporal Dean Bradbury, Corporal Vince Udall, Private Clint Spain, and Private Brad Thacker into the hands of the hospital's chief surgeon, Dr. Glen Lyles, who examined them immediately upon arrival.

Udall had been shot in the back and the bullet had lodged in his lung. He was prepared for surgery immediately, since he was in the most danger. Bradbury had a bullet in his shoulder and would be operated on by a second surgeon within a few minutes. Private Thacker had been creased in the side by a Yankee bullet that had passed on through. Another doctor would clean the wound and patch him up. Private Spain had a tattered ear, which was bandaged upon his arrival at the hospital. The doctor who worked on Thacker would do what he could for Spain once he had stitched up Thacker.

McGraw and Rawlings stayed until all four had been attended to and the doctors had reported their condition. Udall would be the longest of the four to recover, but Dr. Lyles pronounced him out of danger after doing the surgery.

After talking to Lyles in his office for several minutes, the two Sharpshooter officers thanked him for the good care he was providing their wounded men and made ready to leave. The doctor walked them to the office door and stepped into the hall. He chatted with them about the festering situation at the mouth of Mobile Bay, then returned to his office.

Corporal Udall was in a private room with a special nurse to look after him. McGraw and Rawlings went to the room to see how he was doing. The nurse would not let them in, but said she would tell Udall they were inquiring about him. McGraw asked her to convey the message that he would be back in a day or so to see him. She assured him she would pass it on, and closed the door.

Bradbury, Spain, and Thacker had been placed in a four-bed room together, along with another wounded soldier who had lost his left arm in a battle on the Alabama-Mississippi border a week previously. He was Sergeant Marvin Staples of the Ninth Alabama Cavalry.

Upon entering the room, McGraw and Rawlings found Bradbury and Thacker asleep, still feeling the effects of the laudanum. Spain was awake and glad to see them. He was also glad to hear that Udall was going to be okay.

Spain introduced the captain and the lieutenant to Sergeant Staples. The sergeant had heard of McGraw. He shook hands with both officers, saying that he was glad the Sharpshooters were going to be at Fort Morgan when the Union navy decided to make a move on Mobile Bay. McGraw and Rawlings felt sorry for the man, who had only a bandage on his shoulder where his left arm had been, but they did not show it. No wounded soldier wanted to be pitied.

Telling Spain he would be back as soon as he could and to pass the message on to the "sleeping beauties," McGraw headed for the door with Rawlings on his heels. Pausing before moving into the hallway, he said, "Clint, I don't want you chasing any pretty nurses around this place. Understand?"

Grinning, Private Spain cupped a hand to his bandaged ear

and said, "Eh? I'm deaf, Captain. Cain't hear a word you're sayin'!"

McGraw laughed, waved him off, and moved into the hall.

As the two Sharpshooters moved along the hall, they were noticed by a nurse working on a patient in one of the rooms. Near the front door of the building, they ran onto Dr. Lyles, who was in conversation with the surgeon who had operated on Dean Bradbury. McGraw and Rawlings spoke briefly to them, then passed through the door and climbed into the army wagon that waited for them.

Dr. Lyles turned to walk back to his office. He was almost there when he looked up to see one of the nurses trotting toward him. He saw that she was excited and said, "You look like one of your patients just had a miraculous healing, Dixie."

"It's almost as good as that, Doctor," she said breathlessly, brushing a lock of honey-blond hair from her forehead. "I just saw you talking to Captain Ryan McGraw!"

SEVEN

Dr. Glenn Lyles noted the dancing beads of light in Dixie Quade's eyes, and said, "You know Captain McGraw, I assume."

"Yes sir," Dixie replied, realizing how excited she had sounded. Clearing her throat, she covered her elation a bit and said, "The captain was a patient of mine at the Birmingham hospital about a year and a half ago."

"Got pretty well acquainted with him, eh?"

"Well, he was under my care for several weeks. We did get to know each other. Why is he here?"

"He and his famous Sharpshooters have been assigned to Fort Morgan because of the Union naval buildup off the Gulf coast. While coming down here from Montgomery on a special train, they were ambushed by Union cavalry. Three of his men were killed, and four were wounded. He and his lieutenant brought the wounded ones in for treatment. Couple of them had to have surgery."

"I recognized Lieutenant Rawlings, too," smiled Dixie. "Are the wounded Sharpshooters all in the same room?"

"Three of them are. Room twenty-seven. The other one is in worse shape. He's in room fourteen."

"I see. Thank you, Doctor. Well…I have to get back to work."

Dixie's heart fluttered as she made her way along the hall and entered a room to change the dressing of an elderly woman who had been burned severely with boiling water. The patient was under heavy sedative and was barely aware that the nurse was working on her. With no one to interrupt her thoughts, Dixie let her mind run to the handsome Rebel captain. She recalled the day he was brought into the Birmingham hospital. She had watched over him like a mother hen for four days after his surgery while he lay under the influence of laudanum, wondering what color his eyes might be.

While dabbing the elderly woman's burns with ointment, Dixie smiled to herself, remembering the morning Ryan awakened and opened his eyes. When she saw they were a magnificent pale blue, she told herself they fit perfectly with his sandy hair and mustache.

Dixie had also wondered for four days what his voice might be like. She was sure it would be strong, deep, and masculine…his entire makeup was so manly. And sure enough. When he spoke, he sounded exactly as she had imagined.

Was that when she fell in love with him? She thought so. If not, it came the next morning when she made him think she was going to give him a bath. *He was so darling,* she thought. *His face turned such a deep shade of red. Then when I made him think it had been me who had bathed him every day since he had been in the hospital, he went white as a sheet!*

One thing Dixie knew for sure—she had fallen head-over-heels in love with Captain Ryan McGraw almost from the first moment she met him. She thought of how it had bothered her when he began to get better and they had less time together. During their all-too-infrequent visits, they had experienced some precious moments together. At least they had been precious to Dixie.

While wrapping new dressing on the elderly woman's burns, Dixie recalled many of the moments she had enjoyed with Ryan until the very day they had to say good-bye. She remembered how she had looked for some sign in his eyes…anything that would tell her they had become more than just nurse and patient. For a moment there seemed to be an indication that he wanted to take her into his arms, but it quickly faded.

Feeling a sharp disappointment, she could only lay a hand on his arm and tell him to take care of himself, then remark that maybe someday they would meet again. He was kind enough to say he would like that, but gave her no hope that it would come to pass.

Dixie discarded the old dressing and put things away in the small cabinet. Making sure her patient was comfortable, she left the room and hurried down the hall to the nurses' "powder" room. Finding it unoccupied, she let herself recall that last moment, when at the hospital door she had kissed Ryan's cheek to show her affection for him, then waved good-bye through the window as he rode away.

Tears filled Dixie's eyes as she remembered how she wept that night in her bed—and many nights thereafter—missing the handsome captain who had unknowingly stolen her heart and realizing that she might never see him again.

Using a hanky to dry her tears, Dixie thought, *But here he is…assigned to Fort Morgan, less than thirty miles from me, and no doubt intending to return to the hospital to see his men!*

Pulling herself together, she returned to duty. Ryan was on her mind constantly for the rest of her shift. When her day was over in late afternoon, there was one more thing she had to do. Maybe some of the wounded Sharpshooters had been with the outfit when Ryan was in the Birmingham hospital. If this was so, she wanted to know it. Maybe she could learn a vital thing or two.

Dixie made her way to room twenty-seven and opened the door. The first face she saw belonged to the man with one arm. She had tended to Sergeant Staples the first couple of days he was at the hospital. When her gaze met his, she said, "Hello, Sergeant. How are you doing?"

"Fine, ma'am," grinned Staples.

"Good. I've been working the other end of the hospital and haven't had time to stop and see you."

Before Dixie could scan the faces of the three Sharpshooters, one of them exclaimed, "Well, I declare! Miss Dixie, is that you?"

The owner of the voice had a familiar face, and by the fact that he recognized her, she knew he had to have been among the Sharpshooters a year and a half previously. Moving up to his bed, she smiled and said, "I know your face, soldier, but the name escapes me."

"I'm Corporal Brad Thacker. Well...I was *Private* Brad Thacker when you knew me."

"Congratulations on your promotion."

"Thank you, ma'am." Turning to his comrades, who lay looking on, Thacker said, "Fellas, I'd like you to meet the most beautiful and charming nurse in the business. Miss Dixie, this is Corporal Dean Bradbury next to me, and that guy over there is Private Clint Spain."

"Pleasure to meet you, ma'am," said Bradbury and Spain.

"The pleasure is mine," smiled Dixie. "You'll have to excuse the corporal's accolades about me. As I recall, he thinks any young lady in starched white dress and nurse's cap is beautiful and charming."

"Aw, Miss Dixie," Thacker retorted mildly, "that just ain't so."

"Dr. Lyles told me about the ambush you Sharpshooters had on your way down here," said Dixie. "Looks like you tough guys will survive, though."

"Sure we will," said Thacker. "We've got another Sharpshooter here, too. He got shot up a little worse than us, so they've got him in a private room."

"So Dr. Lyles told me. Is he anyone I know?"

"No, ma'am. He's like these two guys here. He came along after our esteemed leader had been in the hospital." Eyes widening, he said, "Did you see the captain when he was here earlier?"

"Well, yes and no. I saw him from a distance—he and Lieutenant Rawlings—but I didn't get to talk to him. I asked Dr. Lyles what Captain McGraw was doing here, and he told me about the ambush and you men being brought in."

"Well, he'll be back in a day or so, ma'am," said Thacker. "He'll sure be glad to see you, that's for sure."

Dixie's heart thudded against her rib cage. Hoping to hear Brad Thacker say that the captain had mentioned her often over the past year and a half, she queried, "Oh? Why do you say that?"

"Because when Captain McGraw was in the hospital there in Birmingham, he mentioned lots of times that your smile and cheerful ways were hastening his recovery."

A feeling of disappointment washed over Dixie like cold water. "Oh. I see. Well, I'm glad to know that." She paused, then asked, "Does his shoulder wound bother him any more?"

"Sometimes. I've seen him rubbing it quite often. S'pose maybe it'll always give him pain now and then."

"It could." There was another question she had to ask. Mustering up the courage, she braced herself and asked, "Brad, has the captain...has he...well, has he gotten married since I saw him last?"

Grinning, young Thacker replied, "No, ma'am. He ain't even got a girlfriend. I guess the war's been keepin' him too busy."

Dixie masked her relief and said, "That's probably it. He'll no doubt find a woman and get married once this horrible war is over."

"I hope so, ma'am. The captain seems like sort of a lonely man sometimes. What...ah...what brought you down here? Run out of sick people in Birmingham?"

"Not quite," she giggled. "It's the Union naval buildup on the Gulf. As you know, General Lee is working hard making preparations for Mobile's defense. You Sharpshooters are part of those preparations. The general is confident the Federal forces are planning an all-out effort to destroy Fort Morgan and Fort Gaines and to capture Mobile. With the potential warfare pending here, experienced medical help will be needed. Like myself, many nurses are being brought in from Confederate hospitals all over the South to beef up the staff in this one."

"I bet they're not all as pretty as you, Miss Dixie," Private Spain said. "I wish they'd let you take care of me. I'd get well faster."

"Aren't you sweet?" she said, blushing.

"Not sweet, ma'am. Just honest."

Brad said, "You still are Miss Dixie, aren't you, ma'am? I don't see a wedding band on your finger."

"Yes," she sighed. "It's still Miss Dixie."

Thacker grinned broadly. "Good. Tell you what. Maybe when I get out of here, you and I could take a Sunday walk together, or somethin' like that. Maybe have dinner some night, too."

"That's a nice thought, Brad," she said warmly, heading for the door. "But once you knew the truth about me, you'd run away like a scared rabbit."

"The truth about you?"

"Mm-hmm," she hummed, pausing with one foot in the hallway. "I turn into a frog at midnight."

Thacker snickered.

Spain grinned and said, "I'll bet you're the prettiest little girl frog a feller ever saw, though."

Dixie laughed, said, "See you *fellers* later," and vanished.

The afternoon sun shone down on the rippling waters at the entrance of Mobile Bay as Captain McGraw and Lieutenant Rawlings stood on the deck of the small ferry and watched Fort Morgan come into view. With the chug of the steam engine in their ears, they surveyed the two-thousand-yard-wide mouth of the bay, letting their eyes sweep southward. Visible on the gleaming horizon of the Gulf of Mexico was the Union fleet, waiting for more vessels to join them before they launched the attack.

"Like a bunch of blood-hungry vultures," Rawlings said bitterly.

"Yeah," nodded McGraw.

The ferry was moving southward about a mile off the eastern shore of the bay, and began to angle to the left toward the tip of Mobile Point, where Fort Morgan's lighthouse lifted its towering head against the azure sky. Letting his gaze rove westward to Dauphin Island where Fort Gaines lay in the heat of the sun,

McGraw ran the two-thousand-yard expanse to massive Fort Morgan on the east. "Morgan's a lot bigger than Gaines," he commented.

"I'd say so!" Rawlings reacted with enthusiasm. "I never realized Morgan was so large."

"General Maury said Morgan's got some plenty big guns, too."

"They'll need 'em," responded Rawlings, lifting his hat and running splayed fingers through his dark-brown hair.

Fort Morgan was an old brickwork fortress built in the shape of a pentagon. Its formidable walls were topped with six feet of sod, which added to their strength. Grass even grew from the sod. Notched in the thick, five-angled parapets were rectangular slots where the muzzles of the big cannons loomed, waiting for Union targets.

With the warm sea breeze caressing his face, McGraw pointed toward Dauphin Island and said, "According to Maury, General Page's men have driven wooden pilings beneath the surface from just off shore to some spot out in there. Any ship trying to come through that area will find its hull being ripped up."

"Good thinking," remarked the lieutenant.

"I told you about the torpedoes. They'll protect the rest of the entrance."

"S'pose he's already got them in there?"

"Don't know, but if not, I'm sure they will be soon."

The ferry, which also bore the army wagon and driver, was gliding up to the dock. The pilot told McGraw and Rawlings to brace themselves. Seconds later, the ferry bumped the dock, and a soldier on the dock caught the rope tossed toward him by the pilot.

As the officers stepped onto the dock, the soldier saluted and said, "Captain McGraw, General Page is waiting for you. I'll take you to his office."

McGraw and Rawlings followed the soldier up the sandy slope, past the lighthouse, and through the heavy gates. Inside the walls, the open area was pentagonal shaped. The commandant's office, the dining hall, and the barracks were located on the eastern side of the impressive structure. Their guide led them to the open door of the commandant's office, halted at the threshold, and knocked on the wooden frame.

A voice inside said, "Yes?"

"I have Captain McGraw and Lieutenant Rawlings here, sir."

"Well, show them in, Williams!" blared the gusty voice.

McGraw and Rawlings entered the relatively cool office to find Brigadier General Richard L. Page on his feet, coming around his worn and faded desk.

Page was a stout man in his sixties with a thick head of silver hair and a handlebar mustache. He stood five feet nine inches tall, but his breadth and booming voice made up for whatever he lacked in height. After introductions and handshakes had been taken care of, Page said, "Gentlemen, I guess I don't need to tell you how glad I am that you and your Sharpshooters are with us. I've got a hundred and twenty good men here, but an additional ninety-four sure looks good. Your presence here has raised the morale of my men."

"So my men told you about the ambush and our casualties, I see," said McGraw.

"Yes. I'm sorry about that. Too bad the engineer was killed, too. How's the fireman going to get home?"

"Don't know for sure, General. He's staying at a Mobile hotel right now. Said he'd get himself back to Montgomery one way or another. Can't take the train back with the bridge out, that's for sure."

Stepping outside with the two officers following, Page gestured toward the barracks and said, "I've given you and your men separate quarters, Captain. At the end of the barracks. I thought it would make it more convenient for you to command your men."

"Thank you, sir," smiled McGraw. "It will."

Page called to a corporal passing by and asked him to find the fort's other officers and send them to his office. Taking McGraw and Rawlings back inside, the general sat them down and eased into the chair behind his desk. He was commenting on all the good reports he had heard about the fighting prowess of the B Company Sharpshooters when three men drew up to the open door.

"Come in, gentlemen!" boomed Page, rising to his feet.

McGraw and Rawlings also stood, and were introduced to Colonel DeWitt Munford, who was second-in-command at the fort, and Lieutenants Wilson March and Frank Cooley.

As the group sat down, General Page eased back in his chair, which groaned from his weight, and said, "We also have a captain attached to the fort. His name is…ah…Lex Coffield."

McGraw and Rawlings both detected a distaste for Coffield in the way the name came off Page's tongue, but neither commented.

Proceeding, Page said, "Captain Coffield is on assignment right now upriver…Tuscaloosa. He'll be back in a few days."

The mention of Tuscaloosa brought Dixie Quade to Ryan McGraw's mind. He felt a sharp pang in his heart at the thought of her. He hoped she was well and happy.

General Page discussed the chain-of-command arrangements with the officers, as stipulated in written orders by General Lee. The Sharpshooters were to remain under the jurisdiction of Captain McGraw and to be commanded only by him. The Sharpshooters were a separate fighting unit and would act as such. Page explained to his officers that this was the reason he had given McGraw and his men a separate section of barracks. Page ran his gaze over the faces of the men and said, "Naturally, because of my rank and position, B Company will follow my orders, but only as I give them through Captain McGraw." Pausing briefly, he asked, "Any questions?"

When there were none, the beefy general looked at McGraw and said, "Now…something that I find it necessary to do."

"Yes, sir?" said McGraw.

"I must warn you and Lieutenant Rawlings about Captain Coffield. The captain is very short-tempered and all business. He's not always easy to get along with. Has a lot of pride. He's a West Point graduate, a distinction none of the rest of us in this room can boast about. He's got a sharp mind…very intelligent. I just wanted to raise a red flag about his temper. If he'd learn to control that thing, he'd be a general."

"I see," nodded McGraw.

"So, what I'm asking, Captain, is that you and Lieutenant Rawlings work at trying to get along with Coffield, and please stress the same to your men."

"Will do, sir," said McGraw.

After breakfast the next morning, a group of men were standing around in the open area inside Fort Morgan, waiting for assembly time. General Page had put out word that he wanted to meet with all the men, including McGraw's Sharpshooters, shortly after breakfast. At the moment, Page was outside the walls in the lighthouse, having taken Captain McGraw with him. With the coming of dawn, the watchmen in the lighthouse had reported seeing new ships in the Union fleet on the horizon. Page wanted to take a look for himself.

A few Sharpshooters were talking with Fort Morgan men, getting acquainted. When Noah Cloud introduced himself to a couple of men, one of them smiled and said, "You say your name's Cloud...C-L-O-U-D? Like them white cottony things in the sky?"

"That's it," grinned big Noah.

Hap Hazzard chuckled, "Only with him, it's not always white. Most of the time, it's like *storm* clouds—you know, dark and ugly."

Noah gave Hazzard a sharp look. "Says you, carrot-head!"

"Yeah, says me!" snapped Hazzard. Looking around at the men in the group, he said, "You fellas all know the Bible story about the big flood. Must've been some kind of dark ugly storm clouds when all that rain was falling, wouldn't you say?"

A few of the men nodded their agreement, not knowing whether to smile or not.

"Well, let me ask you fellas," continued the redhead, "what was the gentleman's name who led his family and all those animals on that big boat?"

"Noah," came a quick reply from the group.

Hazzard reared back and gave a big belly laugh. "See? What'd I tell you? Ol' Noah Cloud here may have hair the color of straw, but like those clouds in the day of his namesake, he's dark on the inside and ugly on the outside!"

"Oh, yeah?" roared Cloud, swinging a haymaker and connecting solidly on Hazzard's ruddy jaw.

Hap's feet left the ground and he landed on his back. Mumbling words that no one could understand, he got up shaking his head, and growled, "You're gonna be sorry for that!"

While the Fort Morgan men looked on askance, the Sharpshooters in the group showed no surprise or excitement.

Taking a boxer's stance, big Noah rasped, "And just how are you gonna make me sorry, carrot-head?"

Spitting into his palms, Hazzard doubled up his fists and hissed, "I'm gonna mash your face into a bloody pulp and make you better lookin'!"

"Bah!" bawled Cloud. "Do it, *then* talk about it, big mouth!"

At the same instant, Lieutenant Wilson March appeared and said, "Hold it, you two! The general doesn't allow fighting amongst the troops!"

"I respectfully submit that we're McGraw's men, sir," said Cloud. "We *gotta* fight. Especially now, because that mutton-brained big mouth has asked for a good lickin'."

"General's coming, Lieutenant!" came a voice from the fringe of the group.

March swung his gaze to the front gate. Page and McGraw were moving through the wide opening with the blue waters of the Gulf of Mexico behind them.

Keeping his voice low, Lieutenant March said to the would-be combatants, "That will be enough. You two break it off right now."

Cloud dropped his hands to his side and said to the big redhead, "We'll finish this later, pal."

"We sure will," Hazzard said through his teeth.

Brigadier General Page assembled the troops and informed them that three new warships had just joined Admiral Farragut's fleet, making a total seventeen. He voiced his opinion that the Yankees would not attack until they had strengthened the fleet a good deal more...especially with ships equipped with greater fire-power than those he had just viewed through a telescope. Farragut was no fool. He knew his fleet would have to bowl its way into Mobile Bay under the heavy guns of Fort Morgan, as well as those lighter ones at Fort Gaines. He would not make a move until he felt he had the firepower to make a successful attack.

Assuring the men that the attack was probably at least two or three weeks away, the general said, "Men, I want to explain the function of the Sharpshooters as I have laid it out for Captain McGraw. It is three-fold. First, they are to plant explosive mines known as 'torpedoes' in the bay. We don't have them on hand as yet, but I planned this so as to coordinate the arrival of B Company with that of the torpedoes. From what I know about Captain McGraw's men, I feel such a task will be to their liking."

"We can handle it, General!" called out one of the Sharpshooters.

Page smiled at him, then continued. "The torpedoes will be planted under the direction of Captain Coffield, who is in Tuscaloosa where the explosive devices are being assembled. Coffield will soon be returning. He is bringing a healthy supply of the torpedoes down the river in small boats."

Adjusting the gray campaign hat on his silver head, the bulky general proceeded. "Second, when the Union fleet moves in, the Sharpshooters will position themselves on the east side of the bay so as to snipe at sailors on the decks of the Federal boats. You are all aware that we have driven huge pilings into the bottom of the bay from Dauphin Island to a point just two hundred yards from where we stand. We'd have done it all the way across, but the water's just too deep at that point. We can't do it. The torpedoes will have to take care of the two-hundred-yard channel.

"Admiral Farragut no doubt is aware of the depth of the bay's mouth, so he's probably figured out that we're using pilings. If he hasn't, he'll know it when he sees some of his ships hung up on the pilings while they're taking in water. Our Fort Morgan men will be firing their big cannons at the Union fleet as it approaches the channel. Even if we're highly accurate, the blue-bellies are going to get some ships into the bay. You Sharpshooters will be there to open fire and take out their deck crews."

One of the Fort Morgan sergeants lifted his hand for recognition.

"What is it, Sergeant Clary?" asked Page.

"Sir, I don't mean any offense at all, but are these B Company Sharpshooters really that good? I mean, if very many ships get past our big guns, some of them will get into the bay, then turn rudder and head toward the other shore to get out of rifle range. Granted they'll be slow-moving, but can these men be accurate, shooting three, four, five hundred yards?"

"Let me assure you that they are the best riflemen in the world, Sergeant," said the general. "They'll do their job. However, let me explain that those waters will also be infested with torpedoes. If they do as you say, they won't get very far before they find themselves in a fourth of July celebration. Those devices will be going off all over the place."

Rubbing the back of his thick neck, Page said, "Let me say to all of you Fort Morgan men—according to General Lee, no army on the face of this earth has an outfit as tough and capable as these McGraw men."

There was an outbreak of cheers from the men of B Company. A man didn't have to be too observant to see that this was a close-knit, hard-fighting bunch. Fort Morgan's troops were impressed.

"Furthermore," continued Page, "let me inform you what else General Lee has reported about these men. He says that not only are they the very best with rifles and pistols, but they are equally skillful at fighting with knives and bare hands. I would advise all of you not to rile them."

Laughter swept through the crowd.

Smiling broadly, the general said, "Now, I want to get back to the three-fold function of the Sharpshooters. General Lee believes the Yankees will also come along the narrow strip of beach to the east that leads to the mainland and hit us from behind. I've asked him to give us more men, but the way the war is going, he is not promising to do it. Our Confederate troops are in short supply on so many fronts. So—function number three—I have asked Captain McGraw to give me a couple dozen men to help guard the rear of the fort. We've got plenty of cannon power, but it sure won't hurt to have some dead-eye riflemen on the parapets putting bullets into blue uniforms."

A Fort Morgan private lifted his cap over his head, waved it, and shouted, "Three cheers for the Sharpshooters!" Waving their gray hats and caps, the entire force of Fort Morgan's troops joined in a rousing cheer.

EIGHT

Morale was running high at Fort Morgan as General Page dismissed the men. Captain McGraw reminded his Sharpshooters to clean their guns, then turned to General Page and said, "Sir, I've noticed that there are some riding horses in the corral behind the fort, as well as those that pull the wagons. Would you mind if I borrowed a horse and saddle?"

"Of course not. You need to go somewhere?"

"Yes, sir. I need to go to Mobile. I realize you've made the ferries available, but I could ride up the shore on horseback a lot faster. I'd like to check on my wounded men at the hospital, and I also need to send a wire to General Maury."

"Of course. Certainly Maury needs to know about the ambush."

"Yes, sir. General Lee wants my unit to always be brought back to a hundred men plus myself when we have losses. General Maury has to know about my losses so he can send replacements."

"Take the bay gelding with the white stockings. Good horse. You'll find McClellan saddles in the feed shed."

"Thank you, sir. I'll be back as soon as I can. I've already made it clear to my men that anything you need done, they are to do it."

"Fine. See you when you return."

McGraw found his lieutenant at the barracks, making ready to clean his revolver and rifle. Most of the men had gone out into the open area to do their gun cleaning.

Rawlings was sitting on his cot, removing cartridges from his revolver when he looked up to see McGraw standing over him. "I'll clean yours, too, Captain, if you want me to," he offered.

"That's okay," smiled McGraw. "I'll do it myself when I get back from Mobile. I'm going to ride one of the horses up the shore and see the men at the hospital. Have to wire General Maury, too. Let him know about the ambush and that he needs to send us some replacements."

"Tell you what," said Rawlings, punching the cartridges back into the cylinder. "I'll just borrow one of the other horses and ride up there with you. I'm sure the general wouldn't mind."

"No need. I think I can find the way by myself."

"I don't doubt that," said the lieutenant, shoving the loaded revolver into its holster as he stood up. "I just think it's best that you not go alone."

"You think I need a nursemaid, is that it?" McGraw chuckled.

"Call it what you want, but I'm going with you."

McGraw shrugged his wide shoulders. "Okay, nursemaid. Let's ask the general for another horse."

When McGraw and Rawlings stepped out into the sunshine, they spotted General Page standing at his office door, talking to one of his colonels. The colonel turned and walked away just as McGraw and Rawlings were drawing up. The captain explained that they would need another horse. Page smiled and said, "Take your pick, Rawlings. The red roan's a good one. You gentlemen have a nice ride and I'll see you—"

The general's words were cut off by a bellowing voice across the sunbaked yard. They turned to see Hap Hazzard and Noah Cloud mixing it up in a furious fight. Page's men were forming a circle around them.

"Looks like a couple of your boys are in some kind of dispute," said Page. "Better stop it."

"It's best that I don't, sir," replied McGraw. "You have to know Hazzard and Cloud to understand, but they're the two toughest men I have. They're fighters by nature. If they don't have Yankees to fight just about every day, they'll fight each other. That ambush didn't last long enough. Just as well let them get it out of their system."

The general rubbed a hand over his mouth and said, "Well, I've got a hard and fast rule about my men fighting each other, but since you're our guests so to speak, I'll leave your men strictly to you on this." Grinning, he added, "I like a good fight, myself. Since you're going to let them go at it, I just as well watch."

McGraw and Rawlings exchanged glances and smiled. Knowing none of the Hazzard-Cloud bouts lasted very long, they walked with the general to where the fight was in progress and joined the Fort Morgan men as they looked on. The Sharpshooters had seen more than their share of Hap and Noah battering each other. They were paying no attention to the fight. The Fort Morgan men were divided as to whom they wanted to see win the contest. Half were shouting encouragement to Hazzard, and half were doing the same for Cloud.

The two combatants were locked in a hand-to-hand struggle, rolling in the dirt. When they slammed into the legs of the excited spectators, Cloud came up on top. Gritting his teeth, he popped Hazzard square on the jaw. Hap took the punch as if it were nothing and arched his back, bucking Noah off him.

Cloud rose to his feet, balled his fists, and breathing heavily, said, "C'mon, big mouth! Get up!"

Hazzard came off the ground as if catapulted and drove his head into Cloud's belly, knocking the wind from him as they both hit dirt and rolled about, stirring up dust. They came up on their knees and Hap quickly threw an arm around Noah's neck, grabbed his wrist with the other hand, and compressed it with every ounce of his strength.

Noah's face turned beet-red. It was a hot day, and both men were sweating profusely. Noah rammed an elbow into his opponent's ribs. Hazzard grunted, but kept his hold on Noah's neck. Noah dug his elbow into the ribs again, harder this time. It hurt enough to cause Hazzard to ease up slightly on his hold. Cloud twisted within Hazzard's grasp, putting his back to him, reached behind him, took hold of Hazzard's head, and flipped him over his back.

Hazzard was on his feet quickly and went after Noah. He missed with a roundhouse right, and caught a hard fist on the chin. They stood there toe-to-toe, trading blows. Finally, Cloud took a step back and said, "I've hit you with everything I've got, you big ugly ape! Why don't you go down?"

"Me?" gasped Hazzard. "It oughtta be *you* goin' down!"

"Hah!" roared Cloud, moving in and punching him on the jaw again. "You're the ugliest, not the toughest!"

Hazzard staggered slightly, then lunged in and returned the blow. "Oh, yeah?" he boomed, knowing he was going to be hit again, and not even attempting to dodge it.

The men of Fort Morgan were dumbfounded. They had never seen the like. It was as if Hazzard and Cloud enjoyed being punched.

"Use some of that Oriental stuff on him, Hap!" shouted one of the soldiers.

Hazzard gave him a dirty look and said, "I don't want to maim the man, I just want to make him prettier!"

The crowd laughed, and the combatants began laughing. Hazzard and Cloud each put an arm around the other and stood there, heads thrown back, roaring with laughter.

General Page turned to McGraw and asked, "Does it always end this way?"

"Always. Those two are the best of friends. They just have to let off steam once in a while. If they can't let off steam on the enemy, they work each other over. What you just saw will last a day or two, then it'll happen again."

Page chuckled, shaking his head. "Those two are crazy."

"I've told them the same thing, sir, and they always have the same answer. Watch." Speaking to Hazzard and Cloud, who still stood there with an arm hooked over the other man's neck, McGraw said, "Hap! Noah! You two are crazy!"

"We know, Cap'n," laughed Hazzard, "that's what keeps us from goin' insane."

There was a big round of laughter, then the soldiers went about their business. McGraw and Rawlings saddled the bay and the roan and headed for Mobile.

Receptionist-secretary Rebecca Worley was working on a stack of papers at her desk, enjoying the slight breeze coming through the open window. The early afternoon sun had just gone behind a bank of clouds, easing the summer heat a little.

Rebecca allowed herself a moment to watch the dozen or so recuperating Confederate soldiers as they sat in the shade a few yards away. She wondered how many more Southern men would be brought in to Mobile's hospital before the horrible war came to an end. She had seen several hundred come and go…some to the local cemetery. Many had returned home missing arms and legs. Others had left blind or maimed. Still others had walked past her desk and out the door to return to combat.

Rebecca's heart was heavy as she beheld one young soldier with bandages over his eyes, walking across the hospital grounds, being led by a nurse. Suddenly her attention was drawn to a young mother plunging through the door, carrying a small boy in her arms. There was a bloody makeshift bandage on the child's right arm and a look of apprehension on the mother's pale features.

Rebecca stood up and stepped around the desk to meet the woman. As she drew up, Rebecca said, "Looks bad, ma'am. Is the cut deep?"

"Yes," she gasped. "Can a doctor see him right away?"

"Of course. Follow me."

The bleeding boy immediately had the attention of nurses in the examining room, and a doctor was summoned. While the worried mother stood close, the nurses removed the bandage and examined the four-inch gash on the child's upper arm.

The boy's eyes showed fear, and in an attempt to calm him, one of the nurses said, "Don't you worry, little fellow, the doctor will be here shortly and get you all fixed up. What's your name?"

"Tommy," came the reply, riding a whimper.

"How did you get this cut, Tommy?"

"Fell out of a tree and hit the picket fence."

"He sure did," spoke up another nurse. "I can see some tiny splinters in the cut."

"Oh, I thought I'd gotten them all out," the mother said shakily.

"It's all right, ma'am," said the nurse. "Dr. Bentley will do a thorough job on it." She looked toward Rebecca, who stood near the door. "Rebecca, I'm sure you need to get some information from this lady. Why don't you take her to your desk?"

"Right," nodded Rebecca. "Please come with me, ma'am. Tommy is in good hands."

Brow furrowed, the mother moved close to the table and said, "Tommy, you'll have to be Mommy's big brave boy now. Okay?"

Lips pulled tight, the boy nodded.

"I'll be just down the hall, honey. When the doctor gets you all fixed up, these nice nurses will let me know, and I'll take you home."

A bit frightened but wanting to show his mother that he was made of brave material, Tommy nodded, but showed no inclination to cry.

As they walked together down the hall, Rebecca said, "That's a fine boy you have there, ma'am."

"Thank you."

Rebecca, who was rather plain and had mouse-brown hair, looked on the attractive woman with envy as she gestured for her to sit down on a chair in front of the desk. She wore a pale yellow dress that held her tightly at waist and breast, and her glossy black hair dropped in a long fall behind her stately head. Her eyes were like ebony bits of marble, giving a hint that they could spark with anger or mesmerize a man with innate power. Her features were clear and exquisitely formed.

Taking a printed form from a drawer, Rebecca picked up a pencil and said, "Okay, I need to get some information from you."

The woman told Rebecca her name was Victoria Manning Coffield, that Tommy was her son, and that she was the wife of Captain Lex Coffield of Fort Morgan. The Coffields had a house in Mobile so the captain could be close to his family.

While telling the receptionist that Tommy was five years old and giving his birth date, Victoria glanced anxiously toward the closed door down the hall where her son was being treated.

Rebecca noted it and said, "Mrs. Coffield, I understand that you are concerned about Tommy, but really you needn't worry. He'll be fine. Dr. George Bentley is one of the very best."

Victoria smiled and replied, "I'm sure of that, Miss—" her eyes dropped to the small name plate on the desk—"Miss Worley. It's just that I've been upset about some other things lately, and…well, this sort of came at the wrong time. I'm afraid I'm not handling it very well."

"I'm sorry, ma'am. I hate to bother you with all of these questions, but it's routine, you know."

"I understand."

At that instant, Victoria's attention was drawn to the front door of the hospital as two Confederate officers entered, looking sharp in their gray uniforms. Her mouth fell open when the officers removed their campaign hats, and she recognized the tall, handsome man with the sand-colored hair.

Rising to her feet as the captain and the lieutenant drew near, Victoria Coffield felt her heart thundering in her breast. It took the captain only an instant to find her familiar face. Shock registered in his eyes. He stopped quickly, his face slightly losing color.

Ryan McGraw had not seen his ex-wife for over six years. She was twenty-one when she walked out of his life, and had matured a great deal. She was still beautiful, and her maturity somehow made her beauty more clearly defined.

Victoria's hands shook as she said with dry mouth, "H-hello, Ryan."

The captain felt a tremor run through his body. He struggled to control his emotions. He thought he had his ex-wife out of his system, but even though she had torn his heart out six years ago, he found something deep within him responding to her presence. Forcing a calm into his voice, he said, "Hello, Tori. You're...you're looking well."

"You...you, too," she responded, looking him up and down. "You really do a lot for that uniform. And...you're a captain, I see."

"Army's desperate," he said shyly, looking uncomfortable.

Judd Rawlings, who knew the story on Victoria, took a step closer, and said, "Captain, if you need a little time to talk, I'll go on and visit the men."

Pulling his gaze from his ex-wife, Ryan set it on Judd and replied, "Sure. Do that. I'll be along shortly."

As Judd walked away, Victoria cast another anxious glance toward the door down the hall.

Rebecca realized an awkward situation had befallen the distraught mother. Rising to her feet, she said, "Mrs. Coffield, if you and the captain need to talk privately, there's a waiting room two doors down the hall to your left. It is unoccupied at the moment. We can finish up with these details on Tommy when you're through."

The name "Coffield" rang a hard bell in Ryan's mind. Was Victoria married to this Captain Lex Coffield who was in Tuscaloosa gathering torpedoes?

Setting expressive black eyes on her ex-husband, Victoria asked, "Would you like to talk for a few minutes, Ryan?"

"I guess maybe we should."

"If there is any word from the doctor before you're through, I'll let you know, ma'am," spoke up Rebecca.

Victoria thanked her and walked slowly down the hall with Ryan. When they entered the room, Ryan closed the door and pointed to a couch, telling her to sit down. As she dropped onto the couch, he took a straight-backed wooden chair and sat down facing her.

"Tommy…" said Ryan. "Is that your son?"

"Yes," nodded Victoria, clasping her shaky hands. "He…he fell out of a tree and cut his arm. I've told him a thousand times to stay out of that tree, but you know how boys are."

"Yes. I used to be one. Trees just seem to beckon to a boy. Not much he can do if he's all boy but give in."

"I suppose," she said, relieved that he was not unleashing a tirade of scorn upon her. "Tommy's that, all right."

"I heard the receptionist call you Mrs. Coffield. Your husband happen to be Captain Lex Coffield?"

"Yes," she replied, looking surprised. "You know him?"

"No. My men and I just arrived at Fort Morgan yesterday, and General Page told us about him. I understand he's up in Tuscaloosa right now, collecting torpedoes for the upcoming naval battle in the bay."

"Yes. I…figured you'd be in the army, with the war and all, but I never dreamed you'd be a captain. Lex is a graduate of West Point, and that's as high as he has gone. You've done all right for yourself."

Ryan shrugged his wide shoulders. "Like I said, the army's desperate."

"You lead a unit of men?"

"B Company. First Alabama Sharpshooters. You heard of us?"

"No," she replied, wringing her hands. "I don't pay much attention to the war. Are you at Fort Morgan because of Admiral Farragut's gathering fleet? I know about him because Lex talks a lot about him being out there in the gulf."

"Yes. We're here to bolster the defenses. Some of my men got shot up in a Yankee ambush while we were traveling to Mobile from Montgomery. We left them here at the hospital yesterday. My lieutenant and I decided to ride up and check on them."

"I see," Victoria said, brushing at a lock of hair that had fallen on her forehead.

There was a heavy, blank silence. Victoria could hardly breathe.

Ryan's memory was torturing him. He was picturing the raven-haired beauty in her exquisite white wedding dress and remembering how utterly happy he had been the day she became his bride.

Feeling the pressure to break the silence, Victoria said, "Ryan, I know I was wrong to just leave a note when I ran off with Lex. At least I should have told you face-to-face that I was leaving you. It's just that...well, I did it in that sudden manner, feeling it was best to make it quick and clean."

Fixing her with ice in his pale blue eyes, Ryan said acidly, "Leaving the note wasn't where you were wrong, Tori. It was leaving *me*. You stood at the altar the day of our wedding and vowed before God and man that you would keep yourself only unto me as long as we both lived. You broke your vows."

Victoria avoided his gaze.

"So you married him at Fort Payne, eh?" pressed Ryan. "That's where the divorce papers came from."

"Yes," she replied, staring at the floor. "That's where he was stationed when we happened to meet in Hattiesburg. Do you want to know how we met?"

"No. I don't care."

A pained look pinched her face. Still avoiding his gaze, she said, "The reason we're here is because when the war broke out, Lex declared his loyalty to the South. He was immediately assigned to Fort Morgan. We've maintained a home here in Mobile so Tommy and I could be close by."

"I guess that's as it should be."

Raising her eyes to meet his, Victoria said, "This will sound inane, Ryan, but I'm going to say it anyway. It's good to see you...and I'm glad to know you're at the fort. It will be nice having you so close."

Ryan wanted to hate her, but he couldn't. Memories of their sweet times together were racing through his mind. Part of him felt the desire to lash out at her for daring to say it would be nice to have him so close, but another part wanted to show her kindness. He was reading something in her eyes...something that told him she was under a heavy strain.

"Tori, are you happy?"

Tears surfaced and her anguish etched itself on her face. Her lower lip quivered as she replied, "Not that you should even care, but I am very *un*happy. Lex is not at all what I thought he was."

Leaving the couch, Victoria fell to her knees at her ex-husband's feet. Tears were now spilling down her cheeks as she laid a hand on his forearm and said with breaking voice, "Oh, Ryan, the last several months I have thought of you constantly. I have relived so many wonderful memories. I...I made such an awful mistake! You're right. The worst thing I did was break my vows. I deserve anything bad that happens to me. You have a right to hate me."

Breaking into sobs, Victoria pulled a hanky from the sleeve of her dress and dabbed at her eyes. Struggling to gain control of herself, she looked up at Ryan from her kneeling position and said, "Oh, darling, you don't hate me, do you?"

Victoria's use of the word darling tore at Ryan McGraw's heart. He was wishing their paths had not crossed in the hospital. Barely moving his lips, he said, "No, Tori, I don't hate you."

Swallowing hard, she closed her eyes and willed herself calm. Speaking with a level voice, she said, "Ryan...?"

"Yes?"

Victoria was looking into his eyes searchingly. "Have you remarried?"

"No," he replied flatly, rising to his feet and towering over her. "I'm not married, but you are. I had best be going."

Jumping up, she clutched both his arms. "Ryan, I need your help!"

"You've gotten along without my help for six years, Tori."

"Please!" she begged. "Living with Lex is unbearable! He's a hot-tempered brute! He mistreats Tommy. He's mean and selfish. He wants everything his own way."

Ryan looked at her blandly. "That was your problem, too, Tori.

At least it was the last year we were married. You changed from what you were when I married you. Suddenly everything had to go your way, or you threw tantrums and pouted like a spoiled brat. Remember?"

Victoria did not reply. She just stood there gripping his arms and looking at him through a wall of tears.

"I suppose that's why you left me for this Lex Coffield," continued Ryan. "You thought he would give you your way all the time. I can see why you're miserable. Two selfish, self-centered people in a marriage can put a strain on things. There's nothing I can do to help, Tori. You made your bed, now you'll have to lie in it."

Shaking her head and struggling to keep from losing control of herself, the troubled brunette sniffed and said, "I deserve anything you say to me, darling, but you can't just walk away and leave me. I need your help!"

"You're asking the impossible, Tori. I can't butt into your marriage."

Abruptly, Victoria wrapped her arms around him, laid her head against his muscular chest, and said with trembling voice, "It will help me immensely if we can just see each other now and then."

Ryan was about to say that they could *not* see each other when there was a knock at the door. Pulling away from his ex-wife, he went to the door and opened it.

Rebecca Worley said, "Excuse me, Captain. Dr. Bentley is about finished with Tommy. He wants to speak with Mrs. Coffield."

Dabbing at her eyes with the wet hanky, Victoria moved up beside Ryan and said, "Thank you, Miss Worley. Tell the doctor I'll be right there."

Rebecca nodded and walked away.

Turning to Ryan, Victoria said, "I want you to meet Tommy."

"Maybe some time later, Tori. Right now, I need to look in on my wounded men."

Laying a hand on his arm, she gave him a certain tender look that had been something special to Ryan when they first fell in love. "Do you still feel something for me?"

"Tori, I must get to my men," said Ryan, and moved into the corridor. "I hope your son is all right."

With that, he walked away from her and did not look back. As he moved briskly down the hall, he was troubled by his encounter with the woman he had once loved with all his heart. When he neared room twenty-seven, he slowed his pace and drew a deep breath. Pausing a moment in front of the closed door, he composed himself, then pushed it open and entered the room.

Lieutenant Rawlings was sitting on a straight-backed wooden chair in the middle of the room so he could talk to all four men at once. When the captain entered, he stood up.

Grinning at him, McGraw said, "Sit down, Lieutenant. I'm not a general yet."

Rawlings grinned back and said, "I wasn't standing up for *you*, Captain, but for the lady behind you."

McGraw turned around to see a pretty redheaded nurse on his heels, carrying a tray with four spoons and a large bottle containing dark liquid. She smiled and said, "So you're the famous Captain Ryan McGraw."

"I don't know about the famous part, ma'am, but I do answer to that name."

"I'm Betty Wells," she said, setting the tray on a small table next to Brad Thacker's bed.

McGraw was carrying his hat. He quickly placed it on his head, then removed it, bowed, and said, "I am so glad to meet you, Miss Wells. It is *Miss* Wells, isn't it?"

"It better be, Cap'n," spoke up Clint Spain, who was propped up in his bed. "If she's got a husband, your lieutenant here is in deep trouble."

"Oh?" said McGraw, arching his eyebrows and setting his gaze on Rawlings.

"Aw, Captain, I haven't done anything but talk to her."

"And drool over her," interjected Dean Bradbury, who was also sitting up in his bed.

Rawlings' face tinted.

"He also chased her down the hall, Captain," put in Brad Thacker, who lay in his bed on his good side.

"I didn't do any such thing!" blustered Rawlings. "All I did was follow her down the hall so's I could get some water for Sergeant Staples."

Betty stuck out her lower lip, looked at Rawlings, and said, "Is that all you were following me for? Phooey. I thought you *were* chasing me, Lieutenant!"

There was a round of laughter in the room, then Betty said to McGraw, "Your boys told me a lot about you, Captain, but they neglected to tell me that you were so young."

"What do you mean?" asked the captain.

"Well, they said you were sort of like a father to them. I pictured this tottering, silver-haired old man."

"It was Lieutenant Rawlings who gave her the old man idea, Captain," said Spain. "He really worked on it. Of course, we know why. He wants her all to himself."

McGraw laughed. "Guess you're not the only one I should have cautioned about chasing the pretty nurses, Clint. Sounds like I should also have given the word to my gruesome lieutenant!"

Again there was laughter, then Betty said, "I'll let you gentlemen visit without interruption in a moment, but first I must give my patients their regular medicine."

"Oh, no!" gasped Sergeant Staples. "Not that awful stuff again!"

"Yes. This awful stuff again."

"We haven't had any of it, ma'am," spoke up Dean Bradbury. "What is it?"

"Exactly what I said—it's your *regular* medicine. It'll keep you that way. Good old syrup of pepsin," chuckled Betty, picking up the bottle and one of the spoons. "Who wants to be first?"

An argument ensued as to who should take the black liquid first. Taking control of the situation, the pretty nurse started with

Staples and moved methodically from bed to bed. When it was done, she picked up the tray and said, "All right, gentlemen, I'll be out of your way now."

"You're not in the way," said Rawlings. "You can stay longer if you want."

"Sorry, but I'm leaving early today, and it's time for me to go. One of the other nurses will see to these fine gentlemen when they have any needs."

Rawlings walked her to the door and said, "Would it…ah…be possible, Miss Betty, for a gruesome fellow like me to take you to dinner some time?"

"Maybe. Next time you're here at the hospital, look me up and we'll talk about it."

"You really mean it?" asked Rawlings, his heart aflutter.

"Try me," said Betty, and moved away quickly.

When Rawlings turned back into the room, McGraw asked, "Have you looked in on Vince Udall yet?"

"Yes, sir. He's not too alert, but he knew who I was. The nurse that's staying with him said he's doing all right. She let me say a few words to him, then chased me out."

"I'm glad to know he's doing well. I'll look in on him myself in a little while."

The captain talked to each of his wounded men, showing sincere interest in their condition. He was standing next to Brad Thacker's bed with his back toward the open door when Thacker looked past him and saw someone in a starched white dress standing in the corridor.

Looking up at McGraw, Thacker said, "Captain, you'll never guess who's here at the hospital."

"What do you mean?"

"I mean, there's somebody here that you really like."

Brow furrowed, McGraw asked, "You mean as a patient? Some soldier friend of mine who's been wounded?"

"No, it's not a soldier, sir. It's a nurse."

"A nurse?"

"One that took real good care of you at the hospital in Birmingham."

The other men followed her movements as Dixie Quade stepped up behind McGraw and said, "The captain probably doesn't even remember me, Private Thacker."

Ryan McGraw knew the voice instantly. He whirled around and looked into Dixie's sparkling eyes above a warm smile that emphasized her dimples. The shock of seeing her momentarily blocked his throat. By this time his emotions were totally in a whirl.

Ryan had just seen his ex-wife, and suddenly here was the young woman he had carried in his thoughts and dreams for over a year. He had given up ever seeing Dixie again.

Unaware of Ryan's emotional strain, Dixie was expecting more of a reception than a stunned look. Her smile slackened as she said, "Captain, aren't you glad to see me?"

"Yes, of course!" he exclaimed, taking both of her hands in his. "I am *very* glad to see you, Miss Dixie. It's just that...that...well, you've taken me totally by surprise! I never...I never...well, I never—"

"Expected to see me here?" she finished for him.

"Yes! This is such a pleasant surprise, it's just left me speechless."

"Your men tell me you still have some pain in your shoulder now and then," said Dixie, allowing the captain to regain his composure.

"Uh...right," he nodded. "Sometimes. What—how—why are you here?"

"To beef up the medical staff for the battle in Mobile Bay. I was certainly amazed to learn that you and your Sharpshooters had been assigned to Fort Morgan. Maybe we will have a chance to spend a few moments together and talk over old times."

"That would be great," he said, releasing her hands. "I'll be back in a few days to check on my men again. Is this your normal shift?"

"It switches around every week, but if you're back by Saturday, I'll be on duty at this time."

"Then I'll make it a point to be back by Saturday," he grinned.

"See you then," she chirped, and left the room.

As the captain turned back to his men, Judd Rawlings gave him a wolfish grin and said, "You tried to get the little nurse out of your system, didn't you, O dauntless leader? But your ol' pal, here, can tell. There's still some Dixie in your blood, isn't there?"

NINE

On June 20, 1864, thirteen hundred Union soldiers of the Sixth Illinois Cavalry First Battalion were bivouacked in a dense Mississippi forest some sixty miles northwest of Mobile, Alabama. They had been there for three days, camped on the Black River, waiting for Major General Edward R.S. Canby to arrive.

The forty-eight-year-old Canby was commander of the Union Military Division of West Mississippi, and was to arrive on that day from his main camp in western Mississippi near Natchez.

It was midmorning, and the birds were singing in the trees overhead while most of the Union soldiers were washing their clothes in the sun-dappled river. In charge of First Battalion was Colonel Perry Stone, who sat in his tent with his five officers, smoking a pipe and discussing their most recent battle. Amid the officers was Captain Leonard Whittier, a fierce and rugged fighter on the battlefield.

The conversation was interrupted when one of the sentries looked through the opening where the flap was laid back and said, "Colonel Stone, General Canby is here."

Stone rose from his chair, thanked the sentry, and while the officers stood, said, "Gentlemen, let's go give a warm welcome to our commander."

The Union officers filed out of the tent into the warm sunshine. A light breeze was coming from the north, softly washing through the treetops.

On his long-legged chestnut gelding, General Canby threaded through the thick trees, followed by some forty-five riders in blue uniforms. Once Canby and his escort had dismounted, the men of First Battalion welcomed them, offering hot coffee from a series of steaming pots at the cook site near the river's edge.

After chatting for a few moments about how things were looking in west Mississippi, General Canby said to Stone, "Colonel, as my messenger told you, I have a plan concerning Fort Morgan. It will involve Captain Len Whittier. I need to get down to business on it so I can head north of here on some other matters."

"Certainly, sir," nodded Stone. Turning about, he let his eyes roam amid the deep surrounding shadows until he spotted Whittier in conversation with two of the men who had ridden in with the general. They each held a steaming tin cup of coffee.

"Captain Whittier!" the colonel called out.

"Yes, sir?"

"General Canby wants to meet with the two of us at once."

Whittier excused himself and hurried to where the general and the colonel waited.

"We can talk in my tent, sir," said Stone as Whittier drew up.

"You have a table in there?"

"Yes, sir. There are two, in fact—a small one with my lantern on it, and a larger one I use for my meals."

Canby turned to a young corporal who stood a few feet behind him and said, "Corporal Burris, I need that map in my left saddle-bag."

Burris hurried toward the general's horse while Stone and Whittier walked him to the tent.

As they entered the tent and sat down at the table, Canby said, "I've worked out a plan concerning Fort Morgan, and it's been approved by General Grant and Admiral Farragut. As you know,

Farragut is gathering his fleet off the Gulf coast at Mobile Bay. I don't have to tell you that it is absolutely necessary that we take Mobile and plug up the bay."

"Yes, sir," chorused Stone and Whittier.

Corporal Burris arrived with the map, placed it in the general's hands, and moved just outside the tent to be at Canby's beck and call. While the general spread the map out on the tabletop, he said, "Captain Whittier, I picked you specifically for this mission because I believe you are the best man for the job."

"Thank you, sir."

"Of course, Colonel Stone has to be in on this because he is your commanding officer, and the men who go with you are under his command."

Whittier nodded.

"Before we look at the map," said Canby, "let me explain what I have in mind. You gentlemen know that when Admiral Farragut leads his fleet into Mobile Bay, his greatest obstacle will be Fort Morgan. According to our latest intelligence report, they've got some plenty big guns in that place."

"What about Fort Gaines, sir?" queried Whittier.

"It won't be much of a problem. Farragut says he can level it in short order. He figures General Page will drive pilings into the mouth of the bay near Dauphin Island to force his ships to draw nearer to Morgan. So it's Morgan we're concerned about."

Colonel Stone eyed his pipe on the small table, which had gone dead. "General," he said, "do you mind if I smoke my pipe?"

Canby, who was a no-nonsense type, eyed him levelly and clipped, "Yes, I do mind. Can't stand the smell of tobacco in any form. You ought to give that stuff up, Colonel. Bad for your health."

"Yes, sir," nodded Stone, smiling weakly.

Whittier knew the rebuke had cut. He avoided looking at Stone.

"The latest intelligence report also informs us that Page has about a hundred and ten, maybe a hundred and twenty men in the fort," continued Canby. "So here's my plan. Captain Whittier, I want you to take a hundred and seventy men and capture Fort Morgan."

Without blinking, Whittier replied, "You want this done when, sir?"

"As soon as possible." Looking at Stone, he said, "Give him the best men you have, Colonel. This won't be an easy task. What you'll have to do, Captain, is build some rafts and transport them in wagons by land as far as the little town of Chickasaw. You know where that is?"

"I think it's due east of here on the Mobile River, sir."

"Correct," said Canby, running his finger across the map. "Right here."

Leaning close to get a good look, Whittier nodded. "So we float down the river on the rafts all the way to the bay, then paddle the rafts down the bay to Fort Morgan. Right?"

"Yes. You'll have to travel at night with the wagons and hide yourselves as much as possible during the day. You and your men will be on foot. I figure three wagons ought to be able to carry the rafts you'll need. Stash the wagons when you reach the river. You'll have to do all your floating at night, too. If the Confederates find out you're headed for the fort, you're in trouble."

"Yes, sir."

"You'll make your attack at night, also. I'd like to have a larger unit make the assault, but it's going to be hard enough to keep a hundred and seventy from being spotted. At least with that many, you'll reasonably outnumber the force at Morgan. You've got to go in there and take it, Captain. With Fort Morgan in our hands, Admiral Farragut will be able to move into the bay and on to Mobile with ease. President Lincoln and General Grant have both emphasized how important it is that we plug up the bay and capture the city. If we're successful, it could mean the beginning of the end for the South. They won't be able to fight us if we cut off their final means of supply. With General Sherman's march on Atlanta coming in a few weeks, this war could be over before autumn."

"You say, General," spoke up Stone, "that Farragut will be able to move into the bay with ease if we occupy Fort Morgan. But what about the Confederate fleet?"

"They don't have much. I'm sure they'll bring what they can down the Mobile River against us, but I don't think it'll amount to much. I did hear that Admiral Buchanan is trying to get some kind of ironclad ram put together, but that will take time. I hope we'll have the fort, the bay, and the city in our hands before he gets it done."

Captain Whittier was studying the map. Pointing to Mobile Bay, he said, "I figure we'll have to paddle down the bay just off the east shore. It's close to thirty miles according to the legend, here. It'll probably take all of one night and part of another. We'll have to go ashore at dawn after the first night and stay in hiding till dark. We should arrive at the fort in the middle of the next night."

"That's the way I had it figured," nodded Canby. "The element of surprise will give you a sharp edge. I want that fort under your control by sunup. You are to fire three cannons at fifteen-second intervals. That will tell our navy out on the gulf that Morgan is in Union hands. Farragut will move in immediately and bombard Fort Gaines."

"Is Farragut ready for such an assault?" asked Colonel Stone. "I thought he was still building up his fleet."

"He is, just in case this little project should somehow be foiled. But he won't need more and bigger ships if Fort Morgan is vanquished. This is why Captain Whittier and his men must not fail. Admiral Farragut can have Mobile Bay locked up for our side in a hurry."

Whittier was scrutinizing the map again. Without looking up, he said, "General, I estimate that it will take us about five days to get down there, take the fort, and have things ready for the fleet to move in. That is, if we don't run into trouble on the way."

Canby nodded. "Okay. Set your sights to have the fort in hand by no later than the twenty-ninth. Colonel Stone will send his best men with you. If you do run into trouble, you should be able to squelch it in a hurry. I want this job done by sunup on the twenty-ninth."

"We'll do it, sir," Whittier said with a note of confidence.

"That's the kind of attitude I like," smiled Canby. "One other thing."

"Yes, sir?"

"Since you're going to enter the fort at night, it would be a good idea to have all of your men wear white arm bands. That way you won't be shooting each other in the battle."

"I've heard of that tactic being used before, sir. Thanks for reminding me."

Canby rose to his feet and said, "You can keep the map. It'll be of use to you."

"Yes, sir, it will."

When the general had ridden away with his escort, Colonel Stone and Captain Whittier sat down with a list of the men in First Battalion and began picking out names.

During the ride back to Fort Morgan on June 28, Lieutenant Judd Rawlings could tell his friend was deeply disturbed. They had ridden at a steady trot for some fifteen miles without a word between them when they reached a stand of heavy trees and were forced to weave their mounts among them at a walk.

With only the muffled sound of hooves on soft earth in their ears, Rawlings said, "Ryan?"

McGraw turned his head and set troubled eyes on him. "Yes?"

"Want to talk about it?"

"About what?"

"Come on, friend. I hit the nail on the head when I said there's still some Dixie in your blood, didn't I?"

A half-grin curved McGraw's mouth. "You think so, eh?"

"I don't *think* it, I *know* it. The only way it could've been plainer is if you'd blurted out that you were in love with her right there in front of everybody."

"You think you know everything, don't you?"

"Oh, I guess there are a few things I don't know, but there's not much about you I don't know. We've been friends long enough that we read each other like a book, and that's the honest truth. Now, c'mon. Spill it. You'll feel better. You're in love with her, aren't you? Been carrying that torch all this time."

McGraw was quiet for a long moment. Then he said, "She deserves better than me, Judd. That's why I didn't pursue anything with her when we were at Birmingham. I already messed up one marriage. She doesn't need a man like me. She deserves the best."

"Aw, quit kicking yourself. You didn't mess up your marriage. Victoria did that." Rawlings paused, pulled at his handlebar mustache, then said, "Did Victoria do or say something that got to you? Must've been difficult for you, seeing her after all these years."

"Wasn't the easiest thing I ever did," admitted McGraw.

"I hope you told her off good. She deserves it."

"What would that accomplish? It's all over and done with."

Shaking his head, Rawlings said, "Good ol' Ryan McGraw. Tough as rawhide on the outside...soft as a feather pillow on the inside. She needs to be told off but good."

"I was firm with her about breaking her marriage vows, Judd, but there's no sense in trying to hurt her. Besides, she had her son in there getting a bad cut stitched up. She was under stress already."

"Her son, eh? You find out who she married?"

"Yeah. And when I tell you who her husband is, it'll knock you right out of the saddle."

Looking down at his saddle, Rawlings said, "This is a McClellan, so it doesn't have a saddlehorn. Nothing to get a grip on."

"Tori is Mrs. Lex Coffield."

Judd's jaw slacked. "Coffield! Mr. Popularity? I hope she likes him better than I think they like him at the fort."

Ryan thought of Victoria's miserable plight, but decided to keep it to himself. "I hope so, too. Be pretty miserable for her if she didn't."

"This'll put some strain between you and the illustrious captain, won't it?" remarked Rawlings.

"Not unless he chooses to make it that way. What's done is done. Let dead dogs lie. That's my philosophy."

"Well, I sure hope the dead dog stays dead. A resurrected dog might be plenty mean."

At midnight, Captain McGraw lay on his cot wide awake. He and his lieutenant had been given a private room adjacent to the long room where the Sharpshooters were sleeping. A closed door separated the two rooms, but the captain could hear a discordant chorus of snores through the door. More prominent was the reedy, nasal sound coming from his friend in the cot beside him.

McGraw's emotions were strung tight as a fiddle string. He thought of Dixie Quade and the joy he felt at seeing her. She certainly showed that she was glad to find him there. She seemed even more beautiful than ever...if that was possible. *What a sweet, unselfish, lovely flower of femininity,* he thought. *Any man would be plenty fortunate to have her as his wife.*

Wife! The word snapped his thoughts to Victoria. *What kind of fateful hand had brought her back into his life? Why did her husband have to be stationed at Fort Morgan?*

Ryan McGraw had been so certain that everything he ever felt for Victoria had long since died. But now—having seen her—he was not so sure. Even though she had become so greedy and self-centered that last year of their marriage, he still had loved her. After what she had done, Ryan felt he should despise her. But that emotion was not there. He only had that strange, unnamed *something* stirring within him for having been in her presence.

It was a warm night, and the room's two windows were open. The soft sound of the gulf's waves washing up on the beach met his ears as his thoughts drifted back to the first time he laid eyes on beautiful Victoria Manning. He was twenty. She was eighteen. Both of them were attending a community ball in Hattiesburg, Mississippi. Their dance partners were friends. The two friends decided to dance a number together, which left Ryan and Victoria on the sidelines. Ryan asked her if she wanted to dance, and she coyly accepted. They whirled across the floor to Johann Strauss's *Donaulieder* waltz.

While the music played, Ryan and Victoria became fascinated with each other, and they planned a time to meet again. Within a short time, they had fallen in love. Soon an engagement was announced, and they were married a few months later, in September of 1856. At their wedding reception, they danced again to what had become "their special number," the *Donaulieder*.

The first year was a happy one. Then Victoria began to change. Ryan's father, Thomas McGraw, was a wealthy land developer in the Laurel-Hattiesburg area, and had taught his son the business. Ryan had established his own just before he and Victoria were married. The area was growing, and the young firm was getting a good start by the time Ryan and Victoria celebrated their first anniversary. The business took a great deal of Ryan's time, but the future looked promising. Ryan was beginning to make a decent living, but little by little, he found he was unable to satisfy all of Victoria's wants. She was developing rapacious tastes and began to demand things he could not afford. She also insisted that he devote more time to her than his young thriving business could allow.

In an attempt to give his demanding wife more of his time, Ryan took in a partner. This satisfied Victoria for a while, but soon she became more demanding. She wanted a larger, more expensive house, better furniture, and more costly clothing. In a serious discussion with her, he made it clear that she was asking for too much. Victoria must learn to live within the limits of his income.

Almost immediately, Victoria began to grow cold toward Ryan. As time passed, he suspected she was seeing another man, but since he could come up with no proof, he never accused her. Then one day in June of 1858, he came home and found the note. Victoria had run off to some unknown place with an unnamed man.

Sweat beaded Ryan McGraw's brow as he lay in the dark, re-membering what Victoria had done to him. He rose from the cot and dressed while Judd Rawlings snored. He would get some cool night air in his lungs.

There was a pale, hazy moon as he stepped out into the yard. Four sentries walked the walls, silhouetted against the sky. Moving across the yard with the sound of the surf in his ears, McGraw reached the gate, where a sentry stepped out of the shadows and said in a half-whisper, "Good evening, Captain. Going for a walk at this hour?"

"Yes. Can't sleep. Thought a little fresh sea air might help."

"All right, sir," said the sentry, opening the gate. "I'll be watch-ing for you to return."

"Thank you. Probably be a half-hour or so."

McGraw's boots crunched on the sand as he walked toward the beach at the southern tip of Mobile Point. Fort Morgan's lighthouse loomed over him, standing some fifty feet in height. The glass-en-closed turret at its top was dark. General Page knew that with the Union fleet off shore, a beacon would only be a tempting target for Admiral Farragut.

The captain was bareheaded, and the sea breeze toyed with his sandy locks as he shoved his hands in his pockets and walked a circle around the towering stone structure. Breathing deep, he let the salty air fill his lungs. While circling the lighthouse, McGraw glanced southward where he could make out the shapes of Union ships on the watery horizon. He wondered when Admiral Farragut would make his daring move into the mouth of the bay. Would the Confederate forces be able to stop him?

Soon the captain was moving along the shore, heading north. With the soft surf washing close to his feet and the dull moonlight dancing on the surface of the dark water, he tried to sort out his feel-ings. Was that the old tingle he had felt today when he looked into Tori's eyes?

McGraw argued with himself. Of course it was not the old tingle! Whatever was once between himself and Victoria was over and done with. And even if it was the old tingle, she was married to this Captain Lex Coffield. Unhappily married to him for sure, but still married to him. And now she had that little boy, too. He had no desire to meet the child. Why should he care about some little boy who—"

Suddenly Captain McGraw stopped in his tracks. Movement in the distance upshore had seized his attention. He dashed to a large rock and hunkered down, peering over its top. A mile or so northward, several dark objects were floating toward him, barely off shore. Squinting to bring them into focus in the soft moonlight, he realized they were rafts, carrying men in dark uniforms. *Yankees!*

Quickly, McGraw darted into the shadows of the heavy brush near the shore. His heart pounded. The Yankees were coming under cover of darkness to swarm Fort Morgan and take it! Peering toward the rafts again, he tried to count them, but they were too closely knit and too far away for him to be sure. He estimated that there were about fourteen of them. How many men would each raft carry? That, too, was impossible to figure. The only thing he could do was run into the fort, alert the men, and get them ready to fight.

Leaving the shadows and praying the Yankees would not see him, McGraw made a mad dash for the gate. As he drew near, the sentries on the wall were watching him. Holding his voice low, but making himself heard, he said, "Yankees coming on rafts! Get everybody up!"

Within five minutes, the ninety-four Sharpshooters and Fort Morgan's one-hundred-twenty-man force were dressed and ready for action. General Page stood with McGraw and Lieutenant Rawlings near the gate as the men crowded close, weapons ready. McGraw had strapped on his knife and revolver and was working the lever of his Henry repeater as Page said, "We may just have the edge here, Captain."

"What do you mean, sir?"

"I doubt Federal intelligence could have reported yet that you and your Sharpshooters are here in the fort. Whatever force is on those rafts probably is numbered according to how many men are usually here in the fort. If that is correct, they are in for a surprise. We'll give them another little surprise, too. While you were going after your weapons, Captain, I ordered two of my cannon crews to get ready. Colonel Munford is up there on the wall with them. Lieutenants March and Cooley will lead our men behind you and the Sharpshooters. Just before you rush out to meet them, those two cannons will each fire a shot directly into the rafts. That ought to shake them up and give you a chance to start mowing them down before they can return fire."

"Good!" exclaimed McGraw. Then turning to his battle-hungry bunch, he said, "Okay, men! We'll lead off, and General Page's troops will follow. We'll wait in the shadows of the walls until Colonel Munford fires two cannon shots. The instant those cannons roar, we give off a Rebel yell and attack. Let's go!"

TEN

Clustered tightly on the dark waters of Mobile Bay, the fifteen Union rafts glided steadily southward, hugging the shoreline. On the lead raft, Captain Leonard Whittier adjusted his white arm band and spoke in a low voice to Lieutenant Chet Noltey, "I'm glad General Canby thought of using these. It's going to keep us from shooting our own men."

"I'm for that," nodded Noltey. "In an operation like this, we're going to have casualties. We for sure don't need to cause any to ourselves."

Whittier ran his gaze over the obscure faces of his one hundred seventy men, then squared himself with the raft and looked on the walls of Fort Morgan in the distance. In the hazy light of the moon, he noted the towering lighthouse looming against the night sky. Moonlight glinted vaguely from the glass panes atop the tall stone structure.

The sound of numerous paddles slapping water filled Whittier's ears as he studied the pentagonal-shaped Confederate bulwark, now no more than a half-mile away. He could make out the Confederate flag waving lazily in the sea breeze above the fort's southernmost corner.

The captain's blood was racing as he anticipated the honor it would bring him to be the man who led the capture of Fort Morgan, which would result in the downfall of the last Rebel seaport. What Whittier accomplished tonight would ring the death knell for the Confederacy. With Fort Morgan under his command, Admiral Farragut could level Fort Gaines and steam up the bay toward Mobile. Ground forces would be alerted and move in from the north. Soon the city would be in Federal hands. When the last avenue of supply was cut off, the Confederacy would be forced to surrender.

Whittier smiled to himself as he envisioned the coming day of glory when at the war's end he would stand at attention before President Abraham Lincoln and General Ulysses S. Grant. Thousands of admirers would look on as Captain Leonard Whittier received a presidential commendation for capturing Fort Morgan, and they would applaud when he was given a promotion to major.

Turning to Noltey, Whittier said, "Lieutenant, pass the word along that we'll haul up and go ashore about two hundred yards from the fort. According to the map, the shoreline curves inward about fifty or sixty feet at that point, and there's plenty of brush. We should be able to get ashore without being spotted. We'll move into the brush and go the rest of the way on foot."

Noltey quickly turned and gave the message to the soldiers at the rear of the raft, telling them to pass it to the other rafts, which followed closely three and four abreast.

Corporal J. B. Burris, who sat directly behind Whittier, patted his Henry repeater rifle and said, "I can't wait to get me some more Rebels. So far in this war, I've killed exactly forty-seven of 'em. I'm goin' for at least three tonight."

"Hog!" chuckled Private Bill Temple, who sat next to him. "There's only a hundred and twenty or so. If you kill three, that'll mean some of our bunch won't get to kill any."

"So what? If the rest of you guys don't want me killing that many, then get to 'em before I do!"

"That's enough talk," said Whittier over his shoulder. "Get ready. We're going ashore in about thirty seconds."

A half-minute later, the captain gave signal for the rafts to haul up on the beach. His raft was first to touch ground. Just as he jumped ashore, a huge cannon roared from the wall of Fort Morgan. The ball plowed into one of the rear rafts and exploded, throwing bodies in every direction. Whittier was about to bark a command for his men to head for the brush further up the beach when a second cannon boomed. Another raft was blown to bits, with bodies scattered into the water and onto dry ground.

"Captain!" shouted Lieutenant Noltey. "How'd they spot us?"

"I don't know!"

Just as the captain shouted for his men to follow him into the brush, a blood-curdling Rebel yell came from outside the walls of the fort, and what seemed to be a huge swarm of enemy soldiers came from somewhere in the deep shadows.

As Rebel rifles barked, their muzzles blossoming orange in the gloom, Whittier raised his rifle and fired, then ran toward the brush for cover. Lieutenant Noltey was beside him, with Corporal Burris on their heels. Just behind them was Private Temple.

Temple heard a bullet whiz past his head at the same instant Burris took a slug in the chest and went down. Guns were booming all around as Temple knelt beside the fallen corporal. Burris's face was buried in the sand. When Temple took hold of his shirt and turned him over, it was evident that he was dead. "No more Rebels for you, J. B." he breathed. "I'll get your three and a couple for myself!"

As the Sharpshooters led the way around the fort's wall and pierced the night air with their Rebel yell, Captain McGraw raised his rifle and fired first. Instantly, the men-in-gray who followed opened fire, and men in dark uniforms with white bands on their arms were falling like flies.

With less than fifty yards between them, Rebels and Yankees

fought it out in the pale moonlight. Rifle fire was a thundering roll, punctuated with loud commands, cheers, yells, and the cry of wounded and dying men.

Soon repeater rifles and revolvers were empty. With no time to reload, the battle became a hand-to-hand conflict. The Yankees found to their amazement that they were outnumbered, and when they clashed with the Sharpshooters, they were outclassed in fighting prowess. Knives flashed in the moonlight, and the smell of blood permeated the air.

Lieutenant Rawlings stayed close to his captain, using his knife, feet, and fists to stun, wound, and slay the enemy. At one point, Rawlings had used an Oriental-style kick to crack the jaw of a Yankee and drop him hard, when he saw another dash up behind McGraw, ready to drive a knife in his back. The captain was busy, battling two men.

Rawlings yelled and pounced on the Yankee. When their bodies collided, they rolled down the sandy beach to the water's edge. The Yankee swore at Rawlings and tried to stab him, but he was too slow. Rawlings drove his own knife into the man's heart full-haft, killing him instantly. Yanking the knife out, the lieutenant charged back up the slope to help McGraw. It didn't surprise him to find that the captain had already killed one of his assailants and was just finishing off the other one.

The Yankee whose jaw Rawlings had cracked was sitting up, groaning, and loading his rifle. When he saw the Rebel lieutenant coming, he tried to close the chamber, but Rawlings was on him with his knife. The Yankee lay dead as McGraw drew up and said breathlessly, "Thanks, pal. That blue-belly you took out a minute ago would've had me for sure."

"Don't mention it. You've saved my hide plenty of times."

Suddenly they saw a couple of Fort Morgan men in trouble, and dashed to their aid.

At the water's edge, Sergeants Noah Cloud and Hap Hazzard were fighting side by side. The Yankee soldiers were no match for them. Five Yankees were already dead on the shore. Four more had lunged in to put down the two husky Rebels. Hazzard sidestepped a hissing knife blade, kicked his assailant in the groin, and met the second man with a hard left, driving his knife into the Yankee's side as he staggered from the punch.

The two men-in-blue who were after Noah Cloud were swinging their deadly knife blades in wide arcs, but found the big man to be surprisingly agile. Noah dodged them three times, then drove a swift kick into the chest of one, putting him down with the wind knocked out of him.

The second Yankee lunged at Noah with his knife. Noah adeptly evaded the hungry blade, then slashed him across the back with his knife as the man attempted to regain his balance. He yelped with pain and pivoted, just as Noah rammed his knife into his chest, burying it deep. He was dead before he hit the sand.

Noah was about to jerk the knife out when he saw the first Yankee coming at him, his knife poised for the kill. The big Rebel leaped aside, jumped the Yankee, and put a lock on his head with powerful hands. One sharp twist, and the Yankee was dead of a broken neck.

As the battle raged, Captain Whittier faced the grim fact that he and his men would all die unless they surrendered. He was on his knees near a thick bush with a cut on his upper left arm when he whipped the white cloth loose and began waving it wildly over his head, shouting for his men to stop fighting and surrender. Three more Yankees were dead before they all heard and complied.

The Yankees, many of them battered and bloody, threw their hands over their heads in surrender. Whittier looked around at the great number of his men who lay dead on the beach and whose bodies bobbed in the water near the shore. His heart sank. They had failed to accomplish their mission. His visions of glory were gone. They were now prisoners of the hated Rebels.

Still holding his bloody knife in a death-grip, the Sharpshooter leader approached Whittier and said, "I am Captain Ryan McGraw.

In the name of the Confederacy, I am taking you and your surviving men as prisoners of war. You will be treated as such."

Whittier was holding his slashed arm. Tiny trickles of blood were running between his fingers. His jaw slacked as he said wide-eyed, "You are McGraw as in McGraw's Sharpshooters?"

"The same."

"But...but we had no idea you and your men were in the fort. We thought—"

"You thought that you'd outnumber General Page's men?"

"Yes. As a matter of fact, we did."

"Good military strategy, but your source of information must be a little slow. Too bad for you. What's your name, Captain?"

"Leonard Whittier. First Battalion, Sixth Illinois Cavalry."

Running his gaze over the Rebel soldiers who now surrounded the Yankees, McGraw said, "All right, men, let's escort Captain Whittier and the rest of our prisoners into the fort."

"What about my wounded men?" asked Whittier.

"Have some of your soldiers carry them," replied McGraw. Then to Lieutenants March and Cooley he said, "Will you two see that our wounded men are brought in?"

"Yes, sir."

"Have some of the men count our dead and identify them, too, will you? General Page will want a report as soon as possible."

Five miles due south of Fort Morgan, in the moon-glazed waters of the Gulf of Mexico, the Union fleet huddled in silence. Aboard the flagship USS *Hartford*, Fleet-Captain Percival Drayton entered the admiral's quarters carrying a lantern. The ring of light showed him Admiral David G. Farragut asleep in his bed. He was snoring, and the yellow glare reflected off his balding head.

Gripping Farragut's shoulder, Drayton said, "Admiral, sir...Admiral..."

The sixty-three-year-old navy veteran snorted, rolled his head, and opened his eyes. Blinking against the bright lantern, he focused on Drayton's face and asked, "Did we get the signal?"

"No, sir, but I thought I should awaken you anyhow. I think something must have gone wrong at the fort."

Farragut threw back the light covering and sat up. "What do you mean?"

"Well, sir, at exactly 2:40, there were two cannon shots. They were about fifteen seconds apart, but since there were only two, I knew they couldn't be the prearranged signal. Not only that, but there has been a battle going on ever since those two cannons were fired. Up until a minute ago, so many rifles were firing, it sounded like a Chinese new year's celebration. You know, firecrackers going off all over."

Farragut glanced at the bell-shaped clock on his dresser, and saw that it was ten minutes after three. Lifting his trim six-foot frame off the bed, he crossed the room in his long-johns and began dressing. Without looking at his fleet-captain, the admiral said, "Go keep an eye toward the fort, Drayton. I'll be there in a moment."

The sea was calm and the night breeze light when the admiral joined Drayton and two other officers on deck. All three were looking toward shore through telescopes. No sounds could be heard coming from the fort. Farragut noted that officers aboard the ships that flanked the *Hartford* were doing the same thing. One of them called across the fifty-foot space between the ships and said, "What do you make of it, Admiral?"

"Only one thing *to* make of it," replied Farragut. "Those rafts weren't carrying cannons. Drayton said there were two cannons fired before the gun battle began. Captain Whittier and his men were obviously discovered before they were able to pull their surprise attack on the fort. Since no signal shots have been fired since the gun battle stopped, I must assume that Whittier and his men are now dead or prisoners of General Page. Looks like we have no choice now but to steam into Mobile Bay and take what Page throws at us."

Drayton lowered his telescope and asked, "How soon will we launch the attack, sir?"

"I'm not sure. I want more ships than we have at the moment. When we go in there, I want to be dead sure we can overcome all obstacles and converge in full strength on Mobile. We *must* take Mobile if we're going to win this war."

At Fort Morgan, General Page ordered lanterns lit and crowded the beaten Yankees together in the open yard. There were only twenty-nine survivors. Of that number, seven were wounded, five of them seriously.

Three of General Page's men were dead, and eight were wounded seriously, including three of McGraw's men. Others among the Rebel soldiers had minor cuts and bruises. The wounded men on both sides were carried into the fort's small infirmary. Rebel soldiers did what they could to stop the bleeding of wounds, and used what medical supplies were available to make the battered men as comfortable as possible.

As General Page looked the wounded men over, he concluded that most of them could not stand a boat trip to Mobile. He quickly dispatched two soldiers to ride to Mobile and bring medical help.

When the riders had gone, Page took Colonel Munford, Captain McGraw, and Lieutenants Rawlings, March, and Cooley into his office. As they took seats, the general eased into the chair behind his desk and said, "Gentlemen, I'm proud of you and the men in this fort. My heart aches for the brave men who died in battle tonight, and for those who were wounded, but the enemy was defeated. Fort Morgan is still in our hands."

"Wish I could see Ulysses S. Grant's face when he receives word of it," Munford chuckled.

"I'd give a month's pay to see that myself," grinned Cooley.

Lieutenant March asked Page, "General, what are we going to do with the prisoners? We don't have room for them here."

"How about the jail in Mobile?" spoke up Cooley. "It could probably hold them."

Shaking his head, Page said, "No. We can't ask the law in Mobile to be responsible for that many men. They'll have to be taken to the nearest prison camp, which as you know is at Jackson, Alabama, sixty miles north of here."

"It'll have to be in wagons, sir," spoke up Colonel Munford. "What about their wounded men?"

"Once our medical people have patched them up and done what they can for them, the wounded Yankees will have to make the trip. If they're in real bad shape, they'll have to be taken to the Mobile hospital as soon as possible. But the rest of them will be placed in wagons and taken to Jackson, along with their comrades."

While Page and Munford were discussing what to do with the wounded Yankees, Captain McGraw thought of his three wounded men, hoping they would be all right. Suddenly it came to him that he had forgotten to wire General Maury at Montgomery and ask for replacements. He had been so emotionally shaken after seeing Victoria and Dixie, it had completely slipped his mind. He would need to ride to Mobile at sunup and get it done. However, instead of asking Maury for seven new men, he would now need ten.

McGraw waited for a break in the conversation, then he said, "General, with my ranks being cut down some more, I'll need to ride into Mobile come daylight and wire General Maury for additional replacements."

"Fine," nodded Page. "We want your unit to be up to full measure. If you and your men hadn't been here tonight, this fort would be in enemy hands."

"That's right," said Munford. "We're mighty glad you're here, Captain."

McGraw thanked them, then asked, "How soon will you be sending the Yankees to Jackson, sir?"

General Page rubbed his chin. "Well, as soon as I know how many of their wounded—if any—can't possibly make the trip. We've got to get all of them out of here. I have enough on my mind with Farragut out there on the Gulf gathering gunboats. Since this little Yankee venture failed, he'll no doubt choose to steam his way in here in spite of our big guns."

"You think he'll come right away, sir?" asked Lieutenant March.

"Hard to tell," Page replied, pulling at an ear.

"You going to call off the dance, General?" The question came from Colonel Munford, whose wife was living in Mobile.

"Nope. I don't think ol' 'fair-guts' will come that soon."

"What dance is this?" Ryan asked.

"Guess I forgot to mention it since you and your men arrived, Captain," said Page. "I felt like our men needed a little boost in morale, so about ten days ago, I made arrangements for Mobile's small orchestra to come out here tomorrow night and play for us. Many young ladies of the town are planning to come. Your men will have to share dance partners with my men, but I think everybody will get a dance or two during the evening."

"General," spoke up Lieutenant Cooley, "how many of our men will you be sending to take the prisoners to Jackson? We don't dare cut ourselves too low here."

"I hate to cut any at all, but it has to be done. They could run into Yankee patrols, so I'll have to send at least a dozen. I wish Captain Coffield was here. I'd send him to lead the wagons."

"He's due back in another four or five days, sir," said Cooley. "Can't it wait that long?"

"No. Those Yankees have to be out of here before that."

"If you would like, General," put in McGraw, "I will be glad to take a dozen of my Sharpshooters and deliver the prisoners to Jackson."

General Page smiled. "I appreciate that, Captain, and I will take you up on it. I mean no disrespect to my own men, but a dozen of your Sharpshooters will be more likely to handle trouble than a dozen of any other Confederate soldiers. We'll know when to plan for the trip once the doctor from town has seen their wounded men."

The general stood up and said, "Well, gentlemen, I'll dismiss you so you can go get a little rest before sunup."

McGraw waited until the other men were gone, then said, "General, I need to talk to you for a moment."

"Certainly," nodded Page, easing back into his chair.

"What can you tell me about Captain Lex Coffield, sir?"

Page's face froze. "Why do you ask?"

"It's important that I know, sir."

"You'll be working with him, placing the mines in the bay. His personal traits won't matter that much. I've already warned you and your men that he's a bit hard to get along with."

"That's not what I mean, sir. What do you know about him as a family man?"

The general's brow furrowed. "Why are you interested in that?"

"Because his wife, Victoria, used to be *my* wife, sir. I have never laid eyes on the man, but six years ago he took Victoria from me and they ran off together. She sent me my divorce papers and a brief note saying she was marrying someone else. I never knew who he was until I ran into her at the hospital in Mobile yesterday. We talked for a few minutes and she told me the man is unbearable to live with. She even said he mistreats their son."

General Page scrubbed a palm over his face and sighed. "Sit down a minute, Captain. Since Victoria has told you this much, I'll fill you in a little."

As McGraw settled his muscular frame on a chair, Page said, "It is common knowledge both in Mobile and here at the fort that Captain Coffield is rough on Victoria and Tommy. It is a concern to me, and to the men of this fort, but there's nothing we can do about it."

"Does he beat on them?"

"I know he causes a lot of mental anguish. And I assume he abuses them physically, but I don't know it for a fact. There have been bruises on both of them, but Victoria always gives some explanation for them…an explanation that absolves Coffield from guilt."

"What would you do if you had proof that such a man under your command was beating on his wife and son?"

"I haven't given it much thought. But with proof, I'd probably have him court-martialed and thrown out of the army."

"That wouldn't keep him from beating his wife and son. Wouldn't it be better to keep him in the army so he's under government authority, and lock him up?"

Nodding, Page said, "Well, yes. It would. I guess that's what I'll do if I ever get proof. Lex Coffield is an enigma, Captain. He is courageous and tough in battle. He's got a sharp mind and is a good soldier. But he's got a couple of quirks that play against him. With his West Point training and military experience, he should be a colonel by now. But his dogged stubbornness to do things his own way and his short-fused temper have kept him from being promoted."

"Did you know he was like this before he was assigned to your command?"

"Only just before. The army sent him to me to get him out of the way at Fort Payne. A letter of warning preceded him by twenty-four hours. They said that in spite of his bad traits, he was good with explosive devices. I'll give him this much—the man does know his stuff about torpedoes."

"Too bad he doesn't know his stuff about wives and children. Even though Victoria hurt me when she ran away with him, I don't like to see her miserable, nor do I like to hear of that little boy being mistreated. I can't stick my nose into their business, but if he ever abuses either one of them in my presence, I'm not too sure I'll be able to just stand by and watch."

"Well, I hope that won't ever happen. By the way, yours truly is escorting Victoria to the dance tomorrow night. Captain Coffield is ordinarily quite jealous over any man who even goes near Victoria, but since I'm a widower and old enough to be her father, he asked if I would take her to the ball."

"I see," nodded McGraw, recalling the night he met the beautiful brunette at a ball. Crowding the memory from his mind, he stood up and said, "Thank you for filling me in on Coffield, sir. I'll go check on my wounded men now."

The Alabama sun was detaching itself from the earth's eastern edge when Dr. Ralph Bender, one of Mobile's prominent physicians, and nurse Betty Wells arrived with the two soldiers who had gone after help.

The wounded men—Rebels and Yankees—had spent the night on cots in the fort's crowded infirmary. As Dr. Bender and nurse Wells were led through the gate, there were whistles and catcalls. Lieutenant Rawlings happened to be in the infirmary talking to the three wounded Sharpshooters when the sounds met his ears. He knew immediately that medical help had arrived, and that at least one nurse had come.

Stepping to the door, Rawlings felt his heart leap when he saw Betty Wells heading toward the infirmary with General Page and a tall man carrying a black bag. Rawlings stepped out to greet her and saw a broad smile capture her face.

As they drew up, Rawlings touched his hat and said, "Good morning, Miss Betty."

"Good morning to *you*," she replied. Betty had already inquired of the two messengers concerning Lieutenant Rawlings and was secretly thankful he had not been one of the casualties.

Betty introduced Dr. Bender to Rawlings, then said, "We might need some help while working on the wounded men, Lieutenant. Would you be available?"

Rawlings had planned to ride into Mobile with Ryan McGraw, but the prospect of being close to Betty for a few hours was too inviting to pass up. "Why, of course," he replied warmly. "I need to talk to Captain McGraw for a moment. He's about to ride into town. I'll be right back."

Rawlings hurried across the open area to the room he and McGraw occupied. The captain was strapping on his holster and knife sheath. Grinning at his best friend, he said, "I know. You want me to find somebody else to ride to town with me."

A puzzled look came over Judd's lean face. "How did you know?"

"Simple. When I heard all the whistling out there, I took a look. The instant I saw that cute little redhead, I knew you'd want to stay here."

The lieutenant's features crimsoned. "Aw now, Ryan, it isn't like that at all."

"No?"

"Of course not. I was still planning to ride with you until Betty up and asked me if I could help her and the doctor with the wounded men. They need me pretty bad. I mean…how can a true son of the South refuse to help patch up his wounded comrades?"

"Why, he can't," grinned McGraw. "That'd be dishonorable." Clapping on his hat, he said, "It's all right, pal. I understand. I'll be in town for a while. Got to send the wire to General Maury, then spend some time with our boys at the hospital. If I'm not back by the time Betty and the doctor are ready to go, why don't you ride to town with them? That way, you can escort me back to the fort from town, or wherever we happen to meet on the trail."

"How about you taking Hap or Noah along?" insisted Rawlings.

McGraw shook his head. "I'll be fine. Those two need a rest after the way they fought last night. Tell Betty 'hello' for me."

Rawlings made his way to the door and watched McGraw cross the open area, taking long, swift strides. When Ryan had passed through the gate, the lieutenant hurried toward the infirmary, his heart drumming his ribs.

ELEVEN

I
t was nearly nine o'clock when Captain Ryan McGraw left the telegraph office, mounted his horse, and rode across Mobile toward the
hospital. As he observed children playing in their yards and people
moving about the streets he felt heavy in his heart. If somehow the
Union fleet out there on the gulf was able to steam past Forts Morgan
and Gaines—and if Union land forces were able to converge with
them—this happy town would be plunged into the depths of despair.
There would be no joy in Mobile if it fell into enemy hands.

Dismounting in front of the hospital, the captain observed several soldiers sitting in wheelchairs with nurses nearby. None of them
were his men.

Just as he reached the door, he met a wheelchair bearing a soldier with bandages over both eyes. He held the door open and smiled
at the nurse who was pushing the chair. She smiled in return and
thanked him. As the chair moved past him, McGraw said, "Good
morning, soldier. Captain Ryan McGraw. How's it going?"

The bandaged face lifted upward and the wheelchair stopped.
"Captain Ryan McGraw? Of the B Company First Alabama
Sharpshooters?"

"That's right."

Reaching up a pale hand, the soldier said, "Am I glad to meet you, sir! I'm Private Ollie Mears, D Company, Third Alabama Infantry."

McGraw took the hand gently, squeezed a little, and said, "The pleasure's mine, Private Mears."

"Thank you, sir, but it's really mine. I've admired you from afar for a long time. I was planning on getting some experience under my belt, then asking to join your Sharpshooters."

"Well, maybe you still can, Ollie," said McGraw, looking at the nurse. She slowly shook her head.

Mears smiled. "Yeah, maybe I can," he said with a lilt in his voice. "Dr. Lyles is good. He's gonna make it so I can see again."

The nurse was still shaking her head, her eyes misting.

"Well, you just keep believing that, Ollie," said the captain. "And when you're seeing good once more, look me up and we'll pull a few strings. Okay?"

"Okay—thanks!"

The nurse rolled the chair away, moving around the corner of the building. McGraw kept his eyes on them until they vanished from sight, then stepped inside. Just as he was passing the receptionist's desk, Rebecca Worley called out, "Captain McGraw!"

Halting, he said, "Yes? Good morning, Miss Worley."

Rising, Rebecca smiled, "Good morning," and extended an envelope toward him, saying, "Mrs. Coffield was in earlier. She left this for you. She said you'd be back to look in on your men sometime soon, and when you did, I was to give it to you."

Accepting the sealed envelope, Ryan thanked her, then proceeded down the hall. When he saw there was no one in the waiting room where he had talked with Victoria the day before, he stepped in and opened the envelope. He removed the folded note and read it silently.

Ryan Darling,
I live at 124 E. Evans Avenue. Please come to the house

while you are in town. I have something very important to
tell you.
All my love,
Tori

Ryan McGraw was once again troubled as he continued down the hall. His old flame for Victoria was struggling to rekindle itself. He placed the note back in the envelope and stuffed it in his shirt pocket just before turning into room twenty-seven. When he shoved the door open, the disturbance he was feeling over Victoria subsided at the sight of Dixie Quade, who was standing at Private Clint Spain's bed, facing the door.

The beautiful blonde's face lit up when she saw Ryan. She was changing the bandage on Spain's head. Smiling, she said, "Good morning, Captain."

"And a good morning to you," McGraw smiled in return. "Are my boys being good?"

Dixie pursed her lips, looked at the ceiling, and said, "Wel-l-l-l…"

"I don't like the sound of this, boys," the captain said, running his gaze from face to face.

Each of the three was grinning.

Settling his gaze on Dixie, McGraw asked, "Okay, nurse Quade, what have they been doing?"

"They've been giving the other nurses and myself a hard time about taking their syrup of pepsin. I think a lecture from their commanding officer would be appropriate."

Sergeant Marvin Staples spoke up. "Now, Miss Dixie, you shouldn't tattle on these boys."

Dixie gave him a mock glare. "It's for their own good, Sergeant. If they don't take it, they're in for real trouble."

McGraw gave each man a stern look. "You Sharpshooters had better take your medicine and not give the nurses a hard time about it, or you'll answer to me. Understand?"

"Yes, sir."

"All right," said the captain. "Now, on a more serious note, I need to tell you about a sneak attack the Yankees tried to pull on Fort Morgan last night."

The Sharpshooters, Sergeant Staples, and Dixie listened intently as McGraw told them of the battle and its results.

Private Brad Thacker asked, "Do you think the Yankee navy will still try to get into Mobile Bay, sir?"

"General Page seems certain they will. It's just a matter of time. Probably a few weeks yet. Farragut's still building up his fleet."

Dixie completed Spain's fresh bandage and said, "Well, gentlemen, I have some other patients to tend to. I'll see you later."

As she rounded the bed and moved toward McGraw, he said, "I'll be here a while, ma'am. I've got to look in on Corporal Udall, also. I'd like to talk to you for a few minutes before I ride back to the fort."

"Of course," she nodded, showing her twin dimples in a warm smile. "I'll be here till four o'clock. Look me up, and I'll take a few minutes off."

"Will do," grinned McGraw, feeling a warm sensation wash through him. Forgotten for the moment was the old flame toward Victoria that had been struggling for life within him. Dixie's sky-blue eyes had him enthralled. He watched her till she passed from view, then turned back to his men.

After spending an hour with Bradbury, Spain, and Thacker, the captain went to Vince Udall's room and spent an hour with him. He was glad to see Udall feeling better and in good spirits. After giving him the story of the foiled Yankee attack, McGraw headed down the hall, glancing about for any sign of Dixie. He was almost to the front door when she came out of a room carrying a medicine tray.

"Hello, again," he said, feeling the ecstasy of her presence.

Dixie's heart was beating hard. "Hello, yourself," she smiled. "Are you leaving?"

"Not until I have a few minutes with you."

"Okay. Let me take this tray to the supply room. I'll be back momentarily."

Dixie was back in three minutes. Drawing up to Ryan, she said, "I can take a few minutes now. Would you like to take a walk outside?"

"Sure," he nodded. "I'd like that."

Ryan and Dixie strolled slowly over the hospital grounds keeping to the shade of the giant oak trees as much as possible. The summer sun was bearing down, and the shade felt good. As they walked together, Dixie asked, "Was there something special you wanted to talk to me about, Captain?"

"Yes, ma'am. I assume you're aware of the dance at the fort tomorrow night."

"Yes. Quite a few of the single nurses who are on days this week are planning to go. I'm one of them."

"Oh, good! General Page hadn't thought to tell me or my men about it until early this morning. As soon as I knew about it, I thought of you."

"Oh?"

"I...ah...didn't know if you'd be going or not, but I was going to...well, I'd like to be your escort when you arrive at the fort. Would you honor me?"

Inwardly, Dixie was all aflutter. Outwardly, she showed calm and replied with a warm smile, "I would be delighted to have you as my escort, Captain."

"Wonderful! I'll be the envy of every man in the fort!"

"I doubt that," she giggled, "but as long as you think so, that pleases me."

Ryan walked Dixie back to the hospital door, thanked her for giving him the time, and told her he would see her at the ball.

Dixie watched him walk to his horse, mount up, and trot away. Just before passing from her sight, he turned and waved. She waved back, sighed, and went inside, trying to calm her heart.

Captain McGraw road away from the hospital thrilled that Dixie so readily accepted his request. He turned around in the saddle, expecting to glance at the spot where he had last seen her, and was surprised to find her still standing there watching him. He raised his hand and waved. Just before the horse carried him beyond her line of sight, Dixie waved back.

Ryan memorized the sight of her standing there in her white nurse's dress with the white jumper apron. Beneath her small cap, the sun shone on her golden hair. There was a feminine grace about Dixie that he found hard to describe. She had a delicate elegance and charm flowing out of her that influenced everything and everyone she touched.

As McGraw rode southward through Mobile, he thought of the note in his pocket. Though the image of sweet Dixie was still fresh in his mind, there was something deep inside him, urging him to stop and ask someone how to find 124 East Evans Avenue. What important thing could Tori want to tell him?

Ryan shrugged it off. He must not let himself get involved with his ex-wife. Tori was married to another man. What could be important between them now?

At dusk on July 1, 1864, final preparations for the dance were being made in the dining hall at Fort Morgan. The men had come up with a few decorations to brighten the place, and even a clean galvanized bucket to serve as a punchbowl. The crude tables had been moved out into the open area to allow space for couples to dance.

At the same time, General Page and Captain McGraw were in Page's office finalizing plans for the journey to Jackson. McGraw had chosen a dozen of his Sharpshooters to take with him. There would be six privates, plus Lieutenant Rawlings, Sergeants Hazzard and Cloud, and Corporals Alex Zale, Chad Ewing, and Bobby Brinson.

Rising to his feet, McGraw said, "I guess that about does it, sir. Three wagons will be plenty. I figure the wounded men can make do in one wagon, and the rest of them can cram into the other two."

"I'm glad we're getting rid of all of them," said Page, standing up. "My conscience won't bother me since Dr. Bender said he'd patched up the wounded ones so they could travel, too."

"We'll pull out at dawn in the morning, then."

"Fine. McGraw, I want to thank you for volunteering yourself and your men to do this."

"Glad to do it, sir. We'll make the trip as fast as we can, just in case ol' 'fair-guts' decides to come in sooner than we're thinking."

"I appreciate that."

"However, let me say this sir…if the Yankees come steaming in here before we get back, the men I have left you are all tough, resourceful, and capable."

"I don't doubt it for a minute. I'm hoping, though, that Captain Coffield will get back here with those torpedoes, and we can get them in place before 'fair-guts' comes barging in here."

"Yes, sir. Me, too," McGraw said, running his fingers through his mustache. Turning toward the door, he added, "I'll go advise Whittier of the plan so he and his men will know what's in the making."

McGraw strolled across the open area to the crowded barracks where the Yankee prisoners were being kept under guard. Entering the lantern-lit room, he found Whittier standing over his wounded men, talking to them. There was a bandage on his left arm. Lieutenant Chet Noltey stood beside him.

McGraw said, "Captain, I believe you are aware that Dr. Bender said your wounded men can travel."

Whittier's eyes narrowed into angry slits. "That's what I would expect from a Rebel doctor. What does *he* care if they die along the way?"

McGraw's cheeks reddened. "He used *Rebel* medicine and *Rebel* bandages to patch them up, didn't he? I didn't hear you complain about that. Maybe I should remind you, Captain, that you and your men are trespassers! You invaded *Southern* territory, paddled your way down here on *Southern* waters with the intent of taking over a *Southern* fort. Three of our men are dead, and eight of them are wounded because of your assault. You want a hug and a kiss for that?"

Whittier lanced McGraw with red-hot eyes, and sneered, "You'll never get us to Jackson, Rebel! The woods are infested with Union troops. When they see you hauling us in those wagons, they'll annihilate you!"

McGraw stepped close to Whittier and growled, "I assure you, we'll get you to Jackson. You'll rot in that *Southern* prison till this bloody war is over. You and your men will be fed breakfast at four-thirty in the morning, Captain. We're pulling out at dawn."

McGraw winked at two of the Rebel guards as he passed through the door.

It was almost eight o'clock when four ferries docked at Mobile Point, bearing several carriages. Forty-three young ladies alighted from the vehicles as they pulled up to the gate at Fort Morgan. Sentries looked on from the top of the walls, knowing that halfway through the evening, they would be replaced so they could attend the ball.

The eleven-piece orchestra had arrived an hour earlier by ferry and were set up in the dining hall. Their instruments were tuned, and they could be heard playing as the soldiers gathered at the gate to greet the women. Extra lanterns had been placed around the fort's open area to provide plenty of light.

General Page stood just inside the gate and welcomed the women as they filed into the fort, then turned and offered his arm to Victoria Coffield, complimenting her on her hair and her dress. Victoria smiled, thanked him, then took his arm. As they moved toward the dining hall, her eyes roamed through the crowd for a glimpse of her ex-husband.

Ryan fleetingly saw Victoria take the general's arm as he elbowed his way through the crowd, for just behind her came Dixie Quade and Betty Wells, side by side. Judd Rawlings had informed his friend that Betty was to be his partner for the night. Ryan stood transfixed as he beheld Dixie while Judd and Betty joined hands and walked away.

This was the first time Ryan had seen Dixie in anything but her white nurse's dress. She was in a high-necked, cream-colored, full-skirted dress with ruffles on the sleeves. The high top was fringed with soft lace, and above it she wore a delicate cameo on a black ribbon that encircled her neck, emphasizing its slender gracefullness.

Dixie had done her long golden hair with tiny ringlets across her forehead and an upsweep that ended in long curls on the back of her head. When she saw Ryan, her eyes glowed and her lips parted in a warm smile.

Dixie's appearance took the captain's breath. As he moved toward her, she held out both hands. He took them in his own, bowed, clicked his heels, and lightly kissed them both. "Miss Dixie, there's no doubt about it. If they were electing a queen of the ball tonight, you would win hands down. You are absolutely the most beautiful sight I have ever beheld."

"Why, thank you, Captain. That is the nicest compliment I have ever had."

Victoria Coffield was standing at the door of the dining hall with General Page as he introduced her to every Sharpshooter who came near. She nodded idly at each man, but her attention was on Ryan McGraw and the honey-blonde he was greeting near the gate. She felt her blood heat up when Ryan bowed and kissed both of the woman's hands.

Victoria had dolled herself up exclusively for Ryan's sake. She fixed her hair his favorite way, and wore a pair of diamond earrings he had bought her for their first anniversary. Lex Coffield was not aware that she had kept them. Ryan had never liked her in a low-cut dress, so she had worn one with a high neck that was frilly and extremely feminine. Victoria told herself Ryan would get a gander at her pretty soon. When he did, that blonde hussy would look like a ragamuffin in comparison.

The music was light and cheerful coming through the door. When there was a break between Sharpshooters who were filing by, the general said, "Shall we go in now, Victoria?"

Ryan's ex-wife wanted him to see her as soon as possible. From the corner of her eye, she saw that he and the blonde were drawing near, moving arm-in-arm toward the dining hall's only door. Glancing quickly at Page, she said, "Let's wait just a few more minutes, General."

Page nodded, then noticed that Ryan and Dixie were almost to the door. A quick look at Victoria told him why she was reluctant to go inside. Though she was trying to conceal it, he could tell she was concentrating on the handsome couple.

As Ryan and Dixie drew up, Ryan felt his throat tighten. Victoria had inched away from Page and was practically blocking the door.

Flashing her ex-husband a toothy smile, Victoria breathed, "Hello, Ryan, darling. Did you get my note?"

Dixie blinked at the word darling.

"Yes. I was at the hospital today. Miss Worley gave it to me."

Victoria laid a frigid glare on Dixie, then looked back up at Ryan and said, "It *is* important, darling. Make it soon."

Visibly uncomfortable, Ryan said, "Victoria, this is Miss Dixie Quade. She is a nurse. She brought me back to health a year and a half ago at the Birmingham hospital when I was seriously wounded in battle. She's stationed now at the Mobile hospital because of the impending invasion of the Union navy. Miss Dixie, this is Victoria Coffield. Her husband is Captain Lex Coffield. He's part of the fort personnel here, but is away on assignment."

Showing a dimpled smile, Dixie said, "I'm happy to meet you, Mrs. Coffield. I'm sorry your husband couldn't be here for the ball."

Ignoring her, the brunette looked up at McGraw and said, "Ryan, darling, don't call me Victoria. You have always called me Tori."

Miffed at his ex-wife for the way she was snubbing Dixie, Ryan chose to ignore *her*. Turning to Dixie, he said, "Miss Dixie, this is General Richard Page."

The general took Dixie's hand, clicked his heels, bowed, and touched it to his lips. "I am very happy to meet you, Miss Quade," he said in a dignified manner. "Welcome to Fort Morgan, and welcome to the ball."

"Thank you, General," she smiled. "I am very happy to be here."

"Well, Victoria," said the general, "let's go inside."

Victoria's gaze clung to Ryan's for a brief moment, then she gave Dixie a feline smile and walked into the dining hall on Page's arm.

When they were out of earshot, Dixie looked up at Ryan and said, "Captain, I assume Mrs. Coffield is someone you know quite well."

Ryan cleared his throat nervously. "Yes. Quite well." Taking a deep breath, he said, "Come on, Miss Dixie. There are some Sharpshooters in here that you'll remember...and some you need to meet."

Ryan escorted Dixie to the punch table first, where Corporal Bobby Brinson was filling a cup for one of the young women. Bobby greeted Dixie warmly, and found quickly that she and the young lady already knew each other. From there, Ryan moved around the room with Dixie on his arm, introducing her to Sharpshooters she had not met, and allowing her to renew her acquaintance with those she had not seen in a long time.

Soon the music stopped, and General Page stepped up beside the orchestra conductor. When he had welcomed everyone once more, he thanked the men in the orchestra for donating their time on behalf of the men of Fort Morgan, and said, "All right, ladies and gentlemen, let the dancing begin. Maestro! Music, please!"

As the evening progressed, Dixie was ecstatic about being whirled around the floor in the arms of Ryan McGraw. She noted, however, that though Mrs. Coffield was dancing with General Page and other men, she kept looking at Ryan.

After an hour of dancing, Ryan went to the punch table and poured two cups full. Carrying them to where Dixie was sitting, he handed her a cup and sat down beside her. Taking a sip of punch, he smiled and said solemnly, "Miss Dixie, I meant what I said."

"You've said many things tonight, Captain," she replied softly. "To what do you refer?"

"I refer to what I said when you first came into the fort tonight. You are absolutely the most beautiful sight I have ever beheld."

Dixie swung her eyes to Victoria, who was on the floor with General Page, and said, "Even more beautiful than your friend Mrs. Coffield? She *is* striking, Captain."

"Yes she is," he admitted, "but she can't hold a candle to you."

Dixie looked deep into his eyes, loving him, but unable to say it. "Thank you. To hear such words coming from you means more to me than I can begin to tell you."

Neither Dixie nor Ryan noticed that the song had come to an end, and that seconds before the next one started, Victoria spoke briefly to the conductor, who nodded in assent. This was the most intimate moment they had experienced together. Ryan's heart hammered in his chest as he touched her hand and said, "Miss Dixie, I—"

"Well!" Victoria's voice cut across Ryan's words as she suddenly appeared, standing over them. "I see you two are sitting this one out." Fixing Dixie with hard, penetrating eyes, she said, "Miss Quade, you won't mind if I borrow the captain for a dance, will you? I mean, since you are not using him for the moment."

"Tori," Ryan said in a strained voice, rising to his feet, "Miss Dixie is my partner for the evening. It isn't proper for me to leave her here alone and dance with you. I've noticed that you've had an abundance of partners. Surely if General Page is growing tired, you can find someone else." With that, he sat down.

Putting on a pout, Victoria took hold of his arm and whined, "But, darling, the orchestra is going to play something special when this number is over. I want to dance it with you for old times' sake. Ple-e-e-ease!"

Graciously, Dixie patted Ryan's hand and said, "It will be all right, Captain. I'll give you up to Mrs. Coffield for just one number."

"See?" said Victoria. "You have permission, now. Come on."

Ryan's brow furrowed as he gave Dixie an "I'll get this over with and be right back" look. Standing up, he said, "All right, Tori. Just one."

Victoria took the cup from his fingers and handed it to Dixie, saying, "You can hold this while I hold *him*, sweetie."

Dixie had the sudden urge to lash out, but suppressed the desire for Ryan's sake. She wondered what kind of hold this woman had on him. What did she mean, "for old times' sake"? Was she an old girlfriend?

Bobby Brinson and his partner drew up to Dixie as Victoria led Ryan away by the hand. They sat down and struck up a conversation about how good the orchestra was. Dixie entered the conversation, but kept one eye on the man she loved.

Victoria held Ryan's hand at the edge of the dance floor, waiting for the present number to finish. While she waited, she said, "Darling, you must come to the house tomorrow."

"I can't. I'm busy."

"Well, get unbusy," she insisted. "It is very important."

"Why can't you just tell me about it right now?"

"Huh-uh," she said, shaking her head. "I have to tell you at the house. You'll understand when it happens. Trust me. Just please come tomorrow."

"Tori, I—"

"Oh, Ryan, the song is ending," she blurted, dragging him onto the floor. "Come on. Let's get ready for the next one."

Victoria took hold of both his hands as the orchestra started to play the *Donaulieder*.

Ryan looked down at Victoria and said stiffly, "Tori, you shouldn't have asked them to play that."

Victoria laughed flirtatiously, reached up and stroked his cheek in a tender manner, and said, "Darling, there's nothing wrong in stirring up a few old memories." Taking her stance for a waltz, she laid her left hand on his shoulder, placed her right hand in his left, and said, "Come on."

Ryan and Victoria were unaware that many of Fort Morgan's soldiers were watching them. Dixie also watched as they whirled round and round the floor. Bobby Brinson and his partner were back amid the dancers.

Presently, General Page sat down beside Dixie, holding a cup of punch. He noted that Dixie was following every move Ryan and Victoria were making. Assuming that Dixie knew who Victoria was, he said, "I see she took him away from you. Victoria *is* a bit forward, isn't she?"

"To say the least."

"Does it...ah...bother you to see them together like that?"

"Not really," she replied, pulling her eyes from the whirling couple and placing them on Page. "It's only for one number. Guess I can give him up for a few minutes to an old flame. That's what she is, I assume—a girlfriend from his past?"

The general realized that Dixie had not been told of Victoria's previous relationship to Ryan. Rising quickly, he said, "Excuse me, dear. I see a man I need to talk to."

Dixie watched the general move away quickly and approach one of the fort's officers at the punch table. Her line of sight soon strayed back to the dance floor.

When the waltz was over, everyone on the floor applauded the orchestra, which then began to play a slow, moody song. Ryan turned to leave the floor, and Victoria grabbed his arm. With a strange look in her eyes, she half-whispered, "One more, darling. Please."

"Victoria," he said firmly, "Dixie granted us one number. Now, I must get back to her."

As Ryan spoke, he glanced toward Dixie, who politely looked away when their eyes met. At the same instant, Victoria pressed against him and said, "Hold me close, Ryan. Like you used to. Our old song touched your heart, even as it did mine. I know it."

"Victoria, I—"

"Don't call me that," she clipped. "My name is Tori to you. It always has been and it always will be. Hold me, darling. Hold me tight."

"Tori, don't," he said, taking a step back. "There's no sense in this."

Forcing herself close again, she stood on her tiptoes and whispered, "Be honest, darling. It's still there, isn't it? You still love me, don't you?"

Gripping her shoulders and pushing her back, he said, "This has to stop, Tori. We mustn't see each other any more. You have a husband and a son. There is nothing between us any more."

Taking hold of both his upper arms, Victoria's black eyes bored into him as she countered, "You *are* still in love with me. I can feel it. And you can see it in my eyes. I am still in love with you. I made a mistake, darling...an awful mistake. Leaving you was wrong...terribly wrong. Please help me. I want to be yours again."

"Tori, two wrongs never made a right. Think of your son. Think what a broken home would do to him."

Victoria dug her fingernails into his arm. Eyes flinting, she said, "I wrote that note to you because there is something very, very important you need to know. Whatever you have planned for tomorrow, shorten it, or cancel it, but come to my house!" With that, she broke away from him and threaded her way among the dancers to where General Page was in conversation with Colonel and Mrs. DeWitt Munford. Within seconds, she had Page on the dance floor.

Approaching Dixie and sitting down beside her, Ryan said, "I'm sorry, Miss Dixie. Mrs. Coffield is a troubled woman right now. Her husband has been away for some time. She's lonely."

True to her nature, Dixie smiled sweetly and remarked, "The way she clung to you, it's evident that she's *quite* troubled. Can something be done to help her?"

"I'm sure it can, but I'm not the one to do it."

Cautiously, Dixie asked, "Captain…how well do you know her?"

Ryan took a deep breath, looked squarely into Dixie's eyes, and said glumly, "Mrs. Coffield is my ex-wife."

Dixie was stunned. Since Ryan's ex-wife had disappeared so long ago from his life, she had not thought of that possibility. All she could do was release a weak, "Oh."

Rising, Ryan took her by the hand and said, "Come on. The music is going to waste."

On the dance floor, Dixie said, "Captain, I don't mean to pry, but I have to ask you something."

"It wouldn't be like you to pry unnecessarily, ma'am," he said, holding her gently. "Ask your question."

"Are you still in love with her?"

"No."

Relieved at Ryan's prompt reply, Dixie was able to enjoy the rest of the evening. When the last dance was over, the orchestra and the female guests began boarding the carriages outside the gate. The ferries waited at the dock below.

Ryan walked his partner to her carriage, and before helping her in, he took hold of her hand and said, "Thank you for letting me be your escort tonight."

"You're welcome," she smiled. "It's been my pleasure."

"Not half as much as it's been *my* pleasure," he said softly.

"When will I see you again?"

"It'll be a few days. A dozen of my Sharpshooters and I are taking our Yankee prisoners up north to the prison camp at Jackson. We're pulling out at dawn in the morning. We have to take them in wagons because the railroad tracks between Mobile and Jackson have been destroyed by the Yankees. We can't float them up the Mobile River without making ourselves perfect targets… so the safest way is to move through the thick forests all the way up there, where at least we will have some protection."

Dixie frowned. "But even that is going to be very dangerous. Couldn't the prisoners just stay here?"

"No. General Page wants them out of his hair when Farragut comes in here, guns blazing.

Dixie nodded. "I can understand that." Ryan was still holding her hand. She squeezed his fingers and said, "Please be careful. I don't want anything to happen to you."

The captain's pulse picked up pace. "I'm glad for that. I promise I'll do my best to take care of Mrs. McGraw's boy."

Dixie smiled at his homespun way of expressing himself. The carriage driver spoke up, announcing that all the ladies should get on board.

Ryan took both of Dixie's hands in his and said, "When I get back, I'll be in to see you. Could I...could I take you to dinner?"

"Of course," she said softly.

Pulling her hands close to his chest, he said, "If it's all right with you, I want to see a lot more of you in the days to come."

Now it was Dixie's pulse that was beating faster. "Yes, it's all right with me."

At that instant, Victoria brushed past them and said, "Tomorrow, Ryan. I'll be waiting for you." She moved on to another carriage, not giving Ryan time to tell her that he was leaving for Jackson at dawn.

Dixie boarded her carriage, told Ryan she had had a wonderful evening, and waved as the carriage pulled away. Captain McGraw stood watching the carriage carry Dixie down the gentle slope toward the dock, and wrestled with his emotions. He could almost swear he was falling in love with the beautiful blonde. He had even come to the point that he wanted to be in love with her and make her his wife.

Yet, he asked himself, *how could I be feeling true love for Dixie when I am so stirred by the presence of Tori?*

TWELVE

efore dawn the next morning, several Rebel soldiers prepared the wagons while the Confederates and Yankees who were going to make the trip to Jackson were eating breakfast in the dining hall.

Captain Leonard Whittier ate quickly, then made his way to the table where Ryan McGraw was eating with Judd Rawlings and Bobby Brinson. Standing over the Confederate officer, Whittier said with grit in his voice, "You shouldn't be making my wounded men take this ride, McGraw."

"We've already been over that, Captain. They're going."

"I'm telling you again, Johnny Reb. You'll never get us to that prison camp. There are plenty of Union troops out there in those forests. They'll cut down every man in a gray uniform in short order."

"You'd better hope not," was McGraw's blunt reply.

"And why is that?"

"Because you and your men are going to be wearing gray."

Whittier's jaw slacked. "What're you talking about?"

"When you made your little threat yesterday about the woods being infested with Union troops, you said, 'When they see you hauling us in the wagons, they'll annihilate you.' Remember?"

"Yeah. So what?"

"You planted an idea in my head. I happened to know that there were several old and tattered Confederate uniforms in a store room here in the fort. General Page was glad to let me have enough to dress each of you blue-bellies in gray. All of you will be wearing Rebel uniforms on the way to Jackson. We'll put your wounded men in gray, also. They'll ride in a wagon together, and the rest of you will fill up the other two."

Whittier's eyes bulged. "You can't do this!"

"Oh, but I can. Your men will drive the wagons while my men and I ride horseback. Every one of your able-bodied men will have a rifle...but no ammunition, of course. With all twenty-nine of you in gray uniforms, we'll look like a detachment of thirty-five Confederate soldiers hauling seven of our wounded men somewhere. Since the Union scouting units are always made up of a dozen men or less, your blue-bellied comrades won't want to tackle a squad of thirty-five."

Whittier measured McGraw with a look of cold fury. "If our troops *do* attack, me and my men will be helpless! They'll cut us down—"

"This is war, Captain Whittier. You threatened me with Union troops coming after us in the woods, so I came up with a way to try to ward them off. If they open fire on you and your men, that's the way it is in war."

"If it happens, it'll make you a murderer."

"It won't be *me* pulling the triggers. You'd better pray your blue-bellied friends leave us alone. I might also add, Captain, that if any of your men try to escape, they will be shot. They're all listening over there right now. You better make sure they understand I mean what I say."

Just before dawn, Captain McGraw led the procession out of Fort Morgan, heading northward along the edge of Mobile Bay. Captain Leonard Whittier rode on the seat of the wagon that bore his seven wounded men. It galled him to see his men humiliated by having to wear Confederate uniforms, and he especially hated the one on his own body. The Rebel who had worn it had been shot in the chest. The ragged bullet hole was still there. He gripped the empty Henry repeater he was forced to hold and cursed Captain McGraw under his breath.

McGraw's dozen Sharpshooters surrounded the three wagons on their horses. Each man wore a sidearm and knife, and carried a repeater rifle. Private Bus Williams was sent ahead to ride point. Lieutenant Rawlings rode beside the captain, with Sergeants Hazzard and Cloud directly behind them. Corporal Bobby Brinson rode directly behind wagon number three. The other privates and corporals chose their places on both sides of the procession.

As the sun began to rise in the sky, it gave promise of a hot, humid day. Soon the procession was deep in the woods, veering away from the bay. They had been traveling for some three hours when Noah Cloud adjusted himself in his McClellan saddle and griped, "I wish I had a good western-type saddle with a saddle horn. I hate this dumb thing some lame-brained Northerner invented."

"General George B. McClellan designed it," said Hap Hazzard. "That's why it's called a McClellan saddle."

Cloud looked at Hazzard askance and said, "You're plumb crazy. That numskull McClellan was the first guy to use it. He didn't design it. They call it McClellan because he endorsed it, and he's a hot-shot. That's all."

"Talk about bein' a numskull. Don't you ever read anything but nursery rhymes? I'm tellin' you…McClellan designed this here saddle back in 1858. In 1859 the United States War Department adopted it as the army's official saddle because it takes less leather than the western kind, so it's cheaper to make."

Noah spit in the well-shaded dirt and guffawed. "Hap Hazzard, do you think everything you read is true? When would McClellan have time to invent a saddle? You got it wrong. It's like I said—he only endorsed it."

The driver of the first wagon, who was directly behind the arguing sergeants, spoke up. "The big redhead is right. I've been in the U.S. Army for a long time, and I know General McClellan personally. He *did* design that saddle in 1858, just like he's telling you."

Noah jerked around in the saddle and spat, "Shut your mouth, Yankee! Nobody gets in on our arguments! Understand? If my friend here wants to believe everything he reads and be told what to think by someone else, let him! But you butt out! The war between me and him is a private one. Got it?"

"Okay," shrugged the Yankee, turning to look at his captain, who sat beside him.

Whittier's face was like solid granite as he glanced at the two Rebel sergeants and said, "Don't bother with them, Oates. Save your energy for more important things."

Victoria Manning Coffield busied herself about the house all morning long, keeping it straightened up in spite of the continual litter left about by her five-year-old son. From time to time, she found herself going to the front door or the parlor window and looking toward the street.

After a while, Tommy noticed her frequent glances outside and asked, "Is Lex coming home today, Mommy?"

Turning away from the front door, which stood open because of the heat, Victoria looked down at the sandy-haired boy, thinking how much he looked like his father, and replied, "No, honey. It'll be three or four more days before Lex comes home."

"Good. I wish he'd never come home."

Tommy had voiced Victoria's own feelings. She did not reprimand him.

"Why do you keep looking outside if Lex isn't coming home? Is someone else coming to see us?"

"Somebody very special, honey. Somebody I've wanted you to meet for a long, long time." She cast another glance out the door, then turned back and said, "Tell you what. I'm trying to keep the house neat for our guest. Why don't you go out and play in the back yard? Maybe Eric and Rollie are in their back yards and will play with you."

"Naw, they ain't. Both of 'em left a while ago with their dads."

Frowning at him, Victoria said, "Tommy, I told you not to use the word *ain't*. You say 'They *aren't*.'"

"Yes, ma'am," replied Tommy, ducking his chin. He paused a moment, then unwittingly ripped at his mother's heart by saying, "I wish I had a *real* dad, like Eric and Rollie. They're always asking me why Lex doesn't take me boating on the bay and other stuff like their dads do. I keep telling them it's because Lex ain't—aren't—*isn't* my dad. He doesn't want to do things with me 'cause I'm not his son."

Victoria bit her lower lip as she saw the hurt in Tommy's pale-blue eyes. There was a tiny tear in the corner of the left one.

Clearing her throat, she said, "Honey, go out back and ride your stick horse that Grandpa Wiley made you."

"Okay," the boy said. He started toward the rear of the house, then halted and looked back at his mother. "Mommy, Grandpa Wiley isn't really my grandpa, is he? And Grandma Wiley really isn't my grandma, is she?"

Clarence and Myrtle Wiley, the elderly couple who lived next door, had taken a special liking to Tommy, and had asked Victoria if they could "adopt" her son as a grandchild. Their own grandchildren lived in Tennessee and South Carolina. Victoria's parents had been dead for over ten years, and since Tommy would never meet his paternal grandparents, she granted their request. To their delight, Tommy was even allowed to call them "Grandma" and "Grandpa."

"No, honey," the young mother answered, fighting a lump in her throat, "they're not your real grandparents, but they love you as much as if they were. Go on, now. Play in the back yard. I'll call you when our special guest arrives."

Wheeling, the boy broke into a run. He was almost to the kitchen when Victoria called, "Tommy!"

Skidding to a halt, he looked back. "Yes, ma'am?"

"Don't get dirty. I want you presentable when he gets here. And be especially careful with your bandage. We have to go to the hospital later this afternoon and get it changed. I don't want Dr. Bentley to see a dirty bandage. Understand?"

Tommy said he understood and was quickly out the back door.

When Ryan had not shown up by noon, Victoria called Tommy in for lunch. To her dismay, he was covered with dust and the sweat on his face and neck had turned to mud. Amazingly enough, the bandage on his arm was relatively clean. She washed him up, changed his clothes, combed his hair, and fed him lunch. One of the neighbor boys had returned home, and Tommy was eager to re-join him in play.

The hours dragged by. Twice Victoria heard the sound of hooves on the dirt street out front and ran to the door expecting to see her ex-husband. Disappointment gripped her when she saw it was not Ryan.

Four o'clock came. Frustrated and a bit angry, Victoria called her son in and washed him up again. Together, they walked the three blocks to Mobile's hospital. Approaching the receptionist's desk, Victoria said, "Miss Worley, I have Tommy here to see Dr. Bentley."

"All right, Mrs. Coffield," smiled Rebecca. "Just have a seat. The doctor is with a patient now, but will be able to see Tommy shortly."

"Thank you," nodded Victoria. Before turning toward the waiting area, she asked, "Has…ah…has Captain Ryan McGraw been in today?"

"Not that I know of, ma'am. I was away from my desk for about twenty-five minutes while I had lunch, but I didn't see the captain earlier or later, so I doubt that he's been in. He stays quite a while when he comes to see his men."

"Is nurse Quade in?"

"Yes. She's about to leave, but someone called for her to help with a patient down in room forty-one a couple of minutes ago. It's straight down the hall and to the left. She should be coming out momentarily."

"All right. I need to talk to her briefly. I'll take Tommy with me so you won't have to watch him. If Dr. Bentley is ready for him before we get back, come and let me know."

Rebecca nodded with a smile.

Leading her son by the hand, Victoria reached the hall and turned left. Just as they rounded the corner, Dixie was coming out of room forty-one, along with another nurse. When Dixie saw Victoria, she could tell by the look on her face she was wanting to speak to her. Dixie excused herself to the nurse, who proceeded on down the corridor, and waited as mother and son drew up.

Dixie's attention was drawn to the boy immediately. There was no doubt who his father was. She wondered why Ryan had never told her he had a son.

Dixie smiled at the boy, then looked up at his mother. Face stolid, Victoria asked sharply, "Miss Quade, are you expecting Captain McGraw to be here at the hospital today?"

"No, Mrs. Coffield. He left Fort Morgan at dawn this morning. He's taking some Yankee prisoners to the prison camp at Jackson. He'll be gone for a few days."

Anger flushed Victoria's face. "Why didn't Ryan tell *me* he was going to Jackson? I've been waiting for him to show up at my house all day!"

Dixie did not reply. She simply turned and started down the corridor in the opposite direction.

The move infuriated Victoria. "Wait a minute!"

Dixie kept on walking.

Tommy watched with wide-eyed concern as his mother ran ahead of the nurse and blocked her path. Dixie stopped abruptly, fixing the furious woman with an impassive look and struggling to keep her composure.

Fiery rage flashed in Victoria's black eyes as she blared, "Don't you walk away from me! I'm not through talking to you!"

Dr. Glenn Lyles emerged from a room a few feet down the corridor. His brow furrowed as he stepped close and asked, "Is there a problem, nurse Quade?"

"Nothing that I can't handle, Doctor," Dixie answered calmly.

"Is this lady upset about something that's happened here in the hospital?" pressed Lyles.

"No, sir. It's a personal matter."

Turning to Victoria, the doctor said, "Ma'am, if you have some personal dispute to settle with Miss Quade, it shouldn't be done here at the hospital while she is on duty."

Victoria had to bite her tongue to keep from snapping at the doctor. Suppressing her anger for the moment, she said, "I...I didn't come to the hospital for the purpose of having a confrontation with Miss Quade, Doctor." Gesturing toward Tommy, who stood where she had left him, she added, "I came to have Dr. Bentley examine my son's arm and change the dressing."

Lyles glanced at the boy, then said, "It might be best if you take your son to the waiting room until Dr. Bentley can see him."

"I will, Doctor, but it is very important that I talk to Miss Quade while I am here."

"Then do it privately and when Miss Quade has the time," said Lyles, and walked away.

When he was out of earshot, Victoria was about to speak to Dixie again when two nurses came out of a room a few doors down and headed their direction. When they had greeted Dixie and passed on by, Victoria put her face close to Dixie's and said, "You know who I am, don't you?"

Dixie knew what she meant, but said tartly, "You are Mrs. Coffield. Captain Lex Coffield's wife."

The cold insinuation was wasted on Victoria. Acidly she snapped, "Did Ryan tell you he was once married to me?"

"Yes, he did. You'd best remember that you're not married to him any more."

"You're in love with him," Victoria said levelly. "I saw it in your eyes when you were in his arms on the dance floor last night."

"That's really none of your business."

"Oh, really? I have a right to know what's going on in Ryan's life."

Temper flashed in Dixie's sky-blue eyes. "No you don't! You forfeited that right when you ran out on that wonderful man and divorced him. But since you brought it up, *Mrs. Coffield,* I will tell you straight. Yes, I am in love with Ryan, but why should you care? You've got a husband."

Ignoring Dixie's heated words, Victoria asked pointedly, "Do you think Ryan is in love with you?"

"It's none of your business, Mrs. Coffield. None of this has any connection with you."

"Well, let me tell you, miss blond prissy, Ryan McGraw is still in love with me! And I'm serving notice right now...I am going to have him back!"

Dixie's temper grew hotter. It shook her throat as she spoke. "What is your husband going to say to that?"

Looking around to see if anyone was in earshot, and seeing no one, Victoria put her nose within inches of Dixie's and hissed, "I'll handle Lex in my own way and my own time! And if you tip anything to him, or try to stand between Ryan and me, *I'll kill you!*"

While her words hung threateningly in the air, Victoria spun around and stomped down the corridor. Grabbing Tommy by the hand, she led him into the waiting room, making sure the receptionist saw them. When they sat down, the boy said, "Is that nurse a bad lady, Mommy?"

Patting his head, Victoria replied, "Yes, honey. She is a *very* bad lady."

The day wore on as the three wagons and their mounted escort wended their way through the dense Alabama forests. The sun beat down mercilessly, and though they were in deep shade most of the time, every man's shirt was stained with sweat.

Private Williams was some fifty yards ahead, his eyes carefully searching the woods. McGraw and Rawlings were still riding side by side ahead of the lead wagon. Hazzard and Cloud had dropped back and were chatting with a couple of other Sharpshooters.

Raising his hat and mopping sweat with a bandanna, McGraw observed two squirrels chase each other around the base of a giant oak tree, then dart up its trunk and disappear into the thick foliage overhead. Giving his lieutenant a sidelong look, he said, "I happened to observe you and Betty off and on during the dance last night. Seems to me things are thickening up pretty fast between you two."

Judd grinned and said, "Does that statement require a comment, sir?"

"Well, I guess you wouldn't say a comment was *required*, but since I am your superior in rank, I do request a comment."

"Okay. I won't beat around the bush. I'm falling in love with her."

"Really? What about Betty? She showing signs of feeling the same about you?"

"Mm-hmm. *Good* signs."

"Yeah? And what are they?"

"Unless I get a direct command to answer, sir, you ain't gonna find out."

"Guess I'll leave it alone."

"Thank you," grinned Rawlings. He waited a few seconds, then said, "Captain, are you aware of the talk among the Fort Morgan men after the dance last night?"

"No. What kind of talk?"

"Well, some of them were discussing the way you and Victoria danced awfully close there at the last. They said that when Captain Coffield returns, he'll no doubt hear about it."

"Probably will," McGraw said dryly.

"They're saying you'll probably have a fight on your hands."

McGraw stuffed his bandanna back in his hip pocket, but said nothing.

Judd proceeded. "The men at the fort say Coffield has a

wicked mean streak. They say he has a hot, hair-trigger temper, and that he's insanely jealous over Victoria. He has already maimed two civilian men in Mobile for being too friendly with her."

When the captain still did not reply, Rawlings said, "None of the men at the fort like Coffield, Captain, and to a man they said they won't tell him about the way—as they put it—you and Mrs. Coffield were cuddling. But they're sure he'll find out about it. Could be real trouble."

"I've faced real trouble before. The hot-headed captain can come after me if he wants to, but the cuddling was Victoria's doing, not mine."

"None of those fort men know she used to be your wife," said Rawlings. "The women who attended don't either."

"That really shouldn't enter into the picture, Lieutenant. Victoria's very unhappy in her marriage and is trying to win me back. I shouldn't even have danced with her. She was so insistent, and Dixie was nice enough to tell me to go ahead and give Victoria one dance. After that one dance was over, she threw herself at me. I should have shoved her away the instant she moved so close, but she'd have made a scene. I know her too well."

"So what are you going to do about her?"

Before Ryan could answer, Private Donnie Jim Michaels pulled up on his opposite side and said, "Captain, you told me to ride up and relieve Williams on point at three o'clock. It's time."

"Fine," nodded McGraw. "Go right ahead."

"I wanted to tell you something, first, sir."

"Yes?"

Leaning close and lowering his voice so Captain Whittier could not hear him, Michaels said, "There's a lot of whispering going on in the last wagon, sir. Corporal Brinson asked me to tell you he thinks those blue-bellies are going to make a run for it. We both think maybe you'd better tell them one more time we'll shoot them down if they try to escape."

"I told them once. They're not children. I'm not telling them again. I gave all of you men your instructions. One warning shot if they try to run. If they don't stop, you shoot to kill. Remember?"

"Yes, sir."

"Brinson and the others will remember, too. Go on up and relieve Williams."

Michaels said, "Yes, sir," and touched heels to his horse's flanks. The animal went into a trot.

As Michaels drew close to Williams near a creek up ahead, Rawlings said, "I think I'll drop back and join Brinson for a while…just in case those blue-bellies decide to make a run—"

The lieutenant's words were cut short as the report of a rifle split the hot afternoon air. McGraw and Rawlings turned to see the eleven Yankees in the last wagon peeling over the sides and running in two directions. Corporal Brinson's smoking Henry was cocked and ready to fire a second time as he shouted to the fleeing men, "Halt! Halt or you die!"

The warning shot had caused most of them to stop, but two of the Yankees were still running to the left, and one to the right. Brinson, Hazzard, and Cloud fired, dropping one, and at the same instant, six more rifles barked, cutting the other two down.

Captain Whittier was swearing at the Rebels and started to get out of his wagon. Jerking on the reins, McGraw wheeled his mount in a tight circle and shouted at Rawlings, "Make him stay in the wagon!"

As McGraw headed back along the line, Rawlings swung his rifle on Whittier, who was halfway to the ground and blared, "Back in the wagon, Captain, or you'll get what those three men of yours just got!"

Whittier froze, eyes blazing. As he moved back into the seat, he swore and bawled, "Murderers! They just murdered my men!"

The Rebel captain rode past the second wagon, telling his men to shoot the first Yankee who threw a leg over the side. When he reached the last wagon, four Sharpshooters were holding rifles on the would-be escapees who were fearfully climbing back into the wagon.

"Good work, all of you!" said McGraw, turning his horse so

each of his men could hear him. "Corporal Zale, you and Private Stelling take six men from the second wagon and escort them as they pick up their dead comrades and carry them back here."

Suddenly Whittier stood up in his wagon and screamed at the top of his voice, "McGraw! The whole bunch of you are murderers! You'll pay for this! I guarantee it! You'll pay for this!"

"Shut up, Captain!" Rawlings shouted, urging his horse closer to the first wagon."

Corporal Zale and Private Stelling were collecting the six Yankees from the second wagon, and Corporals Brinson and Ewing were holding guns on those in the last wagon, along with Private Koop. Hazzard and Cloud positioned themselves so as to cover troublemakers in any of the wagons.

Captain McGraw trotted up to the first wagon, reined in, and said to Whittier, "Nobody murdered those men, Captain. I remind you that all of you were warned that if you tried to escape you would be shot. Corporal Brinson fired a warning shot, and even called out to them, but they still kept running. They were fools for trying to escape."

"My men are just scared, McGraw. They're spooked about being sitting ducks in these gray uniforms! They're also worried about being locked up in one of your filthy Confederate prison camps. Who can blame them for gambling an escape? Your men didn't have to be so eager to cut them down. They didn't have to kill them! They could've shot them in the legs."

"Sure," snorted McGraw. "Like you would have done to us if the tables were turned. They were duly and properly warned, and were given two chances to halt. They kept running. It was their own fault they got killed. I don't want to hear any threats from you."

"I don't care what you want to hear!" Whittier roared. "You'll never get us to Jackson. In spite of these stinking Confederate uniforms, we'll find a way to overcome you. And when you're *our* prisoners and I have the upper hand, I'm going to give you some of your own medicine. You're going to rue the day you were born!"

McGraw did not see Sergeant Hazzard dismount and head

toward the lead wagon as he nudged his horse close to Whittier and said, "Do as Lieutenant Rawlings told you, Captain. Shut your mouth. Now, sit down and cool off."

Whittier's cheeks were red as brick dust in the dappled sunlight that filtered through the trees. There was insolent contempt in his voice as he snarled, "I'll sit down, shut up, and cool off when I'm good and ready, McGraw!"

Suddenly big Hap Hazzard yanked Whittier from the wagon seat and let him drop to the ground. Whittier's empty rifle clattered on the seat, then fell to the floor of the wagon. The Yankee captain gasped for breath and started to rise. Hap sank powerful fingers into his sweaty shirt, lifted him to eye level, and growled, "You can forget trying to make my captain rue the day he was born. By his own medicine, I assume you mean you would kill him. Let me tell you something, big-mouth! Captain Ryan McGraw don't kill easy! A lot of men have tried…and a lot of men have died. Are you listenin' to me?"

Whittier clamped his mouth shut, giving his countenance an insolent mien. Hap's face grew redder. He shook the man and said, "I asked you if you're listenin' to me!"

Whittier swallowed hard. "I'm listening," he choked.

"Okay, you listen good. Even if somehow you succeeded in killing my captain, you'd have *me* to face. You know what I'd do, big-mouth? Do you?"

Whittier's face was paling. He was helpless in the hands of the muscular sergeant and was embarrassed in front of his men. Licking his lips, he said, "No."

"I'd tear off both your arms and beat you over the head with 'em. Then I'd tear off both your legs and stuff 'em down your stinkin' Yankee throat. Then you know what I'd do, Whittier?"

"No," came the weak reply.

"Then I'd kill you!"

The Rebel soldiers burst into laughter. Captain Whittier eyed them with hatred as Hazzard dumped him back on the wagon seat in a heap.

THIRTEEN

The blazing sun made its arc across the sky and dropped toward the western horizon. The horses' ears were drooped from the heat, and the sweaty men rode in relative silence.

Captain Leonard Whittier sat glumly on the wagon seat. Confederates and Yankees alike let their eyes roam the woods around them, aware that Union soldiers could come at them any time. The thought of dying under the guns of their own army was almost more than the Yankee prisoners could bear.

At sundown, Captain McGraw and Lieutenant Rawlings saw Private Michaels trotting toward them from his point position. Reining in, Michaels said, "Captain, there's a bubbling spring just ahead, and it's at the edge of a small clearing. Be a good place to camp for the night."

"Sounds good. We'll do it."

As the wagons hauled up in the clearing and the Rebels dismounted, the able-bodied prisoners were allowed to stretch their legs and drink from the spring. Canteens were filled and the wounded men were given water. When they had taken their fill, they were helped out of the wagon and laid out on the ground.

One of the wounded Yankees looked up at McGraw, and said,

"Captain, riding in that wagon is killing us. Every time it hits a hole or runs over a rock, it jars us and shoots pain through our wounds."

"Soldier, I'm sorry about your pain, but there's nothing I can do about it."

"You could just leave us here. Wouldn't be long till some of our troops would come along. They'd take care of us."

"You ought to know I can't do that, soldier. It's my duty to deliver you to the prison camp. I don't enjoy seeing anyone suffer…not even Yankees. You and your wounded pals just have to face it. War is made of pain and discomfort."

Together the enemies ate a cold meal. McGraw did not want to draw attention by building a fire. Lieutenant Rawlings took charge of assigning sentries for the night. Three men would be on duty at all times, and would work in shifts. The Yankees were huddled together in one spot and lay on the warm ground. McGraw and his men encircled them, and as darkness fell, everyone in the camp was asleep except the sentries.

Dawn came. Privates Southard, Barnes, and Koop awakened the other Sharpshooters, then began rousting out the Yankees. As a matter of caution, Koop began a head count of the prisoners. Coming up one man short, he counted again. When it was confirmed that one prisoner was missing, Koop dashed to McGraw, who was in conversation with Sergeant Hazzard and said, "Excuse me, Captain, but I've got some bad news."

"What bad news?"

"One of the Yankees is missing."

Frowning, McGraw asked, "Are you sure?"

"Yes, sir. I counted all of them. Dead ones, wounded ones, and the rest of them. We're one prisoner short. Somehow one of them slipped past the sentries during the night and got away."

McGraw turned toward Alex Zale and Doug Stelling, who stood near the spot where the horses had been picketed, and called, "Alex, are all the horses there?"

Zale turned, and began a quick count. After a few seconds, he called back, "Yes, sir. They're all here, including the wagon teams."

"Thanks," said McGraw, and wheeled, stomping toward Leonard Whittier with Hap Hazzard on his heels. Koop followed close. The rest of the Rebels caught on that something was up and began looking toward their leader.

Whittier was on his feet, checking the bandage on his arm as McGraw drew up and said, "One of your men is missing."

Whittier had heard McGraw asking his men about the horses, but had paid little attention. His head jerked up. "What?"

"I said one of your men is missing. I want to know who it is."

A wide grin split Whittier's face. "Really?"

"Really. Who is it?"

"Did he take a horse?"

"No. He's on foot."

Looking around with the grin still wide, the Yankee leader said loudly, "You hear that, guys? One of our men was smart enough to get away!" There was an instant cheer from the Yankees.

Fixing McGraw with hard eyes, Whittier smirked, "Well, Captain, it won't be long now. My man will bring Yankees swarming down on you like mad hornets! They'll know about us being in these gray uniforms, too."

"Who is it, Captain?" queried one of the wounded Yankees who lay on the ground.

Whittier ran his gaze over the faces of his men for a few seconds, then replied, "It's Bill Temple."

"He take a horse, sir?"

"No. He was probably afraid if he tried it, one of them would nicker and give him away. He's on foot."

"That'll be no problem, Captain," spoke up another wounded Yankee. "Bill's a fast runner. He'll bring help soon!" There was another cheer from the prisoners.

Bus Williams was standing near. "What shall we do, Captain?"

Before McGraw could reply, Hap Hazzard said, "I'll go after Temple on horseback. I know a little about trackin'. If I can run him down before he finds some of his blue-bellied buddies, this whole episode will be over before you can bat an eye."

"I'll go with you," nodded McGraw. "Lieutenant Rawlings, you're in charge. Don't let anybody move till Hap and I get back."

While a couple of the men were saddling McGraw's and Hazzard's horses, the captain followed Hap as he walked the perimeter of the camp, studying the ground. It took him only a minute to find footprints leading through the trees eastward. Kneeling down and examining the prints closely, he said, "By the way these blades of grass are pressed down, I'd say Temple hasn't been gone more than an hour, Cap'n. Probably made his move just before dawn."

"Let's go," breathed McGraw.

As the two Rebels rode out at a trot with Hazzard's keen eye tracking the escapee, the captain said, "Stands to reason that unless Temple knows of a Union camp somewhere around here, he'll find himself a horse to ride."

"I was thinkin' the same thing," replied Hazzard. "If he spots a farm, he'll beeline for it."

Moments later, they broke out of the woods into open country, and spied a farmhouse with barn and outbuildings about a mile away. "C'mon!" said McGraw, goading his mount.

Their horses' hooves threw up turf as McGraw and Hazzard put them into a full gallop. Just as they were thundering into the yard, they saw an elderly man bound out the front door of the weather-worn farmhouse. He stumbled and fell as he jumped off the porch, and at the same moment, a revolver boomed at the door. The bullet chewed dirt next to the old man's head. The gunman saw the two army officers closing in, and ducked back, slamming the door. In the second or two that it took for him to do it, McGraw and Hazzard recognized Bill Temple in the gray uniform.

Skidding their mounts to a stop, both men vaulted from their saddles, rifles in hand, and picked up the old man. Hurrying, they dragged him behind a huge oak tree close by and sat him down. Sensing danger at the house, the horses followed and stood by the tree.

As the elderly farmer looked into their faces, eyes wide, McGraw said, "Sir, I am Captain Ryan McGraw of B Company, First Alabama Battalion Sharpshooters. This is Sergeant Hap Hazzard. You probably know by now that the man inside your house is not a Confederate soldier."

"Yes," gasped the old man. "That devil Yankee fooled me at first. He knocked on my door and told me he had escaped from a Yankee camp where he was bein' held prisoner, and needed a horse. He couldn't find one in the corral or in the barn. He got angry when I told him I don't keep horses any more, that my son down the road does the farmin' for me with his horses. Then he points that rifle at me and enters my house. Once't he's inside, he grabs my revolver off'n its hook on the wall and points it at me. Come to find out, his rifle is empty. I figure he's a Yankee in disguise an' he admits it. 'Bout that time, he heard you men gallopin' in. I made a dash out the door and he took a shot at me."

"Is there anyone else in the house, sir?" asked McGraw.

The old man drew in a raspy breath, his eyes widening. "Yes, my wife! But she's bedridden. He...he wouldn't hurt a crippled old woman, would he?"

Before McGraw could comment, Temple's voice cut the air. "Captain! Can you hear me?"

McGraw removed his hat and peered cautiously around the tree. The Yankee stood in the doorway, holding the revolver to a small, elderly woman's head. He was supporting her entire weight with his free arm. A look of terror was on the woman's face.

"I can hear you," replied McGraw. "Put the woman down!"

"I will! All you have to do is throw out your guns. I want those horses. I'll ride one and take the other one with me so you can't follow. Do as I say, and nobody will get hurt."

"Can't let you do that, Temple. The lives of my men are at stake. You'd bring your blue-bellied friends down on us."

As he spoke, McGraw levered a cartridge into the rifle's chamber, edged the muzzle around the rough-barked trunk and lined it on what he could see of Temple's head behind the woman's.

Hazzard did the same thing on his side of the tree. "Cap'n," he said in a low tone. "I think you've got a better angle than I do."

"Mine's pretty good," said McGraw.

"Hey!" boomed Temple. "Are you listening to me out there? I said throw your guns out and nobody will get hurt!"

"What's he doin' to my wife?" asked the old man, his voice quavering.

"He's got your revolver to her head, sir," said McGraw, "but in the excitement, he's forgotten to cock the hammer. He's an infantry-man and doesn't handle revolvers much."

"Oh, don't endanger her life, Captain, please! Don't try to shoot him if he's using her as a shield!"

"What's your name, sir?" Hap asked.

"Clive Holman. Wife's name is Elsie."

"Mr. Holman, the Yankee *is* using your wife as a shield, but he's exposing half of his head so he can see us with one eye. Captain McGraw is an expert marksman. When he thinks he's got a clear shot, he can take the man out. If we wait too long, that Yankee is going to realize the hammer isn't cocked. Once he cocks it, even if Captain McGraw drills him perfectly, his reflex could pull the trigger on that revolver."

Clive Holman started praying in a half-whisper.

"McGraw!" bellowed Temple. "My patience is running out!"

Elsie could be heard whimpering.

Voice low, McGraw said, "Hap, tell him one more time to put her down. I'm holding my breath to steady my aim."

The old man was weeping as he prayed.

Looking at the Yankee down the barrel of his Henry, Hazzard shouted, "Temple, give it up! Ease Mrs. Holman down carefully and drop the gun."

"You stupid Rebs are gonna get her killed!" shouted Temple. "Now, throw those guns out or—"

Ryan McGraw's rifle barked and the slug tore through Bill

Temple's right eye. Elsie fell backward on top of the dead man.

"See to her, Hap," said McGraw, reaching down to help the old man to his feet.

"Is she all right?" choked Holman.

"Yes, sir. She's fine."

"Oh, thank you dear Jesus!" the old man sobbed as McGraw steadied him and helped him around the tree.

Hap was standing over Temple's body and cradling Elsie in his arms as the captain and the farmer drew up. Tears were dripping from her chin and staining her cotton nightgown. Reaching past the big sergeant's muscular arm, Clive Holman hugged his wife's neck as they wept together.

A cheer went up from the Rebels when they saw Captain McGraw and Sergeant Hazzard ride up with the dead Yankee's body draped over Hazzard's horse. The prisoners eyed each other with dismay and looked toward their captain, who walked up to the corpse as Hazzard and McGraw were dismounting and eyed the gaping scarlet hole in the back of Temple's head.

McGraw had moved up behind him. Before Whittier could vent his wrath, McGraw met him with a cold stare and said, "Don't say it, Captain. He forced his way into the home of an elderly farm couple, took their revolver, and shot at the old man when he ran from the house. We arrived just as the old man was coming out the door. Your big, brave soldier, here, dragged the farmer's crippled wife from her bed, put the gun to her head, and demanded we give him our horses. He was going to kill her if we refused."

"I don't believe it!"

"Well, that just cuts me deeply," retorted McGraw. Shoving his way past the Yankee leader, he called to the prisoners, "Okay, we're pulling out. Put your wounded men in their wagon and pile in your own. Let's go!"

The dead Yankees were carried in wagons one and two, with

nothing to cover them. McGraw figured it was best that way. Maybe the sight of the corpses would be a constant reminder of what it cost to attempt escape from McGraw's Sharpshooters.

Travel was resumed. The wounded men complained of their discomfort, but to no avail. At noon, when they stopped beside a babbling brook to eat and fill the canteens, McGraw announced that they were halfway to Jackson. By sundown the next day, they would be at the prison camp. Soon they were on the move again. From time to time they caught a glimpse of the Mobile River glistening in the harsh sunlight a mile or so to the west.

Some fifteen miles southeast of Jackson, a squad of a dozen Union soldiers was camped in a wooded thicket as the sun was going down. They were clustered in a tight circle, sitting on the ground, as Sergeant Eli Garrett stood over them.

"So what do you think our assignment will be, Sergeant?" asked one of the soldiers.

"I could guess two or three things," replied Garrett, who chewed on a dead cigar. "But no sense in going through them. Just be a waste of breath. We'll know for certain when Lieutenant Blake gets back."

"I'd like to go over there to that stinking Confederate prison camp at Jackson and free our men in there," spoke up a corporal.

"Take more men than we have here to do that," said Garrett. "I understand it's a virtual fort."

The sound of a horse blowing met everybody's ears. Grabbing their guns, they leaped to their feet. They were traveling on foot and had no horses; the sound meant someone was coming. Seconds later, five riders in blue uniforms emerged from the dense woods and greeted them. Amongst them was Lieutenant Erven Blake, their leader.

After exchanging a few words with the four men who had escorted him from Major General Edward R.S. Canby's camp in Mississippi, Blake bid them good-bye. When they had ridden out of sight, Blake tied his horse to a bush and told the men to gather around.

When everyone was seated on the ground, Blake stood before them and said, "I know you're all eager to find out our assignment, so here's the story. Within the last day or two, a special unit made a night assault on Fort Morgan at the mouth of Mobile Bay. There is no word as yet as to the result of that mission. The unit was to capture the fort and hold it, which would eliminate most of the danger Admiral Farragut and his fleet would encounter upon entering the bay. I say *most* of the danger, because there's also Fort Gaines to reckon with, but it is held by only a few men and can be overcome by land *or* sea quite easily."

Blake lifted his campaign hat, mopped sweat from his brow with a dark-blue bandanna, and continued. "If General Canby learns that the Fort Morgan mission was successful and that the fort is now in the hands of Union forces, he will hasten to send a large number of troops toward the city of Mobile by land. This is where we come in. Our assignment is to move from here toward Mobile and rendezvous with a couple hundred of our troops bivouacked about ten miles north of Mobile."

"Sir," spoke up Sergeant Eli Garrett, "where will General Canby obtain enough troops to capture Mobile? It'll take a whole lot more than two hundred plus us."

"General Canby is working on that right now. From what he said, I think he's going to send Major General Gordon Granger and his Cumberland Fourth Corps. They've got over five thousand men. Right now, Granger's bunch are in a hot battle somewhere north of here, but it looks like that one will be won shortly."

Garrett spoke again. "Lieutenant, what's the time schedule, then? If Fort Morgan is now in our hands, how soon does General Canby plan to move on Mobile?"

"I'd say it'll be about two weeks."

"But what if that assault on Fort Morgan didn't come off as planned? Then what?"

"General Canby and I discussed that. He figures that without control of Fort Morgan, Admiral Farragut will want to beef up his fleet some more before steaming into Mobile Bay. If Fort Morgan is still in Confederate hands, we're probably looking at the first week of August for the big move. So that'd be about another four weeks." Blake paused to mop sweat again, then said, "If the mission was successful, then as I understand it, Admiral Farragut has already run his fleet into Mobile Bay and overpowered Fort Gaines, too. He'll wait until our land forces are ready to close in on Mobile from the north, then move on the city from the bay. This will give the Union a sure-fire victory, and Mobile will then be in our hands."

"So we won't know about all this until we get word from General Canby," said Garrett.

"Right," nodded Blake. "Once Canby hears from Farragut, he can plan accordingly. Our job is to be at the spot ten miles north of Mobile whenever word comes."

"So we move out at dawn. Right, sir?"

"Right. Now let me say something else. General Canby told me that the war is definitely turning in favor of the Union. We're winning more and more battles everywhere. President Lincoln and General Grant are in agreement that once we occupy Mobile and the bay, the end of the war can be hastened."

There was instant joy among the soldiers. They shook hands, patted each other on the back, and laughed heartily, saying they could soon go home.

Blake proceeded. "The reason it'll hasten the end of the war is because having the use of the Mobile seaport will enable the Union to bring in troops, weapons, ammunition, and supplies to the degree that we'll have what it takes to overpower the already weakening Confederate forces."

With spirits running high, Lieutenant Blake and his men ate their evening meal and talked of going home. Soon darkness surrounded them, and they bedded down for the night. At sunrise Blake mounted his horse and headed southwest with his men following on foot. Blake sent Corporal Benny Middleton to move out ahead and walk point. Middleton stayed in sight of the others about fifty to sixty yards ahead.

It was nearly midday when the sun-blistered Yankees saw Middleton waving at them from the top of a heavily wooded rise. He had seen something and wanted them to hurry. Lieutenant Blake trotted on ahead.

When the others arrived, they found Blake and Middleton looking at movement in a shallow valley about two thousand yards below. The lieutenant was leaning against a tree, using binoculars to study the faraway scene.

As the men gathered close, keeping well within the shadows, one of them squinted down into the valley and asked, "Is it Rebs, sir? Looks like gray uniforms, but with the heat haze, it's hard to tell."

Without taking the binoculars from his eyes, Blake replied so that all could hear, "It's Rebels, all right. There are three wagons loaded with them, and thirteen of them on horseback. Can't tell exactly how many are in the wagons, but I'd say at least twenty-five …maybe thirty. They're all bearing what look to be repeater rifles."

Sergeant Garrett stood at Blake's shoulder and said, "They're headed due north across that open meadow, sir. They'll be in the woods ahead of them in a short while. Are we gonna go after them?"

"There's no way we can just rush them. Be foolish to try to swap lead with that many men. We need to hasten on ahead of them, lay wait for them in the forest, and take them by surprise. Without the element of surprise, we'd be committing suicide. We'll try to avoid a gun battle if possible, since we're so outnumbered. If we can get the drop on them, we can take them as prisoners. Looks like they just might be coming from Mobile. I'd sure like to squeeze some information out of them."

Corporal Ken Southard was riding point as the blazing sun neared its zenith. The wagons and mounted Rebels were some eighty yards behind him, moving steadily across an open meadow. Southard studied the dense woods ahead of him and wished for more open spaces. The forests were extremely dangerous because it offered the enemy a place to hide and spring an ambush.

In the procession, Captain McGraw rode alongside the lead wagon, listening to the Yankee leader complain while he gripped his empty rifle.

"You should've let us bury our dead, McGraw," griped Whittier. "It isn't good for my men to have to ride with those bodies. Pretty soon they'll start to stink."

"We're not taking time to bury them, Captain. That'll be taken care of as soon as we arrive at the prison camp. Besides, as I said earlier, having those corpses in the wagons will be a good reminder of why they died. Nobody is going to get away from us. My job is to deliver all of you to the prison camp. I'll do that whether it's dead or alive."

"I'm wondering if dead isn't best," mumbled Whittier.

"Certainly prison camp is better than death, isn't it?"

"Since it's a Confederate prison camp, that's debatable. I've heard some pretty bad things about your prison camps."

"Well, I've heard some bad things about yours, too."

Ignoring McGraw's comment, the Yankee captain said, "You know the South is licked, don't you? There's no way you can win this war."

"That's your opinion."

"It's more than an opinion. You Southerners are short on supply, and you know it. You can't make guns and ammunition out of cotton fields and peach orchards. The North has the advantage. We have factories. We can produce weapons and ammunition in a way the South cannot. Face it, McGraw, the Confederacy is doomed. It's only a matter of time."

Captain McGraw was nobody's fool. He knew what Whittier was saying about the factories was right. This was what made Mobile Bay and the city of Mobile so important. A few foreign countries were shipping in needed supplies via the Gulf of Mexico for the Confederacy's use in the Western Theatre. If the Union navy was allowed to capture the bay and the Union land forces found a way to capture Mobile, all necessary supplies would be cut off.

The Confederates had managed to last this long because of the foreign supplies and the fact that after so many battles in which the stubborn Rebels had been victorious, they were able to confiscate Union guns and ammunition. Confiscation by itself, however, would never keep them in the war. They had to have the supplies that came up the bay to Mobile.

The procession moved into the heavy timber, and the deep shade cast by the foliage overhead was a welcome relief from the heat of the sun.

Having true Southern doggedness in his makeup, McGraw would have the last word of the discussion. Leaning slightly from the saddle, he held Whittier with a penetrating stare and said, "Don't count your chickens before they're out of the eggs, Captain. We've still got Mobile Bay. Never underestimate the South's determination to wear you Yankees down till you turn tail and run back home. We've got grit you haven't even seen yet." With that, McGraw nudged his horse forward and rejoined Judd Rawlings at the front of the procession.

A half hour later, the wagons were rattling amid the thick trees when suddenly a dozen men-in-blue leaped out from the shadows, guns ready, surrounding the procession. Riders and drivers pulled rein.

A single Yankee up ahead jumped from behind a tree, threw his gun on Ken Southard, and commanded sternly, "Drop the rifle, Reb!"

Southard reprimanded himself for being taken by surprise, leaned over and carefully dropped his Henry repeater. When it hit the soft forest floor, the Yankee snapped, "Okay, out of the saddle!"

Southard looked around for more Yankee soldiers, but saw

none. As he slowly dismounted, he wondered why the Yankee hadn't shot him out of the saddle. When he touched ground, the enemy soldier said crustily, "Okay, Reb. Turn around and head back where you came from."

What Southard saw in the thick woods some seventy yards behind him filled him with fear. The wagon procession was stopped and surrounded by blue-bellies, wielding repeater rifles.

"Let's go," said the Yankee, prodding him with the muzzle of his weapon.

Standing his ground, Southard said over his shoulder, "What about my horse?"

"Don't fret," replied the enemy soldier, prodding him again. "We'll be taking him for ourselves."

Lieutenant Blake planted himself in front of the two lead horses, holding his service revolver on McGraw and Rawlings, whom he recognized as officers. "You two dismount!" he directed sharply, waving his gun with authority.

McGraw hated that the Yankees had gained the advantage on them, but knew it was impossible to totally protect themselves when traveling in dense timber. He and his men had been in tight spots before. If a natural opportunity didn't quickly present itself for them to turn the tables, the Sharpshooters would create one. As McGraw and Rawlings were throwing their legs over their saddles, the natural opportunity came unexpectedly.

Eager to identify himself and his men as Union soldiers, Captain Whittier stood up in his wagon, holding the empty rifle, and said excitedly, "Lieutenant, these men in the wagons are Union army! I'm their Captain! My name is—"

The sudden move startled Lieutenant Blake. He raised his gun and eyed him skeptically, expecting a trick. "Sit down, soldier!" he snapped, "and drop that rifle! Union soldiers don't wear gray uniforms!"

Men on both sides tensed.

Frustrated that the Union officer did not believe him, Whittier looked down at the rifle he held and stammered, "It…it isn't loaded, Lieu-Lieutenant." In his frenzied eagerness to prove his point, he jerked the rifle up for Blake's inspection.

A tense Union soldier misunderstood the quick move, reacted by natural reflex and fired his rifle, hitting Whittier in the chest. There was instant bedlam.

Sharpshooters went into action. Guns roared. McGraw and Rawlings had their rifles in scabbards on their saddles. There was no time to grab them. Instead, they hit the ground and whipped their revolvers out of their holsters, firing at the first blue uniforms they saw. They both fired once, and two Union soldiers fell dead. McGraw caught a glimpse of Captain Whittier hanging over the edge of the lead wagon with his head down and a foot caught under the seat. There was a bullet hole directly over his heart. His eyes stared vacantly into space. The empty rifle lay on the ground beneath his head.

Rawlings saw a Yankee dive under the wagon for cover. He trained his revolver on the man's face with the hammer cocked. A split second before he dropped the hammer, he saw the knowledge of death in the surprised Yankee's eyes. The gun bucked against his palm and the Yankee died instantly with a slug in his forehead.

The woods clattered and echoed with the harsh gunfire. Bullets hissed and hummed deadly songs, hitting men and splintering the bark off trees. Horses were neighing and stomping their hooves as the battle progressed. Smoke filled the air, giving off its bitter odor.

Captain McGraw rose up on one knee, hunting for a target, when through the smoke he saw Noah Cloud and Hap Hazzard fighting side by side, using rifle butts to crush Yankee heads. Suddenly a Union corporal dashed through the smoke and vaulted into the saddle of McGraw's horse. McGraw swung his revolver on him just as he took hold of the reins, and fired. The Yankee jerked with the impact as the bullet plowed into his chest and fell to the ground like a rag doll.

The Yankee who walked behind Private Southard kept prodding him with the muzzle of his rifle as they moved toward the wagons. Captain McGraw had taught his men how to take the gun away from an assailant who had it pressed against your back. Southard waited to feel the hard metal against his backbone one more time. They were some thirty yards from the wagons when it came simultaneously with the shot that killed Captain Whittier. Southard moved with the quickness of a cat, taking the Yankee by surprise. When he jerked the rifle from the Yankee's hands, it discharged, sending the bullet into the trees.

Southard planted his feet and swung the rifle by the barrel, cracking the Yankee's head with the butt. The Yankee hit the ground, and Southard brought the rifle around in a second arc, connecting with his head in a savage blow. The man in blue fell flat with a cracked skull. For him the war was over forever.

Flipping the rifle in his hands, Southard worked the lever and ran toward the fight.

The battle was less than a minute old when the Sharpshooters began to take control. In another three minutes, it was over. When the smoke cleared, ten of the men in blue were dead, including Lieutenant Blake and Sergeant Garrett. The other three were seriously wounded. Two Sharpshooters had minor cuts and scratches.

Captain Whittier's body was placed in a wagon with his own dead men, and the procession moved out, carrying the dead blue-clad Yankees and the three wounded ones.

Late that afternoon, Captain McGraw and his men delivered the prisoners to the prison camp. The wounded ones received medical attention, and the dead ones were buried.

At dawn the next morning, the Sharpshooters headed back for Mobile, some on horseback, and some driving the wagons. The impending battle at Mobile Bay was on their minds.

FOURTEEN

Ryan McGraw and his dozen Sharpshooters had been gone from Fort Morgan four days when Captain Lex Coffield returned at noon from Tuscaloosa. The torpedoes were being unloaded onto the dock by the boatmen, who would quickly begin their return trip.

Coffield walked briskly up the sandy slope and was greeted without enthusiasm by the guards at the gate. He cursed at them under his breath as he headed for General Page's office to report his return with the torpedoes. His attention was immediately drawn to the unfamiliar faces intermingled among the regular men of the fort.

A private named Hank Webb noticed Coffield's puzzled expression and said, "We got some help while you were gone, Captain."

"So I see," nodded Coffield. "Who are they?"

"B Company, First Alabama Battalion Sharpshooters."

"B Company?"

"Yes, sir!" exclaimed Webb, grinning from ear to ear. "We done got us the famous McGraw's Sharpshooters!"

Lex Coffield stiffened. His features went pale and stony as he breathed through tight lips, "Ryan McGraw? *He's* here?"

"Well, not at the moment, sir. Right now, Captain McGraw and a dozen of the Sharpshooters are on a mission to Jackson. We had some excitement here while you were gone. I'm sure General Page will tell you all about it."

Without a further word, Coffield stomped away, unaware that every eye was following him. When he disappeared into the general's office, the soldiers went back to what they were doing before Coffield made his entrance.

General Page looked up from his desk at the sound of rapid footsteps approaching the open door. Without waiting for permission, Captain Coffield entered and said stiffly, "General, why wasn't I informed about B Company Sharpshooters being sent here? Certainly you knew they were coming before I left for Tuscaloosa."

"I didn't think it was necessary to tell you."

Dark eyes flashing, Coffield snapped, "I'll bet the other three officers knew, didn't they?"

Page cleared his throat. "Yes. Yes, they did."

"What is it with you, General?" Coffield boomed. "Why am I the step-child in this place? Why do I have to learn what's going on around here from the lowly enlisted men?"

The general rose to his feet, his own features flushed. "When you start acting like you're a captain and like you're one of us in this place, Coffield, you'll be treated as such! Now, come off your high-horse and tell me how many torpedoes you brought with you."

Coffield pulled a bandanna from his hip pocket, took a deep breath while wiping sweat from his face, and said, "Almost two hundred. A hundred and ninety-one to be exact. They're being unloaded on the dock right now."

"Good," nodded Page, sitting down.

Coffield dropped onto a chair in front of the desk, clutching the bandanna.

The general asked pointedly, "Is your ire stirred because I didn't inform you that we were getting additional men...or because the additional men are led by Captain Ryan McGraw?"

The captain studied him for a moment, then said, "I take it you know about Victoria having been married to McGraw."

"Yes."

"She tell you?"

"No. He did."

"I see. So I'm even lower in your estimation than I was before."

Page did not comment. Easing back in his chair, he said, "I have informed Captain McGraw that his men will be helping you place the torpedoes in the bay."

"All right. We'll begin after lunch. Hank Webb said we had some excitement around here while I was gone, and that McGraw and a dozen Sharpshooters are in Jackson on a mission. I assume the excitement and the mission are related."

Page told Coffield of the Union attack on the fort and that McGraw had volunteered to take the prisoners to the prison camp. He added that they should be showing up soon.

The general impressed on Coffield that it was important to get all the torpedoes in the water as soon as possible, since he was expecting Farragut to come steaming in once he had built his fleet sufficiently. Coffield said he would work with the Sharpshooters all afternoon, then ride into Mobile in time to eat supper with Victoria.

Page noted that Tommy wasn't mentioned. He had assumed that the boy was Coffield's son until he learned that Victoria had been married to Ryan McGraw. It didn't take the general long to recognize that Tommy was the spit and image of McGraw. From that moment, he understood why the self-centered Coffield showed no love for the boy.

After lunch, Captain Coffield changed his clothes and led the Sharpshooters down to the dock. They worked until the sun was lowering in the sky, then Coffield dismissed them for the day, saying they would begin again in the morning. Planting sea mines was a slow and tedious task.

Coffield made his way to the stables and was saddling his horse when he overheard a group of the fort's regular men talking on the other side of the thin wooden wall. One of them said, "Did you see the look on his puss when he heard Hank say 'B Company, First Alabama Battalion Sharpshooters'?"

Laughter followed. Then another chuckled, "Yeah! And did you notice his eyes when he said, 'Ryan McGraw? *He's* here?' "

"One thing for sure, fellas," said another. "Coffield and McGraw know each other. And unless I'm mistaken, they ain't pals."

"Well, from what we saw at the dance the other night," put in a fourth voice, "Mrs. Coffield knows McGraw, too."

"I'd say real well," agreed one of them. "Maybe McGraw was her beau and Coffield came along and stole her away."

"I'll bet that's it!" the one who had spoken first said with elation. "The way the two of them were cuddlin' on the dance floor, it was like they'd done it before."

Another laughed and said, "Coffield would've swallowed his tongue if he'd walked in on that! With his temper, he would probably have shot both of them!"

"He might yet if he finds out about it," said another.

"Well, he ain't gonna find it out from *me!*" laughed another.

Victoria Coffield and her son were just finishing supper in the kitchen of their two-story house when they heard a horse blow in the back yard. They looked at each other, knowing what it meant, and Tommy said glumly, "It's Lex."

Victoria rose from the table and looked through the open back door. Coffield was leading the horse into the small corral beside the barn. Victoria had acted bravely in front of Dixie Quade when she snapped that she would handle Lex in her own way, but in truth she was terrified of him. He was big, strong, and could be dangerous when his temper was riled.

Tommy pushed away from the table and said half to himself, "I wish he'd never come home." As he spoke, he hurried toward the parlor, wanting to be absent when Coffield entered the kitchen.

Victoria stood at the door, dabbed at her hair, smoothed her dress, and forced a smile as the captain approached the porch. She waited till he passed through the door, then threw her arms around his neck, saying, "Hello, sweetheart. I missed you! I'm so glad you're home."

As she turned her lips toward his, Coffield exploded. Face beet-red, he sank powerful fingers into her hair, jerked her head back until he knew it was hurting her neck, and growled, "Don't *sweetheart* me, Victoria! Missed me, did you? Glad I'm home are you?"

"Please—you're hurting me!"

"Don't lie to me!" he hissed. "You didn't miss me…not with Ryan McGraw around!"

"Lex, it's not my fault he was assigned to the fort. You can't blame me—"

Shaking her head violently, he spat, "I can blame you for dancing with him the other night! And I can blame you for cuddling close when you did it!"

"Lex, I—"

"Don't deny it, woman! I overheard some of the men talking about it at the fort!"

"Please!" she begged. "You're hurting me!"

"You think I don't know that? I'm hurting you on purpose. You're *my* wife, Victoria! I gave you permission to go to the dance as partner of the fat old man. You knew I meant for you to stick with him only. So did you and your ex-husband step out into the moonlight? Did you kiss him? Huh? Did you?"

"No, we didn't go out into the moonlight, and no, I didn't kiss him," she said, her voice shaking.

Shaking her head by the hair, he asked, "Why'd you dance with him, Victoria?"

Wincing, she said, "I tried to avoid him, Lex, but he followed me around till he cornered me at the punch table. He wanted a dance 'just for old time's sake,' he said. Your fellow-soldiers were there. I would have had to be rude to refuse. None of them know he's my ex-husband. I didn't want the wife of Fort Morgan's captain to appear rude. So, to be polite in front of everyone, I told Ryan I would, but for only one number."

"Yeah? Then what about the cuddling? Why didn't you make him keep his distance?"

Victoria gasped, "I don't know what those men you overheard were talking about. There wasn't any cu—"

"Stop lying, Victoria!" he shouted, snapping her head back again. "I heard those soldiers say if I'd walked in on you two, I probably would have shot both of you. Now tell me the truth! You were snuggling him, weren't you?"

At that moment, Tommy appeared, weeping, and cried, "Let go of my mommy! You're hurting her!"

"Shut up, brat! Go back to wherever you were! Go on!"

Tommy's cheeks glistened with tears and his breathing was ragged as he backed slowly toward the door to the parlor.

Turning his attention back to his wife, Coffield railed, "You *were* snuggling him, weren't you? Tell me the truth!"

"No! I mean…it wasn't me who did it! Ryan surprised me by suddenly pulling me close. I tried to push him away, but he's stronger than I am. I—"

"Liar! Those soldiers I overheard said the way you and him were cuddling, it was like you'd done it before. That doesn't sound like you were fighting him off to me!"

Coffield let go of Victoria's hair and slapped her. She went down hard, screaming. Leaning over, he began slapping her repeatedly. When she raised her arms to protect herself, he batted them away and slapped her harder. She whined and wept, jerking with each blow.

Suddenly the maddened captain felt a sharp pain in his right thigh. Looking down, he saw Tommy gripping his leg and biting him through the pantleg. Swearing, Coffield struck the boy across the top of the head, breaking his hold and flattening him on the floor. The child sprang to his feet, showing hatred in his pale blue eyes and screeched, "Leave my mommy alone! Leave my mommy alone!"

When Lex turned and slapped Victoria again, Tommy lunged at him and sank his teeth in another spot on his thigh. Coffield swore again and struck him with his fist, knocking him loose. The boy struggled to his feet. Coffield placed his foot against Tommy's chest and gave a hard shove. The five-year-old sailed across the room, slammed the wall hard, and slumped to the floor.

Victoria dashed to Tommy and gathered him into her arms. Looking up at Coffield with her nose and mouth bleeding, she screamed, "You've killed him! You've killed him! You beast! You killed my son!"

There was a knock at the front door. Coffield pointed a stiff finger at Victoria and warned, "You stay here!"

While Coffield hurried toward the parlor, Victoria looked down at Tommy. He was limp in her arms. She opened her mouth to wail, but checked it when she saw his eyes roll under the lids. "Tommy!" she gasped, shaking him mildly. "Tommy! Speak to Mommy!"

The lids fluttered, then the eyes that were exactly the same color as Ryan McGraw's looked up at her. They were glassy, but he focused them on her as he spoke with slurred tongue, "Did…did he go away, Mommy? I want him…to go…away."

Victoria held him close and wept. Suddenly she noticed that the gash on his arm had been torn open. Blood was trickling down his arm in two thin streams.

Lex appeared, standing over them. "What's the matter with you?" he said harshly to Victoria. "The kid isn't dead."

Rising to her feet and sniffing at the blood oozing from her nose, she glared at him and said, "It's not your fault he isn't dead! He's got a big knot on his head, and his arm's bleeding again. We've got to take him to the hospital so they can stitch it up. Who was at the door?"

"Our big-nosed neighbor, old man Wiley. He heard you carrying on and decided to come see if there was anything wrong. I had to placate him a little, but he's satisfied everything's all right. We aren't taking the kid to the hospital. You can fix him up."

Victoria's concern for her son overshadowed her fear of Lex. "The wound is torn open, Lex. I can't stop the bleeding! He's got to have a doctor's attention—I'm taking him to the hospital!"

Moving to block her way, Coffield grunted, "I said *you* can fix him up. If the Wileys see you carrying the kid out of here bleeding, the old man will think I lied to him."

"Well, didn't you?" she rasped as she stepped around him, her jaw set in grim determination.

As the inflexible mother headed for the front door, Lex shouted, "Victoria! Come back here!"

She never broke stride. When she opened the door, he bellowed, "Victoria! I'm commanding you to come back here!"

Pausing halfway across the threshold, she turned her bleeding face toward him and said tightly, "I'm not one of your lowly privates, *Captain*. Don't command me!"

Victoria heard the angry man call her a vile name as she moved swiftly across the yard to the street.

A soldier on crutches with his right foot bandaged was coming out the hospital door as Victoria arrived, carrying Tommy. Quickly he hopped out of the way and held the door open, eyeing the blood and purple marks on her face and the blood on the child's arm. She thanked him and hurried to the reception desk. An older woman Victoria had not seen before greeted her. When the receptionist saw the blood on both mother and son, she quickly ushered them down the corridor, saying that Dr. Glenn Lyles would see them right away.

Victoria thanked her and followed her into the examining room. Dr. Lyles was in conversation with Dixie Quade at a desk. Both looked up at the same time. When Victoria saw Dixie, she cursed under her breath.

"Dr. Lyles," said the matronly receptionist, "this lady and the little boy need your attention."

Lyles immediately recognized Victoria as the woman he had

reprimanded for giving Dixie trouble in the hospital corridor. He scrutinized them quickly and gestured toward the examining table. "Put him right over here, ma'am," he said.

As Victoria laid Tommy on the table, Dixie headed for a cupboard to fetch the necessary materials. The anxious mother quickly explained to Lyles that Dr. George Bentley had stitched up a bad gash on her son's arm several days earlier, and that the boy had fallen and reopened it.

"Did *both* of you fall?" queried the doctor, focusing on Victoria's blood-caked nose and mouth.

Dixie was carrying a tray toward the table. The eyes of the women met fleetingly. "Uh…no," Victoria replied.

The doctor looked down at his small patient and touched the bloody bandage. As he examined it closely, he said without looking up, "Miss Quade, see if you can help Mrs.——" He looked around and said, "I don't know your name, ma'am."

"Victoria Coffield. Captain Lex Coffield of Fort Morgan is my husband."

Lyles nodded. Then to Dixie he said, "I'll need that dried blood cleaned off Mrs. Coffield's face. Looks like her lip may need a stitch or two."

"I don't think so, Doctor," said Victoria. "It's cut on the inside, but it doesn't seem too bad."

"We'll know when your face has been washed," said Lyles, then he turned back to the boy, who was studying him with wide eyes, and asked, "What's your name, son?"

"Tommy," the boy said softly.

"Tommy Coffield, eh?"

"No, sir. Tommy *McGraw*."

Lyles shot a glance at Victoria, who had turned to look at Tommy. When her eyes swerved to the doctor's, she said calmly, "Captain Coffield is my second husband."

Lyles nodded, then said to the boy, "Did Dr. Bentley hurt you when he sewed up your arm before, Tommy?"

"A little bit."

"Well, I might have to hurt you a little bit too, but you're a big boy, aren't you?"

"Yes."

"Good. Nurse Quade and I will have you fixed up here in no time."

Tommy's mouth pulled down. He glared at Dixie and said, "I don't want her to help you. She's a bad lady."

"Why would you say that, Tommy? Did nurse Quade help Dr. Bentley when you were stitched up before?"

"No, she talked real bad to Mommy once here at the hospital. She's a bad lady. A *very* bad lady."

Dr. Lyles said he believed Miss Quade was a very *nice* lady, and that if Tommy knew her better, he would think she was nice too. He then noted the knot on the boy's head and asked, "How did you fall, Tommy?"

"I didn't."

"I thought your mommy said you fell?"

"Lex kicked me and I hit the wall."

Lyles set quizzical eyes on Victoria.

Her face pinched. She looked at Dixie, then at the doctor. "My…my husband…he…he has a bad temper. He—"

"Lex is a mean man!" Tommy cut across his mother's words. "He hurt my mommy!"

Dr. Lyles asked, "Why did your daddy kick you against the wall, Tommy?"

"He's not my daddy! I hate him! He hit me on the head, then kicked me against the wall because I bit his leg. He was hitting Mommy. I bit him to make him stop hitting her."

There was a moment of silence. Then Dixie broke it by saying, "Dr. Lyles, Mrs. Coffield won't need any stitches. The cut is on the inside of her mouth as she said. It has stopped bleeding, and so has her nose. I'll put some salve on these bruises, and she'll be all right."

Lyles was pressing firmly on the boy's reopened gash to stay the bleeding while cleaning around it. "Good," he said. "As soon as you finish, we'll take care of Tommy." Then he spoke to Victoria. "Mrs. Coffield, we've found that it's best to work on children without their parents present. You can go down to the waiting room. Once I've closed the wound, nurse Quade can complete the work on Tommy. I'll come to the waiting room. I'd like to talk to you for a few minutes."

"All right, Doctor."

Dixie was finished within a few minutes. Victoria did not thank her for the treatment. She stepped to the table and said, "Tommy, you be a brave boy, won't you?"

"Yes, Mommy," he replied shakily.

"That's my big boy," she said, patting his shoulder. Leaning over, she kissed him on the forehead, then headed toward the door. Opening it, she looked back, waved to Tommy, and stepped into the corridor.

She was halfway to the waiting room when she saw a rather homely young nurse coming toward her. As they drew close to each other, the nurse noticed Victoria's battered face. Stopping, she said, "Hello. Aren't you Captain Lex Coffield's wife?"

Victoria halted and nodded. "Yes. Do I know you?"

"Not really," smiled the nurse. "My name is Florence Dillon. I was one of the girls who went to the fort for the dance the other night. You probably didn't notice me."

The inelegant face was suddenly a bit familiar to Victoria, so she said, "Come to think of it, I do remember you."

Studying Victoria's bruises, Florence asked, "What happened, ma'am?"

Victoria knew it was none of the nurse's business what had happened, but since she just might talk to Dixie or the doctor, she decided to tell her the truth. "My...my husband has a bad temper, Miss Dillon. He got angry over something and batted me around a little."

"Oh, I'm sorry," said Florence. Then in a catty voice, she asked, "Was it because of the way you and that handsome Captain McGraw were holding each other at the dance? I'll bet someone tattled to your husband, didn't they?"

Victoria realized too late that Nurse Dillon was nothing but a busybody. "It really doesn't concern you!" she snipped, and walked away. When she reached the door of the waiting room, she looked back and saw Florence Dillon enter the examining room where Dr. Lyles and Dixie Quade were working on Tommy. *Oh wonderful,* she thought. *Now the busybody will find out that Lex beat on Tommy, too.*

Florence Dillon stepped into the examining room, unaware that the doctor had a patient, and said, "Oh, excuse me, Dr. Lyles. I didn't realize you were busy. I'll come back later."

"Fine," Lyles told her without looking up. He knew Florence's grating voice quite well.

Dixie was intent on what she was doing and did not bother to look up, either.

Florence glided up close and eyed Tommy. "Who's this cute little guy?"

When neither doctor nor nurse answered, the boy said, "My name's Tommy."

"What happened to you, Tommy?"

Dr. Lyles knew Florence could be an irritating snoop, and was about to tell her to go find something to do, but Tommy let it out before he could speak.

"Lex kicked me against the wall."

Dixie and the doctor exchanged glances.

"Oh," said Florence, realizing who the boy belonged to. "I just saw your mother in the hall. She told me about your daddy beating up on her, but she didn't say anything about him beating on you, too."

Tommy was about to say that Lex was not his daddy when he felt a sharp pain and winced.

"You're doing fine, Tommy," the doctor said calmly. "Sorry this has to hurt, but we're almost done."

Unable to subdue her curiosity, Florence said, "Tommy, your daddy was angry about the way your mommy was acting with a man at the dance, wasn't he?"

Tommy's attention was on his arm. "Yes," he said, hoping the nosy nurse would quit asking him questions.

Dixie flashed a hot glare at Florence.

Dr. Lyles was disgusted with the way Florence was pumping Tommy. Pausing in his work, he set hard eyes on her and said in a stern voice, "Nurse Dillon, you must have work to tend to elsewhere."

Florence stiffened and said, "Well I guess I could find something to do."

"Then do it."

Florence walked to the door and disappeared into the hallway.

During the repair work on Tommy's arm, Dixie smiled at the boy frequently and made sure he knew she was doing everything she could to ease his pain. She even held his hand while the doctor was finishing up, which was the most painful part.

Telling Dixie to bandage his arm while he talked to Mrs. Coffield, Lyles left the room.

Dixie stood over Tommy and took his hand again. "You're a brave young man, Tommy," she smiled. "You were real good for Dr. Lyles."

Tommy did not reply. He was confused. The bad lady didn't seem bad at all. She had talked sternly to his mother that day in the hospital hallway, but she didn't do that today. Maybe she had changed. He liked the way she looked at him and the way she held his hand.

In the waiting room, Dr. Lyles sat down facing Victoria Coffield and said, "Ma'am, I have to tell you that I'm quite concerned with this situation."

Victoria had developed a severe headache. Pressing the fingertips of both hands to her temples, she asked, "Will Tommy be all right, doctor?"

"The gash stitched up fine. You'll just have to make sure it doesn't get opened again."

"I'm thinking more of that big bump on his head. I don't know whether it came from when my husband struck him on the head or when he hit the wall. It really frightened me. I thought he was dead. He was unconscious for probably a minute, and he didn't breathe, either. Could there be any serious damage?"

Lyles rubbed his chin thoughtfully. "I doubt it. His eyes are quite clear, now. If he should show any signs of abnormality, bring him in immediately, but I think he'll be all right. What I'm concerned about is his being subject to this kind of treatment...and yourself, too, for that matter. Has this happened before?"

Victoria set her gaze on the floor. Rubbing her temples again, she nodded without looking up and replied shakily, "Yes. Not to this degree with Tommy, but Lex has manhandled me many times and slapped the boy around. He...like I said, he has a bad temper."

"Well, he's going to have to get control of it, Mrs. Coffield, or something serious is going to happen. I'd like for him to come in and let me talk to him."

"He'd never submit to it, doctor. Lex is a proud and stubborn man."

"Are you aware that if the army learns that he is beating you and your son, they will take action?"

"No."

"Well, it's so. The captain could find himself in the brig for quite a long spell if they learn about it. Such conduct is looked at as very unbecoming for any soldier, but much more for an officer. If this kind of thing happens again—even if you don't care about yourself—for Tommy's sake, you'd best report it to General Page."

Victoria nodded, thinking that her best solution was to let Ryan know he has a son and alert him to the kind of treatment Lex Coffield was giving him. She thanked the doctor for his help and advice, and took Tommy home.

FIFTEEN

Captain Ryan McGraw and his twelve men arrived at Fort Morgan at one-thirty in the afternoon on July 5. General Richard Page welcomed them back. He congratulated them when he learned of the attack and how they had handled it.

Page explained to McGraw and the others that the rest of the Sharpshooters were out in the bay planting torpedoes with Captain Coffield, who had returned from Tuscaloosa the previous day. He told them that the Union navy had added more ships to their fleet on the Gulf. A naval invasion was imminent, and he felt certain that a ground attack would come, if not simultaneously, shortly after the ships began their assault. Every man in the fort must stay alert.

General Page advised the weary Sharpshooters to rest for the remainder of the day and plan to join the others in the bay the next morning. Captain McGraw said he wanted to ride to Mobile and check on his men in the hospital.

Arriving at the hospital shortly after four o'clock, the captain was happy to see that his men were doing well. Private Brad Thacker and Corporal Dean Bradbury would be released to go home for further recuperation within a week or so.

When McGraw looked around for Dixie Quade, he was told it

was her day off. Leaving the hospital, he went to the apartment building a half-block away where the nurses lived. By asking a couple of nurses he met in front of the building, he learned Dixie's apartment number. Hurrying to the door of the apartment, he removed his hat and knocked lightly.

There were soft footsteps inside, then the latch rattled and the door swung open. The lovely young woman with the golden hair showed him a warm smile and said, "Well, hello, Captain! I'm glad you're back safely."

"Thank you," he grinned, feeling a fiery sensation wash over him at the sight of her. His arms ached to embrace her and his lips longed to kiss her, but he made no move to do so.

"Would you like to come in and sit down?" she asked.

"I'll be glad to come in, Miss Dixie," he said, drinking in her beauty, "but if it's all the same to you, I won't sit down. I've been sitting in that saddle for so long, I just need to stand for a while."

"I can understand that," she said, stepping aside so he could enter. When he passed her, she closed the door and asked, "Can I get you something?"

"No," he said raising a palm. "I'm fine. Please. Don't stand just because I am. Go ahead and sit down."

"Actually I was standing when you knocked. I was putting new paper on the shelves of my cupboard above the counter. Mind if I finish while we talk?"

"Of course not."

Ryan followed Dixie into the kitchen of the small apartment and watched as she resumed her work. "Can I help?" he asked.

"No, that's not necessary." She used a pair of scissors to cut the paper to size. "When did you get back?"

"We arrived at the fort about one-thirty."

"Run into any trouble?"

"Yes."

Turning to look at him, she asked, "What happened?"

"Small unit of Yankees caught us flatfooted on the way to the prison camp. We were in thick timber, which is always risky. Thing that saved us was that I had put all the prisoners in gray uniforms and made them carry empty rifles. Gave the illusion that there were about thirty-five Rebels in the bunch."

"Smart idea."

"It worked, anyway. The Yankees figured since we outnumbered them, they wouldn't start shooting, but rather, would jump us with their guns ready. That way, they'd disarm us and we'd be their prisoners. But the Yankee captain we had captured was so eager to let his fellow blue-bellies know he was one of them that he made a sudden move to show them his rifle was empty. The Yankees were jittery, and one of them shot him. It was instant gun battle…and the Sharpshooters, as you know, are good at what they do. Anyway, we delivered the prisoners—some dead and some alive—and came back to the fort."

Cutting paper again, Dixie asked, "Did you see Captain Coffield at the fort?"

"No. He and the rest of my men are planting sea mines in the bay. Explosive devices we call torpedoes."

"I've heard of them. So you've yet to lay eyes on Coffield."

"That's right. And to be honest, I wish I never had to."

Dixie had thought a lot about the situation that had developed between Ryan and his ex-wife. There was no question in Dixie's mind that Victoria had been pregnant with Tommy when she ran off with Lex Coffield, but did not know it. When the baby was born, Ryan was never notified. This was why he had never told Dixie he had a son. He was not aware of it…and still did not know. Dixie felt he had a right to know, but it was not for her to tell him. She would leave that to Victoria. One thing for sure, she thought, if Ryan gets one look at Tommy, he'll know he has a son.

"I sure can't blame you for that," she said. "Lex Coffield has to be just about the lowest—"

Dixie's words were interrupted by a knock at the door. Laying the paper and scissors down, she said, "Excuse me, Captain. I'll be right back."

Ryan gave her a warm smile as she left the kitchen.

Dixie opened the door to see Florence Dillon standing there, holding an empty sugar bowl. "Hello," she grinned. "I'm out of sugar. Could you spare some?"

Dixie was not happy to see the nosy nurse, especially with Ryan in her apartment. Florence was also a long-tongued gossip. She would make something juicy out of it if she knew he was there.

Taking the bowl from Florence's hand, Dixie said, "My kitchen's a mess. You wait here and I'll fill the bowl for you."

Florence nodded and leaned against the door jamb, folding her arms.

Ryan had heard every word, though he could not see the apartment door from where he stood. When Dixie came in, she gave him a "you don't want to meet this woman" expression. He smiled at her, nodding that he understood.

While Dixie was filling the bowl from a cloth sugar sack, Florence's loud, grating voice came from the front door, "What did you think about that poor little Coffield boy, Dixie? Sad, huh? How could a father be so mean to his son? I mean, maybe Mrs. Coffield deserved the beating he gave her, but that little boy...I'll never understand it."

Dixie's nerves tightened. A glance at the captain told her he was taking it all in. She knew if she didn't answer immediately, Florence would come traipsing into the kitchen to repeat what she had just said.

Over her shoulder, she called back, "Terrible thing, Florence. Such a sweet little guy. A brave one, too. He took a lot of pain last night. He'll be okay, though."

"I hope so. Somebody oughtta take that Captain Coffield out behind the barn and give him a good threshing."

Hurriedly placing the lid on the sugar bowl, Dixie headed back to the unwanted guest, saying, "I agree, Florence. Somebody ought to give him some of his own medicine."

Florence thanked Dixie for the sugar and was gone. Dixie

closed the door and returned to the kitchen. "Whew!" she sighed. "That mouthy woman makes me nervous."

"A fellow-nurse, I assume?"

"To my sorrow, and the sorrow of the rest of the hospital staff."

"Mind telling me what happened?"

Returning to the cupboard, Dixie picked up the scissors. "Of course not. You'd no doubt learn about it from Victoria one of these days, anyway. I...didn't think it was my place to tell you. That's why I didn't say anything about it."

"Certainly. But since your loudmouth friend told it to everyone in the building, I'd like to know the details."

Dixie finished cutting a length of paper and placed it on a shelf, adjusting it to fit. "It was about seven...maybe seven-fifteen last evening when Victoria carried Tommy into the hospital. She had some pretty bad bruises on her face and was bleeding from the nose and mouth. She admitted to Dr. Lyles and me that Lex had lost his temper and beat her. Tommy had a large knot on his head and a cut on his arm from a few days ago that had been reopened. Dr. Lyles had to stitch it again. Nosy Florence was on duty last night, and apparently had a talk with Victoria in the corridor."

"So this is how she knew about it."

"Plus she came into the examining room and began pumping the boy while Dr. Lyles and I were working on him. Tommy told her—and us—that Lex had kicked him against a wall. Tommy had told us earlier that Lex had also hit him in the head."

"Dirty bully."

"To put it mildly. From what Tommy told us before Florence showed up, he had bitten Lex's leg to stop him from hitting his mother. This was no doubt when he got clobbered on the head and kicked against the wall."

"Did you learn why Lex was beating Victoria?"

"Not until Florence questioned Tommy. You see, Florence was at the dance the other night. I never did see her on the floor, so she had plenty of time to gawk around from the sidelines. Before Dr. Lyles finally ordered her from the room last night, she asked the boy if his daddy was angry at his mommy because of the way she had been acting with a man at the dance. Tommy said yes."

"Me, right?"

"She didn't snuggle close to anyone else."

"And somebody told Coffield about it when he returned to the fort yesterday."

"Must have."

Ryan rubbed the back of his neck. "Victoria shouldn't have pressed me into dancing with her, but no harm was done. Certainly it didn't call for a beating from her husband." Sighing, he added, "In a way, I'm responsible. I did dance with her."

"But the snuggling wasn't your doing."

"I know, but I let her get me in a position so it could happen. Some of the blame is mine. I'm going to their home and see about Victoria and the boy....and express my regret that I've been a source of trouble."

Dixie moved close to him, laid a hand on his arm, and said, "Captain Ryan McGraw, you are a good man."

"You could get an argument on that from some people."

"I mean it. If that no-good Lex Coffield hadn't stolen your wife in the first place, none of this would be happening. And still you're going to go over there and take your share of the blame for this."

Ryan shrugged his wide shoulders. "Just something I have to do."

"God bless you."

"He did, Miss Dixie. He brought you into my life."

While she blushed, Ryan asked, "Could I take you to dinner tonight?"

Dixie's pulse quickened. "Well, yes...of course."

"Know any good restaurants?"

"The Mobile Arms Hotel has an excellent one."

"Okay. The Mobile Arms it is. Seven o'clock all right?"

"Sure."

"Pick you up at seven."

"I'll be ready," she replied sweetly, and thought to herself, *with bells on!*

Mixed emotions stirred within Dixie as she watched the captain swing aboard his horse and ride away. She was thrilled that he wanted to take her to dinner, but felt the strain of knowing that Victoria had set her sights on ridding herself of Coffield and getting Ryan back. She also felt a twinge in her heart. Ryan McGraw was about to find out he was a father.

The sun was setting behind a bank of long-fingered clouds in a fiery blaze of color as Ryan dismounted in front of the two-story house at 124 East Evans Avenue. His nerves tightened as he stepped onto the porch and knocked on the door. Only seconds passed before the door came open, and in the orange light of sunset, Victoria appeared, smiling, and said, "Ryan! I'm so glad you've come!"

Ryan cringed at the sight of her bruises. Then she was embracing him before he knew it. She held him tight for a few seconds, pulled back, took his hand, and said, "Come in."

Ryan was only a couple of steps inside the house when he stopped and said, "Tori, I can only stay a minute. I…I found out about you and the boy being at the hospital for treatment last night, and that your husband had laid into you for the way we were acting at the dance. I just wanted to come by and tell you that I'm sorry to be the source of a squabble between you and Lex. It was you who pulled close to me that night, but it's as much my fault for letting you. I'm truly sorry."

Victoria frowned. "How did you find all this out? Couldn't have been from that…that blonde prissy or the doctor. I didn't tell them why Lex had beaten me."

"Dixie is not a prissy, Victoria," he said firmly. "She is a wonderful, unselfish, sweet young lady."

Victoria did not comment.

"There's an obnoxious nurse at the hospital who had also been at the dance. She saw you and me when we were close. She was on duty last night. Florence is her name."

"Yes," nodded Victoria. "I met her in the corridor. Florence Dillon. Has a big nose, if you know what I mean."

"Exactly."

"I talked to her there in the corridor for a few minutes while Dr. Lyles was stitching Tommy's arm. But I didn't tell her why Lex had beaten me."

"No, but Tommy did. She got it out of him that Lex was angry over the way you acted toward some man at the dance. Florence knew that man was me. I just want to say that I'm sorry my weak moment on the dance floor got you and your son a beating." Starting to turn toward the door, he said, "I have to go, now."

Taking his hand again, Victoria said, "Before you go, I want you to meet Tommy. He's upstairs in his room." Moving to the bottom of the staircase and pulling Ryan with her, she called loudly, "Tommy! Tommy!"

A small voice responded, "Yes, Mommy?"

"Come here, honey! There's someone I want you to meet."

There was the sound of running feet, then a diminutive form appeared at the landing above. The brilliant sunset flowing through a window near the bottom of the stairs cast a shadow above. The boy could not be seen clearly.

When Tommy remained in the shadows, Victoria said, "Come down, honey."

There was a pause. Tommy asked, "Is this the person who was supposed to come that other day, but didn't?"

"Yes. It's that very special someone I told you about. He couldn't come then because he was away on a trip. I didn't know it."

Slowly, Tommy moved to the head of the stairs and began to descend. Before he was halfway down, the glow of the sunset illuminated his face and hair.

Ryan McGraw's jaw slackened. A chill rippled through him.

His mouth went dry. Seeing the express image of himself in Tommy stunned him.

While Ryan was attempting to find his voice, Victoria waited for the boy to reach the bottom step, then took his hand with her free one and said, "Ryan, I would like you to meet Thomas Manning McGraw. I gave him his first name after your father."

To the boy, she said, "Tommy, when you got old enough to understand, I told you Lex is not your father. I explained that you had a real father somewhere, but that you would never be able to see him or know him. Remember?"

"Yes."

"Well, honey, that has changed. This man is your real father."

Tommy's face lit up and a wide smile captured his mouth. "This is my dad?"

"Yes," nodded Victoria, tears welling up in her eyes. "I think it would be proper for you to give your dad a hug."

Ryan choked out hoarsely, "Tommy, until this moment, I didn't even know I had a son," and bent down with open arms.

Father and son stayed together in a long embrace. When Ryan released him, Tommy looked up and asked, "How could you have me and not know it?"

"When you get older, I'll explain it to you, honey," interjected Victoria. "But I want you to know that it isn't your dad's fault that he didn't know about you. It's mine."

Tommy smiled at the tall man who towered over him.

While Ryan thumbed away tears from his cheeks, Victoria said, "When I ran off—when I went away with Lex, I was carrying Tommy, but didn't know it. When Lex found it out, he was terribly angry. At first he was going to send me back to you. Then he had second thoughts and decided he loved me enough to marry me in spite of the baby."

"That was big of him," mused Ryan bitterly.

"When Tommy was born, Lex didn't want anybody to think the baby was his. He insisted he have his real father's name. I gave him my maiden name for his middle name. So he's Thomas Manning McGraw. Ever since I explained that Lex is not his father, Tommy has called him Lex."

"Dad," said the child, looking up with bright eyes, "are you gonna move in and live with us? Then the other kids who live around here will know that I have a real dad, just like them!"

Ryan felt a pang of sadness run through him as he knelt down, looked his new-found son in the eye, and said, "Your mommy and I used to be married, Tommy, but we aren't any more. She's married to Lex, now. That means I can't live here."

"Then mommy can send Lex away and be married to you again," said the innocent child. "I don't like Lex. He's mean to Mommy and he's mean to me. *You* wouldn't be mean to us, would you, Dad?"

Ryan laid a tender hand on Tommy's head. The lump was still quite large under the boy's thick hair. Indignation toward Coffield welled up within him. He had to swallow hard to get the words to come out. "No. I wouldn't be mean to either of you, Son, but I just can't live with you."

Tommy's eyes glistened with tears. "Won't you ever come and see us?"

Ryan folded him into his arms, saying, "Sure I will, Tommy. I'll come see you often."

"Yes, he will, honey," said Victoria. "Now, I want you to go back upstairs to your room and play. I need to talk to Dad by myself."

"Yes, ma'am," replied the boy. He hugged Ryan's neck hard, then charged up the stairs.

When Victoria heard Tommy's door slam, she moved close to Ryan and said in a soft tone, "With Tommy looking so much like you, it has been a little bit like having you near, darling."

Still stunned from learning that he had a five-year-old son, Ryan's guard was down. Before he realized it, Victoria had her arms around his neck, and her warm breath was on his lips. In spite of the black and purple marks on her face, she was still beautiful.

Memories flooded Ryan's mind. He thought of the myriad times he had held her next to him...the times he had looked into those deep, meaningful eyes and kissed those lips. Suddenly they were locked in a fervid kiss. Victoria clung tight, digging her fingers into the thick hair on the back of his head. Though she felt pain from the cut inside her mouth, she held her lips to his with hungering force.

When they parted, Victoria laid her head on his chest with her arms around his slender waist and breathed, "Oh, Ryan you *are* still in love with me, aren't you? Say it, darling. It was in your kiss. I know it. Tell me you still love me."

Ryan loosed himself from her, his mind whirling. "Tori, I...I'm sorry. That shouldn't have happened. I've got to go."

Moving close again and looking deep into his eyes, Victoria said, "It can be us again, my love. Like old times. We have a child, you and I. Tommy is both of us. He needs you. Lex is mean to him—he resents him because he's *your* son. He puts marks on his head and face often."

Ryan let his gaze stray up to the spot at the top of the stairs where he last saw his son. Already his heart was full of love for the boy. Confused and upset, he shook his head and said, "I really must be going."

Realizing she could detain him no longer, Victoria said, "You told Tommy you'd come see us often. How soon will you be back?"

"I can't say right now, Tori. This is Lex's home. I'll have a talk with him. We'll work out some kind of agreement so I can visit Tommy on some kind of regular basis." Pausing, he said, "But it's not *us* I'll be visiting. It's *Tommy.*"

Victoria's face paled. "But what about me?"

"I remind you that you are Lex's wife, not mine. I have no right to be seeing you."

Victoria broke into tears, gripping both his arms. "Please, Ryan!" she begged. "You've got to help me. I want to divorce Lex, but I'm afraid of him! With his violent temper, he could kill me! He might kill Tommy, too!"

Attributing such extreme fears to her emotional state, Ryan said, "You ran off with him and married him, Tori. You'll have to make the best of a bad situation. However, I will talk to Lex about his treatment of Tommy."

"But you don't understand!" she sobbed. "I want to be your wife again!"

"Tori," he said, heading for the door, "the water's already run under the bridge on that count. Tell Tommy I'll be back once I've worked it out with Lex."

Victoria stood at the door, her breath coming in tiny jerks as she watched through a wall of tears while Ryan McGraw rode away.

Less than a half-hour after Ryan was gone, Captain Coffield came home, tired and irritable. Victoria was cooking supper. He entered the kitchen, pecked her purpled cheek, and grunted, "What's for supper?"

Victoria was quiet and moody. "Grits and gravy," she replied without looking at him.

"Well, I hope there's plenty," he said crisply. "Being in and out of that water all day, planting those torpedoes, is hard work. I'm hungry."

"There'll be enough," she said coldly.

Coffield eyed her with disdain and went to the wash basin.

During supper, there was thick silence. After a few minutes of it, Lex set penetrating eyes on his wife and growled, "What's the matter with you?"

Putting a pained look in her eyes, Victoria met his gaze and replied, "You ought to know the answer to that. You beat me up last night, remember?"

"That was last night. This is tonight. Don't pout for the rest of your life over it."

Tommy looked up at the captain and said, "You're mean. You treat Mommy mean, and me too. My dad don't treat us mean."

Victoria's heart leaped to her throat. She had not thought to warn Tommy not to say anything about Ryan being there. She wanted Ryan to be the first to break it to him.

Coffield's heavy dark eyebrows arched. "Your dad?"

"Yes—he said he'd never treat us mean."

Fire leaped into Coffield's eyes as he looked at Victoria. "Ryan McGraw was *here?* At *my* house?"

Victoria's voice trembled as she said, "He learned from a nurse at the hospital that Tommy and I were there last night. He simply came by to see if we were all right. All he needed was one look at Tommy to know whose son he is."

One look at Lex's face and Victoria knew a storm was coming. Her heart sank into abysmal depths.

While the rage within him festered, Lex spat, "You didn't have to let him in the house!" Eyes bulging, he spewed out a string of profanity and demanded, "Why did you let him in my house, woman?"

Struggling to maintain her composure, Victoria answered, "Tommy has a right to know his father."

"It hasn't bothered you for over five years that he didn't know his father! So what's so important about it now?"

"Ryan wasn't near him then. He is now."

Victoria was seated directly opposite Coffield. Leaning halfway across the table and breathing raggedly with fury, he hissed, "I want to know if he touched you while he was in *my* house!"

Victoria's mind was racing. Ryan McGraw was twice the man Lex Coffield was. If she made Lex angry enough to go after her ex-husband, Ryan would handle him and would see what she was dealing with. Ryan would help her get rid of Lex.

Meeting Lex's glare, she said coolly, "I couldn't fight him off. He took me in his arms and kissed me with such passion, I was helpless."

Coffield swore vociferously and overturned the table, shoving it against a wall. Food, dishes, and silverware bounded, splattered, and rattled on the floor. Tommy was screaming in terror, and Victoria was trying to get to him when Lex stomped out of the house, slamming the front door.

Swearing to himself, the furious captain walked down the street at a fast pace. He walked for a half hour until his wrath had cooled, then headed back to the house. He had been gone a full hour when he entered the house and found Victoria on her knees in the kitchen, doing the finishing touches on cleaning up the mess. Tommy was up in his room.

Victoria rose from the kitchen floor with a rag and pail of water, glanced at him, and went to the cupboard, turning her back to him.

Holding his voice calm, Lex said, "Ryan McGraw is never to set foot in this house again."

Turning around, Victoria eyed him levelly. "You'll have to tell Ryan that yourself."

Jaw jutted and teeth clenched, he said, "I will!"

SIXTEEN

As Dixie Quade and Ryan McGraw dined together at the Mobile Arms Hotel restaurant, Ryan did his best to show his interest in Dixie's childhood, her parents and family, and her years in nursing.

Dixie did not doubt his interest in her, but she could read through the facade. After they had finished the meal and she had answered for the third time why she had gone into nursing, she gave him a warm, dimpled smile and said, "Captain, your mind is somewhere else tonight. You're such a kind and good man. You're trying to make me feel important, and I appreciate it, but something's bothering you. All you told me when you came to pick me up was that you had learned that Tommy was your son. Did something else happen?"

Ryan took a deep breath, let it out slowly through his nose, and ran his fingers through his hair. "Miss Dixie," he said, thinking how beautiful she looked by candlelight, "you are important. I very much value the times we've had together...especially this one. The more I see of you, the more important you become in my life."

"Thank you," she said softly. "That means more to me than I can tell you. But I think I know you well enough to sense that there's something under the surface that's eating at you."

Ryan sighed again, looking at the candlelight that danced in her eyes. His heart was warmed by the tender, beautiful young woman. She was everything he wanted. He wished he could take her into his arms and tell her he was in love with her, and if she'd have him, he wanted to marry her. But he couldn't bring himself to do it.

Then Dixie, seeing the affliction in his eyes, leaned across the table and took hold of his hand. Setting her compassionate gaze on him, she said, "Captain, are you still in love with Victoria?"

He was shocked that Dixie could read him so well. He was fighting the inward battle over the way Victoria still rang a bell down deep within him. Until he could settle the dispute within himself, he couldn't pursue what he wanted with Dixie. She deserved better than that.

Placing his other hand on top of hers, he said, "This has been an emotional day for me, Miss Dixie. The way I'm churning inside, I don't even know what day of the week it is. I guess I'm still so stunned at learning about Tommy that I can't answer any question intelligently."

"I understand," she replied tenderly. "We'd better go. You've got a long ride back to the fort."

Dixie's heart was heavy as Ryan walked her home along a dimly lit Mobile street. She was in love with the man as much as any woman could be. She wanted him with everything that was in her, but she was afraid Ryan might still be in love with his ex-wife. Maybe he always would be.

At Dixie's door they talked briefly about the buildup of the Union fleet in the Gulf and the possibility of General Canby launching a land attack on Fort Morgan and the city of Mobile. Before leaving, Ryan said, "Miss Dixie, we don't know when the Yankees are going to come at us, but if they hold off a little longer...could we have another evening together soon?"

A cold hand seemed to squeeze her heart as she asked, "Do you really want it, Captain?"

Ryan felt his pulse quicken as he looked into her tender eyes by the light of a lantern that burned on the apartment porch. He wanted desperately to take her in his arms and kiss her, but refrained. He must not let himself go that far until the struggle over his feelings toward Tori was ended. If it would ever end.

"Yes, I really want another evening together," he assured her.

"Then I'll be at your beck and call," she smiled. She started to turn toward the door, then came back around and said, "Captain?"

"Yes, Miss Dixie?"

"Would you do me a favor? Would you drop the Miss and just call me Dixie?"

"If you'll drop the Captain and just call me Ryan."

Extending her hand, she said, "Let's shake on it."

Ryan took her hand, squeezed it for a moment, and said, "It's a deal, Dixie."

"Yes it is, Ryan," she breathed, then stood on her tiptoes and surprised him by touching his face with her fingertips and planting a kiss on his cheek.

As the sun was lifting itself from the earth's eastern edge the next morning, General Page had nearly all the men of Fort Morgan gathered in the open area for a briefing. The only men missing were two privates who watched the Union fleet out on the Gulf from the top of the lighthouse, and Captain Lex Coffield, who had not yet arrived from Mobile. He was often a few minutes shy of reporting in on time. Page explained that reports had come to him from Richmond that the war was not looking good for the South. The Union had blockaded vital seaports along the Atlantic coast and the Gulf coast. By fighting back at Savannah, Georgia, the Confederates had been able to reopen their seaport and had received arms shipments from England. The government of Great Britain had taken the Confederate side in the war and was sending arms and supplies as fast as possible.

Confederate intelligence reported that plans were being made in Washington, D.C., to send General William T. Sherman and a massive land force to capture Atlanta, then move on to Savannah and capture it. The only other seaport not already in Union hands was Mobile. President Lincoln had ordered that Mobile be taken, if at all possible, even before Sherman began his march against Atlanta and Savannah.

Page told his men that three small gunboats were now on their way down the Alabama River from Selma: the *Gaines*, the *Selma* and the *Morgan*. At Selma's shipyards, the Confederates were working around the clock to build a huge, well-armed ironclad ram. It would be called the *Tennessee*. If Farragut held off another three weeks, the *Tennessee* would be ready for battle, and could mean the difference between victory and defeat. The *Tennessee* was being built under the supervision of Admiral Franklin Buchanan, Commander of the Confederate Navy.

The general explained that the torpedoes were all in place in the bay, but that the Yankees would be coming with many boats. The torpedoes would stop a few, but once they had exploded and done their damage to the first boats entering the bay, those behind them would have smooth sailing. The few men at Fort Gaines would unleash what fire power they had, but it was going to be up to the men at Fort Morgan to carry the load. They must be ready to fight a full-scale battle.

While Page was talking, Lex Coffield appeared and stood at the rear of the group. Noah Cloud was standing next to Ryan McGraw and saw Coffield come in. Elbowing McGraw, he whispered, "The almighty Captain Coffield just showed up."

Ryan turned his head slowly and found the dark-haired man who wore the captain's bars. He pictured Coffield abusing Tommy and felt a tinge of anger.

General Page was reminding the men that the danger of land attack was also imminent. This was one reason the Sharpshooters were there. Page would lean heavily on them when it came.

When the briefing was over, McGraw waved a hand and said, "General, I have an announcement."

"Yes, Captain McGraw?"

From his place at the rear of the group, Coffield swung his hard gaze on McGraw.

Lifting his voice, McGraw said, "All Sharpshooters meet me over there by the north wall in five minutes! It's calisthenics time!"

Noah Cloud drifted toward the designated spot with McGraw as the men of B Company began to slowly gather. Cloud looked across the open area to catch another glimpse of Coffield, and said, "Cap'n, Coffield's coming this way." Ryan saw the man weaving his way through the milling soldiers.

From the side of his mouth, Noah said, "Workin' with that man is a real bucketload of agony, Cap'n. He thinks he's Robert E. Lee."

"He does, huh?"

"Yeah. He was bossing all us Sharpshooters around like he owns the world. Me and Hap got into one of our fights, and he threatened to put us under arrest if we didn't quit. That's rough on me and Hap. You understand, Cap'n. We just gotta blow off steam once in a while."

"Sure," nodded McGraw. "And Coffield hasn't the authority to arrest you, anyway."

"No?"

"No. This is a special setup here. The Sharpshooters are under General Page in the sense that he's commander of the fort, but even he can give you orders only through me. You boys are directly responsible to me and me alone. Remember our very first briefing? The general explained it so the men in the fort would know the situation."

"Oh, yeah," nodded Cloud, rubbing his chin. "Coffield wasn't here. Well, great! I'll tell Hap. Next time the almighty Captain Coffield tries to stop us, we'll just keep on fightin'."

Coffield drew up to McGraw with fire in his eyes. With a rasp in his voice, he said, "McGraw, I'm Captain—"

"I know who you are," cut in McGraw. "Noah pointed you out to me. What do you want?"

Nostrils flared, Coffield replied stiffly, "I want a private conversation with you."

"I want to talk to you, too," came the quick response, "but it'll have to be after calisthenics. I always work out with my men."

Coffield knew by the look in McGraw's eyes it would be useless to argue. "All right," he said. "How long will that be?"

"Exactly two hours."

"Meet you out at the lighthouse in two hours and three minutes."

"It's a date," McGraw said evenly.

For the next two hours, Captain McGraw led his men in a strenuous workout, including hand-to-hand combat practice. He wanted them to be in top physical condition and to keep their fighting skills sharp.

When it was over, McGraw made his way out the gate and found Coffield standing in the shadow of the weatherworn lighthouse. Knowing the structure was tall enough that the men in the glass compartment above could not hear them, Coffield spoke first. "I know about you and Victoria cuddling at the dance, McGraw, and I don't like it!"

"You probably got an enlarged version of it," countered McGraw. "It wasn't that much."

"Well, did I get an enlarged version of you going to my house and kissing her?"

"I don't know, but maybe I should remind you of what *you* did in Hattiesburg when Tori was *my* wife. Don't tell me you never so much as held her hand until the divorce was final and you two were married."

Coffield's face blanched and tiny sweat beads moistened his forehead. His tongue seemed to freeze to the roof of his mouth.

While Coffield was mulling that one over, Ryan said, "Now that I know Tommy is my son, I'm going to say something, and I'm only going to say it once. *Don't you ever touch that boy again.* You've put your last bruise on him, mister. Victoria is your wife, and I can't interfere there, but if I ever learn that you beat on that boy again, I'll pound you to a bloody pulp."

Coffield's tongue came loose. Bristling, he snapped, "I don't like threats, McGraw!"

"And I don't like men who beat on women and children! Only a low-bellied, cowardly snake would manhandle a woman or a child."

Coffield's natural impulse was to send a fist to the man's mouth, but Ryan's size and his reputation as the tough-as-rawhide leader of the Sharpshooters caused him to check it.

McGraw was ready if Coffield threw a punch. When it did not come, and neither did a retort, he said, "Now, I want to discuss Tommy with you, Captain."

"What about him?"

"He lives in your home, and I respect the sanctity of it. I would like your permission to see my son on a regular basis."

"Not in a million years."

"If you had respected the sanctity of *my* home, I wouldn't be asking your permission to see my own son in your home."

For the first time since stealing Victoria, Lex Coffield felt a pang of guilt. He took a step back, removed his hat, and sleeved away the sweat. While the sea breeze toyed with his dark locks, he pondered McGraw's request.

Seven or eight seagulls flew in from off the Gulf, swooped low over the heads of the two Confederate officers, then continued on to the top of the lighthouse. Coffield watched them in their flight, then looked at the rugged leader of B Company and said, "You're sure it isn't Victoria you want to see on a regular basis?"

"I'm sure."

"What about this kissing that went on in my house…and the romance on the dance floor at the fort?"

"Victoria was lonesome for you. We hadn't seen each other in a long time…and she reached for me in your place. I had a couple of weak moments. It won't happen again. Especially if you quit beating on her and show her some love and tenderness."

"You're sure you don't want her back?"

"I've had some old feelings surface. I can't really describe them. But I don't want her back. She's your wife now. I'll leave it at that."

"If I give you permission to see Tommy, will you let him meet you at the door? I don't want you inside alone with Victoria again. By alone, I mean without me there."

"I'll stay outside if that's your wish."

"That's my wish. You can take Tommy wherever you want to. Just don't go in the house with Victoria."

"All right."

"Then you have my permission. I'll talk it over with Victoria and we'll work out some kind of visitation plan."

"Fine," said McGraw, relieved that he would be able to see his son without resistance from Victoria's husband. "Just let me know."

Coffield nodded, placed his hat back on his head, and walked toward the gate of the fort. McGraw turned and set his gaze on the sunlit waters of the Gulf of Mexico. His heart throbbed with love for Thomas Manning McGraw...the son of his own image. He hoped the day would come when his parents could meet their fine little grandson. It would mean the world to his father that the boy was named after him.

Moving down the sandy slope to the water's edge, Ryan stood there gazing at the foaming shoreline for a long moment, then lifted his eyes heavenward and said, "Lord, I don't always understand Your ways...but in spite of all this confusion going on inside me, I want to thank You for letting me learn about Tommy. Already I love him as much as a father can love his son."

Ryan soon found himself focusing on the fleet of Union ships that seemed to hover like vultures on the horizon. How soon would they come, bringing death and destruction with them?

Just after breakfast on Saturday morning, July 9, General Page met in his office with Colonel DeWitt Munford, Captain Ryan McGraw, and Lieutenants Wilson March, Frank Cooley, and Judd Rawlings. Captain Lex Coffield had been informed of the meeting, but had not shown up.

Page stood over his desk where he had laid out a large map of Mobile Bay, and the officers gathered close. Using his index finger as a pointer, he showed them just how the torpedoes had been moored in the mouth of the bay by Captain Coffield and the Sharpshooters. Stretching from the pilings that covered the westward portion of the mouth at Fort Gaines all the way to a red buoy that bobbed in the water within a few feet of the shore under the ramparts of Fort Morgan was a triple line of the deadly torpedoes...a hundred and ninety-one in all.

"Looks like Captain Coffield did a good job," mused Munford.

"Yes," said Page. "Coffield does know his stuff about explosives. The way he has them situated, they'll take their toll on quite a few Union vessels." The general ran his finger to a spot up shore on the east side. "The *Selma*, the *Gaines*, and the *Morgan* are anchored right there, just beyond sight of the fort. They'll be ready to open fire on the ships that make it past the torpedoes."

McGraw ran a finger over his mustache, shook his head, and said, "That doesn't give us much fire power, does it, sir?"

"Not when you take a look at the number of ships and boats Farragut's got out there. Last count was twenty. We're going to have to rely a whole lot on those big guns out there on our walls."

"Even then, sir," spoke up Lieutenant Rawlings, "we're looking at a task that's next to impossible. Our B Company can snipe from the shore and kill a lot of men aboard those Union vessels, but we can't sink them. We need more sea power. Even if the *Tennessee* gets here in time, we're still horrendously outnumbered in the water. How about those rams I've seen docked at Mobile? Can't they be used?"

"No. Not a one of them is seaworthy. Their engines are shot. It would take more time, engine parts, and men than the Confederate navy has to put them into service. The *Tennessee* will do us more good than all of them put together. She's ironclad and well armed."

"I understand she looks a lot like the old *Merrimac*, sir," said Lieutenant Cooley.

Nodding, Page pulled a drawer open and produced a sketch of the *Tennessee*, which also listed the ship's specifications. Laying it on the desk in full view, he said, "You'll see she resembles the *Merrimac* in configuration. See? The sloping sides of her barn-like superstructure are very much like the *Merrimac*. However, the *Tennessee* is the most powerful casemated ironclad ram ever built by the Confederate navy."

"She looks like a floating fortress, all right," said Rawlings.

"See what it says here," commented Page. "The superstructure is plated with three courses of two-inch wrought iron armor, giving her a six-inch composite shield capable of resisting the heaviest fire that could be brought to bear against her. And look at this. Her battery consists of six heavy guns...four six-inch Brooke rifles in broadside—two on each side—and two seven-inch Brooke rifles on pivot mounts, one at each end of the casemate."

"That's some kind of gun vessel," said McGraw. "I just hope they get it down here before ol' ' fairguts' comes steaming in."

"Me, too," agreed Page. "The *Tennessee* is calculated to reduce any Union ships to charred flotsam in a head-to-head battle." The general paused as he placed the drawing back in the drawer, then sighed, "However, she does have one big problem. There wasn't time to build new engines for her, so I understand they cannibalized engines from a Yazoo River steamboat that are quite underpowered for her weight. She'll be slow in maneuverability."

"I guess that's where our other three boats will have to shine, sir," put in Colonel Munford. "At least they're quick and maneuverable."

The general nodded. "They'll have to shine *real good*. And so will the guns of Fort Morgan."

While the discussion continued in General Page's office, Captain Coffield arrived at Mobile Point, took his horse to the stables, and approached the gate. He could hear excited voices as the sentry swung the gate open. Moving inside, he saw a cluster of the fort's men looking on as Sergeants Hap Hazzard and Noah Cloud were whaling away at each other in a bloody-nose fight.

Coffield knew he was late for the meeting in the general's office, but decided he would just have to be a little more tardy. He had forbidden Hazzard and Cloud to ever fight again as long as they were at Fort Morgan, and was irritated to see them defying his orders. Coffield rushed to the battle zone, elbowed his way through the clot of spectators, and shouted, "Hey, you two! Stop this instant!"

Hazzard had just taken a blow to the mouth and countered with a roundhouse punch. Cloud's feet left the ground, and he landed on his back. Neither paid any attention to Coffield's command.

Hazzard stood waiting for Cloud to get up, breathing hard and wiping blood from his lips. As Cloud was scrambling to his feet, the angry captain moved between them, and waved his arms, shouting, "I said stop this fighting!"

One of the excited spectators said, "Aw, let 'em finish it, Captain!"

When Coffield turned to see who had just spoken, Hazzard stepped around him to meet Cloud, who was charging in. The two combatants came together, swinging wildly.

Unable to tell who had spoken, Coffield turned back again, only to find that the two big men were stumbling his way. Suddenly Hap Hazzard's meaty right fist caught him flush on the jaw. The captain went down like a decayed tree in a high wind and lay still. He was out cold. The spectators looked on open-mouthed and wide-eyed, wondering what would happen now.

Big Hap ran thick fingers through his mop of red hair, eyed the unconscious officer, then looked at his friend, and said, "Maybe I oughtta go make a quick report to Cap'n McGraw and the general."

Cloud sleeved moisture from his face and replied, "Yeah, I guess that'd be the thing to do."

"You guys are gonna be in trouble for sure," interjected one of the soldiers. "Coffield will have your hides for this."

The sergeants exchanged glances. Lying flat on his back, Coffield began to stir, rolling his head and moaning.

Hap looked toward the general's office, then back at Coffield. To the men around him, he said, "Maybe I better try to soothe the captain before I report to Cap'n McGraw and General Page. Somebody get a cup of water."

While one of the men ran to a water pail nearby, Hazzard knelt down, using his bulky body to shade Coffield's face, and asked, "Captain, are you all right?"

Coffield batted his eyelids, rolled his head some more, then focused on Hazzard's face as the sergeant was wiping blood from his own mouth. Eyes a bit glazed, Coffield put a hand to his jaw and grunted, "You're under arrest, Sergeant! You struck an officer of the Confederate army!"

As Coffield raised up to a sitting position, the soldier arrived with a cup of water and handed it to Hazzard. Hap took it, extended it to Coffield, and said, "Here's some water, sir."

Coffield swore and batted the cup from Hazzard's hand. Eyes blazing, he snapped, "Don't try to appease me! You're under arrest and so's your friend. Since Fort Morgan doesn't have a guardhouse, you're going to rot in the jail at Mobile!"

Suddenly two shadows were cast over Coffield as General Page and Captain McGraw drew up. The other officers had arrived on the scene also.

"What happened here?" demanded Page.

Struggling to his feet as he spoke, Coffield said, "Hazzard and Cloud were fighting, sir." He swayed unsteadily and jerked his arm from Hazzard's hand as he tried to help him. After burning Hap with hot eyes, he looked at Page. "I've warned these two before about their ridiculous fighting, General. I commanded them never to do it again as long as they're in this fort. When I arrived a few minutes ago, here they were fighting again. I commanded them to stop, but they ignored me." Gesturing toward the gray-clad spectators, he added, "These men can testify to that."

No one affirmed that they would.

Rubbing his jaw, Coffield went on. "Since they disobeyed my

order to stop fighting, I stepped in to stop it myself. Next thing I know, I was lying on the ground. Hazzard knocked me unconscious, General. I have put both of them under arrest. I'm sure you will back me in that, sir."

General Page could not show it, but he was extremely glad the captain had been punched out. Though he wanted to grin, he kept a sober look and said levelly, "No, I won't, Captain."

Coffield shifted his stance to better steady himself and looked as if he had been slapped in the face. "Wha—"

"You have no jurisdiction over any of the Sharpshooters, Captain. B Company is strictly under Captain McGraw's command. Even I can command them only through Captain McGraw."

Coffield gasped, "But I—"

"These fine men are here on special assignment by General Robert E. Lee, and the stipulations are as I just told you. You have no authority to place Sergeants Hazzard and Cloud under arrest."

Coffield's features darkened. "But Hazzard struck me, General! You know what the book says about an enlisted man who strikes an officer!"

"You're thinking of the book you studied at West Point," Page countered quietly. "You ought to know there hasn't been time since the war began for a book to be written for our army. Besides...I'm sure it was an accident. You said that you stepped in to stop the fight. Apparently fists were flying. Sergeant Hazzard wouldn't strike you deliberately. Now, let's drop it right here."

Captain Coffield looked as though he had just swallowed a mouthful of dill pickle juice. "Yes, sir," he managed to say.

"Now, let's get back to our meeting, gentlemen," Page said to the officers. "Captain Coffield, I remind you that you are tardy."

Coffield did not reply. As he walked beside McGraw toward the general's office, he said in a low tone, "Victoria and I have worked out a visitation plan. You can see Tommy anytime and take him anywhere you want as long as Victoria says so...and with the stipulation that you never enter the house."

"Agreed," said McGraw.

When the officers were gone, Hap and Noah went to the water pail and washed their faces. The men gathered close. One of them said, "Hap, we're all curious."

"About what?" Hap said, wiping water from his face.

"Was it really an accident?"

The big redhead gave them a furtive smile and walked away. The men looked at Cloud, who shrugged his thick shoulders, grinned from ear to ear, and followed his friend.

SEVENTEEN

While the Union ships sat quietly on the watery horizon day after day—observed closely from the lighthouse at Mobile Point—Ryan McGraw made frequent trips into town to divide time between his son and Dixie Quade. He took Tommy for walks and ate meals with Dixie.

Each time Ryan went to the house for Tommy and Lex was absent, Victoria tried to lure him inside. Remaining true to his word, he reminded her that he and Lex had an agreement. He would not violate it.

On Sunday, July 17, the devoted father picked his son up after Tommy had eaten lunch. As they stepped off the porch with Victoria and Lex looking on from the door, Tommy said, "Dad, how about instead of us walkin', we take a ride on your horse? I've never been on a horse before."

Pausing, Ryan turned toward the boy's mother and asked, "Is it all right if he rides the horse with me?"

"Certainly," she smiled, "but don't take him too far."

"We'll just ride over to the hospital. I need to see my men who are still there. All but two have gone home. I'd like for them to meet Tommy."

Victoria wondered if Dixie was on duty. She didn't want Tommy being around her, but if she protested in front of Lex, he would question why. She dare not ripple the waters until she had Ryan ready to take her back and help her get rid of Lex. With Ryan on her side, she would not be afraid of Lex.

"Have a nice time," Victoria said, forcing a cheerful note into her voice.

Tommy giggled and squealed when his father hoisted him into the saddle, then swung up behind him. As they rode away at a trot, the boy laughed and said, "This is fun!"

Arriving at the hospital, Ryan led Tommy down the corridor and introduced him to Private Brad Thacker and Corporal Vince Udall, who were now in the same room. After chatting with them for a few minutes, he left and led the boy toward the nurse's station. He knew Dixie was on duty and would get off at five o'clock. They were to have dinner together that evening after attending a church service. Every church in Mobile was holding special services, invoking God's mercy in light of the impending invasion by the Union army and navy.

Dixie was just leaving the nurse's station as father and son drew up. She warmed Ryan with a dimpled smile, then kept it on for the boy, as she looked down at him and said, "Hello, Tommy. I see you're not wearing a bandage on your arm anymore. When did the doctor take it off?"

Tommy looked up at his father and beckoned with his finger for Ryan to bend down. Dixie looked on as Ryan put his ear next to the boy's mouth. Tommy's whisper was louder than he realized as he said, "I'm not supposed to talk to her. Mommy said she's a bad lady."

Ryan looked up, realizing Dixie had heard every word. "Why is she a bad lady, Son?"

"'Cause she talked mean to Mommy one day. Mommy says she's bad, and I shouldn't ever talk to her."

"Let's take a little walk," Dixie said, casting a glance at two nurses who were bent over a desk in the station.

As they moved down the corridor, Dixie said, "Victoria and I had a heated discussion here at the hospital the day after the dance. She… she doesn't like the fact that you and I see each other. It got a little hot. So I guess I'm a bad lady." Dixie would not tell Ryan of Victoria's death threat.

"I see." Kneeling down and looking his son in the eye, Ryan said, "Tommy, wasn't it this lady who helped Dr. Lyles fix up your arm the night Mommy brought you in here after Lex kicked you into the wall?"

The child's memory took him back to that night and he recalled how kind she was to him. He remembered thinking that she sure seemed nice. He also remembered how he liked the way she looked at him and the way she held his hand. "Yes," he nodded.

"Wasn't she nice to you?"

"Yes."

"Do you think she's bad?"

The boy raised his pale blues and set them on Dixie. There was a brief moment of thought, then he answered, "No. I think she is nice."

It was Dixie's turn to kneel down. Looking tenderly at the child, she said, "Tommy, I don't want to make you disobey your mother, so you don't have to talk to me. But I want you to know that I wasn't trying to be mean to your mother. We were both angry, so we didn't talk very nice to each other. I also want you to know that I think you are a very brave little boy…and I like you a lot."

Tommy smiled. "I like you a lot, too."

Standing up, Dixie asked, "How old are you, Tommy?"

He held up five fingers and said, "This many."

"Five?"

"Yes, ma'am."

"Well, it just so happens that we had some nice people come here to the hospital and leave us some candy to give to boys and girls who visit us. Do you like horehound candy?"

"Yes, ma'am!"

"Well, the pieces are small, so we give children one for each year they are old. So I'll get you five!"

As Dixie was turning away, Tommy said quickly, "I'm almost six!"

"Oh, is that so?" she laughed. "When is your birthday?"

Tommy looked at the floor. "Um…August…August…"

"August first," Ryan finished for him.

"I guess that's close enough to deserve six," Dixie said, laughing again and heading for the nurse's station.

With one piece of horehound in his mouth and five in his pocket, Thomas Manning McGraw left the hospital with his father…but not before volunteering a kiss for the nice lady. As Ryan watched the two together, he wished they could be a family. Dixie would make a wonderful wife and mother.

Admiral David Glasgow Farragut stood on the bow of the flagship USS *Hartford* at sunrise on Friday, July 29, 1864. With telescope in hand, he peered toward Mobile Bay and watched the CSS *Tennessee* steam down the bay and drop anchor just off the beach at Fort Morgan.

The long weeks had passed slowly for Farragut while he waited for the Union ships that would make up his attack fleet to arrive one by one. He now had twenty-one ships, but as he studied the ironclad *Tennessee* through the telescope, he knew he dare not engage the seemingly unconquerable vessel in shoal water without ironclads of his own.

The admiral had learned about the *Tennessee* being built at Selma just before the land attack on Fort Morgan a month previously by Captain Leonard Whittier and his unit. When Farragut received word that the assault had been a failure, he knew he must add more ships before attacking. Now with the new threat of the *Tennessee*, he would have to bring in at least four ironclads (also known as monitors) to feel secure about steaming into the bay.

The admiral had sent word to Washington, asking for the monitors to be sent as soon as possible. When ship number twenty-one, the USS *Lackawanna* had arrived in mid-July, it bore a message that three monitors would be sent within a few days. They were the single-turret *Manhattan* from the Atlantic and two twin-turret river monitors, the *Chickasaw* and the *Winnebago* from the Mississippi. They were due to converge on Farragut's fleet around the end of July. The same message also informed Farragut that the fourth monitor, USS *Tecumseh* was docked at Pensacola for repairs and would arrive no later than August 3.

When Farragut lowered the telescope, he found Fleet-Captain Percival Drayton standing next to him. "How's it look, sir?" queried Drayton.

"Like a formidable bulwark of iron and big guns," sighed the admiral. "It'll take a lot of firepower to overcome the *Tennessee*. It's everything we were told it was, and more."

"We can still capture the bay once our monitors join us, sir," Drayton said with confidence.

"We can and we *will,*" remarked Farragut, raising the telescope to study the *Tennessee* some more.

Farragut had all the sagacity of an old sea-dog. At sixty-three, he had been a sailor for fifty-four years. When just nine years old, he became a midshipman in the United States Navy, and during the War of 1812—at the age of eleven—he was prizemaster of the USS *Alexander Barclay.* Thereafter, until the outbreak of the Civil War in April 1861, he held ship commands on various stations, fought in the Mexican-American War, and was the instigator for establishing the Mare Island Navy Yard in San Francisco Bay.

In December 1861, with fifty-one years of service under his belt, Farragut was appointed admiral of the newly formed Federal Western Gulf Blockading Squadron. During the next two-and-a-half years, his fleet developed into a primary strike force in the Gulf of Mexico and Mississippi Delta, carrying the war to the Confederates and capturing New Orleans, Galveston, Corpus Christi, Sabine Pass, and Port Hudson.

His next and primary goal was Mobile Bay.

At nine-thirty that same morning, monitors *Chickasaw* and *Winnebago* were seen on the western horizon of the Gulf, and within an hour had been welcomed as part of the fleet. Later that afternoon, the *Manhattan* steamed in from the east, and except for the promised *Tecumseh*, Admiral Farragut's floating strike force was complete. Once the *Tecumseh* joined the fleet, the Union commander would not hesitate to enter the bay and fight it out.

The *Manhattan's* captain delivered a message from Washington that Major General Canby was experiencing a heavy drain on his manpower, a result of having to send troops to the Virginia theatre. Canby could not yet release Major General Gordon Granger and his five thousand troops for the assault on Mobile. When Farragut's twenty-fifth ship—the *Tecumseh*—arrived, he was to proceed into Mobile Bay at once. His task was to bombard Forts Gaines and Morgan until they were defenseless, then pull out of the bay, leaving enough men and ships to occupy the forts and guard the bay. Land forces would move on the city of Mobile as soon as Canby could spare them.

Farragut's original plan called for a simultaneous attack on the forts by both land and naval forces. With this message from the Navy Department in Washington in hand, he sat down at a table in his quarters and worked out a new plan. When he had it complete, he called for the captains of all the ships gathered around him to come to the *Hartford* for a meeting.

With twenty-three captains and his Fleet Captain Percival Drayton assembled, Farragut used little wooden blocks to represent the Union ships and laid out his plan of attack. He carefully prescribed the position of each vessel in the task force and explained various tactical arrangements he wished to be observed.

The fleet was to form in two columns, the wooden ships in couples running side by side and the monitors in single file. Fourteen wooden ships were assigned to the main column, the number being equally divided between heavy battleships and lesser vessels. Each battleship was paired with a gunboat. Farragut had observed the Confederates installing torpedoes. He knew some of his vessels would sustain severe damage, but this did not deter him. They must go ahead in spite of the deadly explosive devices.

Once a number of his ships had moved past the pilings and those vessels slowed or stalled by the torpedoes, the gunboats were to separate from the battleships to do their own damage to the forts. Some of the fleet would remain outside the mouth of the bay and bombard the forts from the south.

Originally, the admiral intended to lead the fleet into the bay in the *Hartford*, but when he saw the Rebels placing the torpedoes from the red buoy by the shore all the way to the pilings, he changed his mind. The battleship *Brooklyn* was equipped with four "bow-chasers"—cannons on special swivels that allowed them to blow up torpedoes before the ship struck them. The *Hartford* would run in behind the *Brooklyn*.

When the admiral was satisfied that his captains all understood the plan of attack, he said, "Gentlemen, once we have the forts in our hands, Mobile Bay is ours. General William Tecumseh Sherman will take Savannah, and we'll have the Confederacy totally blockaded. Without supplies from England and the other countries that've helped them, they can't last very long. We know they've got a lot of supplies stockpiled in Mobile, but once General Granger and his troops move in and take the city, those supplies will be out of reach. Within a few more months this war will be history."

"I'll vote for that," spoke up one of the captains.

"Me, too," said another. "I haven't seen my wife for nearly a year."

"It's been almost that long for me, too," put in another. "And I've got two grandchildren I've never seen."

Farragut smiled, then said, "Gentlemen, I have set the time of attack for one week from today…Friday, August 5th. We'll go in at dawn to take advantage of the early morning high tide."

The admiral, who was fond of red wine, had his cabin attendant break out tin cups and personally filled them from his well-stocked wine cabinet. While each man held his cup, Drayton poured for the admiral. Farragut then lifted the cup, swinging it in a half-circle toward his fleet leaders and said, "A toast, gentlemen. To the end of the war…and, of course, a Union victory!"

On the first day of August, Captain McGraw appeared on the porch of the Coffield house at dusk bearing birthday presents for his son. Victoria met him at the door, smiled, and said, "Mercy me! You're going to spoil that boy!"

"That's the idea," grinned Ryan. "He's the only son I have."

Tommy's father noted that Victoria was dressed up and had her jet-black hair styled in his favorite way. "You can come in," she said cheerfully. "Lex isn't here. He won't be home for a couple of hours."

The grin faded from Ryan's lips as he replied, "No, Tori. Lex and I have an agreement. I won't break it."

Tilting her head back and lowering her eyelids, she said, "Well, that's too bad. You won't be able to see your son on his birthday."

"Why not? He can come out on the porch."

"No, he can't. Tommy's got a fever and I've got him lying down."

"A fever? What's the matter with him?"

"Nothing serious. This happens to him once in a while. It's that way with some children. He'll outgrow it, I'm sure." Extending her hands, she said, "I'll take the presents and give them to him."

Frustration showed on Ryan's face. "Tori, I—"

"Yes?"

"Will you make sure Tommy understands that I didn't come in and see him because of the agreement I made with Lex?"

"I'll try, but he's only six years old. What does he know about a gentleman's agreement? He'll probably think you don't love him anymore."

"Aw, now, Tori, I can't have that. Can't you just bring him to the door long enough for me to explain the situation and assure him that I do love him?"

"No. When he stirs around, it makes his fever rise."

Ryan's love for his son outweighed even his sense of honor. "All right," he sighed. "I'll come in...but only for a couple minutes."

Carrying the packages, he followed Victoria into a small room at the rear of the house where Tommy was sitting up on a couch. His pale blue eyes widened and danced with glee when he saw his father and the armload of packages. Bounding from the couch, he laughed and said, "Hi, Dad! Mommy told me to stay back here and I'd have a big surprise. Oh, boy! Are those presents for me?"

"They sure are!" said Ryan, kneeling down and laying them on the floor. "Happy birthday! How about a big hug?"

When Tommy wrapped his arms around Ryan's neck, the concerned father placed an open palm against his brow. Letting go of Tommy and rising to his feet, he said, "Go to it, son. Open your presents."

While the excited child was tearing paper, Ryan looked at his ex-wife. "Tori, you lied to me. He doesn't have a fever."

Tears filmed her eyes as she lunged at Ryan, flung her arms around his neck, and planted a kiss solidly on his lips. Tommy looked up, then returned to his presents.

Breaking Victoria's hold, Ryan took a step back. The beautiful woman once again struck a nameless chord somewhere deep within him. "Tori, why? You tricked me."

Blinking to start the tears flowing down her cheeks, Victoria grasped both his hands and said, "I can't stand this marriage of mine any longer, darling! You've got to help me break free from Lex!"

"Oh, boy! A drum!" Tommy shouted.

Both parents looked down to see the child, eyes dancing, holding the toy drum. He beat on it for a few seconds, then laid it aside and reached up to hug his father. Tommy thanked him over and over as he squeezed hard on Ryan's neck.

When the excited boy returned to the other packages, Victoria took Ryan's hands again and pled, "Please, darling...you must help me!"

"Tori, I didn't help you marry Lex. I can't help you unmarry him."

"Oh, but you *can!*" she cried. "You can and you will because you're still in love with me. I know you are, Ryan! Why won't you admit it?"

Again, she lunged for him, attempting to wrap her arms around his neck. Ryan adeptly stepped back and seized her wrists. "No, Tori!" he said sharply. "We mustn't be in each others arms. You are Lex's wife…not mine."

"But I want to be your wife again."

"It's no good. I've got to go." Turning to Tommy, he said, "Son, I have to leave now. You have a good time with those presents, okay?"

"I will, Dad. Thank you!"

"You're welcome. Could I have another hug before I go?"

"Sure!"

Holding the boy, Ryan said, "Tell you what. If the Yankees don't attack the fort tomorrow, I'll come by and take you for another horseback ride. Would you like that?"

"Yes, sir! I really like riding with you, Dad."

Tommy went back to his packages, and Victoria stood at the door and wept as she watched Ryan ride away.

Later that evening, Lex Coffield entered the house and found Tommy playing with his new toys in the middle of the parlor floor. Standing over him, Lex asked, "Where'd you get all this stuff?"

"From my dad for my birthday!" Tommy answered, reaching for his drum. "See my neat drum?"

"Where's your mother?"

"Upstairs."

Checking the staircase to make sure Victoria wasn't on it, Lex leaned close to the boy and asked, "Did your father come inside the house to give you your presents?"

"Yes," Tommy said without looking up.

Coffield's temper flared. "You're sure? You're sure he didn't just give them to you on the porch?"

"Hmp-mm. He brought them back into the sitting room. Mommy told me to wait there 'cause I was gonna get a surprise."

Lex heard Victoria coming down the stairs. Turning toward her, his anger showed. Victoria felt a fear pang as she reached the bottom of the stairs and moved toward her husband. "What's wrong?" she asked.

Lex's breath was hot. "I understand from your son that his father came inside the house to give him his presents."

Tommy stopped his playing, sensing Lex's anger. He looked on as the man moved close to his mother and said, "Well?"

Victoria's hands trembled as she said, "Ryan didn't think you'd care since it was Tommy's birthday. I told him Tommy could open the presents on the porch, but he thought it would be better if he was in the parlor."

Lex's dark eyes were suddenly savage. Victoria felt their striking power as he rasped, "Somebody's lying here! Is it you or the kid? He told me you had him waiting back there in the sitting room, promising him a surprise…and that his father brought the presents back there."

Victoria's lower lip quivered as she stammered, "It…it was m-me who invited Ryan in, Lex. I…I told him Tommy had a fever, and…and if he wanted to see him, he'd have to come in. I'm…I'm sorry. I just wanted Tommy to have a few special moments with his father on his birthday."

Looking down at the boy, Lex asked, "Tommy, when your father was in the house, did he and your mother hug and kiss?"

Tommy's fearful gaze shot to his mother. When he observed the terror in her eyes, he swallowed hard, looked up at Lex, and managed a weak, "No."

Jerking his head around to his wife, the furious husband blared, "The brat's lying! I can see it in his eyes! You and your lover boy were carrying on, weren't you?"

Before Victoria could make a reply, Lex hit her with his fist, knocking her across the room. She bounced off the railing at the staircase and tumbled to the floor. The maddened Coffield moved in and kicked her in the stomach. Swearing, he drew back his foot to kick her again when Tommy grabbed his right hand and sank his teeth into it. Coffield cursed him, jerked his hand free, and slapped him hard. Tommy fell to the floor, dazed, his mouth bleeding.

The anger-crazed captain kicked Victoria again, then wheeled and began stomping on Tommy's toys, cursing the name of Ryan McGraw. When he had destroyed the toys, he threw them out in the front yard. The last to go was the little toy drum. It was battered and broken.

On the way to Dixie's apartment, Captain McGraw rode slowly, wrestling with his emotions. He was having stronger feelings toward Dixie all the time, but there was still that strange, unexplainable stirring within him when he was with Tori.

How can I be in love with two women at the same time? he asked himself.

Ryan knew that even if Lex Coffield was out of the way and the road to Tori was clear, he could never take her back again. But as long as those powerful feelings toward his ex-wife were still alive, he would never be free to marry Dixie. It would be unfair to her.

But the way he felt toward Dixie, he couldn't just break it off with her. He was sure that if he never laid eyes on Tori again, the strange feelings would go away, and he could tell Dixie he loved her and ask her to marry him. But there was no way to avoid seeing Tori when he went to visit Tommy. *That* he could never give up. He had a sudden dreadful thought that once the Mobile Bay battle was over, he would be sent elsewhere to fight. When would he ever see Dixie or his son again? And what was Captain Ryan McGraw, who made fast and firm decisions in the heat of battle, going to do about his divided heart?

An emotional maelstrom was churning inside him when he arrived at Dixie's apartment. She had prepared a delicious dinner, which they sat down to eat by candlelight. While they ate and discussed the coming Union assault, Ryan found himself enchanted by Dixie's beauty of character and form. They were finishing up on apple pie when Dixie asked, "Did you visit Tommy today?"

"Mm-hmm. It's his birthday." He saw no reason to tell her

about the way Tori tricked him into entering the house.

"Oh, this *is* the first! Bless his little heart. This had to have been his best birthday ever…having his daddy to celebrate it with him."

"I hope so," smiled Ryan. "I bought him some toys, including a drum."

"A drum?" she giggled. "I'll bet his mother appreciated that!"

"She didn't say," Ryan shrugged.

"You'll probably hear about it later."

"Probably."

Shoving her empty plate aside, Dixie set her soft gaze on the man she loved and said, "Ryan, there are a couple of things I want to do this evening while you're here."

He hurriedly chewed his last bite of pie and said, "Yes, ma'am."

"First, I have a present I want to give you, then I want to have a serious little talk."

"Okay," he said, blinking.

Leaving the table, Dixie went to a small table nearby and picked up a white envelope eight by ten inches in size. It had a slim pink ribbon tied around it, topped off with a fancy pink bow. She handed it to him, then returned to her chair on the opposite side of the table.

Giving her a suspicious look, Ryan opened the envelope and pulled out a daguerreotype of herself in the very dress she was then wearing.

Dixie could tell by the look on his face that Ryan was pleased, and as his eyes dropped to the handwriting in the lower right-hand corner, she said, "I had it done especially for you."

Ryan's heart was in his throat as he read the words, *I will always love you. Dixie.*

He was overwhelmed with the moment. "Dixie," he breathed. "It's…it's beautiful. I'll treasure it always. I—"

Dixie reached across the table and took hold of his hand. Suddenly they were on their feet, drawn together by a force so strong they had neither the will nor the way to resist. There was pure ecstasy in the room as their lips came together in a lingering kiss. When their lips parted, Ryan looked down into her expressive eyes, but could find no words. Dixie laid her head against his chest and embraced him for a long moment, then looked up and half-whispered, "Now for our serious little talk."

She led him by the hand into the apartment's small parlor where two lanterns burned low and sat him down on an overstuffed sofa. She eased down beside him, folding one leg under her so as to face him, and said, "Ryan, I meant what I wrote on that picture." Her eyes misted. She looked toward the ceiling and placed a hand over her quivering lips.

Reaching toward her, he said, "Dixie, I—"

Shaking her head, she threw up a palm. He waited.

After a moment, Dixie cleared the lump from her throat and began again. "I really meant what I wrote on the picture." She drew a deep breath, then said, "I must bare my heart to you."

Ryan opened his mouth to speak, but she cut him off by saying, "Please. Let me tell you what's on my heart, or I'll never get it out."

Ryan's love for her was expanding by leaps and bounds. "All right," he nodded.

Dixie thumbed away tears from both cheeks and said, "Ryan, I've been in love with you since the first time I saw you at the Birmingham hospital. I knew it almost instantly, and I've never doubted it since. Even when we didn't see each other for so long and I didn't know if we ever would cross paths again, I knew you were the only man I would ever love. No one but the Lord in heaven will ever know how happy I was the day you showed up here. I thought maybe somehow we'd get to see each other, and maybe…just maybe…you would fall in love with me."

As she spoke, Dixie could read in his eyes the desire he felt toward her. It warmed her heart.

He started to speak again. "Please," she said, motioning him silent. "I must get it all out before you say anything."

"I'm sorry. Go ahead."

"Ryan…I…know you are fighting an inward battle. I can see it in your eyes, and I felt it in your kiss that you have strong feelings for me. You've shown it in other ways. I…I want you to know that I understand what's going on inside you."

"You do?"

"Yes. You're not sure of yourself with Victoria. There is something down deep that won't let you quite let go of her, now that you've seen her again after all these years. Tell me I'm wrong."

Ryan said nothing for a brief moment, then nodded. "You're right."

"Thank you for giving me a straight answer. Now, the picture I gave you a little while ago is…is something to remind you of me. I'm leaving Mobile, Ryan," she said quietly. "I've asked for a transfer and it has been granted. I've been assigned to the hospital in Chattanooga. As you know, there is heavy fighting in that area. They are in dire need of more nurses."

"But…with the battle that's coming here—"

"I know. But I must leave, Ryan. I want to give you a chance to sort things out in your own heart. I love you with everything that's in me, but I have to know it's the same with you. If, when you get it sorted out, it's me that you want, you can contact me at the hospital in Chattanooga."

After a pause, Ryan asked, "May I speak, now?"

"Yes. I'm through."

Looking her square in the eye, he said, "Dixie, you don't know it, but I fell in love with you at the Birmingham hospital, also. I wanted so much to reveal it to you, but of course I didn't know how you felt about me. I told myself you probably showed the same warmth and kindness toward all the soldiers you attended. I thought of you constantly during that long period we were apart, and considered looking you up just to tell you that I loved you. But…but I couldn't bring myself to do it because…well, because I felt that since I had been married before and had somehow messed it up, I wasn't good enough for you. I felt you deserved better than me. And I still do."

"Oh, Ryan," Dixie whispered. More tears were surfacing. "There *is* no better than you."

Ryan leaned forward, looked at the floor, and rubbed the back of his neck. "You are the kindest person I know," he managed at last. Lifting his head, he set loving eyes on her. "Dixie, in the past few weeks I've started many times to tell you that I'm in love with you, and that if you'd have me, I want you for my wife. But I just couldn't bring myself to do it. This thing with Tori, I—"

"If Lex was out of the way, Ryan, would you take Tori back?"

"No. My problem isn't that I want her back. My problem is that there's a haunting *something* that I feel when I'm with her. I can't describe it, and I can't put a name on it. I guess...I guess it's the embers of a love that once was a blazing fire. But until it's gone, I can't come out and say, 'Dixie, I love you. I'll never think of Tori again, and I'll never feel a tingle for anyone but you...ever.' Do you understand?"

Laying a hand on his, the tearful Dixie said, "Yes, I understand. You have an honest streak in you a mile wide. I love you, Ryan McGraw. I always will. I would love to be your wife...but not with the ghost of an old love between us."

Ryan nodded silently, then asked, "When are you leaving?"

"Early in the morning. There's a medical team taking a boat up to Selma. I'm going with them. From Selma I can take a train to Chattanooga."

Squeezing her hand, Ryan said, "You're the most wonderful person God ever made. I mean that."

"Thank you." Dixie smiled, blushing.

Rising to his feet, Ryan said, "I'm sure you've got packing to do. I'd better get out of here and let you get to it."

They held hands while she walked him to the door. With his free hand, Ryan turned the knob and swung it open.

"Remember," she said, fighting tears, "I'll be at the hospital in Chattanooga."

"Don't worry, I'll remember," he assured her. There were a few seconds of silence, then he looked down at her and asked, "May I kiss you good-bye?"

"I wish you would."

The kiss was long and tender.

Dixie stood in the doorway, shedding silent tears as she watched the man she loved ride into the night.

EIGHTEEN

L ate in the afternoon on August 2, Ryan McGraw rode into
Mobile, feeling an empty spot in his heart.

Dixie Quade was gone.

Ryan had hardly slept the night before. He had tossed and
turned, wrestling with his dilemma. For the time being, Dixie had
solved her portion of it for him. Her absence would allow him time
to give plenty of thought to the strange battle over his feelings for
Tori. Somehow he would solve the mystery and free himself so he
could hurry off to Chattanooga at the first opportunity and tell Dixie
that the ghost of his first love was gone. He would marry the beautiful woman with the golden hair.

The Coffield house was third from the corner. When McGraw
turned his horse onto Evans Avenue, his attention was drawn to the
front yard. Tommy's toys were scattered about, battered and broken.

Dismounting, Ryan noted the little toy drum, lying off by itself. Only one person in the Coffield household would have
destroyed Tommy's birthday presents and thrown them in the yard.
Heading toward the porch, McGraw hoped Lex was home.

McGraw was mounting the steps when the door came open
and Lex Coffield appeared. Moving halfway out the door, he rasped,

"Get out of here, McGraw! I don't want you on this property ever again!"

"I promised Tommy I'd come by today and take him for a ride on my horse. I'm here to fulfill my promise."

Coffield cursed, backed up, and started to close the door.

Before the door could close, McGraw had his boot against the jamb, blocking it. Coffield swore again and threw his weight against the door, attempting to hurt McGraw's foot. Ryan lunged hard, hitting the door with his shoulder. The blow threw Coffield off balance, and McGraw was inside the house looking for Victoria and Tommy.

"Where are they?" demanded McGraw.

"Get out of my house!" bellowed Coffield. When he spoke, he inadvertently glanced toward the stairs.

Ryan saw it and bolted for the staircase with Coffield on his heels. McGraw took the stairs three at a time. Coffield followed, shouting for him to stop.

McGraw checked two rooms and found them empty. He threw open a third door and found himself in Tommy's bedroom. Victoria was sitting on the small bed holding Tommy in her arms. McGraw's first glance told him the story. Victoria's face had fresh bruises, and the scarlet color of iodine was on Tommy's swollen lower lip, covering a cut. There was also a black-and-blue mark on his cheek. Fear was evident on their faces.

Before mother or son could utter a word, Coffield barged in, blaring at the top of his voice, "Get outta my house, McGraw! I'll have you arrested!"

Wheeling, Ryan shouted, "You'll have *me* arrested? Do you know what the army does to officers who manhandle women and children? They lock them up and throw away the key!"

"You'll never make that happen," Coffield hissed.

"Don't bet on it. But for right now, I think I'll just keep the promise I made you. I told you if you ever laid a hand on my son again, I'd beat you to a bloody pulp. I'm going to give you some of your own medicine."

Even as he spoke, McGraw seized Coffield by the front of his shirt and yanked him through the door. Off balance, Coffield swore and tried to break free. It was useless. McGraw's grip was like spring steel.

"C'mon!" growled McGraw, dragging him toward the stairs. Stumbling helplessly, Coffield unleashed a string of profanity, calling the angry leader of B Company every vile name he could think of, and demanding that McGraw let go of him. Victoria and Tommy moved into the hall and watched the scene.

When they reached the top of the stairs, McGraw halted, still gripping the shirt, and breathed hotly, "Now, *Captain*, you can go down the stairs quietly, like a gentleman, or you can go down the hard way. Choice is yours."

"I'm not going down those stairs at all! Let go of me!"

McGraw swung him around so his back was to the stairs and the first step at his heels. "Oh, but you *are*," McGraw said. "You want me to let go of you? All right." With that, McGraw released his hold on the shirt and gave the man a hard shove.

Coffield sailed halfway down, struck stairs, rolled head-over-heels, banged his head on the banister, and fell in a heap at the bottom. Moaning and swearing, he was trying to gather himself when McGraw grabbed him by the shirt again and began dragging him toward the door. Seconds later, the two men were in the yard, amid the broken toys. Coffield had lost his footing while being pulled down the porch steps, and was on all fours.

McGraw stood over him and said, "Get up."

Coffield's head was throbbing and his whole body hurt from tumbling down the stairs. His face was heavy with hate as he looked up at McGraw. There was no question that McGraw was planning to give him a bloody threshing. Lex decided he might as well fight back.

Coffield swung a foot as hard as he could at McGraw's ankles. It happened so quickly, Ryan couldn't avoid the kick and it knocked his feet out from under him. When he hit the ground, Coffield was on top of him like a panther. He grabbed McGraw's throat with both hands and tried to crush his Adam's apple with his thumbs. McGraw brought his knees up violently under Coffield's rump and sent him sailing head-over-heels.

Coffield landed hard and rolled over, shaking his head. By the time he could get to his knees, McGraw was standing over him again, saying, "C'mon, big tough woman and child beater. Get up!"

The urge to destroy Ryan McGraw was a living thing in Lex Coffield. He leaped to his feet, ejected a wild animal-like roar, and charged him. The adept Sharpshooter dodged him. Coffield skidded to a halt, swore angrily, and spun around. The lust for battle flushed his dark features. He held up his fists and charged again.

McGraw drove the point of his elbow into Coffield's throat, setting him back, gagging and choking. He followed up with a lashing right to the jaw. Coffield was down again.

Shaking his head to clear the cobwebs, he cursed McGraw and got to his feet. Ryan glanced up as Tommy and Victoria came out onto the porch. The half-second his eyes were off Coffield was enough to allow Lex to barrel in and chop him high on the cheekbone. The blow was hard enough to throw Ryan off balance. He stumbled backward, and Coffield was after him like a wild beast.

Ryan brought his elbows up, blocking the barrage of blows. A quick punch through the barrage caught Coffield flush on the nose and staggered him. Water filled his eyes as he fought to stay on his feet.

McGraw eyed Coffield's lower lip at the exact spot where Tommy's was split. The child-beater would now get some of his own medicine. Coffield saw the fist coming and tried to avoid it, but the swiftness of the blow caught him on the targeted place. Skin split and blood spurted. The impact snapped Coffield's head to the side and a crimson spray also came from his nose. He went down once more.

This time, Ryan grabbed his shirt and lifted him to his feet. "Let's find out how you look with black and blue marks on *your* face, Captain!" he rumbled, and cracked him on the cheekbone. Coffield's knees buckled, but Ryan held him by the shirt and hit him three times more before letting go.

Captain Lex Coffield was down again. His face was red from the smarting blows and crimsoned with blood from his nose and lip. Rolling to his knees, he glanced at Victoria and Tommy on the porch. Tommy was standing beside his mother, clinging to her skirt. Lex tried to summon something from deep within him. He had to get up and give McGraw more of a fight. He must show Victoria that he had the courage to battle back. Spitting blood, he grunted and rose to his feet, raising his fists.

McGraw came after him, dodged Lex's haymaker, and popped him solidly on the jaw, purposely pulling the punch enough to avoid knocking him out. He meant to give Coffield the bloody pulp beating he had promised, but wanted him conscious when it was over.

Lex swung again, but missed. Another McGraw fist snapped his head back, opening a cut above his left eyebrow. His bloody mouth sagged open and he stood there groggily swinging his fists. Ryan stepped in and slapped him hard over and over, rocking his head back and forth with each smarting impact. When he saw Coffield's eyes glaze up, he stopped. Lex Coffield's face was a bloody pulp, and Thomas Manning McGraw's father was satisfied. He stepped back and lowered his fists.

Coffield sank to his knees.

Neighbors were looking on, as they had been for some time. Ryan walked to the battered toy drum, picked it up and went back to Lex. Towering over him, he shook the drum in his face, and growled, "You're going to buy my son a new drum exactly like this one, Captain, and you're going to replace all the other toys you smashed. If you don't, you'll think what you and I just did was play a game of patty-cake compared to what'll happen next."

McGraw went to the porch and held out his arms to his son. Tommy reached for him, and Ryan hugged him. While he held the boy in his arms, he asked, "Do you feel like taking that horseback ride?"

"Sure do!"

Looking at Victoria, Ryan said, "Okay?"

"Of course, as long as you're back by dark."

"We'll be back in half an hour."

Victoria watched as father and son rode away, then turned and went into the house. The neighbors went back to whatever they had been doing before the fight began.

Captain Coffield struggled to his feet, wiped blood from his mouth, and began gingerly to pick up the broken toys.

On Wednesday morning, August 3, Ryan McGraw was sitting on his bunk after a strenuous workout with his men. Judd Rawlings was outside in a discussion on battle tactics with Colonel DeWitt Munford and several of the Fort Morgan men. Having a few moments of privacy, McGraw held Dixie's daguerreotype, looking at it dreamily, and missing her.

A dark form appeared at the door, silhouetted against the stark sunlight. "Captain McGraw, your new men have arrived."

Turning toward the voice, McGraw recognized one of the sentries. He thanked the man, then rose from the bunk and placed Dixie's picture under his pillow.

Emerging into the brilliance of the Alabama sun, McGraw followed the sentry toward the gate. Already, Sharpshooters and Fort Morgan men were welcoming the new recruits. As McGraw drew up to where the new arrivals were clustered, a rugged-looking sergeant smiled and moved forward, extending his hand. McGraw recognized him. They had fought together in a battle McGraw could not name at the moment. Returning the smile, he said, "Hello, Sergeant! I remember fighting side-by-side with you, but you'll have to jog my memory."

"John Grove's my handle, Captain," said the sergeant as their hands clasped. "Those cold three days in December of '61 up at Muscle Shoals near Wilson Lake."

"Oh, sure! Now, I remember. You got separated from your unit during the battle and fought with us."

"Right! You probably don't recall, but I told you then that if I ever got a chance, I'd do my best to get assigned to B Company.

Well, here I am!" Handing McGraw a brown envelope, he said, "Here's the official papers from General Maury. He sent a dozen of us to give a little overlap. Said General Lee gave him permission."

"Fine," grinned McGraw, opening the envelope. "With the battle that's coming here, we can use every one of you." Pulling out the papers, he silently read the letter signed by Major General Dabny H. Maury. As the letter stated, on a separate sheet in the envelope were the names and ranks of the new men. Eleven were listed, then at the bottom of the sheet, this note: "One man in the dozen I'm sending you has no combat experience. I realize this is unusual. I have always given you men who have proven themselves in battle. He's also eighteen, younger than any Sharpshooter has ever been. I'm including him in the dozen for two reasons. First, he is the best marksmen I have ever seen. He'll do well as a Sharpshooter once you toughen him up. Second, he showed more enthusiasm for fighting under your command than any potential Sharpshooter has ever shown. I think you know him. His name is Johnny Ray Griffin."

The name brought McGraw's head up with a snap. Quickly he scanned the faces of the new group. At the rear of the knot of men was the boyish face of Johnny Ray. He was looking straight at McGraw, grinning from ear to ear. The grin faded when McGraw did not grin in return.

The Sharpshooter captain welcomed the new men, introduced Lieutenant Judd Rawlings, and informed them that Rawlings would see that they were bunked properly. There would be calisthenics and hand-to-hand combat instruction at three that afternoon. Just before dismissing them to follow Rawlings, he said, "Private Griffin, I want to talk to you immediately."

Griffin remained, looking sheepish as McGraw approached him. A slight smile curved McGraw's mouth as he said, "Johnny Ray, General Maury's note here says you're eighteen. Now, if memory serves me, you were fifteen when I met you. Correct?"

Johnny Ray's face tinted. He lowered his chin. "Yes, sir." Then raising it, he said, "I turned sixteen since then, Captain. And...you gotta admit, I'm tall for my age. I *look* eighteen. The sergeant at the induction center in Montgomery didn't question my age."

"What about your mother? I know she didn't give you permission to lie about your age and join up."

"Well…she got married a couple weeks ago. I…I don't like my stepfather. He sent Ben Rice away, and me and him don't get along. So I decided to run off and join up. When I showed them how good I could shoot and told them I wanted to fight in your company, they talked it over with General Maury. As you can see, he gave me permission to become a McGraw Sharpshooter."

McGraw sighed. "Johnny, General Maury gave his permission because he thinks you're eighteen. You know he wouldn't have if he knew your true age. Right?"

The boy bit his lower lip. "Yes, sir."

Laying a hand on Johnny's bony shoulder, McGraw said, "Johnny, I appreciate your willingness to fight for the Confederacy, and I double appreciate the fact that you want to fight under my command. But Confederate law says you have to be eighteen. Since I know the truth about your age, if I say nothing and let you stay in uniform, I'm breaking the law. Do you want me to break the law?"

"No, sir. I didn't think of it that way. I figured if I told you about my awful stepfather, you'd let me be a Sharpshooter anyway."

"I can't do it, son. You're too young to be out there in combat."

"I captured them Union soldiers. You know about that."

"Yes, and I commend you for it. But that has no bearing on this situation. You are under age, and I've got to send you home."

Johnny Ray looked like he was going to cry.

"There are some civilian clothes in our store room," McGraw continued. "I'll get you into them and take you to Mobile with me next time I go. Probably be tomorrow. I'll find a way to send you home from there."

"But I want to fight the Yankees, Captain McGraw. At least let me go back to Montgomery and get signed up in a unit where nobody knows me."

"Can't do it. I'll have to see that you travel with a military unit of some kind so I know they'll take you home."

Stubbornness showed on the youth's face, but he knew there was no hope of changing Ryan McGraw's mind. "Yes, sir," he replied dejectedly.

"For today, kid," said McGraw, patting his shoulder, "you can watch the Sharpshooters work out. You can bunk with Lieutenant Rawlings and me tonight. Now, let's get you out of that uniform."

Five minutes later, McGraw and the youth emerged from the store room with Johnny Ray carrying shirt and pants. They headed for the captain's quarters, and when they entered, they found Lieutenant Rawlings at his bunk, cleaning his revolver. "Hello, Johnny Ray," smiled Rawlings.

"Hello, sir," Johnny Ray responded glumly.

"Get your clothes changed," McGraw said. Then to Rawlings, "You get everybody situated?"

"Yes, sir." Judd set his curious gaze on the civilian clothing in the youth's hands and said, "I take it you're being sent home."

"Yes, sir."

"Can't let him stay," Ryan said. "He had a birthday since we saw him, but he's still only sixteen."

"Your ma didn't give you permission to do this, did she?" asked Judd.

"No, she didn't," Ryan answered for him.

"Bet she's plenty worried about you."

"No, she's not," replied Johnny Ray. "I don't matter to her anymore. She got married and she's got my dumb ol' stepfather."

Rawlings and McGraw exchanged glances.

"Just because she got married again doesn't mean your mother doesn't love you or care about you, kid," put in McGraw. "She's probably beside herself with worry right this minute."

Shrugging his narrow shoulders, the slender youth said, "Maybe."

There was a rap on the frame of the open door. It was a sentry from the gate. "Captain, General Page sent me to get you. He's in the lighthouse. Wants you immediately."

Captain McGraw hastened up the spiral stairs in the lighthouse to find General Page standing between two soldiers, looking south on the Gulf of Mexico through a telescope. Page lowered the telescope, turned to McGraw, and said, "Take a look at this, Captain."

Placing the telescope to his right eye, McGraw focused on the Union fleet. He saw that instead of bobbing on the water in loose fashion as they had been for weeks, they were lining up in formation. "Oh-oh," he said, still looking. "I think they're getting ready to come in."

"That's the way I see it," responded Page. "Looks like *we'd* better get ready."

"I would say so, sir," said McGraw, lowering the telescope.

"My men, here, spotted a new ship arriving out there about an hour ago," said the general. "It's a monitor. This gives Farragut a total of twenty-five vessels. Four are monitors. He must figure he's got enough, now."

"I agree, sir. You think they'll hit us right away?"

"I'd say they'll wait till tide and come in at dawn."

"Makes sense."

"You're not going to have but one session with your new men if I'm right about the attack coming at dawn.".

"We'll have to make do with that, then, sir. All but one of the new men have combat experience. That one is a sixteen-year-old I know personally who got past the induction center in Montgomery, lying about his age. I've already got him in civilian clothes. I was going to take him to Mobile with me tomorrow, but that's out. He'll just have to stay in my quarters during the battle."

Page nodded. "He's one of many hundred sons of the South who've lied their way into a uniform. That's all you can do with him, now." As he started toward the spiral stairs, Page said to the two men on duty in the lighthouse, "Let me know immediately if they should happen to start this direction."

"Yes, sir."

As general and captain walked together toward the fort gate, Page asked, "Have you seen Captain Coffield?"

"You mean, has he come in today?"

"Yes."

"Not that I know of, sir. But I...ah...I probably should tell you that he might not show up."

"Oh? And why's that?"

"I told you that I learned about Tommy being my son."

"Yes."

"Well, sir, I learned that Captain Coffield is known to manhandle Tommy and leave him black and blue at times. He does the same thing to Victoria."

"I'm aware of how he treats her, but I didn't know about him beating on the boy."

"Have you talked to him about beating on Victoria, sir?"

"No, because whenever I've seen the marks on her face, she won't admit he did it. If I ever get proof, I'll lock him up till the war's over, no matter how long it goes on. As you know, the Confederate army frowns hard on such a thing, especially when the guilty party is an officer. So what happened that Coffield might not be in today?"

"I saw marks that he put on Tommy, sir. I had warned him never to touch my son again. I lost my temper and worked him over pretty good. He's no doubt got a mighty sore carcass about now."

They were nearing the gate. General Page hauled up so they were still out of earshot from the sentries. Smiling, he said, "May I say something in response to what you just told me—just between us?"

"Of course."

"You have my utmost praise and admiration!"

"Thank you, sir," grinned McGraw.

Page cleared his throat and headed for the gate, saying, "Well, Captain, we've got to get ready to take on the Yankees, Coffield or no Coffield."

The Union monitor *Tecumseh* was sighted on the east horizon just before eight o'clock on the morning of August 3. An hour later it steamed in to the cheers of men on the decks of the other ships and drew up beside the *Hartford.* The *Tecumseh's* captain, Tunis A.M. Craven, was an old and close friend of Admiral Farragut. The balding fleet commander stood on the deck of the *Hartford* and invited Craven aboard.

When Farragut had filled his friend in on the attack plan over a glass of red wine, Craven returned to his ship. The *Hartford's* flag man then signaled for the entire flotilla to move into their assigned positions.

Standing next to Farragut on the deck as they watched the massive strike force line up, Fleet-Captain Percival Drayton said, "I like your idea, Admiral. We know they're watching us take formation. And I think you're right—since we're forming up now, General Page will figure us to come riding in on high tide at daybreak in the morning. When we don't come, it'll sure enough give them something to think about. Time they've sweated it out till dark tomorrow night, we'll really have them wondering. They'll be a little shaken when we do come in on high tide the next morning."

"Maybe not much," grinned Farragut. "But even if it's a little, it'll help."

NINETEEN

Like many of the men in Fort Morgan, Captain Ryan McGraw found sleep hard to come by on the night of August 3. It was well after midnight when he rose from his cot, dressed while Johnny Ray Griffin and Judd Rawlings slept restlessly, and walked out into the cool night air. A strong wind was coming in off the Gulf, and it felt good.

Greeting the sentries at the gate, McGraw passed through and walked past the lighthouse to the beach. There was enough moon for him to be able to tell that the Union fleet had not come any closer. The enemy ships were lying in wait, dark and menacing shapes on the horizon. Standing just shy of the foamy line where the surf washed the sandy slope, McGraw let the wind ruffle his hair while he thought of Tommy, wishing the child had a better home life. Even greater than the fear he held for his son living with Lex Coffield was the fear that Union forces would move in and capture Mobile.

What would the Federals do to him? Tommy needed him, but duty would keep Captain McGraw at Fort Morgan until the battle in Mobile Bay was over. He could only pray that Tommy would not be harmed if Granger and his troops did take the city.

And then there was Dixie. He wondered if she had made it to

Chattanooga safely and what kind of fighting was going on around that part of the South. His heart ached for her. "Someday, Dixie," he whispered. "Someday this horrible war will be over. Someday I'll get myself squared away and come for you with a marriage proposal on my lips."

Ryan lost all sense of time. He didn't know what time it was when he headed back for the gate, but a few men were stirring around the cannons at the parapets. When he moved inside the walls, he saw the vague forms of General Page and his three officers huddled together a few feet away. Page called to him.

Stepping to them, Ryan said, "Yes, sir?"

"You couldn't sleep, either, I see," said the general.

"No, sir. I've got Tommy on my mind, as well as what's about to happen here. I'm concerned about what could happen to him if Granger's troops move on Mobile."

"I understand," replied Page.

"Maybe if we whip the Yankees here in the bay, Lincoln will call off his dogs up north," put in Lieutenant Wilson March. "If we can sink enough of their ships to send what's left hightailing it out of here on the Gulf, Granger may not want to venture into Mobile. We could all rush up there and defend it."

"I'd like to believe that myself, Lieutenant," said Colonel DeWitt Munford, "but if Granger's got five thousand men like we've been hearing, our little handful here wouldn't scare him."

"All we can do is take what comes and make the best of it," said Lieutenant Frank Cooley. "Your wife's in Mobile, too, Colonel. I'm sure you're as uneasy as Captain McGraw is."

"Maybe more so," replied Munford. "The Yankees have been known to ravage our Southern women, but not harm the children."

"Well, there's one Yankee leader who doesn't mind harming children," said March, "and that's William Tecumseh Sherman. When he decided to take Pittsburg Landing over near Corinth, Mississippi back in March of '62, he blasted farm houses, knowing there were children as well as women inside. People in Atlanta are scared out of their wits with word that Sherman's going to march down there with blood in his eye this fall."

General Page realized the conversation was only serving to put a pall in the minds of McGraw and Munford, and that talking about the danger would not eliminate it. "It's almost dawn, men," he said. "I'm going to the lighthouse. Get the rest of the men up and in place. Farragut could be coming in here real soon."

When dawn broke, Captain McGraw and his Sharpshooters were out of the fort and positioned along the shore of the bay, beginning just below the lighthouse and strung along toward the north side of Mobile Point. They were spread out enough so they could begin sniping before the Union vessels had even broken the line between the two forts. While Fort Morgan's big guns fired over the Sharpshooters' heads, they would be blasting away with their rifles, shooting Union sailors off the decks. The Tennessee sat in the water some two hundred yards from the mouth of the bay, sided by the small gunboats, *Selma, Morgan,* and *Gaines.*

Inside the fort, General Page's men waited at the big guns to open fire on the Union fleet the instant they came within range. Nerves were stretched tight.

In Captain McGraw's quarters, Johnny Ray Griffin looked on the scene from a window. McGraw had ordered him to keep the door closed. In the youth's hands was a .44 caliber Henry nine-shot repeater rifle. On his waist was a sheath bearing a ten-inch knife. If the Yankees were able to get into the fort, Johnny Ray was ready to defend himself.

A heavy mist hovered over the Gulf. The men in the lighthouse strained their eyes to peer into the vaporous curtain, watching for any sign of movement.

The eastern sky came alive with a pink flush that soon turned orange, but no enemy ships could be seen steaming into the mouth of Mobile Bay. Soon the mists were gone, and in the lighthouse, General Page peered southward through a telescope to find that the Union fleet had not moved since lining up in formation the day before.

When Farragut's armada had not moved by nine o'clock, General Page called for his signalman on the wall to beckon the Sharpshooters back inside the fort.

Meeting with all the men at nine-thirty, except for those on the walls and in the lighthouse, Page stood before them with his officers and Captain McGraw beside him.

"I know you're all wondering why our enemy didn't ride the tide in with guns blazing," said the general. "You were ready to do battle, and no battle came. You're feeling rocks in the pit of your stomachs, and your nerves feel like they're going to snap. Well, gentlemen, this is what is known as psychological warfare. Ol' 'fairguts' is playing games with us. We mustn't let him rattle us. He may decide to come in here at midday without the benefit of high tide...or he may just wait and come at us at dawn tomorrow. Whenever he comes, we've got to be ready and be in control of ourselves. Now let's gird up our loins as the saying goes, and be ready to fight at any moment. What do you say?"

There was a rousing cheer, and a portion of the Fort Morgan men returned to their guns while the rest went to breakfast.

The day dragged on, with no movement out on the Gulf.

When night fell, the Rebel force talked of blasting the Yankees out of the Gulf at dawn. Certainly Farragut couldn't wait another day. Yankees didn't have steel for nerves, either.

At an hour before dawn on Friday, August 5, 1864, a heavy fog lay on Mobile Point and its surrounding waters. The Sharpshooters were back in place along the shore, the men of Fort Morgan were in their places, General Page was in the lighthouse, and Johnny Ray Griffin was in Captain McGraw's quarters.

At 5:45, a light breeze began to stir the fog, causing it to swirl about on the surface of the water in thin tendrils like filmy ghosts. Once again, Rebel nerves were strung tight.

Suddenly, high in the glass compartment of the lighthouse, General Page peered through the thick mists and said to the two men on duty beside him, "They're coming!"

The dim outlines of the Union vessels were slowly emerging like phantoms in the fog. A lantern was lit and waved from the top of the lighthouse to signal the three gunboats and the CSS *Tennessee* to get ready. The long-dreaded battle was about to commence.

The Union fleet approached with the ships lined up two-by-two. As they drew nearer in the fog, the *Brooklyn* forged ahead of the *Hartford*, her bow-chasers fully manned.

Captain McGraw had placed Lieutenant Rawlings at the head of the line of Sharpshooters just below the lighthouse, and had placed himself in the middle of the long, curving line. He would fire the first shot, which would signal his men to unleash a barrage of rifle fire. From that point on, the Sharpshooters were to fire at will.

The fog began to lift at the same time the eastern horizon came alive with light. The Union fleet was closing in, with the *Brooklyn* in the lead. The Confederates naturally assumed the *Brooklyn* to be Farragut's flagship.

In the bay, just north of the minefields, the CSS *Tennessee* and her three gunboats were lining up, ready to begin firing once the Union ships breached the line between the forts.

General Page was now inside Fort Morgan to direct the firing of the big guns. His orders were that they would open fire when the first shot came from a Union ship or when the first enemy vessel struck a torpedo.

The tension grew stronger. Nerves were on edge. Every man knew this could be his day to die, but tried to shove that thought to the back of his mind while he waited...and waited.

Suddenly the Union monitor *Tecumseh*, commanded by Admiral Farragut's old friend Tunis Craven, broke from the line and forged ahead at full speed. There was surprise on board the other Union vessels, including the flagship. At the same time, the *Tecumseh* opened fire with two of her fifteen-inch guns, aiming for the walls of Fort Morgan.

There was a strange feeling of relief among the Confederates the instant the first two shots were fired.

Along the shore, Captain McGraw drew a bead on one of the gunners in the bow of the *Brooklyn* and fired. The man stiffened, then fell to the deck in a heap. Instantly the Sharpshooters cut loose, aiming at other men aboard the *Brooklyn*, which they thought was the Union flagship. Bullets began dropping men all over the starboard side of the deck and were crashing through the glass windows of the captain's cabin.

At the same time, cannons from Fort Gaines and Fort Morgan were thundering and belching fire. The battle of Mobile Bay had begun.

The mouth of the bay was instantly bedlam. Guns roared, rifles barked, and men shouted at the thrill of battle. The bombardment blasted the walls of the Confederate forts and tore into the hulls of Union ships. The CSS *Tennessee* and her three gunboats stood ready to rake the advancing enemy vessels with cannonballs when they broke through the minefields.

The *Brooklyn* was suddenly stalled in the water only a few feet from the red buoy. Its captain and crew had been cut to pieces by McGraw's men. The *Tecumseh* sped past the *Brooklyn* and immediately hit a torpedo. The vessel shuddered with the explosion. At the same time, a barrage of cannon fire was unleashed on it from Morgan. As shot whistled through the monitor's hull and shells exploded around her, the *Tecumseh*'s propeller churned the black water to white foam as it began to list to the starboard side. It was sinking fast. The torpedo had blown a gigantic hole in its bottom.

While the deafening thunder of the battle grew louder and the sky filled with black smoke, the crew of the *Tecumseh* was abandoning ship. Twenty-two of her men were dead. The others were leaping into the water and swimming frantically to avoid being sucked into the ship's whirlpool as it plunged beneath the surface. The last to leave her was Captain Craven.

The USS *Metacomet*, being the closest, steamed toward the *Tecumseh* crew, and under a deadly storm of shot and shell, began picking them up.

It was a critical moment for the Union navy.

The *Brooklyn* was lying across the narrow channel between the pilings to the west and the red buoy under the fiery guns of Fort Morgan. McGraw's Sharpshooters had reduced the *Brooklyn*'s crew to a handful. There were bodies strewn all over the deck. Her engine had since died, and all her surviving crewmen could do was lie low on the port side and try to keep from being hit.

With the *Brooklyn* dead in the water, the whole Union fleet became a stationary target for the guns of forts Morgan and Gaines and the deadly rifles of the Sharpshooters.

Because of the *Hartford*'s position, only her few bow guns could be used. A destructive rain of enemy fire was falling on her, and her men were being cut down by the guns of B Company. In the captain's cabin, Admiral Farragut was swearing at the situation, trying to get a clear look ahead amid the heavy smoke that clung to the water's surface like fog.

At the same time, the captains of Union ships *Monongahelah, Kennebec, Lackawanna,* and *Ossipee* were blasting away at Fort Gaines. The guns in the small fort were doing little damage to the Union fleet, but the four captains, through flag signals, agreed to knock it completely out of commission while they were waiting to move into the bay. It took only a matter of minutes to silence the guns of Fort Gaines.

Aboard the CSS *Tennessee*, Admiral Franklin Buchanan decided to get into the action while the Union vessels were stalled under the guns of General Page. Signaling for the three gunboats to follow, he steamed his huge ironclad forward. Soon all four vessels were firing into the bottled-up mass of ships whose masts were flying the Stars and Stripes of the United States.

At one forward gun on the *Hartford*'s deck, a shell came crashing down and killed several men, blowing their bodies every direction. Some sailed over the edge and fell into the churning waters. Inside the *Hartford*'s cabin, Admiral Farragut swore and said to Fleet-Captain Drayton, "We've got to move, but I can't see for the smoke! I've got to get out there and climb the rigging."

"But, sir, you'll be killed!"

"We'll *all* be killed unless we get moving," snapped Farragut, and charged out the door.

Drayton followed him, hunching low. The sixty-three-year-old admiral scurried up the rigging of the main mast hand-over-hand with the agility of a man in his twenties. He stopped at the futtock-shrouds, just under the towering top. Fearing for the admiral's life, Drayton stood below, observing him on the swaying mast. He was glad when he saw him coming back down.

When Farragut touched deck, he ran to the pilot at the wheel and shouted, "There's space enough for us to pass the *Brooklyn* on her port side. We'll take the lead. Hard a-starboard! Full speed ahead!"

"But, sir, with all that smoke, I can barely see the *Brooklyn*. I may ram her!"

"I said *hard* a-starboard!" snapped Farragut. "Do as I tell you, and you'll miss her. From what I saw up on the mast, once you're alongside the *Brooklyn*, you'll be able to see clearly."

"Yes, sir."

Drayton swallowed hard and faced Farragut. "Sir, I beg your pardon for speaking to you like this, but the smoke isn't the big problem. It's the torpedoes. You saw what happened to the *Tecumseh!*"

The admiral's deeply lined face turned to granite. With a steely look in his eyes, he bawled, "Damn the torpedoes! Full speed ahead!"*

Amid the fire, smoke, thunder of guns, and the sight of many of his men lying dead, General Page paced back and forth behind the guns of Fort Morgan, shouting encouragement. From time to time, the gunners answered back with a Rebel yell.

Down on the shore, the Sharpshooters lay flat and fired at the Union fleet as it moved forward into the bay behind the *Hartford*.

---

*This famous quotation is included for historical accuracy

Torpedoes were exploding and more Union vessels were being damaged and stalled, but many were steaming through. It was evident that their plan was to fire at Morgan from every possible angle.

Six Union ships remained outside the mouth of the bay to bombard the fort from the south side. The lighthouse was taking a beating. The glass was shattered in the compartment at the top, and two bodies hung on the edge. About halfway up, a large chunk had been blown out of the lighthouse's side.

Behind the *Hartford* came the *Octarora*, the *Metacomet*, the *Port Royal*, and the *Richmond*, with several small gunboats in their wake.

The tiny Confederate "fleet" of the *Tennessee*, the *Selma*, the *Gaines*, and the *Morgan* was firing at the approaching enemy vessels as rapidly as possible.

Sergeants Hap Hazzard, Noah Cloud, and John Grove found themselves shoulder-to-shoulder on the shore, alongside Captain McGraw and a half-dozen other Sharpshooters, including Bobby Brinson. The Union ships were moving in rapidly.

McGraw turned to Brinson and said, "Corporal, take four of these men and hurry farther north. Keep them sniping away at crewmen when they've passed us."

"Yes, sir," nodded Brinson. Quickly he chose his men and was gone.

Moments later, as McGraw was reloading his repeater, he heard a rifle firing rapidly from behind him and saw a Union sailor fall aboard the *Metacomet*—which was directly in front of him—for each shot that was fired. Some Sharpshooter, McGraw told himself, was really finding his targets.

Looking around to see who the marksman was, McGraw was surprised to see young Johnny Ray Griffin. Griffin fired again, and another crewman of the Metacomet went down.

"Johnny Ray!" shouted McGraw. "I told you to stay in my quarters!"

Grinning, the boy levered another cartridge into the chamber of his Henry, took aim, and blew a Yankee sailor into the water.

"Johnny Ray!" McGraw shouted, punching the last fresh cartridge into the magazine of his own repeater. "I want you back in the fort! Now!"

"Please, Captain! I'm killing Yankees. Isn't that what *you're* doing?"

"Yes, but I'm a soldier. You're a civilian. Now do as I tell you. Get back inside the fort and stay in my quarters till this is over!"

The boy shouldered his rifle and took aim at a gunner aboard the next ship in line. The rifle bucked in his hands, and the gunner went down. "See, Captain!" argued Johnny Ray. "You need me!"

"I'm going to whip your britches, kid!" bellowed McGraw. "Now get out of here!"

Pouting, Johnny Ray got up and hurried away.

After firing at the Union crews for another fifteen or twenty minutes, McGraw found that he was taking the last cartridges out of his ammunition sack. Turning to John Grove, who was next to him, he said, "I've only got four bullets left. Can you give me some?"

"I'm almost out, Captain, but you can have what I've got."

"I don't want to take all of yours," said McGraw. Looking past Grove to the others nearby, he called, "Can you guys spare me some ammunition?"

To his dismay, he learned that every man near him was running low. Somebody would have to run back up to the fort and bring a fresh supply. Donnie Jim Michaels was on the far side of Noah Cloud. Calling to him, McGraw told him to dash to the fort and bring more ammunition.

Donnie Jim hadn't been gone more than a couple of minutes when McGraw was out of bullets. He emptied his revolver at the passing ships, but with little effect. Soon the others were also out of ammunition.

Hazzard looked back through the clouds of smoke toward the fort and said, "Cap'n, I sure hope Donnie Jim hurries up. We're losin' time!"

McGraw noted a small gunboat with *Loyal* printed on the bow. "Tell you what," he said, removing his hat. "We could come by some fire power if we took over one of those gunboats."

"Novel idea!" exclaimed Hap.

Pulling off his boots, McGraw said, "Hap…Noah…come with me. Let's take the *Loyal,* right there." Leaving the others on the shore, the three men secured their knives in their sheaths and dived into the dark waters.

The *Tennessee* and her gunboats continued to fire at the enemy ships, and the fire was being returned. The guns of Fort Morgan continued to send screaming shells into the hulls and onto the decks of Admiral Farragut's fleet, though some of General Page's big guns had been put out of commission.

McGraw and his chosen partners swam under water until they reached the side of the slow-moving *Loyal,* then bobbed to the surface so close that the crew—who were firing at the *Selma*—could not see them. The deck was barely four feet above their heads.

McGraw blinked the water from his eyes and pulled his knife. Sticking the dull side of the blade between his teeth, he said, "Okay, boys, let's take us a Yankee boat!"

Suddenly a fourth head bobbed to the surface. It was Johnny Ray Griffin. He showed McGraw his long-bladed knife and grinned.

The noise of the battle was loud enough to cover his voice, as McGraw scowled and said, "Johnny Ray, I told you to go back to the fort!"

"I don't have to obey you, Captain. I'm a civilian, remember?"

"I'm telling you to get out of here! You're going to mess up this mission!"

"You have no authority over the bay, Captain," grinned Johnny Ray. "Anybody who wants to can swim in it. That's what I'm doing. Only I want to help you kill Yankees while I'm doing it."

There was no time for further argument. "Okay, kid," sighed McGraw. "You'll have to carry your own weight."

Johnny Ray flashed another grin and nodded. "Let's go."

The four Rebels—knives between their teeth—reached up, laid hold of the deck's edge near the stern, and pulled themselves aboard. The crew of five had their backs to them. The pilot was at the wheel and each of the others manned the four eight-inch iron rifles that were built on swivels and positioned at the bow. Two of the guns boomed seconds apart. The other two were ready to fire.

Cloud dashed across the deck, threw an arm around the pilot's neck from behind, and drove his knife into his heart. At the same time, Hazzard and Griffin went after the men who were just aiming their guns at the *Tennessee*. Being taken by surprise, they had no time to react. It took Johnny Ray two stabs to finish his man, but the Yankee was dead before he hit the deck.

At the same time, McGraw slammed one Yankee on the back of the head with an elbow hard enough to stun him, and as the other one wheeled around, he drove his knife into his heart. As he jerked the blade out, he shoved his victim overboard, then turned to find that Hap had already disposed of the dazed one. He was just heaving the lifeless form into the bay. When the entire crew was dead and overboard, Noah took the wheel and began turning the boat so they could fire at the Union ships.

While McGraw began reloading one of the guns, he shouted, "Hap, show the kid how to fire one of these things! Both of you be ready! We'll be squared around in a minute!"

"C'mere, kid," said Hazzard, planting himself behind one of the guns.

Johnny Ray obeyed quickly. The cannon was mounted on a small platform built on a swivel with thick round springs underneath to allow for recoil. There were small holes in the deck where a steel rod would drop in to steady the gun once it was aimed and ready to fire. Hap showed young Griffin how to aim it, drop the steel rod, and yank the strong, slender cord known as the lanyard to fire the gun.

As the *Loyal* was coming around to face the Union ships, Noah Cloud glanced at the Confederate vessels, hoping the *Loyal* was not in their gun sights. The gunboats were busy blasting away at ships nearer to them, and the *Tennessee* was firing at the *Hartford*.

McGraw had his iron rifle ready to fire just as the *Loyal* squared with the Union fleet. A gunboat called the *Oneida* was bearing down on them at a distance of about forty yards. McGraw's heart leaped when he saw her guns seemingly aimed right at them. When they did not fire, he knew the crew had not seen the takeover.

"Okay, fellas!" shouted the captain. "Aim right down those big hungry-looking barrels and let 'em have it!"

While Hazzard and Griffin prepared to follow the order, McGraw aimed his gun at the *Oneida*'s bow, just above the water line. He could make out the faces of the gunners on the bow just before he yanked lanyard. They had picked up on the gray uniforms and, too late, realized they were now facing their own guns in enemy hands.

The *Loyal* shuddered as all three eight-inchers roared. McGraw's shell split the bow at the water line, but it wasn't needed. One of the other shots blew up the cannon and its men; the other one found the store of gunpowder. The *Oneida* became a huge ball of fire.

"Yahoo!" shouted Johnny Ray, shaking a fist over his head.

"Load up again!" shouted McGraw. Then to Cloud, "Noah, make a circle! We're too close to those other enemy ships coming in!"

The water in the bay was churning and the small gunboat bobbed as if it were in a storm at sea as Cloud gave it steam and began a wide circle. The three iron rifles were loaded before the circle was complete. McGraw, Hazzard, and Griffin each stood at his gun, ready to fire at the first enemy vessel that presented itself a likely target.

Suddenly from the west side of the bay, McGraw saw the battleship *Manhattan* coming at them. Her crew had spotted the Rebel uniforms on the *Loyal*'s deck and watched the destruction of the *Oneida*.

Johnny Ray was sighting in on another Union gunboat steaming their direction from the mouth of the bay. "Look, Hap!" he shouted. "Let's get that one!"

McGraw saw the *Manhattan*'s gunners swing two fifteen-inch Dahlgrens on the *Loyal*. Quickly he cried, "Jump, men! Jump!"

The other three looked and saw the Dahlgrens lining up on them. All three wheeled toward the edge of the deck. Ryan bounded for the water and dived in. While Hap and Noah dashed after him, Johnny Ray abruptly stopped and ran back to his gun. Maybe he could put a cannonball down the mouths of the *Manhattan* crew like he did the *Oneida*.

When McGraw, Hazzard, and Cloud surfaced and were swimming furiously toward shore, they looked back to see young Griffin still on the deck and aiming his gun at the *Manhattan*. Hazzard shouted something indistinguishable just as Johnny Ray yanked the lanyard. In the same split second, the big Dahlgrens boomed. The shells hit the *Loyal*'s deck and exploded, sending the guns into the bay and Johnny Ray Griffin into eternity.

McGraw and his two sergeants exchanged sorrowful glances and swam for shore. When they reached it, they looked back and saw the *Loyal* afire and sinking, but beyond it, the *Manhattan* was stalled in the water. Johnny Ray's shell had exploded directly between the Dahlgrens. They were off their bases, lying on their sides, and underneath a rising cloud of smoke, the gunners lay dead on the deck.

Hazzard stood dripping wet and said with choked voice, "For a civilian, the kid was quite a soldier."

McGraw swallowed the lump in his throat and said, "Yes, Hap. He was quite a soldier."

TWENTY

The sun rose into the sky as the battle continued on Mobile Bay, but it was obscured by a heavy pall of black smoke.

It had become apparent to the tiny Confederate fleet that the *Hartford* was Admiral Farragut's flagship. The *Tennessee* had unleashed a merciless barrage on the flagship, and was preparing to hit it some more when the monitors *Chickasaw* and *Winnebago* moved past Morgan's guns and made a beeline for her. Admiral Buchanan gave his pilot orders to wheel about and meet both ships head-on.

Seeing the *Tennessee's* sudden sharp turn toward the two monitors, the captain of the Confederate gunboat *Selma* swung directly in front of the Union flagship and raked her bow. At the same time, the other two Confederate gunboats were on the Hartford's starboard side, blasting away, but they received more damage than they were able to inflict.

The thick-ribbed *Tennessee* stood "toe-to-toe" with the *Chickasaw* and *Winnebago*, guns booming. Strange metallic sounds rang across the bay as cannonballs struck the heavy armor of the monitors. Some of the Union gunboats had spotted the Sharpshooters on the shore and began to train their cannons on them. When the guns belched fire, the men of B Company dived for cover and slowly made their way to the fort, where they found Captain McGraw carrying Lieutenant Rawlings up the sandy slope toward the gate. Rawlings had taken a chunk of shrapnel in his shoulder.

Inside the fort, the Sharpshooters gathered around their leader as he laid Rawlings on a cot and a couple of the fort's medics went to work. McGraw told his men they had done a magnificent job of sniping. Now that most of the Union fleet was inside the mouth of the bay, they would join the men of the fort at the cannons that were still operable and help keep them firing.

Several of the Sharpshooters were unaccounted for. A few were reported dead by their comrades, but there was still hope that the others would soon come into the fort. Captain McGraw prepared to go out and look for them.

The six Union ships outside the bay continued to bombard Fort Morgan as the day wore on. Captain McGraw moved along the shore, looking for his missing men, and the sea battle between the four ships of the Confederacy and the Union fleet remained hot. From the flagship, Admiral Farragut signaled for his destroyers to continue gunning the fort, while the gunboats and monitors stayed after the four Rebel ships.

Just before noon the Confederate gunboat *Gaines* took a series of shots from three Union ships and ran aground north of the fort, its hull filling with water. The crew jumped onto the shore and ran for the fort. They were barely out of danger when the small Rebel gunboat exploded. What was left of it lay on the shore burning.

The *Metacomet*, Farragut's fastest vessel, turned its attention on the *Selma*. A brief exchange took place, but the Union ship's guns were bigger and soon rendered the *Selma* unable to defend herself. She wheeled about and headed north up the bay. The *Metacomet* overtook her, firing relentlessly. When the *Selma's* captain was seriously wounded, a white flag was run up, and the crew surrendered. They were taken aboard the *Metacomet* as prisoners and the *Selma* was sunk.

Several Union ships converged upon the *Morgan*. The crew knew they had no chance. Running the boat to the shore under the booming guns of Fort Morgan, they hit the beach and dashed to the safety of the fort.

The *Tennessee* was now the target of all the Union monitors and gunboats still in action. Cannons thundered against her, but she fought on gallantly. Soon the bombardment against the invincible Confederate ironclad ram began to take its toll. While the battle raged, the *Tennessee's* flagstaff was shot away. Soon the smoke stack was riddled with holes, and finally disappeared.

Aboard the *Hartford*, Admiral Farragut commanded his pilot to pull back. The Union monitors and gunboats would soon have the *Tennessee* in hand. Standing on the deck of his battered flagship, the admiral watched the dramatic finish.

The monitor *Chickasaw* came up astern of Buchanan's ironclad and began pounding away with eleven-inch shells. At the same time, the fifteen-inch guns of the *Manhattan* pounded her port side, and the twelve-inch guns of the *Winnebago* blasted her starboard side. The *Tennessee* continued to fight back, blasting away at her attackers and maneuvering expertly in the water.

Suddenly the *Chickasaw's* shots cut the rudder chain of the Confederate ram, and the pilot no longer had control. The *Tennessee* began to spin in a tight circle. At the same time, the gunboats *Ossipee, Monongahela,* and *Lackawanna* joined the monitors, firing relentlessly at the *Tennessee*, bent on her complete destruction.

Inside the *Tennessee*, Admiral Buchanan was severely wounded when an iron splinter pierced his side. Immediately the ram's captain displayed a white flag, hoisted on an improvised staff through the grating over the deck. When Admiral Farragut saw the white flag, he commanded his signalman to flash a quick message of cease fire to all the ships.

Abruptly the thunderous cannonade began to diminish until even the guns concentrated on the fort went silent. The afternoon breeze carried the smoke away, and as the six ships outside the bay steamed around Mobile Point to join the fleet, cheer after cheer resounded from the decks of the Union vessels.

Inside the fort, the Rebels looked on dejectedly as the *Tennessee's* crew emerged into the sunlight. A wounded Admiral Buchanan surrendered his sword to the captain of the *Ossipee*, and was taken aboard as prisoner, along with his crew.

Captain McGraw stood with General Page and his two lieutenants and watched glumly as the *Tennessee* was towed across the bay to where the *Hartford* had dropped anchor.

"Looks like we're whipped, General," Frank Cooley said with a break in his voice.

Page stared at the Union fleet gathered in the bay. Though a few of their vessels lay on the bottom of the bay, and many of the others were severely damaged, he knew the fort was now under siege. Without commenting on Cooley's dismal remark, he said to McGraw, "Captain, I want you to take your men to Mobile under cover of darkness tonight. You can have the horses and wagons you need. We'll bury your six dead men for you. Since none of your four wounded men are in danger, take them with you. They'll get proper care at the Mobile hospital. I have six wounded men to send along with you."

"Sir, we can't go off and leave you and your men to face Farragut's guns. You need us."

"We'll be all right," Page replied, looking McGraw straight in the eye. "What I said was not a request. It is an order. We'll hold the fort as long as we can, but Mobile will be President Lincoln's next target. There'll no doubt be ground forces moving against it shortly. The people of Mobile need you and your Sharpshooters more than we do. Lieutenant Cooley is right. We're whipped, here. All we can do is grit our teeth and hold off the enemy as long as possible. The people of Mobile aren't whipped. Go do all you can to see that the Yankees don't take Mobile."

A solemn look etched itself on Ryan McGraw's face. "Yes, sir. We will."

Page scratched at an ear. "And when you see Captain Coffield…"

"Yes, sir?"

"Tell him to stay in Mobile and fight the enemy there. That's an order."

"I will convey the message, sir."

Travel in the darkness was slow. B Company and the fort's six wounded men arrived in Mobile at dawn. The wounded men were taken immediately to the hospital, where McGraw learned that General Maury had sent three hundred men of A Company, Third Alabama Infantry to defend the city. They were under the command of Captain Andrew Garrison and bivouacked just outside Mobile on the north side.

McGraw left the wounded men at the hospital and took the Sharpshooters to the army camp. He was glad to know that Judd Rawlings was under the personal care of Betty Wells.

Captain Andrew Garrison listened intently as McGraw told him of the Confederate defeat at Mobile Point. He welcomed the Sharpshooters, saying he and his men would be honored to fight alongside them. Garrison explained that though General Maury was expecting the Federals to send a massive force against Mobile, he could send no more than the three hundred men of Third Alabama A Company to defend it.

McGraw asked if Garrison had any idea when General Gordon Granger and his troops would come. Garrison told him he did not. All they could do was send scouting patrols northward and hope that once it was learned that the Yankees were on their way, there would be time to evacuate the civilians from Mobile.

McGraw thought of Tommy and asked why they didn't evacuate the civilians now. Garrison explained that the waiting period could stretch into months. Being displaced for an extended time would work a hardship on the families, and if the bulk of Mobile's citizens were gone too long, it would destroy all the businesses.

McGraw then asked if Garrison had seen anything of Captain Lex Coffield. When Garrison replied that he had not, McGraw told him he would be back later. He must go and check on his son, who lived in Mobile.

Word was spreading fast over the city about Fort Morgan's defeat when Ryan McGraw knocked on the door at 124 East Evans Avenue. When the door came open, Victoria broke into tears and threw her arms around him, sobbing, "Oh, darling, I'm so glad you're all right! Our neighbor was here a few minutes ago to tell me that he heard about our defeat at Mobile Point. I was so afraid...so afraid you might have been killed!"

Ryan took hold of her shoulders and eased her back so he could look at her face. There were more bruises, and her left eye was puffy. Scowling, he said, "Another beating?"

Victoria's fingers went to the swollen eye. She nodded silently, tears spilling down her cheeks.

"Tommy?"

"He beat him again, too," she said weakly.

Ryan pushed past her and saw the boy standing in the middle of the parlor floor. The cut on his lower lip had been opened again and was covered with fresh iodine. The whole lip was swollen. There were also purple marks on both cheeks. Ryan dashed to Tommy, took him in his arms, and held him. While the boy sniffled, Ryan turned to Victoria and asked, "Where is he?"

"I don't know for sure. Probably at his favorite saloon, the Rusty Lantern. He got drunk Tuesday night after you brought Tommy home, and has stayed in a half-drunk condition ever since. When he didn't go to the fort on Wednesday, I asked him why. He swore at me and said he was hurting all over from the beating you gave him. He spent all day Thursday at the Rusty Lantern, came home in a stupor, and laid in bed till noon yesterday. When he did get up, he demanded breakfast. I had already fixed Tommy and me some soup for lunch, and I asked him in a nice way if he couldn't just eat some soup. He threw a tantrum and said if I didn't fix him pancakes and bacon, he would beat me up."

"So you refused his demand?"

"No. I fixed him pancakes and bacon. It was when I asked him if he shouldn't get back to the fort that he acted like a madman and started beating on me. Tommy…Tommy tried to stop him, and you see what he did to him. After he worked us over, he stormed out of here. Hasn't been back since."

Ryan put Tommy down, speaking soothing words to him.

Victoria asked, "Tommy, did you finish your breakfast?"

"No, ma'am. When I heard Daddy's voice, I wanted to come and see him."

Patting his head, she said, "Okay, you've seen him. Now go finish your breakfast."

As soon as Tommy was out of the parlor, Victoria pressed close to her ex-husband, clutched him by the arms, and said, "Ryan, I want to divorce Lex. You've got to help me. I'll need protection when I do it."

"Tori," he said, shaking his head, "there's nothing I can do. I'm going to be tied up who knows how long with this impending attack on the city. I—"

"What?"

"I just had a thought. As a Confederate officer, I can put Lex under arrest for beating you and Tommy again. I'll take him to the city jail and have him locked up till the war's over. General Page affirmed that it can be done. With Lex behind bars, you won't be in any danger."

"Wonderful!" Victoria exclaimed, throwing her arms around his neck.

"Tori," he said, reaching back and breaking her hold, "we mustn't be embracing. I'm not your husband anymore."

"But all that can be changed after I divorce Lex," she said, taking hold of his upper arms. "We can be married again."

"No, Tori," Ryan said, shaking his head. "It's no good."

Tightening her grip on him, she looked deep into his eyes and half-whispered, "Darling, it *is* good! It can be us again, just like it used to be. Don't you remember what we once had? Doesn't that mean anything to you?"

Certain words that had just come from Victoria's mouth echoed through Ryan's mind. *Just like it used to be...what we once had.*

That's it! he thought. *That's it!* The mystery of the strange stirring he had been feeling in Victoria's presence was solved! He *was* remembering what they had once had. His subconscious was latching onto what Tori *used to be* when he first met her and fell in love...before she became selfish and self-centered.

Ryan knew then that he had been in love with a *memory*. But that was past and gone forever. Relief washed over him. He was now free to unleash his love for Dixie...the love he had kept bottled up within him.

With this settled, Ryan McGraw's next move was to throw Lex Coffield in jail for the duration of the war. Breaking Victoria's hold on his arms, he said, "I've got to go find your husband."

"But Ryan, you didn't answer me. Doesn't what we had mean anything to you?"

"I have some good memories, yes, but you ran off, divorced me, and married another man, Tori. I can't just erase that out of my mind."

Tommy was chewing his food gingerly because of his split lip as Ryan entered the kitchen. Bending over, he kissed the boy's forehead and said, "I'll see you soon, Son. I love you."

"I love you, too," Tommy said around his food.

"Good-bye," Ryan said to Victoria and headed for the front door.

She followed him, saying, "You won't say you love me, Ryan McGraw, but I know you do. Why won't you say it?"

Ryan did not answer. His temper was white hot. Lex Coffield was going to pay for what he had done to Tommy.

That night, Captain McGraw was in his private tent just outside of Mobile, where the Sharpshooters were bivouacked with Captain Garrison and A Company. By lantern light, he sat down to write a letter to Dixie Quade. Ryan was feeling good. He had found Lex Coffield at the saloon and dragged him off to jail. Mobile's chief constable would keep Coffield confined until further notice.

Ryan was feeling even better about something else. Now he could tell Dixie he loved her with his whole heart. It was no longer divided.

In the letter, he told Dixie that he had sorted it all out, explaining that he had been in love with a memory. The link to the past was now broken. There was no ghost to come between them. He was head-over-heels in love with her, and was asking her here and now to marry him.

When he had finished the letter, Ryan wrote another one. It was addressed to Mrs. Mabel Griffin, General Delivery, Brewton, Alabama. He knew that even though she had remarried, everyone in Brewton knew her. She would get the letter. Wording it carefully, Ryan paid tribute to young Johnny Ray, telling her of the outstanding courage her son had displayed in the face of enemy fire. He had died a true soldier and a hero.

The next morning, Ryan posted the letters with a Confederate courier who was leaving immediately to carry messages for Captain Garrison.

The days passed slowly as the city of Mobile waited for word from army patrols of the enemy's approach. The patrol units were out one at a time, usually staying four or five days.

On August 24, Captain McGraw and his patrol unit of four Sharpshooters came riding in after a five-day tour to learn that General Page had finally surrendered Fort Morgan to the Federals the day before. The general and his remaining men were prisoners of war. Mobile Bay was now in the hands of the Union.

On September 12, word came from General Maury in Montgomery that Confederate intelligence had confirmed a report that General Gordon Granger's Fourth Corps had been whittled down by Rebel forces in battles a hundred miles north. Granger was now waiting for reinforcements before marching for Mobile. Maury cautioned Captains Garrison and McGraw to stay on the alert and keep the patrols out. There was no way to tell when Granger would get his replacements.

On Thursday, September 15, Captain McGraw was sitting in his tent, talking to Judd Rawlings, who had reported for active duty. His shoulder wound was sufficiently healed. Rawlings had also announced to his best friend that he had proposed to Betty Wells, and she had accepted. A wedding date had not been set. The circumstances of the war would affect that.

Ryan was congratulating Judd on the engagement when a shadow crossed the tent opening. Recognizing the regular courier, he stood up and said, "Hello, Wally. Got some mail for me?"

"One letter. It's from Chattanooga."

Ryan's heart pounded. "I'll take it!"

Returning to the bunk where he had been sitting beside his friend, he said, "I sent Dixie a letter better than a month ago, asking her to marry me. This will be my answer."

While Ryan tore the envelope open, Judd said, "As if there's any question that she'll say yes."

Ryan laughed, but his laughter faded as he pulled out the familiar envelope with his own handwriting, addressed to Dixie at the Chattanooga hospital. A small slip of paper was attached.

Seeing the look on Ryan's face, Judd said, "What's wrong?"

"The letter I just told you about…"

"Yeah?"

"It's been returned unopened. There's a note here from an official at the Chattanooga hospital."

Judd observed Ryan's countenance fall as he silently read the note. "Bad news?"

Ryan nodded, without lifting his eyes. When he finished, his face was ashen. "Dixie was serving in a tent hospital near Fort Oglethorpe, Georgia...just south of Chattanooga. On August 14, enemy artillery shelled the tent. Dixie's been wounded, but it's not known for sure what happened to her."

"Oh, no!" gasped Rawlings.

"Goes on to say that the Yankees took about fifty Confederate soldiers as prisoners, leaving our wounded behind. The wounded men said the gallant nurse continued to help them while she, herself, was bleeding. When the Yankees and their prisoners were gone, so was Dixie. They assume she was also taken prisoner."

Ryan lowered his head. Judd stood up, laid a hand on his friend's shoulder, and said, "It'll be okay. I can feel it in my bones. If Dixie was still helping wounded Rebels after she was wounded, it couldn't have been too bad. The Yankees have probably got her somewhere taking care of their wounded."

"Which means she's a prisoner."

"Yeah, but certainly they won't hurt her. They need her."

Ryan was silent for a long moment, then said, "Thanks for the encouragement."

"You're welcome."

The lieutenant stayed with his best friend for a good while, then excused himself, sensing that Ryan wanted to be alone.

Alone, Ryan McGraw battled with the helpless feeling that gripped him. There was no way to find out where Dixie was, or just how seriously she had been wounded. He was also grieved that she had not received his letter. If he never saw her again, she would never know the truth about his divided heart and that she had all of his love. Nor would she know he proposed marriage. Dropping to his knees beside the bunk, he wept and prayed.

The war raged on.

Months passed as scout patrols out of Mobile rode the hills and valleys, watching for Granger and his troops. The army and the citizens of Mobile prepared as best they could for the inevitable. The civilians prepared to evacuate on short notice and the soldiers prepared to fight.

News came to Mobile that the South was slowly but surely being beaten by the North.

In January, word came from Confederate intelligence that General Granger had been engaged in more battles without additional reinforcements. The cold weather had his army holed up some eighty miles northwest of Mobile, and they would not move on Mobile until Granger could muster more men.

During the agonizing wait, Ryan visited Tommy often, having to ward off advances from Victoria. He knew her temperament and dared not antagonize her. She might prevent him from seeing his son. So he avoided her advances, but in a way that made her assume he was preoccupied with the threat of attack on Mobile.

On January 31, word reached Mobile that Savannah had fallen into Federal hands under the leadership of the indomitable General Sherman. Things were looking bad for the Confederacy.

On March 28, Ryan went to the Coffield house to visit his son, and was told by Victoria that she had hired an attorney a few weeks earlier and had just learned that the divorce was granted. She would receive her official divorce papers within a week to ten days.

Victoria was hurt when Ryan did not show excitement about the divorce. She told herself that using Tommy as leverage at just the right time, and stirring Ryan's old longing for her, she would eventually be Mrs. Ryan McGraw once more.

As warm weather came, the people of Mobile waited apprehensively for General Granger and his beefed-up army. News continued to come that the South was losing ground fast. The Yankees were making greater inroads into Southern territory.

Victoria had known that Dixie Quade was gone almost from the time it happened, having learned it from hospital sources. Victoria thought Dixie's absence meant she had a clear shot at winning Ryan back. Although Ryan had not spoken of Dixie to Victoria, she had never left his thoughts. Many a time, in moments of privacy, he had held her picture and prayed for her safety. Someday the bloody war would end. When it did, he would find her.

On the morning of April 6, 1865, Captain McGraw rode out of the army camp with Sergeants Hap Hazzard, Noah Cloud, and John Grove for four days of scout duty. Three hours later, under a cloudy sky that threatened rain, Lieutenant Rawlings was patching a hole in the tent he shared with one of A Company's lieutenants when he looked up to see a familiar figure moving toward him. Dropping his needle and thread, he ran toward her saying, "Dixie! Dixie, how are you?"

She embraced him like she would her brother and said, "I'm fine, Judd."

"But...but we heard you had been wounded."

"I was, but I'm all right, now. Took some shrapnel in my left shoulder."

"I did the same thing in the Mobile Bay battle," he laughed.

Dixie's eyes were roving the area. "Does that make us twins?" she giggled.

"Not exactly. You're too good-looking to be my twin."

Still searching among the soldiers of the camp, Dixie asked, "Is Ryan here?"

"No. He left early this morning on scout patrol. Won't be back until the tenth. That is, unless he sees General Granger coming."

"They told me all about the evacuation plan over at the hospital," she said. "They also told me that Ryan had survived the bay battle and was stationed here."

"Guess you'll just have to wait a few days to see him. What brings you back here? And what happened to you? We heard you had been taken prisoner."

"Well, what brings me back here is that I've been assigned to the Mobile hospital again. I...ah...requested it. I didn't know if Ryan was alive, or even if he was whether he'd be here, but I figured this would be the place to come. I knew somebody here could tell me about him."

"So tell me what happened…I mean your being captured and all."

Dixie explained that she had been taken prisoner by the Yankees after the battle near Fort Oglethorpe and taken to a Federal camp near Dayton, Tennessee. There she was forced to care for wounded Yankees. On March 19, the camp was stormed and captured by Rebels. She returned to the hospital in Chattanooga, asked for the transfer back to Mobile, and it was granted. She had been traveling since then with some news people, who were coming to Mobile, planning to cover the coming attack.

The wind whipped up, and tiny raindrops began to fall. Bending her head against the wind, Dixie said, "Judd…has Ryan spoken of me any?"

Looking up at the falling rain, Judd said, "Step into my tent. Let's get out of this weather." Soldiers all over the camp were scattering for cover as Judd and Dixie moved beneath the canvas shelter.

"Now, to answer your question, young lady—Ryan talks about you constantly. The man is madly in love with you."

Dixie's heart leaped. Then she frowned and asked, "What about Victoria?"

"Oh, he still has to see her in order to see Tommy, but he's not interested in her, Dixie. That's as plain as a black wart on the face of an albino polar bear! It's you he loves. In fact—wait here a minute. I'll be right back."

"Where are you going?"

"To Ryan's tent. He has a private one since he's a hotshot captain. There's something I know he would want me to give to you."

Judd was gone but a moment, and returned with the unopened letter and the note from the hospital in Chattanooga. Pulling the envelope from under his shirt where he had placed it to keep it dry, he said, "Read the name and address on the envelope, then read the note. After you've read the note, open the letter Ryan wrote to you."

Dixie gave Judd a quizzical look, then examined the envelope. When she saw that it was addressed to her, she bit her lower lip and began reading the note from the hospital official. Glancing at Judd, she asked, "Do you know what's in the letter?"

"Sort of, but I never read it, of course. Go on. Read it."

Carefully, Dixie opened the envelope and took out the letter. Angling it toward the open flap to get better light, she read it slowly. By the time she was halfway through it, tears brimmed her eyes. She finished and tears flowed freely as she said with quivering lips, "Oh, Judd, he *does* love me! He *does!* And he wants me to marry him!"

"I know," Judd said with elation. "And I can't wait to see you two in each other's arms."

"I'll be living for that moment. Please...when he comes back, tell him I'll be at the hospital or at my apartment. It's number nineteen. I want to see him as soon as he comes in. Tell him, won't you?"

"Of course," grinned Judd.

Dixie looked outside at the falling rain and said, "I need to be going, Judd. Would you have something I could wrap this envelope in to keep it dry?"

"Sure, I've got a leather pouch over here I use in my saddlebags. You can take it."

Dixie took the pouch from his hand, thanked him, and placed the envelope inside.

As she did so, Judd said, "I've got some good news about Betty and me. We're engaged!"

"Wonderful! I'm so happy for both of you. You make a beautiful couple. Have you set a date?"

"No. The war and all, you know."

"I can't wait to see Betty and tell her how happy I am." Placing the leather pouch under her arm, Dixie said, "Well, I'll be going."

"Don't you want to wait till the rain eases up a bit?"

"No," she chirped happily. "I don't care how wet I get. I'll just sing in the rain all the way home! Good-bye."

"Bye," grinned Rawlings.

Dixie stepped out in he rain and started away, then stopped and turned back. "Judd!" she called, blinking against the rain.

"Yes?"

"I want Ryan to know how things are as soon as possible. Tell him my answer to the marriage proposal is *yes!* And tell him that I love him more than ever!" With that, she was gone.

TWENTY-ONE

On Saturday, April 8, Lex Coffield was pacing the floor in his cell, cursing Ryan McGraw and cursing Victoria. Rage burned within him, firing the desire to kill them both. His mind was racing, trying to pick up some glimmer of an idea of how to escape and take care of both of them. *McGraw would die first.*

The sound of the cell block's door rattling halted Coffield in his tracks. Turning, he saw the door swing wide and the daytime jailer enter. The jailer, a short, fat man of fifty waddled up to the barred door with an envelope in his hand.

Coffield's dark eyes glanced at the revolver on his hip, then met his gaze and asked, "What's that?"

"Some gorgeous doll just came into the office and asked me to deliver it to you. Since I didn't nose into it, I don't know what it is."

Shoving the envelope through the bars, the fat man grinned and said, "You're in here for wife and child beating, Lex. That doll couldn't have been the wife you beat on, could it? Maybe this is a 'good-bye forever' letter."

Coffield scowled and took the letter. "Shut up!" he snapped. "It's none of your business." Without a word, the jailer grinned wolfishly and left the cell block.

Lex looked at the envelope. It was sealed, but nothing was written on it. Ripping it open, he found two folded sheets of paper. One was official-looking. Reading it first, he learned that Victoria had divorced him on the grounds of his mental and physical torture. His being in jail for that very thing had been enough for Victoria's attorney to convince the judge that a divorce was necessary.

The second sheet was a hastily scribbled note in Victoria's handwriting:

> Lex—
> *The enclosed will document that you and I are no longer married. And I say good-bye and good riddance. I should never have left Ryan for you in the first place. That mistake has been rectified, now. We got married again yesterday.*
>
> *V.*

Coffield crumpled the paper and swore, his breath coming in short spurts. A cruel manifestation of diabolical hatred spread slowly over his face like some shadowy creature coming out of its lair. His pulse pounded in his temples as the thought froze in his mind, *No. Victoria dies first.*

Late afternoon the following day, Sergeant Hap Hazzard galloped into the Confederate camp just outside of Mobile and skidded to a halt in front of Captain Andrew Garrison's tent. Garrison stepped out immediately, and gray-clad men began to gather around.

Sliding from his saddle, Hap said breathlessly, "Captain, our scout patrol met up with a small Rebel unit about thirty miles north of here late this morning. They're on their way to some Confederate camp in southeast Mississippi. They told us they spotted General Granger and his troops about fifty miles due north of where we ran onto them. This was Friday morning, they said, and the Yankees are coming this way."

"They estimate how many?"

"Yes, sir. At least five thousand…maybe more. Most of them are on foot. They're bringing lots of wagons and cannons." There was a buzzing among the soldiers who were pressing close around Hazzard and Garrison.

The captain nodded solemnly and said, "That many men on foot, with the wagons and artillery you describe, can only move in that terrain at the rate of about fifteen miles a day. Since your friends spotted them on Friday morning, they'd be some forty-five miles closer by now. You say Captain McGraw's patrol is thirty miles from here?"

"They were when I left them, sir."

"Okay. That would mean Granger has to be about thirty-five miles from here right now. They'll be in here by sometime Wednesday. That means according to our evacuation plan, the hospital patients who are able to travel and the medical staff chosen to go along with them must pull out of here before sundown. We should have everybody gone by noon on Tuesday."

"Should be plenty of time," Hazzard said. "I assume you're still planning to send them all to Hattiesburg."

"That's right. Hattiesburg is the closest city with a good hospital, since New Orleans is in enemy hands. I hate to have to make those patients ride for ninety miles, but there's no choice. Since we're sending them there, I felt it's best to just send everybody to Hattiesburg."

"Captain McGraw said to tell you that they'd keep an eye on Granger from a distance today, and if there were any significant changes, he'd send another rider in to advise you. He and the patrol will be in here by dawn tomorrow morning."

"Good. We'll pretty well know about Granger's progress by then, and can plan accordingly."

At dawn the next morning, Captain McGraw and his two scouting companions rode into camp. McGraw went immediately to Captain

Garrison's tent and made his report. Granger's army was two days away.

As McGraw left Garrison's tent for his own, Hap Hazzard rushed up and said, "Cap'n! Lieutenant Rawlings is in town saying good-bye to Betty. He told me if you rode in to tell you to come to him with all haste. He has something really important to tell you."

"He give you any idea what it's about?"

"Naw. He looks like the cat who swallowed a canary, but he wouldn't tell me nothin'."

McGraw would see what Judd had to tell him, then head for 124 East Evans Avenue. He was eager to see his son. Tommy was an early riser. He would be eating breakfast shortly after sunup.

Trotting his horse into Mobile, Ryan spotted the long line of wagons and soon caught sight of his best friend, standing beside a wagon talking to Betty. The occupants of the wagon were obviously hospital patients.

Judd saw Ryan coming and smiled broadly as he rode up and dismounted. The captain greeted Betty, then said to his friend, "Hap said you had something you were burning up to tell me."

"To say the least. I've got some terrific news. Would you like to sit down before I hit you with it?"

"I can take it standing. Hit me."

Ryan McGraw was stunned by the news that Dixie Quade had returned to Mobile. He was elated to learn that her wound was not serious and to hear the story of her escape from the Yankee prison camp.

Judd was saving the best till last, when Ryan said, "So long, Judd. I'm heading for the hospital. I've got to see Dixie right now!"

"She isn't there. She left last night for Hattiesburg with several patients, other nurses, and a couple of doctors. I assume you know about the order of evacuation."

"Yes. Captain Garrison told me. Tommy and Victoria don't leave until this afternoon." Frowning, Ryan said, "Oh, I wish I hadn't missed Dixie."

Betty spoke up. "I was supposed to stay here myself, Ryan, but the doctors decided these patients could make the trip to Hattiesburg after all. So I'm going along to care for them."

Judd was about to explode. "I have something else to tell you."

"Okay. Shoot."

"Dixie requested to be assigned back here because she wanted to find you."

"Really?"

"Mm-hmm. You…ah…you know that letter you sent to her that came back? I took the liberty of giving it to her. Hope you don't mind."

"You did? No—no I don't mind. How did she react when she read it?"

"Cried like a baby. She thought she'd be here when you returned, so she asked me to send you to her the minute you rode in. Said she wanted you to know her reaction right away. I was supposed to tell you, and I quote: *Tell him my answer to the marriage proposal is yes! And tell him that I love him more than ever!*' She repeated it last night just before she left, and told me to tell you she's sorry she couldn't be here when you got back. She tried to be one of the nurses who will be staying here, but the hospital officials insisted she go to Hattiesburg."

Ryan's heart was pounding his ribs. Suddenly it hit him. *Hattiesburg!* Dixie had been sent to his home town! The wagon train was about to pull out. Turning to Betty, he said, "You'll be seeing Dixie as soon as you get to Hattiesburg, right?"

"Yes."

"Tell her…tell her that I meant every word in that letter, and I'll do my best to come to Hattiesburg when this battle is over. Tell her to go to my parents' house and stay with them. Mr. and Mrs. Thomas McGraw. Everybody in town knows them. They can direct her to their house. It's just outside of town on the southwest side on top of a hill. It's white with two stories, and a huge porch that runs the length and breadth of the house. There are honeysuckle bushes all along the porch, and there are four big oak trees in the front yard. Got it?"

"Got it."

"Okay. Tell her to tell my parents our story and show them the letter…and that I asked that they take her in and let her live with them. She's also to let them know about Tommy. Since Victoria and Tommy will be going to Hattiesburg also, they'll get to meet him."

"Will do," smiled Betty.

Ryan thanked her, then said, "I know you two need to kiss good-bye or something, so I'll be on my way. Got to go see my boy."

The eastern sky was pink, but the sun had not yet put in an appearance when Victoria Coffield descended the stairs and headed for the kitchen. She would get breakfast going. Tommy was dressing himself in his room.

As she entered the kitchen, Victoria's heart lurched in her breast and a gasp escaped her mouth. Lex was sitting at the table with a revolver lying near his hand. His eyes glittered and she saw madness there. A venomous smile parted his lips as he said gratingly, "I had to strangle the jailer to come to you, Mrs. McGraw. But here I am."

Horror crawled up Victoria's spine and over her head, tingling her scalp. Thinking fast, she said shakily, "Ryan's upstairs, Lex. You'd better leave right now. If he finds you here, he'll tear you apart." Turning her head toward the kitchen door, she shouted, "Ryan! Lex is here! He escaped from jail and he's got a gun!"

"Won't work," Coffield said coolly. "I already looked in on you while you were asleep. He isn't here."

Eyes bulging, Victoria gusted, "I want you out of this house right now, Lex!"

"Well, you haven't always gotten everything you want, have you, dear?"

Victoria knew Lex Coffield could be a dangerous man, but she had never seen him like this. She knew he was there to kill her. He would kill Tommy, too. Her heart thundered, shaking her whole body. "Lex," she warned, mouth suddenly dry, "if you harm me, Ryan will kill you!"

The madman laughed. "This is your day to die, sweet Victoria. And after I've killed you, I'm gonna kill your new...or should I say your *old* husband."

Lex's hand was not touching the gun. In desperation, Victoria lunged for it with both hands. Her sudden move took Lex by surprise. She had a firm hold on it before he could stop her. He quickly closed his hands on her wrists and began twisting them to make her let go. His superior strength won out. Victoria yelped as the gun was jerked from her hands.

At the same instant, Lex was aware of sharp pain in his right thigh. Tommy, missing one shoe, was biting into flesh as hard as he could. Lex swore and swung the barrel of the revolver against the child's head. Steel met flesh and Tommy collapsed on the floor.

Victoria was on Lex like a mother cat, clawing and screaming at him. The angry man slammed her jaw with an elbow, then followed with a fist to her stomach. Victoria doubled over and fell to her knees. Lex eared back the hammer of the revolver, aimed at Victoria's head, and squeezed the trigger.

Trotting his horse, Ryan McGraw rounded the corner onto Evans Avenue, wondering where the shot had come from. It was a handgun and sounded as though it had to have come from inside a building.

Suddenly he saw an elderly man leave the house next door to Coffield's and dash toward the front porch. Digging heels into the horse's flanks, he sped into the yard just as Clarence Wiley pushed open the door. On his heels, Ryan bolted inside and caught up to the old man before he reached the kitchen. Charging past Wiley, he entered the room first.

Victoria's lifeless form caught Ryan's attention a split second before he saw Tommy lying a few feet away. Another quick glance at Victoria showed him the bullet hole an inch inside her hairline and the tiny trickle of blood that moistened her forehead. There was no question that Victoria was dead.

Clarence was saying something that was not registering in Ryan's ears as he moved to Tommy. When he found the boy breathing, he whispered a prayer of relief and examined the gash on his temple. It had only been a glancing blow and had not damaged his skull, but it was bleeding heavily. Tommy was beginning to stir.

"...her husband, Captain!" the old man's words finally penetrated.

"What did you say?"

"I said it was her husband! Lex! I heard the shot and came out of my house. I saw him charge out of the back of the house with a gun in his hand, and run down the alley!"

Ryan headed for the back door, saying, "See if you can stop the bleeding. I'm going after him. Which way did he go?"

"West."

Ryan dashed to the alley and looked westward just in time to see Lex Coffield cut into a back yard a block away, heading in the direction of Evans Avenue.

Wheeling, he ran to the front yard, leaped on his horse, and put it to an instant gallop. Up ahead, he saw Coffield plunge toward the street from between two houses, then skid to a halt and look at him. When Lex realized the galloping horseman was Ryan McGraw, he pivoted and disappeared quickly in the direction he had come from.

McGraw drove his horse between the houses and saw a man standing next to his back porch. Pulling rein, he asked, "You see a man go through here?"

"Yes. Is there trouble, Captain?"

"He just murdered a woman. Where'd he go?"

Pointing, he replied, "Across the alley. Into my neighbor's b—"

The hayloft door of the neighbor's barn came open and a shot was fired, barely missing McGraw, who dived from the saddle. The bullet chewed into the man's back porch. He yelped and flattened himself on the ground.

McGraw had his revolver out and was crouching low as Lex Coffield's face appeared at the loft door again behind a menacing weapon. A split second before the gun discharged, Ryan hit the ground, rolling. The slug hissed and struck earth where Ryan had just been.

From his prone position, the leader of the Sharpshooters took aim and waited for Coffield to show his face for another shot. His wait was brief. Victoria's killer had to see if he had hit McGraw. Using both hands to steady his gun, Ryan squeezed the trigger.

The slug plowed into Coffield's forehead. The revolver sailed earthward first, followed by Coffield's body.

At one o'clock that afternoon, Captain McGraw carried his son out of the Mobile hospital toward the line of wagons. The last of the civilians were about to depart for Hattiesburg. There was a bandage on Tommy's head.

Approaching the Clarence Wiley wagon, Ryan smiled at the elderly couple and said, "I sure appreciate this, folks."

"Glad to do it, Captain," smiled Clarence.

"We'll take good care of him," Myrtle Wiley said.

Looking into the boy's pale-blues, Ryan said, "Tommy, when Mr. and Mrs. Wiley take you to Grandma and Grandpa McGraw's house, you tell them I'll be along shortly, okay?"

Hugging his father's neck, the boy said, "I want you to come with me, now."

"I can't, Son. I've already explained it to you. I need you to be a big boy for me."

"I miss Mommy."

A lump rose in Ryan's throat. "I know," he said, squeezing Tommy hard. "You're so young to try to understand. Remember I told you a little while ago that when God lets someone be taken from us, He has a very good purpose, even though we don't always know what it is?"

"Yes."

"And remember…God loves little boys like you. He loves Tommy McGraw so much that He is going to give him someone else to love and take care of him. Right?"

"Yes."

"And who is that someone?"

"Miss Dixie."

"Right. You like her, don't you?"

"Yes. She's nice. And she likes me, too."

"That's right, Son. When you see her, be sure to tell her you like her, won't you?"

"Okay."

"Okay. Give Dad a big hug, now. It's time for you to go."

Ryan McGraw wiped tears as the line of wagons rolled out of Mobile. When the Wiley wagon passed from view, he took a deep breath and turned away, breathing a prayer of thanks that Dixie and Tommy would be waiting for him together in Hattiesburg. "Of course, Lord," he said audibly, "it's up to You whether I ever get to go to them or not."

TWENTY-TWO

The sun had been up about an hour on Wednesday, April 12, 1865, when the little band of less than four hundred Confederate soldiers and about a hundred and sixty townsmen looked northward over their crude handmade barricades and saw the Yankees appear in the distant grassy fields, moving like a swarm of ants.

Captain Ryan McGraw hunched behind an old wagon that had been flipped on its side. On his left was Lieutenant Judd Rawlings, and to his right were Sergeants Noah Cloud and Hap Hazzard. The rest of the Sharpshooters were scattered among A Company and the handful of civilians who had stayed for the fight.

Hazzard eyed the blue uniforms lining up two hundred yards in the distance and said, "Fellas, this is gonna be a tough one."

"Yeah," nodded Cloud, noting the cannons that were being set in place in the woods off to the east.

McGraw looked along the line of Rebels and focused on Captain Andrew Garrison. The captain raised a fist and shook it, indicating that he was ready to fight. McGraw gave him the same signal, then turned back to watch the enemy getting ready to attack.

Ryan thought of Tommy for a moment. He hoped the boy would not have to grow up and fight in a war.

As Ryan beheld the number of blue uniforms, he told himself it would take nothing short of a miracle to bring him through this battle. They were outnumbered more than ten to one…and they didn't have any artillery. His mind went to Dixie. It was the war that had brought them together…for a short time. Now it was the war that was going to tear them apart…forever.

Judd was having the same thoughts about Betty Wells.

Noah laughed hollowly, slapped his friend on the back, and said, "Sure wish we had time for one more good fistfight."

"Yeah, me too," chuckled Hap. "I've never told you this, ol' pal, but all these years I've just been playin' with you. If I'd wanted to, I could've whipped you till you could never fight again."

"Hah! It's the other way around, fella! I could've—"

"That's enough, men," cut in McGraw. "Here they come."

The Yankees were coming in a steady march, spread across the field in a phalanx, shoulder-to-shoulder. It appeared that the cannons were going to hold off firing until they were really needed. Their crews stood idly beside them and watched.

Captain Garrison stood behind the line and shouted, "When I give the signal, fire away, men!"

Every man in the line had his rifle ready. The enemy drew closer and closer. When they were within forty yards, Garrison cried, "Fire!"

The barrage unleashed by the Rebels took its toll. The front line of Yankees began to fall like flies. Abruptly, the swarm of soldiers fired back. Bullets hissed and whined, men shouted, and the battle was under way.

So gallantly fought the Rebels that the Yankees found it impossible to close in for hand-to-hand fighting. Though men behind the crude barricades were falling, they were taking a greater toll on the men in the field. After more than an hour of being held in check, General Gordon Granger gave the order for the cannons to open up.

McGraw had a bullet burn on his right cheek and a nick on his left shoulder. Rawlings was untouched. Hazzard was down with a bullet in his right leg, and Cloud had been creased in his left side, but was still firing.

When McGraw saw the cannon crews making ready to fire, he shouted along the line, "Cannons! Stay as low as you can!"

Captain Garrison looked around at the wounded and dead men and made a dash for McGraw. Hunkering next to him, he said above the din, "Captain, those cannons will finish us off. In my estimation, it's time to surrender. I hate to do it, but it's suicide for the rest of us if we don't."

Surrender went against McGraw's grain, but he nodded and said, "You're right, Captain. I hate the thought of a Yankee prison camp for the duration of the war, but the way it's been going the past few months, the end may not be too far off."

"I think you're right. We'll run up the white flag."

Garrison hoisted a large white cloth on the end of a long stick and waved it so General Granger could see it. "Stop firing, men!" Garrison shouted to the men on the line.

Almost simultaneously, Rebels and Yankees ceased firing.

General Granger rode in on horseback with six officers and dismounted. Under the watchful eyes of the Rebels along the line, Captains Garrison and McGraw stepped over the barricades and walked to meet him. When they both saluted, Granger saluted in return.

"Sir," said Garrison, "as the white flag indicates, we are surrendering."

A Confederate flag was flying on a mast at the end of the homemade barricade. Granger nodded, pointed to it, and said, "Please have your men haul down the flag."

The Rebels wiped tears and saluted as their flag was lowered by two of Garrison's men. Their hearts went cold as immediately a Union flag went up in its place.

A soft breeze blew across the fields and through the empty city of Mobile as General Granger said to the Confederate officers, "Gentlemen, you are now prisoners of war. In the name of the

United States of America, I claim Mobile, Alabama, as Union territory. Before we take you and your men to our nearest prison camp, there is something I want to say."

Garrison and McGraw were standing at attention. "Yes, sir," they replied.

Granger lifted his hat from his head and said with emotion, "To you and your gallant men, I take off my hat. I have never seen soldiers or civilians anywhere who have fought with as much courage, valor, and determination as you have today. You are to be commended."

"General Granger," came the shout of one of the Union officers.

The general turned to see the officer pointing to a lone rider who was riding hard on a lathered horse across the field from the northeast. The rider was shouting and waving his hat. When he thundered to a halt, his blue uniform was flecked with foam.

Granger moved to him as he was dismounting and said, "What is it, Corporal?"

Breathing hard, the Yankee corporal said, "Sir, I've just come from our camp forty miles northeast of here. We got word this morning that General Robert E. Lee surrendered to General Grant at Appomattox Court House this past Sunday afternoon! The war has been over for three days!"

On April 18, 1865, the Mississippi sun was shining brightly in an azure sky as Captain Ryan McGraw and Lieutenant Judd Rawlings rode onto the hospital grounds in Hattiesburg. Betty Wells happened to be on the lawn in the shade of a large cypress tree, sitting on a bench. Next to her was an elderly person in a wheelchair.

When Betty saw the two riders approaching, she jumped to her feet and said something to the patient. She then moved into the sunlight and met the man she loved as he dismounted.

While Judd and Betty held each other, Ryan left his saddle and waited for them to finish their greeting. When they parted, Betty went to Ryan and gave him a fond embrace, saying she was glad both of them had lived through the awful battle. The news of the war's end had reached Hattiesburg on April 13.

Anticipation danced in McGraw's pale blue eyes as he asked, "Where can I find her, Betty?"

Smiling as she held Judd's hand, she said, "Dixie's on the night shift this week. Right now you'll find her at the big white house on the hill."

"Okay," he grinned. He paused a few seconds, then said, "I assume she and my parents have taken to each other all right."

"Oh, have they ever! They adore each other. Your mother can talk about nothing but the wedding, and your father keeps hugging Dixie and telling her how happy he is that she is going to be his daughter-in-law."

Betty anticipated Ryan's next question, and before he could ask it, she said, "And Tommy! Your parents say you and Dixie can't have him. Tommy has to stay and live with them!"

"Oh, no he doesn't!" Ryan laughed.

"I've been out to the house four times now, and it's so sweet to see Tommy and his grandfather together. Your dad thinks it's wonderful that Tommy was named after him. The two are inseparable."

Running her eyes between the two officers, Betty said, "How...how did it go in the battle with the Sharpshooters?"

Ryan replied sadly, "We lost some. A few were wounded and are in the Mobile hospital."

"How about...how about Hap and Noah?"

"They're among the wounded, but they'll be okay. In fact—" Ryan laughed—"they're in the same room, and when Judd and I left, they were arguing and building up to a fight."

"Well, at least if they hurt each other, they'll have medical help close by!"

The three friends laughed together, then Ryan excused himself, saying he needed to get going.

As he mounted up, Judd said, "Hey, how about a double wedding?"

Ryan smiled down at him. "If the girls like the idea, it's a deal!"

The happy couple waved as they watched Ryan ride away.

Birds were singing in the trees and squirrels were chattering as Captain Ryan McGraw emerged from the dense Mississippi forest, drew rein, and lifted his gaze up the long, green slope to the big white house on the hill. Standing a hundred and fifty yards away like a royal castle, it looked mighty good to the boy who had grown up there.

He nudged his horse forward at a slow walk. Within a couple of minutes, he could make out four people sitting in the yard in front of the long porch, enjoying the shade of the huge oak trees. Two of them had silver hair. There was a small boy sitting on the lap of his grandfather, and a beautiful young woman with hair like spun gold was laughing at something that had been said.

Ryan's heart drummed his ribs. He put the horse to a trot.

Seconds later, the elderly man pointed down the hill and stood up with the boy in his arms. The women rose to their feet, and the younger one started running down the hill amid the wild flowers that grew in the grass.

When Ryan was within fifty yards of Dixie, he slid from the saddle and ran toward her. Tears streamed down Dixie's face as she opened her arms. As the distance between them narrowed, the grass and flowers disappeared, the surrounding forest vanished, and they were floating in a remote and wonderful paradise on heavenly clouds. Far away and forgotten was the world of war and bloodshed and loneliness.

With outstretched arms, they reached for each other...and toward a future, bright with the promise of happiness, contentment, and unending love.

EPILOGUE

The Battle of Mobile Bay was Admiral David G. Farragut's greatest victory, but it was bought at great cost. Union casualties were 319, including 145 men killed. The sinking of the *Tecumseh* and the destruction of several battleships and gunboats was the greatest single U.S. Navy disaster until World War II.

The fall of Fort Morgan had a crippling effect on the South. The Confederates were thrown back on their already overstrained and inadequate resources, and the resulting shortages weakened their strength of resistance. Coupled with other devastating losses all over Dixie, General Ulysses S. Grant's forces drummed the South's battered, hungry army into surrender.

As for the city of Mobile, her men fought gallantly alongside the courageous Confederate troops to the bitter end. The Yankee assault on Mobile cost the Union 1,417 casualties—dead and wounded combined—and caused General Grant to lament, "I had tried for more than two years to get an expedition sent against Mobile when its possession by us would have been of great advantage. We waited too long. It cost many lives to take it, but when its ultimate possession came three days after the war was over, it was of no importance."

The Battle Continues...

ISBN: 1-59052-946-4

Volume 2

Beloved Enemy (Battle of First Bull Run)
Faithful to her family and the land of her birth, young Jenny Jordan covers for her father's Confederate spy missions. But as she grows closer to Union solider Buck Brownell, she's torn between devotion to the South and her feelings for the man she is forbidden to love.

Overwhelmed by pressure to assist the South, Jenny carries critical information over enemy lines and is caught in Buck Brownell's territory. Will he follow orders to execute the beautiful spy... or find a way to save his beloved enemy?

Shadowed Memories (Battle of Shiloh)
Critically wounded on the field of battle, one man struggles to regain his strength and the memories that have slipped away from him. Although he cannot reclaim his ties to the past, he's soon caught up in the present and the depth of his love for Hannah Rose.

Haunted by amnesia, the handsome officer realizes he may already be married. And so, risking all that he knows and loves, he turns away to confront his shadowed memories, including those of "Julie"—the mysterious woman he thinks he left behind.

ISBN: 1-59052-947-2

Volume 3

Joy From Ashes (Battle of Fredericksburg)

While fighting to defend his home and family against Union attack, Major Layne Dalton learns that enemy soldiers have brutalized his wife. Tragically, the actions of three cruel-hearted Heglund brothers have caused not only the suffering of his bride, but also the death of Layne and Melody's unborn son. Thirsting for vengeance, the young major vows to bring judgment upon those responsible, yet surprising circumstances make Dalton—presumed dead by his wife and fellow soldiers—a prisoner of the very men he swore he would destroy.

Season of Valor (Battle of Gettysburg)

As teenagers, Shane Donovan and Ashley Kilrain promise to love each other forever. But when Ashley's parents decide to return to Ireland and take their daughter with them, the sweethearts sadly bid each other farewell and accept their fate.

After several years, both have found other loves and married. So when Ashley returns to Maine and the friendship between the two is rekindled, Shane and Ashley find that a new kind of love is needed to overcome the sprouting seeds of tragedy in their freshly intertwined lives.

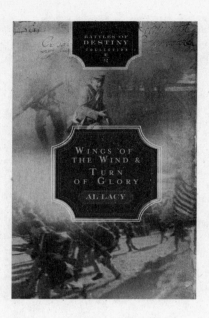

ISBN: 1-59052-948-0

Volume 4

Wings of the Wind (Battle of Antietam)
Early in his life, tragedy and hardship caused young Hunter McGuire to lose everyone he loved: his parents, his little sister, his best friend. Years later, Dr. Hunter McGuire grieves once again after being separated from the young nursing student who has stolen his heart. This time, however, a tender reunion takes place after Jodie returns unexpectedly and helps Hunter tend the wounded at the battle of Antietam. Yet their struggles have just begun, for their life together is threatened by more than they realize. And only One can save their love: the God who walks "on the wings of the wind."

Turn of Glory (Battle of Chancellorsville)
Confederate Major Rance Dayton is wounded on the battlefield and fears he will die until four friends risk their lives to save him. The courageous four are honored and live as heroes until, in the confusion and darkness of a nighttime battle, an unthinkable tragic accident changes their lives forever. The four, so recently renowned as heroes, are now despised and hounded as miscreants, and soon they desert the army and head west to live as outlaws. It is there that Rance, a newly commissioned U.S. Marshal, meets the four again, this time in very different circumstances, but with the knowledge that he owes them his life.

Travel along the Trail of Tears
A Place to Call Home series

By Al & JoAnna Lacy

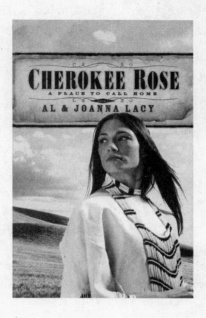

Cherokee Rose—BOOK ONE
ISBN: 1-59052-562-0

It's late summer 1838. President Martin Van Buren issues an order that the
fifteen thousand Cherokee Indians living in the Smoky Mountains of North
Carolina are to be evicted from their homeland. Forced to migrate to Indian
Territory, the Cherokees begin their tragic, one-thousand-mile journey
westward. Most of the seven thousand soldiers escorting them along the way
are brutally cruel. But Cherokee Rose, an eighteen-year-old Indian girl,
finds one soldier, Lieutenant Britt Claiborne, willing to stand up for them.
Both Christians, Cherokee Rose discovers that Britt is also a quarter
Cherokee himself. It's upon the Trail of Tears that they fall in love,
dreaming of one day marrying and finding a place to call home together.

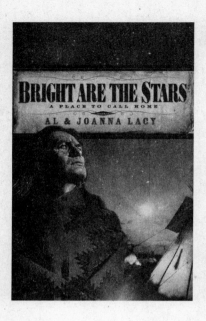

Bright Are the Stars—Book Two

ISBN: 1-59052-563-9

1839. The North Carolina Cherokees are settling into their new home in Indian Territor and Britt Claiborne and Cherokee Rose are settling into married life. Britt, a quarter Cherokee Indian, is released from the United States army and joins the Cherokee Police For where his position takes him into fearsome an heart-gripping dangers. They raise two childr with much love and delight. They also lean o God through the trials of their day—includir the death of the popular Cherokee Chief Sequoyah, who had translated the Bible into their language. Follow the historical events th punctuate their lives until 1889, when Presid Harrison announces that whites are free to en Indian Territory, now known by the Indians a home.

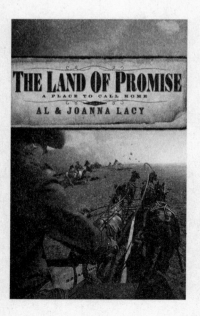

Land of Promise—Book Three

ISBN: 1-59052-564-7

1889. Cherokee Rose and police chief Britt Claiborne are forced onto reservations along with their descendants and the five "civilized" tribes in the Oklahoma District. The U.S. government has told them that because of its rich, productive soil and sufficient water supp the Oklahoma District is now white man's lar of promise. With indescribable sadness and anger, the Indians look on as thousands of prospective settlers and their families enter th district and claim 160-acre sections of land in the Oklahoma land rush. This third book in A Place to Call Home series masterfully inclu the compelling stories of three white prospective-settler families introduced in Brig Are the Stars: Craig and Gloria Parker; widow Martha Ackerman with her parents and three children; and Lee and Kathy Belden with thei two sons.